MW00440037

THE REDWING SAGA

BOOK FOUR

REALMS OF STONE

SHARON K. GILBERT

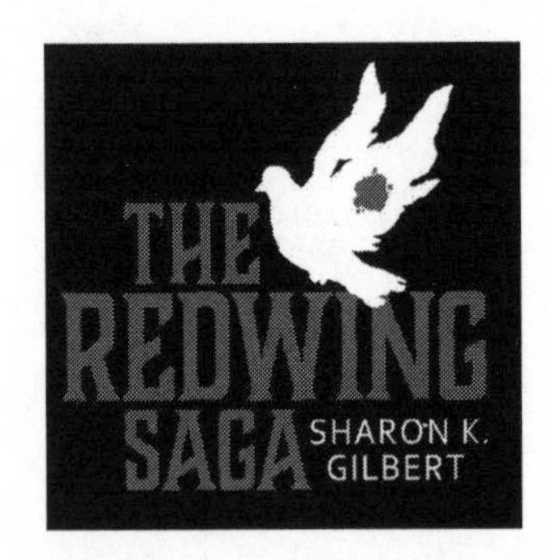

REALMS OF STONE

BOOK FOUR OF THE REDWING SAGA

BY SHARON K. GILBERT

WWW.THEREDWINGSAGA.COM

First Print Edition May 1, 2018
Kindle Edition May 1, 2018

All Content and Characters © 2018 Sharon K. Gilbert
All rights reserved.

ISBN-10: 0-9980967-4-1
ISBN-13: 978-0-9980967-4-2

Published by Rose Avenue Fiction, LLC
514 Rose Avenue, Crane, MO 65633

TABLE OF CONTENTS

FROM THE AUTHOR

It's been such a thrill to spend time with these characters once again. Many of you have written to me, telling me how you've read the books again and again, even taking notes, and it both humbles and encourages me. The first three books of the series laid out the basics of the plots and characters, and so this next trio of books will further develop those relationships whilst unveiling some of the mysteries of the hidden realms.

I'll not spend more than a few lines in this section, for I pray you're anxious to delve into the meat of this installment, but I would like to quickly remind everyone that the English used in all my books employs 19th century British spelling. I've learnt a great deal about the differences during the course of the first three novels, and I'm learning still. I use the Oxford English Dictionary as reference.

I'd originally hoped to release this book on the 8th of April, which is Elizabeth Stuart Sinclair's birthday, but life got in the way (imagine that), and I was unable to finish the manuscript in time. Thanks for your patience, dear readers.

Now on to the story!

Sharon K. Gilbert
23rd April, 2018

For my wonderful readers.

It's your love for
Elizabeth, Charles, and Paul,
for their continuing stories,
their many challenges,
and their victories,
that keeps me going.

You have blessed me beyond all measure.

For I have a word that I would say to you,
a message that I would repeat to you
a word of tree
*and **a whisper of stone**,*
a word unknown to men,
and which multitudes of the earth do not understand:
the coupling of the heavens with the earth,
of the deeps with the stars.
I understand the lightning which the heavens do not know:
come, and I shall reveal it
in the midst of my divine mountain Saphon,
in the sanctuary, in the rock of my inheritance.[1]
—Baal Cycle

He setteth an end to darkness, and searcheth out all perfection:
***the stones of darkness**, and **the shadow of death**. – Job 28:3*

*But thou art cast out of thy grave like an abominable branch, and as the raiment of those that are slain, thrust through with a sword, that go down to **the stones of the pit**; as a carcass trodden under feet. – Isaiah 14:19*

*By the multitude of thy merchandise they have filled the midst of thee with violence, and thou hast sinned: therefore I will cast thee as profane out of the mountain of God: and I will destroy thee, O covering cherub, from the midst of **the stones of fire**. – Ezekiel 28:16*

1 Baal Cycle - Quoted by Nicolas Wyatt, p. 199, *Word of Tree and Whisper of Stone;* Gorgias Press, 2007

PROLOGUE

Somewhere, in a Timeless Land

Charles Sinclair had no idea where he was, nor precisely how long he'd been in this very strange place. His head ached, and his eyes felt painful and dry as he wandered, lost and alone, through the dreamlike landscape. He stood upon a broad road, paved in stones worn smooth by fierce winds and heavy use. The sides of the path were littered with ancient armoury: swords, helmets, shields, spears, bows and arrows—all lying upon a field of shattered, human bones.

I must be dreaming, Charles reasoned, though a part of him doubted that conclusion.

He turned to look behind, hoping to discern his location, but a dense fog descended without warning, as though a curtain of grey muslin fell across the haunted realm. This phantasmagoric mist clung to the skeletal trees like iridescent spiders' webs. Here and there, the mist swirled upon the rocky ground, rising up into a legion of vaporous ghosts exhaled by an invisible dragon, slumbering beneath the cairn of bones.

These faceless apparitions climbed along leafless branches and up ropey bark like translucent, undulating snakes of smoke. Beyond the sentient trees, lonely rings of oddly shaped, standing stones congregated into rock choirs painted in living haze. The sharp-edged silhouettes bore an eerie resemblance to petrified humans with vague approximations of heads, trunks, and limbs. Each weathered face was transfixed into a rictus of pain, and the arms and legs splayed into impossible stances portraying a variety of actions. Some looked as though they'd frozen in mid-stride, whilst others appeared to recline or slumber fitfully upon the intransigent land. A few stared upwards, their stony profiles gazing hopefully towards a starless, midnight sky.

This unyielding firmament grew even darker from time to time, as thousands of ravens and raptors flew past the indifferent moon. One by one, the birds gathered upon knotted branches within the humanoid trees, and one particular bird, larger than all its brethren, watched the newcomer with curious, blinking eyes.

No sound penetrated the adamantine fog, not even the dull tapping of the visitor's footfalls, but as he continued through the nightmare landscape, Charles Sinclair slowly began to notice a welcome and rhythmic pulse within his ears.

It was the soft whisper of his own breathing.

"At least, I'm alive," he spoke aloud.

"Are you?" the watchful raven asked from a thick branch, just over his head. "Alive, I mean. What makes you so certain?"

The marquess looked up at the impertinent blackbird. "Logic tells me I am alive. I'm material, solid. Neither ghost nor spirit," he argued, slapping at his arms, thighs, and midsection to prove the point.

"Logic is somewhat unreliable hereabouts," the creature answered. "Life is death, up is down, black is white, and grey—well, *grey* could suddenly choose to portray itself as any colour or anything it wishes. If you trust only in logic, then your adventure here will fail before it even begins."

"I see," Sinclair remarked politely, though he hardly saw at all. "Tell me, Creature, do all birds speak here, or are you unusual?"

The bird flapped its glossy wings proudly and fluttered to the ground near the human's feet. "I am most unusual, but talking is hardly the accomplishment you might think. After all, *you* are talking, and I rather doubt you could stake claim to anything beyond the ordinary. Although, there is something decidedly different about you," the bird mused as it made an anticlockwise circle 'round its prey. "A different look and smell from all the others. Those who failed, I mean. Why is that?"

"I cannot say," Charles answered.

"Cannot or *will* not?" the bird squawked in irritation.

"That remains to be seen. Just who are you?"

"That, also, remains to be seen," the bird replied in an oily voice. "I'd give you my name, but it's against the rules. However, I might offer a hint in exchange for a small favour. I'm trapped here, you see. Have been for ages, but not for anything I've done. It's all a misunderstanding, I assure you. Perhaps, you've come to free me."

"I rather doubt it. If you are innocently trapped, then how did you arrive here in the first place? And where, precisely, are we, if you please?"

"Telling you is not permitted."

"Telling me what?" Charles asked. "Where we are, or how you came to be here?"

"The latter. Each of us has a tale regarding our presence in this place, human." The bird stood nearly as tall as Sinclair, and it moved to within an inch of his face, staring at him most curiously. "You *are* human, are you not?"

"Yes, of course, I'm human. What a ridiculous question!"

"Caw! Stupid human! No wonder you've been sent here. No doubt, one of your relatives decided you're simply too dense to allow at family gatherings. It is often the way amongst your kind. Useless uncles, conniving cousins, and malicious mothers-in-law; they all end up here eventually."

"Nothing you say makes a whit of sense."

"So you might think, but I assure that everything I say makes perfect sense. You simply lack the wisdom to comprehend it."

The creature shook its wings as though preparing to perform a conjurer's trick. "Now, let me see if I remember how to do this," the disagreeable bird said as it stretched even taller. The avian form slowly elongated into a man's silhouette—or rather a partially humanoid shape. His head was dotted in feathery spikes, and his back, also. The creature's eyes remained an unsettling amber yellow, and the sharp nose protruded outward in a curve like a bird's beak.

Gazing down at himself, the peculiar bird-person frowned in dismay. "It's been over a thousand years since I last wore these skins. It seems I've forgotten how to arrange them. What am I missing?"

"Clothes for one thing," Sinclair wryly observed, then pointing to the chimera's perplexing feet, added, "shoes, for another. However, I'm not sure any cobbler makes footwear to fit three-toed feet."

"Three toes? Ah, I see. Do I require six, then?"

"Five is the usual number, actually."

"Only five? How very dull. Well, then, how is this?"

The birdman shook its legs vigorously until a pair of five-toed, human feet emerged, quickly followed by black boots, which popped onto the newly formed feet from out of thin air. The chimera reached up and felt along the crown of its head, and noticing the errant feathers, snapped its fingers, and before you could say Tom Thumb, transformed the thick plumage into spirals of raven black hair. Clothes of green and black silk wove themselves onto its transformed body, although of a fashion from many centuries earlier. A sable cloak, trimmed in matching plumes, fell across the birdman's broad shoulders. The final picture was almost handsome, if one found yellow-eyed humans attractive, that is.

"Oh, this is quite nice. Particularly, the cloak," the creature said, admiring the new clothing and boots.

"Yes, I suppose it might be, if one lived in the seventeenth century," Charles observed. "Why a thousand years?"

"What is the seventeenth century? Is it a place?" the creature asked. "Wait. A thousand years, you say? Surely not! Have we been talking for so very long?"

"You're the one who mentioned it, not I," the human answered.

"No, you're quite mistaken. *You* mentioned it, but you're wrong. We can't have been talking for a thousand years, as you arrived only a short while ago. Do you like it thus far?"

Charles had grown weary of the inquisitor's methods. "Not particularly. I might find it more interesting, if I knew just where I am, assuming this strange land has a name."

"Of course, it has one! Every place has a name."

"And every creature as well, I suppose," Charles probed. "And yours?"

"I have already told you; I am not permitted to reveal my name to the uninitiated."

"And this place, then?"

"It is *Sebet Babi*," the chimera replied. "The Seven Gates, entrance to the Seven Realms. Do you know nothing, human?"

"I suppose not," the marquess muttered, his left brow arched in defiance.

"Then how did you get here? Did someone bring you? Thanatos perhaps? Or Hypnos, his traitorous brother? Those two are always making trouble for me! I shall have to call a meeting. Disobedience and surprise visitors, no matter how pleasant the conversation, must be dealt with immediately, you know."

"That is your own problem, I suppose, but I'm not sure how I came to be here," Charles answered, glancing down at his hands as though he might discover an answer written there. Though the dismal world had little illumination, he beheld the gleam of a shining, gold band encircling the fourth finger of his left hand.

"A ring?" he asked aloud. "I don't recall wearing a ring like this... Wait, I know what this ring means. It means I am married. How could I have forgotten that? Forgotten her?"

"Forgotten whom?" the birdman asked greedily.

"Elizabeth," Charles whispered, closing his eyes to shut out the oppressive gloom so that he might picture her sweet face. "My Beth. This ring is the token of our promise. She is my wife."

"Apparently, this wife makes you happy. You say her name is Elizabeth? That is a very odd name," the birdman observed, cocking its head to one side. "Who is this Elizabeth? Is she a bird? Is that why she is able to make you happy? Does she fulfill your wishes?"

"All of them, but she is a woman, the great and everlasting love of my life. Our wedding was—it was today," he realised. "Or, at least, I believe it was today. How could I have forgotten that? Where is she? Why isn't she with me? Did we come here together?"

"I cannot provide answers to questions that makes no sense," the creature complained, growing bored. "What is *your* name? Do you have one, human?"

"Yes, of course, I have a name. It's Charles Sinclair. You say this place is the entrance to *Sebet...*"

"*Babi*," he finished. "It is the ancient tongue. You speak it, of course."

"I'm afraid not. By ancient tongue, do you mean Egyptian?"

"Hardly!" the bird creature cawed, the feathery trim of its cloak ruffling in irritation. "The pharaohs are latecomers by my reckoning. I refer to the oldest of all tongues. The original. The one spoken at the dawning of time, when these realms were born. And with them, the Seven Kings, who sleep beneath the living stones."

"None of that makes any sense," Sinclair muttered. "Seven realms containing living stones? You speak nothing but babble!"

"Hardly," the birdman stated, grinning. "That place was abandoned long ago."

"Very droll," the marquess said, "but as I'm speaking with a nonsensical bird creature, I must also assume these realms are equally nonsensical. Ergo, I am dreaming, which explains why Beth isn't here."

"Dreaming is but a journey taken through a door within ourselves. If you think you are dreaming, then try to awaken."

"It cannot be done," Charles declared. "Sleepers do not wake themselves."

"Nor do they perceive that they dream. Your previous logic attested to your own substantiality. If I told you that you are truly, materially in this land, how would you feel? Angry? Curious? Dismayed?"

The marquess had no ready answer, but he meditated upon the problem as he and the birdman walked side by side along the broad path, moving amongst the massive rocks and trees in silence. Enormous shadows shaped like spiders followed their progress, scuttling up and down the trunks of the sleepy trees, whispering to one another in brackish language. Charles perceived crimson eyes within the stalkers' dark faces, and he counted over six dozen of the arachnid soldiers. Off in the distance, booming sounds like thunder mixed with the roaring of lions caused the ground to quake, and each time, the spider army halted as though obeying a command.

After many minutes in this fashion, Sinclair stopped, his eyes on the spiders. "We're being followed," he told his guide.

"Of course, we are!" the yellow-eyed birdman gloated. "We're never alone, human. Not here. Never here. Our citizens grow hungry. It's been so very long since they last fed."

"I don't suppose they eat birds," the human dared suggest.

"Only those who disobey, and I am immune to such rules, anyway."

Sinclair turned to stare at the creature. "Wait just a moment. You're speaking to me in English. How is that, if you speak only the ancient tongue? Or do I merely hear it as English?"

The birdman laughed, though it sounded rather like a cackling sort of chirp. "You know, that is a very perceptive question! So few of your kind ever come here now, that I'd quite forgotten how your limited minds work. There was a time when the great men of old walked here at will, entering our realms through the recitation of magical phrases and incantations. Wisely, they sought me out, and

I communed with them, teaching them many of my secrets. How I miss those days! One grows lonely, you know. Are you here for instruction, Charles Sinclair? Are you on a quest for knowledge?"

"A quest?" Charles asked wearily, searching through his foggy memory. He found himself with significant gaps, but the more he tried to summon up the past, the more his head ached. "I'm not sure why I'm here, to be honest. Assuming this isn't all a dream, I'm quite certain I did not arrive by magical means. It is a pagan practise, forbidden by God."

"Which god?" the birdman challenged the human.

"Almighty God, of course. The Creator of all."

"So he claims!" the other complained, its feathers bristling into spikes. "I know of only one who deserves such a title, and it is not the pretender to whom you refer, Englishman! Clearly, you require instruction, but you are far too stupid to waste my energies upon, Charles Sinclair."

The hybrid creature rubbed its hands together, bending low and speaking in a whisper. "However, I like you, human. You are decidedly different from others of your kind. Therefore, I shall bypass the usual rules and recommend a highly respected tutor who'd work well for a man of your capacity for thought, but it will cost you a little. What have you to offer?"

"I've no idea," Sinclair replied as he searched all his pockets. He still wore the beautiful ensemble Martin Kepelheim had created for the wedding, and nestled within the shallow watch pocket, the marquess discovered a woman's hairpin. "Why do I have this?" he asked himself. Then, as though whispered into his thoughts, the sweet memory returned. "The pin was in Beth's hair to secure her coronet. She removed it at the reception."

"*Re-cep-tion?*" the creature echoed, purposefully lingering on each syllable. "What is a re-cep-tion? Tis a nonsensical word. I'm sure you just made it up!"

Holding the pin up to what little light emerged from the strangely coloured moon, Sinclair smiled as the delightful memory played through his thoughts. "She looked absolutely radiant. More lovely than any bride in history," he said dreamily. He then turned to the strange creature to explain. "A reception is a sort of party, given in honour of a person or persons. This one followed our wedding, you see. As a duchess, Elizabeth had worn the Branham coronet, but after a while, it grew intolerably heavy for her, poor thing. My wife's neck is slender and quite delicate. The crown is solid gold and decorated with a great many, large stones."

"Stones? What sort of stones?" the birdman prodded. "Are they living or dead?"

Sinclair blinked as he snapped out of the pleasant reverie. "Living stones? What on earth do you mean? There is no such thing."

"Earth? Bah! Your stupidity grows by the second, human!" it cawed. "You left the place you call *earth* long ago, and of course, there are living stones. They're all about you, fool! These fixed stones are the ancient travellers who failed to answer the questions correctly. Have you no eyes to see?"

"Apparently not, and I'm afraid I have no money, if that's what you want."

"No money at all? Then, what is that upon your waistcoat?" the creature asked. "It's so very shiny."

"Do you mean my watch?"

Charles opened the Sir John Bennett timepiece and pressed the release latch. Within the gold case, the inscribed words glowed in the darkness as though touched by fire: *To my Captain, whom I shall ever love. Your Beth.*

Seeing Elizabeth's engraved promise, the memory of her abduction flooded into his mind with the force of a million regrets, and Sinclair dropped to his knees as though the weight of every rock and tree in this mad world pressed down mercilessly upon his breaking heart.

"She's gone! My beautiful Beth, I failed her completely, and she's gone!" he wailed. All the forgotten moments crystallised with cruel clarity and fused into a mass of pain: the wedding, the reception, the abduction, and the desperate chase into Whitechapel to rescue his wife—only to arrive too late.

"Trent stole her," Charles whispered as he twisted the gold ring upon his left hand.

"Trent?" the bird echoed. "Now, that is a name I know. What did this fellow do to you?"

"He stole the most precious heart in all the world, for he is a fiend with no heart of his own!" the marquess shouted. "He spent years torturing her; years planning his revenge. I should have seen it. I should have stopped it!"

"Seen what? Stopped what?" the birdman asked hungrily.

"I should have stopped *him*. I should never have allowed Elizabeth to leave my sight. As soon as I looked away, Trent abducted her through a mirror. We rode to her rescue, but his wolf creatures attacked, trying to stop us. And then the house was on fire—Beth was trapped inside it! Dear God in heaven, I think she may be dead!" he cried out in anguish. "No, please, Lord, please! Let this be a nightmare. I beg you! Let me open my eyes and find she's sleeping beside me and that all is well. That she is safe and unharmed. Please, oh, *please!*"

The bereaved husband fell prostrate upon the ground, all strength leaving him, his hands clutching at the sparse tufts of dry, yellow grass that grew amongst the rough stones. He sobbed in agony for a very long time until not one tear remained. At last, he lay motionless, hardly breathing, as though willing himself to die.

The yellow-eyed birdman crouched beside the inconsolable human, listening to the slowing of his heart, trying to discern the reason behind the very odd behaviour. The gnarled trees bent low, their branches drooping, and even the bones and harsh rocks seemed to grow moist in sympathetic response to the human's agony.

The silvery mist thickened, and soon, the entire unearthly realm was cloaked with an impenetrable shroud of deep sadness and endless sorrow.

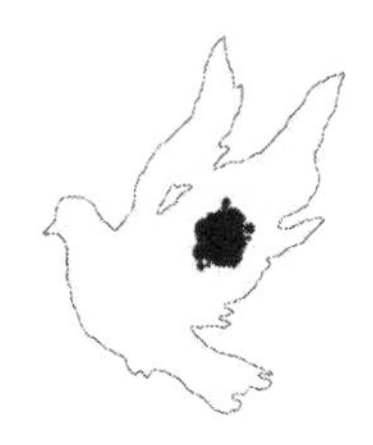

CHAPTER ONE

19th November, 9:13 pm, Montmore House Sanitarium

"Do forgive the interruption, my lord," said a stylishly liveried butler as he entered the library. "A very well-dressed gentleman with a foreign accent insists upon seeing you without delay. He will not take no for an answer."

Dr. Henry MacAlpin glanced up from his book, a densely worded treatise on the cathartic method by Josef Breuer. The physician took the embossed calling card, his dark brows rising.

"I see. Show Prince Anatole in at once."

The handsome alienist straightened his waistcoat. MacAlpin briefly considered putting on the formal coat he'd removed after finishing his evening rounds, but decided against it. The Scotsman had not one whit of trepidation when it came to meeting royalty, for he descended from the bluest of blood, with direct lineages that could be traced back to nearly all the ruling Scottish Houses: Alpin, Dunkeld, Bruce, and Stuart. Despite this remarkable pedigree, the 7th Viscount Salperton smiled respectfully as the tall Russian entered the drawing room.

Henry possessed unusually keen observational skills and an intuition about people that seldom missed the mark. With a mere glance, he instantly summarised the man before him. First of all, Anatole Romanov stood taller than any other man Henry had ever met. Six-and-a-half feet at least, and his ears had a peculiar shape. MacAlpin had made a study of auricular morphology and developed a theory of inheritance based upon similarities amongst siblings. This man had ears that nearly came to a point, and his almond-shaped eyes emphasised the unusual anatomy. His broad, muscled shoulders and slim waist implied diligence and training.

He used both hands equally well, though he favoured his right. His clothing revealed a love of fine fabrics and access to wealth, though he took no thought for flashy trends but dressed to please himself, choosing colours that enhanced and complemented pale skin and raven hair. His eyes were of a peculiarly light shade, and the tight pupils caused the large irises to shimmer all the more. And those eyes were sharp and alert. The serenity in his face and manner exuded a sense of calm. He smiled often and thought deeply. All told, this was a formidable and most unusual man.

Salperton shook the visitor's hand. "Welcome to Montmore House, Your Highness. How may I help you?"

"Thank you for seeing me at so late an hour, Lord Salperton," Romanov began. "Forgive my brash intrusion. I hope I do not interrupt."

"Not at all. I've already seen my resident patients for the evening and was catching up on the latest medical theories. Please, won't you sit?"

"Thank you, but there is no time. I came to ask if you might accompany me. It is my understanding that you keep watch on Dr. Alfred Simon's patients whilst he visits America."

"I do. Are you ill, sir?"

Romanov shook his head, the movement causing a long strand of raven hair to dislodge from the scarlet ribbon that secured it at the back of his head. He tucked the strand behind his ear with such grace that the movement appeared choreographed.

"I am never ill, Doctor," the prince explained. "However, a houseguest is. She is dear to me, and I called upon Dr. Simon this past hour only to learn of his trip to New York and that you had promised to act in his stead. My home is not far, a few minutes by coach. I pray that you will accompany me, for my guest's condition worsens by the hour."

"Is your guest injured?"

"Feverish and unable to awaken," the prince replied, his tone revealing deep concern. "She was caught in the sudden snowstorm last night, and her attire left her unprepared to ward off so deep a chill."

Instantly, Henry made up his mind. "Saunders!" he called to the butler as he stepped into the brightly lit foyer.

The tall servant emerged from a nearby office with his master's medical bag in one hand and a brown tweed overcoat in the other.

"I've taken the liberty, sir," he said offering the coat to Salperton.

"Still reading my mind, it seems," the viscount laughed. "Saunders, tell Mrs. Winstead that I may be away for some time. Ask her to keep an eye on our patients for me, particularly Mrs. Crossfield as she's still somewhat melancholy."

"Of course, sir. Will you be travelling with the prince, or shall I ask Goddard to bring your coach to the front?"

"No need to bother Goddard. I'll go with His Highness, and I can hire a hansom for the return trip, if need be. Prince, shall we?"

Taking the red leather bag in his right hand, the viscount followed the enigmatic Russian to a magnificent coach bearing the Romanov coat of arms. He stepped into the plush interior, settling into its leather seat. "I'd never realised a Russian royal lived so close to me," he said as the midnight black horses began to trot southward.

"Very few are aware of my presence," the prince explained. "I've many residences throughout London, but the castle is my favourite."

"Castle? Surely, you don't mean Ghaist Castle. Do forgive me, I'm sure it has a far nicer name, but that's what the Fulham villagers call it. Ghaist Castle."

"Ghaist? Does it mean guest?"

"I'm afraid not. It's an old Scots word meaning ghost. Forgive me, if it insults you, Your Highness. It wasn't my intent."

To Salperton's relief, Romanov began to laugh, and his light eyes crinkled at the corners. "Ghost, you say? I had no idea my home bore such a curious name! Why is it called this?"

"My mother grew up in Fulham at Montmore House, which now serves as a refuge and place of healing for those with problems of the heart and mind. When I was a boy, we'd often visit here, and I asked my late grandfather about the castle. He told me to avoid it, for it had a dark reputation. Honestly, I'd no idea anyone even lived there, for it's always struck me as uninhabited. Fulham's villagers insist that it disappears from time to time, but surely that is mere fairy tale. Buildings do not vanish any more than people do."

"Such a notion is, of course, impossible," the prince said evenly, but Salperton noticed a hint of sarcasm to his tone. "I believe your father is the Earl of Lasberington. Is that right?"

"Yes, do you know him?"

"We met a few times, long ago, when he was attached to the British Embassy in St. Petersburg. Imagine my surprise at discovering his son is a physician who lives so close to me! Sir, this guest of mine is also of your class. An English peeress. Her presence at my home must remain a secret. May I rely upon your discretion?"

"Yes, of course," Salperton replied, assuming the woman was the prince's mistress. "I do nothing that might injure or distress my patient, if I can help it. However, if I believe her in danger of any kind, then I reserve the right to act on her behalf. My patient always comes first, regardless of who hires me."

"I should expect nothing less," Romanov answered. "May I ask something rather unusual?"

The Scot smiled, his eyes sharp. "More unusual than a Russian prince appearing on my doorstep late at night? What might that be, sir?"

"It is but a trifle. I should like to touch you, if you'd allow it. Tis, perhaps, a vanity, but I consider myself able to learn about a person through touch. A gift inherited from my creator, you might say."

"That's an odd way to refer to one's forebears, but if it assists you, then I'll allow it. Must it be bare skin, or are you able to conduct this ritual through cloth?"

"I admire your direct nature, Lord Salperton. Or do you prefer that I call you Dr. MacAlpin?"

"Whatever you wish to call me is fine. I use the medical title with my patients. For to some, my peerage titles are rather offputting." The Scotsman removed his right glove and extended the hand. "Will this do?"

"Admirably." The prince placed two fingers upon the back of Henry's hand and closed his eyes. Many minutes passed before Romanov spoke again, but when he did, it was a strange series of observations.

"Your mother's name was Catherine Marie. She called you 'little Hal'. She died of consumption when you were six years old. You watched her pass, and she smiled as she crossed over. She told you about an angel who came to take her to God, a beautiful man with golden hair and iridescent skin made of light. When she died, your father entered a state of deep and endless mourning, and you were left to find your own way. Your governess, Miss Vera Abernathy, kept you company for two hours a day, but you spent the remainder alone, wandering the woods and streams near Inverary. Your father is a kind man, but he never quite understood the extreme bond 'twixt you and your mother. You're related to the Drummond dukes through her, for your maternal grandfather, the 6th Viscount Salperton, married the current duke's Aunt Eleanor Stuart. Your father married your mother in his later years. I believe, he is eighty-three presently and seldom travels due to weakness of the limbs."

The viscount listened patiently without comment, his warm brown eyes still. Not even a blink betrayed any emotion he might be feeling, though internally, the words regarding his mother's death struck him deeply. *Help me, Henry! Please! Tell me that I'm not alone. You see them, too, don't you? You see the angels?*

Despite his resolve to remain aloof, Salperton involuntarily shuddered, as though someone had walked across his grave—or hers. *Your mother's insane, Henry. You must keep away from her! She will infect you with her madness!*

"Your mother was not mad," the prince continued, his eyes boring into Salperton's. "Despite what your father feared, she was quite sane. He refused to send her to an asylum—out of love, not neglect or shame. This is why you defied him and abandoned a career in politics to pursue medicine, is it not? You feel closer to your mother, when you help those with similar problems. I admire that."

Salperton drew back the hand and donned the calfskin glove once again, feigning disinterest. "You could have learnt most of that through any peerage history book."

"But not all of it. And none of those books mentions that your dear mother saw angels. One in particular called upon her, and she sketched him many times, did she not? He called himself Shelumiel, peace of God, and his presence calmed your mother as few things in life could. If I told you that Catherine MacAlpin is happier now than she ever thought possible, would it bring you comfort?"

"Forgive me if I appear doubtful, sir, but I could find similar claims from any Cheapside palmist. Speculation and keen observation render almost anyone a prognostic."

"I agree, but as you doubt my gift for telling your past, allow me to offer a glimpse into your future. Neither peerage annual nor observation may enlighten me thus. To begin, you have failed in love, but that is about to change. Twice, you have been engaged to be married, and twice you have been abandoned. I daresay that you will fall in love with the woman you are about to meet, but guard your heart, for hers is taken. However, she will bring you joy beyond your wildest imagination. You will become important to her, also, and even save her life—three times. She will play an important role in your life from this night forward, and through her, you will meet your future wife. I would say more, but I cannot foresee everything. My vision is limited by free will, you understand."

Henry remained unconvinced. "One might say that all vision is limited by free will, meaning the future is ever in flux. I fear your prognostication skills show no keener insight than most who claim to be mystics," the doctor said simply as the coach slowed. "It's true that I've been twice affianced, and as you've implied, both women failed to keep to their affections. One abandoned her promise to follow a worthless poet to Venice, whilst the other chose marriage to a man she perceived had more riches than I. Neither woman is happy at present, though I wish them well."

"As you say, neither is happy, but allow me to escort you to a woman who will forever make you see all others as pale and insignificant. Remember, you have promised to keep her secret. I assure you that doing so is in her best interest—and in that of her husband."

"Her husband?"

"All will become clear soon."

They left the coach, and Salperton followed his host to the main entry. The entire area was lit by torches, and only now did Henry realise that the ruined 'ghost castle' had transformed into a magnificent edifice set amidst jewelled and glittering gardens that whispered of music and springtime. "You must give me the name of your gardener, Highness. I've never seen lilacs bloom in November!"

"Have you not? They are ever in bloom here. Indeed, you will find my home a wealth of impossibilities, Lord Salperton. This way, sir. This ancient door leads to your future."

Shortly before the prince's return, two old friends greeted one another in a comfortably furnished drawing room within the imposing and ghostly fortress known to its inhabitants as Istseleniye House.

"Good evening," Count Riga said cheerfully as he took a chair near the crackling fire. "Has our guest yet awoken?"

"I'm told she sleeps," replied Blinkmire, glancing up from his book. "Miss Ross sits with her. Such a tragedy! Perhaps I am mistaken, but Prince Anatole seemed quite angry about it all, and who can blame him? How dare these Redwing fellows treat a woman of such repute in so callous a manner? Seldom have I seen him so enraged, save when Countess di Specchio left us, of course. I wonder where she's gone, Riga. Do you know? Have you heard any rumours regarding the conniving Italian?"

"Nary a whisper," the hunchback answered. "Though, if there were news, we'd be the last to hear it. The prince's rule, you know."

"Ah, yes," the giant nodded, setting the book aside and removing his spectacles. "Newspapers are anathema. As are any periodicals or journals published within the last six months. Tis a pity, but I suppose I shouldn't complain. After all, our library offers a wide variety of Regency literature and classics, but I'd love to read some of those wonderful stories like the one in *Beeton's Christmas Annual* last year. What was it called again? *A Study in Crimson?*"

"*Scarlet*, I believe," Riga corrected. "A perspicacious fellow, that Holmes. He reminds me of our prince in some ways. Insightful, inscrutable, and wary of women."

"I'd not thought of that!" Blinkmire laughed. "Do you think the author might know our prince?"

"Dr. Doyle? That's a very good question. It's possible, I suppose. After all, Romanov does live a life outside these walls," the count observed.

"I imagine that the prince lives a very interesting life," Blinkmire sighed wistfully. "I understand that he advises the British government on Russian affairs and attends all manner of soirées. Ah, but his is a handsome countenance, and—alas!—ours are not. Twould be nice to have a party now and then, though. Distractions are sorely lacking in our little company, Riga. Since I arrived here many years ago, we've had little to entertain us, save your magnificent cello, of course, and more recently, Miss Kilmeade's light soprano."

"Nonsense, Blinkmire!" the count insisted. "Your voice is admirable, though many of your lower notes are imperceptible to my dull ear. Our Mr. Stanley plays the piano quite well, did you know that? He's promised to perform a duet with me at Christmas. I've asked the prince if he might purchase some new music, and he promised to order a variety of modern choices. I wonder, is he joining us this evening?"

"According to Vasily, His Highness had a call to make elsewhere, but hopes to share a late supper with us. He's very worried about our guest, and I imagine his errand is connected to her welfare in some way. I was asleep when the two of them arrived last night, and she's not come down since. Did you meet her, Riga? Is she as beautiful as I've heard?"

"The duchess is exceedingly beautiful. I'd met her before, though I doubt Her Grace remembers it. I was newly arrived in England, and she was but twelve years old. My, she's certainly matured in those eight seasons!"

"And so she should," Blinkmire agreed, "but why hasn't she come down, I wonder?"

"I fear Duchess Elizabeth may be ill. The dear woman looked quite feverish to my eyes, though my medical knowledge pales to your own. Speaking of medicine, I know yours has been adjusted again. Are you sleeping any better, Stephen?" he asked, using Blinkmire's Christian name.

"How kind of you to ask, Viktor. Yes, it's been an ordeal, of course, adjusting to the prince's new formulation, but I shall master it. The new powder makes me restive, but it has already made a difference. This morning, I measured almost quarter of an inch shorter, and it's only been a fortnight since starting the new regimen. I'd begun to fear that the continued growth would leave me unable to fit through my own door!"

Count Viktor Ardelescu Riga smiled. "You are a man of great stature, my friend, and I do not refer to your physicality, but rather to your heart. Oh, I hear Miss Kilmeade."

Brona entered the parlour, finding both men standing politely, as was their custom. "Ya really don' have ta do tha' fer me, ya know," she told them. "I never go' such from anyone afore comin' here, though it's real nice tha' ya think o' me. I been wonderin' if anyone's seen the prince?"

"Not since eight o'clock," Riga answered. "He had an errand to run, as so often happens. But I wonder, Miss Kilmeade, have you met our newest guest?"

"I did indeed. This mornin' after breakfast. Poor thing's all a-fever."

"Oh, I do hope the lady isn't ill!" Blinkmire fretted. "Fevers can mean so many different things. I do not profess to any formal medical training, but my books inform me of an entire roster of maladies conjoined to fever! Typhus being one of the worst. Perhaps, we should ask Vasily or Antony to speak with Cook. I'm sure she would know of herbs that might bring down our guest's temperature."

The sound of men's voices and the dull clatter of leather heels on flagstone interrupted their discussion, and all eyes turned towards the broad, drawing room doorway. The lights always remained dim in deference to Kilmeade's peculiar ocular condition, but the foyer now brightened slightly as the butler lit a pair of sconces. Romanov entered the parlour, his generally serene features lined with worry.

"Oh, sir, we're relieved to see you!" Blinkmire blurted anxiously. "Our guest may be ill. Shouldn't someone fetch Dr. Simon?"

"I've already taken care of that, Mr. Blinkmire," Romanov replied as the viscount stepped into the opening. "Dr. Simon is away, but this gentleman is keeping watch on all his patients whilst Simon expands his horizons in America. This is Dr. Henry MacAlpin, who also happens to be a viscount in his own right and son of a prominent earl in Scotland. Doctor, allow me to introduce my most esteemed friends, Mr. Blinkmire and Count Riga. The lovely lady in their midst is our Miss Kilmeade. Brona, is Ida upstairs?" he asked, handing his cloak to the footman.

"Aye, sir, tha' she is," the pale Irishwoman answered. "An' it's a good thing, too, for the lady's forehead's warm as a stone in summer!"

"We'll go up at once," the prince said. "Vasily, set another place for our physician."

"That's thoughtful of you, but unnecessary, Your Highness. I ate an hour ago."

"Nonsense! Mrs. Aslanov and her assistant prepare foods to tempt any palate. But as we may be tending to our guest for some time, the others should eat without us," he added, referring to Kilmeade and the men. "Come, Doctor. Your patient awaits."

Romanov led the physician towards a wide, stone staircase, and the two wound their way upwards to a grand apartment that dominated the northwest side of the castle. As they entered the bedchamber, a willowy woman with strawberry blonde hair curtsied politely. "Your Highness, I'm very glad you're home, sir."

"Miss Ross, this is Dr. MacAlpin. He is Dr. Simon's partner."

"Sir," she greeted with a polite curtsy.

"A pleasure, Miss Ross," the physician replied with a formal bow. Then, noticing a woman asleep beneath the carved canopy of a four-poster bed, he asked, "Is this is my patient?"

The prince crossed to the bed and took the sleeper's hand. "She is indeed. Ida, has she spoken?"

"No, my lord," Ross answered, "though, she does whisper now and again in her fever. She keeps askin' after a Captain. I cannot say who that might be, but I do know her, sir. As I told you this morning, I've met her before."

"Yes, I'm aware of your history with this lady, Ida. Now, if you will close the door, please? Supper awaits downstairs. Go eat, my dear. You look worn through."

"I shall, my lord. Thank you." Ross curtsied and left the chamber.

MacAlpin began unpacking instruments from his bag. "Why do you wish this woman's name to be secret, sir? Is she here against her will?"

"The answer is more complicated than you might imagine, Lord Salperton. The lady is married, though not to me. I shall return her to the gentleman, but not yet. For the present, she is safest here."

"Safest? That is a curious word implying danger. By whom is she endangered?"

"Again, the answer is complicated. Even Dr. Simon is unaware of all that occurs within this house. Is it pneumonia?"

"I cannot say. Tell me her history. How did she arrive here, and what precipitated the illness? And do not repeat your unsatisfying answer of complication, sir. I am intelligent enough to apprehend intricacies of the mind; I rather think I can handle any perceived depths to your reply."

Romanov smiled broadly. "You are a man of very interesting temperament and conviction, Lord Salperton, which makes me trust you all the more. Do you not recognise her?"

"Should I?"

"If you read British or French newspapers, you should. Even the Americans have published her photograph many times in recent years. The lady married on Sunday morning."

MacAlpin used a stethoscope to listen to her heart, his mind already sorting through observed signs: moist, flushed skin; extreme fatigue (for the lady did not so much as twitch when touched), and shallow breathing, punctuated occasionally by dry coughs.

"Sunday?" he mused, only half listening. "Why would that mean anything to me? Oh, wait," he added, turning to stare at the Russian. "Good heavens, are you telling me that she is the Duchess of Branham? The woman who was abducted from her own wedding celebration?"

"I am saying that very thing. Can you now appreciate why I wish her presence to remain a secret? I tell you, sir, that she is in grave danger from the same group that abducted her."

MacAlpin paused as he counted his patient's radial pulse. "It is far too quick and weak," he muttered to himself, and then glanced up. "How am I to know that *you* are not her abductor? The press have said nothing about her rescue. In fact, they despair that she is even alive. I dare not imagine what her poor husband must be going through!"

Romanov sat upon the bed and took her hand. "Twas I who rescued her, Lord Salperton," he whispered, his deep voice steeped in agony. "You cannot begin to imagine the horrors she faced. And so bravely. So very bravely," he added, kissing the pale palm. "I shall return this dear lady to her husband as soon as both are well enough, and their enemies subdued."

"*Both?* What of her husband? Is he also ill?"

"The marquess lies in a grave condition," the Russian answered. "I fear for his mind as well as his body."

"That is more than the reporters of London are aware, Your Highness. Nothing in any of the papers indicates that Haimsbury is anything other than bereaved and desperately worried. Where do you obtain your information?"

"I am a friend to the family," the prince answered obliquely. "In time I shall reveal more, but for the present, tend to the duchess. I wish to return her to her husband in the bloom of health."

"Then, you must explain how she came to be in this condition and why she resides here and not in hospital. Explain these dangers to me, if you expect me to be your accomplice."

"Finish your appraisal, and then you and I shall speak further."

The prince left and shut the door. Alone now with an ailing woman, known to be abducted, Henry wondered why he shouldn't simply summon the police and be done with it.

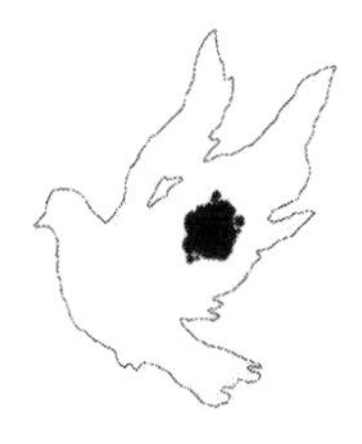

CHAPTER TWO

Early morning, 21st November – Haimsbury House

The room lay in semi-darkness, lit only by a small, electric lamp. A beautiful bed dominated the chamber, a faithful reproduction of one from a famous French palace. A fireplace surround, formed out of carved white breccia and black Campan marble, protected a cheerful fire, fed by two rows of gas jets beneath a cast iron plate. Bookcases and closets dominated the walls on either side of the elegant fireplace, and standing before this warm sentry, two sofas, upholstered in striped blue silk, beckoned visitors to sit.

However, the girl did not sit beside the fire, nor had she chosen to lounge upon a sofa. She sat beside the bed, weary but vigilant, reading aloud from a periodical. Her voice was small but sweet, and her diction crisp. A pair of clear blue eyes rimmed with dark brown lashes darted back and forth, moving rhythmically from left to right, as she pronounced the lines; telling a story, whilst her smooth-skinned hands turned each page of the colourful magazine.

"*Holmes was certainly not a difficult man to live with,*" she read out softly. "*He was quiet in his ways, and his habits were regular. It was rare for him to be up after ten at night, and he had invariably breakfasted and gone out before I rose in the morning. Sometimes he spent his day at the chemical laboratory, sometimes in the dissecting-rooms, and occasionally in long walks, which appeared to take him into the lowest portions of the City.*"

Adele Marie Stuart sighed, for she could see no change in the sleeper who dreamt upon the broad bed. "Are you listening, Cousin Charles? Do you hear me?"

The eleven-year-old set aside the magazine. "Perhaps, you'd rather I talk instead of read. I don't know if you're aware of your surroundings, but you've been here since Sunday night. You're in your own house, within a spectacular bedchamber, but then it was you had it redecorated, isn't it? As I said, you came here Sunday, when my brother and the others brought you in the police wagon. I think Paul called it a maria."

She adjusted the brightly patterned quilt to make sure both the sleeper's arms were covered, and that he was warm.

"Better? Your hands had gone cold. Now, what was I saying? Oh, yes! Sunday night. After you and Paul left with Uncle James, Mr. Baxter called a prayer meeting, and every servant gathered and joined hands in the foyer to pray. Auntie Tory, Aunt Mary, Miss Jenkins, Mrs. Alcorn, and all of us ladies prayed with them, too. I don't think I've ever experienced anything like it before. We prayed and prayed, and it seemed like an eternity passed before Paul sent word of what had happened. But you mustn't worry about that. Cousin Beth will come home. My brother is making sure of it, and Paul is quite fierce when he puts his mind to something."

Adele paused, realising she'd promised not to mention Elizabeth, just in case Charles could hear.

"You've not awoken since then. It's Wednesday morning now. Just after eight. I spent most of yesterday in here, learning basic nursing care from Dr. Emerson. He says you might sleep for days yet. He called it a concussion, I think. Did I tell you already about the magnificent owl? He was quite amazing! He's watched from a branch outside your window every night since you were injured. He has snowy feathers and very large eyes, and the most regal bearing. He must be the king of owls, I suppose. Oh, and this morning, I saw a little bird at the window sill," she said sweetly. "It was quite small, but it sang very beautifully and made me think of Cousin Beth. Aunt Mary called it a greenfinch. Mary knows a lot about birds, and we plan to put out some berries and seeds for it later—and water, of course. All living creatures must have water, mustn't they?"

The girl gulped nervously, unsure just what to say next. She reached for the water carafe that sat upon the marquess's bedside table and poured four ounces into a small glass. "Will you drink this, if I help you?" she asked him.

Sinclair made no reply. Unconscious since Sunday night, he lay quiet and still, all alone in the carved mahogany tester bed he'd had specially built for his bride.

The inner door to the chamber opened, admitting a tall man with shoulder-length, chestnut hair and clear blue eyes. He wore a wing-collar shirt, grey trousers, striped waistcoat and paisley cravat but no coat. The sleepless earl had dressed early and spent the past two hours meeting with his London agents.

"Allow me, Della," Stuart told his sister as he neared the bed. "Has he spoken?"

"Not a word," she answered sadly, "and he hasn't moved at all, though his pulse is regular. I check it every hour, just as Dr. Emerson taught me."

The earl smiled proudly. "You shall make a very fine doctor one day, darling. He'll speak soon. Here now, I'll steady his head whilst you hold the glass," he told his sister as he carefully placed one hand beneath his cousin's head. "Put the glass to his lips and gently tip it. His reflexes will take over, and he'll swallow automatically, but it must go into his throat quite slowly."

Obediently, the willowy girl held the water glass up to the unconscious man's mouth. "Please, drink it, Cousin Charles. Dr. Emerson says you must have water, if you're to return to us. Won't you, please, take a sip? Just a tiny one, for me?"

The earl put a finger against his cousin's chin and pushed down to force the dry lips apart. As the water trickled into his open mouth, the unconscious marquess swallowed reflexively, and the prominent Adam's apple slid up and down his long throat.

"He's drinking it!" Adele exclaimed, spilling half the contents in her excitement. "Oh, I am sorry, Cousin Charles. I've made your shirt all wet. Paul, I'm sorry. Shall I ring for Mr. Baxter?"

"Yes, I think that's a good idea, and then, you should go down to breakfast. Victoria's asking for you. That new Christmas music we ordered last week arrived in the morning post."

"But I've only just started reading the story to him," she pleaded. "Cousin Charles told me that he wanted to read about Sherlock Holmes, but didn't have the time. May I come back after I eat? I promise to do nothing more than read."

"Yes, of course, you may. I'm sure he hears every word you read to him, Della. There are few voices in this world that mean so much to Charles as yours. Go on, now. He might even be awake by the time you return."

She kissed the marquess's shadowed cheek and quietly left the room. Once the door had shut firmly, the earl began unbuttoning the yellow silk shirt, talking to his cousin as Emerson had instructed the family to do.

"You've missed all sorts of excitement whilst enjoying your dreams," he told his sleeping cousin. "You have an entire city praying for you, Charles. The queen sends a messenger to the house twice daily, asking about you, and Salisbury has stopped by as well. Most in the circle have paid their respects, of course. Kepelheim has moved into one of your guest suites, and he's diligently working on your father's coded journal; that is, when he's not sharing tea and biscuits with Baxter and Mary Wilsham in the kitchens. Mary's been a source of great comfort to all of us, and she's become like a mother to Della."

Aubrey paused, trying to find news that wouldn't alarm his cousin. He decided to avoid any mention of Elizabeth, just in case Charles could hear.

"Let's see, what else?" he continued. "Bob Morehouse's widow sent a letter, which I've put on your desk along with all the others. Sir Charles Warren called yesterday afternoon. He and his wife sent a basket of flowers. In fact, the foyer of your house begins to look rather like a flower stall. Scotland Yard detectives and uniformed men from all across the city ask after you, and there are hundreds of telegrams from all over the world, Charles. All are praying for your recovery."

The door opened, and Cornelius Baxter entered. "Allow me to do that, sir," the butler insisted.

Aubrey handed him the damp shirt. "Has there been any news?"

"No, sir. However, Inspector Reid sent a wire. He said nothing about my lady, but asks if you could join him at Leman Street at quarter till eleven. He's arranged to speak with the fire brigade captain regarding the marquess's East End house. I'm sure that the duchess escaped, sir, and before long my lady will be back here with us."

"Yes, of course, she will. And when she does return, we must make certain her husband is awake and ready to put his arms 'round her."

The earl stepped to the northeast window and pulled the blue silk draperies to one side. Instantly, the shadowy bedchamber cheered, each wall painted with bright shafts of sunlight.

"Charles spared no expense when he remodeled his house, and this room is a showpiece! It's everything Beth ever wanted. Even this bed. When she was a girl, our little duchess told me that when married, she wanted a golden tester bed, just like the one in the queen's chamber at Versailles. Apparently, she told Charles as well. This is a perfect reproduction, only Charles had carved doves added to each of the corners. He did it all to make Elizabeth happy."

"It is the equal to any in France by my reckoning, sir," Baxter agreed. "Not even Her Majesty has such a magnificent bed, I'll wager!"

Paul sat on the bed's edge, moving the blue and yellow chintz coverlet to one side. "He will wake up, won't he, Baxter?"

"Of course, he will, my lord. Perhaps, even today. Now, why don't you join the others for breakfast, sir? I can remain with his lordship until Dr. Emerson arrives at ten. You're worn through from lack of sleep and worry."

"How can I sleep, when I've failed them both so miserably, Baxter?" the earl whispered, his eyes on his cousin's pale face. "I was supposed to protect them, but instead I allowed my attention to wander, and look what happened!"

"You did not fail them, sir. Not at all. Now, you must cease this melancholy. Twill do not one jot of good to either of your cousins," the butler said, placing a supportive hand on the earl's shoulder. "You work far too hard, if I may say so. Enjoy some time with your aunt and sister. Allow me to look after his lordship. I'll send word should anything change."

"Very well," he answered, grudgingly leaving the bedchamber.

The aging butler found a clean pair of blue silk pyjamas in the wardrobe next door and began to dress the sleeper with tender care. Once he'd made Sinclair comfortable, Cornelius Baxter sat into the upholstered armchair left empty by Lady Adele. He dearly loved Charles Sinclair, and his heart felt heavier than it had in many years.

"Where are you, sir?" he whispered. "Do you hear us when we speak to you?"

Sighing, Cornelius Baxter picked up the copy of *Beeton's* from which Adele Stuart had been reading.

"Shall I continue where Lady Adele left off? Let's see, if I can find the page she has marked. Ah, yes. Page eleven." Baxter cleared his throat and settled back into the chair, reading aloud, "*As the weeks went by, my interest in him and my curiosity as to his aims in life, gradually deepened and increased. His very person and appearance were such as to strike the attention of the most casual observer. In height he was rather over six feet, and so excessively lean that he seemed to be considerably taller. His eyes were sharp and piercing, save during those intervals of torpor to which I have alluded; and his thin, hawk-like nose gave his whole expression an air of alertness and decision.*"

The marquess never so much as twitched the entire time, but though the butler had no way of knowing it, Sinclair did hear some of what was said. However, to his dreaming mind, it played as a sort of background noise to a very peculiar conversation...

CHAPTER THREE

"What did you say your name was?" Charles asked the birdman.

Proudly fluffing up the feathers trimming his cloak, the creature stared at the visitor, blinking rapidly. "Name? Another stupid question. Names mean nothing, unless, of course, you know their true significance, which I very much doubt you would. It is clear to me that you require a tutor. That shining watch will do for payment. If your instructor agrees to work for nothing, then I shall return it to you. If not, then he and I shall share it."

"I will not bargain away the only connexion I have to my wife!" the confused human declared angrily. "As to names, I presume you have none, since you are loath to offer it. I'll find my own way, thank you!"

Sinclair turned a hundred and eighty degrees, hoping to escape the creature's taunts by returning the way he'd come, but to his dismay the movement offered no such thing. He still faced the same direction with the birdman standing in front of him, just as before.

"I do have a name, though you would never comprehend its meaning without instruction. I might offer several lessons, on *credit*," the bird creature suggested slyly. "When you've learnt enough to find your way home, then..."

"Home? Are you saying there is a way out of this horrid place, back to my own world? Back to my wife?"

"Yes, but what if she is dead?" it asked. "You seemed to think her dead not that long ago. All that senseless weeping over a woman! What will you do next, I wonder? Sing?"

"She cannot be dead," he whispered. "She must not be."

The bird thing's yellow eyes grew round and glassy. "Is she pretty?" it asked, stepping closer. "She must be, otherwise, why would you care about so dull a thing as a wife?"

"She is anything but dull. Elizabeth is the most beautiful woman in all of creation."

"Prettier than Eve?" it asked, the lips twisting oddly. "It has been a very long time ago, but as I recall Eve was quite lovely, though somewhat naive. Such soft skin and hair."

"Who *are* you?" the marquess insisted, his eyes narrowing. "You do nothing but spout nonsense! How do I know that I can believe anything you tell me? Perhaps, *you* have her! What have you done with Elizabeth? Where is my wife?"

"Done? *Done!*" the birdman screeched in irritation. Its peculiar head bobbed up and down like a child's might when trying for an apple on All Hallows Eve, and it hopped from one foot to another as though stamping out a fire. "I have done nothing with your wife, human! If you must know, the traitor took her. She lies in a fever, calling out the name of some fellow named Captain. Since your name is Charles, then I must presume this Captain is her lover. Typical behaviour for a woman! They have no loyalty. Why would you wish for a wife who is unfaithful, human? Can you not get yourself another? You're not all *that* ugly."

Charles's heart leapt. "Beth is alive? No, wait a moment. What do you mean the traitor took her? Took her where? How can I get there? I must find her!"

"I have no idea where he took her," the gatekeeper said, growing bored with the game. "There is a cottage not far from here. Perhaps, you will find your answer there, providing you can reach it."

"Which direction?"

"Now that is the right question at last! It lies behind one of Seven Gates," the gatekeeper explained. "However, without instruction one is likely to choose poorly and end up in a most disagreeable place. How confident are you of your ability to navigate a complicated maze?"

"If this maze leads to my wife, then I'll do it, though I might die trying. Tell me, Creature, where do I begin?"

"The best place to begin any quest is with knowledge. Since you refuse to accept instruction, fool of a human, your task is made all the harder."

The birdman snapped his fingers, and the thick mist parted, revealing a curving stone wall. It rose high into the night air, soaring to seventy feet or more. Its stones were of every shape and size. The smooth surfaces glittered in the peculiar moon's pale light as though encrusted with diamonds, but as the human looked more closely, these winking diamonds revealed themselves to be thousands of tiny eyes.

The contours of the stones followed irregular shapes, yet each had been placed against its neighbour with such precision that no mortar could be seen. A narrow opening stood just to Sinclair's right, and within its black portal, the hideous eyes of hundreds of ravenous birds blinked as though waiting for the marquess to enter so their feast might commence.

"What is this?" Sinclair asked, approaching the massive structure.

"This is the first of the seven *preliminary* gates," the gatekeeper spoke, his voice drenched in deceit.

"Preliminary?"

"Do you never listen, human?" it complained. "This is a maze! Navigating it requires skill and tutelage; endless lessons in the deeper mysteries of truth and near truth. Failure to make even one correct turn will lead you into a morass of spiralling doom and despair. Are you certain you wouldn't barter that shiny watch in exchange for a hint? Such information could greatly increase your chance of reaching the cottage at the centre. Your chance of traversing the entire maze without an error is approximately one in eight hundred twenty-three thousand, five hundred and forty-three."

Sinclair stood before the mysterious gate, his eyes on the sighted stones that formed it. "Your calculation is incorrect, Creature. If there are seven gates, then I have a one in seven chance."

The birdman flashed a mischievous grin. "You would, if there weren't seven gates beyond each of these, and seven more beyond those, totalling seven walls with seven gates apiece. But your chances are based upon the hypothesis that the gates remain fixed, which they do not—hence the *approximation* of your chances. I've told you many times now, human: it is a maze of *living* stones. Do you wish to try or not? Make up your mind, for I have other matters to attend. I am a very busy gatekeeper, after all."

Charles gazed down at his wedding ring. "One chance in over eight hundred thousand of succeeding. Beth would do it for me, I know it. What guarantee have I that you speak the truth, Nameless Creature?"

The birdman crossed its long arms; the beaked nose in the air. "Despite your insults, what reason have I to lie?"

"Because there is the slenderest hope that I might choose correctly. In which case, I would escape your hellish prison."

The birdman arched its feathery brows, and a chilling smile crept across its unnatural face. "You *might*. Many have thought to do so, and nearly all have failed. There is always an exception to the rule; or so I've read. A person who cheats the system, so to speak—who escapes defeat. You must choose, human. Which of the first seven will you enter to begin this quest?"

Sinclair considered the forbidding structure. "Not this one," he announced as he turned towards the right. "I very much doubt that you would lead me to the correct portal."

The marquess prayed silently as he followed the curving wall, which stretched to greater and greater length as he proceeded. The birdman bounced alongside the human, saying nothing helpful, merely grunting (or laughing in bird-like fashion) each time Sinclair seemed ready to make a decision. Finally, after a dreadfully long time, the marquess stopped in front of the seventh opening. A pair of etched black pillars formed the gateway, and Charles could see himself reflected in their glassy surfaces.

Obsidian, he realised. *Just like the mirrors Susanna Morgan told Paul about. The ones used to imprison Watchers. Might this be their origin?*

The creature appeared pleased. "This is a fine looking gate, and I believe it is the correct one at last. Do you choose to enter, human, or are you afraid?"

A collection of ravens and other strange birds flocked to the gate as though assembling to consider judgement. *A murder of crows*, Charles thought dismally.

"Enter and be done with it!" the creature shouted.

Charles prayed as he approached the gate. He could hear whispers all about him, some from above, others coming from within the portal, like voices calling him to his death.

Falling to his knees, the desperate marquess folded his hands, the right fingers touching the cool metal of his wedding ring, as he prayed, "Dear Lord in heaven, help me, please. If I make the wrong choice, then I'll never see my wife again! Yet, though I have never felt so terrified in all my life, I trust in you, Lord. Whatever happens next, I trust you and ever shall."

Charles paused for a moment, for he could sense something next to him. A presence unlike any other. The hairs stood up on the back of his neck, and he could hear a sweet voice whispering into his right ear. Tears streamed down his cheeks as he repeated the voice's words:

"*Whither shall I go from thy spirit or whither shall I flee from thy presence? If I ascend up into heaven, thou art* there: if I make my bed in hell, behold, thou *art there. If* I take the wings of the morning, *and* dwell in the uttermost parts of the sea; *even there shall thy hand lead me, and thy right hand shall hold me. If I say, surely the darkness shall cover me; even the night shall be light about me. Yea, the darkness hideth not from thee; but the night shineth as the day: the darkness and the light are* both alike *to thee.*"

"Must you quote from that annoying book?" the birdman complained. "Why would you place your faith in so lax a Saviour? He cares nothing for you."

"Beware of idle words, Creature. Even you are subject to the Almighty!"

"Am I?" it dared ask, stepping close. "If you think the One has sent his Spirit to rescue you, then you are more pitiable than any other who has passed these gates! Deluded and without hope! If God loved you, then why did he send you here? The One has abandoned you, foolish human!"

Charles refused to listen, and he continued the prayer.

"Father of all, I know not where I am, but whither you have taken me, I shall trust in you. If in hell, then you are with me. If in a dream, then you will open my eyes. It makes no difference, for I trust in you to guide me. Help me now to choose, and no matter where this journey ends, I trust you to be there with me and with my beloved duchess."

Charles then lifted his right foot and took the first step into darkness.

CHAPTER FOUR

11:03 a.m. – 21st November

The house at No. 12 Columbia Road looked like a charred husk of its former self. Curious neighbours watched as Edmund Reid stood with Paul Stuart amongst the melting snow and ashes, including a young woman in a green cloth coat just inside the entrance to the Empress Hotel.

Near the edge of the front yard, an iron post, as well as the surrounding grass and paving stones, still showed traces of Sinclair's blood. The earl knelt beside the post, running a gloved hand up the side. "Charles struck this with very great force, Edmund. He should be dead. In fact, I thought he was dead, when I saw him. God help us, what an awful night that was!"

"God did help us, Paul, because Charles is alive," the shorter man observed, pulling his coat collar up against the cold. "Here comes our fireman. It looks as though he's brought his superior."

Two men approached from the opposite side of Columbia. The taller cut a fine figure in a double-breasted coat of dark wool over matching trousers. He wore no hat, and an unkempt mane of silver curled behind a pair of large ears. A scraggly moustache drooped below the corners of his mouth and continued into an equally scraggly chin beard, but the man's bearing reflected military service. The second wore a similar coat and trousers, and a soft felt hat protected his balding pate from the dank cold. He stood a head shorter than the other, with a belly almost as soft as the hat.

"Good morning, Captain Shaw," Reid called to the military-looking fellow. "Lord Aubrey, allow me to introduce Captain Eyre Shaw, Superintendent of the Metropolitan Fire Brigade."

"Captain Shaw and I are old friends, Ed," the earl said as he extended his hand in fellowship. "Thank you for meeting us."

"Happy to help, Lord Aubrey. This gentleman is C-District's Officer-in-Charge Bertie Lintel. His men doused the fire here on Sunday night, and a few of them engaged some of those curious wild animals," he added, casting a strange look at his district officer. "That fellow at *The Star*'s making hay of all that, as you surely know."

"Yes, I'm aware of those reports," the earl replied, exchanging glances with Reid. "Many of the local citizenry suffered hallucinations on Sunday. Poisoned water caused by a granary. Have you determined the cause of the fire yet?"

Shaw had known the Stuarts for over three decades, beginning with Duke James in the Crimean War and later as a Chief Constable in Belfast. He'd learnt when *not* to ask for clarification on a matter, and the former army rifleman instantly recognised the earl's intentional shift in topic as such a moment.

"No, sir, we've found no cause for the fire anywhere within the house. It has gas lines, of course, but there's no piping to the fireplaces—only the sconces. All these appear functional and in good working order."

"Might arson be involved?" Aubrey asked. "Someone broke into the house a week before this happened. He could have disconnected a pipe."

"Perhaps, but then why didn't the fire occur earlier?" Shaw argued.

"The house stood empty for days. No one was inside to light a jet," Reid suggested.

"No, it won't do," Shaw declared. "I cannot believe a leaking gas pipe would take an entire week to ignite, and then do so only when the duchess was inside. Unless, of course, she lit the match."

"I assure you, my cousin would not have done so. She came here against her will. If a match was lit, then her abductor is to blame."

"Perhaps, but this is all conjecture, Lord Aubrey, and I do not like conjecture, only facts. Mr. Lintel here has five years' experience with house fires, and he's as good as any at reading the evidence. He tells me that gas is not involved, and it is his estimation that most compels me. I fear the precipitating factor remains unknown."

"Yet we do not give up, sir," Lintel added, apologetically. "My men are still tryin' to determine the cause of the fire, and who, if anyone, might have been inside when it ignited, my lord. We believe the duchess must have escaped, assuming she was ever in the house."

"We pray that you're right, Mr. Lintel, and that my cousin escaped before it began, or, as you say, was never inside," Aubrey noted seriously.

"As do we all, sir." Shaw added. The elder man stroked his chin beard thoughtfully. "That's a nasty looking bit of evidence," he said, bending to examine the iron post. "Is this where Haimsbury fell? This post?"

Paul nodded. "It is. Mr. Lintel may have told you, but when we arrived at the house, it was already ablaze. Sir William Trent lay upon the ground, clearly dead. You can see the large area of stained grass, just over there," he said, pointing to a section of the yard marked with four, red canvas flags. "He was covered in shards of glass, having crashed through the first floor window. You can see the window up there, Captain."

"Yes. It's smashed rather badly," the Irishman agreed. "I suppose this Trent fellow jumped to escape the fire. Foolish thing to do, but if the stairs had already become engulfed, it may have been the only exit."

"A fatal exit, if that's what happened," Reid observed. "However, we don't believe he jumped, Superintendent. As you can see, Trent's body landed too far from the house, and his other injuries are inconsistent with a mere fall."

Paul looked at Reid. "Injuries? Edmund, is Trent's body in your dead room? I admit that with all the other stresses in the past two days, I allowed that important detail to slip."

"I had my men convey it to Leman Street as soon as you and Emerson left with Charles. Sunders finished the autopsy yesterday. He's included some interesting observations in the final report. I'll show you when we go back there," he said to Aubrey privately. Then glancing at the shorter fireman, added, "Mr. Lintel, here, seems to think the duchess was never inside. I pray he's right."

"As do we all," Shaw agreed, clearing his throat. "Well, it's evident that you three men can handle all this without me. Lord Aubrey, if it's amenable to you, I'll be going. I've an appointment at the palace. I promised the queen I'd bring her up-to-date on the investigation. Then, I fear, I have to meet with several other brigade officers. We've had a string of suspicious fires in recent days. Three in the city alone, including one at Broad Street Terminus and another near the Royal Mint, for goodness' sake! Her Majesty worries we might have an anarchist cell operating in London, and I fear she may be right. I'm available, however, should you have any questions."

"I'll contact you regardless," the earl said, offering his hand once more. "Thank you, Captain Shaw. I'll let my uncle know how thorough you and your men have been."

"Please do, my lord, and remind His Grace that we've not yet finished that chess match. He'll know what I mean." He reached for Edmund's hand. "Good day, Inspector Reid. I wouldn't remain too long, if I were you. Looks like we'll be getting more snow before the day's out."

The thin, former army man turned about and followed Columbia Road towards Birdcage Walk, where he hailed a hansom. The earl and Reid looked at one another and then to the stout fellow in the felt hat.

Unlike the portly brigade officer, Paul Stuart rarely wore a hat, and his chestnut hair blew about in the easterly wind. "Shaw's right. It does look like snow. Tell, me Mr. Lintel, what makes you so certain that the duchess wasn't inside when the fire broke out?"

Lintel had known very few peers in his forty-six years, but what few he'd met were arrogant to the point of extreme frustration. The only exception to that rule was Charles Sinclair, but the police superintendent wasn't raised with wealth and privilege. Lintel assumed that was the deciding factor; therefore, he forced a patient smile, assuming the earl to be nothing more than a spoilt dandy in a hand-tailored suit.

"My lord, I assure you that my men and I have sifted through every particle of ash on both the upper and lower floors. We found no sign of..." He paused, decidedly uncomfortable. "Well, sir, we found no body; nor was there evidence that the duchess was ever inside the house. It looks to me as though your information is incorrect."

Aubrey glared at the man, his clear blue eyes grown cold and still. Reid had seen that same look on the earl's face many times, and it only appeared when Paul Stuart neared the end of his patience.

"Mr. Lintel, to put it simply, you are *wrong*. If you cannot find a solution to this puzzle, then I will. I'm going up there."

"Sir, it is too dangerous," Lintel warned the earl. "The support beams 'twixt the floors are ready to give way. I've told all my men to keep out from this point forward, and they've years of training in how to walk amongst such damage."

"Then you may remain out here, Mr. Lintel, but I warn you, do not try to stop me!" Aubrey declared and pushed past the fireman to enter the ruined home.

Lintel rushed after, intent on removing the foolish peer, but Reid drew the officer back. "Let the man look, Bert. Lord Aubrey is not like others in his class. He has experience that even you and I lack."

Paul stepped carefully through the door frame, where pieces of splintered wood had collapsed into a heap on the narrow porch. The interior was dark and smelled wet and smoky. The charred walls of the foyer to Sinclair's old home were almost unrecognisable. The earl had visited the house dozens of times since '79, and seeing the substantial damage struck him very hard. It was like reaching the end of an era, and he prayed that it held no dark omens regarding his cousin's recovery.

Most of the wall coverings had burnt, but a few fragile scraps of trellised ivy and floral paper remained; each brittle fragment now curled and peeling with blackened edges and water stains. The oak staircase had once been considered beautiful, and Amelia St. Clair had always pointed out the intricate carving on the newel post and balusters. Paul touched the post's figural cap, and the fragile carcass crumbled beneath his leather glove. The floral stair carpet was installed in the summer of 1879 as a gift from Amelia's parents, but its woolen threads now showed evidence of smoke and water damage, spoilt even further by the muddy impressions of firemen's boots. The entire case leaned precariously towards the western wall, and several of the steps were broken; the railing had split into three pieces, two of which lay upon the foyer floor.

"This is terrible, Edmund," Stuart said as they walked through to the kitchen area. "So much worse than I expected. I'm very glad Mary isn't here to see it."

"As am I," the round-faced detective inspector agreed. "I spoke with her yesterday, and all she could talk about was how the old photo albums and books were spared, because Charles removed the furnishings and storage crates to the Haimsbury dower house after the housebreak. Paul, it gives me no pleasure to say this, but it looks as though Lintel is right. There's nothing to indicate the duchess was here Sunday night. Trent must have taken her elsewhere."

"But then why was he here at all?" Aubrey asked, turning to face his friend. "No, Beth was here, Edmund. Trent's taunt to Charles made clear reference to this house. He wanted to hurt my cousin in the worst possible way by making this the site of his crime. But I doubt we'd find evidence on this level. Trent's body crashed through the upper storey window. We could see the broken glass as we arrived. It was all over the yard. No, if Beth was here that night, then he must have taken her into one of the bedrooms."

The fireman had followed them into the house and now bent to pick up a piece of broken crockery. "If the superintendent did have his property moved, sir, then the removal men missed a bit. Looks like the lid of a little butter dish."

"I've seen enough down here," Stuart declared, heading towards the staircase. "I'm going up."

Lintel blocked the earl's path. "Beggin' your pardon, sir, but that is a very foolish idea. I cannot permit it."

"I neither seek nor require your permission, Mr. Lintel."

"Don't interfere, Lintel," Reid ordered the brigade officer. "I'll come with you, Lord Aubrey."

Lintel grudgingly stepped aside, and the Scottish earl gingerly traversed the treacherous staircase, keeping his weight upon the side closest to the wall for better support. Once on the landing, he went straight towards the room with the broken window.

"Charles and Amelia used this as the master," he told Reid. "Albert's nursery is down the hall at the end. Such a sad little room. I remember Charles would sometimes go in there and sit for hours. He's never gotten over his son's death, but then what man could? Did you ever visit?"

"A few times, though I never came up here," Edmund replied as the two of them entered the modest bedchamber. "I was at J Division until early this year, but called on Charles once or twice to report on investigations, most of them related to Ripper."

"A dark reason to call on so gentle a man," the earl answered with a sigh. "Charles and I used to retreat up here, to get away from Amelia quite frankly. She was a considerably disagreeable woman, and she latched onto me like a starving leech each time I visited. Most likely, trying to further ingratiate herself and her family into ours. Charles was never like that. Truly, I think he'd be content, even now, to live a simple life. Though, the Lord has designed him for leadership, he craves solitude. He's like Beth in that way."

"I never met Sinclair's late wife, but if she latched onto you, as you say, it's likely she mistook your naturally polite manner as familiarity," Reid suggested.

"Or an open invitation for something else. I never told Charles, but Amelia flirted overtly with me and with my father, if you can imagine it. My father was too kind a man to say anything, but he was sixty-five at the time and my mother still lived!"

"Charles never noticed?" Reid asked.

"If he did, he chose to ignore it. Charles hated challenging his late wife, not for any lack of backbone, but because he is a thoroughly good and gentle man. Whenever I'd visit, he'd suggest coming up here to smoke. It offered privacy and a relief from Amelia's constant flirtations."

"Charles doesn't smoke," Reid argued. "I have never seen him smoke anything, Paul. Not a pipe, not a cigarette, not even a cigar. Nothing."

"Nor have I, but I'd light one of my cigars to make sure we weren't intruded upon. Amelia was persistent, but she detested smoke. I suspect my poor cousin had to air this room out as soon as I left, but it invariably worked."

The earl began a slow survey of the room, stopping now and then to run a knife blade along exposed wall lath or betwixt floor planks.

"Did you see this morning's *Daily News?*" Reid asked as he conducted a similar search in one corner.

"Do you mean the Berners Street attack?"

"You know about that?"

"Galton mentioned it in my briefing this morning."

"I'd thought you and the duke too busy with the search for Elizabeth to pay attention to other matters. I confess, I'm surprised that you have the emotional presence of mind to consider anything beyond that."

The earl shut his eyes for a moment. He pictured a block of ice and slowly counted to five. It was a long-practised and familiar exercise, taught to him by his father. This simple but effective mind trick allowed him to postpone emotional responses like heartache or despair. *If Beth is dead, then I shall grieve then. Not now. For now, I stay focused.*

"We manage," he told Reid, turning his thoughts towards matters he could control. "The Berners Street explosion merits investigation."

"Special Branch is looking into it, actually. We've been ordered to ignore it. I was referring to the constable found dead in Hyde Park. Suicide, according to the coroner."

"A police constable? I missed that one. Who was it?"

"Alvin Goode. I never met the man," the inspector continued. "The paper said he joined up in '86, and that a witness claimed Goode had been melancholy and moody of late. He purchased a revolver last Thursday, which is considered evidentiary of suicidal intent. However, the weapon was found fifteen feet from the body."

Aubrey stared at the policeman. "Fifteen feet? Surely, a pistol doesn't leap so far once fired, no matter how inexperienced the handler. You say the fellow's name is Goode? Edmund, would you be able to obtain a copy of the report?" Aubrey asked.

"I might. It's E Division's case. Austin Askew's the inspector in charge."

"I know Askew. If I have time, I'll meet with him later today. I don't want to be away from the house too long. Della's very upset about all of this, as you can imagine, and she's losing sleep over Charles's condition. If I don't find ways to occupy her time, she'll spend the entire day at his bedside. In a very short time, she's come to love him dearly. Edmund, if he dies..."

"That won't happen, my friend. Charles Sinclair is a fighter!"

"So he is," Stuart whispered, picturing the ice block once more. "Wasn't Mary Kelly's funeral on Monday?"

Reid leaned over the sill of the broken window and gazed down at the snowy yard. "That's a long way to fall," he muttered. "Kelly? Yes, it was. Fred Abberline and I attended to see who else might be there. Sadly, we were the only mourners. I'd expected George Lusk and his Vigilance Committee to show, or a *Star* reporter, but it was a very lonely service."

"Poor girl," Paul said as he returned his knife to the right pocket of his coat. "When we've the time, I'd like to see the Kelly photographs and review the autopsy results. The duke wants us to meet later today. Are you able to come?"

"He sent a telegram. I'll do my best to make it," Edmund answered.

"Good. If you do come by, bring the Kelly file with you."

The soft-bellied fireman had decided to join them, and he huffed as he entered the smoky room. "I've examined the entire main floor again, my lord, and found nothing new. Have you discovered anything up here, sir?"

"Nothing yet, Mr. Lintel," the earl answered, his manner gentler. "I hope you'll forgive my manners. I'm very worried about my cousins, and this house is our only lead to finding the duchess."

"Of course, my lord."

The Scottish peer moved to the hearth, whose chimney served both bedchambers. Bending down, he raked at the collection of wet ash with his gloved hand. "This room was always cold, when we retreated up here, Edmund, no matter how bright the flame. I'd always assumed it a result of poor chimney design, but knowing what I do now about my cousin, I wonder if it wasn't more. It may have been a spiritual coldness that permeated the room—perhaps even the entire house. Shadows follow him, Edmund, much like they do Beth." His hand stopped, and Stuart collected a handful of ash. "Hello! What are these?" he asked, showing the other men. "See here? Pearl buttons and what looks like a scrap of burnt silk amidst fragments of bone. Not human, though, thank the Lord."

"How can you tell, sir?" Lintel asked. He moved closer and placed a smudged pair of spectacles on his plump nose. "Surely, only a surgeon can determine if a bone is human."

"Not in this case," Aubrey told him plainly. "This is baleen. Commonly called whalebone. I've seen enough to recognise it at once. It's used in corsets."

The inspector smiled at the fire officer's perplexed expression. "Well, you have our attention, Lord Aubrey. Do you care to tell us how you know that?"

"Let's just say I have experience in the production of certain ladies' fashions. You'll get no more from me on that, Inspector. Not today, at any rate, but look here, gentlemen. Many fine coils of steel wire, also used in corset design. Why would steel and baleen be in the hearth, unless her corset burnt here?"

"Which means someone removed it," Reid suggested darkly. "William Trent always had unnatural inclinations towards the duchess."

Aubrey tried to picture the ice block, but it threatened to melt as he fought against the overwhelming rage and dread that began to take root in his heart. "Yes, so he did," he answered through clenched teeth. "Wait, Edmund. Wait," the earl whispered as he rose to his feet. "Trent needed a mirror."

"What, sir?" the fireman asked. "A mirror, sir?"

"Yes, a mirror! Why didn't I think of this before? Lintel, did any of your men recover a broken mirror? Most likely a large one. Six feet or more."

"Sir, most houses have mirrors here and there," the befuddled man replied, scratching his bald head. "Generally, they break in a fire."

"Was there a mirror found or not?" Stuart insisted.

"No, sir. Nor did we find shards that might indicate the presence of one. Didn't you say the superintendent removed all the furnishings?"

"That's correct. The house was empty," the inspector replied.

Lintel sighed. "Then, looking for a mirror seems a fool's errand, beggin' your pardon, my lord. Now, as to these corset materials, I do apologise, sir. I fear we did not look in the hearth, for we'd assumed the remains within it were nothing but burnt logs."

Aubrey took a deep breath, trying to clear his thoughts, but the ice block had turned to a puddle of water. "I hope you'll forgive any impatience on my part, Mr. Lintel. It is not directed at you, but at these damnable circumstances! My cousin lies upon what may prove to be his death bed, and his bride is missing. If I can find her and return her to him, then my cousin may yet rally, but if I cannot, then I dare not imagine what may happen!"

Lintel nodded somberly, turning the soft grey cap over and over nervously. "Forgive me, my lord. You're a good man, much like Superintendent Sinclair. If you believe a mirror might provide answers, then I'll look in the other rooms whilst you and the inspector continue in here. Perhaps, there's other evidence that we missed."

The fireman left the room, and Aubrey crossed to the shattered window. "He seems a decent man, Edmund, but I hesitate to bring too many into our confidence. I'd have preferred to keep it to ourselves, but considering how many brave fire brigade officers and policemen rushed to our aid on Sunday night, it would be thoughtless to preclude them entirely. Now, what is this?" he asked, kneeling before the broken window frame. "Glass?"

"Most likely from Trent's journey through the panes."

Paul had hoped he'd found the second mirror at last. His coping abilities were wearing thin, and he wanted to smash what little glass remained in the splintered frame. He'd come here hoping to find evidence that would lead him to Elizabeth, but other than the bits of corset, the house had nothing to offer.

He turned to look all 'round the small room, praying to discover something he'd missed. "I wish my father were here. His eyes were sharper than any other's for finding what is hidden. There must be something that tells us where she is!"

"Look, my friend, it's nearly midday. Perhaps, we should leave and return to Leman Street."

"It makes no sense," the earl told the policeman. "If there is no mirror here, then how did he do it? I've spoken with Kepelheim and MacPherson, and both men agree that there *must* have been a second mirror inside this house. Every legend that describes the use of mirrors for travel describes an entry and an exit point. He would need a mirror here. It must be why someone broke into the house! Doing so forced Charles to abandon the house and bring Mary Wilsham to Westminster. With the house empty, placing a mirror here would be simple."

Lintel returned, his hands empty. "Nothing, Lord Aubrey. Not a sliver, not a shard. No sign of a mirror anywhere hereabouts."

The earl grew silent, his eyes following the progress of two young women entering a three-storey house across the street. Reid recognised the look. *Aubrey had an idea.*

Suddenly, the earl turned about. "Gentlemen, I'm finished here. Thank you for your help, Mr. Lintel. May I call upon you with further questions as they arise?"

"Of course, my lord," the befuddled officer answered as he shook the earl's hand. "I'd be pleased to assist any time. When we've completed our investigation, shall I deliver any evidence we've collected to Inspector Reid or to you, sir?"

"Tell Reid when you've finished, and I'll send someone to collect it. Thank you again, Mr. Lintel. This visit has been most instructive."

The trio left the house, and once the fireman departed, Aubrey turned to the detective inspector, a wide smile crossing his face.

"I believe I know how Trent emerged with Beth at the proper place, Edmund. I'd assumed it required installing a second mirror inside Charles's house, but all he needed to do was place it *close* to the house, not necessarily inside it. Go on back to Leman Street without me. I'll see you later at the meeting, if you can make it."

Reid watched the muscular earl cross the busy street and then enter the stylish house opposite. He began to laugh as he realised the purpose of the earl's mission.

"Now, why didn't I think of that?" the amiable inspector muttered to himself.

Constable Danny Antram stood waiting beside their hired hansom, and the young man held the wooden doors open to allow his superior to enter first.

"Where's his lordship going, sir? I thought he'd be returning to Leman Street with us."

"Lord Aubrey is conducting his own investigation, Constable. A very pleasant one, I shouldn't doubt. Leave it to our earl to consider such a possibility."

On the far side of Columbia Street, James Paul Robert Ian Stuart, 11th Earl of Aubrey passed through the bright red door of the neighbourhood's most infamous business establishment, the brothel known as the Empress Hotel.

CHAPTER FIVE

Charles Sinclair hesitated before entering the mysterious portal. The ravens and other hideous birds sat above him on the high stone wall as though waiting to begin their hideous feast. The object of their desire gulped, imagining the hellish carnivores holding knives and forks, their black beaks flowing with saliva.

"Why seven gates?" Sinclair asked the peculiar bird creature. "Why not six or eight? Or ten? Why not a million, if your intention is to confuse and confound your victims?"

"Victims? I do not like your implication, human! Twas not I who built the maze, but rather the oldest of the old. I merely keep watch upon it; that is all. Why should I explain its purpose or mechanism to someone as willfully stupid as you?"

"If I'm so stupid, then why do you spend any time with me at all? Why not abandon me to my fate?" Sinclair noticed the creature's eyes fixed upon his watch. "Or is it this that you covet? Why? Surely, you've no need of gold."

"Of course not—not for payment. Our needs differ from your own. Gold is not a commodity but a *key*," he replied slyly.

"How is gold a key?"

"That is considered education. Pay or remain ignorant."

Charles shrugged. "Fine, then. I shall remain ignorant and in possession of this key, thank you."

The birdman moved closer, rubbing its hands together greedily. "It is certainly *shiny*. Grant me one look at it, and I'll offer you a hint—at no cost."

Charles held up the watch, but didn't dare remove it from the waistcoat button to which the chain attached. "You may look, but do not touch."

"Whatever is it?" the creature asked, hopping closer.

"It is a timepiece and nothing more, but it has sentimental value. I shan't part with it, no matter how much knowledge you promise."

The birdman drew closer still, its feather-trimmed cape bristling in anticipation. "So very pretty. I seem to remember timepieces from long ago. I wonder, does it make that lovely ticking sound? The one such mechanisms used to make?"

"Of course."

"Are you *certain?*" it asked, moving two steps nearer.

"Of course, I am," Charles answered confidently. To prove his point, he depressed the latch once again and stared at the hands beneath the polished crystal. The Sir John Bennett featured a second hand which swept along a dial near the bottom, but the tiny bit of metal was stuck fast at the thirty-three second mark. Only now, did Charles notice the minute and hour hands also appeared frozen—at thirteen minutes past one. He shook the idle watch, but with no resolution. Finally, after unfastening the chain from the middle waistcoat button, he held the watch to one ear.

"Odd. I hear nothing."

The bird creature grinned. "And thus my point is proven. Did I not say that you are stupid?"

"I've no idea what you mean, Creature. I must have forgotten to wind it before the wedding."

"Wind it now," it suggested, the sickly yellow eyes round as buttons.

Sinclair had a dread that the bird-thing was setting a trap, but he slowly wound the mechanism, tightening the springs within the eighteen-karat case. However, the hands remained stubbornly fixed. "I may have overwound it."

"Or, perhaps, there is a simpler explanation."

"And what might that be?" the marquess asked, anger and frustration tightening his voice.

"That time has stopped," the bird stated, as though it were the most natural thing in all the world.

Charles started to argue, but something about the suggestion rang true in his mind. *If I am in a dream world, then time may not exist. However, if I am dead, then it would also, likely, not exist.*

"Are you saying I'm dead?" he asked boldly.

"Do you want to be?"

"No, of course not! I want to find my wife! Is she dead?"

"Another stupid question. I have told you that she asks for a man called Captain. Dead women do not generally submit questions regarding their lovers, now do they? Have you no memory at all, human?"

"That's right," he whispered, the back of his head pounding. "I'd quite forgotten. This is a very confusing place, you must admit. Tell me, then, why doesn't time exist here? If I am not dead, that is."

The creature stretched out its arms and used the black-feathered cape to ascend to the top of a large boulder, where it perched. "You can be quite trying, human. Why would I know about time? I did not create it! Lord Kronos might know, but he sleeps elsewhere. Shall I summon one of the old ones to instruct you? I warn you; they do not take kindly to being awoken prematurely, and they charge a much higher price than I."

"No, let them sleep," the human replied. "Who are these old ones? Why are they asleep at all, and if time does not exist here, how does one awaken prematurely?"

"Just who are you?" the creature asked as it hopped down from the rock in excitement. "I've never had any other human persist in such odd enquiries. Are you, perhaps, related to Gilgamesh? Orpheus? Odysseus? Inanna? Dionysus? Are you the son of an elohim? You smell different to me, Charles Sinclair. My nose never lies. I'm sure you're something very special indeed!"

"I am the son of a human, who was himself the son of a human. Tell me about this traitor you mentioned earlier. Is he also an elohim?" he asked.

The birdman's amber eyes blinked rapidly many times, as though counting. Above their heads, the murder of crows and ravens collectively blinked in unison with the gatekeeper. At last, the creature replied, "The answer would be considered instruction, therefore, I cannot reply without payment. However, I can lead you to the observation chamber. Perhaps you will find the location of your faithless wife there."

"Why do I feel as though you're trying to trick me?" Charles asked.

"No trick. None at all. Come, follow me, human. It is nearby. Just beyond these trees." The creature changed back into a huge raven and flew towards a thicket of yew trees.

Sinclair's legs felt heavy, as though bound by lead weights, but he pressed forward, hurrying to catch up with the birdman's quick flight. After what seemed like an endless series of steps, he entered a clearing. The trees' irregular shapes looked black in the moon's dim light. Though evergreens, some of the yews had lost their foliage, and their limbs spread out from the thick trunks like endlessly entwining arms. Charles noticed that the branches moved, despite the lack of any discernable breeze.

"Here," the raven cawed as it landed near his position and transformed back into a human, or rather the semblance of one. "Beneath these ancient boughs stand the *asaru* stones. They see and record everything that is ever done or thought; every moment, every intention, every dream. Is there a particular day you would like to relive?"

"Relive?" he asked, his mind suddenly crowded with pictures from his own life. "I don't know. I want to find my wife."

"Then, look and see," the creature commanded. Sinclair stared into the asaru stone. Its rough grey surface grew fluid and rippled like the surface of a lake. An image appeared within the rippling grey fog, focusing slowly onto Edmund Reid's office at Leman Street—only Reid wasn't sitting behind the desk. It was Bob Morehouse, Sinclair's late mentor. Morehouse was smoking a pipe and speaking with Dr. Alan Dollarhide, who stood beside the desk. Charles could also see himself, and he could hear their conversation.

> *"She's a pretty thing,"* he heard himself say in the vision.

"That was the first time I ever saw her," he told the birdman as tears formed in the corners of his eyes. "I'd never seen a child so beautiful in all my life."

"That, at least, is an honest answer," the creature said. "She looks very young for a wife."

"She wasn't quite eleven," Charles told him softly. "Why have you shown me this?"

"You see what you *want* to see, human. Why is this moment special to you?"

"Because she is special to me; that's why. If we hadn't met, I... I dare not think where my life would be now."

The stone's display rippled again, and when it stopped, Sinclair perceived a small parlour with a coal fire burning upon a small grate. He could see himself, sitting in a wingback chair, gazing at something. No, at *someone*. It was Elizabeth, lying on a velveteen sofa. She'd begun to stir.

The marquess smiled, for he knew precisely what would happen next. "I remember this so clearly. It was the first time I ever saw her eyes. It may even be the moment, when I started loving her."

"So, this is your young wife again, I take it?" the creature asked as it stared at the stone, blinking. "I suppose she's pretty enough."

"She wasn't my wife at that time," Charles explained. "I felt protective, but that bond betwixt us took root so very swiftly... So profoundly that it felt..."

"Planned?" the bird asked him.

"Yes, I suppose so."

"*Mamitu*, goddess of fate, had destined you to be together," the gatekeeper suggested.

"No," Charles argued. "God Almighty brought us together. I believe he designed us for one another."

"Why must you bring up your useless God again?" the bird complained. "You really are rather stupid. Oh, wait, it looks as though she's about to speak."

> *"Captain Nemo,"* the girl said.
>
> *"Captain Nemo?"* his vision self asked her.
>
> *"Jules Verne,"* she explained. *"Second shelf down, third from the left. It's one of my favourites. Captain Nemo is such a lonely man, don't you think?"*

"She thought you were lonely!" the birdman cawed excitedly. "Women always make such claims to men. They insist it is because they are superior, but I find it manipulative. You cannot trust them."

Charles shook his head. "No, her comment was insightful. Even at eleven, Beth could see into my heart as no one else on this earth ever could."

"Did you notice, though? She called you Captain. Is that what she calls all her lovers?" the gatekeeper asked. "As I thought. You are but one of a number."

"Of course not! Beth has no lovers. She is my wife, and her heart has belonged to me for a long time."

"Is that so?" the creature taunted. "Then explain this to me."

The stone's surface shifted again, and when the rippling finally stopped, the Columbia Road parlour had given way to a stylish compartment of a moving railcar.

"It's the Aubrey train," Charles said. "Is this when we travelled to Branham in October?"

"What is an Oc-to-ber?" the birdman cawed.

"It is a month. We had to leave London quickly, because Beth was in danger. She dared not return home. Paul and I guarded her on that journey, and it was when I first met Martin Kepelheim."

"Ah, yes, he's a rather annoying person by all accounts. Why did you wish to see this moment?"

"I'm not sure. Is this when I kissed her? I longed to confess my love for her, but..."

"But she was not yours to love," the gatekeeper said. "However, I do not think this is that moment, human. In fact, I don't see you at all. How very curious."

The angle of the view shifted, and it became clear that the only travellers in the compartment were Elizabeth and Paul Stuart.

"Why am I seeing this? How is this my memory?"

The creature grinned, its inhuman teeth sharp. "Did I say that these are only *your* memories? Hardly! What sort of seeing stone would that be? No, I'm showing you what you most want to see."

"I don't want to see this," the marquess insisted. "Change it to something else!"

"Oh, but you do want to see it. You have always wondered what happened in your absence, haven't you, Charles Sinclair? You'd left with that annoying tailor to have your measurements taken, remember? Let's watch, shall we?"

> *"Do you love him?"* the earl asked Elizabeth bluntly.
>
> The duchess turned away, and Charles could see anxiety etched upon her face, and her lower lip trembled as it always did when she was upset. *"Please, do not ask me that."*
>
> Stuart took her hands and kissed them. "*Darling, forgive me if it sounds as if I do not trust you. I do. Com-*

pletely. It is only fear that drives me. Fear of losing you to someone else."

"But you and Charles have been friends for nearly a decade. Would you imagine him behaving any way that is inappropriate?" the duchess asked Aubrey.

"No. He is a gentleman, but I also think he cares for you, Beth."

"Perhaps. But it is your present that I wear, Cousin. It has not left my hand since you placed it there; nor will it."

"Elizabeth, do you really see us together as husband and wife, or is my hope in vain? No, wait, forgive me, that was unfair. I know you love me—truly I do—but I fear your heart now strays towards another, and it worries me. For many reasons, but most of all because I cannot imagine life without you. I love you so very much."

The vision grew unfocused, and the sound stopped. Charles touched the stone as though willing it to finish the scene. "What happened then?" he entreated the creature. "What did she say?"

"I've no idea," the gatekeeper answered stubbornly. "But he seems a very sad fellow to me. Perhaps, *he* is the one who is lonely. Not you."

"I've seen enough!" Sinclair shouted.

"Did you *steal* her from him?"

"Of course, I didn't steal her! What a stupid question!"

"Now, you lie to yourself," the creature told him, waving its humanoid hand before the stone. "Let us discover the real reason she married you."

"You're trying to trick me."

"How is showing you the truth a trick?" the sly creature asked.

Reluctantly, Charles gazed once more at the stone, and the image revealed the interior of a one-room cottage. A narrow bed dominated the simple space, and a wood fire burnt cheerfully. A woman slept upon the bed, and a man dozed in a rocking chair next to the fireplace.

"This is October the eighth," the human told the birdman.

"That's a very precise memory," it noted, his cruel brows arched in an odd manner.

"It is the night that..." Sinclair started, but feelings of guilt that he'd locked away in his thoughts rose up to accuse him. "I did not steal her."

"So you say," it answered. "Oh, it appears that you're no longer sleeping."

In the vision, Charles had left the rocker and moved to the bed. He bent to kiss Elizabeth, daring to remove the quilts and slip into the bed beside her. "I ask you, human; is that the behaviour of an innocent man?"

"That's enough!" Sinclair shouted, turning away and refusing to watch any longer. "You're twisting the truth! We had both been poisoned by some concoction, and our actions were dictated by that."

"I see, but it looks to me as though *your* actions are suspect, not hers. Some might say you forced yourself upon her. A policeman might even call it a criminal act."

"No! That is not what happened!" the human shouted. "Switch this thing off, I will not participate in your games any longer. I want to go home to my wife!"

"Your wife?" the creature asked, its head tilted. "Yes, I suppose she is, but had you not interfered, she'd be *his wife*. Hence, you stole her from your ever faithful cousin."

"For the last time, I did not steal her! Elizabeth loves me. We were meant to be together!"

"My, but you're very defensive for a man claiming to be in the right," the gatekeeper observed.

"I needn't explain myself to you, Creature. You mentioned a cottage that would lead me home. I insist you lead me to it now!"

The birdman's yellow eyes fixed on the marquess's gold timepiece. "I'd be pleased to help, even delighted, but the rules restrict me, you see. From this moment forward, I require payment."

"I've no intention of giving you this watch, whether it works or not! If you cannot be more helpful, then begone!"

"As you wish," the creature answered with a chilling smile—and with a loud pop, he vanished.

Sinclair sighed and closed his eyes, praying silently. He had never felt so alone, never so helpless. His head throbbed, his feet dragged, and his heart ached. Slowly, the despondent traveller made his way out of the yew trees and back to the paved road.

The mist had thickened again, but he could still make out one of the first gates of the monumental, outer wall. "I must find my way to this cottage. I will find my way! Beth, my darling, wherever you are, I shall find the path back to you," he whispered as he faced the daunting task of navigating the impossible maze. "Father in heaven, I ask you to send me a sign that you are here. Please, help me to find my way home—to find my beloved wife."

The ravenous birds still cawed and chirped in hellish discord overhead, but floating above this hideous cacophony, he perceived an indescribably sweet song. Charles felt a fresh breeze whisper against his ear, and then the rushing of soft wings. Within the blackness of the yawning portal, a tiny light appeared. This bright spot drew nearer, growing evermore distinct as it slowly took shape.

It was a dove.

The beautiful, white bird emerged from the darkness and rose up high into the air of the strange world, its radiant feathers a welcome contrast to the midnight sky with its peculiar moon.

A sense of peace washed over the desperate marquess, and he bowed his head, a tear sliding down his face.

"Thank you, Lord. Thank you!"

Believing the bird to be a sign, Sinclair stepped towards the gate, but it was like moving through a raincloud made of anger. He feared he'd misunderstood the dove's message; that he'd made a fatal error. Just as all peace left his soul, a small hand emerged from out of the cloud bank of rage and fury, and a sweet voice spoke.

"Are you lost?" it asked.

It was a girl. She stood no taller than four feet, with raven curls and dark eyes. She looked exactly like the little duchess had when she and Charles first met in '79.

"Beth?" he asked, tears filling his eyes as he knelt down to take her small hands. "Can it be you? Have I drifted back in time, or is this another dream from one of those seeing stones? I don't understand. How can you be here?"

"Beth?" the child asked. "Do you mean Mother?"

"Mother?" he repeated, utterly confused. "I'm not sure... What is your name, little one?"

"Don't you recognise me, Father? It's Georgianna. Of course, you and Mother always call me Georgie. I've come to help you. I know the way through."

"Georgie?" he whispered. "You call me Father. You're my—my daughter?"

"Of course, I am!" the beautiful child giggled. She looked so much like Elizabeth at that age, that it caused a rush of memories that both cheered and broke his heart all at once, and the exhausted marquess nearly collapsed.

The child put her hand on his shoulder to steady him, imparting strength. "Never fear, Father. The Lord is ever with you. Come with me. Let's find our way together."

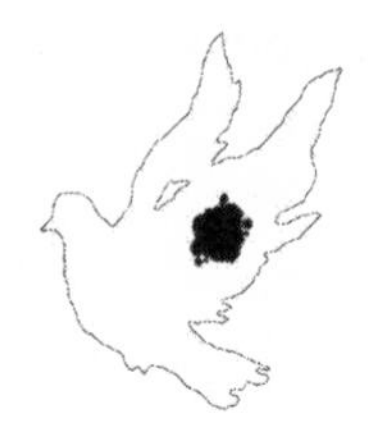

CHAPTER SIX

11:14 am – Friday, 23rd November

"Has he been drinking water regularly?" Michael Emerson asked the butler. "His skin seems a bit dry."

Cornelius Baxter stood nearby, worry accentuating age lines at the corners of his eyes and mouth. "We do our best, sir, but as you can imagine, it's somewhat difficult to achieve. May I give him a bath today?"

"Yes, I think so, but be careful of the head wound. I'll dress it again before I go. Is Lord Aubrey still staying here?"

"His lordship sleeps in the room next door. Lord Haimsbury's chamber. As you know, this is my lady's chamber. I doubt the earl has slept much since Sunday. He is vigilant—as are we all, but I worry about him, Dr. Emerson. Might you speak with him? Perhaps, suggest a soporific to calm his mind at night?"

"I'll see what I can do, but the earl is stubborn. A family trait, it seems."

Baxter smiled. "Yes, sir. That is a fact."

"I understand that your normal household is in Kent," the physician noted.

"That's right, sir. Branham Hall, but as I'm serving here in Mr. Laurence's stead, Mr. Kay has taken over for me for the time being. I shall remain here so long as Lord Haimsbury needs me."

Emerson had been taking his patient's pulse, and he glanced up, smiling. "If only every man took his job as seriously, Mr. Baxter. You're a rare man, sir."

Someone knocked on the closed door. Baxter answered and found Victoria Stuart waiting on the other side.

"My lady, it is not appropriate for you to enter just now. His lordship is not presentable, if you understand my meaning."

"What sort of nonsense is that?" Tory asked the butler. "Is he awake?"

"No, ma'am. He is not, but we must finish preparing him."

"Preparing him for what?" she asked, pushing into the bedchamber.

However, the forceful aunt stopped immediately when it became clear that the butler had spoken correctly. Charles Sinclair had sustained cuts and contusions all over his body, and his pyjama shirt had been removed for Emerson's examination. The unconscious peer lay upon the broad bed, bare to the waist, revealing a muscular and very male torso. Also, his legs were exposed from the knees down, so that Emerson could inspect and re-bandage several lacerations Charles had received after landing amongst a field of broken window glass.

Without so much as a whisper, the duke's sister quickly turned about and faced the marble fireplace. "I see what you mean," she muttered. "Carry on, Dr. Emerson. I merely wish to know if my nephew is improving."

Emerson laughed softly as he and Baxter removed a swathe of cotton gauze from the marquess's head wound. "Lady Victoria, it is a sign of breeding, I suppose, that you exhibit such delicacy, but nurses see sights like this every day, be they maiden or married. Any woman who tends the sick must overcome her natural sense of shyness."

Victoria remained turned, but her back straightened defiantly. "I have never been accused of shyness in my entire life, Michael! Never. Not even once. I have turned my back because it seemed the polite thing to do. For Charles. I'd appreciate an answer, if you're capable of more than laughter. Has my nephew shown any improvement? Yes or no? It is not so difficult a question!"

"I cannot offer a yes or no reply, Tory. I am encouraged, however. The swelling at the back of the head continues to lessen, and the wound begins to close. I should be able to remove the stitches in a week's time. I consider it a miracle, to be frank. When we brought Charles here on Sunday night, both Dr. Whitmore and I feared he'd require trepanning."

"Trepanning? What is that?" she asked, her back still turned, but both the butler and physician noticed that she'd begun to tap her foot impatiently.

"It is a surgical procedure to relieve pressure within the skull," Emerson answered, stepping away from the sleeping patient. "Baxter, if you'll provide the marquess a warm bath, Lady Victoria and I shall move into the parlour to allow Charles some privacy. If he were awake, I rather doubt that he'd appreciate an audience."

Grumbling to herself, Tory followed the physician into a fashionably furnished parlour that dominated one corner of the Haimsbury House master apartment.

Emerson closed the door. "Do sit, Tory. I should like to discuss your nephew's condition."

Victoria took a seat near an elegant Belgium blue and mixed Campan marble fireplace. The fixture was flanked by filled bookshelves and overhung with an oil painting of Rose House, the Sinclair family seat in Cumbria.

"His condition? But you just told me that he improves, Michael. What is there to discuss?"

"He does improve. However, I remain puzzled."

"Puzzled by what?" she asked, her dark eyes narrow. "Surely, not by his wounds. Any surgeon would consider cuts and bruises an ordinary thing, would they not?"

"No, those don't worry me. Even his head injury improves daily. I'm puzzled because he is still unconscious."

She stared at him as though he'd just spoken in a foreign language. "What on earth does that mean? Isn't that considered normal after such a blow? Paul tells me that Charles struck that iron post with great force. In fact, he thought it a miracle Charles survived at all," she continued, her mouth dry. "I find it all very frustrating, Michael. If you've something to say, just say it! These past few days have been a trial for all of us, and frankly, my nerves wear thin to the width of writing paper!"

"Forgive me, Victoria," he answered gently. "What I mean to say is that Charles should have awakened by now. I can find no physiological cause for his prolonged sleep. Yes, he sustained numerous cuts and bruises from the glass and the fall, but there is no infection, praise the Lord. His pulse grows stronger, his heart is sound, lungs clear. There is no perceptible swelling in his brain. No fever. All appears quite normal, yet he remains unconscious."

"He is hardly normal, Michael! Good heavens, must I send for George Price or Reggie Whitmore to get a straight reply from a medical man? You modernists speak volumes yet say nothing."

"That is not my intent," Emerson answered patiently. He had dealt many times with discouraged family members and learnt to soften his tone as required. "Forgive me, Tory. I sometimes forget how much Charles means to all of you. And the lack of news regarding the duchess surely causes you worry."

"Worry?" she echoed, her hands shaking. "That is far too pale a word for what I feel, Michael. Beth has been like my own child! If we learn that she is dead, then I dare not think how it will affect us! Poor Charles must not awaken to find his wife has died, Michael. He cannot! And Paul—have you seen him? He wanders about this house like a pale shadow. Never in my life have I seen that man in such a state. I believe he will go mad with grief, if he loses both his cousins. Please, tell me that this puzzlement you mention holds no darkness to it."

"Would that I could reassure you, Victoria, but do you prefer honesty or palliative lies?"

"I prefer good news," she said, her hands itching to light a cigarette, "but as you cannot offer that, then tell me what puzzles you. Are you saying that Charles will remain asleep?"

"I pray he does not, but it is a possibility. It's a state known as coma, based on the Greek word for deep sleep. Patients who enter this state can remain in a twilight world for many weeks."

"Weeks? How can a man sleep for weeks?" she asked, her dark eyes rounding. "That is quite impossible!"

Moving closer, Emerson reached for her trembling hands and gently took them into his own to calm her. "I wish my news were better, but it is possible, and science is unable to explain it. Victoria, I should like permission to consult with a colleague whom I trust. You and the duke are Charles's next of kin. I considered asking Paul, but as the family's elders, I believe it correct to speak with you first."

She shook her head. "No, Elizabeth is the one who should make this decision. She is his wife."

"If Elizabeth were here, then I'd ask her, Tory, but she is not."

"No, she isn't," the woman sighed, fighting tears. "Very well, then. Beth lived with me for over four years, and I believe I can speak for her. My niece would insist we do everything to return her husband to full health. Bring in your colleague—in fact, consult with as many as it takes. Charles must be well and alert when his wife returns!"

Baxter emerged from the bedchamber and bowed to the duke's sister. "His lordship is ready to receive you now, Lady Victoria. Shall I ask Mrs. Alcorn to come up and sit with you? Or perhaps, Mrs. Wilsham?"

"No, thank you, Baxter. That's thoughtful of you, but I promised Della that I'd listen to her practise the new music after luncheon, so I shan't remain long. My niece intends to play this new Strauss waltz, *Rosen auf dem Süden*, the moment Charles is able to come downstairs again. It's in honour of Rose House, I think." Stuart bit her lip to stop it quivering. "I do hope that day will arrive soon. It's already been six days."

Baxter nodded. "So it has, my lady, but we must let the Lord do his mighty work. Six days to him are enough to create the entire universe."

Tory finally smiled, though her face showed lines of exhaustion written upon it. "Baxter, has my brother mentioned whether we're to have another meeting today? I've not seen the duke since last night."

"His Grace asked that we set the library to accommodate a dozen members, as usual. Will there be more?"

"I very much doubt it," she replied, standing. "Nearly every member is occupied searching for the duchess. Do forgive me, gentlemen. I'm out of sorts. Thank you, Michael. Will you be joining us for the meeting?"

"Yes, assuming no emergencies arise. What time will it begin, Baxter?"

"Seven, sir."

"Very good. That gives me ample time to speak with a colleague about the marquess. I'll see you both later. Lady Victoria, send for me at the first sign of any changes. I'll be at Queen Anne for the next hour, and then I plan to speak with several physicians in the city."

"Thank you, Michael. Baxter, I'd like to look in on Charles before returning downstairs. You're certain he's ready?"

"All ready, my lady," Baxter answered.

The two men left, and Victoria Stuart quietly entered the bedchamber, where she took the wingback chair next to the beautiful bed.

"Charles," she began, reaching for his hand, wondering just where to begin. "My dear nephew, I'd like to say a few things. Emerson tells us that we must talk, you see, just in case you're able to hear us." She paused, searching her thoughts for what she could say that wouldn't upset him. "Charles, because you cannot remember most of your early years, you probably don't remember much of me. Those Christmas memories Martin helped you recover are but a small portion of the countless hours you and I spent together when you were small. My dear, I've loved you," she continued, wiping her eyes as tears welled up. "I've loved you since you were an infant. It's a strange thing to say to a man who's well over six feet tall, but it's true. Charles, you were such a beautiful boy! Even as a baby, those large blue eyes and black lashes caused all the ladies in the household to swoon!"

She drew a handkerchief from the pocket of her silk day dress and dabbed at both eyes to stop the tears. "Your mother adored you, Charles. Angela conceived almost immediately after marrying your father, and she had a very difficult time with you. In fact, at six months along, she nearly miscarried. It was in early 1855, shortly after Twelfth Night. I'd been staying at Rose House during Christmastide, but Abigail and Robert hadn't been able to leave Briarcliff due to heavy snow in the Highlands. They arrived on the tenth of January. We three sisters had gathered together to celebrate the promise of a new generation. Angela, Abigail, and I. Both my sisters were expecting, you see, though Abigail had only confirmed it a few weeks earlier. Four months apart. That's what you and Paul are. Four months. It was the excitement that did it, you see. Angela was so very happy to see our sister, that she ran to meet Abby and tripped, striking her head against the base of a flower pedestal. Angela was unconscious for nearly an hour, and the doctors feared she'd miscarry. As a precaution, Dr. Jensen confined your mother to bed for the remainder of the pregnancy. It all turned out well, though, and when you were born—after many hours of labour, I might add—my dear, you were perfect."

She took a deep breath, touching his hand. "Most babies are born crying, but not you, Charles. They delivered you, and you very calmly looked up at the doctor and midwives in all seriousness, eyes wide, as if to ask the time of day. Your serene expression caused us all to gasp. You weighed nearly ten pounds, and I remember you measured just under twenty-three inches—destined to be quite tall, so the doctor said. You had a perfectly shaped head, beautiful skin, and those remarkable eyes! Even then, their blue had a most unusual tone. I've never seen their equal in any other person."

She stopped, noticing a large white owl sitting outside the window. To her surprise, the bird had blue eyes.

"I must need my eyes tested," she muttered, wiping her face. "Anyway, you have charmed all the ladies since that first breath, my dear. After Patricia's death, James wrote to me and mentioned that he thought he may have found you. I assumed he was mistaken, for how could we even imagine that the boy we'd thought long dead had come back to us? I didn't meet you when Beth's mother was laid to rest, else I'd have recognised you then, but when I saw you for the first time last month, I knew immediately. Those eyes! What is it Beth calls them? Sea blue? She's right. They look like the sea in the south of France. Just at the shoreline, it takes on a shimmer of turquoise mixed with cobalt blue. I thank God for sparing you, my dear! It's why I must believe he will bring you through this, as well. My only worry is that you'll awaken to discover Beth isn't yet here."

His hand twitched in hers, and she wished she'd said nothing. "Perhaps, you can hear me. Then, hear this, my darling nephew. Beth is well and waiting for us to bring her home. I know it! Now, your only job is to recover. She mustn't return to find you sleeping. She must see those eyes, my dear. Her handsome Captain's sea blue eyes."

The stalwart peeress bent to kiss his stubbled cheek, and a tear dropped onto his shirt. "I love you, Charles Robert. My beautiful Charley Bob. Get well now, and open those remarkable eyes."

She left the chamber, and Sinclair's head moved slightly, his hands clenching. His breathing quickened, for in his dreams, a very strange conversation was taking place.

CHAPTER SEVEN

"You are my daughter?" Sinclair asked the child. "Forgive me, but I find that rather confusing."

"Is it?" the girl asked. "One day it will all make sense, I imagine. This may be one of my dreams, actually. I often have vivid dreams like this—about this place, I mean—but I've never encountered you before, Father. Not until now. You used to tell me that a day would come when I'd lead you through a very dark place. I suppose that day is today. Don't worry, darling Father. Follow me, and we'll find our way together."

"And your mother?" he asked as he took her small hand.

"I've not seen her. Only you." Her dark eyes widened. "Is this when Mother was missing?"

"I suppose that is one way to describe it," he replied cautiously. "You know about that?"

She stopped and looked at him. Charles observed the calm expression, the soft contours of her heart-shaped face and the posture of her petite body, and it struck him very hard how this child was a perfect copy of Elizabeth when he'd first met her in 1879. The girl who claimed to be his daughter possessed the duchess's nose, chin, brows, ears, and mouth. Even her laughter and voice sounded so much like Beth's that it brought him great comfort, though it also made him weep.

"You're sad," she said plainly. "I hardly ever see you sad, Father. Only a few times, and even then, you usually try to keep me from seeing it. Why are you sad today? Have I said something wrong?"

He wiped his face and knelt beside her, searching for a way to explain the impossible situation to a child. "No, darling. If I seem sad, it's because I've been so very alone, and quite honestly frightened. Yet, seeing you gives me great hope. You're so very much like your mother."

She giggled and kissed the tears from his cheeks. "I wish I had a penny for every time you've told me that, Father. It must be a thousand or more by now. What day is this?" she asked him. "Did you and Mother just marry?"

"Yes, we did. Why do you ask?"

"Then, I know all about this. You've told me the story many times. I'm sure this is why I've dreamt of this world so often. So that I could help you. Come now, my darling Father. Keep to this path. A few more steps, and then we'll pass through another gate," she instructed him as they neared a dense thicket of yew trees. "Stay close to me. There are traps all along this section. The trees can move, and those that aren't asleep can be quite cross."

He followed alongside her, pondering the implications of her statements. "Darling, may I ask a few questions?"

"Of course. I'd expect nothing less from someone like you."

"Someone like I?"

"You're head of the most important intelligence gathering organisation in Europe. You advise the prime minister daily, and you visit the queen almost as often. I don't think anything in government is ever settled before you offer an opinion. Everyone says the Duke of Haimsbury is the most influential man in all the realm."

"I see," he answered, still wondering if he dreamt. "Wait. Did you just say *Duke* of Haimsbury?"

She stopped, her dark eyes growing thoughtful, and she bit her lower lip. "Oh, dear. If this is your wedding day, then I may have misspoken. You made me promise never to reveal future events to you."

"Not even this one?" he asked.

Her expression reminded him of Beth's whenever she felt torn betwixt two decisions. "I'm not sure, but as I've already said it, I suppose the harm is done. The queen raised you to a duke long ago, even before I was born."

"Did she?" he asked, laughing, for the notion struck Sinclair as altogether improbable. "Why on earth would she elevate me from marquess to a duke?"

"I cannot say, for there are many secrets in our family, but it may have been when the queen asked you to join the Privy Council.

Oh, wait," she sighed, "that is another secret. Perhaps, we should just forge on ahead rather than talk."

Deciding to leave off interrogation for the moment, Charles asked a less probing question. "What year is it—for you, I mean?"

"1899, of course. It will be 1900 soon, a brand new century! Tomorrow is Christmas Day, and we shall take our trip."

"Where do we plan to celebrate?" he asked as she led him around a gnarled and rather angry looking yew. The tree's branches quivered, and a pair of knots widened, the scaly bark stretching like wooden eyelids.

"You there!" the girl shouted, facing the strange tree. "Do not stare at us! We have permission to walk here, and if you continue to spy on us, I shall poke out both your eyes!" Without another word, the small girl retrieved a long branch from the ground, and despite the fallen limb's fierce objection (for it screamed rather like a peacock might), she waved it at the menacing yew. "Do not think I won't do it! You know better, old man! Don't you remember what happened the last time you defied me?"

The ocular knots blinked twice, and then the bark eyelids snapped shut. The spiral leaves rustled angrily, but the youngster waved the branch again. "Quiet! I'm trying to think!"

The tree fell silent, and the girl set the branch upon the ground. "That's better. Now, I shall return this branch to you, but tell all your brothers to let us pass. This is my father, and I will not allow you to harm him! Do you understand me, old man?"

Charles gaped at his daughter. "It seems as though you inherited your mother's temperament and bravery, Georgie."

"So you've told me many times," she answered proudly. "What did you ask me?"

"When?"

"Before that annoying tree started watching us. Was it about time?"

Sinclair found it difficult to maintain a clear head, but he seemed to recall asking her about the year. "Yes, I think so. It's all rather strange here, and I'll admit to some confusion. That gatekeeper creature claimed that time doesn't exist here, but surely it still passes for you. I'd asked you what year it is, and you mentioned it was almost 1900."

"That's right. You asked where we intend to celebrate. That's what it was. It's a strange question for you to ask me, Father, for we celebrate the same way every year. First at Branham, and then we take your special train to Rose House. We arrived here three nights ago. Tomorrow we'll travel to Great-Grandfather's castle and then go to Briarcliff for the New Year. I always love celebrating holidays, but especially Christmastide. Doctor and Mrs. Emerson will join us with their children, and Della is bringing her new baby, and..."

"Wait," he pleaded. "Emerson is married? And he has children? But Della is, as well, and has a baby?"

She stopped. "Oh, I've said far too much, haven't I? You made me promise not to tell you things you didn't already know, and I felt sure I could manage it. But surely you know that Della and her husband always share Christmas with us! And Uncle Paul as well. He's been in New York for the past month, but he's joining us at..."

"*Uncle* Paul?"

"Of course, we've always called him that. He acts more like your brother than a cousin, which is why we call him our uncle. It's perfectly sensible, you know."

"We?" he asked, blinking to clear his head. "You and others?"

She shook her head. "I rather doubt that I'm allowed to answer that. I'm sure you don't know about that part, yet. You did make me promise, and though I've not been very good at complying, I must try, you know."

"Well, then, you must do as I ask."

The child grew thoughtful, and her dark eyes swept across his face as though trying to memorise his features.

"What?" the marquess asked. "Do you find something irregular about my face?"

"No," the girl answered, smiling softly. "It's just that I've never seen you like this. Not in a very long time. Your hair has no grey in it. I'd forgotten that it used to be completely black. And it's much shorter than I remembered it."

Charles laughed. "My hair is now long and grey? Is this new ducal title so very hard on me that I've completely fallen apart?"

"I should never have told you that," she pouted. "You'll most likely be cross, when I tell you about it today."

"When you tell the future me, I assume. Perhaps, I shall simply tell you that I knew it all along, because you told me when I had short hair and no grey. How long?"

"What?"

"The hair. Do tell me that I've not let your Uncle Paul convince me to wear it at my shoulder! I wonder that your mother allows it, actually."

She laughed, and he bent to offer her a kiss. "Uncle Paul's hair is shorter than yours, if you must know. I've seen photographs and paintings of him with long hair, but that all changed when... No, I mustn't say more. I've said far too much already."

"Very well, Daughter, but may I ask when you were born?" he enquired as they continued along the gloomy path.

"1889, of course. On your birthday, in fact. We turn right at this next tree. One of those awful shadow spiders sits in it, and it will try to talk to you, but you mustn't listen, Father. It is a shameless liar."

"I shan't listen," he promised, looking up into the dense evergreen foliage of the gnarled yew. He perceived a set of red eyes within a nebulous, shifting shadow, but nothing more. However, a voice whispered into Sinclair's mind, and it felt like a sharp knife entered, probing for weakness.

"It's difficult to avoid hearing its voice," he admitted. "And it's decidedly uncomfortable."

"Yes, I know, but the pain will stop in a moment. There's a very large stone up here, Father. We go through it."

"Through it?"

"Yes. The stone isn't really there," she told him. "Trust me, Father. I've spent years walking this land in dreams, and I know it quite well."

He pulled at her hand gently, forcing her to stop. "You say your name is Georgianna?"

"Yes, of course it is, but you and mother call me Georgie," she answered patiently.

"You're how old now?"

"Ten. Well, Ten and a half, actually. You told me that I'd find it rather confusing when we finally met in this place, but I hadn't realised how very confused *you* would be, Father."

The back of his head ached, and Charles struggled to retain his link to reality, if indeed, such a thing existed for him now. "Darling, tell me the truth. Is your mother still alive?"

"Of course, she is! Why would you ask me such a very strange question?"

Though he suffered from shifting upheavals in his mind that caused memories to rise and fall, Charles had the distinct impression that Beth had been caught in a great fire, and that he'd failed to rescue her.

The girl reached up and touched his cheek, and that simple act caused the marquess to break down weeping.

"Don't cry, my darling Father," she told him. "I think I know why you're so very worried. You and Mother have told me a little of the many troubles you suffered during the early years of your marriage, but all is happiness now. I wish I could tell you more, but you made me promise. Now, we must push on, Father. We're nearly to the cottage. You'll be all right once we get there. I promise."

He wiped his face and decided to place all his trust in the remarkably bright child.

"You are so much like your mother," he told her proudly. "And I'll give you a penny for that once I see you again, my darling daughter. Now, lead the way."

Georgianna Sinclair didn't hesitate at the rock's rough face, but walked straight into it, and the two of them passed through the massive stone, disappearing from view.

CHAPTER EIGHT

Istseleniye House – 23rd November, 11:03 pm

"She dreams," the prince told the physician. "I can see it in her face. Note the eyelids, Doctor. How they dart back and forth. It is a sign of deep sleep and active dreams."

Lord Salperton yawned as he removed the stethoscope from his ears. "Five days and still no change. I don't understand it. She should be awake by now."

"And her fever?"

"It ebbs and flows," the Scotsman answered, "but her lungs have become congested. I believe she's on the brink of pneumonia, Your Highness. Why on earth was this woman permitted to go out in unsuitable clothing on such a cold, snowy night?"

"It was unavoidable," Romanov told him. "The alternative would have been far worse. Have you no remedy?"

"Not for the extended unconscious state, but I might have a therapy that would aid her lungs. The ingredients are back at Montmore. I'll need to return there for an hour."

"I'll send Vasily to fetch the medicine. I prefer you remain here with the duchess." Romanov said, his tone making it clear that it was an order, not a suggestion.

"Regardless, Your Highness, I must return to my clinic eventually. I've four patients to look after. My nurse may be proficient, but she expects me to make rounds periodically. Ordinarily, Dr. Simon would cover for me when I'm called upon to remain with a critical patient, but as you know, he is in America."

"I appreciate that you've kept to your bargain and remained here," Romanov answered, "but I beg you not to abandon the duchess! She is in desperate need of your ministrations."

Henry stared. In the five days since arriving at the castle, he'd spent many hours in the strange prince's presence, but he had never heard such anguish in the Russian's voice. "You're afraid for her."

"I am terrified for her! You cannot imagine the struggles she's enduring just now. Please, if you will remain here, I promise the effort will be rewarded."

"I'm not interested in money, Your Highness."

"I do not refer to material gain, Doctor, but to greater rewards."

Sighing, the viscount conceded. "Very well. I might be able to arrange for a colleague to look in at Montmore."

"I could arrange for someone to visit your patients."

Salperton gasped in irritation. "Forgive me, sir, but if your connexions within the medical community are so vast, why the devil did you come to me in the first place? There are many experts with more experience than I, and some with far grander titles!"

"But none with so great an interest in the lady's welfare. Nor in her husband's."

"I insist you explain that!" Salperton shouted. He'd had very little sleep, and his patience had begun to wear thin.

"Hush, please, my friend. I appreciate your ire, but I prefer to keep the atmosphere of this room less strident. Let us adjourn to the lady's drawing room, and I shall be pleased to answer any questions you may wish to ask."

The weary viscount found himself thoroughly vexed and confounded, but he forced himself to concentrate on his patient's welfare. After all, the duchess knew nothing of this conversation—she needed him. Henry returned the instruments to the large bag and snapped it shut. "Very well. Lead on, for I have a great many questions."

They moved into the adjoining sitting room. Since arriving on Monday night, Salperton had made this room a temporary bedchamber so that he could hear the duchess should she cry out or awaken. The curved damask sofa where he spent fitful nights held a rumpled red and gold quilt and a small embroidered cushion that served as a pillow. Henry sat into the couch's soft embrace, tempted to fall asleep, but he dared not lose this opportunity to question the Russian. Romanov had a habit of disappearing for hours at a time, and even when present, skillfully evaded all attempts at lengthy conversation.

This was Henry's first chance to learn about his host.

The enigmatic prince took a chair near the fire. "I am yours to command, Lord Salperton. Ask me anything you wish."

"Very well. To begin with, why did you call upon me, Your Highness? I insist you explain yourself clearly. Otherwise, I shall leave this house and go straight to the police."

Rather than react with anger, the prince seemed amused by the physician's threat. "As always, Henry, your heart rules your head, despite what you may wish to believe."

"What the devil do you mean by that?" Salperton shot back.

"Merely, that you are a man of deeply held convictions. I admire that. As to the police, even if you succeeded in reaching the authorities on your own, they would find it difficult, if not impossible, to find this castle. Our household is veiled."

"Veiled? What sort of nonsense is that?"

"You said yourself that my home is known to the villagers as Ghaist Castle. Though I feigned surprise, it was not the first time I'd heard that rather quaint expression. I imagine that this most descriptive name is due to the veil that shrouds the property. I have placed a special type of lock upon all our gates to make it difficult for my enemies to find us."

"And what enemies might those be, sir? The British government? The police?"

Romanov smiled patiently. "Not the police, no, and your government considers me a valued advisor where foreign policy matters are concerned. I refer to a different class of enemies, my friend. Spirits."

"Ghosts, you mean."

"Hardly. Not in the sense by which most mean that word. I told you that your mother could see angels, Lord Salperton, but you also see them, do you not? Only, you perceive angels that are far different from those who interacted with your dear mother. Your visions are darker. Heavier. Surely, you've noticed an absence of these spirits here, within these walls."

The viscount found his mouth suddenly dry, and he longed for a glass of water—or better yet, something stronger.

"There is brandy in the decanter to your right," the prince said, reading his thoughts. "Or do you prefer whisky? I've a cask of Drummond Reserve in the cellar. Shall I have Vasily decant it?"

"How do you know that I... That I see spirits?" the Scotsman asked, his voice cracking.

"I know a great deal about you, Henry, and I confess that it did not arise solely from touching you in the coach on Monday night. You ask why I chose you from amongst all the physicians in London. The answer is simple. It is because of your ability to see these troubling spirits. The duchess needs far more than medicine, Dr. MacAlpin. She needs someone on whom she may rely to help her sort through her own terrifying visions."

"Are you telling me that she also sees these... These hellish creatures? Is she like my mother?" the young physician asked, his brown eyes wide.

"She is like you, Henry. The spirits the duchess perceives—the entities that have surrounded and pursued her for the greater part of her life—are not the loyal *elohim* your mother saw. They are deceitful, entirely fallen, and openly rebellious to God. Elizabeth can see these rebel princes, but also their demonic helpers. Had I told you all this when we first met, would you have come with me?"

Salperton smiled nervously, swiping at his curly black hair with a lean hand. "Most likely not. Most likely, I'd have deemed you demented at best, a liar at worst. Or a charlatan. Would I have been wrong?"

Romanov laughed, and Salperton thought he perceived a faint hint of wings behind the prince's straight back. The Scotsman squinted, certain he'd imagined it.

"Your eyes do not deceive you, Henry. You already suspect that I am not human, and you are correct."

The visitor shot to his feet, angry with himself for allowing this stranger to manipulate him, but also suddenly fearful. The temperature in the room dropped twenty degrees, and the candles actually dimmed. The prince was speaking, but simultaneously, other voices from the doctor's past joined Romanov's, the layered sounds multiplied in different pitches and whispered in dissonant echoes that repeated inside Henry's mind—the experience both pleasant and terrifying, all at once.

"Henry, do you see them? The beautiful angels?" he heard his mother's voice ask. *"Are they real? Tell me they're real, please! Such lovely wings, they have, Henry! Can you see them? They ask if you can see them... They tell me that you have an important task*

ahead. A woman will need you. A woman who sees that which is unseen. Can you see them, my darling Hal? Can you? Please, tell me I'm not mad! Please!"

And along with this came a dissenting and discordant voice, an oily coat upon a grating hiss—one Salperton had heard many times as a boy.

"Do you think it mere chance that you see spirits, Henry? No, indeed, we come to you because you are unlike other boys. You are very special, Henry. Your blood is unique. And we shall keep you from harm and teach you... All you need do is follow us and do as we ask!"

These and a thousand other, ancient memories crowded the Scotsman's mind whilst his ears strained to hear the prince's spoken words beneath the complex strata. Finally, when on the cusp of screaming in agony, the auditory torture abruptly ceased. Henry wiped at his eyes, his breathing quick, head tilted in an effort to dampen the maddening, aural assault.

"Forgive me," he muttered, expecting to find his host in the opposite chair, but the seat was empty.

Instead, Romanov now stood beside the door to the duchess's chamber. Salperton had not seen him move from the wingback, much less cross to the other door.

"Sir?" he asked tensely, wiping his brow. *Why is the room so stiflingly hot suddenly?* "I didn't notice you move, but I heard voices. Not only your own, but others."

"Yes, I know," the Russian whispered, his ear to the bedchamber door as if listening. "The voices you heard came from the seven realms. Keep watch on the duchess in my absence, and do not follow me! A shift in power takes place, and I must leave. Vasily will see to your needs. I promise to answer all your questions at a later time."

Prince Anatole did not open the door; he *passed through it*, and Henry MacAlpin, 7th Viscount Salperton was left alone and wondering if he'd lost all his wits and become a madman.

CHAPTER NINE

"There's the cottage," the girl told Sinclair. "That's strange, I've never seen smoke coming from the chimney before. Sometimes, I see a smiling woman in the window, and she waves to me, but the chimney never has smoke. I wonder why it's changed now."

"Is this the first time I've walked here with you, darling?"

She nodded. "Yes, it is. Perhaps, that's the reason for the difference."

They walked along a fieldstone path that led towards the thatched cottage. It was timber-framed and clad in creek rock. A single shaft of warm yellow light shone down upon its roof, causing the entire building to glow. It had a blue door that bore a pair of entwined carved hearts upon it, and within this carving, he perceived two additional hearts adorned with gold, and these glowed as though lit by fire.

"This is where I must leave you, Father mine. You always told me that I'd help you to find your way and that the cottage was your destination. That's why I've worked so very hard to find the quickest path through the maze. There are evil birds and spiders all about the house. You can see them at the wood's edge, but don't let them worry you. It will be fine, so long as you don't linger too long. Keep watch on the moon. The woman says it is too late, when the moon begins to change."

"Darling, why must you go?" he asked, wishing to know his daughter better. "I've so many questions!"

"I know you do, but you made me promise not to answer them. You said that you mustn't learn too much about the future, as it might affect my past. That I was to tell you only enough to get you here. I've done that." She put her arms around his neck as he knelt beside her. "I love you so very much, darling Father. You make me very proud. You are the most wonderful father in all the world!"

"I love you, too, Georgianna," he whispered. "And I look forward to meeting you again soon, though you'll be just a baby at the time. But I shall tell you all about this miraculous adventure when you're old enough. It's been quite strange, being led by my unborn child. You make me very proud, little one."

She began to laugh, deep dimples forming in her smooth cheeks. "You always call Mother that! Though, you sometimes call me that as well. I'll tell you a secret, Father. I've always loved hearing you say it, so please don't ever stop. Even when I'm grown and married."

"I promise," he said, kissing her small hands, tears glistening in his eyes.

"Go inside now, Father. I'm starting to wake up, but I'll tell you all about it, when I see you at breakfast."

"You will tell the future me, you mean?"

She nodded. "Yes, I suppose it is the future you, though to me, you're just my wonderful, remarkable father. I'll see you again in a few minutes!"

The girl continued to smile at him even as her body thinned into nothingness. In less than two heartbeats, Georgianna Sinclair had completely disappeared, leaving her somewhat confused father all alone.

Charles put his hand upon the door's iron handle, depressing the thumb latch and pushing. The hinges creaked, and he could smell bread baking upon a wood fire. As he entered the cottage's interior, Sinclair could hear the clatter of pans from another room, and a woman singing softly in a thick, Highland accent:

The wild-rose blooms in Drummond woods,
The trees are blossom'd fair,
The lake is smiling to the sun,
And Mary wand'ring there.
The pow'rs that watched o'er Mary's birth,
Did Nature's charms despoil,
They stole for her the rose's blush,
The sweet lake's dimpled smile! [2]

2 Poem by Archibald Stirling Irving, originally published 1841.

"Hello?" he called softly as he inspected the main room. It felt vaguely familiar, and it struck Charles that the furnishings reminded him of another cottage, one he'd just seen in the asaru stone's visions. The hearth stood nearly as tall as the marquess, and an iron kettle simmered upon the crackling fire, suspended from a long hook. A sizzling pan of Bannock bread cooled upon a nearby stool.

The singing had stopped, as had the clattering of the pans, and Charles turned to see a plump woman with a wooden ladle in her hand. "I didn't hear anyone knock," she said in Scots Gaelic. The marquess simultaneously heard the language and translated it inside his head.

"You're Scottish," he said, also speaking Gaelic, much to his surprise.

"Aye, that I am," she replied, laughing merrily. She was round as an apple and dressed in a wool tartan skirt. The homespun blouse had billowing sleeves turned up to the elbows. Charles recognised the tartan's pattern as an older version of the Stuart hunting design, for he'd seen it in several of the oil paintings at the duke's London home. The woman's clothing appeared new but reflected attire worn by Highland peasants from centuries earlier. Sinclair wondered if he'd moved backwards in time.

"Forgive me," he said. "I was told to come in. I should have knocked first."

"You were told to come in? By whom, my lord?"

"By my daughter," he answered. "She had to leave, however. It's all rather strange, actually. She's not yet born, you see, but she proved to be my rescuer. It's odd how the Lord works."

"Aye, our Saviour works his miracles in ways we'd nary expect," the amiable woman answered, her fleshy cheeks rounding above a wide smile. "I reckon you'll be stayin' for supper, then? Just like the other one."

"The other one?"

"The lady, sir. Surely, you know about the lady! I found 'er on my doorstep not half an hour ago. She's powerful tired, though. The boy brought her. You probably knew that as well."

"No, I'm rather ill-informed regarding this strange land. Forgive me, madam. I wonder if I might sit?" he asked, suddenly overcome by weariness and fearful that he might collapse.

"Oh, o' course, sir! Such a poor welcome I'm makin' for ye, an' me havin' waited all this time. Take the rocker by the fire, now. You look nigh ready ta fallin' down! My manners've sure gone rusty! I'll fetch a cup o' tea, or would ye be needin' somethin' a wee bit stronger?"

"Just water, if you have it handy," he said as he sat into the hand-hewn rocking chair. "Where am I?"

"It's called *Fasgadh Bothan*, sir. It means House o' Refuge, though you surely know that, as you're a Scotsman. I can tell from the look o' ye, an' ye speak a wee bi' o' the Gaelic, though wi' an accent, o' course. This house is safe from all those foul creatures. The spiders and bird people, I mean. And you're safe from the Shadows. Evil things they are, sir, but the Lord's own light keeps this house protected. You say that the wee girl brought you through the maze? Aye! I've seen 'er about now an' then, but she nary comes in. She must be a bright child, indeed, for the way is quite confusin' and very dangerous."

"She is a brilliant child," he professed with pride. "Wait, you said that a boy brought this woman you mentioned?"

"Aye, sir, he did. I've seen the lad hereabouts now and again. Tall and quite nice. Black o' hair an' long o' limb. We've spoken a few times, through the window or when I'm in the garden, but he nary comes in neither. Said he's not supposed to. The lady told me 'bout him. The children never come in, sir. This place is only for you."

"For me?"

"And the lady, o' course. Here's your water, sir. It's clean and clear. I'll plate up some soup and add a crust o' bread. It's made from me own recipe. Heavy on the butter an' oats, but light on the sweet. I use honey from me own hives. Tis a blessing ta have bees about; they keep the birds away, ya know. God's own little guardians, I think. Once you've eaten, I'll leave you and the lady ta yourselves."

"Thank you," he said, taking the cup of water. "What is your name, dear lady?"

"It's Hope, sir." The woman added two ladles of the thick stew to a brown and white crock, topped it with a large piece of oat bread and handed it to him. "This'll soon fortify you, my lord. Now, if there's naught else, I'll be goin'. Enjoy yer time, but don't overstay. The birds'll try to get in, but they canno' so long as you don't remain here too long. Keep watch on the moon. When it changes, you must go. It's been real nice meeting you at last, sir. The Lord's blessings be with you."

"And with you," he said as she left through the front door.

Sinclair set the simple meal on a nearby table and crossed to the window, expecting to see the curious woman upon the path, but saw no one. He did, however, see many dozens of the birdmen standing at the edge of the bordering woods and staring at the house. The creatures appeared to be speaking to one another as though plotting, and Charles found himself wondering just how long before they would attempt to breach the door.

Then he heard the sound, soft, like a faint sigh, coming from elsewhere within the cottage. Only then, did he notice another door. Praying the birds hadn't found a weakness and entered, he opened the brightly painted door. It led into a small room, which stood in semi-darkness, lit only by a tiny pinpoint of light from a candle, which burnt upon a washstand beneath a circular window. The narrow bed was formed of willow branches, twisted into a heart shape over the head. The quilt was patchwork, and each colourful scrap held a stitched pair of entwined hearts. Within the overlapping portion of these hearts, two tiny hearts had been embroidered in golden thread. Upon the bed, beneath this beautiful quilt, slept a woman with curling dark hair that spilt across the feather pillows in waves of gleaming sable.

"Beth!" he cried out, rushing to her side. He sat upon the bed, taking her pale hand into his. It felt quite warm to the touch. He put his palm against her forehead, noting that it, too, seemed overly warm.

Charles found a towel in the kitchen and poured cool water into it, wrung it out, and then returned to place it upon his wife's feverish brow.

"There now," he whispered. "Can you hear me, darling?"

She didn't move, but her breathing seemed regular and deep.

"Beth, are you ill?" he asked, worrying. The marquess felt her pulse and found it quick and somewhat weak. "Can you hear me? Elizabeth?"

She turned slightly, her eyes darting back and forth rapidly behind the dark lashes. Charles bowed his head and folded her hand into his as he prayed aloud, petitioning the Lord for mercy.

"Father in heaven, you are the author of all creation; the designer of realms, both seen and unseen. I've spent my life studying mathematics and design, criminal intent and evidence, logic and calculation. However, as I learn more about you, I find myself noticing the internal workings of creation, those hidden complications and mechanisms behind what we call reality. If this strange place does exist, then you are here. If it is only in my mind, then you are still here! No matter where I might travel, you are there, my King, and I thank you for that assurance."

He kissed her hand, weeping as he continued. "Father, I believe with all my heart that you formed the bond betwixt myself and this incredible woman, and that you designed us to become one. I cannot say just why I am here, but whilst I originally thought myself dreaming, I begin to think otherwise. How can we both be here, if it is but a dream? Rather, I think us here as part of some great plan, and so, I ask you to help me to help her. Are we both ill? Am I lying beside her somewhere, or worse, are we separated? Wherever she is in the real world, I ask you to protect her. If she is lost somewhere, then allow me to find her, please!"

He kissed her small hand once again, the tears falling like rain upon his cheeks. "How I love this woman, Lord! She is my life! Please, do not take her from me!"

As though in answer to his petition, the duchess sighed, and he saw her eyelids twitch.

"Lord, thank you! Oh, my King, thank you so very much!" He gently lifted her into his arms, grateful to feel her breath against his cheek. "Beth, open your eyes, darling. Please. Open them for me."

The lids flickered, and she inhaled deeply then exhaled, the lashes parting. "Captain Nemo," she whispered.

Sinclair smiled through a veil of tears. "Yes, dearest heart, it's Captain Nemo. Your Captain is here."

"Where are we?" she asked, trying to sit.

"Be careful now," he warned her. "You're feverish. I think you may be ill, Beth. Can you tell me what you remember?"

"Very little," she told him. "I don't know this house. Where are we? Why are we here?"

"I cannot answer that, not fully. I suspect that you and I are actually asleep somewhere, though not together. Beth, can you tell me what you remember? After the wedding. Anything at all."

"I'm thirsty," she told him.

"Of course, you are. Forgive me! I should have thought of that before forcing these questions. Stay here."

He retrieved a cup of water from a wooden bucket he found near the front door and helped her to drink.

"Thank you, Captain," she said, smiling. Sinclair continued to weep, and she touched his face, wiping the tears away. "How I love your gentle spirit, Charles, but don't worry. You'll soon figure it all out. You're brilliant at this sort of thing. Now, you asked what I remember. Not very much, I'm afraid, but I hear voices now and then. Does that make sense?"

"Yes, it does, actually. Do you know them? Are they male or female?"

"Both," she answered. "A woman and two men, I think. One known to me; the other not. The familiar voice speaks in whispers, and he sounds worried. I'm not sure about the words. It's as though only part of my mind hears them."

"If you're sleeping, or even partially so, then you might not comprehend clearly. Can you smell anything?"

"Smell? Oh, I see what you're asking. Yes, I do. Bread."

He laughed. "That is from our hostess. She made stew and a pan of oat bread. I can bring you some, if you're hungry. What else?"

"A wood fire."

"Also from this cottage. Any perfumes? Soaps? Tobacco?"

She shook her head. "None—no, wait! There's a sort of medicinal smell, like camphor mixed with peppermint."

"It's likely that you're being tended by a physician or nurse. Once I'm free of this place, I'll commence with hospitals. Although, it's possible that you're in our home."

"No, I don't think so," she told him. "I'd recognise all our doctors' voices, and wouldn't you or Paul be near me?"

"I wouldn't be, unless, of course, I'm sleeping nearby. Perhaps, I'm merely exhausted, and I've come to lead you out of this place. I cannot say, but Beth, I *will* lead you out. Here now, let me help you to stand. Are you strong enough?"

"Yes, I think so. I'm very hungry."

"Then, I'll fetch you some of our hostess's fine stew." He brought the bowl prepared for him and sat beside the duchess, feeding her. Within minutes, she began to brighten. "You look much better now, my darling. Can you stand if I help you?"

"Yes," she said.

Together, they walked into the main room, and Charles set her into the rocker. "Here's more water," he said, passing her the cup. "Drink as much as you can, Beth. If you're ill, then this may only nourish your mind, but then how are we to know?" He thought about Georgianna, and how she'd told him that she was born in June, 1889. "Our daughter depends on us."

"Our daughter?" she asked. "What if this child is a son?"

"I do not think so," he told her, smiling. "I'm quite certain of it, in fact."

She shook her head. "Charles, I rarely disagree with you, but in this case, I must. Allow me to explain. I've no idea how I came to be here, but I awoke to find myself standing in a terrifying field of sighted stones and moving trees. A horrid birdman kept insisting that I give him my ring as payment for instruction, but I refused. He told me that the only way home was to enter a maze of stone gates, and I despaired of ever finding you again."

"Until a child appeared and helped. Is that how it went?" he asked her.

She nodded. "Yes! How did you know?"

"Because she also helped me."

Her dark brows pinched together. "She? No, Charles, it was a boy. He looked very much like you. Tall, well-proportioned, exceedingly handsome, and he had sea blue eyes."

Sinclair stared. "A boy? Now, that is strange! What else did this young man say? Did you ask his name? His birthdate?"

"I did. He was born in June of 1889. His name is..."

"Robert," the marquess answered.

"Yes! How did you know?"

"I know it, darling, because you have told me many times that you intend to name our first son after me. That he would be Charles Robert Arthur Sinclair IV, and to avoid confusion, we would call him Robert, or Robby. Remember, how I told you that I wanted to name our first daughter after you? And you said she shouldn't be called Beth or any diminutive of Elizabeth, because that might also be confusing? We decided to call her Georgianna."

"Yes, I remember. Charles, are you saying that the girl who brought you here was named Georgianna?"

"Yes," he answered, smiling. "She said that we call her Georgie. She was born in June of '89. Beth, does this mean what I think it does?"

She began to laugh, and the effect lit up her eyes. "I think it explains many things, Captain! Have you noticed the imagery all about us? Carvings, stitches, even the stencils painted upon the wood trim? They appear to tell a story."

Sinclair walked all around the cottage, examining the motifs present everywhere. Sure enough, the entwined hearts he'd noticed upon the exterior of the door were repeated throughout the interior, but as with the quilt, inside each twin-heart image rested two, much smaller hearts, wrought in gold.

"Twins!" he exclaimed, shaking his head in amazement. "Good heavens, darling, you're carrying twins!"

"Yes, I believe that may be right. Mrs. Alcorn mentioned it to me only this morning—or what seems like this morning. I'm all mixed up, but assuming this is still our wedding day, then it was this morning."

"What did she say to you, darling?" he asked, deciding to refrain from any mention of the abduction, for it was possible she'd forgotten this dreadful truth, as she often did with terrifying experiences.

"She said that my extreme symptoms and early expansion, as she called it, reminded her of a woman she knew some years ago on the Branham estate. A farmer's wife who gave birth to two sets of twins, if you can believe it."

"At the same time?" the marquess asked, sitting upon the stone apron to the hearth.

"No," she laughed. "Not at the same time. Two babies apart, actually. She had twin boys, followed by two singletons, and then a second set of twin girls. Each twin birth caused her to suffer terribly very early on, and her waistline grew quickly, just as mine does. Charles, perhaps, we have a son and a daughter on the way."

"And they are both quite remarkable and brilliant," he said, kissing her hands. "Beth, if true, then I couldn't be happier, but it's all the more reason we must find our way out of this place. I fear that Georgie offered no clue as to how we might accomplish that."

"Nor did Robby," Elizabeth answered, setting the bowl aside. "However, we might have the information already."

"How so, my love?" he asked.

"That hideous bird creature tried endlessly to convince me to give him my ring. Might there be a reason why he would do this?"

"I suppose so, yes. He wanted my watch. I've no intention of ever parting with this timepiece, Beth, for you had it engraved for me in Glasgow. The inscription heartens me as no other message could."

"Your watch? Charles, this may sound quite odd, but does the watch work?"

"Of course, it works, darling. It's an excellent timepiece, although it has been overwound," he said, removing it from its pocket and clicking the latch to the cover. "See? The hands remain fixed at one-thirteen and thirty-three seconds. An ominous set of numbers, if I remember Kepelheim's dissertation on occult numerology."

"On what?" she asked, puzzled.

"Never mind. How might this watch be important, Beth? You think this creature wanted to take it for a reason?"

"I think that all the birds in this awful place are devious, but most especially that one! Perhaps, the watch holds the key to our escape. Might that be it?"

"Key?" he repeated. "Now that is odd. The gatekeeper called gold a key, or I'd assumed he meant gold. Is it possible he meant this gold watch is a key?"

Before Beth could answer, Sinclair felt a heavy shadow of gloom invade his thoughts. He rose and looked out the windows. The birds had left the woods and started towards the cottage. Row upon row, they marched like soldiers, their chatter silenced. They had made their plans, and now they'd begun to implement them.

"What if we cannot escape? Beth, I've no idea how to use this watch, even if it is the key! It may already be too late. We may be imprisoned here forever."

"Charles, my darling husband, you seem to have lost all hope! Is there something you're not telling me?" she asked.

He wondered if she could bear hearing the truth. "Beth, I think you are incredibly strong. If I tell you something quite awful, can you endure it?"

She smiled and took his hand. “Think about it, Charles. If our unborn children exist in the future, then no matter what you have to tell me, it means that any trouble we face now is only temporary. Yes, tell me. I can endure it.”

His heart lightened at her simple words. “My remarkable wife! How very brave you are. All right. The night of our wedding, something quite dreadful happened. But, as you say, our children will one day be born and will thrive and even come here to help us. We mustn’t see this is as the final event of our lives. It is but one small hurdle on a long and wonderful journey.”

“Yes, it is, husband. So, let us leap over this hurdle together,” she whispered. “Tell me, Charles. What happened?”

CHAPTER TEN

24th November, 11:03 am - The Empress Hotel

Paul Stuart had tried to visit with the owner of the Empress several days earlier but was told by the steward that Meg Hansen was indisposed. Though the earl had pressed again and again, the stubborn man refused to allow him to move past the foyer, but suggested the peer return in a few days, when the proprietress would be well enough to receive his call. The earl left his card, scribbling a quick message on the back: *Let's talk business. Send word to me at Haimsbury House.*

That Saturday morning at half past nine, Paul was called from breakfast to greet a middle-aged commissionaire, who bore a message from Hansen: *My lord, I shall entertain all offers today at eleven. Please, be prompt.* After informing Duke James and Emerson of his plans, the handsome Scot dressed in his most expensive morning suit, added diamond cufflinks and the Aubrey watch and chain, and then took one of the new, Haimsbury-Branham coaches drawn by a team of four to Whitechapel. His intent was to put on a display of great wealth and power, using these as a fulcrum to prise open the influential madam's closely held secrets.

Sitting now in a finely upholstered chair opposite Hansen, Stuart offered his most dazzling smile as he accepted a delicate teacup from the hands of a waifish servant girl.

"Thank you," he said. The girl held onto the saucer, as though unwilling to let go of his hand. "That's very helpful of you, Miss..."

"It's Mary, sir. Mary Idlewyld. I can fetch you cakes as well. Or sandwiches. We've lots of sandwiches, my lord."

Meg Hansen cleared her throat and stared at the servant. "Thank you, Mary. That will be all."

The earl sipped the tea thoughtfully. "A lovely child. She looks quite young."

"Mary's nearly thirteen," the brothel-keeper answered. "Do you like them young, sir?"

"I prefer someone with experience," Stuart answered with a wink. "It's kind of you to speak with me, Mrs. Hansen. I know you're a busy woman, so I shall get to the point of my visit."

Hansen poured herself a cup of tea, added two splashes of gin, and glanced at her guest, offering a smile so wide that it nearly caused her face powder to crack. "It keeps out the chill. I wonder, have you a chill, Lord Aubrey?"

"Not at the moment, but thank you all the same. My uncle would insist that only whisky can provide such lovely warmth, but it is a debate for another day."

Stirring the ingredients, the aging madam took a small sip and then set the cup into a matching saucer. "Your uncle is the Duke of Drummond, is he not? Duke James is a very handsome man, as are you, my lord. That business last Sunday night was just dreadful! Our East End newspapers talk of little else. How is Lord Haimsbury, sir? It distressed all of us to learn of his injuries. I do hope he has recovered," she probed.

"My cousin is much improved," the earl lied. "I suspect he will pay a call on your household before too many days have passed—to make certain of your welfare, of course."

"Of course," she parroted back, thoughtfully.

Reporters had been told that Sinclair suffered a blow to the head, but little else. Thus far, no journalist had managed to breach the strict security at Haimsbury House to learn any different. Thankfully, the strange attacks by Trent's wolfmen kept their dull wits and even duller pencils busy scraping paper.

At Aubrey's command, inner circle agents had quickly spread throughout London, to every policeman, every publisher's office, every gentlemen's club, every public house to whisper the 'true' explanation for the monstrous bloodletting, attributing it to water pollution caused by the dumping of spoilt grain into East End cisterns. The entire tale was fabrication, but no one bothered to question it; such was the state of journalism in London's fourth estate.

Hansen's plucked and painted, auburn brows arched in mild surprise and frank relief, for the proprietress had often daydreamed about the handsome policeman, beginning when Charles had first moved into No. 12 with his late wife, Amelia Winstone St. Clair.

"I'm so very happy to hear that the superintendent's accident did not cause any longlasting mischief! And that incident with the water, well, it was quite a shock to learn that a granary could be so careless."

"Indeed it was. Did anyone here suffer the effects of the polluted water, madam?"

"Thankfully, no. The Empress is blessed to have a patron, who's kind enough to send us two barrels of water each day from pumps near his business in Westminster. But I doubt that you called merely to discuss water, Lord Aubrey. A busy man such as yourself hardly visits one such as I without an urgent *need*, shall we say? How may I assist you?"

Very few men could have done so convincingly, but the earl actually batted his eyelashes, pretending ignorance of her overtly sexual suggestion. "*Urgency* is probably not the precise word, my very dear Mrs. Hansen. Perhaps, I called merely to admire one of the most renowned beauties in London."

The effect of Paul's charming display was immediate. Hansen giggled like a schoolgirl. "Oh, my dear Lord Aubrey, you tease me!"

"On the contrary, I speak truth. I do have one other, small question, Mrs. Hansen."

"Meg," she insisted. "Short for Margaret, you know."

"Meg it is, then," he answered, offering a dazzling smile. "My dear Meg, you have an excellent view of my cousin's old house. Through your windows, I mean."

"Lord Haimsbury's house? Yes, I suppose I do. You know, I recall the very day that your cousin moved in. I've been mistress of the Empress for nearly three dec..."

She had started to say 'nearly three decades', which was true, for Margaret Ellen Hansen had come to the Empress as a lithe and lovely, eleven-year-old prostitute, taken from the harsh streets by a wealthy patron. She'd risen quickly amongst the brothel's pecking order until, in 1860, she was offered her current position as proprietress. However, in a profession where experience came only with time, but time eventually worked against you, Hansen preferred her true age remain a mystery.

"What I mean to say," she continued, "is that I've been here long enough to have met the previous tenant at No. 12. He was also a policeman. A Mr. Stanley, I believe. We never learnt what happened, but one morning, there was a 'to let' sign in the window, and our Mr. Stanley had vanished."

"How very curious," Aubrey remarked, storing the information inside his nearly perfect memory. "And how soon after did my cousin move into the house?"

"Almost right away!" she exclaimed whilst pouring a quarter cup of tea, which she then topped to the brim with gin. "I remember that day very well. Early February of '78 and a dismal day it was, too. Cold and rainy. I noticed two wagons drawing up to the house and remarked to Mr. Howard—he was our usher at the time—well, I said to Mr. Howard that it looked as though someone had let No. 12. That house is the jewell of the entire block, or so I've always thought. The other terraced houses are so very plain, but twelve has its own personality. I told Mr. Howard that I hoped someone nice was moving in."

Aubrey smiled, picturing Hansen's face when she first observed a twenty-two-year-old Charles Sinclair, then called St. Clair, descending from one of the moving wagons. His cousin's impressive height and deific physique, coupled with a face that sent many a lady into the fainting room, must have done more than cause the madam's heart to skip beats. Indeed, the prospect of introducing such a handsome and fit young man to her female banquet surely sent Hansen into a financial reverie of Medici proportions!

"And when did you first meet him?" the earl asked his hostess.

"Later that same day," she replied, not surprising Stuart in the least. "I took over a small basket with fruit, a few sandwiches, and a bottle of champagne. One never has the time to prepare food when moving, does one? He appeared to be on his own—a bachelor, so I thought—and I wanted to make sure he had a meal after all that very energetic unloading."

The peer had to work hard not to laugh, but he maintained an outward expression of mild interest. "Yes, I can imagine how such a day might sap one's energies. That was very thoughtful. I'm sure Charles was most appreciative."

"Actually, he was," she answered after taking a deep swig of her 'tea'. "Poor man was all alone. He explained that his wife and son would be arriving that Monday week, and that he'd wanted to arrange the house for them first. To be quite frank, Lord Aubrey, my experience with men has taught me that thoughtfulness such as that is most unusual. The young inspector, for that is what Mr. Sinclair—I mean Lord Haimsbury, of course—well, that was his rank at the time. He explained that he'd wanted a larger home for his growing family, and the house came up quite suddenly for lease. We shared the wine and sandwiches, and I promise you that not one moment of our evening was untoward. Not one!" she added, a hint of regret crossing her powdered face. Sighing, the madam continued, "Mrs. St. Clair arrived the following week with their son. I wonder, would her name now be Sinclair?"

"I rather think it would still be St. Clair, as that was her legal name when Amelia died. My cousin has since had all pertinent records changed to reflect his birth name, of course. But as you and he became instant friends, I imagine any activity across the way must still draw your notice. Recently, there was a break-in at No. 12. Did you know that?"

"In fact, I did!" she whispered, leaning close in conspiratorial fashion. "One of the marquess's own men came by to enquire about that housebreak. I imagine Lord Haimsbury worried that our house might have suffered from the same criminal hand. As I say, Charles Sinclair is a very kind, considerate man."

"Yes, so he is."

"As are you, my lord!" she sang back, intentionally touching his hand. "But this gentleman who called. He told me that No. 12's back door had been forced, and that it was assumed items stolen. The next day, we noticed crested wagons parked outside the house, and that same gentleman, as well as three others, loaded all the furnishings and dozens of packing boxes. His name was Granger, I believe. Hamish Granger."

"You've a remarkable memory," he told her, admiringly. "And you saw no one else? Perhaps, knocking upon the door?"

"No one at all. Of course, I don't make a habit of watching the doors of my neighbours. Sir, am I under suspicion of something illegal? Outside of the obvious, of course."

Aubrey laughed. "Madam, I'm not with any branch of law enforcement. That honour lies with my cousin, but even if I were, the

Metropolitan police rarely pursue the sort of crime in which you and your ladies engage."

"That's a great relief," she told him. "If I may confess, we have a few policeman who call here now and then. Just to make certain all is well, you know."

"Indeed. I'm sure it is gratifying to have their protection. Which leads me to another question. There is a particular lady whom I prefer, but I fear she's gone missing. Miss Ida Ross. She was once one of your own, was she not?"

"Ross," the woman repeated, her mind grappling with why he might ask such a question. "Yes, she did serve here for a few months. Long ago. She became ill and could no longer work, if I remember rightly. In fact, Ida was taken to hospital at Bedlam."

"Oh, that is a pity. I blame myself. I should have kept in contact with Ida. I cannot remember where we met. A party, I believe. In Westminster."

"Might it have been Grosvenor Square, by any chance?"

"Yes. Of course, it was. Clive Urquhart's home."

The madam nodded. "Yes, Sir Clive often orders our girls for his parties. I'm not surprised a man of your distinction and obvious taste for the exotic would attend parties there. I'm told they are riotous!"

"You've no idea," he said, winking. "Tis a pity about Miss Ross, though. She has a particular manner that... Well, let's just say I miss her many talents, and I'd hoped you might know her current location. Whilst here, though, I wonder if I could speak with your other ladies."

She set down the cup and saucer, dabbing her rouged mouth with a lace-trimmed serviette. "Is your interest professional or personal, my lord?" she asked, her eyes glinting with flecks of avaricious anticipation.

Aubrey had spent time in many brothels since becoming a field agent for the inner circle, and he knew precisely how to handle a cautious woman like Margaret Hansen. "It is both, actually," he told her, his dimples deepening as he smiled. "As I say, my peculiar tastes appreciate a woman of talent, but I am also a businessman. It must be exhaustingly expensive to maintain such a beautiful hotel, madam. Investors are surely welcome, are they not?"

Her delighted expression made it clear that his words had found fertile soil. "Investors? Do you refer to others or yourself, my lord?"

"Either and both. Are all of your ladies present today?"

"All but Joanna Marlowe."

"I pray she is not ill. Diseases spread so readily in such houses, and the investors I represent prefer not to expose themselves or their influential friends to illness."

"I understand completely, Lord Aubrey. Joanna is not ill. She is working, enjoying a lengthy visit with a favourite gentleman in the West End. It is but one of the many services we offer, and all with complete discretion! Shall I ask my girls to come to you in here, or do you prefer something more private?"

"Private, I should think," Aubrey answered with a practised smile, and it was as if sunshine entered the dimly lit room.

The thirty-three-year-old earl's beard had begun to grow once again with the pressures of the last week, but the deep dimples in his shadowed cheeks had no trouble penetrating the dark hair. Women had been known to faint when Paul Stuart offered such a glance, and not even the hardened heart of Meg Hansen was immune. On the contrary, it surrendered fully to the earl's considerable charms.

"My lord, I—well, I should be pleased to make any and all of my ladies available for your inspection. Where would you like to begin?"

She stood as did he. "Let's take each floor individually, shall we?" he asked. "That way, there's no danger of leaving anyone out. I shouldn't wish to miss any of the delights your hotel has to offer, madam."

"You promised to call me Meg," she reminded him coquettishly, taking his offered arm and leading Stuart towards the stairs. "We have only parlours on the main floor, of course. Along with our registration desk. Mr. Honeywell keeps the ledger. You did sign, I hope?"

"Of course."

"Well, then, let's begin with Kitty. She's a lovely girl who came to us from Bristol. Her story's rather tragic, but I'm sure it's one you've heard before. So many of our girls descend from poverty, and often their families show little care for them."

Stuart followed her into the upper storeys of the hotel, where they entered a series of rooms and suites, beginning with Kitty Nelson's small apartment and ending with a large suite sometimes used by Redwing members (though the proprietress said nothing of this). Hansen hesitated before unlocking the door.

"We reserve these rooms for special occasions. They are comfortably expansive, suitable for whatever pleasures one might seek, similar to those provided by the West End's finer establishments, but this suite does cost more."

"My dear Meg, there is no finer establishment than your own. Even *Amante Secret* cannot compare to the Empress!" he assured her, his arm through hers.

Hansen's own lashes fluttered in flattered delight. "My lord, how very kind of you! I do not fancy myself equal to Madam Ferrell's remarkable luxuries at *Amante Secret*, but we endeavour to please. A wealthy patron would allow us to rise to the level of the grandest French maisons."

"Money is always the limiting factor, is it not, dear Meg?" he whispered, intentionally placing his hand at the small of her back and then letting it slip, ever so slightly towards her bustle. "Oh, do forgive me!" he whispered impishly.

"Sir!" the whore runner gasped in delight. "You have a very light touch."

"Not always," he teased.

"Really?" she breathed back huskily, patting her upswept hair. Had the mistress been less jaded, she might have blushed, but instead she merely sighed, imagining a long and pleasant night in the earl's muscular arms. Still thinking of his embrace, she turned the key without another thought.

"As you can see, this apartment contains every luxury to which a man such as yourself is accustomed. An *en suite* water closet, three bedchambers for privacy, and two large salons for cards, conversation, drinks, whatever one might desire. The walls were painted by the same mural artist who created the magnificent scenery in many a Westminster peerage home, though our themes are more, shall we say, inspiring? I'm sure you know the artist's name, sir. The room evokes the popular *chinoiserie* enjoyed by so many on the continent, but with a provocative twist. The brocades are the finest silk, the mirrors gilded, and we use only the highest quality beeswax candles in all the chandeliers. We have no gas laid on in this house, as you can tell. I find that it smokes and causes too many fires."

Aubrey smiled, his left brow arched mischievously. "Sparks amongst your guests surely cause fires of their own, madam. Particularly, from someone as *well-rounded* as yourself."

"Oh, sir! You will have me reaching for my smelling salts!"

He kissed her hand and bowed. "I speak only truth, madam. You are fairer than a summer's breeze. Tell me, have I met all your ladies?"

Fanning herself, Hansen breathed deeply, intentionally causing her ample bosom to mound over the tightly laced corset. "Ah, well, there is one other, but she is indisposed today, my lord. A toothache."

"I'm very sorry to hear that. Do you think she would speak to me briefly? I promise to take only a few moments."

The woman realised that she'd given the earl far greater access to the house than her Redwing patrons would deem safe, but as he'd already spoken with the others, how could one more matter?

"Of course, my lord. This way. The young woman arrived only a few days ago from Paris. Her references are quite good, however, and she is lovely. Auburn-haired and fair-skinned. I've many clients who prefer such a combination."

"As do I. Redheads always inflame the passions," he whispered to the aging businesswoman, whose henna-dyed hair shone a fiery red in the corridor's candlelight.

Hansen giggled again as she led him up a narrow flight of stairs to the third storey. "I keep my newest girls up here. Once this one establishes a clientele, I'll move her to an apartment of her own on a lower floor." She knocked. "Miss Fabien?" No one answered, and Hansen knocked again. "She is there, I know it, sir. She might be sleeping. I'll just have a little peek."

Margaret unlocked the door. Inside, the room stood in semi-darkness, and a flowery smell filled the air.

"Typical Frenchwoman. She soaks herself with strong perfume," Hansen explained. "Miss Fabien? Elaine, are you awake?"

The door to a connecting bath opened slightly. "I'm afraid I'm still unwell, Mrs. Hansen," a woman with a thick accent replied from behind the door.

"But this gentleman wishes only a moment, my dear. When you arrived here, you expressed a sincere desire that I should offer you a place. If you wish to remain with us, then you must make yourself available. He is a handsome Scotsman. Titled and with a great deal of influence." She turned to Aubrey. "Sir, I shall leave you to it. Don't remain too long. Ring if you wish for drinks or anything else."

Hansen left and shut the door. Aubrey assumed she'd deliberately abandoned him to the charms of the newcomer, in hopes that the young Frenchwoman might ensure his patronage.

"Forgive me, Miss Fabien," he began sweetly once the door had shut. "I wish to talk, that is all."

Silence.

Aubrey approached the door, standing beside it politely. "If you are ill, I should be happy to take you to a physician, or bring one here, Miss Fabien. Please, will you not speak to me? I assure you, my intentions are honest."

The door creaked as it slowly opened further. "Only if you do not light any candles," she whispered in heavily accented English. "And do not look at me. My face is swollen. I am hideous."

"I shall abide by your rules," he promised. "I shan't keep you long. I wish only to talk."

The woman kept her face turned away as she walked past him into the parlour, taking a seat upon a small, velvet settee. The cold room lay in dense shadow, lit only by a dwindling fire, with all draperies shut.

"What is it you wish to say, and why do you wish to say it to me? I am no one."

The earl paused near a chair. "May I sit, *mademoiselle*?"

"*Oui*."

Stuart chose a comfortable wingback, taking care not to stare or cause her to bolt. "Thank you. Have we met before, Miss Fabien? Your voice sounds familiar. Perhaps, you and I met in Paris?"

"*Oui. Peut être*. Is possible."

"Which maison, may I ask?"

"I cannot say," she insisted, her face turned aside. "Ask your question, m'sieur. I am tired and want to sleep."

The earl said nothing immediately. Instead, he took to his feet again, a series of thoughts tumbling through his mind. A large grandfather clock ticked steadily in a corner of the room, accompanied by muffled traffic sounds from the street below. Wheels of coaches, passersby, costermongers hawking their wares.

"I do not think French is your native tongue," he said at last. "Rather I think it is English, and Elaine is not your name at all."

Lord Aubrey strode deliberately to a silver candelabrum that sat upon a table beside the hearth, where he found matches inside the table drawer. He lit one. The yellow phosphorus tip flared and ignited a series of pinpoints as he touched the wicks of each candle of seven.

He turned and faced her. "Hello, Lorena."

The next five seconds passed like lightning. MacKey rushed towards the bath, knocking over a table to block his path. Aubrey easily avoided the obstacle, chased after, and caught her before she could gain the door. Angered by her deception, he damaged Lorena's shoulder as he yanked her forearm to stop her from slamming the door in his face.

"Demonic hellion!" he shouted, forgetting that they might be overheard. "If you wish to remain alive, then you will tell me where Elizabeth is and why you helped to abduct her!"

"I did no such thing!" MacKey shouted back, but he paid no heed.

"Did Trent post you here to keep watch on the house?" he seethed as he shook her shoulders with both hands. "Was I supposed to meet you on Sunday so that Charles would be left without aid? You are a heartless witch! My cousin may die because of you!"

Lorena began to weep, partially from the pain in her shoulder, but also from the anguish caused by his hate-filled words.

"Say something!" he ordered, his strong hands clenching her upper arms.

"Did you say that Charles might die?" the pale woman managed to gasp.

"He is Lord Haimsbury to you!" the earl shouted. "You have one chance to redeem yourself. Tell me every detail of Trent's plans, now! Or by all that is holy, I will shake it out of you!"

The uproar brought one of the house's burly guards to the door, accompanied by Hansen, who unlocked the apartment and lumbered into the room, all giddiness vanished.

"Sir, you have overstayed your welcome. Do not force me to have Mr. Bertram eject you."

To Paul's surprise, rather than denounce her attacker, MacKey stepped in front to protect him.

"Madam, I've a confession to make. I came to your hotel beneath a shadow of lies. Lord Aubrey is my... He's... He is my cousin, come to take me home, and we argued, as cousins often do, but he is right," she added, turning to face him, "and I beg my family's forgiveness. Cousin Paul, I know you've no cause to answer yes, but may I still come home with you? Please?"

Hansen interrupted. "If you wish to leave, my dear, then you must pay the departure fee. As you agreed when we accepted you, it is one year's earnings. A thousand pounds."

"A thousand pounds!" she gasped. "That is outrageous!"

The earl stepped around MacKey. "Get your coat and anything else you wish to take with you, Cousin. And if Madam Hansen chooses to contest your right to leave, then she can explain her case to the sea of detectives who will descend upon this house by end of day." He reached into his wallet and withdrew a hundred pounds. "For your trouble and any food which my cousin may have consumed. Expect no more, madam. She is done here."

In five minutes' time, he'd put Lorena and her few belongings into the coach, and the two began a long journey towards Westminster.

"Hansen will tell the others of your visit," MacKey began as the wheels engaged. "Redwing, I mean. They meet at the Empress every Saturday, and several of their members play cards there of an evening."

"Why were you there, if you play no part in their deeds, Lorena?" he asked, not bothering to hide his anger.

She rubbed the injured shoulder, the intense pain bringing tears to her eyes. "You wouldn't believe me."

He leaned forward, compassion slowly replacing outrage. "Here, let me," he said, placing his fingers on the shoulder. "I am sorry, Lorena. I may have dislocated the joint. I can fix it, but it will hurt."

She nodded. "Yes, I know what you're about to do. Go ahead."

The earl took her wrist in one hand and the elbow in the other. He gently lifted the arm away from her side until it was at a forty-five degree angle. "All right so far?"

"Yes," she whispered.

"Good. As I said, this will hurt, but once done, the pain will ease considerably. Ready?"

"I think so. I've done this with patients, but never experienced it," she whispered tightly, her words coming in gasps through pain.

"I've experienced it from both sides, more than once. Look the other way now. On three. One, two, three," he warned her. On the third count, he slowly pulled on the entire arm until the head of the humerus repositioned itself beneath the shoulder blade and back into the socket. The process had been almost unbearable, but once done, MacKey felt instant relief.

"Where did you learn to do that?" she asked.

"From the duke. When I was fourteen, we spent a summer in Africa, and I fell out of a *mopane* tree, dislocating my right shoulder. Don't ask me why I was in the tree. It's much more embarrassing than the injury, actually. I'll only say that a snake and a lion were involved. James didn't so much as blink. In fact, he laughed the entire time he was repairing it. It was a hard lesson, but one I've never forgotten." Aubrey found a light blanket in the coach and fashioned it into a makeshift sling. "You'll need to wear this for a few days. We'll put some ice on it when we get to Haimsbury House."

"You're taking me there? Why? I don't understand."

The earl's face hardened again. "Do not think yourself returned to my good graces, Lorena. I want the circle to question you. But as we'll be on the road for thirty minutes, you have time to explain your actions to me first. If you are blameless, then I promise to take that into consideration. And do not count on your beauty to charm me. My cousins have been separated from one another since their wedding day. Charles is in a coma, and Beth might even be dead. If I appear sympathetic at the moment, don't be fooled, for if I think you culpable in any way, I shall see that you hang."

CHAPTER ELEVEN

Sinclair took the empty crockery bowl and set it on a hand-hewn table near the hearth. "Better?" he asked his wife.

"Much," the duchess answered. "Thank you, Captain. It's very quiet here, don't you think?"

"And private, except for those bird creatures in the woods. If we were in our own world, Beth, I'd want to remain here for as long as possible, for it's very nice to have you all to myself."

She took his hand, stroking the bright wedding band. "If only this could be our wedding night cottage, Charles, but you're right. We mustn't linger, no matter how pleasant it might be."

"Pleasant is an odd word for such circumstances as these. Surely, those creatures outside frighten you."

"Yes, a little."

"Only a little?" he asked, a smile playing at his lips.

She laughed. "How could I feel anything but safe in your presence, Captain? From the first moment I saw you, all those years ago, you've made me feel protected and loved. It is strange, I know, for many across the kingdom riot and plot in the name of suffrage and women's rights. They depict men as oppressive and evil, but I think they somehow miss the *good* that men do."

"Darling, the women who protest are generally those trampled beneath the boots of heartless men. Is it any wonder they see nothing good in my sex?"

She sighed. "If that is true, then I'm very sorry for it, Charles. I'd change those awful circumstances, if I could, and I know you feel the same. I wish all women had such brave men to encourage and protect them; for whenever you're with me, I feel as though I could accomplish anything!"

He drew her into his arms. "And so you can, little one. I'll be the first to cheer you on in any endeavour, no matter what, but for the present, we must try to escape this place—as pleasant as it is."

She pointed to his watch. "You said that you tried to wind the stem already and that it failed to work."

"Yes, but it's likely I overwound it. Why?"

"Because properly winding it might require both of us, our combined effort, Charles. These entwined hearts all about us must represent that, don't you think?"

"Perhaps, but it's more likely they represent our physical union, Beth. That which created our children."

"I'm sure that's true, but isn't it also possible it represents our escape? Bear with me. What if both our hands must touch the stem for the watch to start? And what if starting the watch, forces time to move forward again, allowing us to return to our own world? You said, yourself, that the gatekeeper called the watch a key. Perhaps, it is precisely that. Our key to escape! "

He withdrew the watch and opened it. "Please, Lord, let it be so!" he said, considering all the possibilities. "Beth, I've no idea how this will proceed. Whether you and I will leave together, or even return to the same place. If not, then I will find you. No matter where you now linger, I promise you, I *will* find you!"

Still holding her hands, Sinclair closed his eyes and began to pray. "Father, we know not why you've allowed us to come here, but we trust that it is for your perfect purpose. Please, my Lord, I beg you to protect my wife. Wherever she is at this moment, heal her of any illness and keep watch over her welfare. And, please, when she and I return to our world, help me to find her. Help us to find each other."

"Amen," she whispered. "I love you, Captain."

"And I love you, little one," he answered. Charles took her sweet face into his hands and kissed her lips. He fought against the cruel birds' voices that whispered into his mind: *This is your final kiss. She dies now. Here. And you will never see her again.*

"I will find you, Beth," he promised her once more.

"I know, Captain. We'll see each other again very soon."

He took a deep breath. "All right, then. Here we go."

She touched the watch within her husband's palm. The duchess twisted the tiny stem, and instantly, the watch's intricate gears engaged, causing the golden timepiece to tick.

CHAPTER TWELVE

The Haimsbury coach bearing the earl and Lorena MacKey turned right off Bishopsgate onto Threadneedle Street. "What role did you play in Beth's abduction?" he asked his passenger.

Lorena took a deep breath, steeling her nerve. "I didn't want to hurt her, Paul. That was never my aim at all. Trent forced me to assist, and Anatole instructed me to play along."

"Romanov? I knew that Russian had something to do with it!" he shouted. "That smooth-talking meddler has circled about our family like a carrion crow, and he shows far too much familiarity with Elizabeth."

"It isn't what you think. Truly, it isn't."

"Do not make excuses for that creature, Lorena! It does nothing to advance your defence."

"I don't. I merely try to explain. Will you allow me?"

He sighed in irritation. "Go on, but I warn you that I have an excellent memory, and anything I hear is likely to be used in the Crown's case against you, if it comes to that."

She moved slightly to offer her bruised shoulder a moment's respite. "Thank you. It's true, the prince does love the duchess, but I don't believe he'd ever act on it; not in the way you imagine. Anatole Romanov is complicated. Despite your doubts, I choose to trust him."

"I suppose, you would," he answered indignantly.

"Paul, I understand your anger, but allow me a full hearing before you declare me guilty. I've known the prince for a long time. He's always treated me kindly and even rescued me from a terrible and hopeless situation. When you and I first met, I mentioned my family links to Glencoe, near your castle. Do you remember?"

"That seems very long ago," he declared.

"Yes, but only six weeks have passed since you and I first met."

"Six and a half," Aubrey corrected.

She smiled, realising he'd revealed his mind for a moment. "Yes, six and a half. Anyway, the story of the MacKey family is true, but I left out one, very painful part of my childhood. My father died when I was six, and my mother remarried a hopeless and very cruel drunk. Gregory Whitcomb knew every publican in London and enjoyed abusing me almost as much as he enjoyed the taste of cheap gin. My stepfather made a daily practise of beating me, and when not inflicting his belt upon my back, he abused me in less obvious ways," she said softly, her eyes gazing out the window as the coach passed the Bank of England. "By the time I turned eighteen, I'd had two miscarriages, and I thank the Lord each day that Whitcomb never had a chance to hurt the children he created."

"I am sorry, Lorena," he whispered. "No woman should have to endure such abuse."

"No, they shouldn't, but it's far more common than most would imagine, and not only in poor homes. The wealthy of this world engage in sadistic behaviour that makes my stepfather's pale by comparison. I'd grown to hate my life and was considering ending it, when two miracles happened. My stepfather was killed in a pub fight, and Anatole Romanov knocked upon my door. The prince forever altered the course of my life."

"And he taught you to be a witch," Aubrey interjected. "How is that a good thing, Lorena?"

"You're wrong. The prince wanted me to rise above my past. He taught me kindness and altruism. It was William Trent who schooled me in the manipulation of others for material gain. *He* taught me to be a witch. A week after my stepfather died, I received a letter from the London Medical School for Women offering me a place in the next class of students. To my shock, I was told that a wealthy patron had come forward to underwrite my education."

"Anatole or Trent?" he asked.

"The prince. During my first two years, Anatole served as a mentor and tutor. My life took a sharp turn, however, when I met Sir William in the summer of '78."

"'78? You knew that bounder before he killed Beth's mother?"

"Yes, but I had no idea William had any such plans. Remember, Paul, that most of my life had been spent in hardship and under the whip of a cruel man. I never quite understood the prince's kindness, because in my heart, I thought I deserved cruelty from men. William presented himself as a wealthy gentleman with considerable influence."

"And what was Romanov's response?" Paul asked her.

"I believe the prince paid a call on Sir William, for the baronet sent me a letter saying he no longer wished to see me. It sent me reeling, and I wondered what I'd done to disappoint him. It formed cracks in my alliance with Anatole, but then, a very strange thing happened. The prince changed his mind about Trent, and even encouraged me to see him."

"That makes no sense."

"No, but I was only twenty, and I didn't look for life to make sense. From that point forward, the prince seemed to have two different opinions on William. One day, he would deride him and offer warnings, but then the next, he would encourage me to see him. It confused me."

"I imagine it would," the earl told her. "Did you ever learn what lay behind the contradiction?"

"Not until the night before Charles and Elizabeth's wedding. Did you know that Prince Alexei Grigor is actually a spirit being like Romanov?"

"Yes, we'd surmised as much. Grigor has appeared to Charles once or twice, as has Anatole. Their comings and goings make it clear they're not human. Are they angels?"

She shook her head. "I'm not sure just what they are, but if Grigor is an angel, then he is a fallen one. I've never known anyone so diabolically cruel!"

Their coach passed by St. Paul's cathedral, and the earl knew they had little time remaining. "We'll reach the house in less than ten minutes. Tell me more about Trent."

She shifted slightly in the seat, trying to calm her mind. "Yes, all right, but I can tell you more about the fallen realm another time, if you want."

"Fine, but for now, I want to hear about Trent and your part in the abduction. 1878. Trent sent you a letter breaking off your friendship."

"Yes, but not for long. A week, perhaps, ten days passed, and then William called on me one evening at my flat. He brought flowers and chocolates, and he asked if I would go for a short walk along the river. That night we began a new, much different relationship. He lured me into Redwing by promising me power. Looking back on it now, I realise how foolish I was, but at the time, I thought myself wise. William could be very charming, when it suited him. I thought him handsome, and he made me feel as if no other woman compared to me."

"He flattered your pride," Aubrey noted. "He played on your weakness."

She bit her lower lip in regret. "Yes, he did. I became his mistress soon after."

"Yet you knew he was married?"

"He never made a secret of it, but he convinced me that he didn't love her."

"That much is true. William treated Patricia with disdain, controlling her every movement, her every thought. I never understood why any woman would permit a man such power!"

"Women are born powerless, Paul. Don't you know that?"

The coach turned onto Queen Anne Walk. "We'll need to finish this later, but before I leave you, I want to know one thing. Did you assist with the abduction?"

"Yes, but it isn't as simple as you make it."

His eyes turned cold. "Explain."

"Anatole instructed me to participate. He was..."

"There is no reason why I should believe anything you say!" he shouted. "How do you expect me to trust either you or Anatole? Where is he? I would hear these lies from his own mouth."

"I've no idea where he is. After the fire broke out, I..."

"You saw the fire? You saw Charles get hurt? Lorena, why didn't you help? You're a doctor!"

"I was afraid," she admitted, trembling all over. "You didn't see what I saw, Paul! A great battle had broken out over the house, only minutes before the fire started. I cannot see well enough into the other realm to know who was involved, but I tell you that it was two very powerful entities. Possibly Watchers. I ran back into the Empress to seek a place to hide."

"Wait. Did you just say *back* into the Empress? You'd been inside previous to this? That night?"

"Yes. There's a second mirror in the suite used by Redwing for their meetings. Inside a closet. Sir William, the duchess, and I emerged through this mirror, and then he took her across to Charles's house. Paul, I had no idea William would try to hurt her! He told me that he was trying to protect her from the others in Redwing. Yes, I know how foolish that sounds, but I've been a fool about many things in my life. Some more profoundly personal than others."

He looked into her eyes, trying to discern whether or not she lied. In most cases, the earl could spot deception at a hundred paces, but he felt completely lost in MacKey's presence.

"Did you see Trent die?"

"I saw him thrown from the window, if that's what you're asking. He did not jump. Something hurled him through the glass. Meg Hansen was also watching when it happened. We were all standing outside the Empress, and when Trent crashed to the ground, both of us screamed. That's when you and Charles arrived, I think. My attention was on the spirit entities engaged in battle."

"We're here," he told her as they pulled through Queen Anne's main gate.

"I thought you were taking me to Haimsbury House."

"First, I want you to see Michael Emerson. He's the physician who's been caring for Charles. He's been staying at Queen Anne since last Sunday night. Lorena, I want to believe you, but it's difficult."

"I realise that. I don't think I'd believe me. You're far kinder than I deserve. Is Charles really in danger of dying?"

"He's still unconscious, but we're praying for his full recovery. Look, I'm very sorry that I injured your arm. It wasn't my intent. I fear my anger got the better of me."

"I understand," she whispered. "The shoulder doesn't hurt all that much."

"I doubt that's true. Once Michael's seen to your injury, then I hope you'll tell me the rest of your story."

"I'll do my best," she promised as the coach stopped in front of the great mansion. "Paul, even though William is dead, Redwing will continue. They're meeting again tonight at the Empress. When Hansen tells them that you took me from her home, my life is forfeit. I'll be the next woman found in bits and pieces upon the embankment."

He grew quiet for a moment, remembering the bloated remains of Susanna Morgan's tortured body. "Can you give us the names of all the London members?" he asked. "Lorena, I realise how dangerous this is for you, but it's important. The circle has a partial list, but we must learn who it is we've missed."

"Are you aware that William's Round Table has been trying to free some very powerful spirits in recent weeks? Fallen angels who've been imprisoned?"

"Yes, we know a little about that," he said cautiously. "Susanna revealed some details to me. I believe it's why she was killed."

A footman arrived at the door, and Paul could see Eric Miles descending the portico steps. "We'll have to continue this later."

The earl stepped out of the coach and spoke to the butler. "Miles, this is Dr. MacKey, a distant cousin of mine and Lord Haimsbury. She's injured her left shoulder rather badly and requires medical attention and rest. Could you prepare an apartment for her, please?"

The butler bowed. "It's our honour to serve, Lord Aubrey. Mr. Jacks here will see to any bags the lady has. Dr. Emerson is at the other house, tending to his lordship. Shall I ask Mrs. Meyer to see to the injury until he returns?"

"Yes, Miles. Thank you." The earl helped Lorena out of the coach. "Careful now, Cousin. If I'm delayed at the other house, I'll send word. We've a meeting this evening, but you and I will continue to reminisce later."

To Lorena's surprise, Paul kissed her cheek.

"Thank you, Cousin Paul," she whispered.

The physician followed the footman and butler into the mansion, turning one last time to watch the coach depart for Haimsbury House. "Mr. Miles, I wonder, is there a Bible in the house?"

"Yes, my lady. If you'll follow me?" The butler guided her through the foyer, and into the yellow morning room. "We have many copies of the Bible. Have you a preference, ma'am?"

"Whichever is easiest to read, I suppose. And where should I begin? Genesis? Or is there a better place to start?"

Miles answered as though it were the commonest of questions. "Mrs. Meyer might offer a suggestion, my lady. I'll send her in to look after your shoulder. As you're a physician, is there a remedy you'd recommend? Ice, perhaps?"

"Yes, ice, but also truth."

"Our ice cave can provide the first, and God's word will provide the latter, ma'am." The butler left, and Lorena took a chair near the window.

Is this a new beginning to my life, or the first step of the end? Only God knows now.

CHAPTER THIRTEEN

12:43 pm – 24th November

Martin Kepelheim had nearly worn a hole in the carpeting. "Emerson did say that Charles spoke? Is that right?"

The Duke of Drummond had hardly slept in days, and his dark eyes were rimmed in puffy circles, adding age to an otherwise ageless face. "Della told us that she heard Charles whispering in his sleep. Surely, that means he's coming 'round. I wish to heaven Beth were here! He'll go mad when he learns she's missing."

"We mustn't borrow trouble, sir," Cornelius Baxter said as he poured coffee for the two men. "Lady Adele has been keeping very close watch on his lordship. It's no surprise that she'd notice changes before anyone else. If I may be so bold, sir, you've not eaten at all today and very little yesterday. I'm sure the marquess would be most upset if he learns you've allowed your own needs to go unmet during his illness. We've plenty left from breakfast. Mrs. Paget baked those blackberry tarts again, Your Grace. And there are smoked kippers and bacon. I could bring up a tray with a selection of offerings. Shall I, sir?"

Some peers would have called the butler impertinent, but the duke merely smiled. He'd known Cornelius Baxter for over forty years, and in that time, the servant had never so much as hinted at impertinence. Rather, his thoughtful commentary reflected a deep love for the Stuart family.

"You're right, Mr. Baxter. We'd all be lost without your wise counsel. Our Princess will need us strong and able if we're to find her, will she not? Bring trays up here, if it's not too much trouble. Simple fare will do. You know my tastes."

"I certainly do, Your Grace. Will it be coffee, tea, or something stronger?"

"Water for now, but also more coffee. My sister will likely want tea. She's downstairs with Lady Della presently."

"Very good, sir," the faithful servant answered with a bow.

No sooner had the door to the parlour shut than it opened again. Paul Stuart entered the warm drawing room, still wearing his overcoat and gloves. "I came straight up. Miles told me that Emerson was called back here. Is Charles worse?"

"If only we knew!" the tailor complained. "Your dear sister ran to fetch us less than half an hour ago, filled to bursting with the news that our marquess had stirred in his dreams. She claims he said something nonsensical, but it may be that Della mistook it."

"What did he say?" the earl asked as he removed the leather gloves and tossed them onto the nearest table.

"He was counting, or so claims our Della. One, two, three. Most peculiar!" Kepelheim observed.

"He's most likely dreaming," the duke suggested as the bedchamber door was opened by Emerson. "Well?" Drummond asked anxiously.

"I'm happy to offer good news," Emerson told the three men. "Please, do come in. Della's right. I think he's beginning to come 'round."

They hastened into the bedchamber and gathered at the foot of the handcrafted bed, and to the delight of all, Charles Sinclair's eyes were open. He stared at the concerned faces before him, not recognising anyone at first. The dissonant and abrupt change of venue had caught the sleeping man off guard. Though he'd prayed to return to his own world, the new environment seemed both strange and familiar all at once. The back of his head pounded, his mouth and lips felt like sandpaper, and the rest of his body ached as though he'd fought six rounds with a lion.

Slowly recovering his bearings, Sinclair made several quiet observations: He lay in a darkened bedchamber and could hear hushed whispers coming from the faces that surrounded his bed. The smell of liniment and carbolic acid burnt his nose. Then, he realised what bothered him most. Amongst the familiar faces, one stood out—*as missing*.

"Where's Beth?" he asked, his unused voice barely audible.

Hearing this simple question, Kepelheim looked as though he might break out in song; the exhausted earl started to weep from relief; and the duke's ever-widening smile threatened to slice off both his ears.

"Welcome back, son," Drummond answered happily. "We'd thought you might spend the rest of the year sleeping."

Ever the professional, Michael Emerson calmly checked his patient's pulse. "Do you remember your name?"

"That's an odd question," the patient replied. "If I say St. Clair, will you doubt my memory or my sanity?"

"Apparently, the blow did nothing to alter your sense of humour," the physician noted.

"What can you remember, son?" asked Drummond.

"Very odd things, actually. Might I have a drink of water?"

Aubrey had already poured half a glass, and he moved past his uncle and the physician to offer it. "Here," he told his cousin. "Drink it slowly."

Charles's hands trembled as he lifted the glass, but refused Paul's assistance. "I can do this on my own. Just give me time. Time..." he repeated, thoughtfully. "That's it. Time was the key. You ask me what I remember, but I doubt it will make sense to any of you. It made very little sense to me. That annoying birdman and the cottage..." he told them, suddenly wincing in extreme pain. "Oh, my head! Did I take a fall?"

"You might say that," the ebullient tailor said, his grey eyes glistening. "Charles, it is wonderful to hear your voice once more! We've been very worried about you."

"Worried? Why? James, where is Elizabeth? I thought she'd be here. The watch started ticking, and then..."

Charles stopped. The entire scene and its meaning crystallised into a dreadful possibility. "Is Beth dead?"

Paul Stuart sat beside his cousin and took his hand. "Try not to think of it right now, Charles."

"Think about what? Are you saying that she *is* dead?" he asked, worry and dread shadowing his pale face.

"No! Not at all. At least, we pray she is not. Charles, the truth is that we've no idea what happened to Elizabeth or where she is. When we were finally able to enter your old house, we found no one inside. She'd been there, but escaped before the fire started."

Strangely enough, Sinclair actually laughed. "Thank you, Lord! Thank you! She's alive, Paul, I know it. I saw her. She was with me in that awful place, but she's alive. Only, she may be ill. She must be. Why else would she have been there with me? But if I escaped, then Beth can escape, too, can she not?"

"Of course, she can," the earl answered, thoroughly confused but not wishing to upset his cousin.

"But you say I've been sleeping? That may explain my journey. Perhaps, she is also sleeping in a fever. How long?"

"Long?" the earl asked.

"Yes, long," Charles answered as he pushed his way up, finally gaining a sitting position and throwing off the quilts. He wore a blue silk nightshirt, and though his leg wounds were no longer bandaged, he noticed five red gashes along the shins and thighs, three of which still bore stitches. "Now, how did I get these?"

"Glass," Emerson answered as he took the marquess's pulse once more. "Your heart's racing, Charles. Your constitution is strong, but you've been in a protracted coma for days."

"Days? How many?" he asked again. "How long have I been sleeping?"

"A week," the physician replied. "Seven days."

Sinclair's face took on an odd sort of calm. "A week? I see. And you've no idea where Beth might be?"

"We've searched the entire city," Paul told him. "But we will find her. I promise."

"And I'll help," the patient decided, starting to stand.

"No, Charles, you need to remain here for the rest of the day," Emerson ordered, his hands on Sinclair's shoulders.

Paul agreed. "Charles, rest today. Tomorrow, you and I shall prepare a plan."

"No, I've slept long enough. I promised to find her, Paul. I promised! I cannot let her down. I will not!"

The determined patient pushed out of the bed, but the duke and Kepelheim gathered near to hold him, trying to stop Charles from injuring himself.

Esther Alcorn had just entered the room, bringing clean bandages and freshly laundered linen. The efficient Scotswoman quickly assessed the situation and provided precisely what was needed.

Passing through the knot of distraught men, she reached the bed and spoke to her employer in a soothing voice.

"How nice to see your eyes open, sir," she whispered. "I know it must be quite confusing for you, but it will all make sense in a moment."

"Mrs. Alcorn, I've lain in bed far too long already. I will not stay here one moment longer!"

"I understand, my lord. Do you trust me, sir?"

He nodded. "Yes, of course."

"Then, allow me to offer a suggestion. If you must leave your bed, then why not sit by the fire?"

"If it means I can begin to make plans, then fine. Yes, I'll sit."

Alcorn smiled graciously. "We'll do all we can to help you, sir," she said, taking charge.

Esther turned to the earl. "Sir, if you could give the marquess your shoulder, and Mr. Kepelheim, perhaps you'd be good enough to fetch a dressing gown. There should be plenty o' clean ones in his lordship's bedchamber closet."

"I'll get it," Drummond offered, crossing through the connecting bath and into the master chamber. The duke opened the panelled door to an expansive, cedar-lined closet that stretched the length of an entire wall. Since Sunday night, the earl had spent many sleepless nights in this chamber, and his own clothes took up part of one rod. After replacing Matthew Laurence as butler on Monday morning, Cornelius Baxter had taken an entire afternoon to arrange the contents of the closet. He pressed and cleaned dozens of suit coats, trousers, shirts, and waistcoats; organised the items within a built-in bureau, including sleepwear, socks, personal linen, handkerchiefs, ties, and ascots; and even polished and re-ordered the marquess's jewellery into two velvet-lined drawers. A series of shelves stretched from one end of the closet to the other and held a variety of hats and shoes, neatly arranged by colour and occasion. The beautifully ordered closet would have made any haberdasher proud, but Baxter had done it to keep his hands and thoughts busy.

The duke whistled when he saw the interior. "Baxter needs to teach Booth his secrets. My closets look as though a military campaign's run through them. Dressing gowns?"

Alcorn had entered to put away the linen. "There, sir. To your right. The blue one looks quite nice."

"They'd have bit me, if I stood here any longer," he said, removing a quilted dressing gown with velvet trim.

"Here," he told his nephew as he placed it against Sinclair's back and shoulders. "Arms through, son."

"Thank you, James." Aubrey and Drummond helped him through the doorway and onto one of the upholstered sofas near the fireplace.

"Are you satisfied now?" Charles asked his caretakers. "I'm not an invalid, and unless you plan to shackle me, I intend to start searching for my wife."

Aubrey stood nearby. "No shackles. You and I shall spend the afternoon making plans." He turned to the Branham housekeeper. "Mrs. Alcorn, would you be so kind as to tell Lady Victoria that her nephew is awake?"

"Of course, sir," she answered. "I'll fetch a pot o' tea as well."

"I believe Baxter is arranging that, Mrs. Alcorn," the duke informed her.

"Did you say it's Saturday?" Sinclair repeated, his voice slowly growing stronger. "If I've slept a week, then why do my mind and body feel completely worn out? Mrs. Alcorn, I'm surprised to find you still here. Delighted, but surprised. And, James, did you just mention Baxter?"

"Neither our blessed Alcorn nor the formidable Mr. Baxter would leave you, Charles," the earl explained. "They've been very worried about your health, and both have vowed to remain until the duchess returns and you are fully recovered."

Sinclair reached out and took the woman's hands. "My dear Mrs. Alcorn, that is the nicest thing anyone's done for me, I think. I hope Mrs. Partridge has treated you kindly."

Esther laughed. "Aye, sir, she has, and we've become good friends. She's got her own manner o' keepin' a household. I stay out of her way, an' I get ta do as I wish. Mr. Baxter, now, he's taken over as butler. I do hope he didn't overstep."

"My fault," Aubrey explained. "I needed as many men hunting Beth as possible, and I seconded Laurence as an agent. He's scouring Kent County as we speak. A very good man. I'd like to keep him, if I may, Charles. You're head of ICI. It's your decision."

"If so, then, I heartily agree," the marquess answered. "Not only to Laurence, but also to this new arrangement. Mrs. Alcorn, would you consider remaining here indefinitely? As you know, we'll be needing an experienced nurse. Not only for the duchess, but for our children once they're born."

"Children? Did you just say children, sir?" the Scotswoman asked.

"Did I?" the marquess replied, smiling as he thought of Georgianna. "I meant child, of course, though eventually we'll have more than one, I'm sure. If you'd consider staying on, we'll make arrangements at Branham for your replacement. I take it that Mr. Kay has assumed leadership there?"

"He has, sir," she answered, "and I suggested that Mr. Baxter promote Mary Haversham to temporary housekeeper. She's been helping me for a year now and is quite competent."

"Good. Thank you for taking care of all that, Mrs. Alcorn."

"You're welcome, sir. Shall I ask Mrs. Paget to prepare a special tray for you? Clear broth is better than cheese and meats after so long a time without food."

"I'm tired but famished, actually," he admitted. "Michael, is my diet restricted?"

Emerson shook his head in amazement. "I have never in all my years in practise seen a man come out of a protracted state of unconsciousness with such energy, however, I suggest eating sparingly today. Clear broth, porridge, scrambled eggs."

"No bacon?" his patient asked. "Not even one rasher?"

"Your digestive system will be sluggish, Charles. Allow it to catch up to your appetite. Mrs. Alcorn, I'll speak with the marquess's cooks regarding dietary requirements."

"Very good, sir. Lord Haimsbury, I'll see if there's any rashers left over from breakfast," she added with a wink.

Aubrey began to laugh—something he'd not done for many days. "Praise God Almighty! Charles, it's a great relief to see you on the road to recovery!"

"If I'm recovering, it's because I know that Beth is alive, Paul. I've seen her. She's feverish but alive."

"I think you've been dreaming," the earl answered.

Drummond took a chair near the fire. "How can you have seen her, son, if you've yet to find her? I'm confused."

"As was I at first," Sinclair answered. "Imminently perplexed, to be honest, but no longer. She is alive, but ill. Her skin felt hot to the touch, and she thought a doctor stood nearby. She could smell medicines."

"Slow down, Charles," the earl insisted. "You've lost me as well."

"Then, let me tell you where I've been for the past week. It was a strange world, but one connected to all of this. To Redwing, and perhaps to these mirrors Susanna Morgan warned you about. It is an impossible land of talking birds and living stones."

"And Beth was there?"

"Beth and two children who will one day play a very large role in our rescue. My friends, this tale will sound impossible, but I assure you, every word is true."

Lorena MacKey read through the message as she sipped Darjeeling tea from a yellow rose cup. "Thank you, Mr. Miles. Am I to send a reply?"

"The footman didn't say, but he's still here, if you wish to send Lord Aubrey an answer. Shall I fetch pen and paper?"

"Yes, please. Do you know if Dr. Emerson plans to return this afternoon?"

"I'm not sure, ma'am. The doctor generally spends nights here. I'll ask the marquess's footman to enquire."

"That isn't necessary. I can include the question in my note."

The butler left, returning a few moments later with a lap desk containing sheets of paper, a bottle of ink, and three pens. As she opened the desk, she felt a strange chill pass through her body. The cream stationery bore the Branham crest upon it, with the words *Elizabeth, Duchess of Branham* embossed in gold ink. She quickly wrote a note to Aubrey, folded it once, and handed it to Miles.

"May I keep the lap desk? I'd like to write a letter."

"Of course, ma'am," Miles told her, taking the message and leaving the drawing room.

Once alone, MacKey read through the earl's note again:

> Lorena – We shan't be meeting with you today. Charles has awoken, and I prefer to spend the day with him. The circle will gather tomorrow evening instead of tonight, and we'll send for you then. I pray your shoulder

is improved. I am very sorry for injuring you. More sorry than you can ever know.

– Paul

MacKey felt a stab of guilt, not only for deceiving the Stuarts, but for Susanna Morgan's death.

"More sorry than you can ever know," she said aloud. "What does he mean by that?"

The doctor took a deep breath to cleanse her thoughts and lifted the stack of stationery from the box, hoping to find blank sheets. She preferred not to use anything bearing the crest, as it would reveal her whereabouts. To her surprise, she discovered a letter at the bottom, penned by Elizabeth but never posted. It looked as though she'd been interrupted whilst writing, and Lorena wondered why it was never completed.

I shouldn't read this, she thought to herself, but her curiosity overruled reason. The letter was addressed to James Stuart and dated the first of October, 1888.

Dearest Grandfather,

As I'm sure you're aware, I've returned early to London. I suspect that Paul's spies have already informed you of this, but I wanted to explain my reasons. I beg you to understand, my darling friend, for it is never my intention to keep anything from you. The recent crimes in London's East End must surely remind you of my mother's murder. I implore you for permission to explain to Superintendent St. Clair why that murder connects to those done by this Ripper fiend, and how it may also connect to me.

Last week in France, I received a letter that implied a threat to me. I've told no one else about it. There were three attacks on women in the Montmartre area of Paris, and two near Goussainville, which—as you know—is but a stone's throw from Victoria's château. Grandfather, I've a dreadful fear of all this. I'm sure something quite awful is about to happen. I've started suffering from nightmares again, just like in the old days, and Shadows stalk my steps.

I've written to the superintendent and asked him to meet me this week. I'm terrified, Grandpa. Simply terrified, and I want to tell Charles everything. I pray he'll agree to speak with me, though I've no idea if he even remembers the pitiable duchess he once called 'little one'.

I hope that he does, for you know my thoughts. My love for him has never waned—not even the slightest, despite his silence all these years. I don't know if you ever posted my letter to him, but it no longer matters. I am of an age, when I should be allowed to make my own decisions.

Paul will likely be angry, but it is a risk, I must take. Grandfather, do I dare speak to him about it? Will Paul understand? I love him dearly, but I am convinced that Charles is meant to be my husband, though I cannot explain why.

Last night, I had the worst dream so far. Wolves and terrifying bird creatures surrounded me, and spi—

There the letter stopped, and MacKey wondered what it was the duchess had planned to write. Why did she never post it? It looked as though she'd been interrupted whilst writing, and perhaps forgotten about it.

The physician returned the letter to its former place beneath the stationery and shut the lap desk, deciding not to write. She'd planned to send a letter to Margaret Hansen, but even an unmarked message might lead Redwing to find her, and then cause suspicion to fall on Hansen. She could never allow that. Meg had risked her life to help Lorena, despite what Redwing's human and inhuman members might do to her, just as they'd done to Susanna Morgan.

"My lady, there is a caller for you. He asks if you would join him on the portico."

She glanced up. "A caller? Is it Lord Aubrey or Dr. Emerson?"

"Neither, ma'am. The gentleman is well dressed but unknown to me, and he refuses to offer a card. Shall I send him away?"

"No, I'll speak with him, but will you keep watch on me through the window?"

"Of course, ma'am. I can remain with you, if you prefer. In fact, several of us could accompany you."

She smiled. "You and the other men here are certainly kind, Mr. Miles. Kinder than I deserve. No, that isn't necessary. Just keep watch."

Lorena left the drawing room, crossed through the broad foyer, and out the main entry. At first, she saw no one upon the broad stones that formed the high porch. Six enormous, marble pillars supported the great, pedimented roof of the portico, which led down a set of wide steps and onto the circular, gravel park. The summer's willow chairs had been removed to winter storage, but four ragstone benches flanked the entry, and Lorena sat, allowing the warmth of the southern sun to shine upon her face.

"What did you think of the letter?" a male voice asked.

She saw no one, but she did recognise the speaker. "Why didn't you enter the house?"

Anatole Romanov stepped out of the shadows and took her hand. "It isn't because I am prevented, but out of respect. I prefer to be invited by the home's owner."

"And I know this because you tell me?" she challenged him as he sat beside her. "You might be one of your brothers in disguise. A false Anatole."

He kissed her hand. "Bring me a Bible, and I shall prove it. My brothers dare not touch the holy scriptures, for even the printed pages bring them great pain."

"How do I know this? Satan knows the scriptures, and dared to quote them to Christ! No, I no longer trust any of you. If you are Anatole, then why did you force me to work for Trent? Charles may have awoken, but he nearly died, and it would have been my fault! My fault!" she shouted angrily.

He placed an arm around her shoulders. "Do you remember when your stepfather died? I promised to keep watch on you. Lorena, I have not failed to do so, despite what you believe. Only recently, did I learn that Raziel had taken my form. I do not know how often he has done this, but my brother will answer to our Creator for his crimes."

She shrugged, forgetting the injury and wincing at the pain the movement caused.

"Here, allow me," Anatole said, and he gently placed a hand on the injured joint. "The earl did not intend to harm you. His anger overwhelms his reason at times." His fingers moved, massaging the area, and the joint and soft tissues grew warm. The pain lessened and then vanished. "There. It should function normally now."

MacKey rotated the shoulder and abducted the arm, surprised to find all pain and stiffness gone. "Thank you. Anatole—assuming it is you—tell me why you appear to me now, after a week, and show such kindness?"

"Because I care for you, Lorena. I know that my methods confuse and frustrate you, but there is always a reason for my actions. Tomorrow evening, Charles Sinclair will come to speak with you. Tell him the following, and you must be precise. Firstly, tell him that the duchess is with me."

"With you?" she interrupted. "Where? The circle's been searching everywhere! Why haven't you told them? Told Paul?"

"I will not reveal her location to anyone yet. Her enemies keep watch on this house, and some of their spies can hear thoughts. Tell Charles that I keep her safe from all who would harm her. She is being tended by a trustworthy physician and will return to him soon."

"And the rest? What else am I to say?"

"Tell Sinclair that Redwing is at war. The spirits begin to bicker, and loyalties shift. His success within the stone maze has caused the doors and windows of the Seven Realms to shake, their locks now weaken, and some of the prisoners may soon escape. The human members of Redwing will begin to die, and the killer is a wolf in sheep's clothing. The Stone King works with Raziel to break through the barriers and chains placed upon him in ages past. If he and his minions enter this world, then even my powers may not be enough to stop the slaughter. If Ripper's deeds caused London's citizens to fear, then the Stone King will strike terror into the hearts of the entire country. Perhaps, the entire world."

She started to ask more, but the prince had vanished.

Lorena remained on the porch for many minutes, considering the strange encounter. Spies in the house? A wolf in sheep's clothing? Who? Did he mean someone in Redwing? Someone on the circle? Who amongst these two factions might be a devil in disguise?

CHAPTER FOURTEEN

Saturday, 7:10 pm – the Empress Hotel

Sir Clive Urquhart handed his cloak to Meg Hansen and joined the others in the private salon. "Where is everyone this evening? Has Trent's demise caused our members to quake in fear?" he asked as a scantily clad young woman offered the Redwing member a glass of wine. "Thank you, my dear Diana. As with the goddess after whom you are named, you are a delight to the eyes! Mrs. Hansen chose well when she added you to her stable. Speaking of which, my little spies tell me that a certain nobleman visited this morning, madam. Is this true?"

Hansen wore a tight gown of pale green satin, trimmed in black lace. The neckline plunged into a deep teardrop, but the whorehouse keeper had added a scarf of delicate black netting for a modicum of decency. A ruffled bustle created the illusion of a small waist, and its striped silk continued to the floor. The skirting concealed a special pocket, where Meg kept an ivory-handled jacknife and a loaded derringer—just in case.

"If you refer to Lord Aubrey, then yes, he paid a call," she answered. "It was mere curiosity. Nothing more."

Hansen didn't dare reveal her compliance with the earl—allowing him access to the entire hotel, but she'd had reason for the indulgence. No one in Redwing knew that Lorena MacKey had taken refuge in the hotel on Sunday night, and though Meg had made a pretense to Aubrey of thinking her a Frenchwoman, the truth was far more complicated, which the inner circle would soon learn. Margaret Hansen was more an ally than any of the Stuarts dared to guess.

"Lord Aubrey asked nothing about Trent?" Alexander Collins asked pointedly. "Nothing about Sunday's events? Nothing about Sir William?"

"Not a word," Hansen lied. "I think the earl feels at home in my sort of establishment. Perhaps, he merely came to shop. He is, after all, an unmarried man with the usual appetites and drives, is he not?"

"And a right 'andsome one at that," Diana Margate observed boldly. "I'd take 'is lordship as a reg'lar."

"I very much doubt that Aubrey came here for pleasure," Contessa di Specchio noted suspiciously. "Mrs. Hansen, will you leave us? My friends and I have private matters to discuss."

"As you wish," the brothel-keeper answered. "Diana, come with me. Ring should you require anything," she told the gathering.

Hansen shut the door, and Di Specchio waited several minutes before speaking again. "I do not trust that woman. There is a gleam to her eye that reveals much about Lord Aubrey's visit. The earl has a special talent for breaching even the most fortified female portcullis."

Urquhart laughed, twirling the hair of his waxed moustache with one hand whilst holding a wine glass in the other. "A delightful picture, Contessa, but you are correct about our Scottish earl. He is no stranger to Paris's *maisons de passe*. I happen to know that he spent many months in such places in his younger days, and he keeps a secret regarding one particular liaison. I think we might use that, should he ever draw too close to the truth."

"Whatever do you mean, Clive?" asked a younger man, sitting near the window. He had light brown hair which curled at the forehead, a slight moustache (which looked more like a shadow than actual hair), and blue eyes so light in colour that they practically disappeared from his face. "I'd rather thought Aubrey inscrutably dull."

"Oh, but that is so very wrong, *mon ami!*" the builder proclaimed as he replenished the younger man's glass. "You are new to our membership, Sir Albert, but I would never call Aubrey a dull fellow. Inscrutable, yes, irritating to be sure, but never dull. Ask any man who crosses him, assuming that man is still alive. Aubrey is a formidable opponent."

"So everyone keeps telling me, but I simply don't see it. The man is weak. He fawns all over his Cousin Elizabeth. I believe he'd happily lie down as a rug for her to cross, should she ask it! No, the earl is hardly formidable, Clive. *She* is his weakness."

"You may have a point, Sir Albert," di Specchio agreed. "Do we know what happened to her? The duchess, I mean. Surely, she did not kill Trent!"

"The lady might have sliced him with her sharp tongue," Wendaway observed, still stinging from Elizabeth's reproof at the wedding reception. "Why are so many men in love with that spoilt and irritating woman?"

"The duchess is a thorn in your tender flesh, is she not, Sir Albert? Admit it, *mon ami*. Her infamous beauty has captured even your black heart. You are simply angry that she did not fall for your charms."

"Whatever you say, Clive," the baronet replied, feigning boredom. "How can Aubrey be stopped, if he is so very formidable?"

The builder returned to his chair and lit a fat cigar. Once satisfied that it drew correctly, he exhaled deeply, his dark eyes rolling back into his head with pleasure. "These are made by Lord Aubrey's own tobacconist. I can see why he prefers them, which means we can learn from the earl, no? My dear Wendaway, you may be right about his weakness being the duchess, which makes it all the more important that we find her, I think. Serena, my dear, what say your spies inside the world of reflected light?"

"What is that?" asked Alexander Collins. "Is that the place Lord Raziel calls *sen-sen?*"

"Indeed," di Specchio explained. "Sen-sen is a realm similar to this one. It lies beneath us, as a lake lies beneath and reflects the sky. But there are many other worlds beyond sen-sen. What we call reality is but a fraction of what truly exists." She lifted her wine to the candle's light. "This is little better than water! I crave real nourishment. Why does Raziel insist we avoid slaking our thirst? These new rules begin to grate upon me."

"He says we must veil ourselves, and he's right. Trent drew far too much attention to his activities," Collins observed. "Sir William is dead, because his methods were avoidably provocative. I warned him that his hybridisation program produced individuals with enormous strength but little capacity for thought, but he refused to believe me. In my opinion, Trent's own alterations affected his mind adversely. We must improve our methods, if we are to survive."

"To do so requires the retrieval of Trent's body from the police—as soon as possible," a newcomer said, stepping through the closed door of a coat closet. "Good evening, everyone. Is this actually *wine?* How very dull."

"Lord Saraqael, this is indeed a surprise! Welcome to our gathering," di Specchio said, rising to accept the handsome elohim's kiss. "You honour us, my lord."

"I spy upon you, Countess," the unnatural being replied with a wink. "Do you consider that an honour? It seems that I arrive back in London to discover I've missed a great deal of fun. I understand that Trent is dead. Slain by Anatole, no less. I imagine that was a delightful little encounter."

"Alas, the baronet is gone from our midst," the builder bemoaned. "I shall miss him. Not because of his leadership, no, of course not! Trent had little capacity for true leadership. I shall miss his companionship. Few of our members throw so lavish a party as Sir William."

"Yet he lived on the *largesse* of others, did he not?" di Specchio noted. "If he threw parties, they were paid for by his friends. Sir William was a user as well as a fool."

"His carcass is food for crows in the underworld realms," the elohim observed. "A fitting end to so loathsome a man. Not even a man. A petty hybrid with aspirations to greatness! Tell me, Contessa, where are Samael and Raziel? Where are my brothers?"

"Why seek that insolent traitor?" Urquhart seethed at the mention of Samael, known to most as Prince Anatole Romanov. "The Russian does not show his face, because he fears us!"

"Insolent, yes, but I doubt that Sama fears you, Clive," Saraqael answered as he sat beside di Specchio. "I doubt he gives much thought to you at all. Countess, that is a deliciously daring dress. I wonder what treasures lie beneath that tight satin. Shall I investigate further, later this evening, at midnight?"

The vampiress stroked the Watcher's smooth hand. "I am yours anytime you wish, my lord, but our builder makes a point. Why would you expect to find Anatole anywhere near our gathering, when he has so often worked against us?"

"Sama is a complicated creature. I expect to find him nowhere and everywhere," he answered.

The spirit being had dressed himself in handsome human flesh, selecting from a favourite pattern, based on a Wallachian prince, whom he'd slain in Bucharest many centuries earlier. His dark brown hair fell past his broad shoulders in loose spirals; his eyes were dark, his brows thick and arched, and his full lips sensual. As with his brethren, Saraqael always made his form taller than ordinary humans; this particular one stood just over six and a half feet.

"How do you like the new me?" he asked Serena.

"I've seen this one before, haven't I?" she noticed. "At Versailles. King Louis's ball in honour of Pietro Durazzo, Genoa's Doge, no? 1685? Indeed, I remember this body as quite spectacular and endlessly satisfying, my lord! I look forward to reminiscing."

"Then allow me to slake your thirst, madam," he answered laughing.

The false human waved his left hand across the top of the carafe. The red liquid within the cut crystal shimmered as it transformed. "For you, my dear, I change wine into blood, and no need for a priest to mutter over it. Drink your fill." He sat beside her, his long legs crossed, one over the other. "Now, as to Samael, I suggest that human limitations make it impossible for you to understand our motivation. My brothers and I operate within an entirely different set of rules and a broader collection of dimensions, which can make our behaviour inscrutable to those without spiritual eyes. However, there are certain herbs and plants which may be consumed that grant access to these higher dimensions. Why be limited to four, when six or even ten might be accessed?"

"Four? Are there not just three?" the baronet asked boldly. He'd not yet met any of the elohim princes, and Sir Albert had no idea of their capabilities.

Sara cast his dark eyes upon the newcomer. "And you are?"

"Sir Albert Wendaway, and I, for one, liked William Trent. The man is dead, and I will not hear his name slandered!"

"I admire your loyalty, but it is misplaced," the Watcher answered patiently—an uncharacteristic moment for Saraqael. "To answer your question, time is the fourth dimension. One day, your scientists will try to solve its riddles, but they will fail. Without *pharmakeia* and ritualistic communication, humans haven't the eyes to see the beauty of multiple layers. Time is nothing as humans imagine it. But, tell me, who last spoke with Prince Anatole?

I've looked everywhere for my brother, but he has vanished from all the realms!"

The members glanced at one another. The countess started to reply, but a deep voice interrupted—booming into the room as if from another realm. "I saw him last."

The candles flickered, and several paintings depicting gods in congress with human women rattled as though shaken by unseen hands. A low rumble shivered along the walls, and every human shuddered as the voice's owner materialised out of thin air.

Saraqael merely smiled, for he'd heard Raziel coming long before he'd asked the question. The mischievous elohim offered Raziel a sardonic smile. "And when might that have been, Brother?"

The Watcher known to the politicians of English government as Prince Alexei Grigor took his brother's wine goblet and drank it down, wiping his mouth as he sniffed the dregs. "You're losing your touch, Sara. Too much iron."

"Yes, but then I prefer acquiring blood the old-fashioned way. Directly, from the circulatory wellspring," the elohim said languidly as he poured himself another glass.

"As do I," di Specchio agreed boldly. "A beating heart provides the finest wine."

Raziel placed a hand on the vampiress's head, his long nails raking her scalp and drawing blood. "You might discover your own veins providing nourishment, if you do not measure your words more carefully, Serena. Our presence in London grows far too public. Sir William Trent's actions led to his death. Is that what you crave? Eternal night in the Seven Realms?"

Di Specchio refused to be curtailed. "I crave what we all crave, my prince: power and transformation. How can we accomplish that without human blood?"

"We return to my original plan," Raziel explained, taking a chair beneath a painting of Leto with her twin children, Apollo and Artemis. "To achieve it, we must accomplish two things. Release all our brethren, and then use their combined powers to unlock the gates. Sara, did you uncover the locations of the next two mirrors?"

Offering no reply, Saraqael's mind had wandered to a new puzzle. He'd opened the door to the coat closet and was studying the looking glass from which he'd emerged. "Is this what I think it is?

The carvings are very familiar—particularly the red dragon and ravens. Didn't I use this one at the boy's home?"

"He is no longer a boy," the elder elohim argued. "Did you find the French prisons or not? I sent you there to uncover their locations, fool!"

"Of course, I found them," Sara answered, his mind still fixed on the mirror. "They were just where we surmised. One hidden behind the wall of a crypt, beneath the old abbey at Goussainville. The other in Normandy close to that river—what is it called again? French is such a clumsy language."

"Epte!" Raziel told him, clearly annoyed. "What's so difficult about that?"

"I don't know. It bores me, I suppose. Though, there was a bit of excitement whilst there. I saw an old friend of yours."

"What friend?" Raziel glowered as he poured himself a glass of the 'wine'.

"Oh, just a very powerful one," the other teased. "One who once had your favour."

"I know many of Redwing's humans in France. Who?" Raziel asked again, growing more annoyed by the second.

"She is angry with you," Sara told him, grinning. "Very angry."

"She?" the Watcher asked, his interest now piqued.

"I'd not have thought it possible, but she is even more beautiful than the last time I saw her. I believe she's changed her hair."

"Speak you blithering moron, before I remove that sack of flesh from your worthless bones!" Raziel shouted.

The threat had no effect on Saraqael, and he idly ran his hand along the mirror's frame, deliberately ignoring his brother. "I'm sure this is the same mirror. This scratch on the upper right corner happened when that fool of a footman tried to smash it with an ax." He turned towards the other. "Did you just call me a blithering moron? That's rather harsh, Raza. I might even say cruel, but I shall ignore it. And the friend is Antoinette. She wonders why we're digging in her backyard. The woman is so very territorial!"

"Antoinette?" Raziel repeated, his face a mixture of surprise and delight. "What did you tell her?"

"Only that we intend to recover the prisons of two others in our little club. She's quite interested in our endeavours, Brother. In fact, she offered to help us—for a small fee."

"Yes, and I can imagine what that fee entails. No, she will try to control the entire project! I've no intention of allowing Antoinette Gévaudan to ruin this. We'll have to find a way to remove the mirrors without alerting her. Perhaps, a distraction."

"Who is this Gévaudan woman?" the baronet asked. "Is she another of your kind? I'd assumed you were all male."

"Who are you?" Raziel asked. "I don't remember smelling you before."

"*Smelling* me?" Wendaway complained, taking to his feet. "That's a dreadful comment! I'll have you know that I bathe every day, and my *eau de cologne* is the finest money can buy!"

"And the strongest," di Specchio observed. "Who is this woman, my lord? I don't recall hearing mention of anyone called Antoinette."

"No one you need concern yourself about, Serena. I shall deal with Antoinette in my own way. Now, to the events of Sunday. Where is the vessel?"

"Vessel?" Sir Clive interrupted. "Forgive me, Lord Raziel, what vessel? A dish of some kind?"

"You truly do try my patience at times, Urquhart. I speak of the duchess, of course. We've spent centuries perfecting her design and blood, all so she could be mated with the one Sara keeps calling the boy. Sinclair is now a man, and he begins to remember his purpose."

"And Samael serves as his champion," Saraqael added. "I wonder, does Sama know something that we do not? His foresight is very keen. Perhaps, I should go and ask him."

"You will do no such thing! Samael dared to mask himself in *my own form* on Sunday! He has forsaken us—forsaken his own kind to support the paltry humans of the circle!"

"And he slew Rasha, let's not forget that," the other Watcher remarked casually. "Though, it's no great loss. I never liked that little guttersnipe."

Surprisingly, Raziel agreed. "Rasarit was a failed experiment, a rudimentary first attempt. Practise, you might say, for when I assume control of England's next king."

Wendaway seemed perplexed. "Our next king will be Edward, surely. How do you intend to control him?"

Raziel glared at the slightly built human. "Who invited you to attend this meeting?"

Wendaway blinked arrogantly. "Sir William made me a full member over a month ago! It was a very unsettling ceremony, and my clothing had to be burnt, if you must know. Blood everywhere. I must say, I'm hardly impressed by any of you thus far. Trent had style, and I shall miss him."

"Sir William is dead," Raziel answered, his eyes glowing red and fixing on the baronet. "Would you like to join him?"

Wendaway appeared to shrink, and the Watcher continued, his eyes reverting to their normal icy hue. "Trent never understood Samael's plans, but I do. Sama has been a step ahead of us all along, which makes me wonder why he permitted that idiot to steal the duchess in the first place?"

"Our brother plays a long and complex game. His vision of future possibilities has always been sharper than yours or mine, Raza," Sara told his brother. "That vision makes him a master strategist."

Raziel smiled. "Then, we create a new set of rules and ruin his game."

"I could kill him for you," Saraqael suggested, his cold eyes glittering in anticipation. "I've wanted to do away with Sama for a very long time."

"My grievance is far greater than yours, Brother," Raziel told the other Watcher. "Samael imprisoned you for a mere three decades, whilst I was held inside that cruel stone for five millennia! Killing Sama is not an option, for it would allow him to slay us in self-defence. I suggest a better strategy. Let us compromise our brother and coerce him into rebellion against the One. Sama would have no choice but to side with us, then."

Sir Albert Wendaway had imbibed an entire glass of the altered wine and gone completely green. "Who is this Samael?" he asked, half choking.

"Samael is one of the greatest of the warrior elohim. He and I led an expedition to earth many ages ago. At first, he and I agreed on how to accomplish that mission, but we parted ways five thousand years ago. Sama reported my deeds to the One, and my punishment was to be encased within a living stone until the time of the end."

"The time of the end? Do you mean the apocalypse?" Wendaway asked, his stomach heaving.

"Quite so. That time draws near, and my release came in 1871. In the years since, I've learnt that Samael has betrayed me even further, spying upon the humans who seek freedom from the One's strict rules. He pretends to agree with our plans whilst reporting directly to the One. Samael may have ruled our family once, but he is a traitor!"

Wendaway started to laugh. "Family? You're a bunch of fallen angels! How can that be a family? It's ridiculous!"

All patience gone, Raziel struck the insolent human across the face, causing the hapless baronet to disgorge the entire contents of his stomach onto Urquhart's expensive trousers.

"That, *human*, is the first and only warning you will receive!" Raziel shouted. "We are as far above you as man stands above the crawling things of this world. Where were you when I flew across the realms of smoke and fire? When I taught the gargoyles to fly? The *ala* to transform? I have seen civilisations rise and crumble. I designed the sphinx and taught the Egyptian priests to write. I have sailed the seas of oblivion and sat upon the thrones of *Wussuru!* The gods of wind and storm fear me, and those who sleep beneath the stones praise me, for it is I who seek their release! Who are you to ridicule one such as I?"

The baronet wiped his mouth and pushed to his feet, his manner subservient, but his mind aflame with rage. "I beg your forgiveness, my lord."

Raziel shook his head, speaking with disdain, "You are a gutless worm, Wendaway." Then to his brother, he returned to the problem in France. "Tell me more of your meeting with Antoinette. Did she ask after me?"

"She did," Saraqael answered, playfully flicking the baronet's hair with a long-nailed hand, causing the slight man to flinch. "She asks when you intend to repay the three million francs you owe her. Something about a bet, I believe."

Without warning, Raziel threw a reproduction of a Ming dynasty vase into the fire. "I shall eat her heart!"

"Yes, she thought that might be your reaction, Brother. Nevertheless, she insists that you pay her or forget about excavating in her country."

The Watcher opened his mouth to argue, but Saraqael held up a hand and drew him aside. "Let's not squabble in front of the children. We can solve this small matter later. For now, I'd know just how you plan to use the duchess. As she is already with child, the boy is no longer necessary. May I not have him? Please?"

"No, you may not touch him. Not yet. Human babies are fragile and often die, do they not? We cannot risk any harm to him until we have two males of sufficient age. Leave the boy alone."

"Boy?" Wendaway asked. "How can a boy be involved? What boy?"

"Keep out of this," Saraqael told the imprudent baronet. "Children should keep silent when their elders speak." He then turned back to his brother. "Is she carrying a male child?"

"I do not yet know. My vision is limited by many factors, but there is no doubt she conceived. If it becomes clear that the child is female, then we'll simply start again."

"Again?" di Specchio asked, filling her wine glass once more from the transformed decanter. "And how many times do we retry, if she continually conceives a daughter? It took four attempts before her wretched mother finally bore Elizabeth! Three useless sons, all killed and buried. A waste of time and energy, but the risk is greater to the vessel. The duchess looks weak to me. She might not survive even one miscarriage."

"I might have a solution," Collins suggested. "Sir William paid to add a special wing to our facility, designed to provide the duchess round-the-clock care as she enters confinement. We could move her there immediately—if we can find her, that is."

"It's a consideration," Raziel agreed.

"And Sama?" Saraqael asked. "What of our traitorous brother? Are you sure I may not kill him, even a little?"

"I shall deal with Samael in good time, but Dr. Collins has given me an idea. Would you like a new job, Sara?"

"No, actually," the younger Watcher proclaimed. "I prefer play to work. Why?"

"Because it will allow us to keep an eye on the vessel. It's time we found you a more suitable veil of flesh, don't you think?"

"No, I must protest," Saraqael complained. "I'm happy to help with your plans, Raza, really, but human women find this form quite pleasing. In fact, I've become a favourite at many of the East End brothels. They don't even charge me."

"You may continue to wear that form, if you wish, for private pleasures, but I've another in mind that will allow you to move easily amongst the monied of this city."

"Who says I want to walk amongst the higher levels of London society? I prefer the seedy backstreets to those glittering ballrooms. And if I do choose to interact with a countess or duke now and then—or even a queen—I shall follow your example and pretend to be another. I might even pretend to be you, Raza!"

This time, the chief elohim's hand flew against his brother, and the mortals in the room perceived a flash of lightning, as though a weapon of fire had briefly ignited.

Rather than submit, Saraqael drew his own weapon, a curved blade made from a dense metal that grew only in the shadow realms, and for precisely thirteen seconds of human time, the Empress's salon erupted into chaos.

When the battle at last ended, Raziel stood over Saraqael, a sword at his throat. "Submit to me or die, Brother!"

Saraqael had never been one to conform or obey, but he was a consummate schemer. Casting his dark eyes upon his elder brother, the fallen angel smiled. "I swear to you, Raziel, by the blood of the ancient ones, who sleep beneath the stones, I am at your service."

Raziel's ice-blue eyes narrowed. He considered slaying his brother anyway, regardless of the rules amongst his kind, but he stayed his hand only because the fool might prove useful. He could always kill him later.

"Then, bow the knee and swear an oath to me, Saraqael, also known as Sariel. Lover of blood, Sabitu of the East, Possessor of the Salmu Stone, Guardian of Anur, Consort of Sarrat Gula. From this moment forward, you will agree to perform all that I command thee, immediately and without question, and if you fail in this, to forfeit your life to the eternal hunger of the Babu birds of the netherworld, who will consume your heart and blood, even as you have consumed those of others. Do you agree?"

Sara did as commanded. He knelt before Raziel and kissed his hand, feigning humility. "I do so agree."

"Then, arise, Brother! Arise and begin anew! We must find a form that will allow you access to human blood aplenty for your appetites without alerting the inner circle spies to our activities." He turned to Alexander Collins. "Doctor, you once mentioned to me that you lack for scientific oversight at your institute. As Trent's experiments failed to produce a hybrid of superior cognition, an elohim's knowledge would be welcome, would it not?"

Collins shifted in his chair, obviously uncomfortable with the suggestion. "But Sinclair is already suspicious of us, my lord. Would this not cause him to examine us more closely? I'm happy for the assistance, but I've no wish to provide cause for the police to shut us down. The work we're doing is far too important to the final plan."

"So it is," Raziel agreed. "Very well, I shall place this fellow elsewhere and offer my own knowledge to expand yours."

"Thank you, my lord!" Collins grovelled. "I should be pleased to receive any and all help you might offer."

Raziel turned to his brother. "What shall we make you, Sara? French? Spanish? American? Sara, have you a preference?"

"May I be a Scotsman?" Saraqael asked, already plotting how he might destroy Raziel's plans. "And one with royal blood, I think. A descendent of an ancient king with lands and a title—oh, and lots of influence."

"If it pleases, you, but only so long as you do not threaten the Stuarts."

"Of course not," he replied slyly, for it occurred to Saraqael that such a promise allowed a loophole through which he might slither. After all, just what did 'Stuart' actually mean? "Do you have someone in mind?"

"I do. There is a man who exists already, who can provide the perfect vessel for such a deception. To use him as a convincing spy, you must inhabit him rarely and even then, most subtly. He can never know that you are there."

"Rather like wearing a human suit," Contessa di Specchio suggested. "Is this man handsome?"

"Oh, yes, my dear Serena. He is most handsome indeed!" Raziel assured her, walking through the salon as though he owned it. "And you've already met him—in fact, you tried and failed to lure him into your bed several years ago. Twas at a soirée given in Milan hosted by your Cousin Umberto. Shortly after, this Scotsman naively attended a ceremony on the outskirts of Paris, though he fled before the ritual ended. It was then that I marked him for our kind. Therefore, entering him will be a simple matter. But bide your time,

Sara, and keep silent. The human must never suspect he is inhabited by you. If you are shrewd, you can infiltrate the inner circle itself."

Saraqael's mouth widened into a smile. "The Stuart scum will think me an ally?" he asked, almost salivating with glee.

"They will invite you into their homes! You will have access to the inner sanctum, you might say. I'd originally thought to insert myself into this one, but I've far too many other matters to attend at the moment, and Samael is at the top of that list. You must vow never to reveal yourself to the Stuarts, but report all their plans and activities to me. The One's rule stating that we may not enter a blessed house is most irritating and inconvenient, but there are always ways around rules. Clothed in the flesh of one whom the Stuarts trust allows us to circumvent the One, because they will invite you to enter."

"And may I feast upon their blood?"

"Of course not! I'm placing you on staff at a certain hospital in east London. Indigent men and whores aplenty darken those corridors, and no one will notice the deaths of a few, penniless patients."

"And my name?"

"Dr. Anthony Gehlen, who descends from the Stuart line, via James Charles Henry Stuart, the bastard son of Charles the First, whom he sired with a kitchen maid named Maria Watts. The philandering king admitted to fathering the boy, but never made him an heir. He did, however, grant him a noble title and settled upon him one of his many properties, Pencaitland Hall, outside of Edinburgh. Thus, thanks to the adulterous king's generosity, the commoner maid became the wealthy mother of the 1st Earl of Pencaitland."

Sara's smile became a pout. "Must I descend from a bastard line?"

"I find it fitting, considering your character, Sara," Raziel observed. "Mind you, Gehlen's father is the current title holder, and they are estranged, but when the 10th earl dies, the outcast son will inherit all titles and lands."

"And where does this convenient suit of flesh currently abide, my liege?" the rebel asked.

"In Cumbria, but he will soon receive an invitation to teach at London Hospital's Medical School in Whitechapel."

"Excellent! I shall fly to this Cumbria place and make certain the fool accepts. Do I own property in London, or must I find other accommodations? The Empress Hotel is rather nice, and certainly convenient. I'm sure Madam Hansen would welcome a noble fellow such as myself."

Earlier, Clive Urquhart had left the room to clean his soiled trousers in the *en suite* water closet, and he emerged now, still brushing them with a dry towel. "Did I hear you mention Pencaitland? I'm familiar with this family, my lord. As the son of a Scotsman who had the wisdom to marry a wealthy Frenchwoman, I heard many tales of the nobles of Edinburgh. The Pencaitland earls once had riches beyond compare! If still true, then why is this son involved in medicine at all?"

Collins entered the debate. "My question exactly, Sir Clive. Can we really trust anything this Gehlen fellow will do? If he can be controlled by you, might he not also be controlled by the other side? I worry about Anatole's plans. He moves all too easily betwixt worlds, and it's said that he can take on the appearance of anyone and anything. Should we not deal with him first, before trusting to infiltration? Surely, Prince Anatole will perceive Lord Saraqael's possession of this Dr. Gehlen and end it. He may even use him to spy upon us!"

"Silence!" Raziel shouted, his temper short and his eyes turning to flame. "Do you take me for a fool, Doctor? Lord Samael, whom your paltry Round Table calls Anatole Romanov, is far more powerful than you can possibly imagine. *Dealing* with him, as you so clumsily put it, must be accomplished with great care. It is better to coerce him to our side. We would benefit from his abilities. Sama controls the *Bu'idu* Flame and the Sword of *Enir*. His eyes opened even before my own, and his powers and cunning are unsurpassed amongst our kind. Therefore, I choose to overlook his betrayal, but he will not have the chance to betray me again. Samael will have one chance to join us, or he will die at my hand."

Saraqael stood in the corner, quietly observing Raziel's manner and mercurial moods. He could see the inner workings of his brother's mind, and unlike the mortals present, his keen eyes had noticed a faint light that shimmered above their heads, three inches to the right of the chandelier. A third Watcher had concealed himself as a cherub within the brightly muralled ceiling. Raziel had always assumed himself superior to the others who once guarded the One's throne, but five thousand years' imprisonment within the stone of Hermon had weakened him.

Raziel is wrong about Samael. He will never join us willingly, and he's too clever to be tricked into sin, Sara reasoned. *However, his desire to please the One might prove useful and allow me to rise above Raziel.*

"Anatole is indeed strong, my liege, but let's forget about the Russian for now. Tell me about this London house of mine."

Urquhart smiled broadly. "If I'm not mistaken, Lord Saraqael, there's a vast estate called Pencaitland Manor in Westminster, and it sits very close to Drummond House."

"I shall be the duke's neighbour?" Saraqael laughed. "That is quite delicious! I look forward to calling on him and introducing myself!"

Di Specchio poured herself a glass of the altered wine. "It's as though it was all ordained, is it not? Lord Raziel, let us toast to this new member of the Scottish aristocracy, shall we?"

Everyone raised a glass of the transformed wine, now an iron-rich composite of human blood. "To the bastard's descendent, Dr. Anthony Gehlen!" she said. "May he be our Trojan Horse within the castles of the Stuarts!"

Saraqael raised his glass to toast with his fellow conspirators, but his eyes glanced upwards at the cherub's face. The painted eyes blinked, and the shimmer faded and then ceased. Anatole Romanov had departed.

Smiling, the younger Watcher drained his glass.

"Where is the lovely Madam Hansen? I should like to celebrate with all of her ladies at once. And then, we shall have a game of cards, I think. Raza, have you ever played *Calabresella?* It is similar to *Tresette*, but with four players instead of three. I have my own version, which involves punishments for the loser in addition to pleasant rewards for the winners."

"It sounds like fun," the contessa said greedily. "And the punishment?"

"I shall decide that, based on who loses," Saraqael answered as the members gathered 'round one of the tables. "Oh, and did I mention?" he asked in a whisper, his eyes on his brother. "I *always* win."

CHAPTER FIFTEEN

4:09 pm – Sunday afternoon, 25th November

The busy kitchens of Haimsbury House were amongst the most modern in Westminster, and the two cooks who kept them orderly and efficient could not have been prouder. Three primary kitchens, equipped with ten gas-fired cook stoves, dominated the below-stairs areas on the east side of the enormous mansion. A roasting room jutted out from the primary kitchens, where three open fire hearths with six spits apiece provided ample meats and savouries to hungry guests, which, during the early years of the mansion's life, had included high profile businessmen, foreign ambassadors, and members of the British royal family. Three enormous, coal-fired boilers provided hot water to the kitchens, and then percolated upwards throughout the house, bringing comfort and heat to twenty-seven apartments, twelve state rooms, six large drawing rooms, four small parlours, four dining halls, a music room, three libraries, a nursery, two studies, three galleries, servants' quarters, and the largest ballroom in London.

Molly Anderson was a short, squat woman of fifty-eight who'd served the Duke of Drummond for twenty-seven years. Her younger sister, Katy Paget, had served as head cook for the Earl of Granndach for twelve years, and the two had joined the Haimsbury House staff in a sort of semi-retirement. Paget baked breads and cooked breakfast and luncheon, whilst Anderson prepared supper and made desserts.

The mansion's strict housekeeper, Ethel Partridge, had just concluded a long meeting with the newest maids regarding a disciplinary action over immodest communication betwixt the male and female sides of the servants' floor. As the rather sheepish young ladies filed out of the staff dining hall, Anderson clapped her fleshy hands to command their attention.

"Look here, girls!" the Scotswoman called. "Do stop and give me your attention for a wee moment before ya return to your tasks. There's been no formal announcement, but I'm sure most if not all o' you have heard by now that his lordship awoke yesterday from his twilight sleep."

While nearly everyone in the household had heard the wonderful news, two people had not, a new girl named Twila Donovan, who'd been hired as a replacement for the late Gertrude Trumper, and Mrs. Linda Williams, a twenty-four-year-old widow, brought from Branham to supervise the ladies of the master apartment.

The good news caused the unlined faces of both young women to break into wide smiles. Williams raised her hand. "Might I ask a question, Mrs. Anderson?"

"O' course, ye may, dearie. It's Mrs. Williams, am I right?"

"Yes, Missus. I was wonderin' if we're still to keep the same hours with regards to cleanin' the master chambers? When his lordship was still asleep and always accompanied by a caregiver, we never had ta worry 'bout walkin' in and causin' a disturbance. In fact, Mrs. Alcorn performed most of our duties whilst teachin' Bessie and Louisa proper nursing care. Will his lordship remain a patient for a time, or is he now recovered?"

Anderson, a former battlefield nurse in the Crimea, had spent many an hour's turn at the marquess's bedside. The buxom woman answered with conviction. "My dear, it's premature to think that his lordship has returned to health. He has not. If he'd listen to his doctor, Lord Haimsbury would be abed yet, but he's a man with a singular purpose to find the duchess, and we cannot begrudge him such a noble quest, now can we?"

The girl agreed, as did all, but she failed to hear a decisive answer in the cook's reply. "And does his lordship's malady mean he might relapse and return to a long sleep? Forgive my askin', Mrs. Anderson, for I've had no nursin' experience to draw upon, and I worry that we might disturb his lordship during the course of our duties."

"I see what you mean, Mrs. Williams. You're in charge of how many maids?"

"Six, ma'am."

"Is Alicia Mallory about?" Anderson asked.

The duchess's lady's maid had attended the meeting, even though she no longer slept on the servants' floor, but had taken residence in a small bedchamber near the master apartment. She raised her hand. "I'm here, Mrs. Anderson."

"Miss Mallory, you've supervised chamber maids at Queen Anne and at Branham, and you know the marquess as well as most. What answer would you offer to Mrs. Williams?"

The shy young woman stepped forward, clearing her throat before replying. "Well, I do not yet know his lordship all that well, but in the two months since I first had the honour to meet him, he's struck me as singularly focused. I imagine he and Lord Aubrey will keep long hours, rising early and working late, until my lady is found."

Many of the young ladies nodded at this, and several whispered to one another about the 'handsome earl'. Alicia waited until the clamour died down before continuing. "Yes, the earl is indeed handsome," she told the younger maids, "but he is also quite gallant and very kind. I spoke with Lord Haimsbury this morning, and I can report that he does not intend to return to bed outside of normal sleeping hours; though, if I may say so, I wish he would. He looks very tired to my eyes, but then, it's none of my business. But no matter what his lordship chooses, it is our duty to make his life as comfortable as possible, and we must pray that he and Lord Aubrey are successful in bringing my lady home!"

"Well said, Miss Mallory," Partridge agreed. "You are a credit to the household, and you speak for all of us."

Anderson nodded. "She certainly does. Mrs. Williams, I think the answer is this: Tell your girls, and I hope all are present at the moment, that as our business is to make his lordship comfortable in his own home, then we must all make a practise of knocking upon all the master apartment doors from this day forward. When the duchess is found, and she will be found, our lord and lady will commence their wedded lives together. I'm sure that if any of you ladies had only just married, you'd appreciate a bit of privacy. Am I right?"

A few of the older girls giggled at this, but the six chars, all under ten years of age, appeared perplexed. "What does that mean, Missus?" asked eight-year-old Sarah Blundt.

"I'll explain it later," Williams told the girl.

Anderson and Partridge exchanged amused glances just as Esther Alcorn entered the kitchens alongside Mary Wilsham. Alcorn wore a modest day dress of midnight blue but no apron, and her greying hair was braided and wound about her head.

"Did I miss a meeting?" she asked Partridge.

Wilsham appeared somewhat uncomfortable. "I reckon we're interruptin'. Mayhap we should go, Mrs. Alcorn."

"Not at all!" Partridge insisted. "You're just in time. How is Lord Haimsbury, Mrs. Alcorn?"

"Better, but stubborn as ever," Esther replied with a wink. "I wonder, as most of the ladies are down here already, might we gather and pray for his lordship and also ask the Lord to bring our little duchess home?"

Katy Paget had said little, for she'd been supervising a team of four kitchen maids and two sculleries. "I think that's a grand idea, Mrs. Alcorn," the buxom cook said, wiping her brow with a bare hand. "But before we start, do we know how many will be comin' to this meetin' the duke has arranged? I was told no more than twelve, but I keep hearing that number may treble, now that the marquess is awake."

"No one seems to know the exact time or number, Mrs. Paget," Alcorn replied. "Mr. Baxter can give you a full accounting once his footmen return from making their calls, but whenever the circle members met at Branham, we'd sometimes have thirty or more. Mostly men, and all with great appetites. Generally, though, they prefer food that might be eaten quickly. They mainly come together for prayer and making plans, though the food's always appreciated. Men think better when their stomachs do not grumble. Especially, Scottish men."

Paget, a sunny-spirited woman of fifty-three, laughed merrily, her green eyes practically disappearing behind palpebral arcs of freckled flesh. "Aye, tis true. I've seen the duke tuck into a meal with the relish of an ant come upon a basket o' bread and jam! We'll make certain there's plenty. We've three roasts goin' next door, and pies bakin' as well. The dough for tomorrow mornin's loaves is finished and risin' in the larder. All's well. How did his lordship seem ta you, if I might ask? Will he be able ta eat with the others, or should I keep a pot o' broth goin'?" she asked as she demonstrated how to knead dough to a former char, now learning kitchen skills. "Not too quick now, Sadie. Easy does it."

Alcorn smiled at the pretty picture of the girl's hands in the soft dough. "Lord Haimsbury likes his toast sliced thick, Sadie. And I'm pleased to say that he looks much better today. I'd not want him out of bed if he were my patient, but he's always struck me as a man of fierce energy and drive. It'll be a chore ta keep him resting, that's for sure. Mary," she said to Wilsham, "let's find chairs and begin praying, shall we?"

By half past four, the staff dining hall had filled not just with women, but also with half a dozen footmen as well. Word soon spread to the stables and gardens, and those men that could, entered and took places at the back of the large hall, hats in their callused hands, heads bowed. For half an hour, each man and woman prayed silently for the Stuart and Sinclair families, but especially that their duchess might return to them safe and unharmed.

CHAPTER SIXTEEN

5:10 pm – Sunday, Café Royal, Regent St.

Constance Calliope Wychwright ordered a bottle of 1855 Château Margaux Pavilion Blanc to accompany her Marengo chicken with asparagus and carrots *au Beurre*. Her husband flinched when he heard his wife order the expensive wine, but kept his temper in check as he handed the menus to the waiter. "I'll have the same, I think, but potatoes rather than asparagus spears. Can't abide the things."

"The '55 Margaux?" he repeated as the slim waiter departed.

"I'm not made of money, Constance."

"I never said you were, but we come to the Royal to be seen, or so you've always claimed. Now, let me tell you what I've learnt. This is an opportunity that will not repeat itself!"

"Yes, I'm sure it won't," he replied automatically. "And what opportunity might that be? Eating?"

She smirked and shook her head. "Though you make fun, this is very serious, David. I've thought of a way to ensure our future, but we must act soon."

"Act? Act how, my dear? What are you jabbering on about?"

"Aubrey," she said plainly. "It's as clear as day, if you're looking in the right direction. Although, his cousin might even be persuaded."

"You're spouting nonsense again, Connie. What's all this about Aubrey?"

"As a potential son-in-law. Do you never listen to anything I say?"

"Not if I can help it," he mumbled to himself. Then, seeing her stern face, the baron clarified his position. "What I mean to say, my dear, is that Aubrey is not on the cards. No matter what you might believe, he is anything but smitten with our daughter."

"Not yet, he isn't, but he will be. I've sent two baskets of roses to Haimsbury House with cards of good will, but that is hardly enough. Now that the marquess improves..."

"You must leave Haimsbury alone, Constance. The man is mourning the loss of his wife."

"Is it certain then? The duchess is dead?" she asked, her voice rising in pitch excitedly.

Wychwright leaned closer, his hand on hers. "Hush! Constance, temper your voice! Why do you speak with such relish about so awful a possibility?"

"Is it fact or not?"

The baron stared at his wife, completely dumbfounded. "You wish her ill? Why? What has that good lady ever done to you, Connie? I am shocked by the very notion!"

Constance Wychwright cast an indignant glare at her husband; a stony stare that ordinarily sent him spouting line upon line of frantic apologies, but today the visible reproof only caused him to grow evermore concerned for his wife's sanity.

"Connie, I understand that you have ambitions for our daughter, but tell me that you haven't considered so hideous a possibility."

"I said nothing of the kind. I merely asked if she were dead. Is that unusual? Our family is close to the Stuarts, and..."

"I'd hardly call us close, my dear. The duke and I have served together on Home Office committees from time to time, and we nod to one another in public, of course."

"And my sister's theatre box shares a curtain with Aubrey's. Don't forget that."

He sighed. "I could never forget that, Connie. As to the duchess, the rumour at Parliament is that she is *presumed* dead, but there is no proof. Officially, she is listed as missing. We should be praying for her, not looking to prey upon her bereaved family in this dark hour!"

She sipped her water thoughtfully. "You think me a predator? That is a cruel statement, David Wychwright. I do no such thing. All I want is to make a good marriage for Cordelia. Is that predatory? Her beauty is great enough to attract any man, and whilst I'd looked to the earl as a possible suitor, a widower might also make a fine catch."

"A widower? Constance, you cannot mean Haimsbury!"

"Charles Sinclair is one of the wealthiest men in Europe. He is young and looks to establish himself in government, but he must also produce an heir. Cordelia can provide opportunity for both."

The baron shook his head. "You can be heartless sometimes, Constance. The Stuarts are not steppingstones to advancement. I see enough of that sort of nonsense at Whitehall. I will not watch it burrow its way into my family!"

"Steppingstones, no, but opportunities, surely. And our family is in dire need of their aid. Our sons will never provide such an opportunity for us! Three sons. Three chances at wealth and power, and each one has turned out to be a disappointment."

"I wouldn't say that," he argued as the waiter arrived with the wine and a basket of bread. Wychwright tasted a small sip, enjoying the lovely feel in his mouth but dreading the high cost. "Yes, that's quite nice." The waiter poured two glasses, set the bottle into a cooler on the table, and then left.

"Now, what were we saying?" Wychwright murmured, his thoughts now on his bank account.

"We were discussing our future, David. Our sons."

"Ah, yes, so we were. I'm rather pleased with our sons, Connie. Thomas has found success in the Army, and William does well in his studies—or so he claims. Ned's marriage has given us two lovely granddaughters. Why must you be so pessimistic?"

"Thomas and William remain unmarried, and Ned is content to manage a brewery! How is that successful?"

"Yes, I do wish Thomas would marry, but his military service makes that unlikely at this time," the father bemoaned.

"He may never marry, which means the title might eventually pass to another. Neither Thomas nor William has a whit's chance of marrying into money, therefore we must make certain that Cordelia does! We are destitute, David. Only a profitable marriage can save us."

The baron took umbrage at this. "Hmph! My income would suffice if you didn't take so many shopping trips!" Then, seeing her reaction, he grew kinder, taking her hand. "My dear, I would give you the world were it mine to offer, but I was but a poor baron's son when you married me, and now I am a poor baron. When Thomas inherits the title, he will also be a poor baron, and eventually, Windermere will crumble into the dust from our penniless natures."

"Then, let us build up that legacy with one of the Stuart fortunes. If, as you say, it is unthinkable to consider Haimsbury, then let us look at Paul Stuart. If Cordelia were to marry him, then our grandson could become the 12th Earl of Aubrey."

"Does she show any interest in the earl?"

"She likes him a great deal, and I'm sure he'd look her way with the right coaxing," she declared. "It will take a little nudge, but I believe I can make it happen."

"Do nothing unseemly, Constance," he warned her. "And do not ask our daughter to behave contrary to that of a lady."

"I'd never dream of it," she replied, sipping the wine thoughtfully. "There is another possibility, however. A rumour circulating amongst the card rooms of London."

"And how would you know anything about card rooms?"

She laughed. "Not gentlemen's card rooms, David! My dear, I refer to the whist clubs attended by ladies of quality. I played a few hands with Maisie Churchill on Friday, and she commented as to how the duchess had become ill several times at the wedding reception. Now, I have it from another friend, an assistant to Madam du Monde, who designs all the duchess's clothing, that Elizabeth's figure underwent dramatic shifts in the fortnight leading up to her wedding day."

"And your point?" the baron asked as he nodded to a passing parliamentarian.

"The duchess is pregnant. Or rather was, if indeed she has passed out of this life—God rest her soul."

David Wychwright's mouth dropped open, and he set down his butter knife. "That is never to repeated, do you hear me?"

She smiled. "Then you've heard it as well. I know you very well, David Thomas Wychwright. Who told you?"

His hands clenched, and the henpecked baron longed to be elsewhere instead of melting beneath his wife's withering glare.

"It is but a rumour," he said at last.

"Rumours are often rooted in fact. Who told you?"

"Lord Kendrick, if you must know," Wychwright confessed. "After the final session on Monday. He didn't mention who told him, but Kendrick happened to say how dreadful it was that the duchess was abducted, but that her delicate condition made it all the more pitiable. He even said Haimsbury may have lost not only a wife but also a child."

"You see? Rooted in fact. Kendrick is hardly the purveyor of idle chatter. He's a sober man with considerable influence and connexions."

"Poor man," Baron Wychwright observed. "Haimsbury must be beside himself with grief."

She tapped his hand with her forefinger. "Not Haimsbury. Aubrey."

He blinked. "What? Whatever do you mean?"

She leaned in close to offer an explanation. "It is a fact that the earl and duchess planned to marry until their sudden trip to Scotland in October. When they returned, she and Haimsbury were engaged. Isn't that odd?"

"What are you implying?" he whispered nervously.

"Only that the duchess found herself in a bind, and when he learnt of her deception, the earl discarded her. Haimsbury picked up where his cousin left off, and..."

"You go too far, Constance. Too far! The marquess and earl have been friends for nearly a decade. Why would such fine men conspire in such a way?"

"I do not say they conspired, David. Only that one took the place of another. It's done all the time in these old peerage families, but it leaves two openings for Cordelia."

"Two? I don't follow."

"It is simple. If the earl rejected Elizabeth because he thought she'd *dallied*, shall we say, then who performed the dalliance? Surely, it was Haimsbury. That means that he has indeed lost a child."

"And the second opening?"

"That Aubrey was the actual father, but Elizabeth refused to marry him, for she loved his cousin. Aubrey and the duchess spent many weeks together in France, so it is a strong possibility. If true, then it is the earl who is bereaved of a child."

Wychwright felt as though he'd spent the past ten minutes inside a gale—lots of wind with no relief. "Constance, do you ever listen to yourself? My dear, you make no sense. How does any of this help Cordelia find a husband?"

"It's my belief that the earl is bruised and vulnerable, but so is the marquess. Now, if Cordelia plays this hand well, then she can secure a profitable marriage to one of them. Either will do; although, the newspapers imply the marquess has grander titles yet to come."

"That is pure speculation," the baron reminded her. "Speak no more of it! Those tales about the queen's legitimacy slither through London's press every decade or so. I'll hear no more of such idle talk."

"If you say so, my dear. Are you busy tomorrow afternoon, David? I thought Cordelia and I would call on her young friend, Lady Adele, and that you might wish to come along. Maisie mentioned the girl is staying with Haimsbury presently."

Wychwright had lost his appetite, and he pushed back from the table. "Take care, Constance. Lord Aubrey loves his sister, and he will not brook having her used. Not at all—not by anyone! Paul Stuart may be an eligible bachelor, but he is a formidable man. His reputation is without equal. If you cross him, then you're done in government. I will not be a part of such deception!"

"It is not deception, David. Not really. I think only of our daughter's happiness. Cordelia and I will do what must be done. If it means altering the bait to land the greater fish, then I'll make sure our daughter's is the only hook in the water. No matter what it takes, I shall discover the lure required to land that formidable fish. You may rely upon it."

He glowered at his ambitious wife, wishing he'd married her sister Margaret instead. "I'll hear no more of this. No, you will say not one word further, Connie! If you continue with this mad scheme, I shall go to the earl myself and warn him."

She sighed and reached for the bread basket. "You're right, husband. I was wrong even to suggest it."

"Yes, well, that's better then. Now, what shall we do this evening? As you're in London, I could vacate my room at the club and join you at Fitzmaurice Place. Perhaps, we could have the Cartringhams over for a late supper and a game of whist."

"That would be lovely. My sister and her husband are fine company," his wife said automatically, her eyes on a paunched man sitting at a nearby table. She nodded, and the man raised his wine glass. "David, I think I'll take an hour to rest at home before planning for company. This week's left me wrung out like an old sheet."

"Never an old sheet, my dear," he said, recalling why he'd married her in the first place. *She'd been a beauty then.*

The baron reached for his wife's hand. "Shall we put off supper with your sister until tomorrow? If you're worn out, then perhaps an early night is best."

"Perhaps," the baroness sighed, happy to spend the evening without her husband. "Can you stay at your club again tonight?"

"Of course. I'd promised to have drinks with Kendrick anyway."

The waiter arrived with their entrées, and the baroness began slicing into the chicken. "Such a mad time to be alive. Poor Elizabeth! I shall speak to Cordelia and arrange for us both to visit Lady Adele tomorrow."

"Did you say tomorrow? No, can't make it. I've a meeting at the Exchange."

"Well, then," she answered, "I shall write to the earl and make arrangements for a time when we can all go. It's imperative that we show a united front, David. Although, I might call on Haimsbury this week, on my own, just to offer our condolences. See if he needs anything. Offer a bit of comfort."

"I doubt he's receiving," her husband argued as he salted his potatoes.

"Not ordinary people, no, but friends are surely welcome. Lady Victoria and I spent a great deal of time talking at the reception. She's an interesting woman. Dominant, but interesting. She suggested that we include Aubrey in our invitations from now on. She's concerned about him, I think. Poor man must blame himself for the duchess's death."

Wychwright's eyes rounded behind his silver-framed spectacles, and the right corner of his mouth twitched. "Blame himself? What sort of balderdash is that? Constance, do not repeat such a foolish notion to anyone—not ever again," he warned in a whisper. "And stop referring to the duchess as dead. She is nothing of the kind until it is announced. It's vile and heartless! Should anyone overhear, it could have very serious repercussions. Do you want Haimsbury and his family to learn you've made such statements? London has very large ears, and her streets and restaurants teem with reporters and ministers who would make considerable hay of such idle words. I'll not hear one word more, madam. I will not! Am I clear?"

The baroness had heard her husband spout similar warnings often, over the years, and she knew how to handle his temper. "I merely repeat what others are whispering—for your ears alone." She glanced again in the other man's direction, but this time her husband caught sight of it.

"Why do you look at that vile person, Connie?"

"Vile? That's an odd statement. He's an influencer of powerful men. Isn't that what you once told me?" she countered skillfully. "Surely, currying the favour of such a man is helpful to your career."

"Clive Urquhart may be influential, but he is a pot-bellied serpent. He writhes through government offices as though he owns them, spreading his venomous bribes with no thought of the consequences. I wish no commerce with men such as that, and certainly not whilst eating."

"Men such as that have access to great wealth, husband."

"Some do, and others merely pretend. I've yet to discern which category applies to Clive Urquhart. Oh, dear, he's coming this way."

The diminutive half-French, half-Scottish builder pranced towards them wearing a sickeningly sweet smile. Arriving at their table, he kissed the baroness's hand and then bowed to Wychwright.

"*M'sieur le baron, mon ami!* It is fortuitous, no? Meeting here in this way? It saves me steps to your very nice office at Whitehall, or do you still make your deals at the Exchange?"

David Wychwright managed to keep his temper and even offered a pained smile of his own. "Afternoon, Urquhart. If you've business matters to discuss, then it's best to do so at Westminster, or, as you say, at the Royal Exchange. I'm there most mornings."

"Ah, yes, but ministers are so seldom in their chambers. I have a proposal I hope you might pass along to your fellows at the Home Office. A little plan of mine to construct a charity hospital in the east. It is a project that might also open profitable doors to a certain family known to you."

"And who might that be?" he asked, thoroughly annoyed.

"A family that awaits news of a loved one's fate. Whisper the words 'charity hospital' to Lord Haimsbury and see how he jumps!"

"I rather doubt he'd jump at anything today, Urquhart," Wychwright snapped back. "The man's in great distress over his wife's disappearance. Do you not read the papers?"

"*Oui, certainement!* I read them every day, many times a day. And some hint our Haimsbury is *un héritier royal*, no? More than mere marquess."

"I've no idea what you're talking about, Clive. Constance, I think we should be going."

"But we've not finished eating!" she objected. "And even if we had, I plan to order dessert."

The builder clicked his fingers to summon the waiter. "The service here is slow today. I shall speak with the owner. M'sieur Nicols and I are, how you say, old chums! I see you later, eh? At your club." He turned to the baroness. "Madam, if a sweet tooth must be satisfied, then try the *madeleines*. They are iced with *chocolat* and hazelnut. *Ils sont magnifiques!*"

"Madeleines? Is that something new?" she asked hungrily, for the baroness's appetite for sweets seldom had a day's rest.

"*Oui*. Little butter cakes that sit upon the tongue like a beautiful cloud! Henri, the *pâtissier*, adds brandy, eh? Try them, madam. You will not be disappointed. Enjoy!"

He bowed once more, and then the little builder waddled towards the exit where he joined a younger man, who waved to the baroness. Both he and Urquhart disappeared through the dense crowd of diners.

"Who was that fellow?" her husband asked.

"Which?"

"That slightly built chap by the door. The one who left with Urquhart. I've seen him before, but I can't recall where."

"Oh, him. It's Sir Albert Wendaway. Lord Haimsbury's cousin. We met him at the wedding reception. He and Delia have become friends."

"Wendaway? I hope it's not the same Wendaway whose name keeps cropping up at my club. If so, he's a braggart and a gambler, if not worse. Not the sort of fellow we want around our daughter."

"I doubt it's the same man," she said. "Sir Albert's a handsome fellow, though his title and lands are hardly worth Delia's time. One house and only two thousand a year. However, he is cousin to Haimsbury, which makes him useful."

Wychwright said little else during their meal, and by six, they'd parted company. The baron headed to a series of casual meetings at the Carlton Club, and his wife to a house in Grosvenor Square, where she held court with Urquhart and his imminently useful companion.

6:03 pm – Haimsbury House master suite

Charles Sinclair stared into the mirror, examining the cuts and bruises on his bristled chin. Only one week earlier, he'd dressed in bespoke finery, married the woman of his dreams, and then held her in his arms as they led dance after dance on the ballroom floor of Drummond House. He had no way of knowing that within a few short hours, she'd be taken from him.

Shortly, the inner circle members would gather to discuss the events of that fateful night and decide how to proceed, but Sinclair had no patience for meetings. Instead, he wanted to gather a force of policemen and hit the streets, going from house to house if necessary, to find his wife.

A soft step broke his concentration, and he turned to find Martin Kepelheim standing inside the bedchamber. "I knocked, but you didn't answer. I'd feared you might have relapsed."

Charles managed to smile. "No relapse, just frustration. I've lost an entire week, and it's difficult to remain indoors, when I should be out there hunting."

"Let Paul's team do the hunting, Charles. I assure you, they have not been idle. Believe me, when I tell you that our earl has left no stone unturned. Do you think he would? He loves her, too."

"Yes, I know. Forgive my impatience, Martin. It's just so difficult to let another man do what I should! She's my wife, my responsibility."

Kepelheim placed a hand on the marquess's shoulder. "My friend, you think yourself strong, but you are not. Please, I beg you. Sit for a moment."

The marquess sighed and took a chair near the bedchamber's marble fireplace, staring into the fire as he spoke. "It's difficult to keep still."

"Yes, I'm sure it is, but it will aid in healing. We've a little time before the meeting begins. Perhaps, it will help to talk."

"That's kind of you, Martin. I can't imagine what I'd do without family and friends. Victoria's doing her best to cheer me. Yesterday, she gave me a collection of Beth's journals from France. I read a few entries last night. I can almost hear her voice in the words." He shifted position to offer relief to his bruised body. "As you can see, I've left Elizabeth's chamber for this one. I thought it best to have her room clean and ready for when she's found."

"Yes, I noticed this morning that Lord Aubrey had relocated to the next apartment. I've always loved this house, Charles, particularly these rooms. The bedchambers are enormous!"

"They are, and Beth's is even larger than this one."

"You kept your grandfather's bed, I see," he said, pointing to a full tester made of carved mahogany. The arched canopy was softened at the corners by damask curtains in blue and gold silk. "Did you know it was designed and handcrafted by a fellow named Chatsworth? He and your grandfather served in the Peninsula together against Napoleon's forces."

"My grandfather must have been fairly young," Charles noted. "The Peninsula campaign was what? 1810 or so?"

"1807 is when that war officially began, but there were political upheavals for decades leading up to it. Redwing had a hand in those, but then, they're often involved in warfare."

"Are they in control of governments?"

"Not directly, but they influence decision makers in ways you'd never expect."

"How pervasive are they?"

Martin's brows worked their way upwards as he replied. "Well, now that is a lifetime of study on its own! Think of them as shadow governments, is you will. Each country has its own ruler and cabinet, and not all call themselves Redwing. Only the English speaking countries use the term. If you want a full list of names, I'd be happy to share what MacPherson and I have put together. It has over seventy entries, and within each division are multiple subdivisions. Below those, smaller committees and subcommittees. War and the resulting bloodshed fuel their cabalistic machinery. They are a diabolical lot, Charles. Your grandfather fought many a battle against their battalions. I met the ninth marquess the year he died. I was but a youngster at the time, barely twenty. Did you know that your grandfather rebuilt this house because of the ghosts?"

"Did you just say *ghosts?*"

Kepelheim's round face grew serious. "Not humans back from the dead, no, but spiritual entities. The first Haimsbury House was built in the mid-sixteenth century, and some claim the hauntings drove the 4th Marchioness, Katherine Sinclair, mad. I've only scant evidence to back up the claim. However, when your grandfather decided to tear down the old and rebuild, he was forced to retain some of the original foundations, as well as the wine and root cellars. The ninth marquess never lacked for funds, of course, but his architect warned that an extinct underground river made it dangerous to delve too deeply and convinced him to leave the foundations and cellars intact. The marquess died the very year this house was finished. You'll notice motifs throughout that evoke Sinclair history, much of it from France. The *fleur de lis* is predominant, but also other emblems. Charles, are you aware that your bloodline descends from much more than the Plantagenets and Stuarts?"

"I think James mentioned it once. Why?"

"My friend, when Elizabeth has returned, and our lives regain a sort of normality, I should like to revisit your childhood memories. Your father taught you many things about your heritage, and we need the information that's stored inside your brilliant mind! Also, there are several scrolls at Rose House that I should fetch for you. Proofs of inheritance and letters patent from both the English and French crowns."

Sinclair shook his head. "I care nothing for titles, Martin. All I want is Elizabeth. Until I can hold her in my arms, nothing else matters to me."

"Of course, I'll let it go for now, but we must speak of it eventually, because it may explain a great deal about Redwing's plans regarding your future children."

"Beth's having twins," Sinclair said suddenly, immediately wondering why he'd blurted it out. "Or at least, I think she is."

Kepelheim leaned forward in his chair, the firelight flickering across his round cheeks. "How can you possibly know that? She's not yet two months along. I doubt any physician would make such a claim at this point."

"No physician did, but I met my daughter in that place, Martin. You and Paul think I dreamt it all, but I didn't. Both Elizabeth and I were in some hellish land with talking birds and a terrifying maze of stones. My fear is that she's still there."

"If you say you were in such a place, then I believe you, Charles. Heaven knows I've come across many strange things in my years with the circle! If you were held prisoner, that may explain your prolonged state of unconsciousness, but how did you escape?"

"This watch," he said, holding up the Sir John Bennett. "The one Beth had engraved for me in Scotland. It stopped, and I tried winding it, but only when Beth touched it, did the watch start ticking, forcing time to advance. That's when I awoke. I've no idea whether or not she escaped at the same time. Don't you see? If she is also unconscious, then it means she's ill. We must find her soon!"

"My friend, the Lord knows her whereabouts, and he will bring her home."

The tailor poured a glass of water from a delicately painted china carafe and handed it to his friend. "Drink this down. You are a man of fierce convictions and seldom heed advice, if it runs contrary to your instincts, but I beg you to take it now. Your injuries require rest and repose. Charles, you nearly died. How can you help her, if your health fails?"

Sinclair drank the water and set the empty glass on a table. "It won't fail. I'm alive in ten years' time, which convinces me that no matter how I choose, all will be well."

"Alive in ten years? I don't understand."

"Neither do I, actually, but it's true. Despite what all of you believe, Martin, I *did* speak with my daughter. Georgianna Sinclair led me through the stone maze. She and her twin brother Robert will be born in June of next year. They were not a dream. It's for them that I push myself, not just for their mother, but for our children. I cannot fail them. I will not!"

Kepelheim's eyes blinked as he tried to sort through this odd confession. "I do not say you dreamt this, but you must admit it is difficult to understand."

"Yet it happened," the marquess insisted. "Beth experienced it, too, and when we find her, she'll tell you her own story. I've never been so certain of anything in my life, but my wife is ill. We need to find her soon, Martin, before it's too late."

"Yes, and we will, but you must grow stronger to accomplish that task. Have you eaten today?"

"Mrs. Alcorn brought up a bowl of soup about two hours ago." He wiped at his eyes, straining against fatigue. "I promise to eat well tonight, and I'll retire early. I just pray I can sleep. Perhaps, my body's fighting against it. I did sleep an entire week, after all."

"A coma is hardly restful, Charles."

"No, I suppose not," he replied with a slight smile. "Last night, I found myself staring at the ceiling. You'll probably laugh at how I spent the hours, but I sat inside Beth's clothes closet."

The tailor's greying eyebrows pinched together forming twin furrows of thick flesh above his nose. "That is an odd way to spend one's time. May I ask why?"

"To be close to her," he answered softly. "In a way, I feel a little like Samson after Delilah's treachery. His hair was the source of his strength, and Beth is the source of mine. Without her beside me, I'm scarcely able to think, eat, or sleep. So, I sat in her closet, looking through all her gowns and jewels and reminiscing about when I last saw her wearing them. You can still smell raspberry and vanilla scent on some of them. It's Beth's signature soap, milled to her specifications in Paris. I found several bars of it in a linen cupboard, and I placed one beneath my pillow. That's how I finally fell asleep. Somehow, the scent made it seem as though she lay beside me. I need her, Martin. I'd simply stop breathing without Elizabeth in my life."

"We will find her," the tailor promised. "Now, if you're able, I think Della has a little surprise. She's practised several new piano arrangements and wants to play them for you."

The marquess finally managed to smile. "Except for Elizabeth, there is no other person who cheers me like Della Stuart. Thank you, Martin. Thank you for talking to me. You are the best of friends."

A few moments later, Charles entered the music room to the heartfelt refrain of *Auld Lang Syne*, played skillfully by Adele Stuart. She'd originally planned to play a Strauss waltz called *Rosen auf dem Süden* in honour of Rose House, but the duke convinced her that a Scottish air might be more appropriate.

Charles cared not one whit about the selection, but about the hands playing it. He walked to the piano and sat beside her.

"That is a perfect choice," he whispered, kissing the top of head.

The eleven-year-old threw her arms around him, squeezing tightly. "I'm so very glad you're all right!" she cried out, her face against his chest. "I've been ever so worried."

"So I understand," he replied, kissing her hands. "These are very talented fingers. I'm told you sat at my bedside every day. I cannot tell you how much that means to me, Della. I love you very much, little one."

She wiped her eyes, trying not to cry. "That's what you call Beth."

"But also what I call you, if that's all right."

She nodded. "Yes, please, but you had me very worried. You're not ever to get sick again. Not ever! Is that clear?"

He saluted. "As clear as glass, Commissioner Stuart. Will you play me another song?"

"What would you like to hear?"

"Anything, so long as you perform it. I'll sit here beside you, if that's all right. I could turn the pages."

Without warning, her resolve failed, and Della began to cry. "I just want to hug you, Charles. I do love you so very much!" she whispered tightly.

"I love you, too, Della Marie. Very much. Will you help me to the chair, then, if you don't need a page-turner? I'm a little wobbly on my feet yet and could use a shoulder."

Charles had no trouble walking, but he sensed that Adele wanted to keep near him, and he was right. The girl very seriously put her slender arm around his waist to provide support.

"Lean on me," she told him. "Once you're safely in the chair, then I shall bring you water, if you like."

"Not just yet. Mr. Kepelheim insisted I drink an entire glass upstairs. Perhaps, you might read to me? I understand that you've been reading that Holmes story from last year's *Beeton's*. I fear that I slept through it all. Would it be asking too much for you to read it again?"

Adele's face lit up. "I've put the copy with my music. It's right over here!"

She dashed to the lidded basket where she kept many volumes of piano music and found the Christmas annual from the previous year. "Mr. Holmes is very interesting," she whispered as he lifted her onto his lap. "He reminds me of you, Cousin Charles, though he's not nearly so nice. But he solves crimes and mysteries, just as you do. You mustn't worry. Beth will be all right. I promise. We've all been praying and praying. The Lord won't let anything happen to her. Mr. Baxter says she's in the Lord's mighty hand, and there's no safer place."

"You're very wise, little one. That reminds me of a psalm."

"Which one? Is it about the Lord's hand?"

"No, it's about wisdom. Psalm Eight, I think. How does it go again? *Out of the mouths of babes and sucklings hast thou ordained strength because of thine enemies.*"

"I like that one," Adele told him. "Does it mean that God gives children wisdom that adults lack?"

He laughed. "Yes, I think he does. Next summer, Elizabeth and I shall have a baby, and I think she will be quite remarkable."

"Or he," Adele told him. "Babies come in two varieties, you know. It might be a boy."

"Or it might be both," he answered with a broad smile.

"How can it be both?" Della giggled. "That's quite impossible!"

"Not if there are two babies."

"Can there be two?" she asked him, snuggling close.

"Sometimes a woman gives birth to twins. We'll see what happens, shall we?"

The eleven-year-old found the answer satisfying and opened the Christmas periodical, beginning to read sweetly.

As Charles listened, he considered the topic of children. *Twins.* The very word caused him to smile, and he drew Adele close, thinking about Georgie's comment that by 1899 Adele would be married and bringing her own baby to their Christmas celebration.

Out of the mouths of babes...

Charles shut his eyes, listening to the fictional narrative of Dr. John Watson and thinking of his abandoned desk at Scotland Yard—and how a letter penned by Elizabeth in October had forever altered his life.

The memory made him smile, and he fell asleep, thinking of the moment inside Queen Anne House library, when a poor policeman had dared to kiss a duchess.

CHAPTER SEVENTEEN

7:01 pm

Charles was awoken by the gentle hand of Cornelius Baxter, who informed the startled marquess that the inner circle had assembled. At one minute past the hour, Sinclair entered the library to applause and humbly took his customary seat.

"No, son," Drummond told him. "You're leader of the circle now. Your chair is at the head of the table."

"You're sure, sir? But you're the head of our family."

"Yes, but you're the principal guardian of our girl. And the elder heir of the twins. Sit, Nephew. Sit!"

Sinclair did as ordered and assumed his rightful place. Drummond took the chair to his nephew's right, and following the oval table in clockwise fashion from Sinclair were Paul Stuart, Sir Thomas Galton, Dr. Reginald Whitmore, Sir Percival Smythe-Daniels, Dr. Michael Emerson, Dr. Deidra Kimberley, Dr. Simon Allerton, Dr. Edward MacPherson, Lord Malcolm Risling, Edmund Reid, Arthur France, Martin Kepelheim, and Duke James.

Sir Thomas Galton and his team had begged leave to continue searching for the duchess in the outer boroughs of the city. Victoria Stuart chose to spend the evening with Adele, Esther Alcorn, and Mary Wilsham, reading the Bible and praying for Elizabeth and Charles.

Now that all available members of the august fellowship had arrived and settled in, the tailor shut the door. Once he'd returned to the table, Kepelheim held up his glass.

"Our esteemed Mr. Baxter has filled our cups with a lively claret. I suggest, therefore, that we all stand with glasses raised to toast to our marquess's miraculous recovery!"

Everyone stood, but Drummond interrupted Kepelheim before the tailor could pronounce his toast. "If I may, Martin. I'd like to offer the toast." He turned to face Sinclair. "Charles, when I saw your condition last Sunday night, I feared the worst. Son, we thought you were dead or dying, and it was like losing you all over again," he said, his dark eyes glistening. "But our compassionate Lord works in mysterious ways. Your life is a testament to that. Once again, he brought you back from the brink of death. Therefore, I am delighted to raise a glass to my resilient nephew, Charles Sinclair, who makes the enemy quake in their collective boots! May you find our girl quickly, and may the Lord bring you both a long and very happy life!"

Sinclair fought against tears and fatigue, but the gesture touched his heart. "Thank you, James. There is no other fellowship which means more to me than this one. Please, everyone, sit. I try to avoid standing too often. I suffer from lack of sleep, but also a touch of dizziness now and then. I'm told it's normal. I wonder, Martin, would you open us with a prayer?"

The tailor blushed as he took to his feet. "It is my honour to offer a prayer during your first meeting as our leader, Charles. And to be the first to pray in this glorious library since we lost your dear father, well it brings back many pleasant memories. My friends, let us bow our heads, shall we?"

All heads lowered, and the duke gripped Sinclair's hand tightly. Charles noticed it trembled.

"Lord of all, Creator of the universe, and Sovereign King of everything that has ever been or ever will be, we come to you today as a group of flawed humans. Yet, despite our failings, you see us as finished and perfect, because of your Son's covering blood. How marvellous—how very wonderful!

"Father, it is our privilege to call you by such an intimate name. It causes me shame when I think of how poorly I behave as your son, yet you patiently continue to teach me. One such lesson has been to watch the lives of Charles, Paul, and Elizabeth. These three young people shine like beacons in our midst! Their love for one another is a reminder of your love for us, and so I ask you to reunite them quickly. Return our beautiful duchess to us, my Lord. Help us to find her, and when she has returned, I ask that you might grant her and her guardians a season of rest. Redwing and their spirit guides have caused us many sleepless nights, yet you know the end from the beginning. We cannot see where the road leads, but you have always known each twist and turn, every hill and valley, even from the foundation of the world.

"Lead our conversation this night and bind us as a family of believers, so that we might form a circle of protection around our trio, whose lives stand at the centre of it all. Charles, Elizabeth, and Paul. It is a mystery to me just how you've designed them to so undergird one another, yet it is undeniable. Thank you, for allowing me to be a part of this family. Nothing else in life means more to me. In the name of Christ Jesus, I ask all these things. Amen."

Sinclair raised his head and immediately walked 'round the table to embrace Kepelheim, who began to weep on the marquess's shoulder. "Thank you, Martin. I'm honoured to call you friend, but you are family. My talented Uncle Marty!"

Wiping his eyes, the tailor sniffed. "Oh, my, you called me that when you were a boy. Getting to see you, all grown up and serving Christ, has been a great surprise, Charles. You can ask the duke. Am I not right, Your Grace?"

The duke wiped his own, wet face. "Aye. We all mourned for you, son. Paul as much as anyone. He'd lost his childhood companion, but now you're closer than ever."

Charles returned to his chair and eased into the seat, ignoring the pounding at the back of his head. "The Lord had his reasons for allowing me to be separated from my family, and I'm convinced he has reasons for separating me from Elizabeth, though I cannot perceive them yet.

"My friends," he continued, "I know that you've all worked doubly hard this past week to find her, and I pray you'll forgive me for pulling you away from that important task. As a Scotland Yard superintendent, I'm accustomed to taking charge of investigations; therefore, it shouldn't surprise anyone that I intend to take charge of this one. A few of you have suggested I remain idle and rest, but that is not an option. I shall only find rest when my wife is returned to me. James, when you gave me your granddaughter's hand in marriage, I vowed to love her and keep her safe. I've failed in this second. I should never have left her inside that strange cottage. I should have made certain she escaped first, not the other way 'round."

Most at the table found this comment odd. "Cottage?" asked Diedra Kimberley. "I thought the duchess was taken to a house in Whitechapel. Are we misinformed?"

"She was, but Elizabeth and I spent countless hours—perhaps days—trapped inside a forbidden land inhabited by bird creatures and scuttling shadows. No matter what you might think, it was not a dream. I'll explain it more thoroughly, Dr. Kimberley, at a later date, but the essence is that we found our way to a refuge, a small cottage, at the centre of a daunting maze. This cottage was to lead us home, but only I escaped. I'd thought Beth would leave with me, but she did not. Wherever my wife's body is in the physical realm, her mind and spirit may still be trapped inside that cottage."

"I know this sounds implausible," the duke told the gathering, "but I believe Charles and Beth were in a real place." He turned to his nephew. "You did well to escape, Charles, but our girl is resourceful, and we place her welfare into God's hands. Do you think our Saviour would abandon her now?"

"No, he would not." Sinclair took a few seconds to focus by forming a mental list. "Very well, down to business. For the purpose of this meeting, let's deal with facts under our control. To begin, how did Trent abduct Beth from her own bedchamber? I'm sure most of you have already dealt with this, but I need to understand it, so indulge me."

"Allow me," Kepelheim said, taking to his feet. "Whilst you were unconscious, Mac and I spent many hours at Queen Anne looking into this puzzle. Do you recall the mirror?"

"Do you refer to the looking glass in Beth's bedchamber?"

"Yes. Alicia Mallory insisted that Trent took the duchess through that glass. Do you recall that as well?"

"Somewhat. Honestly, some of my memories of Sunday's events are rather disjointed," the marquess admitted.

"It's a common issue after a prolonged period of unconsciousness, Charles," Michael Emerson observed. "I beg you not to overdo, or you risk your health and your mind."

"I promise to rest later. Martin, tell me about this mirror. Explain how Trent used it."

"The mirror is quite unusual," the tailor answered, "but for those who've not seen it, allow me to describe it. Eight feet tall, hinged on a pedestal stand. It is not silver-based, but we've not yet discovered what metal is used. It might be mercury or something more exotic. However, the frame is carved Indian rosewood and ebony, and the imagery is subtle but disturbing. At first glance, it looks like a series of cherubic figures with wings, but using a hand lens, you notice each figure's face is made up of smaller ones—and all are demonic. Rather like the gargoyles used on French architecture. And there are many birds carved along the edges. At the very top, however, is a raven wearing a crown."

Charles shut his eyes, suddenly grown dizzy.

"Are you all right?" Aubrey asked.

"Yes. A slight headache. Go on, Martin."

"The mirror has writing etched along the bevel. It's in a language unknown even to Mac, but he agrees with me that it is similar to Sumerian, which Halévy and Delitzsch think may be a code of some kind, related to Akkadian. We've no idea what the script means, but we've written to Dr. Delitzsch in Leipzig, soliciting his opinion."

Edward MacPherson stood. "Charles, we also believe that the mirror is one of a pair. Probably created or perhaps dedicated at the same time to form two halves of a spirit doorway, entering from one mirror and exiting through the other."

"Then Trent needed a second mirror to exit at my old house?" Sinclair asked them.

Paul answered for both men. "I've already looked for one, Charles. There is no mirror in your house, however, I thought there might be one nearby."

"At the Empress," the marquess declared.

Aubrey smiled. "You're far quicker than I, Charles. I wish I'd thought of that before spending so much time in the ruins of your home. I'd assumed the mirror had to be inside the house, but it only needed to be close enough for Trent to carry Beth to your house without being observed."

"The Empress Hotel?" asked Kimberley. "What is that? I've never heard of it before."

"Allow me to answer," Inspector Reid began, standing. "Most of you have never visited Lord Haimsbury's former house. No. 12, Columbia Road, sits in the middle of a mixed neighbourhood of industry, rail sheds, pubs, and churches, bordering a modest residential block. Opposite No. 12 is a very large house, which originally served as the residence of a brewer named Harold Langley. When he died, the business was sold off along with all his properties. Since then, the house has changed hands a few times, and is currently owned by a French banker, who operates it as an upscale whorehouse under the name Empress Hotel."

"And you allow this so-called *hotel* to operate without limits?" Kimberley asked pointedly.

"We keep watch on it, but our ability to police is limited by numbers and the hours in a day, Doctor."

"Yet, I've heard that the police sometime allow crimes to continue whenever it suits them. I imagine men would find these softer crimes appealing."

"If you imply that we turn a blind eye because it benefits us, Dr. Kimberley, I must object. My men work countless hours to keep the streets safe for all citizens."

Diedra was unconvinced. "Then you are one of the few honest policemen in London, Inspector Reid."

"Are you suggesting most are dishonest?"

"I did not say it," she deflected.

"Yet, you imply it. Doctor, I find that insulting!"

"I imagine you would," she replied, shrugging.

Sinclair slapped the table angrily. "I will not have this circle descend into pettiness! If I'm to lead it, then you will comport yourselves with dignity, or else leave!" He turned his attention to the physician. "Dr. Kimberley, you have implied that some within the Metropolitan Police willfully ignore crime in search of personal pleasure."

She started to object, but Charles held up his hands to indicate silence. "I shall offer you opportunity to reply, but allow me to speak for the police. The officers and constables serving in the east are amongst the country's finest. They've suffered a great deal of abuse and slander in recent months, yet each man continues to do his best to protect those same, abusive citizens, though it might cost his life. They earn very little but are expected to do the impossible. In fact, two brave constables named Donovan and Albrecht died last Sunday night, defending the streets from Redwing's hybrids. There is no finer collection of men on this planet, and I will *not* permit anyone at this table to suggest otherwise!"

The physician stood, her manner softer. "I hope you'll forgive me, Lord Haimsbury. You're right. I was far too quick to judge. Most of what I know of the police comes from newspapers, but that doesn't excuse me. My opinion derives from a different experience than your own, working with the women who serve in these establishments. For five years, I've patched them up following forced abortions; set bones and bandaged wounds, when their clients beat them; and attended funerals, when my medical knowledge fell short of their need. Prostitution is a hideous way for a woman to make a living, yet it is one of the few our city offers."

Sinclair bowed gracefully. "Then, on behalf of these women, Doctor, I offer my thanks. I can think of no other group in this city who needs more charity, save perhaps their abandoned and orphaned children, who beg for scraps or slave in workhouses. I am no stranger to their plight, Dr. Kimberley, and neither is the earl. He and I may not be women, but I assure you that both my cousin and I would change the world, if it were in our power. However, sin makes that an impossible mission. We must, therefore, endeavour to make a difference in as many lives as possible. Your ministry is one I should like to help. When all this is over, I'd like to speak to you about doing just that."

The women blinked, surprised by his statements. "Thank you, Lord Haimsbury. I look forward to it."

Charles turned to the earl. "Paul, if you think this mirror is hidden inside the Empress, then you and I shall return there tomorrow."

"I suspect Meg Hansen will be loath to admit us," the earl confessed. "She's rather upset with me just now, but I did find something else whilst there. Corroboration of the research done by Martin and Edward, but also some new insights."

"Such as?" Ed MacPherson asked.

"I cannot claim your scholarship, Dr. MacPherson," the earl replied. "My ancient language skills are limited, compared to your own, but I have it on good authority that Trent used the mirror as a portal to a realm known as *sen-sen*, a 'mirror world' similar our own, that permits the traveller to cross from one point to another without being observed. I'm told he entered the mirror in Beth's chamber, crossed through this sen-sen realm, and then exited through a second mirror, hidden somewhere inside the Empress."

"And what is your source?" the clergyman asked. "Have you located a hermetic text that I lack? I've never heard of this 'sen-sen' world."

"My source is not a text, but a person. Lorena MacKey."

At the hated name, the entire table erupted into discordant shouting. Some protested that the earl would even consider speaking to the woman, whilst others insisted on hearing him out. Still others suggested interrogating the deceptive doctor in order to force a confession and learn all of Redwing's plans.

The Duke of Drummond held up his hands to defend his nephew. "Please, please, everyone! May we have order? It's true, Lorena MacKey is in league with Redwing, but I trust my nephew's discernment. If Paul believes her, then so do I."

"As do I," Charles agreed. "Paul, when did you speak with her?"

"Yesterday morning. She'd been hiding at the Empress, using a false name. Dr. MacKey shared some of what she knows, but we must question her further. Rather than risk losing track of her again, I brought her back to Westminster. She is, even now, at Queen Anne House."

"You brought that witch into the duchess's home?" MacPherson objected. "That is very dangerous, Lord Aubrey! Mr. Kepelheim and I worked assiduously to rid Queen Anne of evil influences, and now you bring the devil through the front door!"

"She is hardly a devil, Mac," the earl argued. "I'm not saying I trust her completely, but it seems to me that Lorena wishes to change."

"Change whom?" the cleric asked. "Herself or you?"

"Herself, of course, and her circumstances. I considered bringing her here directly, but at the time, Charles hadn't yet roused from his coma. In Beth's absence, I took the liberty of leaving her with Mr. Miles, but if Charles wants her gone, then I'll take MacKey to my home. I will not return her to the Empress. She's in danger there."

Sinclair knew what worried his cousin. "You think the Round Table will torture her?"

"Frankly, yes, but that's not the only reason I want to protect her. I do so, because it's the right thing to do. My friends, I know that we have a duty to keep watch on the bloodlines of all three houses, Branham, Drummond, and now Haimsbury, but does that permit us to lose sight of the great commission? We are called to tell everyone the good news! Some will accept it, others will not, but it is not up to us to choose for them by closing that door!"

Most of the members grew silent, and the earl continued.

"I pray this company does not think me impertinent, for most of you have served our cause longer than I, but I believe Lorena MacKey is as much a victim as Elizabeth is."

Many at the table found this idea completely unacceptable, but it was Charles who called for calm.

"Please! May we show a modicum of kindness? We all want to find my wife, but do you imagine that my concern is any less than yours? Dear God in heaven! I held Beth in my arms and saw the trust in her eyes. Yet, I've seen similar trust in the eyes of those whom we wish to call evil. Perhaps, the world is less black and white than we would like to paint it. Paul, is Lorena still at Queen Anne?"

"She is. I sent her a note yesterday to let her know we'd not meet until this evening. I assume Miles still keeps watch on her. Also, she's injured, and it's my fault. I'm afraid, when I first saw her, I allowed anger to determine my actions."

Michael Emerson stood. "Shall I tend to her injury?"

To everyone's surprise, Charles interrupted. "Before anyone else goes over there, I wish to speak to her alone."

Paul shook his head. "No, Charles, I will not permit it. She may be dangerous."

"I do not require your permission, Cousin. And if she wished to harm me, she's had ample opportunity."

"Then, if you must be foolish, allow me to go with you."

Sinclair placed a hand on his cousin's shoulder. "You can help me most by remaining here and leading the discussion." He turned to Emerson. "Michael, if you'll come along, you can see to Lorena's injury and continue to watch me. Yes, I've noticed your surreptitious stares."

He left the table and headed to the closed doors. "In my absence, I hope you'll study Paul and Reid's reports. It would make smart use of our limited time. I want to know exactly what happened on Sunday night, all details of Trent's autopsy, and every possible location where Beth might be. Also, I want to know what happened to the hybrids we killed that night. Where are their bodies? Have a list ready when I return."

The duke stood. "Son, why must you go at all? If Lorena comes here, then we can all speak with her."

"Yes, sir, that's true, but I suspect this gathering would only intimidate her. Let me speak with her first, and then if she agrees, I'll ask her to attend the next meeting.

"Charles, I really wish you'd sit down," Emerson pleaded as he followed his patient into the foyer of Queen Anne House. "A man's body does not run on determination alone. Your injuries require rest and nourishment."

"I'll obtain the nourishment at supper, and sleep will come when I've found Beth. Miles, would you let Dr. MacKey know I'd like to speak with her?"

"Right away," the butler told his employer. "Would you care for tea whilst waiting, my lord?"

"He'd love some," Emerson answered for Charles. "And soup, if Mrs. Smith has any prepared."

"She's serving cress soup and braised quail with mushrooms, Dr. Emerson. Also, celery *au gratin*, fruit, apple tart, and cheese, sir."

"It all sounds quite delicious, Miles," Charles answered, "but I'm sure the Haimsbury cooks have planned on us. No tea. I'm content with water, and it looks as though the carafes are full. Thank you."

The butler bowed and left, shutting the doors. Michael poured a glass of water from a cut-crystal carafe and handed it to his patient. "Are you always this obstinate?"

"Generally, yes," the marquess answered. "Thank you." He drank half the water and set the glass on a nearby table. "Did I say anything whilst unconscious?"

"Only as you were coming 'round," Michael answered. "Della heard you counting. She's worried endlessly about you. I think the girl has formed a very strong attachment, as a daughter loves a father."

Sinclair smiled, thoughtfully. "She sees me as a father figure? That's lovely. Has Paul noticed it?"

"He's the one who pointed it out. Look, I am not a part of the family, and it's none of my business, but it's my understanding that Adele is adopted. Is that correct?"

"She is, but I don't know if Della's aware of it. She often points out that she has Stuart eyes, and that her hair is just like Paul's. Why?" Charles decided against revealing the real reason for the family resemblance, that Paul Stuart was Adele's father, not her brother. It was Paul's secret to tell, not his.

"My point is this," Emerson explained. "If Della thinks herself a natural member of the earl's family, then it stands to reason that she believes Paul's father was her biological parent."

Sinclair sighed, unable to follow the logic. "Yes. And?"

"Della still mourns the man she considers her father, Charles. You bear a striking resemblance to the late earl, and you have a natural gift for parenting. I've seen you with her. The girl lights up whenever you're nearby. It's important that you acknowledge that affection. Poor Della has been heartbroken, fearing that you, too, would die!"

The marquess started to answer, but the drawing room doors opened before he could, admitting a tall woman with auburn hair and emerald green eyes.

"You asked to speak to me?"

Both men stood politely. Seeing Lorena MacKey caused Sinclair a momentary twinge of anger, but unlike his cousin, he not only overpowered the anger, but even managed to smile.

"Michael, would you give us the room, please?"

Emerson bowed and left, closing the doors.

Sinclair offered her a chair. "Please, sit, Lorena. This shouldn't take much time, and then Dr. Emerson will examine your shoulder." She sat, and he took a seat opposite, not more than a foot away. "I'm very sorry for your injury, and the earl regrets it deeply. He'd tell you himself, but I wanted to speak with you alone first."

Lorena considered her response before opening her mouth. Sinclair surprised her with this display of chivalry and kindness, but despite his gentility, a lifetime of abuse at the hands of men dictated her answer.

"Why is that, Lord Haimsbury? I'd assumed you'd drag me to your meeting and interrogate me there."

Paul Stuart would have answered sharply, but even if he felt it, Sinclair showed no hint of anger, instead he showed remarkable restraint, even sweetness. "You called me Charles in Scotland. May I not be so honoured now?"

"I don't understand. Lord Aubrey insisted I call you by your title."

He leaned closer, so that he might touch her hand. The simple gesture caused her to flinch. "I'm sorry. Is that your injured arm?"

"No, it's my left, actually, but it didn't hurt. The shoulder is fine now."

"I'm very glad to hear it, and I've no wish to cause you dismay. I merely seek answers. Is that agreeable to you?" She nodded. "This may sound far too personal, Lorena, but I require information that only you may provide. Therefore, I must move quickly to the heart of my enquiry. Is that also agreeable?"

"Yes. Ask me whatever you wish. I'll do my best to answer honestly."

She appeared vulnerable, and Charles wondered if the manner were genuine or pretense. "Lorena, the earl told me what your step-father did to you. How he abused you physically and even forced himself on you, when you were young. No woman should have to endure such horrors."

The physician took a moment to answer, and she swallowed hard before doing so, a sign of inner turmoil. Charles noticed her hand shaking ever so slightly—another tell. "I did nothing to invite that abuse, I assure you," she whispered. "Why do you mention it?"

"Only to let you know that I see you as a victim, not a perpetrator."

"That's a surprise," she answered, looking away for a second to hide her feelings. "What is it you wish to ask me?"

Sinclair realised he'd overstepped. "Forgive me for making you uncomfortable. It wasn't my intent."

"Your questions?"

He sighed. "Truly, Lorena, I meant no harm, but it's clear I've offended you. I pray you'll forgive me." She said nothing, and he continued. "Very well. The night Trent abducted my wife, you were in her bedchamber. Is that right?"

"Yes, but not because I chose to side with William. If the earl relayed our previous conversation, then you already know that."

"I do, but I still don't understand why you followed Anatole's instructions. Do you trust him so completely?"

She took a deep breath, her eyes on an snowy white owl near the window. "I suppose I do, yes. The prince warned me that William intended to use me as part of his plot, but assured me that, if I followed his instructions, the duchess would be safe."

"Yet, you tried to warn me at the duke's house on Sunday. Why did you do that, Lorena, if you thought Romanov had it all in hand?"

"Fear, I suppose. No, that isn't right," she told him, glancing away out of embarrassment. "Not fear, really..."

"Love," he suggested, causing her attention to snap towards his face. "I'm right, aren't I? Your affection for the earl is far greater than your fear of reprisal from either Anatole or Trent."

Shock painted her features, but she quickly regained composure. "Love for the earl? I'm sure I don't know what you mean."

"Lorena, it's obvious to me that you care deeply for Paul. Your behaviour in Scotland may have arisen from obedience to Trent, but I think your emotions were genuine, even then."

"You're mistaken," she insisted. "Paul is kind, and I enjoy his company, but I do not love him. Someone else does."

His brows knit together. "Do you mean my wife?"

"No. The duchess does love him, of course, but I meant someone else."

"Who?"

"Susanna Morgan."

Charles stared at the woman. "Morgan loves no one. She is dead."

"Yes, I'm aware of that, but it doesn't change how she felt about the earl when alive."

"How can you know that she loved my cousin? Did the two of you speak recently? Do you know who killed her?"

"Yes, we spoke recently, and I can guess who's responsible for her death. Susanna detested Clive Urquhart, and she'd begun to look for ways to leave him and begin anew. She and I met the same day you attended the Ripper play at the Lyceum. She'd decided to leave Redwing and wanted me to help. That's when she admitted to being in love with the earl."

"Where did you meet? Was it possible Urquhart had her followed?" he asked, his policeman's brain whirring.

"We met at a small hotel near the British Museum. Susanna organised it. She was far brighter than Sir Clive imagined. He thought her nothing more than a harlot who loved gemstones and furs, but the truth of her life couldn't be more different. Charles, she wanted out. She'd begun to suspect her family had lied about the inner circle."

"What do you mean?"

"Redwing members are taught that the circle is selfish and manipulative. After spending time in the earl's company from time to time, she noticed his kindness. It caused her to reconsider and do some research. As I'd only recently spent time with all of you in Glasgow, she asked my opinion. Whenever she spoke Paul's name, it was obvious she loved him. I'd like to avenge her death, if possible. If there is anything I can do to destroy Clive Urquhart and the other Redwing members, I'll do it."

"That's very brave of you," he observed, wondering if she meant it, or if this line was intended to appeal to his gallantry. "For the present, let's return to the night Beth was taken. How does the mirror work?"

"It's a dangerous device, Charles. You have removed it from this house, I hope?"

"I'm told it's in a storage shed near the stable."

Her eyes widened. "It's still on the property? No, you must drop it to the bottom of the Thames, or else bury it! If it is anywhere close to Elizabeth, he'll find her again!"

"Trent is dead, Lorena," the marquess told her. "He can find no one now."

"I'm not sure evil like that can ever die, but even if he is dead, another could use it. Raziel, or one of his hellish brothers. Did Susanna tell you that Redwing plans to free an entire cadre of Watchers? Charles, I was once foolish enough to seek power, but I've come to my senses. Even if they kill me for it, I cannot allow them to harm you or your family!"

"The Lord will protect me," he argued. "And he will protect you as well, Lorena, if you would only allow it."

"I'm past redemption, but even if Paul hadn't discovered me inside Meg Hansen's brothel, I'd have left there to find you. Only two men have ever treated me with genuine kindness. Prince Anatole and you. Charles, you took the time to speak to me that last night in Scotland, and you made me realise that men needn't be cruel or selfish. I've thought about it a great deal since. It's why Susanna asked to speak with me that day. I'd sent her a letter about your kindness, about your gentle manner, and how the inner circle's aim is far different than we'd been told."

"Can you explain?"

"You'll think me foolish, but I was taught that Redwing is noble and scientific; that they seek to liberate humanity from the yoke of religious oppression through scientific enlightenment. The inner circle, they claim, want to enslave humanity beneath the yoke of a false god and create a world government by placing one of their own on the throne of England."

Charles gasped. "That is a patent lie! It is the last thing we want!"

"I realise that now," she assured him. "Redwing teaches lies, Charles. They manipulate their members through tricks and promises of power, but they claim it is all for mankind's good. They convinced me that these occult powers are required to stop the inner circle. They want to control the world. They want to enslave mankind, and they'll start by controlling England. They intend to crown your son, Charles. It's why they forced you and the duchess together."

"I'm painfully aware of that," he said. "That night in Scotland. Was it you who poisoned our tea?"

She nodded. "I'm not proud of it. Trent gave me the powder and told me to add the entire container to the kettle of water. The farm couple were unaware of it. They had nothing to do with Redwing. William had someone paint the group's symbol on their barn months before."

"Months before? How could he know Beth and I would even be in Scotland? She was still in France months earlier."

She took a deep breath, Anatole's words still echoing in her mind. *Tell him, Lorena. Tell Sinclair all.*

"Trent had access to a seeing stone. He claimed it showed him what would happen, weeks, even months ahead of time. He foresaw himself and his friends slaying women in Whitechapel."

"How? You're sure William was Ripper?"

"One of them. Half a dozen or so participated. Shapeshifters like William. The bloodshed had a dual purpose. It provided the energy needed to release the Watcher Saraqael, but it also brought Elizabeth back to England. William even committed several murders close to the château where she lived, hoping it would cause her to panic. The plan worked, and she came straight to you."

"Trent knew she loved me?" he asked.

"Yes, but Elizabeth's love for you is genuine. Trent had no hand in manipulating that."

"I know," he told her softly. "I have never doubted Beth's love, nor will I. And the farm couple's murder?"

"One of William's marksmen shot them and set fire to the buildings after you fled with Elizabeth."

"Did Trent hire Lemuel? Did he cause a trusted physician to turn traitor?"

She sighed. "I can't answer that. You might ask Alexander Collins. He's the head of Castor Institute. He and Lemuel were friends."

"Collins and Lemuel? Yet another reason to speak with him." He mentally ran down a list of questions, ticking off the answers. "There was a wolf pack that chased our coach. Was Trent involved?"

"Sir William had the ability to transform into almost any type of creature, but he favoured the wolf. He'd sold his soul long ago, though he told me it was a bargain meant for the world's good." She laughed. "I really was a fool, for I believed it all."

"He played upon your pain, Lorena. There's no shame in foolishness, only in willful blindness."

"I pray I've learnt to see a little now. I can give you more information about Trent, if you wish, but I don't think he was the leader of the pack that night. I'd thought it was Anatole back then, but I was wrong. The prince isn't to blame for any of this. His brother, Raziel, is."

"Can you elaborate?" he asked, trying to remind himself that he wasn't interviewing a suspect but a broken woman. "If you know anything, it would be helpful."

"Raziel's been pretending to be his brother for at least a decade, but he fooled me and many others. It took me a long time to realise what was happening. I told Paul that Anatole Romanov provided education and friendship to me at a time when I was at my lowest. He taught me to see the world as hopeful, but after I met William, I began to notice changes in Anatole. He grew morose, manipulative, and he encouraged me to spend time with Trent and the other Redwing members. His personality, if you will, seemed at odds with itself. One day, he would urge me to care for the poor and downtrodden; the next, he derided these same people as parasites feeding upon the blood of their betters. This strange dichotomy only made sense to me after I saw Raziel the night of the Kensington Palace ball. He transformed into a perfect copy of Anatole. Charles, I believe Raziel has been impersonating his brother since 1871."

"You know about the Mt. Hermon stone?"

She looked surprised. "Yes! I'm amazed you know about it. I've slowly discerned a little of its history, but you'd need to ask Anatole for clarification. Raziel and Anatole disagreed on a mission they'd been given over five thousand years ago, and Raziel chose to disobey and sin against God. Anatole, who is sometimes called Samael, was ordered to execute Raziel at once. They are brothers, Charles. Can you imagine how you would react if God ordered you to kill the earl?"

"It would be very hard," Sinclair admitted.

"Yes. It would. Samael begged God to allow Raziel to live. The Creator agreed, but as punishment, Samael was ordered to imprison Raziel in a living stone until God chose to release him, near the time of the end. Samael was also ordered to remain on earth until that time, just prior to Christ's return. I've never really believed in a sacrificial Saviour, much less his return, but I've begun to wonder if I've been wrong."

"Raziel is a fallen angel?"

"He's what most think of as a fallen angel, but he and Samael—or Anatole, if it's easier to think of him that way—they call themselves *elohim*. There are different types of these beings with different jobs, personalities, and abilities. Raziel is a very powerful one, but I think he's insane."

"Do you think he used Trent to further the fallen realm's agenda?"

"Of course, he did. Raziel uses everyone, even his own brothers."

"Do you know why Trent abducted Elizabeth?" he asked, fearing the answer.

"You won't like it, Charles. William was a prideful, self-absorbed man, and he only pretended to follow Raziel's plans. William intended to abort your child and replace it with his own, and then he would crown that son."

Sinclair shut his eyes, hands clenched tightly, but a sweet whisper in his mind reminded him that Trent's plans had failed: *Rest in the Lord. He is your refuge and strength, Charles. God's plans never fail. Beth lives. Your unborn children live.*

"It was the Lord who stopped Trent from fulfilling that evil plan, Lorena. He allows the fallen to proceed with their plots for his reasons. His purposes."

She sighed, tears beginning to form in her green eyes. "I wish I had your faith!"

"You can have it, Lorena. You need only ask. Speak to God. I promise you! He is waiting to hear from you."

"I'll try."

He hated leaving, but he knew the circle awaited his return. "I'd speak with you more tomorrow, but I begin to grow weary. Will you remain here at Queen Anne whilst we search for Beth?"

"If you wish it, yes. Charles, I must tell you something more before you go. You can confirm this with Miles, but I had a caller earlier today. Rather than enter the house, he asked me to meet him on the portico."

"Who?"

"Anatole. I asked him why he didn't come in, and he said he preferred to gain permission from the home's owner. There is a tradition amongst Redwing that says spirits may not enter a blessed home without permission. Because of this, I'm not really sure if this spirit was Anatole or Raziel in disguise, but I think it was Anatole, for his manner was far too kind for an imposter."

"What did he tell you?"

"First of all, he told me that he has Beth in his keeping, but you're not to worry. He wouldn't say where, but he insists that she is safe. He says she's remains in danger, and that once the danger is past, he'll bring her back to you."

"Anatole has her?" he asked, amazed. "He's protecting her? From whom?"

"He didn't say, but I'm sure it's Redwing, and most likely the spirits as well as the humans."

"Did he explain just how he found her? Did Romanov kill Trent?"

She sighed. "Probably. He certainly knew about Trent's plans, didn't he? It's likely that he knew Trent's every step. The spirits have access to visions of future events, but their eyes are far sharper than any human's."

"But he will bring Beth home?"

"So he said. Charles, I'm sorry, I didn't think to ask him for more information. I'm not much of a detective. I urged him to speak with you himself, but he insisted that I deliver the message. He knew you would be visiting me this evening."

"Did he say anything else? Where she might be? If she's ill."

"He didn't mention if she is ill, but he assured me that she'd return soon. He did, however ask me to tell you this. Redwing is at war. He says their members will begin to die, and that the killer is a wolf in sheep's clothing. I asked him to explain that, Charles, but he vanished."

"Yes, I know that trick. He often disappears when I try to ask questions. Do you know where he lives?"

"I've a list of his addresses, but if he's hiding Elizabeth, he could be anywhere. He owns a dozen different houses throughout the city, primarily to keep his enemies from discerning his whereabouts. He could be in any one of them."

Charles stood, but fatigue hit him with the force of a stone wall, and he had to catch himself on the chair to keep from falling.

Lorena instantly offered support, placing her arm around his waist. "It's too soon for you to be out of bed, Charles. Please, you need rest. If you won't do it for yourself, then do it for the duchess."

She helped him to the doors, where she summoned Emerson and the butler, who'd been speaking near the staircase. "Mr. Miles, your master requires assistance!"

In a few minutes, the butler and Emerson had secured the marquess into the coach. MacKey watched from the foot of the portico steps, standing six feet from the coach.

"I'll send Michael back right away to examine your shoulder," Charles promised her through the open coach window. "And I'll have men keep watch on the house. If you hear anything, notice anyone that frightens or concerns you, send a footman to my home right away. Do you understand?"

"I do, now go and get some sleep," she told him.

MacKey watched the carriage leave, waving goodbye until it passed through the great stone gates.

As she climbed the portico stairs, Lorena thought through everything he'd said about God, about the circle, about himself. Charles had been honest and open and so very kind.

And she had lied to him.

Not about herself or about Romanov. Not about Trent or anything regarding Morgan or Redwing.

She had lied about one thing only, and its implications meant she dared not remain at Queen Anne House. It was far too dangerous.

Charles had nearly guessed it. Lorena was in love, but not with Paul Stuart. She'd suspected before, but now, Lorena Melissa MacKey knew it for certain.

She was in love with Charles Sinclair.

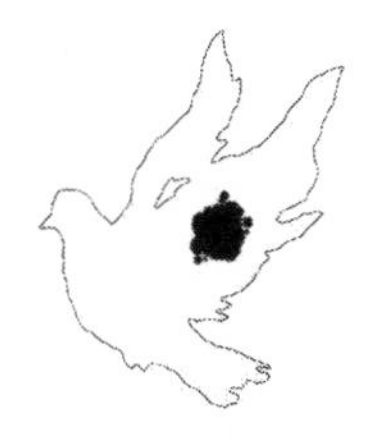

CHAPTER EIGHTEEN

The strange cottage - one second after Charles disappeared

Elizabeth Sinclair began to weep. She could still hear the echo of her husband's voice in her ears, feel the warm touch of his hands, smell the woody scent of his cologne. She reached into the empty space where he'd stood only one second earlier, and the molecules still vibrated.

"Captain!" she sobbed, clutching at the air as if it held his essence. "My darling, please, wherever you've gone, find me!"

All alone in the cottage, the duchess took a deep breath and crossed to the window. The sky in this strange land held no sun, but a sickly moon shone down upon the midnight landscape. The black line of yews and sinewy trees revealed an army of eyes within their dense shadows. Birds. Thousands of them, and Beth could hear their caws and whispers grow evermore bold and strident with each passing moment.

"I must find a way out," she said aloud. "Charles, if you can leave, then certainly I may, also, but how? How do I go about it?"

The cottage's main room held two rockers and a willow settee dotted with plump feather pillows. A single, down quill had wriggled its way out of the corner of one, and Beth noticed that its colour was white.

"All the birds here are black," she said to her absent husband. "Captain, does this mean something? How could this cottage's owner stuff white feathers into cushions, when there are no white birds anywhere?"

Elizabeth sat for a moment, finding herself somewhat dizzy. "This feeling isn't fear," she said, still speaking to her husband. "Or at least, I don't think it is. Oh, Charles, I pray you've found your way home! We will see each other again, Captain, I know it! But I'm so very tired and warm..."

Sitting upon the settee to allow the spell to pass, she studied the surroundings. The entwined heart pattern appeared throughout the cottage's interior, repeated again and again, as if reminding Elizabeth of her living bond with Sinclair.

"Two tiny hearts within our own," she said aloud, a tear tracing her soft cheek. "Can it be true, Captain? Am I carrying twins, or does this mean that there are two possible outcomes to this pregnancy? One a boy, and the other a girl?"

She looked at her left hand, where the Pink Princess diamond sparkled against her wedding ring. The band was set with seven white diamonds cut in the Peruzzi style to add brilliance. During the reception, Charles had jokingly suggested each diamond represented a future son or daughter. Beth had argued that seven would make a fine start.

How long ago was that? Hours? Days? Weeks?

"I must find my way home," she said, forcing herself to concentrate. "Think! What is it Father used to say? Never let fear dictate your actions. Instead, use that fear to sharpen your wits. Charles, you left when I wound your watch. You tried on your own, but failed, and only my touch made it work. Why? Do I require another to help me to escape? Perhaps, but who? No one else is here. The woman left long ago, and neither of our children is here now. I'm so confused and tired, Captain. A part of me wishes you were still here, but another is very glad you've escaped."

Outside, the birds drew nearer to the cottage, and the moon's faint light had grown brighter. The lunar god of *Sebet Babi* was starting to awaken.

"Oh, please, Lord, help me to find a way home!" she cried out, her hands clasped together. "I'm afraid. I'm so terribly afraid!"

"You sound troubled," a man's voice called from the other side of the cottage door. "Let me in, my dear, and I'll protect you. I can help you find your way home."

Elizabeth swallowed down the fear as she moved closer to the entry. "Who are you? Your voice is familiar."

"A friend," the man softly answered. The voice was musical, even hypnotic.

"No one I know would be here. I dare not trust you! I shan't open this door. Go away!"

"You know me well, Elizabeth. I've been your friend for so very long. Don't you remember? I used to stand beneath your window and talk to you. Very pleasantly."

"No, go away!"

High-pitched laughter sailed upon the howling winds like the screeching of a thousand witches, and the duchess feared the carnivorous birds might soon reach the door. The male voice called to her again, its tone altering—the resonance shifting into a slightly different register, as though imitating another.

"Princess," it whispered. "Let me in. It's Paul. I've come to rescue you, but you must hurry and unlock the door! The birds are close behind me!"

For a tiny second, hope replaced fear, and Beth started to unlatch the door. *How can Paul be here?* She hesitated, her fingers on the handle. "Prove to me you're Paul. Tell me something only he would know."

Silence.

"Tell me about the tree room. Where is it? What game did I play there?"

"I've forgotten, Princess. Remind me."

She pictured a high bedchamber in the central tower of Briarcliff Castle. When she was six, Beth visited the castle for a an entire summer and would spend hour upon hour in the magical space. The chamber's bed was made from a gigantic yew tree. The thick trunk formed the posts, and the branches a natural canopy. Whilst home from his Oxford studies, the earl would play knight and princess with her and even pretend to rescue her from dragons. Beth used a wooden sword to dub him 'Sir Paul' as reward. Stuart called her his very own Princess, and she promised to love him forever and marry him.

"Shall I ride my knightly steed and batter down the door, Princess?" the voice asked, turning cruel.

"Go away!" she cried, realising the hopeful voice had been that of a trickster.

"Little one," it spoke again, the voice now a heartbreakingly perfect imitation of Sinclair's. "Let me in. There was a lying spirit at the door, but I've overcome him. He's gone, little one. Trust me. I've returned to help you escape. I've found the path that leads home, Beth. Just open the door."

"Leave me alone!" Elizabeth shouted as she shut her eyes tightly, whispering prayers. But her whispers were lost in the wild, avian cacophony that overflew the cottage. She feared the creatures advanced upon her, and that soon she would be taken.

"The Lord Almighty knows your plans, Creature! He will not allow you to harm me!" she shouted.

The area near the creek stone fireplace rippled as though the entire structure were reflected upon water, and a booted foot passed into the room. Behind that foot, emerged a long leg, then a broad torso, and finally the entire, hideous person stood before the fire. He brushed sparks from his clothing with gloved hands, tendrils of smoke clinging to strands of long, dark hair. His eyes were icy blue.

The Watcher smiled, and the temperature of the cottage fell by twenty degrees.

"Is that any way to greet an old friend?" Raziel asked her.

Beth nearly collapsed from shock, but the fallen angel grasped her arm to draw her close.

"No, no, my dear," he said greedily. "You cannot escape me here. This is *my* domain. The traitor cannot rescue you here, for the way is shut. Oh, but you look feverish," he continued, lifting her into his arms.

Beth resisted, but all strength abandoned her.

"Poor duchess," the cruel Watcher hissed. "All alone, now that your husband is gone. Did you think his timepiece was a means of escape? No, my beautiful prisoner, your Captain has been removed to another section of *Sebet Babi*. He is chained inside one of my cells."

She began to shiver. "You lie," she answered defiantly.

"Would you risk his life to prove it? It lies within your power to free him. You need only yield to me."

Elizabeth heard his voice in a thousand pitches at once, each out of phase with its nearest neighbour, and the overall effect caused her to fall into a light trance.

"That's better. Here, now, let me place you upon this soft bed."

Raziel Grigor carried his victim into the candlelit bedchamber and set her upon the quilts. "How inviting this bed looks. A bride deserves a wedding night, after all. Shall I resurrect my foolish son to keep you company? Rasha is here, you know. I keep his worthless flesh in the lower dungeons, beneath the centre of the maze, just in case I ever need to resurrect him."

"Rasha," she whispered, trembling all over. "Rasha is dead."

"Yes, the foolish Romanian failure is very dead. He believed me when I promised to make him king. I'd hoped to inhabit him eventually, but his blood failed the test. Not to worry! He was but an early attempt. My next son will be perfect."

"I don't understand," she whispered, trying to shut out the trancelike voices.

"No, you don't, but your husband begins to understand. He will remember it all soon. All that he is, and all that he is destined to become. And on that day, every prisoner will be released!"

"You're insane," she dared say.

"Am I?" Raziel laughed. "Shall I show you what plans I have for you? Rasha was meant to tempt you into bed, but his methods were cowardly and crude. Perhaps, I'll use you myself," he hissed into her ear as he crept onto the quilts, his weight crushing her small body. "No, wait, I have it!" he crowed, pushing himself into a sitting position. "I'll assume the form of another. One that you know very well. The hybrid creature who called himself William Trent. That should prove a great deal of fun."

Trent's name snapped Beth from the dreamscape, and the duchess's dark eyes widened in shock. "Trent is dead!" she shouted, trying to break free of his powerful arms. "I saw him die!"

"Of course, he's dead," Raziel answered. "This is the land of the dead. Aren't you aware of that? Your husband is also dead, just as you are dead."

"You lie!" she shouted, twisting out of his hands and stumbling out of the bed. Elizabeth tried to run into the main room, but Raziel slammed the door with his mind, and she cowered near the door, weeping as she slid down the wall.

Two balls of red light popped into the room, and they transformed into a pair of winged reptilian creatures. The face of the taller gargoyle was pockmarked in oozing sores, and he carried a coiling serpent in his left hand. The other held a balance and a sword. "These are my companions," Raziel told her. "They offer their help, my lady. Touch the duchess, Globnick. Let her feel your power."

Beth had nowhere to run, and the scaly creature stepped towards her. She shut her eyes as its burning claw touched her forehead. Instantly, a searing heat branded her head with pain, and she screamed in terror.

"Now you, Shishak. Offer the duchess your special medicinal aid."

"No, please!" she wept, but the hideous demon cackled as it gripped her by the waist. Elizabeth doubled over. Her entire abdomen erupted into waves of intense fire. Nothing the duchess had ever experienced compared to it, and she felt as though she had truly entered Hell's gate.

What if I'm dead? she thought in despair. As consciousness abandoned her, she cried out, "Captain, I love you! Wherever you are, I love you! Find me, please! Find me!"

25th November – 11:59 pm

Inside the northwest apartment of Istseleniye House, Elizabeth Sinclair screamed. Her physician, Dr. Henry MacAlpin, had been taking a fitful rest upon a sofa near the fireplace. At the bloodcurdling sound, the young Scot jumped to his feet and rushed his patient's bedside.

"Duchess?" he asked, feeling for her pulse and finding it exceedingly rapid.

The piercing screams had awakened the other guests, and though it was nearly midnight, both Ross and Kilmeade arrived at the door to the grand apartment.

"What's happened?" Ida asked anxiously as she tied the sash to her dressing gown.

MacAlpin felt like a first-year medical student. He could find no physical cause for the duchess's continued unconscious state, and the screams made no sense to him at all. Her heart hammered wildly, the brow hot as a brand, yet her hands were like ice.

"Fetch brandy and a cool cloth," he ordered Ross.

Brona Kilmeade divided up the work. "I'll fetch the cloth, Ida. You get the brandy. There's a half-filled decanter on a table near the drawing room piano."

The women left to carry out their tasks, and Henry turned back to the duchess. He placed a stethoscope over her chest, listening carefully to her lungs and heart. Brona returned with the cloth, handing it to the physician.

A familiar voice spoke from the open doorway. It was Romanov's. "Brona, you may leave us."

Henry glanced up. "She's worse. I take it Miss Ross found you?"

"Not really. I heard Elizabeth cry out and left off my errands to return immediately," the Russian replied mysteriously.

Prince Anatole Romanov wore elegant evening attire, and a black cape lined in red silk crossed his left shoulder. He looked as though he'd just returned from an evening at the theatre.

"I fear she's developing pneumonia," Henry told him wearily, "but there is something more. Another malady that defies explanation. Though still unconscious, her hands keep clutching at her abdomen. It's possible she's in pain, and this caused her to scream, but I'm confounded as to what's causing it."

"Contractions?" Romanov asked as he laid the cape across the back of the curved sofa.

MacAlpin stared at the Russian. "Why would you use that term, sir? Most would call it a pang or pain. Contraction is specific and implies something altogether different."

"I use the word, because it is correct," Anatole answered. "Understand that this must not be discussed outside this room. You must promise me, Lord Salperton."

"Of course, I promise. How many times must I tell you that my patient's welfare is my only concern? I've done everything you asked of me, and still it seems you place little trust in my promises. Are you telling me that she is with child?"

"I am saying precisely that," Romanov answered flatly.

Henry's expression darkened into one of accusation. "Then she is your mistress, and this is your child! I'd assumed as much when you called upon me with your strange story. And this explains why you'll allow no one to reveal her whereabouts! Does her husband know? I rather think he does not."

Anatole did not smile, but neither did he frown. His face revealed no emotion at all; no hint of his thoughts. "She is not my mistress, Lord Salperton, nor will she ever be. Even if I considered engaging in a physical relationship, which I would not, Elizabeth is deeply in love with her husband. Lord Haimsbury is the father, and he is aware of her condition, as are the inner circle's core members."

"Inner circle?"

"Yes," he answered, his strange eyes filled with worry. He placed a hand on her abdomen, holding it there for a moment. "Someone is trying to cause a miscarriage."

"Someone? What the devil do you mean by that odd comment?"

"Devil is descriptively accurate," Romanov answered. "I may be able to counteract their assault," he continued, his hand moving across her body.

"Do you mind?" Salperton insisted, removing the prince's hand. "I'd like to assess her condition for myself."

"Of course," the other said, walking away from the bed.

The physician pushed gently on her abdomen, his expert hands palpating the area, determining the roundness, position, and elasticity of the uterus. "I'd say twelve weeks, perhaps thirteen. Is that right?"

"Seven, actually," the elohim declared.

"No, it cannot be seven. The abdomen is too round for that. Twelve is more likely right. Fourteen at the outside."

"It is forty-nine days precisely," Romanov declared.

Salperton stared, his dark eyes round. "If you know the precise date she conceived, it implies that you were there, sir, which means you participated. Ergo, you are the father!"

"I am not," the prince said simply. "However, I do know when she conceived. The eighth of October in Scotland."

The doctor's eyes narrowed. "And how would you know that?"

"Because I was there."

"You speak in riddles!"

"No, I speak plain truth."

Henry wanted to throw something at his host, but he managed to avoid it by clenching his fists. "Even if I believed you, she is clearly more than seven weeks pregnant. Unless..."

The prince waited, allowing the truth to seed itself into the human's mind. "Yes? You're nearly there."

"How can you know?" MacAlpin asked. "Is it even possible?"

"I know because I can sense the life inside her, and it is entirely possible. It is the beautiful spark of the One. His breath arises from the moment of conception. There are two lives growing within her body. Two unborn children that will die, if we do not bring her home. See to her needs first, and then, you and I shall talk," the

Russian replied. "Oh, before I commenced with my other activities tonight, I paid a call to your clinic. Your new resident patient, Mrs. Crossfield, was about to jump out of her second storey window. I convinced her that life is too precious to waste. Your nurse soon settled her into bed."

"You called at my home and dared speak to one of my patients, without consulting me first?" MacAlpin asked in irritation. This entire business had begun to grate upon the independent thinker. The viscount hadn't yet decided whether or not Romanov could be trusted.

Is the duchess safe here? Is the Russian lying? Should I remove her to Montmore, or better yet take her home to her husband?

"The marquess mustn't know Elizabeth's whereabouts. Not yet," the Russian said, reading the other man's thoughts.

A soft step caught their attention. Ross entered quietly, a decanter of brandy in her hand. "The wine, sir. Forgive the delay. I had trouble locating it."

"Thank you, Ida. Pour some into a glass and then dip one corner of this into the liquid," the physician ordered, handing her his handkerchief. When he'd taken the brandy-soaked cloth from Ross, the viscount touched it to Elizabeth's lips, pressing just enough to force a little of the strong wine into her mouth. "That will be all, Miss Ross. Thank you."

Ida departed, curtsying to Romanov before closing the door. The prince sat upon the soft bed's edge. "She is all alone and terrified," he told Salperton. "She grows weaker."

"She is not alone," Henry argued. "Why would you say so?"

"Because it's true. Her screams are caused by hideous demons outside this room. Outside this world."

"I imagine the duchess is dreaming. Fevers often cause nightmares."

"Hardly," Anatole said, kissing her hand. "A tormentor has come, and he breaks her will with lies. She calls for her husband, but the marquess cannot rescue her. However, you can."

"What do you mean, I can rescue her? Medically?"

"How strong is your faith, Henry? How firm your convictions? Would you risk being pulled into a nightmare beyond all imagining to provide her an escape?"

"Your words make no sense," he complained.

"Of course, they do. Touch her hand."

"I've done little else!" the Scotsman shouted.

Henry closed his eyes, trying to think through the fog of frustration and fatigue. He'd slept very little since arriving on Monday night, and his usual good temper had worn thin.

"Forgive me, Your Highness, but since you brought me to this strange castle, you have continually made wild statements that make no sense whatsoever! This haunted palace is little more than a realm of ghosts, and I begin to wonder if I've dreamt it all!"

"We are hardly ghosts, Henry. When the duchess has returned, then I shall be pleased to introduce you to our company, but until then..."

"Returned? Returned how, sir? What the devil do you mean by such a peculiar word? She is unconscious, not on a journey!"

"You know better than that. I told you that she is in need of rescue. Will you offer it or not?"

Since the loss of his mother, Henry had never expected to find another woman who deserved all the beauty that life might offer, but if ever such a woman lived, then surely the Duchess of Branham was she. It made no sense, but he felt as if he *knew her*. Had always known her, as though they were connected in a profound way.

"How?"

"By believing in things your eyes cannot see."

"I don't understand. Yes, I've come to realise that you are no mere mortal, but for all I know, I'm hallucinating all of this from a cot inside my own sanitarium! Perhaps, you are the ghost who inhabits this phantom castle, and the residents here nothing more than your fellow spirits. I may even be dead!"

"You do not believe that," Romanov said simply. "I am not a ghost. I am an *elohim*, and my abilities are beyond mortal man's comprehension."

"Then, if you are so very powerful, why do you not rescue her yourself? It's clear to any man with eyes that you love her, sir! If you are able, then bring her home!"

The entity grew quiet, his ice-blue eyes still. "It is not permitted."

"Hang permission, Romanov! If she's in danger, as you claim, then use your powers to help!"

"It is not for me to explain my reasons to you, Henry. Don't you understand? This is why I chose you as her physician. Your blood helps you to see our kind, because it connects you to the spirit realm. It is this which allows her to hear your voice."

"*My* voice?"

"Yes, but we must hurry. Though, time does not exist in *Sebet Babi*, it does exist here. The duchess's body and mind weaken, and soon the fever will overtake her and cause her to miscarry."

Henry felt thoroughly inadequate to the task, but he could not allow Elizabeth or her unborn twins to suffer further harm.

"Very well. I believe you. I've no choice but to believe you. If she needs rescue, then I'll do my best to offer it. What must I do?" he asked, his mind made up.

"You must show her the way back."

He mentally steeled himself. "How?"

"By speaking to her. It will bring you great danger. Are you willing?"

"Of course. I will not leave her there, but first, allow me to prepare. I don't suppose you have a Bible?"

"I have many. The Geneva, Wycliffe, Tyndale, King James. Also, the Septuagint, if you read Greek; Vulgate, should you prefer Latin. There are numerous, original scrolls in my personal library. Which do you prefer? Shall I send Vasily to fetch one, or all of them?"

Salperton managed half a smile, his right brow arched as he considered the absurdity of the situation. A creature calling himself an elohim had just offered him original scrolls from the Bible to rescue a duchess from a spiritual prison!

"That won't be necessary, Your Highness. The King James will do nicely."

Anatole left the room briefly and returned carrying a very large book. It was over five inches thick, and its wooden cover was sheathed in dark leather. Each corner had metal reinforcements that looked like bright gold. Two closures of the same shining metal held the covers shut.

"Is this a reproduction?" Salperton asked as he took the beautiful book into both hands. "I've never seen its like. It reminds me of an antique edition in my Uncle Andrew's collection. My uncle is a rather smug fellow. Thinks he's smarter than anyone else, and I suspect he collects Bibles as one collects art, seeing them not for their spiritual value, but because they are pretty and might fetch a fine price one day." He lifted it, whistling. "It's quite heavy, isn't it? Twenty pounds or more, I'd say."

"Thirty and one ounce," the prince informed his guest.

Henry unsnapped the closures to look inside. "This is incredible! I've never seen a copy with water-coloured drawings before. This looks almost like an original, but it cannot be; though, whoever made it knows his art. The paper is rag linen, like my uncle's 1648 copy, but the print is too clear and bold to be original, and the colours on the binding too bright. The metal looks as though it was added just this morning, and it's fine gold. Surely the original closures were brass, don't you think?"

"This edition is one of a kind," the elohim replied, touching the beautiful book's spine. "The printer, Robert Barker, handed it to me one week before he delivered the finished volume to King James. I hired a team of reformist monks to add colourised illumination to the woodcuts as well as each chapter's initial capital."

Salperton set the thick volume upon the bed. "Like the old Bibles copied by the Catholics. Well, it is magnificent," Henry said, admiringly. "Wait, did you say that the printer handed it to you, himself? Before he delivered it to the king?"

"I am old, Lord Salperton. Very old. Older than you could possibly imagine. Which passage do you search for?"

"Psalm Twenty-Three. My mother loved that psalm. She had me memorise it as a boy. It's a trifle embarrassing, but I asked for the Bible because I like to feel the page beneath my fingers whenever trouble comes my way. It's a strange custom, I know, but the child's notion still lingers in the man."

Romanov waved his hand, and the handcrafted pages turned on their own, fanning past, through books of creation, history, prophecy, and poetic beauty. The paginated ballet stopped abruptly when it reached the Twenty-Third Psalm.

"That's quite a trick," the viscount said, more to hide his own hammering heart than to make a joke. He placed his palm across the page and shut his eyes. Henry had done this hundreds of times in his life, but to his shock, this time, the page grew warm beneath his skin. He could *feel* the words move into his bloodstream, becoming part of him, entering his very soul. The sensation straightened his back and strengthened his heart.

"I'm ready," he told Romanov. "What do I do now?"

"You begin by leaving behind all that you think you know and crossing into the realm of the impossible. The Valley of the Shadow of Death is a real place, Henry, and you are about to enter it."

CHAPTER NINETEEN

Time unknown - Sebet Babi

Elizabeth awoke to find herself lying upon the hard floor of the cottage. In this nightmare land, she wore only a white silk chemise—the last item of clothing left to her, when Trent had ripped away all else in order to force himself on her. Only now, did Beth notice that the silk undergarment was torn. Raziel's trance had left her dazed, struggling to recall where she was for a moment. The one clear memory was of Charles Sinclair's face. Still foggy, she couldn't remember his departure, but knew he'd been with her previously. To her dismay, she could find him nowhere.

"Captain, where are you? I'm sure you were here. Where is this place?" she asked aloud, struggling to connect half a dozen thoughts into a consistent pattern. The gargoyles' attack had left her weak and confused. The duchess coughed as she pushed herself into a sitting position. She paused a few seconds to catch her breath, and then used the bedstead to gain her feet. She wore no shoes, and the rough boards against her tender soles helped to tether her to reality.

"I must keep moving," she said out loud, still speaking to her departed husband. "Charles, I don't know how, but for the sake of our children, I will find my way back to you, my love."

It took a series of starts and stops before she reached the main room. The fire had nearly died, and the coals glowed a reddish orange. Hoping to stoke it higher, Beth searched the room for a wood box, but found none.

"Charles, why am I so cold?" she asked her absent husband. She moved to the window. The unnatural birds still kept watch on the refuge, but they'd left the woods and formed a series of circles, beginning at the edge of the gravel yard. Their formations reminded

Elizabeth of something she'd seen before, but what? She estimated their numbers to be in the thousands, perhaps ten thousand. Each birdlike creature stood as high as a man, some even taller. Their eyes never blinked, and their colour ranged from dull yellow to crimson red. It seemed to Beth that they communicated, for occasionally one would listen for a moment, its head tilted to the side, and then move to a different place, as though following orders from an unseen commander.

"It's an army," she said aloud. "Charles, why would they be forming into ranks unless they mean to attack? I know nothing about military manouevres. Oh, I wish Paul were here! He knows all about these things. Why didn't I pay closer attention when he used to talk of them?"

A series of whispers floated upon the cold night air, as though the avian soldiers were discussing a report or rumour. Then, the foremost circle of creatures parted in a specific place, followed by the next, and then the one beyond that. This continued within each concentric circle of birdmen. Only then did Elizabeth recognise the pattern.

"It's the stone maze come to life!" she gasped. "Charles, they've formed into the same shapes as the gated maze. There's something else, though. Something new is happening towards the very back. It's quite strange to watch. The circles of birds are rotating in alternating directions. I think they're aligning themselves to form an opening for something. Or someone."

She glanced up at the unyielding night sky, and only then did the duchess notice that the moon had disappeared. "Where has it gone? The moon! It's been here the entire time, like some sickly thing, but now it's vanished, Captain!"

Elizabeth ran to the back of the cottage, nearly stumbling on the torn hem of her chemise. A tiny window on the far side of the bed allowed her to glimpse a different portion of the sky and grounds. Sure enough, the moon was nowhere to be discovered. However, she could see inky shadows flying against the cloudless vault—a legion of birdmen with wings that looked harsh and broad, more bats than ravens. These criss-crossed the airspace over the cottage like a company of hateful spies, growing ever nearer as they spiralled towards the solitary refuge.

"Duchess," a voice whispered. "Can you hear me?"

Beth heard the voice, but did not trust it. "Leave me alone! Stop trying to trick me!"

"Please, Your Grace, I mean you no harm. I only want to help. Can you find me? I've no idea if you can even see me, but follow the sound of my voice."

What new torture is this? she wondered. "If Raziel has sent you, then you'll not find me so easily fooled. Go away!"

She left the bedchamber and returned to the main room, looking again through the large window beside the door. The ranks had ceased moving, and now a broad corridor had formed. Every creature faced towards the opening, as though awaiting the arrival of a sovereign or general. Though the dusky panorama had very little light, Beth could make out movement coming from the dense woods. A cracking sound split the air, and she could see the canopies of huge yew trees shivering as the wooden sentries obediently moved aside to make room for the newcomer. Something enormous emerged from the gnarled and ancient trees, and Beth thought she could see some of the yews bowing, as though paying homage to their ruler.

The hideous king wore black armour and rode upon the back of a monstrous dragon, whose leathery wings spread out sixty feet on either side. The creature's body and tail reached higher than the trees, two hundred feet or more, and the ground trembled beneath the stamping of its clawed feet.

The rider also bore wings, but had the aspect of a human, clad in finery decorated with gold and jewels that served as a faint and glittering light in the oppressive gloom.

"Their ruler is here, Charles. If this place is a level of the underworld, then this may be their infernal king. Captain, what do I do? He's heading towards this cottage, and the door is no match for that dragon. Please, my darling, help me! Find me!"

She moved towards the room's only source of light, the dying fire. The voice spoke again.

"Your Grace, I believe I can hear you now. Did you just say that you are in the underworld?"

"Go away!" she pleaded. "Do not tempt me, please. I cannot bear it!" she wept. "Oh, Charles, if only you were here!" she cried out, dropping to her knees from lack of strength. "Please, Lord, help me. Please, I don't know what to do!"

"Duchess, I implore you to listen. I am not a part of any attempt to hurt you or lie to you. My name is Henry MacAlpin, and I've been tending you as your physician. Prince Anatole Romanov hired me, and it's been my honour to keep watch upon you, but you will never recover, if we cannot release you from this prison. I know it's difficult, but I beg you to trust me. The prince tells me that you must leave right away. He says this fellow Raziel left only because he was commanded to do so by a very powerful and wicked fallen angel. That commander is about to enter your refuge. You have but a few moments to escape before it is too late!"

She looked into the fire, for the voice emanated from within its charred stones. "You say your name is Henry?"

"Yes, yes, my name is Henry! Please, Elizabeth, I know you must be terrified, but I beg you, do this for yourself and for the unborn life within you. Will you do it?"

She prayed silently, struggling with the decision. "I can't. I'm too afraid to move," she confessed, tears clouding her vision. "I want Charles. Is he there with you? Have you seen him?"

"I'm very sorry, Elizabeth. Charles isn't here, but the prince assures me that he is well. I'm sure you are terrified, and your husband is your sole source of comfort, but if you hope to see him again, then you must escape! You're running out of time, and your pulse is weakening. I beg you to do as I ask!"

"You say Anatole is there with you? Let me speak to him. If he knows how to help, why doesn't he come himself? Charles says that Anatole isn't human but a messenger from another world. Perhaps, an angel from God. Why can't he come here? Please, tell him to come here. I'm too afraid to move, and the birds will reach the door soon. And there's a dragon!"

"Yes, the prince is here. Give me one moment, Elizabeth. Don't stop listening and stay close to the source of my voice. Can you do that?"

"Yes, I'll stay here, but, please, hurry!"

In the real world, Henry MacAlpin's anger erupted into a tirade of accusations against his host.

"How can you put her through this? She doesn't know me, and it's clear from her voice that she's been through more than any woman can bear! If you're able to help her, then do it!"

The prince seemed to grow taller and his eyes sparked fire as outrage overtook reason. "Do you think I haven't tried?" he shouted. "I have pleaded with the One to allow me to rescue her. His answer again and again has been no. Without the One's permission, the way for me remains shut unless I submit myself to the underworld king's rule. Do you not see? This is an attempt to lure me into rebellion, and I cannot do that. Not now. Not ever."

"What the devil does that mean?" Salperton shouted in return. "If you love her as much as I believe you do, then go there and help!"

"I cannot, and that is the end of it! You must convince her to trust you, Henry. She will. I have foreseen it. You play an important role in her life from this moment forward. Talk to her."

"I *am* talking to her!" he roared, both hands clenched in anger. Shutting his eyes tightly, the viscount forced himself to calm, his heart to slow, his mind to clear. "Very well. As you're unwilling to do it, I shall."

He placed his hand once more on the open Bible, an electric sensation coursing through his body. "Elizabeth, can you hear me?"

No reply.

"Duchess? Please, if you can hear me, I beg you to answer."

Have the dragon and his demons already taken her?

"Elizabeth? Are you there?"

"Henry?" a childlike voice whispered into his thoughts.

"Yes, yes! It's Henry. I'm here."

He could hear her crying now, and it tore through his soul. "She's terrified," he said, tears streaming down his face. "She doesn't know me, and she's afraid."

Anatole sat beside the duchess, all serenity gone from his lean face, replaced with tension and agony. "Call her Beth," he told the viscount. "Ask her if she remembers the time when she was lost in the woods near Branham Hall. Tell her that the same man who rescued her, then, will do so now."

"What?" he asked, completely mystified. "I cannot do that. It is a lie."

"It is not. Tell her."

Henry glared at the prince. "No."

"Tell her, Henry. I promise you. It is the truth. Tell her."

Forgive me for this, Lord. "Beth, it's Henry. Can you still hear me?"

"Yes, I hear you," she answered, her voice small and trembling.

"Do you remember a time as a child, when you became lost? In the woods near your home?"

"At Branham?" she asked faintly.

"Yes, that's right. At Branham. Tell me about it."

"I was five years old," she whispered, her strength failing.

"What happened, Beth?"

She sat beside the fire, staring into the dying coals. "I was with my father. We'd been enjoying our last afternoon together before he left again for India. He'd been carrying me on his shoulders, and we laughed and laughed as he pretended to be one of my ponies, bouncing me up and down. He loved playing that game," she explained, her eyes rimmed in sadness. "But, then, he put me down. His voice turned quite serious, and he ordered me to return to the house."

"Why?" Henry asked her, his eyes still shut to concentrate.

"I'm not sure we ever learnt who it was, but Father saw someone near the hedge maze. A stranger. He called for our chief gardener, and the two of them started towards this person. I could hear Father shouting, and several of the household servants ran into the garden. I should have gone inside, but instead, I must have wandered away. I can't remember why. I may have followed someone. Before I knew it, I'd gotten all turned 'round and become lost in the woods just the other side of the maze."

"You were lost?" he asked her. "How did you find your way out of the woods?"

"A man found me," she answered. "No one I'd ever met before. A tall man with dark, curly hair and brown eyes. He reminded me a little of my father, only not as tall. I'd been warned against talking to strangers, but this man promised to take me home. He seemed kind and trustworthy, and he knew my name. He called me Beth."

"And this man led you to safety?" Henry asked, tears watering his cheeks.

"Yes. He was very nice with kind eyes and a Scottish accent. He took my hand, and I remember that as we walked, he taught me what I thought was a poem, but it turned out to be a chapter in the Bible."

That same electric shock ran from the printed words and up the Scotsman's arm. His entire body felt as though it vibrated, and he could actually *see* her now—pale and frightened, sitting beside a stone hearth inside a farmer's cottage.

"Which chapter was it?" he asked, though he'd already guessed the answer.

"The Twenty-Third Psalm. The man told me his name was Hal. It was what his mother always called him."

Salperton began to weep, and he had to force himself to concentrate. "That's right. Hal. It's short for Henry. That's what my mother always called me, too. Will you follow me out of the woods, Beth? Will you take my hand?"

"How? I don't understand. I hear your voice, but I can see nothing."

"The Lord will guide you. Say it with me. *The Lord is my Shepherd. I shall not want.* Say it, Beth."

He could see her plainly—as clearly as he could see anything in life. Her pale arms trembled, for the thin chemise barely kept her warm, but also terror and cold caused her to shiver. The viscount reached out hoping to touch her.

"Here's my hand, Beth! The Lord will show it to you. Take it! I'm here, and I won't leave you until you are safely out of these dark woods. Just follow my voice and speak the words."

Silence.

"Beth, say the words with me. You can do this. Trust me. *He maketh me to lie down in green pastures. He leadeth me beside the still waters. He restoreth my soul.*"

Elizabeth shivered, for she could hear the cries of the bird creatures. "I cannot see your hand. Where is it?"

"Here," he told her, concentrating and praying silently. "Let Christ's words lead you home. Say it with me. *He leadeth me in the paths of righteousness for His name's sake.*"

She listened to the quoted passage, and it was like a refreshing breeze whispered heaven's own song into her heart and mind. "*He leadeth me in the paths of righteousness for His name's sake,*" she repeated.

"Yes, that's it! Continue, Beth. We'll say it together. Speak it with me. *Yea, though I walk.* Say it. *Yea, though I walk...*"

Henry recited the next few lines, and Elizabeth tried to do likewise, but the reminder of a valley of shadows, caused her to doubt. "I can't!" she cried out. "Please, don't make me say it! I'm afraid!"

"I know, but our Lord is with you, Elizabeth, and he will not forsake you. Neither will I. Say it with me."

Her voice quivered, but she did her best. "*Yea, though I walk through the valley of the—the valley of the shadow—the shadow of death,*" she said, weeping. "No, I can't do it! I'm afraid!"

"I know, Beth, but Christ is there with you. You are not alone. The enemy wants you to fear, for he cringes at the sound of the Lord's Holy Word. Say it, Beth. Speak the words with me. Show the enemy that you will never submit to them! Remind them of who walks beside you as Shepherd. *Yea, though I walk through the valley of the shadow of death.* What comes next? Say it, Beth. Say it so that all those horrid creatures can hear it! Say it so that all the worlds ever created can hear it!"

"*Yea, though I walk through the valley of the shadow of death, I will fear no evil,*" she said aloud, her eyes on the dwindling fire, "*for thou art with me.*"

The light which had shone down upon the cottage suddenly winked out, and the ravens shouted in response. They stamped their feet rhythmically, the dreadful sound like the pounding of a million drums. The army had grown confident, now that the cruel light no longer protected the cottage or its inhabitant.

The enormous dragon bellowed, and its gigantic feet thundered upon the ground as it raced towards the refuge.

Elizabeth could hear the dragon's cries, and horns blasted from all directions. They were coming for her. HE was coming for her.

She began to sob, her shoulders jerking in spasms. "I can't do this without Charles. Captain, please, wherever you are, please help me!"

Henry listened from the other side of reality, his heart breaking in two. "*Thy rod and thy staff, they comfort me,*" he repeated as he silently prayed. "Beth, say it. Say the next line with me."

She lay against the hearth's stone apron, weeping so hard that her entire body jerked. "Captain, please!"

"Elizabeth, I beg you to say the words. Charles needs for you to escape this place! Please, say them! For him!"

She wiped her eyes and swallowed the fear. "*Thy rod and thy staff, they comfort me. Thou... Thou preparest a table before me, in the presence... In the presence of...*" she halted upon the words, for the entire cottage had begun to shake as thunderous cries filled the air outside.

Henry could hear them, too, for their raucous shouts of victory bled through from the underworld into his.

Anatole Romanov also heard and understood the brackish language, perceiving the meaning of the ravens' cries. "The king has broken through the protections placed on the cottage. If she does not leave right now, he will take her."

"Beth, speak the words!" Henry implored, his hand upon the Bible, eyes shut to concentrate. "*Thou preparest a table before me in the presence of mine enemies.*"

"*Thou preparest a table before me in the presence of mine enemies. Thou anointest my head with oil,*" she continued, the fear now replaced with a strength not of her own making. "*My cup runneth over!*" she exulted.

The duchess took to her feet, steadying herself against the fireplace. "Henry, how do I leave?" she asked the viscount. "They're about to break down the door."

"Anatole says you must walk towards my voice."

"But... But your voice is coming from the fireplace! How do I walk towards it, if you're in the fire?"

"You walk by faith. Close your eyes and follow my voice." He concentrated with every last fibre of his being and reached out with his mind—forming the picture of a hand, and 'seeing' her take it. "Look for my hand, Beth. I'm right here. Let me help you find your way home."

"I love you, Captain," she whispered, though she shook all over. "Father in heaven, be my Shepherd now and lead me where my eyes cannot see a path. Show me this hand and take me back to Charles, I beg you!"

Henry waited—listening, his heart pounding.

"Beth? Do you see it? Can you see my hand?"

Nothing.

"Elizabeth? Duchess, talk to me, please!"

A thundering shock ran along his spine, and in his mind, Henry could see the wooden door to the cottage shudder, then splinter into a thousand pieces.

Instantly, a raincloud of gigantic birds spilled into the dark and cold interior, filling it with caws and the harsh rush of gigantic wings. Behind these, he heard the screams of a monstrous creature, probably the dragon. The birdmen ceased their maddened flight and stood still as stones.

The underworld ruler bent to peer through the open doorway.

For an instant, Salperton stared into the infernal king's eyes.

He'd seen him before.

"*You!*" it screamed, the voice like a clap of thunder. "*It's you! How dare you interfere with my plans again!*"

Salperton could feel strong hands shaking him.

"Henry! Wake up!" a voice shouted from somewhere nearby.

"What?" the viscount muttered, trying, but unable to open his eyes.

Many seconds passed—an eternity of seconds. In his mind, the birds circled 'round him, and Henry could hear the harsh speech of the king and his soldiers talking to one another—and now and then to him—but he could not hear the duchess.

She was nowhere to be seen.

"What have you done with her?" he shouted at the infernal king. "Where is she?"

The creature's laughter shook the cottage, and the rafters began to splinter and crack. More birdmen burst through the small windows, shattering the glass and wreaking havoc upon the furnishings. Their sharp beaks tore through the quilt, the pillows, and the mattress. The dragon breathed, and the entwined hearts caught fire. In minutes, the birds and the dragon fire had destroyed everything inside the precious refuge.

Now, they turned towards him with hungry eyes.

The hands shook Henry again, more violently this time, and he felt a sharp slap against his right cheek.

"Release him!" a deep voice commanded. Then in a different language, other commands volleyed back and forth betwixt worlds, as though two ancient kings waged war. The ruined walls of the cottage shook, and lightning flashed against the midnight sky. "Release him now! I command you in the *Name of the One!*"

A mighty crash tore through his mind. Something slammed against the corridor that connected him to the duchess's prison, and Henry MacAlpin collapsed against the bed.

"I do not hear them now. Nor her," he panted, gasping for air, all hope gone. "I failed. I failed! The demon took her!" Henry pushed against the mattress, steadying himself, anguish tearing at his heart and mind. "She's lost."

Moments passed, then a soft voice began to whisper.

"*Surely, goodness and mercy shall follow me*," it was saying.

"*Mercy shall follow me. Follow. Surely, it shall follow me*."

"She's here!" the viscount shouted exuberantly, nearly falling as he rushed to the duchess's side. "Elizabeth, open your eyes. You've made it! You're home!"

"*Goodness and mercy*," she whispered. "*And I shall dwell in the house of the Lord forever and ever. Amen.*"

Her eyelids twitched ever so slightly, and then, for the first time since he arrived at the castle, Henry's patient opened her eyes. They were dark brown with pupils as wide as saucers. Her black lashes contrasted with the chocolate irises, showing off tiny flecks of gold at the rim of each pupil. Henry had never seen such beautiful eyes in all his life.

Recalling the warning Prince Anatole had given during their first meeting, the love-struck viscount wondered just how the Russian had known.

"Hello," he said, his smile as wide as hope itself. "I'm Henry. Welcome home."

Her lips parted, but no sound emerged from the slender throat. Her left hand reached out for his, and he took it.

"Here, now, let me help you to sit."

The duchess gripped his arm, and Henry placed two pillows behind her head. "Thirsty?" She nodded. "Yes, I imagine you are." He filled a small glass to the halfway mark and put the rim to her lips. "Take it slowly. You've been unconscious for many days."

She sipped a little and then pushed the glass away. "You're Henry?"

"Yes, do you remember my voice?"

She nodded, wearily. "Where is Charles?"

"I'll explain in a moment, but allow me to assess your health before addressing that," he stated as he examined her skin colour and eyes. "You're still flushed, and your pupils dilated. Can you breathe?"

She tried to inhale, but it caused a coughing spasm.

"May I?" he asked, showing her the stethoscope. "I'd like to listen to your lungs."

"Why does it hurt to breathe?" she asked.

"You've contracted pneumonia, or something akin to it. I fear you'll be a couple of weeks mending."

"No, I have to find Charles!" she exclaimed, trying to rise from the bed. "He disappeared! The Captain—his watch started working, and he's gone! I have to find him. Please, help me find him!"

"I will. I promise," he told her sweetly, his hands on her hers. "The Captain will want you well, now won't he? Until then, you must do as I ask."

"But will you tell Charles that I've escaped?"

"I will, but allow me to do my job first, all right? Tell me, do you know your name?"

"Yes, of course, I do. I'm Elizabeth Stuart. No, wait. It's Sinclair now. My mind's all foggy, but I think my wedding was...it was..." she said, panic crossing her features as the memories clarified into harsh truth. "Charles was hurt! I remember now! Trent took me. He put a cloth against my mouth, and I think I lost consciousness. When I came 'round, we were inside an empty house, and someone else was there. Rasha, I think. But he—someone killed him!"

Her words came in a rapid-fire stream, like a desperate tide. Elizabeth took a painful breath, sorting through recollections that seemed impossible. "I can't remember clearly, but someone else was there. I could hear them talking. William tried—he tried to hurt me. Force me to yield to him! He climbed on top of me, but someone pulled him off, someone helped me. I can't remember who it was. I'm not sure, but I think he killed Trent. Suddenly, I was flying up in the air, and then the house caught fire, and then I saw creatures on another roof." Her eyes rounded in shock. "Oh, no! Charles was thrown back onto the snow! Blood covered the ground, and... Please, tell me he's all right! Tell me he isn't dead!"

The prince had been quietly standing in the corner of the chamber, out of her line of sight. He had no wish for the duchess to recall that awful night. To stop her, Romanov returned to the bed and reached for her hand.

"Your Captain is well," he told her. "Elizaveta, these memories are too much for you to bear. Think no more on them."

"Anatole?" she whispered. "Where am I?"

"You are in my home. Do you remember how you came to be here?"

"Yes. No wait, I don't," she corrected as the prince touched her forehead. "I cannot remember. I'm so very sleepy. I'm sorry."

"That's right, my friend. Sleep, Veta," he whispered. "Dream of home and your handsome Captain. Soon, you will be reunited."

She closed her eyes and relaxed against the satin pillow as though in a faint. The Scotsman glared at the Russian, anger colouring his cheeks. "What did you just do?"

"I shall explain in due course. For now, come with me, Doctor. Katrina will keep watch on the duchess."

Before leaving the bedchamber, Romanov pulled the bell rope to summon the servant. The lady's maid entered and curtsied.

"My lord?"

"Katrina, our patient will sleep for many hours, but we must still keep watch. I know it is late, but will you sit with her? The doctor and I shall retire to my private drawing room. Send for me, should you require us."

The prince led the physician down a tapestry-lined corridor that connected the northwest apartment to the rest of the castle's first floor. Henry paused to examine several of the beautiful designs near the turning to another apartment. "Medieval histories?"

"Some are," Romanov answered. "Others are much more ancient." They continued past the second apartment and into an extraordinarily beautiful parlour. The room was circular, and the ceiling soared overhead, curving into a dome. Every square inch of the walls bore bright murals, predominately red, silver blue, and gold in colour. The floor tiles were black and white marble, overlaid by a silk rug with an equally beautiful design in shades to match the walls. Though Henry had never visited Russia, the room looked Eastern and ancient and exceedingly opulent to his eyes.

"The word magnificent comes to mind," the Scotsman said as the prince led him to a large sofa. "Is the design Russian?"

Anatole pulled a velvet cord near a carved marble fireplace. "Of course. I may not be of human origin, but my current form is. During these many centuries as a Russian, I've developed a great love for the styles and furnishings of the tsars. Do sit, Henry. I'll have Vasily lay in a selection of food and wine for us. We shan't be disturbed for some time, I shouldn't think."

The viscount sat upon the curved sofa, his back against two brightly embroidered, suzani cushions with gold tassels at each corner. The room was as large as any royal state room and, over the centuries, had hosted hundreds of Russian dignitaries.

"This room has always been my refuge," the prince explained as he sat opposite his guest. "It is a copy of one in my Moscow palace. I hope you are comfortable, Lord Salperton. I appreciate how exhausted you must be after so arduous a task."

"That is an understatement. I'm decidedly weary, but filled with questions. To begin with, just where was I this evening? Hell?"

"No. I told you plainly. You were in the Valley of the Shadow of Death. It has seven levels, the first of which is a complicated maze within the Realms of Stone. The Stone King has many names and many crowns, and he can transform into flames of fire, melting even the hardest of rock. He recognised you."

"So it seemed," Salperton answered uncomfortably. "When my mother died, I had a terrifyingly vivid dream. That Stone King creature was in it, astride a dragon. Surely, a child's fancy."

"Was it?"

Henry had no wish to discuss it further, and he deflected by posing his own question. "What did you do to her? The duchess, I mean. She was trying to explain what happened to her, but you touched her forehead, and all her memories vanished."

"I helped her to sleep. That is all. The duchess is in too fragile a state to recall the tragic details of last Sunday. When she is stronger, I will return the memories to her."

"But she will awaken again? Tell me that you've not consigned her back to that hellish world!"

"Of course not," Romanov answered. "I would never harm her. Did I not send you to rescue her? Why, then, would I return her there?"

"I've no idea. Honestly, I find all this rather disorienting, if not exhausting. What time is it?" the physician asked, swiping damp hair from his sweaty brow. "I feel as though I've run a hundred miles."

"I suspect your body grows heavy with the weight of responsibility and discovery. Few humans have visited the Stone Realms. I do not yet know why the duchess and her husband were pulled into it, but I intend to find out. It may require that I leave you for a few days. If so, I pray you will remain with her until I return."

"Of course, I will. I won't leave her."

Anatole smiled. "Because you love her."

"Because I am her physician!" he answered angrily. "Why do you insist on baiting me?"

"Is it bait to pronounce fact?"

"You enjoy playing with words," Salperton noted, choosing to avoid the trap. "Your Highness, I'm more tired than I've ever been in my entire life, and yet I have a thousand questions swirling inside my head which will keep me awake."

"Then, you must ask them," his host said kindly.

"To own the truth, I'm not sure where to start. I suppose, I'll begin with this place. This ghost castle. How old is it? When was it built?"

Just as Romanov started to answer, Vasily quietly entered with a tray of fruit and sandwiches along with a silver-mounted decanter containing an amber liquid. "I promise to address your question in a moment, but first, I suggest you eat, Doctor. I'm sure you are famished after so arduous a night. Vasily has brought us brandy, but we have a cellar stocked with other options, as well." The prince lifted the cut crystal stopper and sniffed. "Ah, the Bouchard '26. An excellent choice, Vasily."

The viscount showed no interest.

"Perhaps you prefer vodka? Being Russian, I keep several varieties, but I warn you, vodka is much stronger than what you Scots drink."

MacAlpin smiled, wiping at his eyes wearily. "The brandy will do nicely, but you might be surprised what we Scots drink, Your Highness."

"So I'm often told. Thank you, Vasily," he told the servant. "Has everyone else retired for the night?"

"All but Mr. Anderson, sir. He's still adjusting to his medicine. Everyone else has gone up to their apartments. Katrina sits with the duchess, but there is another matter, Your Highness."

The butler bent to whisper, and Anatole's light eyes rounded. "Is that so? Position guards at all the entrances. Come to me at once, if you hear of further news. No other disturbances, however, if it can be helped. Lord Salperton and I wish to speak privately."

Vasily left to carry out the orders, and the prince poured his guest a snifter of brandy and handed it to him. "If I appear secretive, it is not my intent. Vasily whispered that the local police have raided a gambling house on the other side of the cemetery. I've always thought it a curious place to conduct such business, but then the dead experience events different than we," he added mysteriously.

"Yes, very curious," Salperton answered, not the least bit convinced of the explanation. "The castle?"

"Yes, the castle. It is not called Ghaist, of course, despite what the locals choose to believe. Originally, its name was *Vrata Raya.* It is an older form of Russian, meaning Heaven's Gate."

"An interesting choice of names, considering what I've just been through," Salperton observed as he sipped the wine.

"Indeed. The name is based on a local legend, anchored in truth. A fifth century tribe, descended from the Regni, once called this area of London home, and they told a story of divine beings who taught their ancestors the art of forging steel and producing superior weapons."

"Divine beings such as yourself?" Salperton suggested.

Anatole smiled. "Yes, I was there, but I did not teach them these things. I discouraged it."

"Yet they continued to commune with these fallen angels?"

"They did. Therefore, I placed guards over the gate to shut it."

"So you say."

"I do not insist you believe me, Henry. In time, you will decide for yourself whether or not I can be trusted. To continue the story, however, I kept close watch on the portal over the following centuries, and when the Muscovy Trading Company established itself in London, I returned here to broker that venture."

"You returned? But surely not as Anatole Romanov? That family did not take control of Russia until, what?—the early 17th century?"

"1607 to be precise. A most auspicious year, historically speaking. The Bank of Genoa failed, England was severely flooded, Monteverdi's opera *Orfeo* premiered, and Jamestown colony was established in the new world. One might say a new era had begun. My current form is based on a man whom I admired during the reign of Michael I, the founder of the Romanov dynasty. As with all my kind who walk the earth, I create histories for myself, should anyone ever wish to investigate my past."

"You lie."

"No, I merely invent. You would be surprised how often humans encounter my kind, though they are blissfully unaware of it."

"Hebrews 13:2," the viscount noted, smiling. "*Be not forgetful to entertain strangers; for thereby, some have entertained angels unawares*. My mother often quoted it. And this trading company offered you an opportunity to return to the site of this gateway?"

"It did, indeed," Romanov replied. "My attentions had been drawn away to other matters in a distant part of the world, and in that time, someone discovered the covering stone and removed it. The gateway stood open once more. Rather than risk the same occurring again, I built this castle upon the portal."

"How is any of this possible? If you knew the Regni, then that would make you two millennia old!" the medical man argued.

The prince said nothing, merely smiled.

"You're *that* old?"

"Much, much older," the prince whispered.

Salperton inhaled deeply. "Well, then, I may require a sample of that vodka. After all, I can't get any madder than I am already, can I?"

Romanov filled a pair of chased silver cups, decorated along the rim and handle with finely crafted roses. "I think you'll find this outmatches your Scotch whisky for strength, but with a more complex flavour."

"I'll reserve opinion for the moment," MacAlpin answered.

"I like you, Henry. I always told your mother that you would grow up to be a fine man. She was a very beautiful, compassionate woman. Talented, and quite bright. She loved you as few mothers love their sons."

"I loved her in return," Salperton answered softly. "I miss her yet today. That ache never leaves me."

"Until now," Romanov dared suggest.

The viscount cast the prince a sharp look. "Do stop insinuating that I am in love with my patient. I am not."

"If you say so," the prince agreed, though his expression made it clear he hardly agreed at all. "Henry, did you know that one of your mother's paintings was of me?"

"You?" Henry asked in shock. "My mother saw you?"

"She did. We even conversed a few times. I tried to conceal myself, but your mother's eyes cut through my veil. Her eyes were very sharp, much like your own. You will find the watercolour portrait inside the box of treasured memories you keep inside your study. The box is made of carved oak and bears the Salperton crest upon it."

The physician stared. "How can you possibly know that?"

"You keep the box in a safe, hidden within your study wall. Behind an oil painting of a tricolour spaniel dog. Your childhood friend, Droigheann."

"No one outside my family knows about that dog! Even if you broke into my home, that painting bears no plaque."

Romanov smiled. "I had already informed you that I visited your home, remember? Droigheann was a sweet-tempered animal, and very brave, was he not? His name is Gaelic for bramble."

"Yes, it is," the physician answered, his brown eyes softening. "He was a stray, by all accounts. I found him lodged in a thicket near the woods outside Inverary. Poor thing was a mess of briars and nettles. Despite the pain, he never once complained. Our butler spent over an hour cutting thorns out of the dog's fur. Finally, he clipped it all down short. Practically shaved the animal. It grew back, though," he added, smiling as he recalled the childhood event.

"Droigheann was small but fierce. He died protecting you from a wolf."

MacAlpin's face paled. "How can you know that? Just what are you? You claim to be two thousand years old..."

"Older."

"Yes, so you say, but how is that even possible? You're not a spirit. I can touch you. If I put a stethoscope to your chest, would I hear a heartbeat, or are you merely a figment of my mad imagination?"

"I am one who watches, Henry, and I've been watching your family for generations. My human form is real, though I did not steal it. I fashioned it using science unknown to humankind. It is the kind of knowledge my rebellious brethren taught to Adam's descendants. Indeed, they still teach it! Did you ever hear your mother speak of a man named Trent?"

He shook his head. "No. Should I?"

"Did she ever mention a group called the Round Table? Are you sure? What of the great wolf? A red-eyed beast as large as a horse."

The annoyed physician tipped back the vodka in one quick gulp without so much as a blink. "Whisky is stronger," he declared, setting the cup neatly on a marble-topped table with a carved dragonfly base. "Why do you ask about the wolf? What have my childhood nightmares to do with you, the duchess, with any of this?"

"That wolf was not a nightmare, as you well know. Did you dream Droigheann's death? No, he charged the hellish beast and saved your life. Afterward, your mother told you about a man called Trent. She told you that he was evil. You have no recall of this? I rather doubt that, Henry."

Salperton poured another shot of vodka and drank it down, wiping his mouth with his hand. He looked completely worn down and pale, as though the prince had lanced a festering boil and drawn poison from his system.

"When I was at Oxford, a classmate at Queen's College suggested that I join this Round Table group. The fool thought them nothing more than a social club, but I knew better. My mother had warned me of their plots, and I'd spent years looking into their history. They are a fellowship of political miscreants who espouse revolution and riot. They plot to unseat the rightful sovereign and place their own man on the empty throne. Despite my warning, I fear my friend did join. Why do you persist with this, and what has this to do with my mother or me?"

"The Round Table presents itself as an anarchistic gathering of modernist thinkers with money and titles. You might call it an elitist version of Fabianism, but behind that political face is a heinous and very evil group of men who call themselves Redwing."

"Redwing?" Henry asked, finding the suggestion absurd. "They are but a child's tale!"

"Hardly. Not unless that child is haunted by them from a very early age, which is precisely what happened to the duchess. Sir William Trent was her stepfather, and he led both the Round Table and London's Redwing membership until very recently. He also knew your mother."

"That is no surprise, Your Highness. As I'm sure you're aware, the peerage is a closed set. It's not only likely but almost inevitable that the duchess would know a man who once met my mother." He thought for a moment, calculating. "This Trent fellow must have been much older than Beth's mother. Elizabeth looks no more than twenty to me."

"Trent was very old, indeed; stretched and altered through magic and demonic rites. He is now deceased, or rather his current material form is. The demon that inhabited that form has passed from host to host for millennia, but is now trapped inside the Stone Realms. It will not be there for long, if the Stone King escapes."

Setting aside his glass, the Scotsman's eyes narrowed. "How can a demon escape from Hell?"

"I did not say the demon is in Hell. The world is complicated, and there are more realms than you might think."

"You're a vexing chap, Romanov. Do you always speak in riddles?"

"One of your kinsmen asks me that from time to time. No, I do not always obscure facts, but you're not ready to hear everything that I know, Doctor. I teach in increments, building up a knowledge base and then layering upon that base. Would you have understood biochemical reactions without first understanding the structures of carbon and hydrogen?"

"I suppose not. What knowledge base do I lack, then? A belief in fairy tales?"

"You jest, but that would serve you well," Romanov answered. "Do you believe in the old tales? Those that speak of mythical beings with the ability to transform from one species to another? Or the stories of spectres and shades that stand unseen within a room, appearing only to those with the ability to see? Fairies are not imaginary, Henry. They exist, only not as the tales portray."

"I am a scientist, Your Highness. Yes, I believe my mother saw unusual visions when I was young, but I'm not sure just what those were—despite any painting that may vaguely resemble you. These visions may only have been her mind trying to explain a natural phenomenon."

"Such as?"

"I've no idea, but I keep an open mind with regards to truths that science has yet to uncover."

The prince began to laugh. "You see your mind as open? I shall let that go unchallenged for the present, Doctor. I assure you, however, that there is much your human science will never uncover. But let us return to the duchess. She is fragile. You can see that, I am sure. Until she recovers, her mind is incapable of processing all the horrors she has seen. Your mother had the same difficulty. For example, she was threatened by the wolf many times. Duchess Elizabeth has also seen this creature. It is not a natural animal, Henry. Are you a man who reads the newspapers?"

"Sometimes. Do you refer to the hysteria that swept the east last Sunday night? It was nothing more than the unfortunate result of a toxin in the water supply. Mild ergotism caused by mouldy grain."

"You do not believe that."

"Why shouldn't I? The police reported that a granary dumped an entire shipment of contaminated rye into a Whitechapel cistern, and it leeched into the piping."

"Is that what you *really* think happened? That hundreds of people all hallucinated the same thing? No, my friend. Occam's Razor is a concept understood by a man of science. The simplest explanation is most likely to be true, and in this case, the simplest is this: That spiritually altered wolfmen attacked and killed many horses and men near the rail sheds, north of Commercial. I have seen the bodies of those injured or slain. They are not imaginary."

"Wolfmen? Surely, a learned man such as yourself cannot buy into this superstitious claptrap!" MacAlpin argued, but his voice carried little conviction.

"You believe it to be true, Doctor. Admit it. The men these wolves attacked were in pursuit of the duchess's abductor, Sir William Trent. He used a charmed mirror to enter that gracious lady's bedchamber at Queen Anne House, and then carried her off through an ancient doorway that connects to a hidden realm."

"More fairy tales!" Henry snapped angrily. He longed to leave the room, to escape the torment of this strange man's uncomfortable revelations, but a nagging voice in the back of his mind told him to remain and listen, for everything the prince had told him was true.

Romanov showed no hint of irritation. "You think fairy tales are imagined, but they teach truths, though often simplified versions. As I said, Henry, you must learn the foundational aspects of the world before you will understand the depths of the hidden realms. Your mother could see into these other worlds. So can the duchess. And so can you, though you refuse to trust your own eyes. It is why you were able to reach her. Though Elizabeth was held prisoner in a realm far beyond the edge of time, she heard your voice and followed it home."

"What are you? Are you a devil? An angel? A ghost?"

"The answer is complicated, but allow me to simplify it for the present. As I've said before, I am not human. I am elohim. That is a very simple way to describe those who live outside Earth's time constraints. Consider England, if you will. It is a kingdom consisting of many counties. Elohim live within realms that are divided into many domains, as well. The One, that which you call God, reigns supreme over all realms, all worlds, all that exists. He is our Creator and our sovereign Lord. He exists from everlasting to everlasting. The One is not a created being, but he created me and my brothers long before Adam opened his eyes. Consider that your first lesson."

Henry could scarcely keep his eyes open, but he wished to learn more. "Are elohim angels, then?"

"Some are, but the term angel describes a mission not a class of individuals. You've slept very little this past week, Henry. Retire and rest. Tomorrow, the world will look much brighter."

"You're right, but I hope to hear more another time. Before I leave you, I should like your permission to inform Beth's husband that she's here. It's clear she relies upon the marquess for strength. I believe her recovery would progress more quickly, if he would write or perhaps even visit her."

"I cannot allow that," Romanov insisted. "She remains in danger."

"From whom? Those hellions who held her captive cannot cross into our world, can they?"

"They already have emissaries in this realm, Doctor. It is their king who might escape. He is far more evil than any other elohim presently in England."

The viscount took to his feet. "I shan't drop the request, sir, but for the moment, I'll say goodnight. I've spent the past week on the duchess's couch. I wonder, might I avail myself of the bedchamber adjoined to hers?"

"Of course. Sleep long and late. The duchess will not awaken until late morning. I promise."

Henry had no idea just how the prince could make such a promise, but he chose not to challenge it. Instead, he left the opulent parlour and followed the corridor back to the northwest apartment. After making certain that Elizabeth slept soundly and bidding Katrina goodnight, the Scotsman climbed into a soft bed for the first time in seven nights, and in two minutes had fallen into a deep and dreamless sleep.

CHAPTER TWENTY

Haimsbury House – 10:13 pm

It had been a very long day for Sinclair, and he dreaded retiring to the bedchamber. Without Elizabeth's smile to greet him, no room seemed friendly. Paul Stuart, Duke James, Kepelheim, and Michael Emerson remained with him following the circle meeting's adjournment, and all tried to convince Charles to go to bed, but the marquess kept postponing.

"I cannot go up there," he told his uncle. "Not to that room. Not without her."

Cornelius Baxter entered the drawing room with a quiet step and bowed. "Is there anything else you require before we shut up for the night, my lords? Mrs. Anderson has already closed most of the kitchen, but I can boil water for tea or fetch a bottle of wine from the cellars. There's cheese and fruit in the larder, and several meats leftover from supper, if anyone is hungry."

The duke answered for his nephews. "We're set for food, Mr. Baxter, but does the cellar still have that lovely claret the marquess's father put in?"

"The Château Lafite? It does, sir. Shall I fetch a bottle?"

"Charles, does that meet with your approval?" Drummond asked his nephew.

Sinclair stared into the fire. "Whatever you want, James. Nothing for me."

"Son, you have to keep hoping," he said as Baxter left to fetch the wine. "Lorena said the prince has her in his keeping. That's encouraging, isn't it? You've said yourself that you doubt Romanov would ever harm her."

"No, I don't believe he would," Charles answered.

"Because he loves her," the earl observed. "Do you think Romanov killed Trent?"

"Yes, I think he may have. Paul, you told me that Lorena described a battle in the skies that night. How did she put it again?" asked Charles.

The earl searched his eidetic memory and retrieved the conversation, as though turning to a page in a book. "She said it was two very powerful entities. Possibly Watchers. Then, she ran back into the Empress to seek a place to hide."

"Watchers like this Raziel? Is he one?" asked the duke. "And the other. What's his name again?"

"Saraqael," Aubrey replied. "Lorena said Trent's second mirror is inside the Empress. She mentioned a closet. You and I should search through that house tomorrow, if you're up to it. Charles, you look worn through. Go to bed."

"Sleep eludes me, Cousin. Work is the only thing that helps." His head throbbed, his body ached, but he dreaded bidding his friends goodnight. "James, this mirror. Is it still in the shed at Queen Anne?"

"So I'm told. No one has removed it. But there's no need to worry, Charles. MacPherson blessed it with oil and spoke prayers over it, and I had him place a Bible inside the crate."

"Still, I'd like to see it."

"Son, it's past ten o'clock. If you want to see it, we can take a look tomorrow."

Charles stood. "I want to see it now."

The earl sighed, standing. "Very well. I'll go with you, if you're so determined. I'll ask Baxter to call for a coach."

No sooner had the butler's name formed on Aubrey's lips, than the gentle giant returned. "Forgive me, my lord, but shall I decant the wine before I bring it up? We've three types of wine left from the circle meeting, already decanted. If I decant the Lafite, it will require half an hour if not longer."

"Actually, Baxter, the earl and I've decided to take a short walk along the grounds, provided it's not raining."

"A walk?" Aubrey echoed. "Charles, it takes fifteen minutes to cross the park. Are you sure you're up to it?"

"The exercise and night air will do me good."

"Or cause a chill," the duke remarked. Seeing his nephew's stern face, he threw up his hands. "Fine! If you must go, then bundle up. Baxter, fetch the marquess's heaviest coat."

"At once, Your Grace. I'll bring Lord Aubrey's as well."

"That won't be necessary," Stuart told the butler. "It's not all that cold. Not for me."

Baxter made certain the marquess dressed warmly with a wool scarf and leather gloves, and by half past ten, the cousins exited through Haimsbury House's south doors and commenced the long walk to Queen Anne House.

"I've never been much for overcoats and all that, unless they have another purpose," Paul explained as they walked. "One doesn't often have such luxuries when in disguise. I spend half my life as someone else, usually in miserable circumstances. However, I find certain outerwear indispensable. If you ever see me wearing a leather overcoat, you might want to look around you for danger," he added mysteriously.

The cool air actually helped to invigorate Charles, and he managed to smile. "I'll remember that. Truly, Paul, I don't know how you manage it. When I first met you, I imagined you a pampered peer with nothing to occupy your day but riding, shooting, and attending lavish parties. Yet, each passing week brings new insights into how you've actually spent your life. When did you first begin working for the government?"

"Oh, I suppose I was eleven or so when James first took me with him to North Africa. I learned to ride a camel, eat scorpions and locust—very poor fare, I tell you—and to find water in a desert without a map. We nearly died that year, but he insisted it was the best way to learn survival skills. After that, I accompanied James and my father, now and again, to dozens of exotic locales. The American southwest, the Argentine, India, China, Russia—but my formal service began during the latter part of my second year at Oxford, when the foreign office sent me to Paris."

Charles sighed. "How different our lives have been. I was at Cambridge at that time, heading towards a career in mathematics, but I ended up a policeman instead. A good life, I suppose, but I now begin to think it all according to God's design. You know that verse about all things working for good?"

"*For we know that all things work together for good to them who love God; to them who are called according to His purpose.* Romans 8:28. I used to think it meant God could make a silk purse out my sow's ear, if it served his plans, but I begin to wonder if it isn't deeper than that."

Charles kept his gloved hands inside his pockets, pondering how the earl dealt with the low temperatures. "I believe Beth and I were always meant to be together. If I'd made other choices, how God might have worked those choices towards the same end?"

"You could drive yourself mad trying to reason it out, Charles. Look, I know I've told you that this maze world you and Beth were trapped in was a dream, but I admit to being wrong. You've only been part of the inner circle since October, yet your faith in the unseen truths of this world surpasses mine; despite my having grown up with it."

Aubrey grew quiet for a moment, and Sinclair allowed him the silence. The one thing he'd learnt about Paul Stuart was that the earl's silences usually meant his mind was struggling with something. The night breeze blew through Aubrey's chestnut hair as they walked, and overhead a white owl circled.

"All the grain kept for the horses must attract mice," Sinclair said, pointing to the owl. "I'm glad our feathered guardian likes rodents."

Aubrey stopped, his eyes on the sky. "I don't remember ever seeing a white barn owl. Not solid white, anyway. Strange."

They walked further, passing the stables, reaching the halfway point to the other house. "Charles, I'd like to talk about Lorena. I hope you didn't think me presumptuous in bringing her to Queen Anne. I should have asked your permission first."

"Not at all. You did the right thing. After what happened to Morgan, I understand your fears for MacKey. I just want to make sure no one in the circle treats her unkindly. We have to be better than Redwing. Abusing women is not allowed."

"Thank you," answered the earl. "She's a strange one, but I think her more victim than conspirator. Did she tell you that Anatole's brother impersonates him?"

"Raziel? Yes, I'm familiar with his abilities. It may have been Raziel who tempted poor Gertrude into betraying her mistress. She was another woman hurt by Redwing's actions. I pray she's with God now. Tell me what you think about Serena di Specchio."

"The countess? I'm not sure, why?"

"She danced with me at the ball last Saturday, or I think she did. I believe she caused me to fall into a trance of some kind. If there is an evil woman involved with our enemies, then it's di Specchio."

Paul nodded as they reached the edge of the main gardens. "Di Specchio. Funny, her name's Italian for looking glass."

Charles stopped, staring at his cousin. "Why has no one mentioned that before? Paul, I want to know everything you can uncover about the countess. Her origins, family, associations. Everything."

"I'll have Deniau start on it right away. He's returned to France to search for information about Beth, but he has men stationed in Venice. Also, we should learn more about Urquhart. He has Parisian contacts that Deniau can track down for us. Shall I go there myself once Beth is found?"

"No, I prefer you stay here. That is, if Salisbury will allow it; which reminds me, I promised to talk to the prime minister this week. He left me a note when he called last Friday. He and the Home Secretary have some notion of keeping me on with the Yard."

Paul laughed. "Not exactly with the Yard, but a new branch that oversees parts of it. Salisbury asked my opinion when he was here, and I think it's brilliant. He and Matthews received permission to create a new commissioner position that reports directly to the Home Office and sits on the cabinet."

"A *new* commissioner? How can a new commissioner be part of Scotland Yard? It has but one with that title."

"Actually, you'd be the Commissioner of Intelligence for the Home Office, but as such, you'd have authority over the CID."

Sinclair shook his head. "It makes no sense, but if Beth agrees to it, then I'll be happy to say yes. If that happens, then you'll need to see to the day to day running of the ICI. I'll tell Salisbury that my acceptance hinges on the condition that the foreign and war offices no longer take you as their own. I need you here."

"Shall I salute, sir?" the earl teased.

"Only during working hours."

As they neared the back entrance to the mansion, Aubrey turned to a different topic. "One thing, though. If I do have to leave England for any reason, I'd ask a favour."

"Anything. Just name it."

"Keep watch on Della for me. She loves you dearly, and I think you love her as well."

"She's like my own daughter," Charles told his cousin. "I couldn't love her more, if she were."

"Then be a father to her, Charles. I'd considered telling her the truth about her mother—about me—but I've left it too late, I think. She sees me as her big brother, and I'm content with that. I'm not really parent material, anyway. Some men are natural fathers. You're one. I'm designed to spend nights in doorways without a coat. My career leads me into dangers that I prefer remain separate from my daughter. If she's in your keeping, then I know she's safe. And loved."

"Whatever you want, Paul, but Della would understand. She'd love you no matter what."

He shrugged. "Then, let me continue as her brother."

They entered the back doors, surprising the servants, who'd been in the process of closing down the kitchen. The housekeeper was holding a glass of wine in her plump hands, and the butler had doffed his livery coat and loosened his tie.

"Sir! We had no idea you and his lordship were planning to call," Miles explained, hastily bowing and simultaneously tying his tie whilst reaching for the coat.

Paul instantly put them at ease. "Stay as are, please! Mr. Miles, we did not warn you because we decided last minute to call, and it seemed easier to come through the park. Lord Haimsbury and I are here to do a bit of detective work. We plan to take a look at the mirror the duke stored in the garden shed, but first we'd like to examine the duchess's apartment. Is it locked?"

"No, sir. Shall I go with you?"

"We can find it on our own, but if the shed is locked, we'd appreciate the key. Do you mind if we use the back stairs?"

Miles looked surprised, but he followed orders. "Not at all. You're sure, you don't require my assistance?"

"No, I don't believe we do," Charles replied. "Please, you and Mrs. Meyer return to your evening," he told them as he and his cousin started up the servants' staircase.

Once at the landing, Charles paused a moment to find his bearings. "It's this way, I think. Yes, all right, now I know where I am.

This corridor leads to the guest library and main gallery. We turn there, continue past the ballroom and then right. From there, up a half flight to Beth's apartment. Is that it?"

Paul nodded. "The house is a bit of maze, but yes, that's it."

In five minutes, they reached the top of the short staircase, and the two cousins turned into the hallway that led to Beth's private rooms. Charles noticed the door to her bedchamber looked new. "Has the door been replaced?" he asked, turning the knob.

Paul followed Charles through. "You don't remember? We had to break it down to enter. Miles had a carpenter here the next day to install a new one."

The duchess's chamber felt cold, for the fire hadn't been lit in many days. "I miss her," Charles declared. "The room still smells like Beth."

"Raspberry and vanilla," Paul said, wistfully. "I've always loved that scent. The mirror stood just there," he said, pointing to the eastern window, "which put it directly opposite the door. When Beth came up, she must have found her maid right away, but Trent surely stopped Beth from calling out. Chloroform, you think?"

"Most likely."

"Alicia told us that she felt dizzy when she got up here. The girl had one glass of champagne, no more. Someone must have drugged it."

"A reasonable assumption. We'll need to determine who."

"Lorena, I should think."

"Possibly. After we broke into the room, what then?" Charles asked. "The head injury's left my memory rather fuzzy."

The earl sat on the edge of the bed. "We found the note. There was an envelope attached to the mirror's frame. It had your name on it in red ink."

"Yes, I think I recall that. It was from Trent. He told us to follow the map."

The earl nodded. "And we found Reid's map in the library, where Martin had stored it. There were coded numbers on it, indicating Ripper murders, but also others."

"The Victoria Park Killings," Charles said. "Yes, I remember that now, which is how we discovered the number next to my house. When did Trent put the note on the mirror? Before or after?"

"Let's find out," Aubrey told his cousin, pulling the bell rope. "I hate to bother Miles, but he's the one to ask."

In a few minutes, the butler knocked on the open door frame. "Yes, my lord?"

"Miles, we're sorry to interrupt you again, but the earl and I are puzzled about this mirror," the marquess answered.

"The mirror we moved, sir?"

"Yes, the one that stood here on my wedding night. It was not here before the wedding. Do you know anything about its arrival?"

The butler thought hard about the problem. "Well, sir, I believe the mirror arrived that afternoon. It stood inside a large crate and upon the exterior were instructions to remove the gift and install it next to the east window in my lady's chamber. The orders were quite specific, insisting the mirror face the door. I assumed the giver wished to make sure the duchess noticed it right away when she returned that evening. Is it important, my lord?"

"It might be," Charles said. "Was there an envelope already attached to the mirror's frame when it was unboxed?"

"An envelope? I don't recall, sir. We received many gifts that day, although most went to your new home. We usually sent them on, but this one instructed as I have said. Is there any news of the duchess?"

"Nothing more, but she will be found. I'm sure of it. The earl and I are searching for anything here that might offer a clue. Do you have the original crate still? Or the instructions?"

"Mr. Frame placed the mirror inside the crate and removed it to the shed. If there is an envelope attached, or if the instructions remain, I cannot say. Dr. MacPherson supervised its removal. He might offer more information. Shall I send for Frame, my lord?"

"No, if I wish to speak to him, I can do so tomorrow. That's all for now. I appreciate your help. Oh, but we will need the key to the shed. We'll come back down through the kitchen and fetch it on our way out. Thank you, Miles."

The butler bowed and shut the door.

Charles stood in front of the window, picturing the mirror in his mind as he sorted through his imperfect memories of that night. "All right, the instructions specified that the mirror should face the door, but was it to make certain she saw it?"

"Perhaps," Paul answered, crossing to the door and facing Charles. His eyes grew round. "I have it! What if the position of the mirror is part of a spell? Remember that Lorena said the mirror is a gateway to a realm called sen-sen? Perhaps, in order to cast the spell correctly and become this doorway, the mirror must reflect an actual door. Lorena said the second mirror is in a closet, which also has a door."

"Yes, I follow. Mirrors. What am I forgetting? Something Beth said." He paced a moment or two, his eyes on the sky outside. The white owl circled lazily over the park, as though scanning the area. "I remember! At the Kensington Ball last week. We'd thought Anatole had taken her, but it was actually Raziel disguised as his brother. When we found Beth at last, she had fainted, but she said some very odd things on the drive home. She said something about seeing visions in a mirror—wolves and children. But she also mentioned Trent. Is it possible that these visions caused her to faint?"

"If she saw Trent in a mirror, then perhaps he had access to worlds beyond our own. We need to learn more about these pathways, and we must find the second mirror."

"If it's at the Empress, we'll find it tomorrow," Sinclair told his cousin. "Assuming it hasn't been removed."

"Meg isn't likely to welcome me back, but I'm sure she'll allow you to enter, and not only because of your warrant card. Madam Hansen has a soft spot for you, Charles."

He smiled. "Yes, I know. She tried to seduce me—several times. Look, it's close to eleven. We should leave and let Miles get to bed. We'll fetch the shed key and look at the mirror, although, I may stay and talk with Lorena before heading back, Paul. You can go on home."

"And leave you here on your own? Not a chance. We came together. We return together."

Charles looked at the earl as if puzzling out a riddle. "You think me incapable of making it home on my own?"

"I think you're a target, Charles, which means you're in danger, but you're also recovering from a concussion. Besides, I like your company, so no arguing with me."

"You think I require a bodyguard?"

"Perhaps you guard me?" the earl countered.

Charles laughed. "Let's just say we guard each other from now on."

As promised, the *sen-sen* mirror stood securely inside its crate, bound with a chain, pages of scripture, and still showing the cross-shaped oil stain where MacPherson and Kepelheim anointed it. They found neither instruction nor red-inked envelope anywhere inside, but the two cousins decided to have the crate moved to another location as soon as possible.

Charles and Paul relocked the shed, kept the key, and then returned to Haimsbury House. They found the duke snoring in a corner chair of the drawing room, kept company by Beth's two dogs—also snoring. Charles roused the sleeping Scotsman and the dogs, briefed the human regarding the mirror, sent the animals upstairs to guard Adele, and then bid the duke farewell for the night.

Once Drummond's coach passed through the Haimsbury gate, Charles yawned. "Time for bed at last, I think. My brain wants to sleep, but my head pounds," he sighed as the earl walked his cousin to the master apartment.

"Emerson put a vial of white powder beside your bed. It's medicine. Add a teaspoon to a glass of water, and drink it all. He made me promise."

"If it's to make me sleep, I prefer not to take it," he warned his cousin. "If word comes about Beth, I want to easily awaken."

"No sleeping powder, just a pain reliever. It's made from willow bark."

"If it helps my headache, then I'm glad for it. Goodnight, Paul."

The earl shut the door, leaving Charles to face the quiet apartment another night without Beth by his side. He changed into a silver and blue striped night shirt, staring at himself in the large mirror inside the bath. "Mirrors," he said to himself, his hand touching the glass. It grew warm beneath his skin, and an odd sensation shivered through his body. He thought he saw Elizabeth's eyes within the glass, and dread clawed at his heart.

"Lord, please, tell me that my wife escaped that awful place!"

The idea that she remained trapped inside the stone realms drained him of energy, and his legs buckled. Charles caught himself on the edge of the porcelain sink, gripping it with both hands to keep from collapsing, but his hands had very little strength. Just as his fingers started to slip, a pair of friendly arms caught him.

"Gotcha!" It was Stuart, wearing only trousers and a shirt. "I decided to come back and make sure you took the powder. It's a good thing, too," he told Sinclair. "Steady on, Cousin. Lean on me."

Aubrey helped his friend into the bedchamber and started to guide him to the bed, but Sinclair refused. "No, not yet. I can't face it, Paul. Sit with me for a little, won't you?"

"If you insist," the earl agreed, helping him to the sitting area. "Dizzy? Shall I send for Emerson?"

"No, I just need a minute. The spell will pass."

"Charles, you must give yourself time to heal."

"Physically or emotionally?"

"Both. Look, Charles, Beth will return to you. I refuse to believe that the Lord will keep you parted for long. Perhaps, there's a reason why she's still missing."

"What might that be?"

"She may be recovering. The evidence I found at your old house shows that Trent tried to... Well, he tried to hurt her. If she left the house without her wedding clothes, then we have to believe she had help. Perhaps, Romanov told the truth. He may indeed have her."

"But if did he take Beth, why not bring her home? I'm still unable to sort through it all."

"Discerning the prince's motives will keep you awake for weeks, but since Lorena had already gone to bed tonight and asked not be disturbed, we'll have to leave it until tomorrow to learn more from her. I'll stop by and speak with her first thing."

"I'll go with you, and then after, we'll call at the Empress."

Paul sighed, his face revealing an unquiet mind. "I'd rather you stayed here. Let me handle the search."

"It's no easier for you than for me, Paul. You love her just as much as I do. I know it tears at your heart as well."

"I'll think about it, once we find her," the earl answered, picturing the ice block. "Now, go to sleep. I'll help you into bed."

"I can get there on my own."

"Probably, but allow me to make sure you don't collapse again. If not to satisfy me, then do it for Beth."

Sinclair smiled. "Very well. For Beth." He leaned on Aubrey's broad shoulder until reaching the bed. Once beneath the quilts, Charles pointed towards a tall bookcase to the right of the marble mantelpiece. "There's a red leather box on the third shelf. Could you bring it to me?"

Paul fetched the box and set it on the bed. "More of Beth's journals?"

"Yes, I've not finished them. If I cannot have Beth here, then her words offer the next best thing."

"I pray you find sleep, Charles," Stuart said gently.

"I'll sleep once she's home. Goodnight, Paul. And thank you."

The earl shut the door. Sinclair lifted the lid to the beautiful box. Inside, he found stacks of letters, written by Elizabeth to her grandfather through the years. Charles had read all the letters many times over, but Victoria had added several journals to the collection. Since turning six, Elizabeth had faithfully recorded her thoughts into embossed leather books, organised by year, and Charles removed the diaries written whilst she lived in France. He'd made it through many of the entries already and marked where he'd left off with a scarlet ribbon.

29 August, 1885

It's been over a year since I left London and still no word from Charles. I've written to Grandfather, but he will not tell me whether or not he posted my letter. I begin to doubt that he did, for surely Charles would write, if for no other reason than to tell me that he is still my friend but seeks nothing more from me. He's too kind a man to ignore me.

His wife Amelia remains in Ireland, I think, but it's possible that they've reconciled. Would he write to me if they have? Perhaps not. Victoria says I must put him from my thoughts, but it is so very difficult. I cannot explain it, but I feel more connected to Charles than to any other person on this earth.

God, grant me strength to keep on hoping!

15 December, 1885

Tomorrow, I leave for Branham to celebrate the Christmas season with my darling Mr. Baxter, Mrs. Alcorn, and so many others. Whilst there, I might take the train into London and shop for gifts. Perchance, if my carriage strays into east London, should I visit Leman Street?

No, that is too forward and pushy. I must wait, and let him decide.

But it is torture! If Charles would only write! I am sorely tempted to write to him again, regardless of what Victoria tells me. She called me a foolish woman and advises me to set my sights on Paul. He is my future, she tells me. If loving Charles is foolishness, then I shall remain a fool until the day I die.

3pm – Without any warning, Paul arrived at the château. He claims he's been working in Paris (although he'd said nothing previously), and he will travel with me to Branham and remain until I leave for Scotland in January. I suspect Tory contacted him. She either reads minds or reads my journal. I should be cross, but I know she has my best interests at heart. However, I do wish she wouldn't interfere! I love my darling knight, but I can no longer imagine being his wife as I once did. Is that cruel of me?

Paul leaves for America in February, but he's promised to return by my birthday. I shall be eighteen next April. If Paul proposes before I learn Charles's true feelings, I simply cannot say yes to him, but will it break my wonderful cousin's heart if I refuse him? Truly, I do not know the answer. Paul loves me, but I do not think he is *in love* with me.

Oh, my Captain! Please, my love, write!

16 February, 1886

Paul left for America today. Grandfather is also going away on a diplomatic trip soon, and I'll return to France, where I shall be isolated in the countryside!

Charles, my darling, wonderful friend, if only you were here. I know we are to be together. I know it! If only, you knew it, too. Shall I sneak away to London to find you? Would you think me young and foolish, as Victoria and Paul do?

I cannot sleep, I cannot eat. I dream of you each night. This is torture!

8, April, 1886

I am eighteen today, and I am doomed to marry Paul. I try try to keep cheerful about it. I only cry most nights now, not all of them. I shall do my best to be kind to my cousin, for he has shown me a new side to himself. It is odd, for the appearance of a visitor has given rise to a new aspect of Paul's affections.

Indeed, I believe he is jealous!

A young man named Prince Rasarit Grigor is staying with Dolly Patterson-Smyth, and he stopped by to bring me a birthday gift. Paul is visiting as well, and he behaved quite differently from usual. You might even call it 'clingy'. Dolly hosted a musical soirée, and whenever Rasha would ask me to dance, Paul would very quickly cut in, and he kept very close to me all evening.

I've never met anyone like Prince Rasha before. He's an unusual man: very tall, mysterious, and rather likeable, though somewhat full of himself at times. However, no man exists who could replace Charles St. Clair in my heart, but I really must try to forget him. Not one line has ever arrived from him, which must mean he has forgotten me. If I am so very forgettable to him, then I must find a way to leave this love behind and move forward with my life.

But it is so very difficult to do! The more I try to forget Charles, the more I think of him. His name is branded upon my very soul!

I must go to sleep now. I'm so very tired tonight. More tired than I've been in years. I pray for a dreamless sleep. The old nightmares have returned, and sometimes, I hear the Shadows talking near my window.

The one bright spot in my life is that Paul did not propose—but it is only a matter of time. Will I accept? I cannot think about that now.

10 June 1886

Today is Charles's birthday. I've been at Branham since late May for the annual fete, and I decided to make him a card, which I shall deliver to him in person when I go to London in a few days.

Charles, my love, do you think of me? You are thirty-one today. Happy Birthday, my handsome Captain!

14 June, 1886

London has never felt so empty, so devoid of joy. Tonight, I'm to sing at Lord Salisbury's. I suppose the one good thing that happened to me in Paris has been studying with M'sieur Bordelon, for he has worked wonders with my singing voice. Martin Kepelheim, a very kind and energetic man, who's known my grandfather and Paul for many years, will be accompanying me, and he is quite excited about it all. Martin's a very sweet man, and he managed to make me laugh many times, despite the ache in my heart.

Why does my heart ache? Why else? I tried and failed to see my handsome Captain. This morning, whilst Paul's attentions were turned towards Whitehall, I hired a hansom and rode into Whitechapel to visit the Leman Street Station House. Charles was not there! The desk sergeant informed me that his office is now at Scotland Yard. Tis the height of irony, for Charles now works in the same block of buildings as Paul!

Should I try to see him there, I wonder? I dare not. Paul's spies are everywhere, and he'd learn of it and scold me—but worse, he might blame Charles. I cannot risk that. Paul's behaviour of late is very strange, and though he and Charles are friends, I fear his reaction!

I keep praying that my Captain and I might one day be united, but I begin to worry that God's answer is no.

15 June, 1886

Last night's charity ball was a great success, and our musical selections well received. The Royal Opera director, Sir Anthony Delving, so appreciated our selections, that he asked me to sing there tomorrow night as a prelude. Mr. Kepelheim thought it a grand idea, but I said no. Perhaps, I should have said yes. I still could, I suppose. If I sang at the opera house, Charles might see my name in the news and realise I am in London. I doubt it would matter. I fear he has forgotten me.

Paul insists I must return to Paris next month. So I shall. He's to be my husband one day, and I must do as he asks.

Oh, Charles! Why have you not written? If only you'd been at Leman Street—but perhaps you were not meant to be. I have been praying and praying, but my prayers go unanswered.

Then again, the Lord may be saying no. Why does he allow me to love Charles, if we're not to be together? I do not understand it! Please, Lord, please! This is my heart's greatest desire. I beg you to grant it or else remove this love from my soul—for it is killing me!

The journal for 1887 was missing, but he found 1888's and thumbed through the entries. As before, Beth wrote over and over of her love for him, mentioning Paul's continued absence, broken now and again by a quick visit.

Then in April of that year, the Romanian prince made a second appearance.

9 April 1888

I am ill. Victoria has called in a doctor, and he says I have fallen victim to nervous prostration. Tory blames Paul, for he behaved most unusually at my birthday party last evening.

Dolly Patterson-Smythe hosted the party, and Prince Rasarit Grigor attended. Rasha is once again visiting Dolly (I believe Dolly and Rasha's late aunt were friends), and he brought me a gift, a hand mirror and brush made of ebony and layered in gold. The set once belonged to his ancestor,

Princess Erzsébet of Hungary and was given to her in 1658 by King Louis XIV, who'd taken her as his mistress.

The items are quite expensive, worth many hundreds of pounds, and Paul insisted I return them because the set is too intimate a gift and implies a relationship to Rasha which is improper. I've no idea why Paul would make such a statement, for I've received expensive gifts from other admirers—including him. He was so angry that he practically challenged Rasha to a duel over it!

Now, tonight, I am fatigued and can scarcely lift this pen to write, but my heart aches and I must get it all out. This pain and emptiness over Charles never leaves me. The nightmares continue unabated, and Charles often appears in them, but always as my rescuer. Upon waking, I am both happy and sad. A dream is better than nothing, but I miss him all the more for it! Tory says I must forget my handsome policeman and find contentment in marrying my cousin. Truly, I can barely think!

Oh, my sweet Charles! I could bear anything if I knew you loved me. I would walk through a lonely desert, if I knew you waited on the other side! Write to me, my darling. Please, write!

20 May, 1888

Paul and I had a terrible row last night. He is so very jealous of Rasha! The prince spends nearly every evening at our home, laughing and telling stories, and he often rides with me in the woods near Goussainville. Paul was supposed to leave again this week on assignment for the circle, but he's postponed it. He insists I am in danger. How can that be? Rasha is only being polite, and we are always chaperoned, so where is the harm?

Despite my protestations, I may return Rasha's gift to him. The mirror gives me a very strange feeling that is hard to explain. It's as though it looks back at me whenever I use it. Am I imagining it? Probably. I'm not sure. Sometimes, I hear voices, and my fatigue grows ever worse. All my doctors are perplexed. Some say I'm overwrought, others that I've suffered an insect bite, for there's a little wound on my throat that won't heal. It is very warm this summer, and many flies and other insects flitter about of an evening.

A large raven sits outside my window each night, but bats get into the attics and fly throughout the entire château, causing the servants to panic and a few have left us. Many talk of ghosts and something called a 'vampire'. It's all very strange.

I still dream of Charles, and last night, I dreamt we were married with seven beautiful children. On waking, I could still feel his sweet kiss on my lips, and it made me weep.

If only he would write to me, then I would recover! I'm sure of it. I am heartsick and desperate. And alone. I entreat the Lord for an answer, and thus far, the answer remains no. Will He never say yes?

I must keep believing that one day He will. I must!

Charles closed the diaries, glancing down at his wedding ring, the fulfillment of Elizabeth's dreams—and his. *She never stopped loving me. Never stopped hoping and believing, and I must not. Though everyone told her to give up on me, she never did. Not once. Beth trusted that Christ would eventually bring us together.*

"Thank you, Lord, for saying yes at long last," he whispered into the quiet darkness. "Though my darling Beth had no way of knowing it, I loved her all that time and also prayed for an answer. I believe that your plan was always for us to be together, but the timing had to be perfect. I beg you to return her to me, please! I will die without Beth beside me, Lord! I truly will."

He wiped tears from his eyes and turned down the lamp, lying alone in the silent chamber. He placed the bar of raspberry and vanilla soap beneath the plump pillow and lay back against it, allowing the sweet scent to calm his senses and still his aching heart.

Somewhere, his wife—his great and everlasting love—also looked into the darkness, perhaps ill and fearful. He had to stay strong for her.

And for their unborn children.

CHAPTER TWENTY-ONE

7:01 am – Monday, 26th November

Edmund Reid had slept very little. After tossing and turning most of the night, a constable had called at his modest home shortly before dawn. Now, as he arrived at the crime scene, the middle-aged inspector discovered why the matter couldn't wait for him to have breakfast. He passed by two constables guarding the entrance to the house. Both had almost literally turned green.

"That bad?" he asked Sergeant Joseph Meyer.

"Worse," the seasoned detective replied. "The body's this way, Inspector. As you can see from the marks on the hallway carpet, the victim was dragged through to the parlour. Sunders is working the scene, but I'll warn you. It's quite gruesome, sir."

"Worse than Mary Kelly?" Reid asked as he followed his officer into an elegant drawing room.

"I didn't work the Kelly scene, sir, but this one's a right mess."

The room was thirty by forty, width by length, and twenty in height. The pale blue walls displayed a variety of photographs and portraits, surprisingly, most were of women in various states of undress. "Is this a brothel?" he asked Meyer.

"The decor suggests it, doesn't it, sir?" the sergeant replied. "Though if it is, it's a new one."

Before inspecting the body, Reid examined the rest of the room. A trio of arched windows divided the south wall, their sparkling panes offering an unobscured view of George's Brewery. On the walls above each window, the inspector noticed a series of strange symbols, similar to pictographs MacPherson had once shown him. Each image was written in red, using a brush or perhaps a finger; probably, with the victim's own blood.

The floor carpet looked new, and the long drag marks Meyers had pointed to in the corridor continued through the door and across the floral design, ending in the centre of the parlour in a pool of blood.

Lots of blood.

A veritable orgy of blood.

Dangling above this crimson field, hung the dead man, upside down, his throat slashed, eyes protruding from the skull in shock. He'd been stripped of clothing, dignity, and finally his life.

"Good heavens, it's Lord Hemsfield!" Reid exclaimed as he saw the victim's face. "Has anyone notified Lord Aubrey?"

"The earl?" Meyer asked. "Should I have done?"

"Yes! Aubrey's been following crimes committed by the Earl of Hemsfield for over ten years. Send one of those ailing constables to Westminster, quick sharp! If he's not at Aubrey House, he'll likely be at his cousin's home, Haimsbury House. Ask his lordship to come at once."

"Very good, sir," the sergeant replied. "Antram! Over here, Constable. I've a mission for you!"

Reid gingerly stepped around the blood-soaked areas of the carpet and assessed the body. Gerald Dryden, 5th Earl of Hemsfield, hung by his right ankle from the primary downpipe of a cut-crystal gasolier. His hands were bound behind his back, and the left leg bent into an acute angle, the foot tied with electric wire behind his right knee. He wore nothing at all; not one stitch of clothing. The peer's pale, hairless chest was carved with the Roman numeral XII, and the throat slit from ear to ear.

"Choked, then bled dry," Thomas Sunders said calmly from the other side of the victim. "Morning, Inspector. This is one for the books."

"I can see that," Edmund muttered as he studied the corpse. "How do you know he was choked first?"

The physician used a fireplace poker to turn the dangling body around to show Reid the man's back. "See here, sir? Just below the hairline, you see ligature marks. If the purpose was to paint the room with blood, they'd have knocked him out first, then hung him up and slit his throat. But it looks as though the killers wanted to control the flow of blood and force it to pool below the body. Stopping the heart first allowed them to do so. Rather like hanging a pig. Kill it, hang it, then slice it from ear to ear."

"So I see. Why killers?"

"A guess, but a logical one," Sunders explained. "I'd estimate our victim weighs a little over two hundred pounds. If they killed him first as I suggest, he'd be dead weight. It takes a powerful man to lift and hang something that heavy from so high a pipe. You'll notice there are no marks on the carpet, indicating a stool or ladder was used. They might have moved it, of course, but I can find nothing nearby. And the room was found locked."

"Locked?" Reid didn't like it one bit. "The earl will have his work cut out on this one."

"Earl, sir?"

"Lord Aubrey. You remember him."

"I remember him well, sir. Will he be joining us on this one?"

"Most likely. Our victim is an old acquaintance of his. Look, Sunders, I want a thorough examination of this man's stomach contents, and run chemical analysis on the blood. I want to know if he consumed anything poisonous. Take samples from the carpet and also his veins, if you can find anything left."

"I'd planned to perform all those tests, Inspector, but it seems redundant to kill a man by so many methods. Poisoned, choked, and then dragged to a hanging to be bled like a pig."

"It might, but the scene is clearly staged. Also, compare any evidence found on the body to our Victoria Park victims," Reid suggested. "The manner differs, but those women were exsanguinated. It may be our killer expands his method to satisfy some twisted desire."

The weary inspector felt an overwhelming sense of dread. Sunders placed an arm around the policeman, for he'd noticed Reid's complexion pale suddenly, as though all blood left his face. "Sit, sir, next to this window. Did you have any breakfast? A full stomach at such a scene is more a liability than an asset."

"Thank you, Tom. Thankfully, I had no time for food," the inspector said as he took the chair. "Meyer!"

The sergeant had been speaking with a constable near the entry door and responded immediately. "Sir?"

"Send for a photographer. I want everything documented, including the writing above these windows. Be sure to take multiple plates of the man's pose. There's a message in it."

"Right, sir," Meyer answered, jotting the orders in his police book.

"Also, compose a list of everyone who works here, and no one is to leave the house before being interviewed," Reid continued. "Ask the butler what sort of business is conducted here, and if he keeps a record of visitors, either through calling cards or a guest-book. Also, get a list of everyone with a latch key. Oh, and send several constables to canvass the neighbours, especially the brewery. Ask whether anyone has suffered a break-in of late, if anyone noticed unusual activity near Lord Hemsfield's house, any strangers in the area, that sort of thing."

"Sir, I cannot say what business operated here, but this isn't Hemsfield's home."

Reid's eyes widened. "Then, whose is it?"

"According to the butler, the earl leased it a few weeks ago from an estate agency."

A dark sensation crept along Edmund's midsection, like an adder slithering through his bowels. "Don't tell me. Royal Estate Agency. Located on Wormwood in the city."

"Yes, sir. How did you know?"

"I fear that it makes a disturbing sort of sense. Sergeant, this will be a very long day."

8:47 am – Haimsbury House

Still clutching Beth's journal, Charles awoke to the sound of persistent knocking. "Yes? What is it?" he called sleepily.

"It's Baxter, sir. May I enter?"

"Yes, of course," the marquess answered, pushing himself into a sitting position.

The white-panelled door opened, and Baxter's wide face appeared in the dimly lit room. "Forgive me for waking you, sir, but Lord Aubrey insists you come down at once."

"Has my wife been found?" Sinclair asked throwing off the quilts.

"No, my lord, I'm afraid not. It seems there's been a crime in the east, which Inspector Reid considers of interest to you and the ICI. That is the name of your new endeavour, is it not, sir?"

"Yes, Baxter, it is, and I'll want to speak to you about that eventually. Is Dr. Emerson here this morning?"

The butler opened the cedar-lined closet and began selecting a suit for his employer to wear. "Dr. Emerson informed young Mr. Stephens that he had to attend a patient in Marylebone. An emergency, apparently. He hopes to return by midday."

"And my uncle?"

"The duke has not yet called this morning, sir. Lady Adele is practising her piano, most beautifully, I'm proud to say, and Lady Victoria is walking her dog. Shall I run you a bath?"

"No need. I took one last evening, and if I'm visiting a crime scene, I'll likely want one when I return," he answered running a hand across his chin. "I'll need to shave once my wife is found."

"Shall I fetch a bowl and razor now, sir?"

"No, it'll wait for the duchess. She may prefer the beard."

"Very good, sir. Will you be eating breakfast before departing with Lord Aubrey?"

"I rather doubt it, Baxter. Can Mrs. Paget pack me a sandwich or a few boiled eggs?"

"Of course, sir. I rather thought the dark stripe this morning," the efficient butler said, holding up a charcoal coat and matching trousers. The cloth bore a subtle stripe of pale silver through the weave, which Kepelheim deemed 'fit for a marquess'.

"If it's a fabric that's readily cleaned, it's perfect, Baxter. As you'll soon discover, my occupation takes me into environments that are apt to stain rather badly."

"I'd assumed as much, sir. I'm accustomed to removing blood from a gentleman's clothing. However, I pray the blood you bring home from this moment forward is not your own, sir."

"As do I, Mr. Baxter," Charles answered. "I'll carry the Sir John Bennett watch, of course, and I'll need my CID warrant card. For the moment, I'm still a Scotland Yard superintendent."

"I'd already thought of that, sir, and I set out your ICI warrant card as well. Just in case."

Fifteen minutes later, Charles descended to the main floor by way of the newly installed lift. As he exited through the scrolled safety grating, his cousin met him, dressed in finery of his own.

"I'd feared you might try the stairs, despite Emerson's warning. Have you decided to be more compliant?" the earl teased.

Aubrey wore a light grey suit in worsted, Merino wool with a matching waistcoat. A pocket watch of chased silver, hung from a fine chain that ended in a curious fob that looked like an eagle.

His cousin took note of the item. "Is that new? Don't you usually wear your father's watch and fob?"

"Yes, but it's being repaired. This is another of Father's watches, given to him by President Grant during his final week as British ambassador to the United States."

"That explains the fob. Our country owes a debt of gratitude to your father, Paul. And to you as well. Is there any news of Beth?"

"Possibly," the earl said brightly. "Sir Thomas is following its trail, though I doubt it will prove fruitful. If Romanov does have her, it's likely she's in one of his houses."

"And what of this lead?"

"Slender at best. A physician in Bethnel Green told Superintendent Keating at J Division that he'd treated a woman answering Beth's general description, but many women in London have dark hair. The duke put up a five hundred pound reward whilst you lay unconscious, and we've followed many a false trail. Galton will make a thorough search of it. The Lord allowed you to see and speak with her in this *Sebet Babi* realm; therefore, she is alive. Hold onto that truth, my friend. Trust in our Lord to protect her."

"That is my only thought right now, Paul. She'll come home. I know it."

Sinclair paused momentarily at the front door to take a small parcel from Baxter, containing two beef sandwiches, half a dozen boiled eggs, two apples, and a jam tart. "Is all this for me?"

"Mrs. Paget worries you'll go hungry, sir. She suggests sharing with Lord Aubrey should it prove too much."

"She's a dear woman and very thoughtful. Thank her on my behalf," Charles told him as Baxter helped him into a dark grey Chesterfield overcoat.

"I've put your gloves in the right pocket, sir. As you rarely wear a hat, I've not fetched it, but I'd be happy to select one, if you wish."

Sinclair actually smiled. "Baxter, you take very good care of me. No hat, but I appreciate the thought."

With a quick word of goodbye, the two cousins emerged from the main doors of Haimsbury House, bound for Whitechapel.

Inside the crested coach, they exchanged words about Lorena MacKey. "I wish we'd been able to talk with MacKey last night. I hated waking her, though, by continuing to knock. When you stop there this morning, was she awake?"

"I stopped, and I fear we missed our chance, Charles. Lorena's gone."

Sinclair's dark brows rose in concert. "Gone?"

"She must have left during the night, possibly before we called there to look at Beth's room. It may explain why she didn't answer your knock."

"We have to find her, Paul. Lorena's in danger, whether she knows it or not. I will not have her end up like Morgan!"

"She may have run because of me," Paul suggested.

"Regardless of why she ran, we must find her," Sinclair said, a nagging worry creeping along his scalp. *Something very bad is coming.* "Two women now elude us, Paul. Beth and Lorena. It's all connected somehow, but I can't reason why just yet."

"A hunch?"

"A dread. Tell me about this murder in Whitechapel. Reid sent for you, I take it."

"Yes, but the constable explained very little. Poor lad looked ready to lose his breakfast. He said the scene's quite bloody, but then, it may be the boy's first murder. He did know the victim's name, however, which explains why Reid sent for me. He's a man Galton and I have been watching for nearly a decade. Gerald Dryden, 5th Earl of Hemsfield. He served as banker for the Irish branch of Redwing for six years, then suddenly moved to Spain in September of this year to broker an arms deal. I've no idea when or why he returned to London, but Deniau will be annoyed, as its his net that was slipped."

"Was Hemsfield a Round Table member? Is he on Ida's list?"

"No, I'd remember that. However, I've never believed Ross's list is complete. My information indicates London's branch has three tiers. An outer level with seventy members, a middle with thirty-three, and both these lower tiers are directed by a secretive, third tier called The Round Table, acting somewhat like a board of governors. Trent led this exclusive group, which begs the question: who is his replacement?"

"Perhaps, that's the reason for the war," Sinclair said, his eyes on the Bank of England's twelve-pillared portico as they drove past.

"War?" Aubrey asked.

"Civil war. It's what Anatole warned me about. Both in person and through Lorena MacKey. He said the Round Table members would begin to fight amongst themselves, but that the infighting is but a symptom of spiritual battles in the hidden realms. Paul, when I was trapped inside that stone maze, the very air was thick with anger. What if rebellion manifests as more than just warfare against God's throne? What if it's ingrained in the very essence of those who hate the Lord? They'd spy, plot, and make plans like a band of deceitful courtiers. One would betray another, with all choosing a side, leading to uprisings and wars just like in our own world."

The earl smiled. "Your eyes are so much clearer than mine, when it comes to spiritual things, Charles. I envy that."

"Envy is an appropriate word, though I know you mean it well. Envy and greed lie at the heart of all rebellion. Something very dark is coming, Paul. I can feel it. Can't you?"

"Darker than we've already experienced?"

"Much darker," Sinclair observed, his eyes still. "Susanna Morgan told you that Trent and his companions committed the Ripper murders to provide the spiritual capital to free a Watcher from his prison. Lorena told me something similar. Raziel plans to release thirteen of these entities! If Ripper's crimes shocked and dismayed, then imagine what is to come!"

"Elizabeth told me something akin to that recently," answered Aubrey. "She called it moving shadows, scuttling about like spiders with plans. Her dreams return whenever the enemy draws near."

"Shadows," Charles whispered, taking a deep breath to clear his thoughts. "I read through some of Beth's journals last night. She mentioned in several that her nightmares returned, and it always coincided with the appearance of Prince Rasarit Grigor. Do we know what happened to him?"

"No idea, and I shan't miss him. I can have Deniau look into it, if you want. Grigor may have fled to France after what happened to Trent."

"Or he may have killed Trent. If so, then Rasha is stronger than we thought."

Aubrey's smile disappeared completely. "I'd not considered Rasha as a possibility. He always struck me as a coward, but if you think he may have killed Trent, I'll go to France tonight."

"No, Paul, I need you here. Let Deniau search for Rasha. We'll announce a reward and plaster his and Beth's photograph all over Paris. If either is there, someone will report it to the police."

"Perhaps, but I'd feel better if I investigated it myself, Charles."

"Anatole told Lorena that Beth is safe. Somehow, that's keeping me sane. If we've heard nothing more by the end of the week, then you can go to France. In the meantime, let Deniau handle it." The marquess knew his cousin's mind. Aubrey hated the idea of standing idle in England, if there was even a chance Beth might be in France, but Sinclair felt certain she was still in London.

"Rasha isn't the only one mentioned in Beth's diaries, you know. She speaks of her love for you many times. She called you her knight. Paul, I truly believe Beth would have married you, had you asked her two years ago."

"No, she would not," he declared, but showed no sign of anger. "That's kind of you to say, Charles, but our little duchess has loved you, and you alone, for many years. When she comes home to us, I want only for the two of you to find happiness together. Seeing her smile brings my heart greater joy than I can ever express, but I also find peace in your happiness."

The marquess smiled, the words touching his heart. "Thank you. The Lord gave me a great gift when he made us friends."

They turned onto Whitechapel Road, and to Sinclair's surprise, several passersby and costermongers started waving to the crested carriage, a visible sign of the Haimsbury-Branham union. Word quickly spread along the street, and soon a crowd gathered along the sidewalks. Men waved their brimmed hats, women curtsied, and street urchins ran alongside the coach to catch the eye of the inhabitants within its curtained interior.

"What's that all about?" the detective asked.

"Haven't you read any of this morning's papers?" Aubrey asked.

"I had no time. Why?"

"Your picture is on the front page of almost every edition. I'd intended to bring it up at our meeting later today at Queen Anne, but as you ask..."

"Yes?"

The earl began to laugh.

"Is it so funny?" Sinclair persisted.

"In a way, and you'll no doubt find it amusing as well. I haven't a copy with me, but the general sense of the reports goes something like this. Above a fine photograph of you with the queen, taken at your wedding, is a headline that suggests that Victoria is an illegitimate imposter, and you are the rightful heir to England's throne."

"I'm *what?*" Sinclair exclaimed. "That's preposterous! Why would anyone make up such a ridiculous story?"

"It's a rumour that floats now and then, to do with the queen's birth. Even before she was crowned, many at court believed Princess Alexandrina Victoria was actually fathered by Sir John Conroy, not the Duke of Kent. Conroy was personal secretary to the Duchess of Kent and comptroller of the duke's household—an advantageous mix, leading to hints of improper handling of Kent's finances. Conroy and the duchess were close. Very close. In fact, the entire court gossiped about their relationship. Even the Duke of Wellington thought them lovers!"

"Really?" Sinclair asked. "Why have I never heard any of this before?"

"It's circulated once or twice since you and I were born, but you probably didn't notice. James and my father pointed it out to me each time it made the papers. The scandal nearly broke the monarchy early on, but efficient handlers soon made it disappear. Our uncle's father had a hand in that."

"How?"

"James and the queen were born the same year, and when the question of legitimacy arose, Prime Minister Melbourne approached the old duke and asked if he might enact the Drummond-Branham Agreement, referred to by insiders at Buckingham Palace as the DBA."

"The document about the Plantagenet twins, you mean?"

"The very same. As we told you, every prime minister has to sign it upon taking the oath, and Lord Melbourne was no different. Although, our great-uncle believed Conroy was indeed Victoria's father, he had no wish for his son, our Uncle James, to take the throne. Privately, James and the Princess Alexandrina had become close friends, and our uncle was even considered as a possible husband for a few weeks. However, the circle members refused to approve the match, for it would have caused all Drummond properties to be absorbed by the Crown, and it might have violated the agreement, the DBA. The squabbling at the time was quite nasty with everyone taking sides, but with England still rebuilding after the Napoleonic wars, no one wanted instability—or God forbid, another war over who had the greatest right to the throne—and it eventually died down."

"I had no idea," Charles answered in amazement.

"After so long and successful a reign, I can only guess why someone's trotted it out again, but I suspect it's to do with Redwing's plans for your child."

"Or children," Sinclair replied without thinking. "Yes, child, of course."

"Is there something you're not telling me?" he asked as the coach began to slow. "Is this about that dream again? Forgive me. I hadn't intended to say dream. I do believe you, Charles. If you say you travelled, then you did, but just because you met two children there, it doesn't mean they exist here. Does it?"

"We'll discuss it later," Charles replied, his mind already on the crime scene. They'd stopped next to a three-storey terraced home behind St. Mary's Church. It looked relatively smart with freshly painted trim and washed brick. A black police maria stood near the side entry, and several uniformed police constables kept watch from the house's front porch.

Their driver, Hamish Granger, opened the door for the two peers. "Shall I come inside, sir, or wait with the coach?" he asked the marquess.

"Stay out here, Granger, but strike up conversations with the neighbours if you see anyone about. I'd like to know their opinions of our victim. Ask if anyone heard or saw anything."

"Very good, sir."

The cousins entered the house through the main door, and then passed into a wide foyer. Sinclair stopped before going further, closely examining the area. "What strikes you first, Paul?"

"The smell. Blood and urine," the earl answered honestly. "And excrement."

"Those are typical of a murder scene. What else?"

"Out here?" he asked, turning to look at the walls and floor. "It looks like most of the borough's nicer homes, though the photographs are a bit risqué."

"Aside from the photos, the house strikes as odd," his cousin disputed. "It's new. All of it. The wallpaper, the carpet, the furnishings. Even these shameless photographs look recently framed. It's feels like a set from a theatre."

Edmund Reid appeared at the end of the foyer, just at the turning towards the drawing room. "We're back here. I apologise for dragging you from your homes, gentlemen. Charles, I'm sure you'd benefit from a few more days rest, but I knew you and Aubrey would want to see this."

"It keeps my mind occupied," the detective said. "Have you spoken with Keating over at J?"

"About Elizabeth? Yes, he and I talked late last night. It's the reason I had very little sleep, actually. I spoke with the physician myself and showed him several of the duchess's recent photographs. His patient looked similar, but he thought older. Mid-thirties. I'm sorry, Charles."

"Thank you for looking into it, Ed. She'll come home. I know it. I cannot explain the peace in my heart, only to say that is must be from God. Now, as I'm still a Yard detective, tell me about this murder."

CHAPTER TWENTY-TWO

2:06 pm – 26th November, Istseleniye House

Prince Anatole Romanov entered the elegant drawing room to the warm sound of Riga's cello. Not wishing to interrupt, he quietly took a chair away from the main group, remaining in shadow. The prince's thoughts turned towards multiple rivers of possibilities as he closed his eyes, allowing the hypnotic music to usher him into a realm of waking dreams.

David Anderson, the former Mr. Thirteen, sat beside Brona Kilmeade, each enjoying the music's soothing qualities. The count had received the arrangement as a gift from Romanov only the previous week, and he'd originally planned to debut the work on Christmas night with Elbert Stanley accompanying him on the piano, but the others had persuaded the two men to offer a preview of the holiday concert. Called *Le Cygne*, the 6/4 time composition was one of fourteen movements within a greater work, *Le Carnaval des Animaux*. Camille Saint-Saëns had finished the suite in '86, but decided that only this movement, the thirteenth, adequately represented his genius and passions. Though intended for two pianos and a cello, *The Swan* was rewritten for a single piano, and when the prince heard it in Paris the previous spring, he immediately ordered a copy for Riga.

"Do you enjoy music?" Romanov asked Salperton. "I find it to be a river, upon whose mystical waves, my mind journeys to times and places beyond the present."

"That's an interesting way to describe it, Your Highness. I wonder, is such a river capable of transporting those held prisoner within the present?"

"You have a wry sense of humour, which does not escape me. You refer to the duchess, of course, and perhaps to yourself, also. You are not a prisoner, Lord Salperton. You may leave anytime you wish."

"No, I may not. You know perfectly well that I would never desert the duchess whilst she remains here. Sir, may I not speak to her husband? If you will not permit her to leave, then bring him here, or allow me to write to him."

"That is entirely impossible," Romanov whispered, not wishing to interrupt the performance.

"I find that answer insufficient if not deceptive," the viscount answered, his voice low. "I begin to suspect there are other reasons that you insist upon keeping them apart."

"My reasons are inscrutable to you, Doctor, for your discernment lacks refinement and reference."

"What sort of nonsense is that?" Henry asked, growing angrier by the minute, but the last three words echoed in the room—for the music had stopped, and the company paused briefly, before standing to applaud. The physician shut his eyes in embarrassment. "That was lovely," he muttered, as he started to clap.

Mr. Blinkmire failed to notice. He beat his hands together vigorously and jumped to his very large feet in admiration of his friends. "Well done!" the giant shouted. "Oh, very well done! I wonder, would you play it again? That brought me to tears, Count. Indeed, I could hear those dulcet passages every night!"

Riga bowed, careful of the crook in his aging back. He held the cello and bow in one hand as he indicated Stanley with the other. "I owe it all to our fine pianist. Elbert, I'd no idea you played with such delicacy. I shall enjoy working through the entire collection."

Anatole had also taken to his feet, and he offered both musicians a deep bow. "*Bravi! Bravissimi!* Not even in St. Petersburg's courts have I heard anything finer. Mr. Stanley, you are a talent indeed, and, Riga, your interpretation is unsurpassed. Mr. Stanley, how are you feeling this afternoon?"

"Much better, Highness. Not even a twitch these past few nights. Mr. Anderson and I owe you a great debt of thanks for your kindness, sir." The former policeman motioned to the newcomer. "David, my dear friend. Come here, please."

The bashful gentleman shuffled to the piano. "Sir?"

"Your Highness, though my friend is loath to tell you, Mr. Anderson's new medicine caused him a rather distressing side effect. Severe nausea. I wonder if his dosage might need adjustment?"

"Is this true, David?" the prince asked the man. "Have you noticed anything else?"

Anderson shook his head. Until the prince found him wandering along a road near Castor Institute, David Anderson had suffered months of hideous experiments at the hands of Alexander Collins and his assistants, Dr. Crispin Favor and Dr. Theodore Kepler. Any change was welcome, but he feared the side effects meant his wolf attributes might soon return.

"It makes it hard to sleep, sir. It's the moonlight. Though my windows are blacked out, a bit enters in now and then through the corners. I won't change again, will I, sir? I'm ever so afraid I might!"

"You will never return to that state, my dear friend. Never. The medicine may require adjustment. Perhaps, Dr. MacAlpin will agree to examine you."

"I'd be pleased to help," the viscount answered. "You're ill?"

"Not ill, sir. Just altered."

The Scot started to ask what he meant by such an odd word, but every head turned as Blinkmire suddenly thundered across the room towards the window.

The explanation for the outrageous behaviour was this: Kilmeade had been seated, and as the sun's angle changed, pyramidal beams entered through a gap in the drapery. The pale woman had winced at the bright light, and seeing her dismay, Blinkmire—ever the gentleman—rushed to attend the window.

"My dear Miss Kilmeade!" the great man exclaimed as he drew the drapes shut. "Do forgive us, please! We neglected to close them well enough. Moonlight may confound our Mr. Anderson, but sunlight disturbs your delicate eyes. I am so very sorry."

"You're a darlin' man, Mr. Blinkmire, an' there's no mistakin' it. I shoulda picked a chair out o' the light." She turned to Salperton. "So, will ya be takin' over all our treatments, Dr. MacAlpin? If so, me left eye is takin' on a new colour. I dunno if it's a good sign or no', but it's gone a bit bleary, if ya know what I mean."

Romanov glanced at his perplexed guest, who looked as though he had no idea what to say. "That is up to Lord Salperton, Brona, but as I must spend the day elsewhere, it would be a great comfort to me, if he would be kind enough to examine you."

"You're leaving?" Elbert Stanley asked.

"I've important matters to attend in another part of the city, but the house remains shrouded. No one will bother you in my absence, I assure you, Mr. Stanley. Lord Salperton will be here, and I'm certain he'll want to hear all your stories. I hope you will cooperate with him fully."

Kilmeade cast her pinkish eyes upon the viscount. "Sure an' we will. Doctor, would ya care fer a coffee?"

Henry had never been terribly comfortable with women. Two failed engagements had left him careful of entanglements, for they inevitably led to disappointment. "That's kind of you, Miss Kilmeade, but I must see to the duchess first. Perhaps, later. Prince Anatole, if you have a moment, I'd like a word in private."

"Certainly. Good day, my friends," Romanov told the household's company.

The two men left the drawing room, and the Scotsman followed the Russian towards the staircase. "How long do you intend to hold the duchess against her will?"

"Who said she is here against her will?" the elohim asked as Vasily arrived with the prince's cloak and cane. "I may be away overnight, Lord Salperton. As I told you previously, matters elsewhere demand my attention. If you would keep our duchess company until I return, it would ease my mind."

"Seeing her husband would ease her mind, sir!" the viscount exclaimed angrily.

Romanov remained unaffected by the outburst. "I'm sure it would, but that is not to be, not yet. However, as the duchess has improved, you might spend an hour with her in the garden. You'll find it quite delightful. The veil that protects this castle also keeps our gardens warm and ever-flowering, like eternal spring."

The prince tossed the cloak over his left arm, grasped the cane with his right, and departed. Alone with the butler, Salperton fought an overwhelming urge to summon the police.

"I'll be upstairs," he said at last. "And then, as it appears to be a command, the duchess and I shall have tea in the garden. Three o'clock, if that's possible, Vasily. She and I will spend the afternoon talking and enjoying this eternal springtime."

The crime scene near Whitechapel Road took nearly seven hours to process, and Charles sent Aubrey home to attend the circle meeting whilst he followed Reid back to Leman Street.

"It feels like an age since I sat in this office," he told his friend as he and Edmund entered the cramped space. The inspector hastily cleared three stacks of files from the sofa that sat along the wall opposite the desk.

"I'd not planned on guests," Reid said, smiling. "I can imagine the real reason you decided to avoid going home. You've always had difficulty keeping away from work. You're the only superintendent I've ever known who leaves his desk and investigates murders alongside his inspectors."

"I detest desks, and I feel energised in this awful place," the detective answered. "This battered old sofa always makes me think of Beth. It was here that I saw her for the very first time. Have there been many other sightings of her?"

"A hundred possibilities if there's one, and we've followed up on each. You can thank the duke's reward for the high volume, and I'm told you and Aubrey have added to it. A thousand pounds is a king's ransom hereabouts. We'll be up to our eyes in dark hair and eyes before long."

"We didn't intend to make more work for you, Ed."

Reid shook his head. "Overlook me. I'm lacking sleep. Charles, I'd spend a hundred hours a day to find the duchess. Hang the overtime. She'll find her way home. Elizabeth is resourceful, and it's obvious that she had help."

"Why do you say that?" Sinclair asked. "Prince Anatole, you mean?"

"Possibly. Paul told me about the prince's strange visit to MacKey. Why did you insist on speaking to her on your own, Charles?"

"I'm not sure," he admitted. "Perhaps, I felt we owed her a kinder reception than hauling her before a tribunal of circle members. Diedra Kimberley certainly had no kind words for the woman, despite her claims of ministry towards others. She may be genuine, but there's something about Dr. Kimberley that doesn't sit well with me."

Reid grew irritated. "Don't start me on Kimberley! She and I have never seen eye to eye on police matters. She's very opinionated, which you'll soon discover. Beware that one. She'll scratch your eyes out and then send you a bill to repair them. I've never understood why the duke allowed her to join the circle in the first place." The inspector sighed, his stomach growling. "Paul tells me that MacKey's disappeared again. Shall I issue a bulletin with her description?"

"No," Sinclair answered quickly. "We don't want Redwing to learn she's left us. Meg Hansen must have told them what happened. The longer they think she's in our protection, the longer she's safe. The circle will have to find Lorena without police help." He wiped his eyes wearily. "I'd forgotten all about Hansen. I'd planned to go there this morning. I'm too tired to do it now. It will have to wait until tomorrow. Ed, do you still have Trent's body?"

"We do. I could show it to you before you leave."

"I'd appreciate that," Sinclair told him. "William Trent remains a mystery. No one seems to know where he lived or where he came from. Except for a few clues, the man's entire history is blank. I'm sure Sunders has kept busy since last Sunday, but did he get a chance to examine it?"

"It's all in the report I left with the duke last night. Kepelheim may have it, actually. Tom mentioned a theory about the alterations in Trent's brain."

"His brain?"

"I can show you, if you want, but they weren't obvious alterations to my eyes. Sunders has made a study of the human brain and insists Trent's is very different. I'd call him in to explain, but he's up to his elbows dissecting Hemsfield's remains at the moment."

Sinclair leaned against the sofa, his head tilted backward, eyes closing.

"You should go home, Charles."

"I will. Eventually. Am I in your way?"

Reid smiled. "No, but you look as though you could fall asleep any moment. If you won't return to Westminster, let me fetch a pillow and blanket."

"Not necessary. Paul mentioned a series of fires in the city. Apparently, the fire brigade head..."

"Eyre Shaw."

"Yes, Shaw thinks there's an arsonist loose. Is Redwing involved?"

"I doubt it. It's more likely the IRB. The Brotherhood has been conspicuously quiet lately. Special Branch will look into it, I'm sure. Oh, I'd nearly forgotten with everything else. We received further information on the woman's remains found in the Thames. The one we identified as Susanna Morgan."

"Yes?"

"Charles, we may have gotten it wrong. I wired Chicago for a full description for this Cassandra Calabrese. I understand that's her legal name, correct?"

"So Paul tells me. Why?"

"It seems Miss Calabrese has an arrest record for prostitution and gambling. The booking form used by the Chicago Police Department is thorough, listing scars, height, weight, and so forth. If the body we fished out of the Thames is Morgan, then I'll eat my hat."

"The details don't match?"

"Not at all," Reid declared. "When Sunders measured the femur of the only leg recovered, he estimated the victim's height at just over five feet, but the form from Chicago lists Calabrese as five foot eight."

"Paul said she was tall. Go on."

"The form also lists Miss Calabrese with naturally dark hair. Specifically, it says , and I quote: 'red hair with black roots, but other hair also black'. As I said, they're thorough. Our victim had red hair with roots of the same colour, a natural redhead, which leads to me question whether the woman in our cold room is someone else. Susanna Morgan may be alive."

Sinclair stood. "That is news my cousin will want to hear right away. If Susanna is alive, then we now have three women missing in London. Beth, MacKey, and Morgan. There's a pattern here, Edmund, but I cannot yet see its shape. I will, though. God help me, I will!"

3:10 pm - Istseleniye Castle Gardens

Elizabeth Sinclair had recovered enough to sit for short intervals, though her cough returned when she least expected it. The fever had left her, and she'd begun to feel like talking. After discovering the wonder of Anatole's impossible gardens, Henry suggested they spend the afternoon in the orange orchard. Vasily set a table with quartered sandwiches, a variety of cheeses, Russian and French pastries, sparkling wine, tea, and fruit. Above their heads, an impossible sky shone in shades of azure, and the equally impossible sunshine painted the scene with dancing light. Their table stood beneath a canvas canopy, placed there for their picnic, and muslin curtains billowed in the gentle breeze. No real spring day could have been more perfect.

"I feel as though I'm dreaming," Beth told her companion. "Am I?"

"If so, then we're sharing the dream. Tell me, Duchess, how did you meet your husband?" Henry asked her.

"It's a long story, but Charles rescued me. It was in 1879, and I was a week or so shy of my eleventh birthday. He helped me through a very harrowing time. Have you ever heard of a man called Trent? Sir William Trent."

"The prince asked me that only recently. I'm afraid I don't know him, not personally."

"Consider yourself blessed," she told him. "He killed my mother. And he wanted to do terrible things to me," she paused, her mind almost recalling the night of her wedding, but as quickly as the thought arrived, it vanished again.

He noticed the shadow in her eyes. "Beth, are you all right?"

"Yes, I think so. It's probably best I don't speak about Trent. Tell me your story, instead. How do you know Anatole?"

"Does anyone know him, I wonder? As to how we met, it happened only last Monday night, when he called at my home and asked me to treat a guest who'd fallen ill."

"Me?"

"You," he answered, his eyes filled with admiration. "Since that night, I've found myself, alternately, fascinated and outraged by the fellow. More often the latter."

She began to laugh, which surprised him.

"I've never heard you laugh before," he said, a similar effect crossing his own face. "I must say, it's quite pleasing, and it cheers my heart to hear it. Tell me, why do you think it funny that the prince annoys me? He does very little to engender trust in a man."

She continued to laugh, which caused her to begin coughing. Automatically, he left his place and filled a glass with water, helping her to drink it. "You may have left the house too soon. I'm a very poor physician to bring you out here."

"You're a wonderful physician and a very good friend. Thank you," she said, taking a deep breath. "It doesn't hurt quite as much as it did yesterday, and the sun feels so very good. Henry, do you think the prince will allow me to go home soon?"

"I've no idea. The fellow gives no timetable, saying only that you're in danger, but it strikes me as a thin excuse," he answered, clearly irritated.

She smiled softly, her eyes wide. "You don't like Anatole, do you?"

"Not particularly, no."

"Neither does Charles, though he's come to trust him a little. Oh, Charles," she whispered, her face losing serenity. "I'm very worried about him, Henry. If I knew that he's safe and well, it would grant me a great deal of peace. I'd be content to remain here as long as Anatole wishes, but I must know about Charles. Is there a newspaper I might read? I'm sure the press would have written about what happened. I don't recall very much, but I've a vague memory of fire, and there's something else, like a dull ache behind my thoughts that won't go away. I'm sure I saw Charles in Whitechapel, and there was snow on the ground. And wings. Oh, why can I not remember it!" she exclaimed, her hands twisting in despair. "Henry, I fear Charles might be injured. Why was he trapped in that awful place with me, unless he, too, is ill?"

"I'm afraid the castle takes no recent papers. Apparently, they're forbidden. The prince's orders. Still, there might be a way," he continued, leaning in close to whisper. "Vasily keeps watch on the house by day, but retires each night at eleven sharp. I could ask Mr. Blinkmire to safeguard your door whilst Miss Ross sits with you. If I can hire a hansom near the cemetery, I believe I can make it to Westminster and back in two hours. Is there a doctor whom you trust that I could ask about your husband?"

"Yes!" she answered excitedly. "If Charles is ill, then either Reggie Whitmore or Michael Emerson would be tending him."

"I know both those men, and Emerson and I are old friends. He used to see patients at St. Mary's. I could try there. A night porter or nurse might offer information. Does he keep a house in London?"

"He often stays at his father's home in Mayfair, but if Charles is ill, then Michael might be staying at Haimsbury House. Henry, do you really think you could discover what's happened and then return here before Vasily or the prince learns of it?"

"I'll do my utmost to achieve it. I'll go tonight, if you're well enough to manage a few hours without me." She nodded, anxious for any news of her husband. "Good. The prince thought he'd be away all night. If I'm quick, I can find out about your husband and return to my bed well before dawn."

11:17 pm – Haimsbury House

Charles stayed at Leman Street until nearly eight, finally leaving only because Reid insisted he go home and rest. He and Aubrey ate a late supper in one of the home's smaller drawing rooms, a brightly painted parlour called the Cumbria. The duke joined them at ten, and he and Kepelheim played a round of chess, whilst Charles perused that day's newspapers.

"Utter nonsense," the detective muttered, turning a page.

"I take it you're reading about your royal status," his uncle said as he moved a white knight into position. "You're in trouble, Martin. Better mind your queen."

The tailor stared at the board, considering all possibilities. "Yes, I see that, but I might be luring you into making a false move, Your Grace."

Sinclair threw the paper against the cushion of a nearby chair. "Even the *Pall Mall Gazette* ran this ridiculous story! I hope Della hasn't seen any of these."

"She rarely reads the papers. Besides, our girl spent the day making cards for Elizabeth's homecoming. Watercolours or something. Oh, Paul, I received a letter from Baron Wychwright. He asks if he and his family might call this week. I rather think he's heard the rumours."

"Which one?" Aubrey asked. "Those regarding Beth, or the rumours about Charles?"

"Both, I should think. Charles, you mustn't let these reports get under your skin. These rumours regarding the queen surface with regularity."

"But why do they surface now, James?" Sinclair asked. "And with hints that I'm the better choice to sit on England's throne? I do not like it one bit!"

The earl had been making notes for Laurence, Deniau, and Galton, but set the notebook aside. "The conclusion one must draw is your child. Or is it children? You keep using the plural term, which makes me think you know more than you're saying. Have you information beyond this dream—I mean your journey? Which is it? Child or children?"

Sinclair glanced at Martin. "Either and both. I don't mean to be obscure about it, but I can't state it as fact. As you still doubt whether or not I really visited another realm..."

"No, I don't doubt it. I've told you, I simply do not understand it, but neither do you."

"May we, please, change the subject?" Sinclair asked, his head aching.

"Go to bed," the duke told him, a white pawn changing position. "Checkmate!"

The tailor sat back, his grey eyes round. "Your Grace, if I weren't a Christian man, I'd have to wonder just where you've been keeping that pawn."

The duke laughed and began resetting the board. "I never reveal my secrets. Paul, take your cousin up to bed. That is an order."

The earl stood. "Come, Cousin. Our uncle is still head of the family, and therefore master of us as well as master of the chess board. We'll share a brandy and talk a bit. Goodnight, gentlemen," he told the others.

"See you tomorrow, Nephews."

"Goodnight," Kepelheim said, his mind on the new game.

The two cousins left the drawing room and used the lift to reach the upper floor. Once inside Sinclair's bedchamber, Aubrey filled a pair of snifters with brandy and handed one to Charles.

"To Beth," he said, clinking the other's glass with his own. "Our beautiful princess and mother to the next generation."

"To my wife," Charles said, smiling. "May she return to us before another day ends."

"Indeed!" Aubrey said, taking a sip. "Nice bouquet, this. Napoleon may have been an overly ambitious scoundrel, but he knew his wine. Charles, you really think Beth's having twins, don't you?"

"For many reasons, yes, I do, but we'll confirm it once Beth is home. Paul, there's something I need to tell you."

"About Beth?" he asked, sitting into a leather chair.

"About the body that washed up along the Thames."

"Susanna's?"

"No, not Morgan's. Or probably not. I spoke with Reid today, and he no longer believes those body parts belong to Morgan. In fact, he's convinced it's another woman."

The earl's blue eyes widened, and he set the snifter aside. "Why would he think that?"

"Because of a report he received just yesterday from Chicago. That city's police department keeps detailed information on each prisoner. Cassandra Calabrese, also known as Susanna Morgan, was arrested in 1876 for prostitution and gambling. She was bailed out by end of day by her father's solicitor, however, her booking form had already been filed. It describes her as five foot eight with red hair and dark roots."

Aubrey smiled. "I always suspected she dyed her hair. And the height is correct. Why does this alter Reid's conclusion about the embankment body?"

"I'm getting there," Sinclair assured his cousin. "As you know, that body was dismembered, and not all the parts were found. We do have the upper left leg, and Sunders used a mathematical formula to determine the victim's living height, based on the length of the femur. The woman was barely over five feet tall. It's my belief that someone wanted us to think it was Morgan, and probably inflicted the burns and other markings to make the case."

Aubrey's face passed through a dozen different emotions. "If you're right, then Susanna may yet be alive!" he exclaimed, standing. "I'll start looking right away. If she's in London, then she'd hide herself in the darker parts of the city. I'll start with the music halls."

"We'll make a start tomorrow, Paul. I've already put two inspectors on it. James insists I sleep, but I would offer you the same advice. Three women now require that you and I use every brain cell God gave us. Redwing has declared war on us and on its own members. We may not wish to sleep, but our tasks require that we try."

"Then take some sleeping powder, Charles. If you will, then I will."

The detective sighed. "Very well. Just this once."

Aubrey left for his own apartment, and Charles shut the door. He changed into a pair of yellow pyjamas, added a teaspoon of soporific powder to a glass of water, drank it down, and then slipped into the bed. The chamber maid had removed the bar of soap, but placed it into a drawer nearby. He found it and returned the scented bar to its previous spot beneath the pillow. As the powder took effect, Charles drifted into a pleasant dream, his senses filled with thoughts of Elizabeth and the sweet scent of raspberry and vanilla.

1:13 am

Sinclair was torn from the dream by heavy pounding and shouting, just outside his chamber door.

"Charles!" his cousin called, knocking again and again.

Too impatient to wait for a reply, the persistent earl burst into the room and switched on the electric chandelier. Stuart was fully dressed and wearing a dark brown coat of burnished leather. "Wake up, Charles! Wake up! We know where she is!"

The sleeping draught had hit him hard, and Sinclair lost his balance as he struggled against the bedcovering and spilled out of the bed's warmth. Aubrey caught him.

"Where is she?" the marquess asked, shaking his head to clear it.

Stuart set him into a chair and then started gathering clothes from the closet. "It's not an easy place to find, but there's an old friend of mine here, who thinks he can show us. It's turned very cold. You'll want to dress warmly." He handed Charles the same wool trousers and braces he'd worn the previous day along with a clean shirt, socks, shoes, and a suitcoat. "There's no time for anything else. Hurry!"

Sinclair dressed in five minutes, and the cousins took the stairs rather than the lumberingly slow lift. By the time Charles reached the main floor, the sluggishness had worn off, replaced by rising hope. Emerson and a second man, unknown to Sinclair, stood waiting near the north entry.

"Michael, where is she?" Charles asked.

"That's a bit complicated. To explain it, let me introduce Dr. Henry MacAlpin, Viscount Salperton. He and I studied together at Edinburgh, but it seems that Aubrey knew Salperton at Eton and Oxford. Henry tells the story better than I."

The viscount had never intended to reveal the location of Istseleniye Castle to anyone, but he'd blurted it out without thinking when he'd found Emerson still awake at his father's home in Mayfair.

"Sir, it's an honour, and I apologise for calling at this late hour. I've been attending your wife since Monday last, and I'm happy to say that she's mending well."

"Beth's alive?" the marquess asked, his knees weakening.

"She is alive and asks for her Captain hourly, sir."

Charles nearly fell to the floor, but Baxter caught him in a bear hug beneath the armpits. "Let's get you to a sofa, my lord," he said gently. "This is too much for you."

"No, no, we must go and bring her here. Why didn't she come with you?"

Salperton sighed, casting his eyes upon the other men uneasily. "I fear that is rather difficult to explain. You see, Prince Anatole insists that..."

"Anatole?" Charles repeated. "Then Lorena told the truth. Romanov's had her all along. But she's well?"

"Yes, sir, she's on the mend. Romanov's a very strange fellow, and I cannot say whether I trust him, to be honest, however, he did fetch me to look after her. The duchess was quite ill when I first saw her. Feverish and unable to awaken. She had a mild case of pneumonia, but she is, as I say, improving daily."

"I pray I'm not dreaming," Charles said as he took a seat on a carved mahogany bench twixt a pair of potted ferns. "She's alive. My wife is alive." He wiped tears from his face. "Tell me, why hasn't Romanov brought her home?"

"He claims that the duchess is in danger from a group called Redwing. It's preposterous, I know, but he will not back down from it."

Baxter interrupted. "Forgive me, my lord, but why did this prince hire you to tend my lady? Are you known to His Highness?"

The Scotsman laughed. "Hardly! Originally, I'd assumed he brought me in because my clinic lies close to his castle, but it's more complicated than that. I shan't take up our time by getting into all this now. Lord Haimsbury, if you insist on returning with me, I warn you that the prince may not allow you to enter. If he is there, I mean."

"Why wouldn't Romanov be there, Henry?" Aubrey asked his Oxford friend.

"He left early this afternoon, stating only that he had work to accomplish and might be away the entire night. He's frustratingly mysterious!"

"And no one saw you leave?" asked Emerson.

"Not that I noticed. I waited until the household staff retired before leaving. However, even if the prince has not returned, his butler will likely prove unfriendly. He takes his orders quite seriously. Of course, all this assumes we can even find our way back inside! The castle is shrouded by very peculiar mists. It took me the better part of an hour just to find my way out of them."

"Shrouded?" Aubrey asked. "Charles, we might be smarter to wait until morning. If the Russian has placed supernatural wards upon the castle, then it could prove dangerous to enter. Not only for us, but for Beth."

"What do you mean?" Sinclair asked his cousin.

"He isn't shrouding the place from humans, Charles. If I understand the process, passing through these wards weakens them. I imagine that anytime Anatole does, he repairs the wards and locks right away."

Henry grew concerned. "Paul, if you're right, then I fear I may have done a very foolish thing. My own passage through the wards, as you call them, may have caused a breach. The main gates are rather like a maze, and I became lost. I pray I've not bumbled this! I only wanted to see about your own health, Lord Haimsbury, and report back to Elizabeth. She is consumed with worry over your welfare, and I sought only to offer consolation."

"We go tonight, then," Charles announced. "Baxter, fetch my overcoat and several weapons from the armoury. If I know my cousin, he's already carrying a pistol, but I'll require a shotgun and at least two handguns. Michael, you needn't come with us, but I'm afraid we need Henry's guidance."

"Am I not allowed to enjoy a bit of shooting now and then?" Emerson asked, smiling. "I'll take a pistol, if you have an extra. My aim might not match yours or Aubrey's, but I can hit a rabbit when I must."

"I rather doubt we'll be shooting rabbits tonight."

The earl checked the cylinder of a prototype, single-action Remington revolver and added two boxes of .44 Winchester shells to the right pocket of his leather overcoat. "I only pray the targets are material. We may be heading into a repeat of last Sunday night, Charles."

"Then so be it," Sinclair answered resolutely. "I will not leave Beth there one night longer. We bring her home or die trying."

CHAPTER TWENTY-THREE

1:33 am - Istseleniye House

Count Viktor Riga had a reputation as a great and monumental snorer. The Romanian's hooked nose and high cheekbones combined into a magnificent resonance chamber that allowed the sound created by the vibration of his soft palate to proceed from the nasal cavities in an almost musical tone. Riga's apartment sat opposite that used by Blinkmire, and the gentle giant had often mused that listening to the count's nightly concerts was akin to enjoying a solo from the French horn section of a symphony orchestra.

The castle's company had spent most of the evening hours listening to wax cylinders of Wagner's *Parsifal*, recorded earlier that year in Turin under the baton of a young musical genius named Arturo Toscanini. The prince had purchased the cylinders whilst in Italy that August, and the nuances of Wagner's portrayal of the famed tale of Arthur and his grail knights, brought tears to every eye within the castle's fellowship.

After enjoying the entire set of cylinders and watching two games of chess, the duchess had gone upstairs on the arm of Henry MacAlpin. Ida Ross joined them shortly afterward, having already promised the physician that she'd keep watch on the duchess during the night. Ross had warned Salperton that Anatole's rules should never be broken, but the gentle-hearted young woman also worried about Sinclair, a man for whom she still cared deeply.

"Do not delay," she told Henry. "Sometimes, the prince says he will be gone the night through but returns suddenly, with no warning at all. He has the power to hear thoughts and can pop out of thin air."

"Do you trust him, Miss Ross?" Henry had asked her.

"He saved my life, sir. How can I not? Now, go. Mr. Blinkmire has promised to remain in the parlour all the night through. Do be careful, my lord. Beware of all who follow you. The prince has many enemies, and not all are human."

That had been hours before, and Ross now slept soundly in the chair next to the duchess's bed. She'd tried to keep awake by reading Sir Thomas Malory's *Le Morte d'Arthur,* which the count had given her, but Ida had found it tough going. And so, the book of poetry lay upon her lap, open to chapter twelve, titled *How Elven Kings Gathered a Great Host against King Arthur.* The very last line she'd read was: 'And now they sware that for weal nor woe, they should not leave each other, till they had destroyed Arthur.' At that point, the former prostitute shut her eyes as though dosed with a sleeping powder and entered a deep dream state.

Within the warm parlour next door, Stephen Blinkmire also snored; however, the brash snuffles and wheezes produced by his pig-like snout sounded nothing like a French horn, but rather like the dissonant belching of a fishing trawler's whistle. The large man's head tilted back against the curve of the overstuffed chair, lolling from side to side as he slept. His tongue protruded ever so slightly from betwixt his teeth, and a droplet of saliva slowly coursed its way along the curves of his smooth chin.

Elsewhere in the castle, all stood in silence. Not another sound echoed throughout the great halls and drawing rooms. No mice scampered along the trim work, nor bats against attic windows; no windswept branches tapped upon the foundations; nor did a single creak or pop sound from the ever-settling stones. The mystical wards placed around the property shimmered, casting a ghostly air about the ancient castle, and to passersby, it seemed little more than a ruin from ages past.

Then everything changed.

Quick as a blink, an iron spear point, tipped in Greek fire, pierced the shroud just west of the cemetery, precisely where Henry had at last found the exit two hours earlier. Behind the spear, a muscled arm clad in bright armour followed, and behind this, the arm's owner burst through the portal. He stood thirteen feet high, his large head crowned in armour fashioned from black metal and smeared with blood. Every square inch of the battle dress bore inscriptions in an otherworldly script, which described the purpose of the armour, the owner's names, and his place within the hierarchy of the infernal realm.

The warrior elohim's primary name was Raziel, no longer in human form, but clothed in light and shadow cast by the lamps of a thousand elementals. Accompanying the fallen angel, flew an army of demons and gargoyles, teeth champing, red eyes fixed upon the castle and its sleepers. Raziel's gambit to lure Samael into sin by endangering the duchess had failed, and now his anger towards his traitorous brother knew no bounds. He charged at the windows, guided by blind rage and vengeance. The Watcher's plan was to seize the duchess and take Romanov captive.

"Leave only the duchess alive!" he shouted to his minions as they broke through the inner wards. "Find her and then slay them all!"

Inside the castle, Vasily heard the battle cries and animal-like snarls of the demons seconds before they broke through, and he hastily armed himself with two blades and a specially designed pistol, made to bring down demons. Antony, the two cooks, and Katrina also took up arms, and then the lady's maid raced from her bedchamber to warn the duchess.

Riga snorted to wakefulness, blearily wiping at his rheumy eyes. Despite his deformity, the hunchback hastily threw a woolen coat over his nightshirt, and even had the presence of mind to place a medical book in the pocket. He also placed a derringer inside, grabbed a knife from its hiding place inside a small desk drawer, and then rushed into the corridor to meet the invaders head-on.

The onslaught breached the upper floor from three directions at once, led by a trio of demonic lieutenants, each clad in battle armour and brandishing a variety of hellish weapons. Hybrid creatures that resembled sabre-toothed boars ran alongside these three, bursting through the doors so that the demons could search for Elizabeth.

"Burn it to the ground!" Raziel ordered his army, and a team of dog-sized dragons from the middle ranks rushed forward, blasting flame from their gullets. The fire sizzled in tongues of blue unlike anything known to man. Not even Greek or Roman fire could match it, for this flame burnt through supernatural structures and locks. The squeals and caws of monstrous bats and ravens rang in pitches so high that the ears of the frightened occupants of the castle began to bleed.

Ross covered both ears against the terrifying din, and she shouted for Blinkmire, who'd already roused from a strange dream of roaming the world as a three-foot-high man with red hair and spectacles. Now stone-cold conscious, the massive man raced into the room, reaching the duchess, who'd only just awakened.

"Here, my lady. Take this blanket and put it 'round your shoulders," he told her. "There is no time for anything more!"

The duchess did as instructed, and the pig-like gentleman lifted her into his arms whilst Ross placed a second blanket across Elizabeth's body to shield her from the supernatural flames.

"Stay behind me, Miss Ross! Put one of those blankets on yourself now. Don't look to the right or left. Just follow me!"

Carrying the duchess protectively, he led Ross through a secret panel that concealed a back staircase. The prince had taught all who lived there to meet in the brick pavilion behind the west garden wall should the castle's defences ever be breached. Special wards of highest strength were placed all along the passageway that Blinkmire now followed, and he met no intruders until they reached the final turning towards the garden doors.

A demonic dragon keeper and its fire-breathing sidekick had burnt through the final ward that protected the secret passage, and flames of blue pain seared into Blinkmire's thick hide, nearly causing the great man to stumble.

Refusing to drop his precious cargo, the brave man forced his bulky leg muscles to push harder, and he burst through the door and into the night air. The blankets that protected Elizabeth had caught fire, and Blinkmire used his hands to extinguish the hellish flames, scorching his palms and fingers in the process.

"Run to the pavilion beyond the little gate!" he ordered Ross and the duchess as he set her upon the dewy grass. "Do not turn 'round and do not stop—not even once!"

Behind them, the dragon appeared through the opening to the castle, ready to exhale a cloud of blue death into the moonlit garden.

Ross screamed.

The duchess shouted, "No!"

Blinkmire turned to face the monster, willing to die to protect the women.

The next four seconds ticked by in slow motion.

Elizabeth saw the dragon's midsection grow large as it sucked in air until its scales stretched to bursting.

The creature opened its mouth to slay her champion, and Blinkmire, still running, raised his hands to protect his face as he raced towards certain death.

The demon riding upon the dragon leapt into the air, and Beth perceived the glint of a spear. Both the flames and spear assailed the night air, gliding towards the doomed giant.

In the fourth second, a miracle happened. Viktor Riga came running around the corner of the castle's exterior wall, followed by Vasily, Mr. Stanley, Katrina, Kilmeade, and Mr. Anderson. The Romanian brandished a knife, and the butler carried a crossbow loaded with arrows tipped with a poisonous metal created in the mirror world of *sen-sen*. Vasily fired two arrows into the dragon's side and a third at the demon's head, causing the winged creature to sway wildly and then shut its mouth.

Blinkmire stopped when he saw Riga, which caused the hurled spear to miss its mark.

The demon vanished in a puff of smoke.

And to their great relief, the dragon-beast fell to the ground, dead.

"Well done!" Riga shouted victoriously above the riotous noise of the ongoing attack. "Anderson, help Blinkmire! Stanley, carry the duchess! Everyone else, get to the prince's special coach without delay! It's stored inside the brick pavilion! I'll stay with Vasily and fend off the others!"

Blinkmire was badly burnt, but had no wish to leave his friend. "Viktor, you must promise to meet us!"

Riga bowed and offered Stephen Blinkmire a wide smile. "If I do not see you at the pavilion, we'll meet you beyond the cemetery. Near the green. Go with God, my friend!"

An explosion obscured any further exchange of words, and a shower of stone fell all around the Romanian's feet, narrowly missing his head. "Come, Vasily!" the wily count told the butler. "There's a tunnel beneath the orange grove!"

The pair ran together through a narrow corridor of shrubs that ended in a planting of graceful orange trees where Beth had shared tea with Henry MacAlpin. The prince's shroud also kept the gardens in a perpetual state of blossom and fruit, and these mixed upon the branches in an otherworldly fashion. Rings of brick encircled each tree, and a small stone structure resembling a garden shed concealed the entrance to the tunnel. The others had already entered the escape route, and Vasily and Riga followed. As they ran along the tunnel, the butler turned back often to watch for signs of pursuit.

Inside the pavilion, Blinkmire and company had reached Romanov's special coach. Also built in *sen-sen*, the conveyance required no horses, and was operated by thought.

"How do I work it?" Stanley asked as the others found their seats. "I've heard the prince speak of it, but never seen it. Blinkmire, have you any ideas?"

"None at all," the huge man answered. "My lady? Are you all right?" he asked, ignoring the intense pain from the burns that covered his face and hands.

The duchess gave no reply, for she'd fainted from fear and smoke inhalation. Her lungs, which had only begun to heal from the bout with pneumonia, struggled to maintain oxygen flow to her blood and brain, and she'd lost consciousness.

"We have to hurry!" Blinkmire told his friends.

The pavilion door opened again, and the men turned, expecting to engage the enemy, but instead sighed in great relief.

"Riga!" Stanley cried out happily. "Come, quickly!"

The cooks, Katrina, Kilmeade, Riga, Antony, and Vasily piled into the large coach, which seemed much roomier within than it did from without.

"I've no idea how to work it," Stanley told the newest passengers. "Vasily, I pray you've a notion to offer."

"The prince has never allowed me inside it, but I believe it works by desire," the butler suggested.

Ross stared at the controls of the carriage. "If only we could find the police, they'd help us!" she said, thinking of Whitechapel and the officers who worked with Charles Sinclair. The kind-hearted detective's handsome face dominated nearly every corner of her thoughts, and she pictured him as she'd last seen him, smiling at her as she lay upon a cot inside the constables' lounge of Leman Street Station House.

In a flash, the coach began to hum, transporting it and its occupants through the dizzying realm of *sen-sen* and emerging betwixt a hansom and a police maria, stopping just six feet from the door to 76 Leman Street.

The Haimsbury coach arrived at Istseleniye House precisely twelve minutes after the prince's remarkable carriage appeared on Leman Street. Already, Raziel and his minions had fled the remains of their incursion, leaving behind a smouldering heap of stones.

Charles ran from the carriage almost before it had come to a full stop, followed quickly by Paul Stuart. "Where is it? Was it smoking like this when you left?" he asked Salperton.

"No, not at all. It looked rather like an abandoned castle from the outside, but once you passed through the gates, it looked completely normal. I don't understand. I tell you, this place was different only three hours ago!"

Paul withdrew his pistol, ready for battle as he carefully stepped into the stone-covered yard. "I think this devastation just occurred, Charles. See here? Blood, and it's fresh."

Sinclair felt like screaming. "Where is she?" he moaned as he followed his cousin through the smoking ruins. The company of men picked their way through piles of stones, furnishings, clothing, and mayhem. The terrified marquess kept his eyes on the ground, expecting to find his wife's body at any moment.

Aubrey walked ahead and had just turned a corner, when he called to the others. "Back here!"

All three ran, reaching him in seconds. The earl stood over the body of a creature that made no sense in the natural world. Raziel had ordered his captains to remove the fallen and wounded to *sen-sen* immediately, but this one had been missed.

"What is it?" Emerson asked, bending down for a closer look at the sickly green corpse.

"No idea. I've never seen anything like it," Paul answered.

"I never should have left her," Salperton declared, running both hands through his dark hair in despair. "Dash it all! I never should have left! Romanov said she was in danger, and I foolishly broke through his protections. My actions probably let Elizabeth's pursuers inside. Charles, I'm so sorry. Dear God in heaven, it's my fault!"

Sinclair closed his eyes, trying to picture Beth's face, but it proved hard. "Where in the castle did she sleep?" he asked Henry.

"First floor, northwest corner. Up there, where the wall is blown apart," he answered darkly.

The earl left the group once again, his keen eyes focused on the ground. "There are tracks here, Charles. Several that look like men's, but others much smaller. Henry, how many people lived here?"

"Let's see," the frazzled viscount replied, "there's the duchess, of course, but also Miss Kilmeade, Riga, Blinkmire, Stanley. Oh, and there's a fellow who calls himself Thirteen, but I'm told it's actually Anderson. Vasily's the butler, and there's a footman and two cooks."

"Six men and three women, plus Elizabeth?" Charles asked.

"No, wait, there's also a woman who served as lady's maid at times. Katrina. And, of course, Miss Ross."

"Miss Ross?" Sinclair asked, staring at Salperton.

"Yes, a lovely woman, though somewhat shy. Ida Ross." A strange light of relief swept across the marquess's face, which thoroughly puzzled Henry. "Do you know her, sir?"

"I'd thought her dead," Charles answered. "Romanov makes a habit of rescuing women, it seems. How did he let this happen? He seems to foresee all sorts of things. Why didn't he foresee this?"

Aubrey had reached the brick pavilion. "The tracks stop here, Charles, but the building is empty. There's evidence that something sat here. You can see wheel marks on the floor. A carriage, perhaps?"

"If so, then, they hitched up the horses elsewhere," the detective observed. "Let's walk through the castle. I have to believe Beth is safe, Paul. The Lord would not allow her to die—not after he's already rescued her once. Would he?"

"No, Cousin, he would not. Henry, show us where Beth stayed, will you?"

The men started back to the ruins, and high above, a dragon flew upon the thin winds of *sen-sen*. The massive wings outstretched against the moon, obscuring it momentarily, but few in the human realm saw so much as a sliver of shadow. The mirror realm offered a window into earth's material world, but those within it remained unseen. Only certain animals had the instinct to see into the shadows.

And a few humans.

Henry shivered as the moon of *sen-sen* winked out for a second. He looked skyward, perceiving the shimmer from the other realm.

"What is it?" Aubrey asked his friend as they neared the castle entrance.

“Nothing. A ghost, perhaps. A hint of an apparition. Never mind me.”

Raziel Grigor watched from his seat upon the brilliantly hued dragon. “That one has eyes,” he told the beast. “Interesting.”

The dragon turned and descended towards a maze of living stones, three realms below *sen-sen.* The beast could hear his master’s thoughts, and he knew Lord Raziel planned to confer with the Ravens and seek the Stone King’s advice.

It would be a very long night in *Sebet Babi.*

CHAPTER TWENTY-FOUR

4:56 am – London Hospital, Whitechapel

Edmund John James Reid paced back and forth like a caged cat. A constable named Howard Belman had roused the inspector from a much-needed night's sleep at half past three, telling a tale that sounded like something straight out of Grimm's book of fancy. What the experienced detective discovered upon arriving at Leman Street could not have surprised him more if a unicorn had greeted him, bitten him on the nose, and called him Uncle Bob. Now, at nearly five in the morning, he awaited a reply to the message he'd sent to Haimsbury House. The answer arrived in a crested coach, drawn by two matched Friesian mares.

"Where is she?" Sinclair asked as he burst into the hospital's main lobby.

"Treves is with her down the hall. Charles, he asks us to wait out here."

Ignoring the caution, Sinclair pushed through a group of police officers, two nurses, and a porter until he reached a closed door flanked by two sergeants.

"We're not allow anyone inside, Superintendent. Mr. Treves was quite insistent."

"I'm not anyone," Sinclair declared as he turned the doorknob.

Inside the hospital room, three men hunched over a patient, mumbling instructions and opinions as a middle-aged nurse watched. "Sir, no one is to enter!" the woman declared sternly.

"That is my wife. Treves, let me see her, please!"

Frederick Treves turned 'round, his face serious. "Charles, you may see her for a moment, but only that. I appreciate your anxiety, but allow us to finish our assessment."

The physicians left the bed momentarily, and Sinclair approached. "She looks so pale," he said, reaching for her hand. "But she's all right, isn't she?"

"We're worried about her lungs. She's having difficulty breathing. The others mentioned smoke and a fire, but wasn't that fire over a week ago?" Treves asked the detective.

"Yes, but there may have been another one tonight. Others? What others?"

"Her companions. We're also treating several of them. One was burnt quite badly. Two of the women are being looked after for shock. We've placed all the ladies in a room together, and the men in a private ward. Has Reid told you how they arrived?"

"I've not really talked with Edmund. Has she said anything?"

"One word, spoken twice. Captain. Does that make any sense at all?"

"Yes," he said, smiling. "Beth, can you hear me, darling?"

Her face turned towards his, but she gave no reply. Charles took her hand and kissed it. "Thank you, Lord," he whispered. "I'll be outside, Fred. Call me if anything changes. Oh, and the doctor who's been tending her for the past week is here with me. Shall I send him in to you? He mentioned pneumonia."

"That helps a great deal," Treves answered. "Yes, please, send him in."

Sinclair kissed Beth's hand once more, and then left, rejoining his cousin and the others in the waiting area.

Paul brought his cousin a glass of water. "How is she?"

"Pale, but alive. Nothing in this world has ever cheered me more than her face this day, Paul. Seeing her has brought me back to life."

"I understand," the earl answered, for his own heart had leapt when Baxter brought them Reid's message. "Charles, you look as though you might collapse. You'll do her no good if your health fails. If you want to help Beth, then gather your strength."

Sinclair wiped his eyes and drank the water. "You're right. I am tired, but very happy."

The doors to the main entry parted, and the Duke of Drummond strode into the lobby. His powerful presence caused the sea of waiting patients and constables to part as though commanded. James Stuart spread his muscular arms and embraced his nephew.

"Charles, this is good news indeed! Booth woke me half an hour ago."

"Half an hour?" Aubrey asked his uncle. "Your horses certainly made short work of the journey 'twixt here and Westminster. I suppose we should be grateful you took time to dress."

"Did I?" the duke asked, winking. "As one ages, the mind tends to forget mundane matters like clothing. Your aunt promises to visit later, but she and Della await news. Is there a telegraph nearby?"

"The hospital keeps one inside the administration wing, but we have one at Leman Street as well, sir," Reid told the Scotsman.

"You look close to fallin' down, son," Drummond told Sinclair.

"I'm fine, sir. Just tired. Sister?" he called to the charge nurse.

A tall woman approached. She wore the dark grey dress common to nurses, along with a white pinafore apron. Her wheat-coloured hair was bound into a tight chignon and tucked beneath a peaked cap of starched cotton. A pair of white streamers fell behind the cap, and a gold and navy enameled pin bearing the hospital's insignia indicated her position as supervisor. "How may I help you, Lord Haimsbury?"

"You know me, Sister?"

She smiled, nodding her head in deference. "Anyone who reads knows you, sir. Superintendent Charles Sinclair, 11th Marquess of Haimsbury—and perhaps more," she added. "What might I do for you, my lord?"

"I'm told that a woman named Ida Ross arrived with my wife. Could you show me to her room?"

"Certainly, sir. If you'll follow me?"

"James, send for me at once, if anything happens."

"Sure enough, son," the duke answered as Charles followed the tall charge nurse down the corridor to the right. They passed two large wards of female patients, and then entered an area with smaller, private rooms.

"In here, sir. I'll send a porter to fetch you, should the duchess awaken."

Charles entered the hospital room. It had a single window, which faced north, and contained four beds. Three barefoot women in overcoats sat upon wooden chairs and spoke in whispers from a corner. On one bed, lay a very pale female with bright red hair, the coverlet drawn up to her chin, eyes shut. A second bed held Ida

Ross, her strawberry blonde hair loosely braided, her eyes open and watching the detective.

"Sir," she whispered, her lungs struggling to work after the smoke-filled escape. "Mr. Sinclair."

He sat upon the narrow mattress and took her hand. "Miss Ross, I am so very happy to see you. I'd grown terribly worried after receiving your letter."

"I'm sorry for that, sir," she told him, gasping between words.

"Don't try to speak. Dr. MacAlpin found us, and he told me about the duchess. He said that you've been very helpful, Ida. Thank you. If there is anything you need, you're to tell me. Anything at all."

"I'm content, sir," she whispered, her voice barely audible. "Have you seen him?"

"Seen whom?"

"The prince, sir. Did he come?"

"Do you mean Prince Anatole? No, I've not seen him. Did he harm you?"

She shook her head. "No, sir. He's been very kind—to both of us. The duchess and me."

Her eyes shut for a second, and he could see that she wanted to sleep. "Rest, now, Ida. I'll visit you again later. And I'm going to place a guard on this door."

She closed her eyes, and her breathing grew regular. Sinclair turned to the others. "I'm Charles Sinclair. Were you ladies also living in the castle?"

The tallest of the three stood and curtsied. "My lord, I'm Katrina Gulin. These are Lila Brodeur and Maybelle Aslanov, the castle's cooks. Miss Kilmeade sleeps over there. We all lived at the castle."

"You served there?"

"Not Miss Kilmeade, but we three did, sir. I clean a little and help wherever the prince requires it. I've served Miss Ross and the duchess as lady's maid. We're very worried about the prince, sir. He didn't come. He always comes if the enemy draws near, but not this time."

The cooks began to talk to one another in a mix of French and Russian, and the elder of the two, Maybelle, spoke up. "Is most strange, sir," she said in a thick accent. "I blame that witch! The countess. The prince warn us that she might be traitor. Forgive me saying, but is strange. I think she bring much bad to us."

"Contessa di Specchio?" he asked.

"*Oui!* She bad person," the second cook agreed. "*Trés mal!*"

Katrina explained. "The countess lived with the prince off and on for six months, sir. Recently, she began to host visitors that the prince explicitly said were not welcome, and after the last time, His Highness ordered her to leave and never return."

"And she's not been back since?"

"No, my lord. She has not. How is the duchess?"

"We don't know much yet. The doctors are still deciding, but I'm hopeful. Thank you for whatever part you played, Katrina. I'm told that some of your men sustained injuries. What happened?"

"He came, sir. That bad one. Lord Raziel."

Charles felt a chill run down his spine. "We found the body of some reptilian creature outside the castle."

"I've heard the prince call it an *ala*, sir. Raziel uses them in battle. They have the ability to transform into any type of creature, making them perfect soldiers. I've seen them as wind, rain, human-like beasts, snakes, and ravens."

"Ravens?" Charles asked. "Do they speak?"

"Indeed, my lord, they do. You must beware of their lies, for they are quite convincing."

"I can attest to that," he said. "Thank you. I'll leave you all to rest. May I speak with you later? And if you need lodgings, please tell Mr. Treves, and I'll arrange it."

"That is kind of you, sir. We hope to stay close to Mr. Blinkmire and Count Riga until they have fully recovered."

"They're in a private ward?"

"So I'm told, my lord, but we're not permitted to visit them."

"I'll ask a nurse to bring you word of their condition."

He left and shut the door. Once back in the lobby, he left instructions with the sister to deliver news to the women regarding the men. As they waited, Sinclair kept busy speaking to Reid.

"Anything more on Hemsfield's murder?" he asked the inspector.

"Nothing yet. Charles, I'd like to borrow Arthur France, if you can spare him. I've no one presently with as much experience, but if you need him to keep watch on the duchess, I'll find someone else."

"No, you can have him for a week. After that, we'll talk again. He and his wife Brenda are staying in the Haimsbury dower house at present. Once their apartment is finished, they'll move into the main house, and France will commence his regular duties. Beth can be unpredictable at times, but it's unlikely she'll do anything other than sleep for the next few days. If she requires a guardian, I'll keep watch."

"How's your head?"

"Pounding, but I manage to ignore it. I'm sure I'll sleep much better tonight, which should help. Edmund, how well do you know the shop head at T Division, Hammersmith?"

"That would be Bill Fisher, right? I know him well enough to say hello when we meet up at the Yard. Why?"

"I'd like to learn more about this castle where Beth was staying. See what Fisher can tell you about the place. Henry MacAlpin, Beth's doctor, might also know Fisher, if it helps. Henry owns a residential clinic near Fulham, not far from Hammersmith Station House."

"MacAlpin," the inspector repeated. "Is this the same as the Lasberington earls?"

"Yes. Henry's the only child, apparently."

"Ask Kepelheim about the Lasberingtons. If this is the same person, he's a very interesting young man, Charles."

"How so?"

"Martin told me once that the earl's son, Henry, has the ability to see into the spirit realm; somewhat in the way the duchess does."

"I wonder if that's why Romanov drew him into all of this. Where is that Russian? Paul!" he called to his cousin.

Aubrey had been speaking with a porter near the main doors. "Yes? Is it Beth?"

"No, not yet. I'd like you to send word to your government contacts and ask if anyone has seen Anatole Romanov in the past two days. There's an idea growing inside my head, but I require more information to water it."

"It might just be your concussion talking, Charles."

"I rather think it's my intuition finally waking up from a week's slumber. Oh, and have Galton speak with all his contacts. I want every known member of Redwing watched. If anyone so much as sneezes, I want to know it."

"You think Hemsfield's murder is connected to Romanov?"

"The prince told MacKey that members would begin to die, and less than twenty-four hours later, we find the earl dead. Anatole said the killer would be a wolf in sheep's clothing, which either means the killer is betraying his fellow members, or else he sits on the inner circle."

Aubrey stared, the idea of a traitor slowly seeding itself into his brain. "That is a very dark thought. I'll make sure every known member is watched, and I'll wire Deniau to start looking into di Specchio and Trent," he told his cousin. "Here's Treves."

The weary physician wiped his eyes as he, Salperton, and two fellow surgeons left the hospital room. "Charles, forgive us for making you wait. In a moment, you can visit your wife, but I'd like to speak with you first. In private."

Sinclair stepped away from his family and followed Treves into a small registration office, where two porters were arguing over which nursing students were the prettiest.

"Mr. Cross, Mr. Davis, if you'd give us a few minutes?" the chief surgeon asked the gabbing men. Davis shut the door as he left with the other porter. "Charles, I'm concerned about the duchess's condition. There is a complication," Treves told the detective.

"Is it her pregnancy?"

"You already know?" the surgeon asked, obviously relieved. "Honestly, I worried this would be news."

"I've known about her condition since before the wedding. Is Beth in danger?"

"No, not at this time, but I want to keep her in hospital for a few days. It's always a concern when an expectant mother undergoes trauma, but pneumonia can be very problematic. Do we have your permission to keep Elizabeth until Friday at least?"

"May I not take her home, Fred? I could hire any number of nurses, and we've several physicians to call upon. This fellow Salperton's been watching Beth for the past week, and he's already enquired about continuing as her physician. I'm inclined to say yes, if she wishes it. I've spent far too long without my wife beside me, Fred. I need her."

"I understand, Charles, but moving the duchess prematurely is very dangerous."

"I see," he answered. "May I stay here, then? I've no wish to be without her, and I think she may be in danger. Regardless of how many officers I post at her door, I would find no peace."

"Yes, I'm sure we can accommodate that. I'll speak with Sister, and have her alert the female staff and porters. Shall I have a cot moved into the room?"

"Yes, thank you."

"The hospital is already awash with reporters, according to my registering clerk. Everyone wants to know about you and the duchess, which reminds me. I'm to wire the prime minister and the police commissioner."

"I'll take care of both," he said, shaking the surgeon's hand. "I'll have our butler pack a bag for me. I'm not leaving until my wife comes with me."

"Then, have him pack enough for a week, to be on the safe side."

The two men left the office, and the duke approached Sinclair. "You can see her now, son."

Charles entered the quiet room and sat next to his beloved wife, kissing her lips and touching her pale face. "Elizabeth?"

She didn't move, but her breathing appeared less laboured than before. "Thank you, Lord," he whispered, taking her hand. "Beth, I don't know if you can hear me, but please—please forgive me for not being there when you needed me most. I've promised you for so long that Trent would never harm you, and yet he—well, he did. He's dead, though, Beth. I don't know if anyone has told you that, but Trent was already dead when we got to the house. Oh, my darling, I thought you might be—that you might have left me, you know? I'd feared that our strange time together inside that other realm might mean you lingered near death. If you ever did leave me, I don't think I could go on, so you must recover. Promise me, you'll do that."

Her hand moved slightly within his, as if she knew he was there. He struggled with what else to say. If she could hear him, then he must avoid saying anything that might upset her.

"I've got our apartment all ready, darling. I even added the tester bed you wanted, a replica of the one you told me about at Versailles, only I had the furniture maker add a few special touches. And the walls are painted in the shade of blue you selected. I'm not skilled at these things, but Tory chose fabrics to coordinate: upholstery, draperies, cushions, and all that. Your bedchamber gleams with golden touches, and the shelves are lined with your favourite books. Mine is less beautiful, though functional. Oh, and Mary asks about you every day, as does Adele. Your grandfather and Paul are here, and I'm sure both want to come in and say hello. Aunt Victoria will come by later today with Della. Beth, we've all missed you so very much. I've missed you."

Tears slid down his cheeks, as he continued. "Beth, I've never been so terrified in my entire life. When I awoke and discovered that you weren't there, I feared the worst. We had no way of knowing what happened to you. When Paul and I reached the house tonight and saw the fire, I thought that you…that you… But you're here now, aren't you? You're safe, and soon you'll be well. Beth? Darling, can you hear me?"

She slept quietly, her chest rising and falling rhythmically. He lay his head upon her stomach, listening. "I love you," he whispered to his unborn children. Sinclair lingered beside the bed, content simply to look at her, and then at last, he kissed her lips and left, softly closing the door.

"How is she?" the earl asked, a note in his hand.

"Sleeping, but I talked to her a little, and I'm much encouraged to see her sweet face. You've learned something. What?"

Aubrey smiled. "That's the cousin I've missed these past few days. This message is from Sergeant Williams. A man called at Leman Street half an hour ago, entreating you to speak with him. He claims he knows about Hemsfield and insists the murderer is a Russian magician. The note mentions a Tarot card called 'the hanged man'."

"What has that to do with Hemsfield?" Charles asked.

"The positioning of the body and the carving on his chest," Stuart explained. "The way one leg was bent and tied behind the other knee to form an upside down '4'. The twelfth card in the Tarot's major arcana is known as the 'hanged man', and the figure looks just like Hemsfield. The card signifies treason, Charles. Redwing's sending a message to all its members."

Sinclair added this information to the other factors in the equation. "Do you think the mention of a Russian magician refers to Romanov?"

"No idea, but this man asks us to meet him at a nearby hotel. It's neither the finest nor the safest, but it offers food. We can eat whilst there."

Charles hated to leave, but as Beth would likely sleep for hours, he decided to join his cousin. "Are you carrying your ICI warrant card?"

"Do I need it?" the earl asked.

"Only if we must arrest a foreign national."

"I see what you mean. Yes, I have it, but several other warrant cards as well—in a variety of names."

"Now, why doesn't surprise me?" the detective laughed, turning to the duke. "James, Paul and I must see to a matter that may help to solve a Yard case. If Beth awakens, tell her I'll return in a few hours. Edmund, will you join us?"

The inspector's eyes were rimmed with red from lack of sleep, but Reid found reason to smile. "Now, that you and the duchess have found one another again, the world feels right. I'll return to Leman Street and let you and the earl handle this one. Stop by when you're finished. If this solves the Hemsfield case, then you'll make me happier yet."

Charles Sinclair felt energised for the first time in many days. "Cousin, since we are not doctors, let us be detectives and see what this Russian has to tell us. Where are we to meet him?"

"Gloucester Street. A placed called Porter's Inn. It's only a short walk from here, actually. The sun's out at long last. Let's walk."

The pair of cousins turned out into the morning bustle, looking like brothers, their fine clothing and polished appearance causing every head to turn at their passage. A few recognised Sinclair and waved or even bowed.

"I wish they'd stop doing that. It feels very strange," the marquess told his cousin as they journeyed southward. "How did you know Gloucester was a short walk from the London? This is my beat, not yours."

Aubrey laughed, the cold breeze blowing his long hair. "I've made it my beat for years. Even before William's crimes in '79, I often worked these back alleys and crosscuts. Redwing operates everywhere, but London is its heart, and it's to the dark rookeries of the east that their crows gather. After that night in '79—after Elizabeth came into your life—I made the borough a second home. I lived on the docks for a few months, in disguise, of course, and I daresay that even you failed to recognise me. One dark night, I was brought into your cells, and you said not a word."

Sinclair stopped and stared at his cousin. "Surely not! I'd spent enough time around you by then, that I'd have recognised you anywhere, even in a disguise."

Aubrey laughed. "Apparently, not. Look through your records for a longshoreman named Liam Dorsett, a rascally Scotsman found passing snide amongst your Whitechapel citizenry."

"Dorsett? That name is familiar. How is it you escaped our tender care, Mr. Dorsett? Counterfeiting is a very serious crime. Did we not send you to Newgate for your unsociable activities?"

Paul laughed. "Yes, in fact, you did, but the able Mr. Dorsett found an exit that very night. One day, I'll tell you how I escaped, but for now, we're nearing our destination. It's quicker to go through here."

They passed through a shadowy crosscut, littered with debris and scuttling rats. A man and woman haggled over the cost of a 'quick one' near a mildewed brick wall, whilst a scrawny fellow in a threadbare coat sold gypsy curses. A pot-bellied sailor tried to stop Charles, offering to sell him a quivering Chinese boy for six pounds. Sinclair showed his CID warrant card, and the entire assembly of discarded humanity fled the narrow enclosure like a flock of startled birds.

The cousins emerged onto Gloucester, where a boarding house faced east. Above the door, a weathered sign read, 'Porter's Inn' on one side and 'Rooms by the Hour' on the other. A card in the window offered special rates to sailors. The small hotel appeared to have been a fashionable address once, where seamen and travelling businessmen stayed a few nights whilst docked. Much of merchant life had changed once the expanding rail system made the unloading and transportation of imported goods efficient, cheap, and swift. Many of the East End dock owners now found their account books running red with debt, and a few threatened closure, adding to the stresses on seafaring men, hauliers, and longshoremen alike.

Passing through the weathered door, Charles noticed a woman playing with two young boys in what appeared to be a connected kitchen. In the main room, beside a warm charcoal fire, a trio of rough-looking men told ribald jokes as they passed the time in a game of cards.

"A pleasant day to you, good lady," Charles called to the woman, his manner easy.

"And the same ta you, sir," she answered, wiping her hands on a towel. "I'm Molly Porter, an' this 'ere's my place. What might I do fer ya? Room fer the night? A meal? I got a chicken simmerin' what's about done, but kippers and eggs is easy ta fix as well."

The detective shook his head. "Nothing just yet, thank you. Would you have a guest staying here who speaks Russian?"

"Russian, is it? That's real strange. Another asked me the same thing, no' an hour past."

"Another? Can you describe him?"

"Dressed right smart. Short, thin, wore one o' them tall 'ats," she told Sinclair. "Like I told 'im, my guests speak a variety o' languages. Some days, it's like Babel itself hereabouts. Can you describe this Russian gent, sir?" she asked amiably.

Aubrey replied. "Mrs. Porter, the man we seek knows a great deal about cards. Particularly the old ones. There's a mysterious figure that I hope to discuss with him. It's called the 'hanged man'. Does that sound familiar to you at all?"

The largest of the three card players cast his eyes towards the peers. He looked like every other man that worked the docks: rough of face and hands, squint-eyed from too much time in the sun, and wearing every item of clothing he owned upon his back. It was clear to Aubrey that the mention of the 'hanged man' had caught the fellow by surprise, but the earl had spent enough time as a spy to discern mere interest from suspicious guilt. The large man fell into the latter category. It was beginning to feel like he and Charles had walked into a trap.

The proprietress paid no heed, and she twisted her red hair with one hand in an effort to stimulate her memory. "An 'anged man, ya say? Weren't there such a man up on Commercial, found 'angin' from 'is own ceilin'? Two o' them men from the *Juggernaut* come in talkin' 'bout it."

"*Juggernaut?* Is that a ship?" Sinclair asked.

"It is, sir. One o' them steam trawlers what runs out ta Gravesend an' back every week. Big beam an' all fer the nets. Run by a feller name o' Gantry. Real tall fella. Got a limp an' hellish black eyes. Like soot they is."

Aubrey had a tingle near the back of his head, as though his senses screamed for attention. "Tell me, Mrs. Porter, how is this Gantry dressed?"

"Like most men, I reckon. Save you gents, o' course. Never seen such fancy clothes in my place afore. Ain't that a leather coat, sir?"

Aubrey allowed her to feel the sleeve. "It's called a duster, actually. Burnished cowhide. I had it made in America."

"America?" she echoed, whistling. "I ain' never seen nobody wear a coat like that. And made in America an' all! I reckon you're bofe rich, then?"

Charles considered showing the woman his warrant card, but decided to defer—for now. "We're men of business," he explained, bending the truth somewhat, for both he and his cousin owned a variety of businesses, most of them inherited. "Does Mr. Gantry ever stay with you?"

"Now an' then, he does. I could give 'im yer card next time 'e comes 'round, if ya like."

Porter's two boys rushed in and tugged at their mother's sleeve, asking for a penny to buy sweets. She sent the children to another room to play, promising they could share a penny after supper. Paul followed them.

"Oh, sir!" the woman called to Aubrey. "There's naught back there but me own rooms. I can fetch you an ale, if you're thirsty."

Aubrey turned and smiled disarmingly. The woman smiled in return, for the well-dressed gentleman was certainly handsome.

"Good lady, I smell a delicious chicken, do I not? I'm a connoisseur of fine cuisine and a bit of a chef—though I hesitate to boast—and I would see your spices, if you'd not think it an imposition. Do I smell oregano and tarragon? Marjoram?"

The woman blushed beneath her muslin bonnet, completely charmed by her guest. "You do, sir! Oh, now tha' is a gift most men do no' share wif you. Tarragon's one o' me secrets, and I always adds a pinch of marjoram. Oh, go on, then! I reckon there's no 'arm in it, if you've a mind to see me spices."

She turned back to Charles, who'd been thoroughly enjoying Paul's remarkable performance. "Care for a pint sir?" she asked him.

Sinclair offered a bow, smiling. "That would be most welcome, Mrs. Porter. I'll have an ale, and so will my friend."

"Two ales, it is, then. Oh, Mr. Gantry did stay wiv me las' week, but he's not been back since. Paid for a fortnight, 'e did, but stole away on Sunday evenin', just afore them wolves come out."

"Wolves?" Charles asked.

"Oh, yes! I seen 'em. Looked like 'airy men wiv a wolf's face! Like ta scared a year's life righ' outa me, they did. My boys seen 'em, too, no matter wha' the police say. Oh, them ales! I'll go an' fetch 'em."

Charles looked towards the three men, wondering if one might have have sent the curious note. "It's certainly a cold day. Mind if I join you gentlemen beside that most gratifying fire?"

He left no time for them to answer, but crossed to the fireplace and began warming his hands. "It looks like snow again. Early for winter, but it is nearly Christmas. I wonder, did either of you happen to be staying here last week?"

One of the three turned, his face shadowed by a week's growth of honey-coloured stubble. "I were 'ere. Why?"

"Only that I had a business contact who often stays at this inn when he works in London. A Russian fellow. Quite tall."

"I don' know no Russians, an' I ain' never been ta Russia neever. I reckon a toff like you travels all over the world, eh?"

Charles had never been called a 'toff' before in his entire life, and he actually smiled. "Well, sir, in truth, I've not visited Russia either, but my friend has been there many times. You're a fisherman, I take it?"

"I were. Used ta fish the estuary. Now I works the docks 'eavin' cargo when I can get on the rolls. Pete 'ere's been ta Russia, ain' cha, Pete?"

A second man, smaller than the first, glanced up from his cards. "Yeah, I been. It's all right, I reckon. Cold as a witch's wand, iffin ya gets me drift, sir. What's two fancy gents like you doin' 'ere, eh? You lookin' for sumfing special? I knows a few places where Bobby Blue don' go, iffin you've a mind fer exotic entertainments o' the female variety."

Charles considered the absurdity of the moment, wondering what the card-playing dockworker would think if he knew he'd promised to take a Scotland Yard superintendent on a tour of the bawdier locales of Whitechapel.

"That sounds quite interesting," he said as Paul emerged from the kitchen and signalled. "I fear it will have to wait until another time. If you'll excuse me. My friend wants a word."

Sinclair left the fire and joined his cousin at the table.

"The boys had much to say," Aubrey whispered. "Give it a minute, and then follow me."

Aubrey took an ale from Mrs. Porter and drank deeply, wiping his mouth. "Send her up when she gets here," he told her and then climbed the steep stairs to the upper floor.

Charles lifted his own glass, drank two swigs, and then followed his cousin. The three men looked one to the other, and then to the woman.

"What's them toffs up to, Molly?" the largest man asked roughly.

"They got a fella what procures fer 'em, and she's ta be delivered—so they says. They's paid well enough, an' I ain' one to pry. Bite o' chicken, gents?"

Upstairs, Paul left the door to the second room open so Charles could find him.

"In here," he said as Charles arrived. "The boys said a man who spoke fluent Russian slept in here until Sunday night. Tall with a limp and bright clothes. I thought we might see if our mysterious, limping Russian left anything of interest."

"You're a devious sort, Lord Aubrey. Do you often resort to such intemperate subterfuge?"

"All the time," he answered as he searched through the closet. "There's mud on the floor and prints that look as though a man with large feet dried a pair of boots here. You can see the pattern of the toe. It's square like those worn in Russia. Based on the size, I'd say this man is well over six feet tall."

"I never cease to learn from your experience, Cousin."

The earl laughed. "I'm happy to help."

He opened every drawer in a tall chest, stopping at the third. "Charles, look here. A deck of Lubek Tarot cards."

"Just what are Tarot cards, Paul?"

"They're used for divination by gypsies and palmists. Most use the Marseilles cards, but these are in the Lubek style. Lubek is a type of Russian illustration, often used to teach a lesson or tell a story. Lubek decks are popular with gypsies from the Carpathians and have more cards—a total of seventy-eight in most cases." He began shuffling through the deck, and stopped part way through. One card had been turned at the corner to make it stand out. "What are we to make of this? The seven of cups?" the earl asked his cousin.

"Let me," Sinclair said, reaching for the card. The image showed seven ravens, each bearing a gift. One carried a tower, another a snake, the others presented gold, a laurel wreath, a crown, a glowing figure, and a dragon. "What does all this mean?"

Paul shook his head. "As with most Tarot cards, the interpretation varies. Some say the card represents the seven deadly sins; others that it indicates future achievements or even temptations."

The image grew warm in his hand, and Sinclair had a strong sense of dread. "Leave the deck here. I want no part of it."

"But it's evidence," the earl argued. "And this card was left here for us to find."

"It is evil," the marquess declared. "Leave it. Leave the whole deck."

"Tell me what you're sensing, Charles, for to me they're just bits of paper."

"Can't you feel it? Hear it? The birds, Paul. They're talking."

Paul took the card from his cousin and returned it to the deck. "We're leaving and heading straight back to the London. Your head injury needs tending."

"No, it isn't that. It cannot be coincidence. See the raven that bears the crown? It looks exactly like the gatekeeper in its bird form. It even has yellow eyes!"

The earl placed the deck back inside the drawer and shut it. "I believe you, but you're pale and in need of rest. Come, Cousin. Let me take you back to the London. We'll hire a cab, and..."

"No, I'm fine. Let me sit a moment. You keep looking."

He took a seat on the bed whilst the earl continued to search the room. The only other evidence Paul found were two brass buttons from a seaman's coat and strands of black hair. He crossed to the window to see if anyone might be watching from below. The street seemed normal for mid-morning. A bird seller, a girl offering bundles of violets for a penny, a fishmonger, a ragged man who claimed to sharpen knives better than any other, a baked potato and pies wagon, and a myriad of other cart men.

"We should go," he told Sinclair. "I want to learn more about this ship, the *Juggernaut*. Charles, I don't know if you've have much time to review recent crimes along the docks, but a pair of sailors were found dead on North Quay last Sunday night."

"Is that relevant?" his cousin asked.

"I'm not sure. It might be nothing more than roughs picking a fight, but it's worth investigation. Did you speak to the three men below?"

"I did. Typical sort. Called us 'toffs'. I guess we are, though I'd never thought to hear myself called such. I hinted at Russia, but achieved little, I'm afraid."

"Did you see their hands, Charles? Two of them showed fresh cuts on the knuckles. Not atypical for workmen, but it's possible they engage in activities that might offer a police detective a bit of leverage."

"Activities like illegal boxing? There's a bare knuckle ring not far from here. It's run by a man who calls himself Angus Swiss in the old Ludlow Shipping warehouse. I asked Reid to shut the operation down, but the Home Secretary countermanded my decision. Apparently, despite being illegal since '67, these bouts provide an outlet for a great many West End gentlemen of influence, including several MPs."

"Charles, if you accept the position of Commissioner of Intelligence, then you won't be under anyone's authority. Not even the prime minister would interfere with an operation that's funded with off-book funds."

"Off-book?"

"As with my own position, intelligence operations seldom show up on a government ledger. The fewer eyes on these activities, the better, which is probably why Salisbury wants you on the cabinet. He's a wily fellow, our prime minister. And subsequent PMs will relish having access to intelligence that bypasses Parliament. It's a catbird seat, if ever there was one."

"I want to ask Beth first, but it does sound intriguing. For the present, what say you to a short round of question and answer with these three card players?"

Paul smiled. "Happy to oblige. It's a pleasure working with you, Lord Haimsbury."

"And a pleasure working with you, Lord Aubrey."

The two cousins returned to the main level only to find the men had vanished. Molly Porter was just wiping down their table.

"The three who sat there, Mrs. Porter. Where did they go?" Paul asked.

"Out to find work, or so they said. Seemed nonsense ta me, my lords, for them three's been content ta lounge by that fire fer more 'n a week! When they sees there's no work ta be 'ad, they'll be back. I could fetch a full English whilst you wait, sirs."

Paul shook his head. "No, dear Molly, I fear that we must take our leave of you, but it's been a distinct pleasure. I shall ever remember your fair cheeks and the blue of your bright eyes."

She laughed, blushing to a crimson hue that matched the stray hairs that peeked from beneath her bonnet. "Oh, sir! Ya tease, but I thanks yer anyways!" she giggled.

Aubrey offered his best smile, dimples deepening beneath the unshaved cheek. "You're a bonny lass, Molly, but my friend and I hope to find those three men. One looked familiar to me. Thomas Bright, I believe. A barber. The small one with the scar on his cheek."

"Oh, no, sir, that's Eddy Macon. Works up ta the sugar mill when 'e can get on the rolls. Them other two's 'is brothers. Pete and Joey Macon, bofe seafarin' men. They kept company wiv a man name o' Michael Kennery, but he were killed down near the quay last Sunday night. I fear tha' I can say naught good abou' tha' man, and he'll no' be missed by me!"

"My mistake then," Aubrey said, kissing her hand. "Thank you, sweet Molly. I'll be back to examine your kitchens one day soon. Tell your boys goodbye for me. They're handsome young men."

Paul tapped Charles on the shoulder, but the marquess turned back a moment before leaving. "Mrs. Porter, I'm this gentleman's cousin, and I tell you that he is honest and true, and I agree with his estimation both of your charms and of your character. Please, accept this in return for your hospitality and the ales." He handed her two ten-pound notes, and she squealed in delight.

"Oh, sir! Tha' is right gen'rous! Thank you. And I do hope you'll come back soon. Bofe of you!"

Charles and Paul left, and the earl hailed a hansom. "Do you think this Kennery is one of the two men listed by *The Star?*"

"Very likely," the earl answered as a driver pulled up near them. "Where to?" he asked, his cousin.

"Leman Street police station," Sinclair told the driver as he stepped into the cab. "Before we return to the London, I want to see if we can find anything on these men from Porter's."

Paul tapped on the roof, and the cabman headed south towards Commercial. "Charles, if we've time, I'd like to speak with Sunders regarding Hemsfield's autopsy. Is he finished?"

"Probably," Sinclair answered as the bells of Christ Church sounded the hour of ten. "Once we're at Leman Street, I'll wire Baxter with news of Beth's condition. I'm sure he's worried. Should I send a telegram to the queen as well?"

Paul laughed. "It says a great deal about you, Charles, that your first concern is for your butler rather than Her Majesty."

"And why not? To me, his blood is as blue as any royal. I intend to ask him if he'll stay with us in London permanently, and Mrs. Alcorn as well. I've a position in mind that will allow Mrs. Partridge to continue as housekeeper."

Paul laughed as they walked towards Leman Street. "Let me guess. Nursery duty?"

Sinclair smiled, his sea blue eyes twinkling. "You read my mind. Do you think Esther would enjoy that?"

"I think she would leap at the opportunity, Charles. It's a wonderful idea, and with Baxter as your butler, I can keep Laurence as an agent. He's quite good, you know. I might assign him to look into these three men from Porter's."

"You don't plan to do it yourself?" the detective teased his cousin. "Porter is a bonny lass, after all, and she certainly took a shine to you."

"Yes, well, I only spoke the truth. Porter is a lovely woman, though she has the careworn look of a scorned wife left to fend for herself. I've seen far too many with such a look. Adele's mother was one."

"Paul, you did Cozette du Barroux much honour in her final days. Did you love her?"

The earl took a moment to respond, his eyes on the scenery. "I'm not sure. In my own way, I did. I've never been particularly open with my heart, as you can guess. I waited too late to share it with Beth. If love ever comes my way again, I hope I'm better able to recognise it."

"It will come. Just keep your eyes open. Will you ever tell Adele the truth about her mother?"

"Perhaps, but I'm not sure how she'll react to it. She only knows me as a brother. I'd rather she never learns just what a cad I can be."

"Hardly that!" Sinclair declared. "You may not have loved Della's mother, but you never denied your child. Had Cozette told you before you left Paris, I'm sure you'd have done well by her."

"We'll never know, will we?" Aubrey asked, his tone strange. "Still, though I try to maintain the actions of a brother, it gets evermore difficult to keep my protective streak in check. Your cousin, for instance. That pompous baronet at the wedding. It was all I could do to keep from strangling him by his scrawny throat!"

"You won't find me stopping you," Sinclair told him as their hansom turned west onto Little Alie Street. "Albert Wendaway's been a thorn in my side for a very long time. Keep him away from Della. He will only bring her to ruin, and I'll not have that. I've grown to love her dearly."

"Della loves you, too. Tory may have told you this, but whilst you lay unconscious, Della sat beside you each morning and afternoon. Emerson taught her a few basic nursing duties, and my beautiful daughter performed each with efficiency and tender care. She would talk to you, and whenever I'd happen to catch her, I could see the despair on her face, Charles. The last time she looked like that, my father lay dying. She feared you might die, too. She truly loves you."

He smiled. "Della is the brightest star in England—second to Beth, of course. I'm very glad that bright star is now found. Where is Romanov, I wonder? It's very odd that he's not yet appeared. After taking such care of Elizabeth, why would he disappear just hours before the castle is attacked?"

"That is a riddle we must solve, Charles. I never thought I'd say this, but I'd actually feel relief if that Russian mystery walked through our door. When Beth is able to bear it, we'll need to ask her about last Sunday's events and all that happened afterward."

"I'd like to postpone that for as long as possible. I prefer she have a long rest first."

They arrived at the police station, and a young constable rushed to help the superintendent from the hansom's interior. The driver put out his hand for payment, but recognising the marquess, offered a bow instead. "No charge, my lord. Not fer you."

Regardless, Charles handed the man half a crown and thanked him. Four constables and a sergeant sat upon wooden chairs, enjoying cups of coffee and sunshine on a cold day. The sergeant stood and offered a salute. Sinclair waved it off. "This isn't a military unit, Sergeant Brookman. However, I appreciate the respect."

"Much more 'n respect, my lord. Much more."

The two cousins entered the station, Sinclair still puzzling out the odd behaviour. The lobby of the station house teemed with activity. Most of the cells held collections of pickpockets, vagrants, drunks, and various belligerents. The booking sergeant, Alfred Williams, busily scratched entries into a ledger, asking questions of a burly man in a patched greatcoat and a middle-aged woman wearing a velvet cape over expensive, but rumpled, evening clothes. The two made a strange pair, and Aubrey nudged his cousin.

"I know that woman, Charles."

"Personally or socially?"

"Both, actually. She's Lord Finchley's sister."

"Finchley?"

"A lifetime title. He's a businessman who helped to secure British trade in South America. Why would Gemma Finchley be here? And with such a scruffy looking fellow." Intending to find out, the earl walked up to the desk. "Good morning, Sergeant Williams. How's the wife?"

The officer's copper moustache upturned along with the corners of his fleshy mouth. "Lord Aubrey, sir. It's always a pleasure. Mrs. Williams is doing quite well, my lord. Thank you for askin'."

The well-dressed woman gasped at hearing Aubrey's name, and she sheepishly turned her face away, trying not to be seen. The earl refused to allow it. "Gemma? Is that you?"

"Lord Aubrey!" she gasped. "Whatever brings you to Whitechapel? Oh, I see you're with Lord Haimsbury. Do forgive my appearance. I've just come from an overnight stay with a friend."

"Yes, I can see that," Paul answered with a raised eyebrow. "Gemma, is everything all right?"

The burly man at her side pushed forward to answer for the woman. "I reckon she's just fine. Ain't ya, Miss?"

"Yes, yes, of course, I am," the woman chittered nervously.

The earl took Finchley's arm and directed her away from the desk. He then stepped towards the man. "I don't believe I caught your name."

"No, you didn', and ain' tellin' ya!" the brute shouted.

"It's George Malcolm, Lord Aubrey," the sergeant interrupted. "Superintendent Sinclair, sir, shall I inform the earl as to the charges against both or just Malcolm?"

Now Charles became involved. "Charges? Williams, are you saying there are charges against Miss Finchley?"

"Ain't none o' yer business, so clear off afore I belt ya good!" Malcolm shouted. The stench of gin exuding from the man's non-hygienic mouth caused Sinclair to push betwixt his cousin and the brute.

"Mr. Malcolm, I believe we've seen you before at Leman Street. Public drunkenness and procurement, if memory serves. Are you so fond of our cells that you wish to extend the current charges to assaulting an officer of the law?"

"What officer o' the law?" the intoxicated man dared to ask. "I don't see nobody but a toff what's about ta kiss the floor!"

The brute's right arm swung, but to the earl's surprise and delight, Sinclair neatly ducked the punch and produced a quick uppercut to the chin, followed by a left jab and a powerful right hook that knocked the huge man clean off his feet.

"Put that mess into a cell, Constable Andrews," he told a fresh-faced youth standing nearby. "Miss Finchley, if you'll come with us, I'd like to ask you a few questions."

Sergeant Williams looked as though he'd swallowed a crescent moon, for the grin upon his bearded face stretched from ear to ear. "Nice ta see you've not forgotten your trainin', sir. I've not had the pleasure o' watchin' you take down a man since last year's police championship. That right hook never fails."

"Thank you, Sergeant. It felt quite good, actually."

"Cup o' coffee, sir?" Williams offered.

"Yes, thank you. Is Inspector Reid here?"

"He's not returned yet from the London, sir. How is the duchess?"

"Improving hourly, Sergeant. Thank you for asking. We'll be in Mr. Reid's interview room if needed."

Aubrey kept his arm around Finchley as they walked, and he wore a smile not unlike that of Williams. "Police championship? Charles, have you been keeping secrets?"

"I may box now and then," the detective answered with a wry smile. "And won."

The earl laughed. "How often?"

"Always."

Aubrey continued to laugh as he and his cousin led the flummoxed woman up the main staircase to a small, rectangular interview room. Inside, stood a square oak table and four wooden chairs. The partition wall, shared with the corridor, was solid to four feet, and then proceeded upwards to the plastered ceiling with blinds over mullioned windows. A single door provided the only entrance.

"Please, Miss Finchley, take a seat," Sinclair said, holding the chair. Paul sat opposite and Charles beside him. "You know my cousin, I take it. I'm Detective Superintendent Charles Sinclair."

"You're Lord Haimsbury," she whispered shyly. "I've seen your photograph."

"Yes, that's right, but in this station, I represent Scotland Yard. Do you understand?"

Finchley had the furtive look of a woman with secrets. Her pale skin revealed fresh cuts over the left eye, caking face powder, and traces of lip rouge. Her copper hair hung in disarray, and the silk clothing had a wrinkled appearance. She seldom looked directly into the men's eyes, and she consistently chewed her lower lip.

"Yes, sir. I understand. Why am I here?"

Before Sinclair could answer, a boy named Johnny Twitcham knocked on the door. The ten-year-old's father operated the police mews across the way, and Johnny ran for meals, operated the telegraph, and delivered notes within the building.

"Superintendent, sir? Sorry to interrupt, but Sergeant Williams sent this up for you."

Charles took the form and placed it on the table. "Thank you, Master Twitcham. I wonder if you'd run to the Bear and ask Danny to prepare sandwiches for myself and Lord Aubrey? Have him add anything you want to the order." He handed the boy five pounds. "Keep whatever's left."

"Thank you, sir!" Twitcham exclaimed. "I won't be long, sir."

The youth shut the door, and Charles examined the booking form. "Miss Finchley, I see here that your companion is charged with a litany of serious crimes, including public drunkenness, lewd behaviour, procurement, gambling on illegal boxing, and incitement to riot, of all things. With Mr. Malcolm's previous record, it's doubtful he'll see the outside of a prison for a decade or more. May I ask just why you arrived in his company?"

The woman's lower lip trembled, and her upper teeth showed stains of rouge along their edges. "I cannot remember. Really, I can't. The last I recall with any clarity is talking with a few friends at a music hall. We'd gone there to see a magician."

"A magician?" he asked, thinking of the Tarot cards. Can you tell me the establishment's name? Is it in Whitechapel?"

"Yes. It's called the Copper Penny. Over near Bishopsgate."

"I know this place, Charles," Paul whispered to his cousin. "I fear it has a dark reputation. Gemma, why did you go to such a crime-ridden place as the Copper Penny? Surely, you know better."

"I'd no idea that's where we would go," she explained. "My brother's friend said we would see a magic act and have a few drinks. That's all. I thought it would be great fun, but..." She grew quiet, and her thin hands shook like brittle leaves in a gale. "But it wasn't fun at all!"

Charles reached for her hands to help the woman calm. "Are you injured, Miss Finchley?"

She shook her head, and it struck Charles that she reminded him of Elizabeth whenever the duchess struggled to recall troublesome events. "I hope you'll excuse me," he said, leaving the room without explanation.

Whilst his cousin was absent, the earl took over. "Gemma, are you hurt? Did that fellow harm you?"

"I'm not sure," she admitted. "Paul, I don't know, because I cannot remember! I awoke sometime after five o'clock this morning in a sort of fog. I was at a disgusting table filled with even more disgusting people in some awful hole of a place. They stank of gin and cigars and made great sport of my condition."

"Your condition?"

"My clothing was torn, as you can see, and my hair had come down from its combs. I felt thoroughly out of place, and when I tried to leave, that Malcolm person chased after me. A few of the other people there began to call me a slag, whatever that is, and I tried again to leave. Malcolm stole my handbag, and I shouted for the police. I remember music, strangely enough, but also men's voices. There was sawdust on the floor, and a tall wooden post stood in the middle. Paul, a man hung from it! I don't know if he was even alive, but his face looked as though someone had taken a meat mallet to it!"

"What happened then? Did this man hurt you?"

She began to cry. "Paul, I tell you truly, I cannot remember! There was a slightly built fellow with a moustache who tried to intercede, but he changed his mind when Malcolm pushed him. The entire place erupted into shouts and flying fists, and before I knew it, the police were arresting everyone."

"And the officers brought you and Malcolm here? Who else?"

"Dozens of others. The rest had already been locked into cells by the time you and Lord Haimsbury arrived. That awful man told the desk sergeant that he and I spent the entire night together, but I tell you that is patently untrue! Wouldn't I remember it? My head pounds like a demon with a hammer lives inside it, and I've a terrible roaring in my stomach, as though an entire legion of hammer demons have taken up lodging. Paul, I did nothing wrong. It was meant to be an enjoyable night at a music hall. If you don't believe me, you can ask Cordelia Wychwright. She was with us, along with the fellow I mentioned. The one with the moustache. I can't recall his name, but I'm sure one of them could explain it."

Paul's face lengthened in surprise. "Delia Wychwright? The baron's daughter. She was with you at a disreputable place like the Copper Penny and then this fight ring? Why on earth would either of you go to such places?"

Charles returned, and he'd brought Sunders along. "Miss Finchley, this gentleman is our surgeon, Dr. Thomas Sunders. I'd like for him to assess your health before we proceed any further. If it makes you more comfortable, I'll ask a matron to sit with you whilst the doctor examines you. Does that meet with your approval?"

"Must I? May I not send for my lawyer?"

"Do you need a lawyer?" Charles asked gently.

"I don't know. Yes, yes, of course, proceed with your examination, if you think it necessary, but I'd like a matron to be present."

"Certainly," Sinclair answered kindly. "Paul? Let's close these blinds and allow Sunders to work in private. Dr. Sunders, will this room suffice, or would you prefer we move to your surgery?"

"This will do for the present, Superintendent. Mrs. Williams was here earlier to fetch the laundry. If she's still about, I'd be happy to work with her. She has nursing experience."

"Of course. Miss Finchley, I'll return in about an hour. When all is done, Mrs. Williams will show you to a room where you may lie down and rest."

"Not a cell, sir, please!"

"Not a cell. A room with a very comfortable sofa. Use the detectives' lounge, Doctor, and place a 'do not disturb' sign on the door."

"Yes, sir. I will."

Sinclair and the earl left the interview room. They climbed a second set of steps to a large, open area dotted with desks and filing cabinets. Near one end, stood a telegraph room and beside it a private room marked 'Detectives' Lounge'. Just past the lounge, stood Edmund Reid's cramped office.

"Did she tell you anything in my absence?" Sinclair asked his cousin as they entered and closed the door.

"Nothing that makes any sense. From Gemma's description, I think she awoke at a makeshift table in one of those illegal boxing rings we were discussing earlier."

"Good heavens! What's a woman from Westminster doing in a rough place like that?"

"Hard to say, but she may have been drugged. Sunders should take a sample of her blood to test for morphine. But there's another wrinkle to this mess. Gemma mentioned that others were present at the fracas, including Cordelia Wychwright! Charles, I'd like to send a telegram to Galton at Whitehall and ask him to look into this from the other side of the city."

"You want him to call on the baron?"

Paul nodded. "At the very least, Delia's testimony could help provide clarity to poor Gemma's situation. But I'd also like to know how a thug like Malcolm is involved. It's quite vexing, to be honest. I realise that Cordelia is young, but a pretty face and a foolish mind can be a dangerous mix."

"Did you just say her face is pretty?" his cousin asked with a grin.

"Modestly pretty," the earl replied, fiddling with a paper knife on Reid's desk. A stack of files lay scattered across the oak surface, and the earl began to glance through them.

"Only modestly? Admit it, Paul. You're fond of Cordelia Wychwright."

"I'm no more fond of Cordelia than I am of any other young woman in our society. She's annoying, if you must know. What's this?" he asked, holding up a list. "Where did Edmund get this?"

"You're intentionally deflecting, Lord Aubrey. How is it the young woman annoys you? Might it be your feelings towards her are the true source of this annoyance?"

"No," he answered with conviction. "Charles, this is a copy of the list Ida Ross sent to you, but Reid's crossed through four of the names and added this notation: *Deceased*. Hemsfield is included."

"Four? I only knew of Hemsfield's death. Who else is crossed through?"

"Susanna Morgan, but he's now put a question mark beside her name," Aubrey said. "William Trent, of course, Lewis Merriweather, and Sir Christopher Holding. I'd no idea Holding was dead. Reid has a date by each entry, and it seems Sir Christopher died only last night!"

"I'm not familiar with him."

"He ran an ironworks company that contracted with the British Army. Charles, someone is targeting the people on Ida's list. You're right. Redwing has gone to war."

The boy knocked on the office door to deliver their meals, and Charles gave the youth half a crown for his speed and efficiency. "You'll make a fine detective one day, Master Twitcham."

"Thank you, sir. There's a note for you, as well, Superintendent. It come on the wire a few minutes ago. Mr. Williams asked me to deliver it."

He passed Sinclair a quarter sheet of paper, overwritten in a quick, neat hand. Charles read the message and took to his feet, his manner serious.

"It's from Reid. He says Cordelia Wychwright's been admitted to the London in very serious condition. Grab the sandwiches, Paul. We'll be eating on the way."

In another part of London, at the castle known as Istseleniye House, a carriage drew close to the ruins. Contessa di Specchio wore a black lace mantilla over her head and face and a silk cape of claret red velvet. Her companion, a handsome man of modest height and light eyes, helped her from the coach and onto the gravel drive.

"It looks as though Raziel's army practically demolished the place," he said. "So, does this mean Romanov is dead?"

Di Specchio carefully examined the debris, sniffing the air in animal-like fashion. "Lord Raziel failed," she declared.

"How can you tell? He left the place a total mess. You can see where the walls were torn through, and there are scorch marks all across the exterior. It looks to me as though Raziel emerged victorious."

"It's obvious you have no eyes to see! You are blind as well as foolish! The castle may be ruined, but is the duchess ours? No, she is not. Raziel failed."

"You used to say my eyes were beautiful," he pouted, kicking at the fallen stones.

"And so they are, my dear, but those pretty blues have limitations. Now, let us discover what lies inside. With the wards broken, we might be able to locate Anatole's secrets."

"Secrets? Treasures, you mean? Like gold?"

"Finer than gold, my dear Sir Albert. Much finer. Follow me, and I shall usher you into a realm of sublime truth!"

She took his soft hand, and together the two Redwing members entered the castle by way of the north entrance. They searched through the debris, and both complained. Wendaway of his back and new shoes, Di Specchio that the items she'd hoped to find weren't there.

Neither of the self-possessed pair noticed the large white owl that watched them from within the fading blossoms of an orange tree. The bird's head tilted to one side as it observed the vampiress and the hapless human. Finally, when it was clear that their search had yielded no fruit, the owl rose up on the high currents above London and headed towards Westminster, where he perched on the slate roof of a magnificent mansion and listened to an eleven-year-old girl practise the piano.

The owl's astonishingly blue eyes blinked, and its right foot kept time with the Scottish air's fluid melody.

CHAPTER TWENTY-FIVE

Cordelia Wychwright looked pale and tired. To no one's surprise, her mother had insisted she be given the hospital room one door away from Elizabeth Sinclair. Treves had admitted the disoriented and barely conscious young woman less half an hour after Paul and Charles left for Porter's Inn, and in that very short time, the baroness had already replaced the bed's hospital linen with down pillows and a velvet coverlet, embroidered with pink roses.

The earl knocked on the open doorway, his reaction mixed. On the one hand, it was a great relief to see Delia sitting up, whilst on the other, he suspected a hidden agenda to the young woman's appearance at the London.

"Paul," Delia whispered at seeing him knock on the open door. "I mean, Lord Aubrey, of course."

"Are you all right?" he asked as he entered. A nurse had just finished taking the ingénue's vitals, and the caregiver started to walk away. Baroness Wychwright sat in the far corner of the room, reading a newspaper, and she cleared her throat to attract the nurse's attention.

"Miss, you did not take my daughter's temperature. Mr. Treves insisted that she be monitored closely for signs of fever. I'm sure he'll be cross should my daughter decline further. Are you a nurse, or merely a student?"

"A nurse, ma'am, with ten years' experience. I did take Lady Cordelia's temperature, my lady, when I first entered. It is slightly above normal. Ninety-nine, point six."

"A fever! Do you hear that, Lord Aubrey? And see how flushed her poor face is? You see it, don't you?" she asked the earl. "Poor darling, how awful to be out all night in such a chill. I shall have that fellow arrested!"

"What fellow is that?" Aubrey asked as he sat next to the girl's bed.

"No one," Cordelia insisted. "And Mama makes a fuss for nothing. Really, nothing at all."

"Delia, how is it that you find yourself in hospital in Whitechapel? Surely, St. Mary's would be closer to your home."

The young woman started to answer, but her mother spoke before she had a chance. "That horrid baronet brought our daughter to this side of town, Lord Aubrey, and he abandoned her. She told him no, again and again, and still he dragged her from a simple party in Belgravia to this hellish borough!"

"Mama, please!" Cordelia pleaded, her cheeks pinking from embarrassment.

"I say only the truth. Your father will deal with this man's family. Yes, he will see to it that the devil is prosecuted and never has opportunity to endanger you or any other young woman again. You can see the state he left her in, Lord Aubrey. My poor, poor child!"

Paul wanted to throttle the woman. "I wonder, Baroness, would you permit me to speak with Cordelia alone?"

The baroness offered a practised smile. "Certainly, if that is your wish. It will allow me to send word to the baron again. I cannot think why that man isn't here!"

The ambitious woman left, her strident voice echoing in the corridor as she shouted for a nurse. Paul waited several minutes before speaking. He noticed that Delia's hands and fingers never stopped moving, as though providing occupation for a restless mind. Or perhaps, a guilty one.

"Cordelia, I'm very sorry you've been injured," he began. "When Charles and I received the message that you'd been admitted, I feared the worst. I'm relieved to see you're sitting up, at least, but what are those scratches on your face? And your arms show bruises. What happened?"

"I'd rather not speak of it, Lord Aubrey."

"You may call me Paul," he told her. "It only seems right, as I so often call you Cordelia."

"I prefer Delia," she whispered. All the coquettish mannerisms had disappeared, and the earl saw the true Cordelia Wychwright for the first time.

He took her hand. "Delia then. Tell me about this man. The one who dragged you to Whitechapel. Who else came along, and what is his name?"

"You mustn't tell Mother," she whispered. "It's all mixed up and terrible. I sent a telegram to her from the Royal Exchange at six o'clock this morning. I didn't know what else to do!"

"What were you doing at the Exchange so early, Delia?"

"I'm not sure. I walked, you see. I think I wanted to find my father."

"Walked? Why didn't you hire a hansom?"

Her hand trembled visibly, and her eyes cast about wildly. "I don't know."

He soothed her by stroking the back of her wrist. "We'll let it go for now. Do you remember anything else?"

"It started with the party. Mama told me to go, even though I don't like Lydia Marstead. Do you know the Marsteads? They're on Chesham Place in Belgravia."

"Yes, I know them. Go on."

"The party didn't even start until nine, and I was quite tired. Mama made me drink chamomile tea after supper, and I think it made me sleepy. It gets a bit mixed up after that."

"Mixed up?"

"My memory."

Her pupils were large, but that was normal for someone so young. However, her behaviour was anything but normal. "I'll tell you what. We'll speak more later. You look as though you could sleep for days. Did the nurse give you anything? A draught of medicine, perhaps?"

"She had me drink some rather awful water just before you got here. I am sleepy, but will you come back?"

"I will," he told her, starting to rise just as Constance Wychwright returned.

"Did she tell you?" the meddling mother asked him.

"Let's speak outside," Paul insisted, taking her by the arm and leading the baroness back into the corridor. "Over here." He drew her away from the door so that Cordelia might not overhear. "Who did this to her?"

"A reprobate baronet, that's who! She was found at the Exchange this morning in a state of partial undress, Lord Aubrey. I want the man who left her in that condition arrested!"

"His name?" Paul asked, barely keeping his temper in check.

"Albert Wendaway."

"I see," he answered tightly. "Let me take care of this. Do nothing, Baroness. Do you understand me? Nothing."

"I do understand, Lord Aubrey, and thank you for your kindness. I wonder if you and the marquess might convey my heartfelt wishes for a speedy recovery to the duchess? I tried to stop by her room, but she's speaking with others just now. Lady Victoria and Duke James."

"Beth is talking?"

"Yes. So I understand."

"Praise the Lord," he said, leaving her side. Once the earl departed, Wychwright returned to her daughter's room, finding Delia half asleep, turned towards the wall.

"The earl seemed quite concerned, my dear. He insists that he take charge of your protection. Isn't that wonderful?"

"Leave me alone, Mama," Delia whispered.

"You don't mean that."

"I do!" she answered, still facing the wall. "I'm going to sleep. Please, close the drapes. It's too bright."

The scheming baroness drew the thick drapes together, content that the plan she'd concocted with Albert Wendaway seemed to be working beautifully. If the rumours now circulating through the social clubs and card rooms of the city about Haimsbury were true, then Paul Stuart's value as a potential husband had increased almost infinitely, for he stood but a heartbeat away from the man some claimed had the right to be called England's king.

Charles Sinclair had not laughed so much in days. He sat beside his beloved duchess, listening to a rather animated Duke James tell stories from his childhood, and how he'd learnt to shoot a rifle whilst on horseback. Victoria sat in a nearby chair, nodding off now and then, but occasionally waking to add her own touches to the duke's colourful tales. Drummond pranced back and forth, arms raised to demonstrate his very imperfect aim as a six-year-old boy, pantomiming his father's reaction when the shot missed and the deer turned about, causing the horse to rear up and toss his poor shot of a rider to the hard ground.

Elizabeth coughed now and then, and each time, Charles offered her a sip of lemon water. Tory had thoughtfully brought a packed case for her niece, filled with nightdresses, shawls for modesty and warmth, personal linen, slippers, a mirror, brush, comb, and Beth's special soap. Their aunt had also helped to wash Beth's hair and braid it, so that it gleamed against her left shoulder as she lay upon the bed. She'd never looked so beautiful to her husband, not even on their wedding day, for to Charles, Elizabeth was a miracle in flesh and blood. He squeezed her hand, his heart full to bursting.

"We should let you rest," Drummond said after finishing his tale.

Paul watched from the open doorway, his own eyes misty at the touching family scene. His duchess was back and growing stronger, yet his heart felt strangely heavy. What had happened to Gemma Finchley and Cordelia Wychwright? And what role had Albert Wendaway played?

The duke kissed his granddaughter and then spoke to the earl. "Paul, why don't you join Tory and me for luncheon? I imagine your cousin will stay and eat with Beth. Unless, you need to sleep, Princess."

"I'd relish a few minutes with my cousin first, if you don't mind. Paul, will you stay and talk to me?" she asked Aubrey.

"I'd be honoured," he told her.

"Thank you, Grandpa. Tory," the duchess called to her aunt. "Thank you for everything. Please, tell Della that I hope to see her tomorrow."

The short speech caused Beth to cough again. Charles gave her the glass once more and then rose to see his aunt and uncle to the door. "I'll be right back, little one. Drink all of that now. I shall check to make sure you've complied when I return."

The earl watched his cousin leave, and then took the chair left vacant by Victoria. "You certainly look better," he said, suddenly feeling like the odd man out. "Where's Henry? I'd hoped to speak with him about a case."

She finished the water, and Stuart took the empty glass and set it on the table beside her bed. "Come closer, Paul, and tell me what's troubling you."

"Troubling me?" he asked, moving to the chair beside her bed. "Nothing, other than worrying about you."

"And if I told you that I worry about you as well, how would you respond? Paul, you've a look that speaks more loudly than any words. I've seen it countless times before, and it always precedes sudden flight."

"Flight?" he echoed in confusion. "I'm not sure what you mean. Do I sprout wings and fly away?"

"No, but you leave. You're restless and unhappy. Is it because of me?"

Paul had no wish to tell the truth, for she'd struck a sensitive nerve. "Of course, not. I've had very little sleep this past week, and it's been a chore to keep your wayward husband from charging all over London searching for you. I need sleep not a lecture."

"Am I lecturing?" she asked, her smile disappearing. "Forgive me, Cousin. That's thoughtless of me."

"No, Princess, my comment was thoughtless. I'll admit that it's still difficult to adjust to my new role in your life, but so long as Charles makes you happy, then I rejoice in it. Honestly, dear, I'm very happy that you and your Captain are together at long last."

"I want you to find that same joy, Paul."

"I'm content with my life, Princess. I'm a spy, you know. It's how I'm made."

"Then, promise your spying won't cause those wings to unfurl, all right? That you plan no sudden flights to other countries."

He wondered how she knew his mind. In truth, a part of Paul longed to leave London, but he'd promised Charles to remain. Yet, Cordelia's condition nagged at him, and he found his thoughts fixed on finding Wendaway and teaching him a lesson.

"Paul? You're far away already—wingless, yet flying. What is it?"

He kissed her hand. "Nothing. You should sleep. I'm off to join James and Tory for a much needed meal. It's been a very long day, and not a crumb to show for it. Enjoy your rest, Princess. You've a wee one depending on you now."

She smiled, her hands on her slightly rounded abdomen. "Perhaps, two wee ones."

"Two? Is the other one Charles?" he laughed.

"Go eat your luncheon!" she told him as Sinclair returned.

"I'll see you this evening," he told the detective. "Shall I bring you an overnight bag when I visit later?"

"No need. Baxter sent it with Tory. If you see Reid, ask him about that list."

"Of course," Aubrey said. "Until next we meet, Princess. I love you and always will."

He shut the door, and Charles took his former place beside his wife. "Should I be jealous?"

"Of course not," she answered seriously. "Oh, I see that was said in jest. Forgive me, Captain, this visit has begun to wear me down."

He kissed her forehead. "I can see that. Perhaps, I should join Paul and the others and let you sleep."

"Is Henry nearby?"

"He returned to his clinic, but he promised to visit this evening. I like him, Beth. A great deal. Henry's a fine man, and I owe him a debt of gratitude that may take years to repay."

"He reminds me of you," she told him. "Kind, thoughtful, and not inclined to take anyone at face value. He challenged Anatole often."

"I like him all the more, then. Where is the prince, Beth? I'd expected him to visit you by now, or at least send flowers."

"I really don't know," she answered, yawning. "Do forgive me, husband. I must close my eyes."

"Then, do so, if those beautiful eyes require it. I'll be with you tonight. All the night through, and we shan't ever be parted again. That bed felt like an island without you beside me, Beth. A massive, lonely island. I cannot return to it without you."

She closed her eyes, and he kissed her cheek. Charles considered lying down beside her, but his stomach growled. The sandwiches he and the earl had brought with them had gone cold, so he left the hospital room to join his family at the pub across the way. Whilst the duchess dreamt of playing Knight and Princess in the tree room at Briarcliff Castle, Sinclair heard more tales of boyhood prowess from the man he'd come to think of as a substitute father. James Robert Ian Stuart IV, 10th Duke of Drummond.

6:11 pm – A hotel in the city

Contessa Sofia Serena di Specchio gazed into a mirror, admiring her smooth alabaster skin and throat. "Yes, that does make a difference," she said to the young man who lay upon her bed. "Your is such virile blood, my darling boy. You are a wonderful lover, Marcus, but an even better meal."

The youth could barely open his eyes, for she'd taken two pints—more than any other time—and he now teetered on the brink of consciousness, within a twilight dreamland.

"You needn't speak, *mio amore*. Rest now. I shall return to you later." The tall vampiress licked her ruby lips and began looking through a stylish clothes closet for something to wear for an evening out. "Such old things," she complained to the dreaming youth. "I require new dresses with beautiful necklines to showcase all that I have to offer, no?"

She selected an elegant gown of red silk, decorated across the bodice with delicate beadwork formed into black roses. She had long ago ceased using a maid to dress, after three had failed to keep her secrets and died for it. Now, di Specchio let her lovers help with hooks and buttons.

She stepped into the gown and leaned back against the bed. "Use those talented hands and fasten these for me, my love. Good—no, no! You must button them, Marcus! I have an appointment elsewhere, my darling boy. I've no time for play."

Once fully dressed, she turned back to the mirror, and in her side vision, she saw the glint of a glimmering shadow. She smiled, revealing sharp teeth. "Prince, you honour me. How may I serve you this evening?"

Saraqael still wore his new Carpathian, human form. He lay beside the exhausted youth, stroking the boy's dark hair. "A bit young, isn't he?"

"He is of age."

"Is there anything left in his veins for me?"

"A little," she answered. "There was a time when we shared many young men and women, did we not? So long ago, though."

Saraqael kissed the boy, licking the wound on his throat. "Delicious. How the world changes! The men of old knew how to worship one such as I. And the parties! My dear, the parties went on for months."

"Why do you speak of ages past, when the present is so very exciting?"

Sara frowned as he gazed at himself in the vampiress's mirror. "You forget how old I am, Serena. The present is but another moment to me. I saw the world begin, and I watched the birth of the Seven Realms. Long ago is not long for immortals. It is a breath, a wink of an eye, a spark! And how quickly that spark fades into nothingness and endless monotony."

"But Lord Raziel will return us all to those glory days, will he not?" she reminded him.

Sara stared at her, the smile vanished. "Will he? His plans are meant to unchain my kind, but I prefer to keep them imprisoned. Does that surprise you?"

She grew pale, her dark eyes uncertain. *Is this a test? Is he trying to trap me?* "I leave it to you to decide such things, my lord. I merely follow and serve."

"Bah! You serve only yourself, Serena, which is why I like you so very much." His smile returned, and she began to breathe again. "There's a small task I would have you do. One that requires a woman's touch."

"I am here to serve you, my lord."

"Oh, you will serve me, my dear, and as a reward, I shall complete your transformation to glory! You will fly with my kind and have powers beyond that of any other hybrid. Would you like that? To become a goddess of the night?"

"Yes, my lord, I would!" she exclaimed. "I'd give all to achieve such glories."

Saraqael drew her into his arms and began unfastening the buttons of her dress. "Then, we should celebrate. Together, you and I can achieve anything, Serena. We'll finish this one, and then move on to another and another, until all of London bleeds! Then, they shall bow to us and call us gods!"

"But your brother, my lord. Raziel has other ideas. Other plans."

"So he does, but he already weakens. His attack on the castle failed, and his plans for France show little progress."

"Because of this woman you mentioned? Antoinette? She interferes?" di Specchio asked, hoping to gain information that might prove useful.

Sara laughed as he lay upon the bed. “You’re a scheming little witch, aren’t you? Yes, Gévaudan interferes, but I’m glad of it. Raziel will no doubt find some way to circumvent her obstacles, but we’ll not ruin his plans. Not yet,” he winked. “We’ll need his help to uncover and open the next two mirrors, but once done, he will be redundant. Araqiel has the power to find any remaining mirrors we wish to unlock, and Sathariel has the wisdom to decipher Raziel’s codes. Will you pledge yourself to me, and me alone?”

“Anything for you, Lord Saraqael. Raziel thinks me weak and foolish, all because I am a woman, but you see my true worth!”

“It is your womanhood that makes you so very important to my plan, Serena,” he said, stroking her dark hair as she joined him upon the bed. “Now, my bloodthirsty one, this is what you will do for me.”

CHAPTER TWENTY-SIX

6:44 pm - Montmore House

"Lord Salperton?" the butler asked from outside Henry's door. "Will you be overnighting elsewhere, or do you plan to remain here this evening?"

The physician had just finished a hot bath. Wearing only a dressing gown, he stared at himself in the looking glass, realising he'd not shaved for over a week. "Actually, I'm returning to Whitechapel to check in with the duchess, and then afterward, I I'll stay at Lasberington House. I've plenty of clothing there, should I need them, Saunders. I could use a shave, though, if you've the time."

"I'll fetch the razor and towels, my lord."

The servant left, and Henry crossed into the sitting room of his apartment to read the day's newspapers. When he'd inherited Montmore from his late mother, the viscount converted four of the apartments into patient rooms. He added a locked cupboard inside each *en suite* bath, where his nurses kept sharp items as well as chemicals and medicines. No one, save himself, the butler, and a charge nurse had keys. Not even the housekeeper had a key, which grated on Mrs. Newton at first, but when Henry explained it was to prevent a patient from stealing them, the sensitive but efficient woman expressed understanding.

It had been days since the doctor had slept more than an hour at a time, and he looked forward to a deep and peaceful rest. He was glancing through the *Pall Mall Gazette*, when he heard the door open and assumed it was the butler returning.

"Where would you have me sit?" he asked, his eyes on the paper.

"Wherever you wish," a woman answered.

He glanced up and rose to greet the unexpected visitor. She had glossy dark hair, curled into a fussy unsweep and secured with carved ebony combs. Her dress was scarlet, her eyes black as pitch, and her cheeks pale. The white of her skin seemed almost translucent, and for a moment, Henry fancied her an apparition. Whatever she was, the hair on his arms stood up, and a strange sensation passed through his entire body.

"Madam, I hope you'll forgive me, but you've wandered into private rooms," he said, tightening the sash on his dressing gown. "Did my nurse admit you whilst I was away?"

"Hardly," the intruder laughed. "I've no need of your primitive remedies, Lord Salperton, and I'm sure you would declare me mad, indeed, if I told you all that I know."

The butler entered the parlour, but passed by the woman as if she weren't there. "Shall we proceed, sir? If you'd sit in the green chair near the fire, I'll take care of those whiskers."

"I'm afraid I cannot introduce you, as you've not offered your name," Henry said to the woman. "Saunders, will you show the lady to our drawing room, please?"

"Don't bother," she told him. "Your manservant neither hears nor sees me. Our entire conversation takes place in a fraction of unused time. He thinks you're sitting in a chair, actually, and he's already begun lathering up your face."

A chill ran down Salperton's spine.

"That's impossible," he whispered. Despite the sense of foreboding, Henry assumed the woman was mentally disturbed, and most probably a new patient. "Madam, if you would follow me, I'll be pleased to show you into one of our drawing rooms. There you can speak with my nurse, Mrs. Winstead. She will offer you tea, and when I'm finished dressing, I shall be happy to entertain whatever questions you wish to ask me."

"I've no need of your English tea nor any form of human hospitality," she declared. "I came to offer a word of advice. You might call it a warning, but I consider it wisdom."

"Pray, tell me, madam. What might that be?" Salperton asked, bristling at her brash manner. "You make pretense at civility, though I've yet to hear a name. If you wish to enlighten me, then precede your tuition with a simple and courteous reply."

The red lips smiled, but the dark eyes turned cold as steel. "Contessa Serena Sofia di Specchio. I found your medical bag inside Istseleniye Castle, and inside the bag, your name and address, which means you attended the duchess. We can offer you fellowship or enmity, Lord Salperton. I advise against the latter, for enmity with us is a quick road to certain death."

The countess turned to go, but Salperton would not be bullied, and he grasped her by the arm. "Stop right there! I've no idea just who it is you represent, madam, nor do I care. If you think to discourage me in any way at all by these heavy-handed threats, then you'll discover that little in this world shakes me. I've seen things that would shatter most men; yet, here I stand! You think yourself superior to others, but I find you little more than an unwelcome intruder. Saunders, see the countess out."

The woman offered a chilling smile as she leaned in to whisper into Henry's ear. "Beware, Lord Salperton. Treading upon serpents may seem an easy task to those wearing thick boots, but it is a mortal mistake when one's foot is bare."

She glanced down at his feet, which wore neither sock nor shoe. Her left hand stroked his throat and then wandered beneath the dressing gown, along his bare chest, aiming for the beltline, but he grasped her arm firmly to stop any further invasion.

"I admire your physique," she whispered, licking her lips. "Should you ever change your mind and accept my offer, I promise you ecstasies beyond your wildest imagining!"

With that, the contessa returned time to its normal flow, causing the butler to see her for the first time.

To poor Lester Saunders, the woman had popped into existence from thin air. "Madam!" he gasped, just seconds before the countess vanished.

The perplexed butler promptly fainted.

Henry, however, took the parlour trick in stride. The countess had intended to frighten him, but instead her gambit had the opposite effect. Before di Specchio's visit, the viscount had considered bowing out of the duchess's life once she returned home, but now, he had no intention of doing so.

Bending down, he checked his butler for injuries. "Lie still until the blood returns to your head, Saunders."

"I am sorry, my lord," the man muttered. "I've no idea what happened."

"Perhaps, you forgot to eat," Henry told him, deciding to ignore any mention of the strange countess. "I'll forego the shave for the present and leave for Whitechapel as soon as I can finish dressing," he told him. "Lie still whilst I fetch smelling salts. Breathe as normally as possible," he ordered the servant.

In less than ten seconds, Henry returned with the bottle. Saunders coughed, shocked at the harsh ammonia smell. His eyes teared, but the man slowly regained his feet, leaning slightly on his employer. "Allow me to help, sir. I'll lay out your evening clothes."

"Nonsense, I'm perfectly capable of dressing myself. Go to your rooms and lie down. Keep your feet higher than your head for half an hour. Consider that an order. You're to take the evening off and rest."

Salperton finished dressing, but once done, he took his spare medical bag, left written orders for the staff, bade goodbye to the nurse and housekeeper, and called for his driver.

By eight, his private coach and pair turned onto Warwick Road. Salperton pulled the woolen greatcoat's collar tightly around his stubbled chin. Though the woman's threats bore no fruit in his spirit, he felt as though a ghost had walked across his grave. He peered out the window, looking up into the evening sky. The early stars had emerged, and a white moon waxed towards her round form. Silhouetted against the pale face, a great shadow flew, its shape shimmering as though reflected upon water.

Henry could almost hear his dead mother's voice. *You see it, don't you, Henry? You see the monster?*

Henry did see it.

It was a dragon.

At half past eight, Paul Stuart knocked on Cordelia Wychwright's door. "I know it's somewhat late, but I wondered if you're up to talking?"

To Paul's relief, the baroness was nowhere to be found, and her daughter lay upon the bed, turned to the wall as though sleeping. At the sound of his voice, Delia stirred and wiped at her eyes. "Lord Aubrey. Oh, I mean Paul, of course. What time it is?"

"Half eight or so. I could come back tomorrow, if you prefer."

"Yes. I mean, no, don't go. Come in. Mother's gone to speak with Mr. Treves. She only just left, but we might have five minutes before she comes back."

"Good," he said, pulling a chair close to the bedside. "How are you feeling?"

"Tired. Worried. Foolish."

"Which of those might I help with?"

The young woman managed a wan smile. "None, I think. Or perhaps all of them. Lord Aubrey, I owe you a very great apology. I've been an absolute bore, and you must wish you'd never met me."

"Nonsense."

"If it is nonsense, then I'm the one who's nonsensical. It's not my mother's fault, not entirely," she chattered. "You see, I'm the only one who can marry into position. That's what my mother calls it. I know she wants me to marry well, but I want to marry for love. You're rather older than I, and it's not likely you'd ever understand, especially as you're a man, but modern girls have dreams and aspirations. We don't always want what our mothers want. At least, that's what all the magazines tell me. I'm rather confused by it, actually. Mrs. Abbot's advice column tells me to be demure and obedient, whilst Mrs. Spicer's says I should be forceful and provocative. Which is it? One cannot be both, can one?"

"I can't answer to your satisfaction," he said, "for I'm neither a woman nor young, as you've pointed out."

"I've made you angry," she whispered.

"No, no! Of course, you've not made me angry. The fact is I'm of a different age, in some ways. The world changes before my eyes. I was raised to protect and admire women, but it sounds as though you think my ideals rather dull and old-fashioned. You prefer to lead a less constrained life. Am I right?"

"You think me a child."

"No, I do not. Though, you're not much older than my sister, I do not see you as a child. Look, if you don't want your mother to matchmake for you, then tell her."

"You don't understand. She won't listen."

He shook his head, sweeping a long tendril behind his left ear. "I want to understand, Delia. I do, but I fear it's beyond my male brain. Talk with Elizabeth. She's close to your age and has keen insight and a patient heart."

"The duchess cannot understand, for she's never lacked for position or wealth. She inherited hers. If I'm to fulfill my mother's desires, then I must marry well," she insisted.

He kissed her hand. "If you're to marry well, then you must be well rested. I'll leave you to sleep."

"Paul, will you visit me again? As a friend?"

"Yes," he promised. "Sleep now and stop worrying."

As the earl left, he discovered his cousin waiting in the corridor near the duchess's door. "Have you been ejected?"

"Yes, but only whilst a new doctor examines her. He's an obstetrician. It's a new medical discipline, I'm told. They specialise in expectant mothers."

"But she's doing well, isn't she?" he asked Sinclair, suddenly worried. "Why is Treves bringing in this specialist?"

"I've no idea. I find myself wishing your friend Salperton were here. Beth trusts him."

"Where's Emerson? Couldn't we seek his opinion?"

"Gone to Scotland. He received a telegram from his father two hours ago. Michael's brother has taken ill. The doctors don't expect him to live out the month. It's very strange timing."

Paul grew pensive, his eyes clouding with worry. "Charles, this may be nothing more than a natural occurrence."

"Is it? Emerson is Beth's primary physician, as well as mine, and now he's pulled from us! Oh, ignore me," he added, wiping at his face. "I'm tired."

"Charles, why don't I keep watch here tonight?"

"No, I intend to stay with Beth."

"Yes, I'm aware of that, but I worry about you, Charles. Let me do this. I can place a chair near the door and make certain no one enters."

"Do you think someone would?" asked the marquess. "Who?"

"Whoever attacked the castle. This isn't over, Charles. In fact, it may just be the start. I rather doubt these attacks will let up until Beth has delivered your child."

"Or children."

Paul stared, whispering, "Have the doctors diagnosed twins?"

"No. Yet, both Beth and I feel certain of it," his cousin replied. "If you'd send word to Henry, I'd appreciate it. And tomorrow, I plan to investigate the names on that list, as well as Miss Finchley's story."

"I may have something to add to that tale, Charles, but it can wait until the morrow."

The door opened, and Treves exited the hospital room along with a taller, dark-haired man in a tweed jacket and matching trousers. His bearing was easy and true. The cut of the coat hinted at an athletic build, and his features were the sort that caused society ladies to forget themselves: dark eyes, a ready smile, and a mysterious manner.

Treves offered introductions. "Lord Haimsbury, Lord Aubrey, meet our newest instructor, Dr. Anthony Gehlen. He's a Scot, so you might have many things in common."

"A pleasure," Charles said, shaking the physician's hand.

"Scottish? I can't recall any Gehlens," the earl noted.

"We're part of the Pencaitland line. My father's the current earl. I took my mother's maiden name when I entered school. Long story. A rift with my father that's never healed."

"I'm sorry to hear that. May I ask your experience, Dr. Gehlen?" the earl enquired.

"My full resumé is available through Treves, if you wish it, but I studied at Cambridge for chemistry and Edinburgh for medicine, graduating in '78. I've spent the past ten years honing my skills as an obstetrician in a variety of situations in Paris, Milan, and Vienna. I've delivered over four hundred babies, losing only three, and amongst that number, I had the honour to diagnose and deliver seventeen sets of twins and two of triplets. All but one of those babies survived."

"That's an impressive career," Charles remarked. "Forgive my asking, but if you achieved so great a success abroad, why return to England?"

"To bury my uncle," he answered, his eyes taking on a sad expression. "Sudden heart failure a month ago. A very great shock, actually. Uncle Andrew was my late mother's only sibling. He and I grew close after my father cast me out. Andrew practically raised me. He'd been a vital, energetic man right up until the last. He served as Bishop of Carlisle for thirty-six years."

"I'm sorry for your loss, Doctor," Charles said, nodding his head respectfully. "I look forward to visiting Carlisle. My family home is near there."

"Rose House, correct? Overlooking Eden Valley. I've never been inside, but my uncle told stories of remarkable parties held there when he was newly arrived in the area."

"I'm afraid I can neither deny nor confirm, Dr. Gehlen. I've only scant memories of my childhood, but you'll want to speak with the Baroness Wychwright. Her husband's family has property in Windermere, and it's quite likely he knew your uncle. The baron is MP for the Lake District."

Gehlen's dark eyes glinted. "Wychwrights. I've heard that name. Thank you. It's most gratifying to be with my fellow countrymen once again. When, I arrived back in England, I found myself nostalgic for London and its thriving medical community. I've known Treves, here, for years, so I sent him a letter, explaining my desire to teach obstetrics to his students. I'm happy to say that he answered almost immediately."

Treves nodded. "Anthony's been named a visiting professor at both the Women's School and here, Charles, but as his duties do not commence until January, I asked if he would consult with the duchess."

"Then I praise God for his provision," Sinclair told both men. "Dr. Gehlen, have you an opinion on wife's health?"

"A preliminary one," he replied. "The duchess is doing well, considering. I've been told of the ordeal she suffered recently, but despite physical trauma, shock, and probable pneumonia, the duchess recovers quickly. She must be a woman of considerable energy when healthy."

"You might say that," Paul answered glibly. "Considerable drive and stubbornness, certainly. Charles, I'm going to speak with the other residents of the castle, unless Treves objects."

"I've no objection at all," the shorter physician answered. "But do be careful around Mr. Blinkmire. He's dealing with a great deal of pain. A brave man, that. I very much doubt the duchess would have survived without his protection. Miss Ross told me of their flight from the fire. Blinkmire's quick thinking saved the duchess from suffering similar burns."

"We have much to be grateful for," Charles said as he turned to his cousin. "Let me look in on Beth, and then I'll come with you, Paul.

As he entered the room, a strange chill shuddered along Sinclair's entire frame, as though a sharp draft blew throughout the space. Expecting the window to be open, he crossed to it and drew the drapes aside, but found the window shut and locked. Still, the peculiar chill hung in the air as though alive.

"Captain?" she called.

As Sinclair turned about, that same freezing fear clutched at his heart. For the briefest of seconds, he saw her dead. The eyes open but staring, the mouth slack, bloodstains covering the bed and sheets as though she'd just given birth—or miscarried. A blur of motion crossed his vision, like something only half visible had rushed past him. Charles reached out, and he could actually *feel the thing*, the sensation turning his fingers to ice.

Then she spoke again.

"Charles, are you all right?"

It had all been mere thought, a vision perhaps—or a glimpse into the future. The hospital door opened, causing Charles to jump, his nerves raw.

"Sorry, Haimsbury," Henry MacAlpin said cheerfully. "I knocked, but no one answered. I'd thought the duchess might be alone, you see, and... I say, are you all right?" he asked Sinclair, who'd gone completely white.

"Yes, I think so," the marquess muttered unconvincingly.

"Sit down now!" the Scotsman ordered the detective. "Duchess, I wonder, can you reach that water glass to your left?"

Beth found the glass and handed it to Salperton, who had both hands busy keeping Sinclair from toppling over.

"Steady on. Stay right here, Charles. Do not move from this chair."

Henry drained the water carafe, filling the glass almost to the top. "Drink this. Half first, and then the rest." He lifted Sinclair's wrist and checked the pulse. "I assume you're generally in fine condition, but your heart is working far too hard at the moment. I fear your head injury isn't yet healed."

"Is he all right, Henry?" Beth asked.

"He will be, but he must rest. Charles—forgive me, may I call you Charles?"

Sinclair nodded.

"Thank you. Charles, you have accomplished your task. The duchess is with you, and she is recovering. Those lovely eyes now look upon you, wondering at your health."

Sinclair said nothing, but continued to stare.

"My friend, I really do think you require rest. There is a vacant patient room just the other side of this one. I suggest you take advantage of that bed and sleep for a few hours."

"I'll sleep in here," he insisted, his eyes focusing at last. "Henry. When did you get here?"

"A moment ago. Do not stand yet," he warned Haimsbury, who'd started to rise, but grown dizzy again. Charles complied and returned to the chair.

Sinclair blinked to clear his thoughts. *What just happened to me?* "Sorry. Thank you, Henry. You're right. Forgive me, Beth," he told his wife, reaching for her hand. "I've given you a fright."

"That's all right, Captain. Henry, would you ask a nurse to bring us more water?"

"Yes, certainly."

The viscount left, and Elizabeth sat up as straight as she could manage. "Tell me."

Charles sipped at the remaining water, blinking defensively. "Tell you what?"

"Whatever is troubling you, for a start, but also this head injury of yours. It happened last Sunday night, didn't it?"

"Beth, really, it's but a trifle, and I do not wish to speak of it."

"Is that a command?" she asked him stubbornly.

"If it must be, yes."

Her eyes grew still and fixed upon his. "Very well," she said at last. "But you must promise to tell me everything as soon as we return home. Will you do that?"

He nodded and leaned over to kiss her. "I promise."

She ran a finger along the shadowed outline of his cheek. "Your face tells a story, Captain. You've cuts and bruises, and you've not shaved, probably since the eighteenth. No, I'm content to wait! Only do be careful, darling."

"Always," he told her as Henry returned with the water.

"Your colour is much improved," he said, setting the filled carafe on the table. "I rather imagine it's due to the duchess more than anything I may have done. Charles, Mr. Blinkmire and Count Riga have asked to speak with you. Have you a moment?"

"Yes," he answered. He kissed his wife's cheek and whispered, "Sleep, little one. I shan't be long."

As the two men walked along the corridor towards the private ward, Salperton offered an observation. "Look, Charles, I know you probably don't fully trust me yet, if at all, but may I speak frankly?"

Sinclair laughed. "According to my cousin, you do nothing but speak frankly. Paul calls you the most forthright man he's ever known."

"Well, I don't know about that, but there is a strange feeling to your wife's room. It hit me quite hard when I entered and found you collapsing. You felt it, too, didn't you?"

The marquess stopped, a dozen thoughts swirling in his head. "Paul tells me that he once asked you to join the inner circle. How familiar are you with our mission?"

"Only just," Salperton answered. "I asked my father about it after Paul spoke with me, but he refused to answer. My father is a peculiar and insular man, always has been. I'd hoped he would change as I matured, but he grows evermore distant with each passing year. However, I do know a little about the circle. Thomas Galton told me it's about an ancient inheritance or something. And Prince Anatole mentioned it."

"Let's speak more of this after we meet with Riga and Blinkmire. What do you think of them?"

"I think them extraordinary men. They dearly love your wife, but then all men do. We cannot help it. She emits a delicate light which draws us in and holds us there," he said wistfully. "Do forgive me! I mean nothing by it."

"I understand completely, Henry," the marquess answered as they reached the ward. "I think your description is perfect, and I also know how very blessed I am to be married to that beautiful light."

They entered the six-bed ward. It was the same arrangement as the women's ward, where Ida and the other ladies now slept, but this room was slightly larger and had a porter's closet. Riga was resting his twisted back against a plump pillow, his left arm in a sling from a dislocated shoulder. "My dear Salperton! A pleasure to see you again."

"And you, Count," the viscount answered. "Forgive me for not visiting you sooner, but I had some details to work out at Montmore. Have you met Lord Haimsbury?"

Riga extended his free hand in fellowship, a smile illuminating his aged face. "A distinct pleasure to meet you, Lord Haimsbury. I've been reading about you in this newspaper. We've had nothing but library books and year-old broadsheets to read for a very long time. I confess to enjoying my incarceration here, for it offers time to catch up on the news. Tell me, sir, is this report true? Is your blood royal?"

Charles walked past Blinkmire's bed, where the giant lay snoring. He reached out to take the newspaper. "May I?"

"Yes, of course," Riga said as he handed Sinclair that morning's edition of *The Star*. The headline read: THE RELUCTANT PRINCE OF QUEEN ANNE HOUSE, and referenced an unnamed source in the queen's household who insisted that a well-known peerage family had a stronger claim to the throne than 'the Germans' who now occupied it. Though the article did not name Charles specifically, it certainly implied as much, for only two men of 'marriageable age', as the article described this mysterious 'prince', had ever called Queen Anne House home: Charles and his cousin, Paul Stuart.

The latter gentleman entered the ward as Charles scanned through the outrageous article, growing angrier with each line. "Why do publishers keep printing this trash?" he asked his cousin.

Paul reacted in typical fashion. "To sell newspapers, of course. Now that the Ripper murders have subsided, the press looks for new ways to tantalise their readers."

"Ah, yes, Ripper!" Riga interjected. "I've been reading about him. Most distressing! I pray his crimes have ended."

"As do we all," Sinclair agreed.

"That young porter, Lord Haimsbury. The tall one. A Mr. Davis, I believe. He was kind enough to bring me the papers, and we discussed this Jack the Ripper person. His description reminds me of the *dybbuk* creature that haunted Romania when I was a boy."

"We've heard Ripper called *dybbuk* by others, Count," Charles replied. "I wonder, if we might speak of different matters for the moment. Do you mind if I sit?"

"Please! I understand that you also work for the police, Lord Aubrey."

"I do all the work, and Charles gets all the glory," the earl teased.

"Remind me to reduce your wages, then," the detective answered, his brow arched.

"Ah, the two of you jest with one another," Riga said, smiling. "Tis a sign of great affection. I suspect you both work very hard."

"We do our best," Sinclair said. "As you may already know, Count, I'm currently a detective with Scotland Yard, though that position may change soon."

"As you inherit the throne?" the count joked.

"No," Charles smiled, "but because my cousin and I have started our own intelligence organisation. It is under that auspices that we're investigating the fire at Istseleniye Castle."

Riga grew serious. "Ah, so you know its true name, then. Yes, I imagine Miss Ross or Katrina told you. How are Miss Ross and the others?"

"Mending," Sinclair told him. "And you?"

"Healing quickly for an old man. I've nothing to complain about. Stephen—Mr. Blinkmire—is the worst of all of us. His eyes were burnt quite badly. He sleeps from powerful medicines. A blessing, I think. And our Mr. Stanley suffered a dreadful cut to his left leg, but it's healing well, is it not, Mr. Stanley?"

Elbert Stanley had been reading a book in the bed opposite, and he brandished a wide smile. "Very well, I'm happy to say. Superintendent Sinclair, the count's quick thinking is to thank for our state of health. Before escaping, he placed the prince's medical book in his coat pocket. The book contains the chemical recipes for the treatments we've been undergoing. I shudder to think what might have happened without our daily medicinals! Poor Mr. Anderson, most of all. He'd only just begun his treatments. It would have gone very badly, otherwise. But you're all right, aren't you, Mr. Anderson?"

The man once called Thirteen had been sleeping off and on, and he waved from his bed. "So long as the drapes remain shut, I'm well enough. You're Superintendent Sinclair?"

Charles nodded from Riga's bedside. "Yes. I take it that all you men took treatments prescribed by Romanov? I recall someone once telling me that the prince has powerful healing abilities. Countess di Specchio, I believe."

"She is not to be trusted!" Stanley warned the detective. "I don't like to speak ill of others, but she's with *them*, sir."

"With whom, Mr. Stanley?"

"The evil ones. The countess used to bring her friends into the castle, late at night, when she thought us all asleep, but my illness makes me sensitive to light, and I often walked about the castle after dark. My condition improves, and it is not dangerous, but..." he paused, his face serious. "Let us say that I can be quite dangerous in that *other* state."

Stanley looked towards Riga, who offered a compassionate nod. "Never fear, Elbert, you are amongst friends. Speak freely."

"Thank you, Viktor. Well, sir, one night, not long ago, the prince was away for several days, and during that time, the countess changed my medicine and then left my door unlocked. I reverted to my older ways and caused poor Miss Ross such a fright! The prince returned in the nick of time, and he set us all to rights. A few days afterwards, he banished di Specchio from the castle. We've not seen her since, but I know she is at the heart of that attack on us! I do not like saying this, but I find myself hating that woman!"

Paul Stuart, who'd been standing just inside the door with Salperton, asked an insightful question. "Mr. Stanley, didn't you used to live at No. 12 Columbia Road?"

"Yes! Why, yes, I did. Why do you ask, my lord?"

"If Count Riga will notice last Monday's edition of those newspapers stacked beside his bed, he'll see that a house on Columbia caught fire amidst a very strange attack the previous night."

Riga quickly answered, whispering, "I've said nothing yet, Lord Aubrey. Our Mr. Stanley suffered terribly for over a decade at the hands of these demonic men. I've no wish to upset him."

"Upset me how?" Stanley asked innocently.

Blinkmire's snores grew more staccato as he snorted into wakefulness. His large hands wore thick bandages, and his eyes were bound. "What?" he puffed, thrashing about in panic. "Who's there? Where is she? Is she safe? My lady!"

Riga left his bed and crossed the room in his dressing gown to touch his friend's right arm. "There now, Stephen. All is well. The duchess is safe, thanks to you. Sleep now."

The gigantic man with the soft heart sighed and returned to snoring. Riga glanced up, and Sinclair could see tears glistening in his aging eyes.

"This dear man will probably never see his name in a newspaper, yet his is one of the greatest tales known to me. Do you know that his childless parents visited a gypsy necromancer nearly forty years ago in search of a cure for their curse? The gypsy offered them a potion, which the wife consumed every night for a month, and within three months more, she discovered herself with child, despite her husband's having died without ever touching her again. She proclaimed to all in her Irish village that she'd conceived without need of a man. Of course, no one believed her, but when Stephen was born with features that looked both human and, well, non-human, let us say, these same villagers began to whisper of sorcery and a legend called the Moss People. As the boy grew, he demonstrated a remarkable ability for numbers and languages. Lord Haimsbury, my selfless friend has memorised whole sections of the Bible and many other books, and he can recite the value of *pi* to three hundred decimal places! But he'd trade all that mental ability for a normal life. As you can see, he stands close to eight feet tall and weighs nearly four hundred pounds. It is a great improvement over where he would have been, were it not for his rescuer."

"The prince?" Charles asked the count.

"Indeed, and the story is miraculous! You see, at only ten, Stephen had outgrown all the elders of his village. At twelve, he stood seven feet tall, and I'm told at fifteen had reached over eight feet. On his sixteenth birthday, young Stephen had decided to take his own life, for he could no longer bear the taunts and jeers of his fellows. He'd prepared a thick rope and climbed a tall sycamore, but the end did not come as he expected, for that is the day Prince Anatole Romanov appeared and rescued him. He convinced the youth to accompany him and since that day, Blinkmire has been a loyal friend to the prince. In turn, His Highness has continually searched for better ways to counteract the vanishing gypsy's curse. Without these medicines, Stephen would probably grow to monumental heights! It is my belief that the madmen known to some in England as Redwing—but in my country as the Lords of the Black Stone—were behind my friend's curse. Di Specchio is one of their kind, sir. A bloodthirsty witch. It would not surprise me at all to learn that she and her coven of vampires are behind all those Ripper murders!"

Riga's face had crimsoned with anger, and he stamped his feet, which caused his twisted back to spasm. Sinclair and Stuart each took a side and helped the patient back to his bed.

"Here," Charles said gently, "your passion does you credit, but you must rest to heal. I shan't bother you men any longer tonight. If I may, I'd like to speak with you again tomorrow. Also, with the loss of your home, you'll need new lodgings. As the prince is yet to return, I wonder if you'd consider staying with us?"

"With you?" Riga asked, his face lengthening in surprise. "But, sir, you know nothing of us!"

"I know that you saved my wife's life, and she admires and trusts each of you. The Queen Anne dower house has six apartments and two drawing rooms, as well as a small conservatory, music room, a library, and servants' quarters. You'll have access to doctors, books, outdoor and indoor activities, and new friends. There's a very nice piano in the music room, and the house is wired for electricity on all three floors. I've already spoken to the duchess, and we hope you'll accept."

The count looked at the other men. "We're not like normal guests, my lord," Stanley objected. "We'd not want to cause any trouble."

"On the contrary, Mr. Stanley, I believe you may serve a wonderful purpose in our lives. We are ever expanding our families, and with your names added to the rolls, we shall be the richer for it."

"May we give you our answer tomorrow, sir?" Riga asked. "We must confer with the ladies, and we'll want Mr. Blinkmire to have a say."

"Of course. Good evening, gentlemen. On behalf of my duchess, I thank you for your courage and friendship."

They left the ward, and as the door shut, Riga and the others began to weep.

CHAPTER TWENTY-SEVEN

28th November – 10:02 pm

The White's Row public house sat one block north and one west of the London Hospital, and by ten o'clock that Wednesday night was filled to bursting with harried medical students, single nurses looking to impress harried medical students, doctors longing for simpler days when they were merely harried medical students, and on this night, three peers of the realm.

"Henry, I can't thank you enough for what you did for Beth," Sinclair said as the trio shared a simple meal at a backroom table.

"As I said earlier, Charles, it's nothing any other man wouldn't have done. I'm only glad my blundering didn't end badly. I should have assumed the prince had a good reason for insisting I remain in the castle. I wonder where he is, anyway?"

"It's our experience that Romanov appears when he's least expected," the earl noted as a pretty barmaid arrived with a tray of Scotch ales. "Thank you," he said, taking one and handing the others to Charles and Henry. "You probably enjoy working here," he told the maid. The earl had a habit of striking up conversations at the oddest of times, but it usually had a purpose. "Do you see many medical men hereabouts?"

"All the time, sir. Mostly students," the redhead answered. Her henna-dyed locks practically shouted, and her provocative attire followed suit in raucous harmony with the hair. She bent low to offer the handsome peer a closer look at the pillowy flesh above her neckline, causing Paul to wink as though interested.

"I'm happy to meet up with any man what wants a bit o' schoolin'," she teased.

"I've no doubt you've much to teach," he answered with a bright smile. "I fear my mind tends towards other matters tonight, but you might help me with one of them. Have you noticed a dark-haired Scotsman in here of late? Lean of face, tall, dark eyes, muscular build?"

"Would that be the new professor, sir? Real good looker? Six foot tall, if he's an inch. Stylish dresser?"

"That's the one."

She showed disappointment. "I hope you don't work from the other side o' the street, sir. Seems like all the handsome men do nowadays. I don' reckon this doc'd be on t'other side, though. Dr. Gehlen looks right rugged ta me."

"I'm sure he is, but I work from your side of the street, my dear," Aubrey assured her. "Tis a very pleasant side, is it not?"

"My shift ends at midnight, sir. Iffin you've the time, then, I could show you some o' them lessons."

Charles handed the girl five pounds. "This is for the ale and the information, Miss. I fear my friend must decline your kind offer of instruction," he added showing his warrant card. "Besides, he's a very poor student."

"You're blue?" she exclaimed, seeing the police card.

Henry laughed. "This gentleman is as blue as they come. Not only his uniform, but also his blood, according to all the papers. Is that all we need for now?"

"For now," Aubrey said, laughing as he handed her a fiver of his own. "Go buy yourself a pretty frock to wear out with one of these students. On me."

She took the money and left, and Sinclair shook his head. "Do ladies ever stop throwing themselves at you, Cousin?"

"I'll let you know," the earl answered impishly.

"Did you ask about Gehlen for a particular reason?" the viscount enquired as he dipped a spoon into the thick stew.

"Not really. My father taught me to distrust anyone new until he proves his *bona fides*, you might say. The duke is the same, only he makes you think he trusts you, whilst he searches through your pockets and investigates every aspect of your life."

"Keep your enemies close and talking," Sinclair quoted. "I remember hearing him say that more than once. Do you consider Gehlen a possible enemy?"

"I've no idea," the earl said, "but I'd be a fool to abandon a practise that's kept me alive for many years. Actually, now that I think of it, I've disregarded that practise twice since Father insisted I use it."

"Only twice?" Salperton asked.

"Only twice, and I'm looking at both instances. You and Charles. Our little duchess has the finest intuition known to mankind. She can spot a fraud across any ballroom, detect deceit in any crowd, and she does it all with a mix of grace and fire. Grace to all until they cross her, and then you'd best put on armour against the inevitable inferno."

His cousin and the physician smiled at this, and the earl continued, "Let me explain. When Beth was a child and demonstrated an aversion to someone new—assuming myself older and wiser—I paid little heed to her intuition, yet in every case, without fail, her instincts proved to be correct. So, when Elizabeth told me in '79 that she trusted you completely, then I also trusted you, Charles. She knew from the very first moment, that you were worthy of unswerving trust, Cousin. And Henry is much the same. Elizabeth told me that she knew instantly that you're a good and honest man. She trusts you without reservation," he told the viscount, "therefore, even if I hadn't known you since Eton, Henry, I'd have placed full faith in you. Beth is never wrong."

"I pray that I'm always worthy of that trust—from both of you."

Charles had eaten half a sandwich and drunk all his ale, and he pushed away the plate, noticing the beginnings of the headache returning.

"I may have to leave soon," he said. "Lack of sleep begins to catch up with me."

"Charles, your injuries begin to catch up with you!" Aubrey exclaimed. "I should have insisted you go to bed right away."

"No, I'm fine, and I needed to eat. Besides, this fellowship is more therapeutic than all of Emerson's potions, though don't tell him I said that."

The earl had ordered the stew as well, and he broke a crust of bread and dipped it into the steaming broth. "Henry, if you'll recall, I tried to bring you into our circle back at Oxford, and if your spiritual eyes are as clear as I'm told, then you would be a very great asset. You say Romanov knows your history?"

"So he claimed," Salperton said, wiping ale from his upper lip. "I wish now I'd paid more heed to your talk of the inner circle back in school. Better late to the party than not at all, I suppose. This Romanov's a most peculiar man, though man is an improbable noun to use. I think him quite unnatural in his species. As is this di Specchio creature."

"You know the countess?" Charles asked, leaning upon the waxed oak table. "How?"

"The woman had the audacity to show up at my home this evening! I'd returned to Montmore to make sure my resident patients hadn't fallen into neglect during my unanticipated absence. I am grateful to the Lord that they all seemed well. One woman had worried me exceedingly, for the prince claimed she tried to leap out of a window, though how he knew it—well, that is another matter. This countess, though, she did not so much as knock upon my door! Just appeared as though invited, which I assure you, she was not. Then, when she'd made her threats known, vanished from sight without so much as a wink! My poor butler fainted, and he'll probably take days to recover his senses. You'd think that working in a madhouse would prepare a man for unnatural occurrences, but perhaps we're just not mad enough."

Charles said nothing. He held the empty ale glass in his hands, staring at it as though trying to pierce its reflective surface, his thoughts far away.

Salperton cleared his throat nervously, fearing he'd misspoken. "Charles, I meant no offence. I pray you don't think my idle comment about madness had anything to do with you or the duchess."

Sinclair's hands tightened 'round the glass, whitening the knuckles. It seemed as though he wanted to break it.

"Charles, what is it?" Aubrey asked.

"I know you're joking, Henry, but sometimes, I feel as though I'm going mad," he whispered, looking up at his friends. "I try to be strong for Beth. Try to say nothing that might alarm her, but no matter what I do, Shadows follow us like hissing snakes."

"Shadows?" Henry enquired. "Spirits, you mean? Charles, can you see them? I know the duchess often does. Anatole told me as much, but do you also perceive these creatures?"

The detective smiled nervously, and he moved the glass to one side. "Were you any other alienist, Henry, I'd find that question worrisome, but as you also experience such visitations, then yes, I'll admit it. I do see them, but not the way Beth does. When they appear to me, it's as though they *want* me to see them. It's a game to them, I think. In Beth's hospital room earlier, I felt a deep chill, which had no physical source."

"Yes, I felt it as well," Henry observed. "Paul, what about you?"

The earl pushed back in his chair as though distancing himself from the conversation. "No. Nothing. I don't doubt either of you, and I've certainly seen Elizabeth's reaction when she encounters these spirits, but they conceal themselves from my eyes. Charles, you look completely worn out. Let me walk you back to the London. Henry, why don't you come back to Aubrey House with me, and we'll discuss inducting you into the circle at our next meeting—that is, if you're still interested."

He and Salperton took to their feet, and the barmaid started towards them to clear the table. Charles also started to stand, but the ale glass inexplicably shot from the table of its own accord, narrowly missing Sinclair's head by quarter of an inch.

Paul Stuart's reflexes kicked into gear, and he nearly caught the glass, but it smashed against the wooden partition that separated the private area from the main area of the pub. Shards of sparkling glass rained down the wall like glittering ice.

"I think we're not wanted here," Henry observed matter-of-factly. "Let's talk elsewhere, gentlemen, and if there's a Bible in the duchess's room, I think it's time we use it."

Charles made sure of her welfare as soon as they returned to the London and found her asleep. Then, whilst Charles held her hand, Henry quietly inspected every square inch of Beth's small room; opening the closet, looking inside drawers and behind books, even opening each volume to make sure the titles and contents matched. After quarter of an hour and satisfied with his search, Salperton set a Bible upon Elizabeth's side table and opened it to Psalm Ninety-One.

As Henry MacAlpin made his survey, Paul Stuart paid a quick visit to Cordelia Wychwright. She'd fallen asleep, thanks to the soporific ordered by Treves, and the earl kissed her sweetly on the cheek and left.

Paul then wired Kepelheim and asked him to bring as many circle members as he could muster to the hospital for a hastily arranged prayer meeting. It was half eleven by the time their small group convened: Haimsbury, Aubrey, Salperton, Sir Thomas Galton, Martin Kepelheim, and Arthur France, who'd taken up temporary residence with Edmund and Emily Reid whilst investigating the Lord Hemsfield murder. Kepelheim brought with him a collection of journals and papers, and he was the last to join the group.

"Charles, my dear friend, forgive my saying so, but you are a fright! Here I thought you well enough that I could leave London for a day or so, but clearly I was mistaken. Why aren't you in hospital along with your dear wife?"

"Because he is just as stubborn as our duchess, Martin," the earl told the tailor. "But then aren't most of us? Thanks for answering my summons. It's good to have you back. Did you discover anything in Cumbria that might help us?"

"Cumbria?" Henry asked. "Forgive me for sounding naive, but, sir, who are you? Are you a detective?"

Kepelheim laughed, and his round cheeks grew pink with mirth. "Our marquess asked me that once, or something akin to it. As I recall, what you actually said, Charles, was that my abilities might qualify me to serve as a detective, to which I intimated that I've been one all along."

Sinclair smiled at the memory. "Has it only been two months since then, Martin? Not even that, actually. In some ways, it seems like no time at all has passed, but other times, as though we've lived a hundred years."

"Yes, I should think so," the tailor replied. "Your love for Elizabeth must make the days fly past, but these dangers that surround you both weigh you down. I can see it in your face, and in those remarkable eyes. What is it Elizabeth calls them? Oh, yes, 'sea blue'. Now, to Lord Salperton's question, I think I can provide an answer that will surprise him."

"Surprise me?" the viscount asked. "How?"

Arthur France and Galton whispered together at the far end of the table. Two porters had been kind enough to deliver it from storage along with half a dozen wooden chairs. Kepelheim's stack of papers and journals were spread out before him, and each man had a glass of water. France sipped his, still speaking in whispers with Galton.

"Forgive me, sir, but what was that?" the inspector asked the tailor. "Sir Thomas was just explaining who Lord Salperton is. I apologise for bein' rude, Superintendent."

"It's my fault, Arthur. I should have made introductions as soon as you and Galton arrived. Allow me to introduce the membership to a man you'll soon come to know very well. Dr. Henry MacAlpin, 7th Viscount Salperton. Henry, this is an old friend and colleague, Inspector Arthur France. Arthur and I have been friends for more than a decade. He will now serve as part of our investigatory team at Inner Circle Intelligence, when he's not keeping an eye on my wife, that is. Of course, Sir Thomas and you are old friends."

"Indeed. It's a pleasure to meet you, Inspector," Salperton said politely. "I look forward to getting to know you better. Do go on, Mr. Kepelheim. Why would your trip to Cumbria surprise me?"

"Ah, yes," Martin said after swallowing the water he'd just gulped. "Well, the trip *per se* may not surprise you, but what I discovered whilst rummaging through Rose House might. That beautiful home is a fascinating place with deep historical significance. It overlooks Eden Valley, of course, but it is built upon land once owned by Uther Pendragon. Did you know that, Charles?"

"I'd surmised as much, based on hints you've offered, but also the memories of Christmas you helped me recover. The tree was set up in the Pendragon Room. It overlooks Uther's ruined castle."

"It does indeed, but Uther's tale is also connected to our viscount's family. Henry, you're related to Charles through more than just the Stuart line. You also have Sinclair blood in your veins. I discovered it in these scrolls, and I'd no idea that upon my return to London, I'd find you here, back with your family. But then, that is always the way with God's timing, isn't it? He brings us surprises when and where we least expect it. Charles's meeting with Elizabeth in '79 is but one example."

"*And we know that all things work together for good to them who love God, to them who are the called, according to his purpose*," Salperton quoted "It's one of the first verses my mother had me learn. She said it would make sense as I grew older."

"As do nearly all things," Kepelheim observed soberly. "And so it is with our circle. This is what I discovered, and it's written in code, by your father's own hand, Charles. Here is the original, which you may pass around the table. I've translated it as closely as my limited knowledge of your father's complicated ciphers allows."

The tailor handed Sinclair a tanned leather book, wound about with a split leather cord. "This entry is dated the 11th of June, 1855, but before I read it, let me explain that Robby Sinclair rarely wrote down anything in plain English. He had a very strong fear of Redwing spies within his own house. Charles, as you know, your father and mother married in early September of '54, and very quickly after, she conceived you. Robby thought it was on their wedding night, in fact. A miracle, but then your life is filled with them. Here is my translation of the entry:

> 'Not one wink of sleep last night, but it's all been worth it. As I write this, I gaze at my newborn son. Never have I felt such exhilaration nor such anxiety, all at once! Angela did beautifully, despite the long hours of labour. Charles Robert Arthur Sinclair III is the perfect result of that very long night. He has my hair, Angela's eyes, and the doctors say he'll be quite tall. My greatest prayer at this moment is that the Lord will allow me to see him grow and perhaps have his own children one day. Though, I fear that may never happen. The creature appeared again last night, hovering over Angela's birthing bed as if waiting for our son to be born! How I hate that loathsome spirit! I said nothing to Victoria. How could I? Only I can see the demon. Even my beautiful wife could not see it, but I did. Why, I cannot say. I've discussed it with Connor many times, and he believes it is a spirit-tie of the blood. I must speak to Martin about it, when he visits next week.
>
> The drumming began again, hours before Angela's waters broke, as though signalling our son's imminent arrival. They resound from beneath the stones of our home, and whenever they commence, the old ruins below shimmer with a faint light. Locals claim it's the ghosts of Uther's poisoned men. I know better. I only pray my son never sees these creatures.
>
> 'I have written to my Great-Uncle Henry MacAlpin at Inverary. His son Hal was born last year. Uncle Henry once told me whilst visiting here, that the drums cry out at

his castle as well; as though hell itself calls to him. I wrote last month to ask if these shades and spiders ever creep about his halls and upon his ramparts. I await the answer.

'May the Lord keep us safe! This verse provides solace as I listen to my son's soft breathing. Job 12:22, which says: *He discovereth deep things out of darkness, and bringeth out to light the shadow of death.*

'Oh, Lord, may this be your mission here! To bring light to these menacing shadows! Quicken my heart and sharpen my vision that I may protect my beloved son, I beg you, for I fear I shan't see Charles live to manhood. Tonight, I feel as though the drums call me to my doom!'

"And there the entry ends," Kepelheim told them.

Sinclair said nothing, only stared, the leather journal in his hands. His blue eyes closed, and Martin noticed each knuckle whiten upon his fingers.

"My dear friend," he told Charles, "I know how it must tear at your heart to hear these words, but they reveal your father's mind that night. I know of only one other man who matches him for integrity and courage, and that is you, his son."

The table of men had listened with nary a whisper or movement, and the marquess held the bound, leather book to his chest, tears filling his eyes. "This is as close as I'll ever come to knowing my father, this side of eternity, Martin. Yes, it's hard to hear his words, but they also comfort me. Thank you for taking the time decipher them. I look forward to reading more of his entries, when you have the time to decode them."

Henry MacAlpin took a pencil from his pocket and began writing out a series of names on a bit of paper. "He called my father his great-uncle. I'm trying to figure out how that works."

"I can show you, if you wish, Lord Salperton," Martin offered. "I've all the family lineages, dating back to the 9th century, at my home. And partial lineages going even further back in time, extending past Clovis in some cases. However, in Charles's case, I believe I must travel to France for my next clues. Uther's castle provides the starting point."

"I've no idea what you mean," Sinclair said. "Paul, have you a notion?"

"I think it's late," the earl declared, standing. "Charles, you should go sleep. We'll adjourn to Haimsbury House in the meantime and continue, with your permission, of course."

"Yes, of course," his cousin answered. "If Baxter's still awake, he has my permission to raid the cellars."

"We'll ask the good Mr. Baxter to join us, then," Aubrey said. "Henry, will you come?"

"If you don't mind an ignorant fellow tagging along, yes, thank you. Charles, send for me should you require medical advice—or anything else."

The marquess shook the viscount's hand. "I will. Thank you."

Sinclair left the gathering and entered Beth's room. To his great relief, it felt warm and friendly—and safe. Even though the hospital staff had provided him a cot, Charles had no wish to sleep apart from his wife. He removed his coat, waistcoat, and shoulder holster and placed them in a closet along with his shoes and socks. He then slid in beside his wife, still in trousers and shirt, in case a nurse might enter during the night.

How wonderfully warm her body felt, how calming! The bed was quite narrow, forcing the six-foot-three marquess to move as close to his wife as possible, but that only made him happier. She'd turned onto her right side, and he put his left arm around her waist, his fingers touching her abdomen.

"Good night, little one," he whispered. "And goodnight to you as well, Robby and Georgie. I love you all so very much."

In a few minutes, his breathing grew regular, and for the first night in many, Charles Sinclair slept deeply without so much as one moment of fear.

CHAPTER TWENTY-EIGHT

2:45 pm - Monday, 3rd December, 1888

During the next five days, the Stuart clan became a fixture at the busy hospital. The duke visited his granddaughter twice a day, bringing flowers and chocolates for the nursing staff and handing out gold sovereigns and sweets to any children in the wards.

Mr. Blinkmire recovered his eyesight, Riga his shoulder mobility, and Ida Ross grew well enough for release. Charles sent four of his best coaches to collect the Castle Company—as they'd come to be called—and move them into the Queen Anne dower house. Elbert Stanley and David Anderson, formerly called Mr. Thirteen, shared a small apartment on the first floor, whilst Riga and Blinkmire took the slightly larger, corner suite as their own. Ida felt strange living so close to the man she'd admired for years, but Mrs. Alcorn convinced the former prostitute that the family wished only for her comfort, and after much discussion, Ross finally decided to share with Kilmeade. Katrina chose rooms on the second floor. The cooks were hired to provide meals but given their own, private accommodations, and the butler and footman received similar attention. All in all, the castle's former residents quickly settled into a pleasant routine, and the ladies took turns with cleaning duties.

Delia Wychwright said very little during those five days. Her scratches and bruises began to heal, and Treves suggested she might be released. Her mother, however, insisted the chief surgeon keep her in hospital—as a precaution. Sinclair stopped in one morning to visit the eighteen-year-old, for Paul had told his cousin about Albert Wendaway's deplorable treatment of the girl.

"I hope you don't mind if we talk, Lady Cordelia," the marquess said as he brought a wooden chair close to hers.

Cordelia hated lying in bed, even when unwell, and she'd spent many of the tedious hours walking the corridors, visiting the duchess, or working jigsaws. A lap desk covered in pieces of the French countryside sat upon her knees, and a pot of tea steamed beside a half-empty cup on the nearest table. "Oh, hello, Lord Haimsbury. Talk? What about?"

"Is your mother here this morning?"

"No, but I'm sure she'll show up soon enough. Father's at the Exchange, I imagine."

"Isn't he an MP?"

"Yes, but Father conducts business at the Exchange very morning. He seldom misses a day." She tried again and again to force an irregularly shaped piece of sky into a tree branch, despite the colours not fitting in the least. "Is this a friendly talk, Lord Haimsbury, or an official one?"

"I'd rather keep it friendly, but I confess to concern regarding what happened to you last week. We may speak in whispers, if you wish. I have very good hearing. As your mother's not here, I prefer not to shut the door, for reasons of propriety."

She smiled, still pressing upon the ill-fitting piece with her thumb. "You must think me a complete and utter nitwit, Lord Haimsbury. Honestly, when I think of the way I behaved the first time I met you, it causes me intense regret. I'm sure you see me as little more than a pampered girl, but I want to be better than that. Truly, I do! I just don't know where to begin."

Charles had noticed her behaviour with the puzzle piece, and he wondered if she'd been given medication that altered her thinking. He also noticed several other things about Cordelia Jane Wychwright: The loss of colour to her cheeks, the increase in her breathing, and a slight shift in the position of her body. She appeared to shrink, as though trying to remove herself from the conversation. He'd seen many people behave the same way when being interviewed, but those had been criminals. Why would Delia show such reluctance to speak to him?

"I imagine you'd love to go home," he said casually. "I know my wife does. Will Treves release you soon?"

"That's up to Mama."

"I rather think it's up to your doctors, Delia. May I call you that?"

"Oh, yes, of course. Why won't this work?" she complained about the puzzle piece.

Charles gently removed the bit of sky and moved it to the appropriate position. He then found one with green leaves and helped her to place it inside the branch. "Life can be quite confusing at times. I know it is for me. I sometimes feel certain I fit in, and then suddenly I realise I'm all wrong for the job. Did you know I once planned to teach mathematics?"

She looked at him, her eyes round as saucers. "Did you? I can't imagine anything more dull. Oh, forgive me! That was rude."

He laughed, amiably. "No, you're right! It is dull, but then I was dull. My late wife thought so, anyway. She wanted me to become a solicitor, actually, but if I had, I've never have met the duchess. Because I took a job as a policeman, I was there the night she needed me."

"I'm not sure I understand."

"Beth was the victim of a crime long ago, and I helped solve it," he answered, offering a simplistic explanation. "All I'm saying is God's plans for our lives don't always move in a straight line. Mathematics still serves me well, though I'm not a teacher. Have you plans for the future?"

Her hands started to tremble. "I'm not sure I have a future. Not now."

"Why is that? Delia, you have all the things a young woman could desire. Beauty, position, opportunity."

"Do you think I'm pretty?"

"Certainly."

"Mama says I'm fat and useless. She hates me," she said suddenly.

Cordelia's face paled, and Charles glanced out the open door to make sure the baroness hadn't returned. "I doubt that's true. Why would you think she hates you?"

"Because I'm damaged. I cannot prove it, but I think she had a hand in it. Albert, I mean. Why would a mother do that?"

Something about her behaviour set off alarm bells. He'd seen mannerisms like this far too often in far too many young girls. "Delia, what did Sir Albert do?"

"Nothing."

"Was he your escort into Whitechapel last week?"

"Escort?" she repeated, her fingers dancing as though counting. "I don't know. Was it last week?"

"Delia, I want to help you. As a friend. I hope you know that."

To his surprise, her entire demeanor altered. Her facial muscles relaxed, her hands stopped fidgeting with the puzzle pieces, and her constantly moving eyes settled firmly on his. "You consider me a friend?"

"I do," he assured her in a soft voice. "A good friend. Tell me about Sir Albert."

"I thought he was nice," she whispered. "He isn't nice."

"Why not?"

She looked away, her attention on the window. "My friend Davina Southwoood thinks he's dreamy, but he isn't. He's cruel and selfish and quite awful!"

"What happened last week? How did you end up at the Exchange?"

She took a deep breath, and then started working the puzzle again. "Why are men so very cruel sometimes?"

Sinclair considered the question, not only as one related to criminal intent, but to morality. "Delia, did Albert hurt you?"

Her hands tensed. "No."

"I lay no blame on you, Cordelia. If he overstepped with you in any way, then you may tell me. Did he kiss you?"

She nodded, the sinews of her neck tightening as she selected a piece to add to the tree.

"Were these kisses mere affection or something more? Were they intimate?"

"I cannot say," she answered and moved the tree piece to the grassy area.

The marquess slid his chair closer and took the piece from her and set it aside. He then took her hands into his. "I am your friend, Delia. Think of me as your defender, your very own knight, and my job is to vanquish anyone who might wish to harm you. Tell me, did Albert touch you in any way that was improper?"

Her shoulders began to spasm, and her lower lip quivered. "Please, don't tell my parents! Please! I beg you! It's why I had to run away from him, you see. I told everyone it was the noise and blood of the boxing match, but it was Albert. He wanted to... He tried to...! He... Oh, you must think me a terrible harlot! I'm ruined! Ruined!"

He moved the lap desk to the side and drew Cordelia into his arms, holding her as she wept. "You did nothing wrong."

"Why did I let him?" she sobbed. "I tried to fight it, I did!"

"Hush now. Albert will answer for his actions. I promise you. What he did is a crime, Delia. My job as your knight is to see he pays for that crime. I'll find Wendaway and arrest him."

"I hate him!" she wept into his shoulder. "I wish to never see his awful face again! Am I so pitifully useless that he'd think me easy prey? I thought he liked me."

"Delia, have you spoken to my wife about any of this?"

She nodded again. "Yes, and she said I should tell you, but if Paul ever found out, I'd die!"

"He should know, Delia. If you really want a relationship with Paul, then allow me to tell him. Will you do that?"

"He'll hate me! He mustn't know!"

"No, he won't hate you. Now, I think you should rest. Don't worry about any of this. Let me take care of everything. Will you do that?"

"Will you talk with my mother? She mustn't know I told you."

"I shan't say a word without talking to you first."

"Promise?"

"I promise."

"Thank you. You're very kind," she whispered, hiccupping from release of strain. "My own brothers are never as kind as you."

He kissed her on the forehead. "That's a very nice thing to say. Would you like some cocoa to help you to relax?"

"Yes, please. With peppermint."

He smiled. "I'll see to the peppermint. My wife likes it that way as well. Don't let any of this worry you from now on. Let me handle it."

The marquess left the room and shut the door, waving to Sister Reston as he crossed the corridor. "Sister, could you have some cocoa delivered to Lady Cordelia? With peppermint, if you have any. Also, is Dr. Gehlen available?"

"Yes, he is, my lord. In the doctors' library across the park. It's raining, sir. Shall I find an umbrella?"

"No, I doubt rain will hurt me. Thank you."

He left the main building and walked through familiar gardens, winter-weary from the snow, and then crossed the large gravel park until he reached the Medical College. The main foyer was a sea of chattering students, discussing a lecture given by Frederick Treves on when and how to perform appendicectomies as well as indications for post-operative care. The class of thirty students had formed into two groups, one arguing over the demonstration they'd just observed, whilst the other debated the benefits of completely different topics such as gambling, tuition, fine clothing, and most of all—women. Charles passed through the crowd and turned towards the main office. Inside, he found three men: Frederick Treves, an older gentleman in business dress, and Anthony Gehlen.

"Charles, this is a pleasant surprise! What brings you to the college?" Treves asked his friend. "Thinking of adding Doctor to your many titles?"

"You're Haimsbury, aren't you?" the older gentleman asked. "Sir Nigel Willoughby. I'm on the board of governors for the hospital. Your wife is an absolute delight, sir. Absolute delight! She's picked my brain until it's sore about the ways and means of funding a charity hospital. I warned her that it's a very expensive and thankless endeavour, but I don't think she paid me any heed."

"It's a pleasure to meet you, Sir Nigel. The duchess has very definite ideas about that hospital. You'll not dissuade her, and I could not be more proud. Dr. Gehlen, I wonder if you have a moment?"

"Certainly," the tall physician answered. "Here, or would you prefer more privacy? There's a rather cramped office I've been using, just down the hall."

"Yes, I'd like to speak in private. Thank you."

The two men left, and in a few minutes sat together in a tiny office near the west end of the building. "I call this my broom closet," Gehlen joked. "Drink?" he asked, opening a drawer in the desk and removing a dusty bottle of whisky. "It was gifted to me by the closet's previous tenant, a fellow who taught chemistry. I've no idea if this is a good distiller or not, to be honest. I never indulge myself."

"No, thank you."

"Teetotaler like me, then?"

"Hardly. I'm the Duke of Drummond's nephew. He'd disown me. However, I try to avoid spirits when I have important matters to discuss."

"Do you refer to the duchess?"

"No. Actually, it's a possible criminal case. I could call our police surgeon, but I fear that would cause the lady needless embarrassment. Am I right in thinking that you've been tending Lady Cordelia Wychwright?"

Gehlen took a deep breath, leaning against the chair's high back as he pondered the question. "I've seen her a few times along with Treves. Wychwright's mother is one of those social climbers who sees doctors as a form of jewellery. We're there to make her look more impressive to friends, therefore, the more doctors you can show off, the more you impress. Why?"

"Did you examine her?"

"Not really. Treves had me consult, but I never did more than watch. The girl was admitted with superficial scratches and bruises to the face and hands from walking through foliage. So she says. Her reason for hospitalisation was due to catching a chill from exposure to cold. Lord Haimsbury, why do you ask?"

"Could you examine her? It may be too late to find anything evidentiary, but I fear she may have been sexually assaulted."

Gehlen stared at the detective. "Did she tell you that?"

"Not directly, no, but she hinted at it. And her story of why she walked to the Exchange before sunrise, makes no sense, unless she so feared for her safety that she fled. I doubt she's told her parents everything. Girls in these situations seldom do. I prefer not to place her under further duress, but do you think you could conduct a modest examination? Enough to determine if there's legal cause for further action?"

"Yes, I could do that. It isn't the first time I've been asked to conduct this sort of thing, but I pray you're wrong, Lord Haimsbury."

"As do I, Doctor. Now, I shan't keep you. I need to speak to Treves, and then I plan to share tea with my wife."

"The duchess is a lovely woman, sir. If you've time in the near future, I'd like to speak to you regarding her pregnancy."

"She's all right?" he asked, concerned.

"Yes, quite healthy, though suffering with morning sickness and balance problems. Did they manifest before her trauma?"

"They did. Beth's had a difficult few weeks. Is that unusual?"

"Sometimes. Early difficulties aren't always a sign of anything wrong, but it is early for such severe symptoms. With your permission, I'd like to examine her before she leaves the London."

"Yes, of course, so long as Elizabeth agrees to it. Will you get back to me regarding both women? Lady Cordelia and my wife?"

"As soon as I have any information," Gehlen answered shaking Sinclair's hand.

Charles left the room, his mind now mulling over the obstetrician's comments. His head ached, causing his balance to shift without warning, and he had to stop and lean against the corridor wall. *It's just the injury still healing,* he told himself. As he neared the main office, he noticed the older man had left, and Treves now spoke with two students. Deciding to defer his questions for the surgeon until later, Sinclair left the medical college to visit the duchess.

He'd arrive late for tea. A very strange encounter would reschedule all his afternoon plans.

CHAPTER TWENTY-NINE

"Do join me, won't you, Lord Haimsbury?" a portly man in a banker's suit called from a black coach. "We shan't keep you long."

Charles had a peculiar tingling sensation at the back of his neck, like tiny needles dancing across the skin. "Do I know you, sir?"

"No, but I know you. This will take an hour at most, and I assure you that it's worth the time. Please, sir."

Sinclair walked closer. The coach's driver wore a simple overcoat and soft hat, and no other servant or passenger—save the plump-faced speaker—stood anywhere within sight. *Looks can be deceiving*, the voice of experience whispered inside his aching head. *Take care.*

"I'd appreciate a name before I join you."

The rotund fellow laughed, his fleshy cheeks dancing upon the bones. "It's Parsons. Sir Reginald J. Parsons. I'm chief clerk at the Lords, you know. If you ever attended a session, Lord Haimsbury, you'd recognise me at once. Do come out of the rain, sir. You could catch your death. "

Reluctantly, Charles entered the unmarked coach and sat opposite the jolly stranger. "Why is the chief clerk from the House of Lords sitting outside London Medical College? Are you ill?"

"Oh, hardly!" he laughed. "No, sir, I'm fit as a fiddle." He tapped on the roof of the carriage with his walking stick, and the wheels engaged. "As I said, I shan't keep you too awfully long, but I have a duty to perform, which requires your cooperation, and I'm never a man to shirk duty."

"What duty is that, Sir Reginald?"

"A solemn promise to a woman of quality. I spoke with that good lady two hours ago, and she commissioned me to deliver you to a meeting. You needn't worry about the duchess, Lord Haimsbury. I've two reliable men keeping watch on her, from a discreet distance of course, and someone she knows and trusts will inform her that you'll be late for tea."

"It appears you've thought of everything."

"That, my lord, is my job. The title of chief clerk is a misdirection, you might say. A deliberate obfuscation. You'll understand everything shortly."

They rode together through the city of London, past St. Paul's cathedral, past St. James's Park, finally stopping at a three-storey Georgian on the north side of Hanover Square. The white limestone façade and pillared portico gave the place an aged, historic look, as though built by ancient Greeks. However, it had only stood at this spot since 1824, when the Duke of Wellington and General Sir John Malcolm, in cooperation with the East India Company, established a society for servicemen returning from India.

"The Oriental Club?" Sinclair asked as he exited the coach and started up the broad steps. "I've no desire to apply for membership, nor would I qualify, Sir Reginald."

"Neither would I, sir, but we've a very important meeting arranged in the third floor parlour. It is the least smoky portion of the club and will not irritate our good lady's lungs."

"And what lady might that be? The very nature of a men's club is that women are generally absent. Or am I mistaken?"

Parsons managed the steep steps with surprising grace, and he chuckled at his unwilling guest's discomfiture. "I'm sure you're rife with questions, but I promise your patience will soon be rewarded, Lord Haimsbury."

A uniformed usher met them and asked for their membership cards. Parsons handed the youth a note. The boy's face whitened in shock. "Right this way, sirs."

They walked past the club's sergeant-at-arms, a liveried butler carrying an ornate silver tray, and a footman standing on a wooden ladder to dust a chandelier. The walls were of panelled oak, decorated in elaborately carved mouldings, each brightly polished to keep down the smoke stains, and the thick carpet looked recently cleaned. Charles's mind raced to interpret the clues—or the lack thereof—as he tried to decipher why and by whom this mysterious meeting had been planned.

They reached the top of the final set of stairs, and the usher stopped at a rather nondescript door bearing a simple brass plaque which read: The Mauritius Room. He opened the door, his hand out.

"In here, sirs. Ring if you have need of anything."

"After you, Lord Haimsbury," the penguinesque Parsons said with a grin as he offered the lad two gold sovereigns. "For your silence," he told the usher. "Do follow me, Lord Haimsbury. All will become clear once you're inside."

Charles tried to remember if he'd chambered a round into the revolver he kept holstered next to his chest, but with the business of the day, he had no idea if the answer were yes or no.

"Good afternoon, Charles," a woman's voice spoke from a shadowy corner of the parlour. The closed and heavy drapery made it difficult to see the lady's face, but the voice was unmistakable.

"Your Majesty," the marquess said, bowing deeply.

"Don't bother with all that, my dear. Please, sit. Parsons, pour us some tea, will you? Or would you prefer something stronger?" she asked the stunned detective. "I had the club's butler set out a decanter of Drummond whisky. They had none of the Reserve in stock, I fear. More's the pity. I always favoured the '36."

"Thank you, ma'am, but I'm content with tea."

Parsons handed the queen a cup of Earl Grey. "We've other blends as well. Have you a preference, sir?" he asked.

"Whatever the queen is having will be just fine, thank you."

As her guest added sugar and milk to his cup, Queen Victoria explained. "Charles, I asked Parsons to fetch you, because I wanted to keep this meeting very quiet. Salisbury's aware of it, and I invited him to join us, but he has other business today. Matthews knows nothing of it, however. Our Home Secretary's fallen out my good graces this week. I shan't elaborate, but take it as fact. Now, Parsons knows all about this—well, Parsons knows everything there is to know in government—and I've asked him to remain as witness to our discussion. Charles, this story in the papers. The one claiming an informant inside the palace revealed your lineage. Have you seen it?"

"Yes, ma'am, I have. It's hard to avoid seeing them, as nearly every paper has printed it, but I place no stock in these reports. They're spurious at best."

She laughed, her small mouth forming into a delicate oval. "Oh, my dear, you are so like your father! However, Robby Sinclair would never have allowed such a story to continue. He'd have found the reporter and given him a black eye and a swift kick to the rear for his trouble!"

Sinclair didn't know whether to laugh or nod politely, but it soon became clear that the queen hadn't invited him here to scold him, but rather to offer fellowship. "I'd liked to have seen my father do that," he said at last.

"Yes, well, I had the pleasure of seeing your father behave that way many times. Robert Sinclair had a rather short fuse when it came to his personal life, but all the more when it came to me. Albert and Robby were very good friends, and I confess to having a deep fondness for your father. But these rumours, Charles, as a policeman, I imagine you've wondered just who started it all."

"I have, and if you've asked me here to begin an investigation, ma'am, I shall be happy to do so."

She grinned mischievously. "No, Charles, that isn't why I summoned you. Indeed, I already know. It began with a report in *The Star* and sort of gathered steam from there, but *The Star*'s reporter did not fabricate the facts, as some in Parliament claim. He received his information from someone inside government, and I can tell you that informant's name."

"Who?"

"My grandson," she replied simply.

"The Duke of Clarence?"

"Yes, and before you ask, he did so with my blessing."

Charles sat quietly for a moment, trying to process the implications of her statement. It occurred to him that the entire conversation might simply be playing inside his head. He had suffered a head injury recently, and his head still throbbed now and then—and there was that odd tingle dancing across his neck.

I might even be in hospital, for all I know.

"You're trying to figure it all out, aren't you, my dear?" the queen asked. "Do stop being a detective for a moment, and let me share my mind with you, Charles. For weeks now, there've been whispers in the palace and throughout government that someone had obtained a copy of the Drummond-Branham Agreement."

Sinclair didn't wish to speak in front of Parsons, so he feigned ignorance. "What agreement is that, Your Majesty?"

"You needn't worry about Reggie. He knows all about it. I've no idea how he sniffs out all our secrets, but I've come to trust him, as much as one can trust government people."

"That's kind of you to say, ma'am," the plump clerk said with a curious wink. "I do my best to serve."

The queen shrugged and stirred another cube of sugar into her cup. "Reggie is a sort of bloodhound when it comes to finding truth, and I've made use of that nose of his many times during my reign. Haven't I, Sir Reginald?"

"Indeed, you have, ma'am."

"Do stop calling me 'ma'am', Parsons! It makes me feel like an old woman."

"You are hardly that, Your Majesty," the penguin assured her, smiling.

She sighed. "Charles, I'm sure the duke's told you all about the agreement that your forebears signed."

"Yes, he has. Why do you mention it, ma'am...I mean..."

"Call me Drina, Charles. It's what your father always called me." He smiled at this, and the queen's eyes began to tear. "My dear, you remind me so much of your father when you smile. Ah, but time never stops, does it? Nay, it speeds up as one ages. Do forgive the nostalgia. I did not interrupt your day to reminisce. Perhaps, another time."

"I'd enjoy that, Drina."

She laughed. "How very nicely you say it! Yes, well, this agreement with the Duke of York, that is King Edward IV—though some even today refuse to call him that, as you can imagine. That agreement is one of those documents that's set in stone, you might say, and has never been questioned by anyone I know. To those few who are aware of its existence, it's considered England's *pis aller*. Our last resort."

"Last resort for what?"

"Last resort to maintain the monarchy."

Charles shook his head in confusion. "Maintain the monarchy? I don't understand. Is there a threat to it?"

The queen sipped the tea, gathering her thoughts. "That will be all, Parsons. Charles and I shall speak alone from this point forward. We'll ring when we've finished."

The so-called 'chief clerk' rose without another word and left the room. She waited a moment, and then continued. "Reggie's probably listening at the keyhole, for that's his way, but I enjoy the impression of privacy now and then. I seldom get any. My dear, there are a growing number of MPs and lords who regret and even resent the way my children have overtaken European throne rooms. In the past, a monarch was encouraged to marry with other rulers. Such unions generally engendered military alliances, and sometimes even periods of peace. However, because of the current anti-German sentiment in our kingdom, there is a growing concern that my family's interconnectivity might lend strength to a rising German state. It's no secret that the Ottoman Empire is dying, and the next few years will determine which countries inherit the empire's wealth and influence. Germany very much wants that power, as does Russia. France is no stranger to this hunger, and even Spain would like a bite! It may be Britain that serves as the only sensible mediator to a world gone mad with greed and lust. That role would prove very difficult with a German monarch as ruler."

"But, ma'am—I mean, Drina, I don't believe the people of England think of you as a German."

"Oh, but I am! To those who long for the return of the Stuarts or Plantagenets, my heritage is anathema! Good heavens, even the French are preferred by some! My dear, I do not complain, nor do I intentionally slight the wonderful people of our kingdom. I am, at heart, a pragmatist, and I believe this course is best for England."

"What course is that?"

She reached for his hand. "One that you must agree to navigate, Charles. The head of your family is required to sign that agreement each time a new king or queen takes the throne, and as such, it is as binding upon you as it is upon us. Though you have never signed it yourself, Duke James did, and when you were born, he wrote to me and pledged your life to our service should we ever require it."

Sinclair grew quiet, trying to sort through the implications of this startling conversation. "Are you asking our family to take the throne?"

"Yes, I am, but before you answer, Charles, let me tell you three things. First of all, I've discussed this with my son, the Prince of Wales. Edward has never really sought the throne. He sees it as too much work, actually. My grandson, Prince Albert Victor, is more like myself. He wants only the best for England, and his pragmatism foresees a change in royal houses as the best way to prevent Germany's ascension. Secondly, I know that your inner circle fears Redwing's plans." She paused, noticing his look of utter shock. "You show surprise, my dear."

"Frankly, I am surprised," he admitted.

"Redwing tries to camouflage themselves in hues of good deeds, but their true colours always emerge. Snakes cannot help being snakes, can they? Do you really think me so out of touch that I'd not notice them? Charles, I've ejected more of their riff-raff from the palace than I've had dogs! Smooth-talkers always think a woman's ear is tender and eagerly attends to soft words, but not this ear. No, my dear, not this one!" She winked as she refilled her cup. "More?"

"No, thank you." Charles felt a bit numb, and the idea of holding liquid in a cup with any amount of grace seemed completely unachievable.

"Ah, well, then, I'll finish the pot. Now, Charles, you must listen carefully to me. It is known to those within my own 'inner circle' that Redwing hopes to use your royal blood for political and probably spiritual gain, but I do not believe you're the type to fall for their schemes. If my ears are sturdy, then yours are made of iron! Thirdly, I've always felt that controlling a situation is far better than allowing the situation to control me, therefore, it seems prudent to preempt Redwing's plans by mounting our own. That is why I spoke with my grandson and asked him to whisper a few secrets to T. P. O'Connor. Eddy made it clear that these were never to be revealed, which of course O'Connor immediately did. He thinks himself wise to the world's ways, but he is a very useful dupe."

Charles began to laugh. "I do so wish O'Connor could hear you say that, ma'am!"

She put a finger to her lips. "It will remain our private joke," she said, her blue eyes twinkling mischievously. "Now, if you wish to speak to your Uncle James before giving your answer, I understand. But in the meantime, I should like to raise your title to that of duke."

Sinclair put up his hand in shock. "Wait, please! Did you just say you intend to elevate my title?"

"Yes. I do hope that doesn't displease you, Charles. Most peers would leap at the chance!"

"It isn't that, Your Majesty. It's just that someone told me recently that I'd be made a duke. In a dream, or rather something like a dream."

"Dreams can be prophetic, my dear. The world of the spiritual is far more complex and diverse than our imperfect eyes can see, or our hearts imagine. The ceremony will be held at Buckingham Palace, and you may invite as many family members as you like. Of course, Salisbury will attend along with a few of my most trusted advisors. Once done, the news will be leaked to O'Connor or possibly William Stead, of course, which guarantees its release to the public. Also, I should like you on the privy council. We meet monthly, for the most part, which shouldn't interfere with your other duties."

"Other duties?"

She smiled. "Husband, investigator, and soon to be father from what I'm told. The Stuart and Plantagenet lines continue on, and with the addition of your Sinclair blood, that triangle of royalty is fixed and perfected."

"How so?"

"I shall leave that for others to explain, Charles. Will you accept?"

He kissed her hand, bowing deeply. "I have no aspirations to anything other than that of husband to Elizabeth Sinclair, but if it pleases Your Majesty, then I shall be happy to serve you and England in whatever way you deem best."

"Good," she said, smiling widely. "You make me very happy, Charles. This is but the first step in our new direction. We mustn't let Germany know our plans, nor Russia. In fact, it is vital that we keep our agreement quiet for as long as possible. Redwing will think it all their doing, which allows us to use their momentum as our own." The queen's smile turned into laughter, and her eyes danced merrily. "Honestly, I've not felt so free in years! My European relations will most likely balk, but once they see the wisdom of it, they'll come 'round. Except for Wilhelm, of course. Ah, but there's nothing to be done about the fellow—not yet. Now, ring for Parsons. I'd like to have him arrange the ceremony for raising your title. Prince Charles, 1st Duke of Haimsbury, has a very nice ring to it."

"Prince?" he repeated, nearly choking.

"Of course! Your true title has always been Prince, my dear, just as Elizabeth's is Princess. It is in the Drummond-Branham Agreement, remember? You have read it, I hope."

"Yes, I'm aware of that, but is the title officially recognised?"

"It's inherent within the agreement! Of course, it's recognised, though seldom discussed openly. You may ask Elizabeth, if you doubt me. I've called her our little princess from the moment I first met her. You'll see, when you read your letters of patent. They'll list you as His Highness, Prince Charles Robert Arthur Sinclair III, 1st Duke of Haimsbury."

"It's all quite a lot to take in," he admitted. "May I tell my wife about our conversation?"

"Of course. Oh, and Parsons will give you a bouquet of flowers to take to Elizabeth. To make up for keeping her waiting. Does she come home soon?"

"Tomorrow," he answered. "I'll speak with the duke as well."

"Do that. Now, ring for Sir Reginald. My gout worsens, and I must soak the wretched foot. Will you be Christmasing at Branham?"

"Uh, probably. I'm not sure."

"Usually, I spend the season in Scotland, but if there is a corner where you might put me, I'd very much enjoy a weekend there this year. It's been ages, since I enjoyed the festivities at the hall!"

"I'm sure Elizabeth would offer you any apartment you desire, Your Majesty."

"Drina, remember?"

He laughed and kissed her hand once more. "Forgive me. Yes, it is safely Drina."

He rang for the clerk, and she offered him a bright wink. "One day, Charles, *you* may be the one called Majesty."

"That is far more than my overtaxed brain can possibly fathom at the moment, Drina. My fervent prayer is that the Lord in his mercy allows you to remain on our throne for many more years."

"Well said, my dear," she said. "Kiss my cheek, Charles. I should like you to think of me as family."

He did so, and she touched his face, her eyes glistening. "How like your father! Salisbury and Parsons will contact you soon regarding the ceremony for your new title. The press will have a field day once they hear!"

"Yes, I imagine they will."

"And then we'll celebrate Christmas together. Won't that be fun?"

"I look forward to it, Drina," he told her, bowing one last time before ringing for the clerk.

He was leaving the chamber as Parsons entered. The clerk grinned, and it occurred to Charles that the ubiquitous spy had probably overheard every word.

"Congratulations," Parsons whispered. "We'll talk soon."

The usher arrived to escort him to the coach, and Sinclair wondered again if all this were but a dream. The chilly air hit him with fury as he left the building, reminding him that he walked in the real world. His name was Prince Charles.

That's madness!

Now, to find a way to let Elizabeth know that she'd be giving birth to children who might one day be heirs to the throne of England.

CHAPTER THIRTY

5:56 pm

Elizabeth Stuart Sinclair had spent the past hour writing letters. Now that her lungs had nearly healed, the duchess was given permission to sit in a chair for an hour at a time. Parson's messenger, Frederick Treves, had indicated Sinclair might be away for several hours. To fill the time, the duchess threw her energies into productive activities. She'd just finished short notes to her solicitor, Branham's steward, and an estate agent on Finsbury Circus; as well as a long letter to Lady Margaret Morehouse, thanking her for the flowers she'd sent to Charles and expressing gratitude for the widow's offer of support towards the proposed charity hospital. She was sealing the letter in an envelope, when someone knocked on the partially closed door.

"Good day to you," spoke a somewhat hesitant but pleasant male voice as the opening slowly widened. "I hope I do not interrupt."

Beth recognised the halting speech pattern at once, and she began to smile just picturing the remarkable individual who owned it. "My dear Mr. Merrick! Oh, I'd rather hoped you would visit me today. Please, come in!"

Joseph Merrick, who was once exhibited by penny gaff showmen Sam Torr and Tom Norman under the derisive epithet 'the Elephant Man', had lived at the London since the summer of '86. Since then, he'd become a reluctant celebrity. His unusual speech, constricted and muffled due to facial deformities, sometimes made it difficult for visitors to understand him, but Merrick's high intellect and boyish charm never ceased to win him new friends, and in the few days since their first meeting, the young man had come to care deeply for the sweet duchess.

"I bring you a small gift," Merrick said, wheezing as he spoke from just inside the doorway. He held a music box in his left hand, the one with the greatest amount of normality and function. "It is but a trifle."

Elizabeth motioned for him to enter as she set aside the letters. "Mr. Merrick, nothing you might bring me could ever be considered a trifle."

He entered and used his cane to push a small chair towards her position and carefully sat into it, holding the box tightly within his hand as he lowered his oddly balanced body onto the cushioned seat. Once safely down, he set the box upon a nearby table and then unhooked the cane from his forearm, using the stick to steady himself.

"Is this box for me?" she asked. He nodded. "Does it play?"

"It does indeed. Beethoven's *Moonlight*. It isn't new, but does mean a great deal to me. The box was given to me by Mr. Treves when I first arrived at the London. He gave me permission to pass it to you, who are far more beautiful than any moonlight, more lovely than any song."

"That is so very sweet of you, Joseph," she said, leaning over to take the box. "Does it require a key?"

"The key is contained within the design," he said proudly. "I have already wound it for you. You need only open the lid."

The silver box was set with half a dozen garnets, and the lid was carved ivory. Elizabeth lifted the delicate lid, and the tines began to play the sonata, causing her to weep happy tears. Merrick saw her reaction and grew worried.

"Oh, have I mistaken the music?" he asked. "It was thoughtless of me to offer a secondhand gift. Perhaps, another song would be better, if this is not to your liking."

"No, Mr. Merrick, you will do no such thing," she said, wiping her eyes. "The song is perfect. I would not change it for anything."

"But you weep. Does the music make you sad? I had hoped to make you happy."

Beth wiped her dark eyes with her fingertips, and he offered his own linen handkerchief. "Thank you," she said, dabbing the corners of her eyes. "Sometimes, tears stem from both emotions, Joseph. I'm sure you've found yourself experiencing both joy and sadness all at once."

"Yes," he said, glancing out the window into the garden beyond. "That is true. I have. But, may I ask why you feel sad?"

"You're such a gentle soul, Joseph. Much like my father was. This sonata. *Moonlight*. It was his favourite, you see. He used to ask me to play it, when I was a little girl. It was—it was the last song I ever played for him. Only hours before he died."

She began to weep, for memories of her handsome father and how he'd not been there for her wedding, nor would see his grandchildren, tore open an old wound, but the hot tears brought relief, not pain.

"Oh, my dear Elizabeth. Forgive me. Had I known, I should never have…" he began, attempting to rise, but she touched his deformed hand gently to stop him.

"Please, Joseph, you mustn't think your gift has made me sad. It is difficult to explain, but I'm glad to remember him, you see? I only wish he could have lived to meet my husband. And you. And there are so many other things he's missed in my life. But like this music, his memory plays in my mind and heart, and one day, I shall see him again. In heaven."

Merrick nodded. "Yes. That is when we shall all be equal in face and form. Yet, I imagine you will still outshine us all."

Beth shook her head. "No, Mr. Merrick. Outward appearances matter little to God. *Your* spirit shines brightly and ever shall. Thank you so much for the gift. I shall cherish it always. Tell me, what plans have you for Christmas? Will Mr. Treves permit you to travel?"

"I am glad you like the gift," he said, sitting back and relaxing somewhat. "Christmas? Mr. Treves permits me to travel short distances from time to time, and I even went to the countryside once on a train. It was marvellous! I imagine Christmas will be spent here. We had a beautiful tree last year, and we sang carols and had a delicious pudding and punch. I won a most amusing hat in my cracker. Perhaps, you could join us this year."

"I might, but I'd rather hoped you would join us for Christmas. I'm not sure where we'll be. Either here or at Branham. Oh, Mr. Merrick, the hall comes alive at Christmastide! The entire house is decorated from top to bottom, and we play music and games, and the villagers enjoy an entire week of festivities, and on Christmas Eve night, there's a dance with all the servants and farmers. If the weather is cold enough to freeze the reflecting pool, then we ice skate. It's a very merry time! Would you consider joining us?"

"Will your husband permit it?" he asked simply.

"Her husband will insist upon it, Mr. Merrick," Charles Sinclair's resonant baritone answered from the doorway. "I wish I'd thought of it myself, but my wife's ideas are always the best ones. Will you join us?" Merrick started to rise, but Charles sat instead, touching the smaller man's left forearm. "Please, do not stand on my account, old friend. You and I have known each other far longer than I've been a marquess."

Merrick laughed. "It's true. Elizabeth, did you know that your husband once aided me at this very hospital? In the garden, I mean."

Beth took her husband's hand and kissed it. "No, Mr. Merrick, I did not. Charles, perhaps I should ring for a matron to place these flowers in water. They look as if they've been thirsty for an hour or more."

Sinclair laughed. "Forgive me, darling, I received them from a gracious lady who insisted you deserved a bouquet in recompense for delaying me, which you do, but then I stopped to speak with Reid before coming here. I fear the roses have grown rather thirsty. I'll get the water. Is there a vase?"

She pointed to several that Victoria had brought with her the previous day. "Use the blue one. There is a little water in that pitcher. Yes, that's the one," she added, pointing towards her bedside table. "This gracious lady you mentioned knows my taste. China pinks. They're very pretty, Charles, but I think Mr. Merrick's gift is nicer."

"Then I shall have to do better next time," Charles said, picking up the box. "The box is lovely, Joseph. Haven't I seen this before?"

"You have and recently. I kept a message there, given me by a good friend, but I thought it was time to pass it to someone else. Someone who appreciates the music, just as I do."

"Then it plays? Oh, I see it does," Sinclair said as he lifted the ivory lid. "Beethoven's *Moonlight*. Did you know it's one of my favourites?"

Beth reached over and closed the lid. "Then, I have three reasons to love it now."

Merrick's eyes blinked within the misshapen head. "Three reasons? Your husband and your father are but two, Duchess."

"*You* are the third, Mr. Merrick. Now, tell me about my husband's adventure in the garden. When was this?"

Merrick took a deep breath to compose himself, for her words had touched his heart. "It was my first summer here. August of '86. I was still living in the hospital's attic, and it was unbearably hot. I would often climb down the stairs and stroll through the gardens after nightfall. I did not yet know the layout of the park, and I took a wrong turning. That is when two young scallywags decided to make sport of my appearance."

"Oh, no, that is terrible! You must have been awfully frightened, Mr. Merrick. I know I would have been."

"It was indeed frightening, but this tale has a bright ending, Your Grace. Your husband, you see, was walking past, and without so much as a thought, he took the youths by the scruffs of their necks and sent both of them packing! Charles and I spent the remainder of the evening talking. In fact, it was outside this very window."

Sinclair rose and walked to the window on the left. Beneath it, lay a dormant rose bed and two limestone benches, flanking a brass marker for the benefactor who'd endowed the garden. "You're right, Joseph. I'd no idea this was the window. You have a remarkable memory."

Merrick smiled as much as his deformity allowed, but his eyes were merry. "What is it they say about elephants?"

Charles sat down again. "If I didn't know you better, I'd probably fall all over myself apologising, but I do know you. Beth, Joseph has a knack for taking aim at himself, but it's more from a wry sense of humour than lack of confidence. Shall I tell my wife the trick you played on me last spring?"

Merrick began to laugh, and the effort made him wheeze even harder, but he slowly regained his composure and breath. "Yes, well, perhaps not. The duchess will think me infantile."

"Puerile?" Sinclair suggested.

"Quite. But that first night helped to forge a long and lovely friendship, did it not, Charles?"

"It did indeed," Sinclair said. "Beth, the reason I'd gone walking that night was you."

Elizabeth had begun to tire, and she reached for a pillow and placed it behind her back. "Because of me? In '86? Please, I must know how I precipitated a walk around Whitechapel, Charles, when I'd not seen or heard from you in over two years."

"That's just it. I told you on our wedding day that I never received your letter from four years past, but I didn't tell you that I'd considered sending one of my own in '86. That very night, in fact. Amelia had died two months before, and ordinarily I'd have entered a long period of mourning, but in truth I'd mourned the loss of my marriage and her love long before."

She touched his hand, for his face had shadowed with a flitter of sadness.

"Elizabeth, when you were… When you were missing," he continued, his voice lowering to a whisper, as even the memory of those dark days tore at him. "During those long nights, I read through your diaries from Paris. Victoria had brought them with her, thinking I might find them useful, and they became my lifeline. Your words kept me company—kept me sane during those lonely hours. In them, you talked about singing at Lord Salisbury's charity event and how you wished you'd said yes to singing at the Royal Opera, thinking it might make the papers and that I would see it."

"Yes, I did write that," she said, her eyes rounding. "However, I declined. Would you have known about it, if I had sung there?"

"I found out about it anyway," he explained. "You see, Salisbury's charity event made all the papers, and Bob Morehouse showed me your name in the *Gazette*. I rushed out and bought up every paper in London and read every review. I had them memorised. Beth, I had no right to love you back then. I was still legally married, but when Amelia passed a few weeks later, when I was truly free, it set me to thinking of you once more. That night in August, I'd been struggling with whether to write to you or just go to Paris and knock on every door until I found your aunt's home. The dilemma nearly drove me to madness, and I decided to walk and pray about it. That walk took me past the London and the discovery of a new friend."

Merrick smiled. "Your husband came past here night after night in the following months, and we formed a friendship that has continued to this day. That is why, when I learnt that his wife had been admitted as a patient, I simply had to come down and meet you. I feel as though I know you, Elizabeth. Charles talked about you for hours at times. I cannot tell you how pleased I am that you found one another at last! God's timing may not always conjoin with our own, but it is the best and wisest timing."

Elizabeth's eyes had begun to tear again, and she wiped her face. "Yes, it is," she said, her voice breaking. "Well, gentlemen, perhaps you two will wander through the garden once again, for I have overstayed my time in this chair, and I grow weary. Mr. Treves will scold us all, if I do not lie down. Mr. Merrick, you are the dearest man I've known in many years, my husband excluded, of course. Thank you very much for the music box, but also for your friendship."

"You are most welcome to both, Elizabeth. I hope to see you again before you go home tomorrow, but perhaps also at Christmas?"

"Yes, I do hope you will come. Charles, could you help me into bed?"

Merrick rose, leaning heavily upon his cane, and slowly made his way back towards the doorway, but turned before leaving. "Charles, I cannot convey all that is in my heart, but seeing the two of you together—well, it brings me indescribable joy!"

Sinclair shook Joseph's deformed, right hand, clutching it with his. "My dear friend. May you know that same joy every day of your life. God certainly has given it to me. I'll stop in to visit you later, if that's all right."

"I shall look forward to it. And perhaps a game of chess? With Mr. Blinkmire and Count Riga's departure, I lack for challenging partners."

"Very well, but only if you do not cheat," Sinclair said with a wink.

"I promise nothing," Merrick responded with a similar wink. He turned away and followed the tiled floor to his own apartment, and Charles shut Beth's door.

"I'd no idea how you two met," she said as he lifted her into the bed. "Had you really been thinking about coming to Paris in '86?"

"Yes," he confessed. "Elizabeth, I don't know how all of this works, but I suspect that God has established an eternal connexion 'twixt you and me that no assault can ever break. Some might call that fate, but I call it design. You and I were designed for one another, little one. He always intended us to be together, but the timing had to be his. Joseph is the one who convinced me to wait. *He* was the answer to my prayer that night. Merrick assured me that God would make it happen at the right time and in a manner that would allow your grandfather to accept me as your husband. And so the Lord has."

"Indeed, he has. Do you think Treves will let me to go home tomorrow?"

"I'll go and ask him, and then after I must lose a game or two to Mr. Merrick."

"I hope you don't lose intentionally, Charles. He is a bright man, capable of playing against a champion, I should think."

Charles laughed. "I'd say he can! I won the Cambridge chess tournament my last two years, and still Merrick beats me. I shall be happy to achieve a draw."

"Then, we shall plan a tournament for Christmas. Do be careful, Charles."

"At chess? Darling, it's hardly dangerous."

"No, I mean… Well, in general. It's been too quiet these past few days. I've a very strong premonition of darkness on the horizon. I try not to think of it, but will you promise to watch for all the enemy's gambits?"

He stroked her hair and smiled. "I promise. Now, you must fulfil your promise and rest for an hour at least. I've a few last errands, and then I'll return. I love you, little one," he whispered, kissing her lips.

"And I you, Captain. Would you bring me the music box before you go?"

He took the silver box from the table and placed it into her hands. "Here you are, darling. Now, I really must go. I'll speak to Treves."

He kissed her once more and then shut the door as he left. Beth lifted the lid on the music box, the simple melody bringing memories that tugged at something long ago locked behind a dark door inside her mind.

Why did she think of a wolf, when recalling her father's face?

Elizabeth closed her eyes. As the music played, she slipped into a fitful dream, where bird-like Shadows with yellow eyes and curved beaks, overflew London in dense flocks, destroying buildings and slaying thousands by pecking out their eyes. One of these rode upon a monstrous beast that breathed fire. The rider looked like a man with raven's wings, and he whispered to her in hellish speech, offering a warning.

Beware the looking glass. She is poison.

7:15 pm

Sinclair played three games of chess with Merrick, losing two but winning one, and then crossed the gravel park to the medical college, where he knocked on Frederick Treves's office door. The handsome surgeon smiled at seeing the detective and rose to shake his hand. "Please, Superintendent, do come in. I was just marking last week's exam books. May I offer you some water?"

"No, thank you, Frederick. I'm sure you know my question already."

"Yes, I can imagine it," he said with a smile. Both men sat, and the busy surgeon withdrew a file from a cabinet, glancing through the many notes contained within. "It's remarkable how much the duchess has improved since arriving. Her lungs have cleared considerably, but I'd like to keep her another day at least. Now, I see the disappointment on your face, and I understand, but I've a few concerns, which I should like to settle in my mind before sending her home."

"What concerns you?" the marquess asked. "Is she still in danger?"

"I'm not sure," he replied. "Forgive me for being obscure; it isn't my intent. Anthony Gehlen and I have spoken often of the duchess's case, and her condition presents irregularities."

"That is not more clear," Sinclair replied, worry creasing his brow.

"No, I suppose it is not. How can I put this?" he mused, rising to shut the door. Once seated again, Treves folded his hands and leaned towards the detective. "I wish Gehlen were here, for this is his area of expertise, not mine."

"Is he in the building?"

"No, Anthony has already left for the day. We could meet tomorrow morning, if you have the time."

"Fred, tell me!"

"Yes, of course. Let me see if I can explain this clearly," Treves said, clearly uncomfortable. "Charles, can you tell me the precise date when the duchess conceived? Honestly, I would never ask a man this, but your wife insists it is the eighth of October."

"It is," Sinclair replied. "That is not for public knowledge, you understand. The press is already jumping to a lifetime's worth of conclusions with this whole royalty business. They would have a field day with this information!"

"Yes, I'm aware of that. You needn't explain, but if you are absolutely certain that no other date is possible, then…"

"None other is possible, Fred. It is that date, and only that date."

"Very well. Then, I should like to ask Gehlen to conduct a full examination. I realise you and Elizabeth know practically nothing about him, but I've known him for many years. He's discreet and thorough, and I've come to trust his skills and his opinions."

Charles took a breath and counted to ten, for this conversation disturbed rather than comforted. "Just tell me what you suspect."

Treves thought for a moment, looking again at the file. "Ordinarily, I'd not even mention these suspicions, but because of your position and the duchess's trauma, I feel I must. Charles, I think it possible that your wife carries more than one child."

Charles said nothing, for after meeting Georgie and hearing Beth talk of Robby in their strange, shared dream, the news already felt familiar. If he hadn't hallucinated the conversation with the queen, then he'd soon be made a duke, just as his future daughter had told him would happen. The entire stone realm experience was real, meaning his children were real and would be born in June of '89.

"Did you hear me, Charles?" Treves asked, trying to pierce the other man's reverie.

"Yes, of course, I did. Sorry, Fred. Are you saying she *is* carrying two babies? Definitely?"

"I'm not saying it is a fact. I may be completely wrong, but I would keep her here for another day or two, if you'd permit it, so that Gehlen has time to conduct his examination."

Charles sat back in the chair. Believing in the possibility of twins, based on a shared dream was one thing; hearing a well-respected surgeon state it, was quite another. "I don't suppose you have something stronger than water?"

Treves laughed. "No, I'm afraid not. Twins are a double blessing, but they can also bring added risk to a pregnancy. It's imperative that your wife follow all my instructions."

"I'll see that she does," Sinclair promised. "And you may keep her as long as you find it necessary. In truth, she's less likely to make rash choices in your care. Thank you, Frederick. Oh, I'm to ask you if Joseph Merrick might visit us over Christmastide, either here or at Branham."

"I'm sure he'd enjoy that. I'll speak to Joseph about it, and we'll make arrangements regarding transportation at a later date. Thank you for asking him. He's grown quite fond of your wife, and, of course, the two of you have been friends for a long time."

Sinclair rose to leave. "If there's anything I can do to help with the arrangements, let me know. My cousin owns two trains, and we'd hire any medical personnel you deem necessary."

"Excellent. Now, I've an evening lecture to give to my first year students on diagnosing tumours. It's actually more exciting than it sounds."

Charles shook the surgeon's hand once more and left by way of the north entrance, where he hailed a hansom for Leman Street. When he'd spoken with Reid earlier, Charles had asked the inspector to arrange a supper meeting with Fred Abberline for 8:00. As the Yard's new Commissioner for Intelligence, Charles wanted to know every detail of the current murder investigations.

No sooner had the marquess's cab turned onto Whitechapel Road, than a dark-haired woman emerged from a second hansom near the main hospital entry. She paid the driver, asking him to wait, and then entered—bound for the ground floor's private rooms.

Passing by a porter engaged in conversation with a student nurse, the disguised woman approached the constables who kept watch upon the duchess's door. She passed a slip of paper to the shorter one. After whispering together, the pair reluctantly left their post and moved to the east entrance at the far end of the hallway.

Now, with no one observing her movement, the woman entered the shadowy room, where Elizabeth Stuart Sinclair lay dreaming.

8:02 pm

Press coverage of the Ripper crimes had finally begun to wane, thanks to the front page stories of the 'duchess kidnapping' and her sudden reappearance and subsequent hospitalization. But also, tucked 'twixt these major stories, the rumblings of royal rumours had taken hold in eager readers' fertile imaginations. Consequently, as Charles Sinclair entered the station house, several officers near the booking desk saluted, and one actually bowed.

"The next man to do that buys drinks," Sinclair warned the trio. "Despite what Fred Best might imply, I am not, nor ever will be a man to whom you men bow. Is that understood? Even if I were King of England, I'd consider you my comrades. Got that?"

"Yes, sir," the men answered in unison.

"Is Abberline here yet?" he asked, returning to business.

"In with Mr. Reid, sir," Williams told him. "They've ordered supper from the Bear. Sandwiches and ale. Hope that's all right, Superintendent."

"It's Commissioner Sinclair now," Edmund Reid called from the stairwell. "We're up here, Charles."

Sinclair turned to the sergeant. "Sandwiches and ale sound perfect, Alfred. Thanks."

He dashed up the familiar steps and landed in Edmund's office in ten seconds flat. Stepping through the door, he took a seat on the sofa, sighing happily. "I have two hours. Is that enough?"

"Enough for what? Solving crimes or eating a leg o' lamb?" Abberline asked, grinning. "Good ta see you with both eyes open, Charles. How's our duchess?"

"Sleeping, but that's a state that can change without warning. I'd like to be back at the London by ten, if possible."

"I think we can manage that, Commissioner. Or has the new position started yet? Our memo didn't specify."

"Home Secretary Matthews swore me in at nine this morning. It was a lovely ceremony, actually. And I have a brand new warrant card to prove it."

Reid laughed. "Commissioner Sinclair! It has a nice ring to it, but then so does Your Majesty."

"No more of that," the new commissioner chided his friend. "It's bad enough to get it from the lads downstairs. Catch me up on your current investigations. When I meet with Salisbury tomorrow afternoon, I may as well know what I'm talking about."

Abberline handed his superior a thick folder. "We've compiled it all in here, and you can keep it for your fancy new office," the gruff inspector said, his mutton-chop whiskers twitching. "Are we to believe this Trent person was Ripper?"

"I'd thought him the likeliest suspect," Reid admitted, looking at Sinclair. "As did you, Charles."

The detective glanced through the collection of evidence on his lap: photographs of victims, clothing, witness interviews, drawings of wound patterns, and every note taken since the string of hideous murders had commenced the previous December, beginning with a woman, known locally as 'Fairy Fay'.

"We can't prove Trent's involvement unless we can draw a clear line from him to at least one of the victims," he said, glancing at Reid. "As yet, that line does not exist."

Though the circle members were convinced of the late baronet's guilt, English law required more than suspicion. With Lorena MacKey and Susanna Morgan missing—the latter woman, possibly dead—the only hard evidence remaining was Ida Ross's list, which would be tossed out by a judge as inflammatory and possibly even fabricated.

"We may never solve Ripper," Reid declared. "Charles, if you're in a rush, let's discuss the Hemsfield murder. Parliament is up in arms about this one, and the press have discovered some of the more lurid details. I've no idea who told them, but Best intimated as much earlier this evening at the Bear. And speaking of *The Star*, I've more bad news. Michael O'Brien has been released."

"What? Why?" Sinclair asked, setting the file aside in frustration. "Who advocated for him this time 'round?"

"An Irish solicitor named Burns. He's got plenty of friends at the Old Bailey, but it's his city friends that made the difference, I imagine."

"I cannot believe that man escaped us again," Sinclair muttered. "Burns, you say? First name?"

"Patrick. I suspect they're old pals, from the way they conversed on their way out. Shall I assign someone to look into the man?"

"No, I prefer not to use police resources. I'll have an ICI agent do it. Now that Beth's returned to us, we have men sitting idle. Matthew Laurence mentioned a desire to visit Ireland. I'll dispatch him right away."

"Poor lad," Abberline quipped. "He'll soon wish to be back in England. Williams has the solicitor's business card and contact information."

"Thanks, Fred. So, Hemsfield?"

Reid nodded. "Yes, Hemsfield. Sunders found no evidence of torture or intoxication, either through alcohol or drugs. However, France noticed an item we all missed."

"Arthur did? What?" Charles asked.

"A candle."

Abberline harrumphed loudly to make his opinion known to both colleagues. "This is a load o' horse manure, if you ask me! Candles at a crime scene? What's next? Arresting a pub owner for having spirits in his cellar? Every house in London has candles!"

"So they do," Reid agreed. "However, very few have candles like this. I showed it to Martin earlier today, and he recognised it at once. It's a variation on the soporific candles some in this borough claim are made from the organs of Ripper's victims."

"Poppycock!" Abberline sputtered. "Are we policemen or palmists?"

"We're open to whatever the killer believes, Fred," Sinclair chided his junior officer.

"Well, then this killer is a madman."

"I'll not argue with that," the marquess replied. "How is this candle a variant of the other you mentioned, Edmund?"

"Martin called it a Mandragore Candle. We might call it a Mandrake Candle, but old manuscripts refer to it as the Hand of Glory. Typically, so says our tailor, it's a tallow candle made from the fat of a hanged man, preferably a felon found hanging at a crossroads, and it's placed within the desiccated left hand of the same man, using the hand as a candlestick. In this case, the candle stood inside a ceramic hand, bearing the inscription 'The Left Hand Path' upon it. It's a phrase used by a popular occultist named Helena Blavatsky. We found two pamphlets and a book by that lady in Hemsfield's rented house."

"Pamphlets! What kind of evidence is that? Are we to arrest this Blavatsky woman, then?" Abberline grumbled. "I doubt any woman could hoist a man of over two hundred pounds and hang him from a chandelier pipe that's eighteen feet off the floor!"

Charles started to answer, but Arthur France knocked on the office door. "Sirs? I'm very sorry to interrupt, but there's been another one."

All three faces lost colour. "Another murder?" Reid asked the young inspector.

"Yes, sir. Over at the Exchange."

"That's the city's jurisdiction," Sinclair argued. "Sir James Fraser's patch."

"True, sir, but Commissioner Monro insists we send a team over right away, as the method is the same. Another hanged man."

"Isn't the Exchange closed?" Reid asked. "Who found this hanged man?"

"The cleaner, sir. And the victim's a member of Parliament."

Suddenly the tingling at Sinclair's neck began to scream. "Who?"

"Baron Wychwright, sir."

Charles shut his eyes tightly. This would be a very long night.

CHAPTER THIRTY-ONE

The Royal Exchange opened for business on the 23rd of January in 1571. The most recent version of that revered institution stood opposite the Bank of England on the south side of Threadneedle Street. Two previous buildings had succumbed to fire, and this third, designed by William Tite, followed the original, rectangular layout with a large, central courtyard. Architectural elements included pediment statuary, an eight-columned portico, spired bell tower, and multiple entrances. The building housed several restaurants, Lloyd's Insurance, Reuters News Agency, and played host to a babel of multilingual traders from across the metropolis and Europe.

As the four detectives entered the hushed corridors, voices could be heard from the south side of the courtyard. By day, this area would teem with businessmen, reporters, bankers, traders, Parliamentarians, and government workers. A few might stop to purchase a fine clock or watch from one of the Exchange jewellers; whilst others shopped for shares in new or old companies, sold imported goods, or exchanged their inheritances for the modern-day equivalent of a handful of magic beans.

City Police Commissioner Sir James Fraser emerged from a vacant office, his face pale as he approached Sinclair. "Lord Haimsbury, I appreciate the prompt answer to my call. This one's not for the weak of stomach, I can tell you that."

"Sir James, we've been told the victim is the Lake District Minister Baron Wychwright. Is that true?"

"I'm afraid so. Wychwright's a constant fixture at the Exchange, and he kept offices here until last year."

"Kept offices? Past tense. He no longer does so?" Sinclair asked.

"So I understand. You'd need to verify that with the Exchange's chief clerk. A fellow named Calloway."

"I'll do that. Wychwright was a family friend, and I know his daughter rather well."

"She's in hospital, I understand," Fraser said. "This will go down very hard."

"Yes, it will," Charles remarked. "Let me tell her, will you? My men and I will do all we can to aid your investigation, but this is your jurisdiction, Sir James," the marquess added as Fraser led them into the crime scene.

The room was unfurnished, save for a large, freestanding closet. The office's dimensions were close to twenty by thirty, and two windows provided a view of the courtyard, the daylight augmented by a gaslit ceiling fixture and wall sconces. The victim wasn't exactly like Hemsfield, for he'd been stuffed into the cramped closet following what appeared to be a hanging. The MP's short neck showed three rings of gashed impressions, far deeper than a rope might cause, but also multiple stab wounds to the chest and buttocks. Both wrists were slashed longitudinally, and blood had collected inside the closet's interior and onto the floor.

"He bled out," Sinclair observed as he knelt beside the body. "Is this what alerted the cleaner? The blood on the carpet?"

"So we're told. Her name's Alice Marshall. Forty-three, married with two children; both adults. She's worked for the Exchange for twelve years with a spotless employment record. By all accounts, a decent woman. As you might guess, this mess caused her to faint."

"As it might most men," Reid noted. "You say the baron no longer kept an office here? So then, who uses this one?"

"No one presently," Fraser answered. "I've sent Inspector Graham to find the night steward. Apparently, he'd gone to the pub for a quick one when all this happened."

"What time did the maid discover the body?" asked Sinclair.

"Six or so, she thought. It's a puzzle, because Mrs. Marshall had to unlock the office to clean it. Meaning, our killer must have a key."

"Paul's not going to like this at all," Charles muttered.

Reid looked at his friend. "Are you saying this is connected to Hemsfield? Wychwright's not on the list."

"No, but this murder's certainly connected to other matters that concern us, Ed. Sir James, may I examine his pockets?"

"Yes, of course."

Sinclair carefully searched through the dead man's coat and trousers. The interior coat pocket held a scrap of paper, and Charles held it up to the light to read the pencil marks. "I may have to recuse myself from this one, Edmund.'"

"Why?"

"Because, the message says, 'Meet me at five. – A.W.'"

"A.W?" Abberline repeated. "Who in God's green earth is A.W.?"

Charles pushed himself up and handed the note to Reid. "As my cousin is fond of saying, he's a worm in a silk suit. You'll want to issue an arrest warrant for Sir Albert Wendaway."

Beth had been sleeping for over an hour when the woman entered her room. The tall figure stole through the doorway without making a sound. She crept to the side table where the water pitcher sat beside a small, clean glass. Withdrawing a vial from her apron pocket, the woman poured a small amount into the glass, swirled it to coat the clear sides, and then emptied the remainder of both the glass and the vial into the pitcher.

Putting the stopper back into the vial, she hid it within her pocket once more, and then started for the door. "Who's that?" the duchess asked.

"Just a nurse," the intruder whispered. "Hush now. Go back to sleep."

She turned to leave, but a genuine nurse knocked just as the woman touched the handle. For a brief moment, the unwelcome visitor considered assaulting the unwary woman, but fearing the resulting commotion might ruin her surprise, the disguised woman performed an impossible feat: she vanished.

"Your Grace?" the matron softly called as she entered. Beth had fallen asleep again. The nurse stepped softly to the bedside and gently shook her shoulder. "My lady?"

The duchess opened her eyes at the nurse's touch. "Who was that?" she asked, sleepily. "Oh, Mrs. Reston. Is it time for my sleeping powder already?"

"I'm sorry to wake you, my lady, but I must perform my duties."

"Yes, I know. Go ahead."

The sister checked her patient's pulse, respiration, and temperature, and then jotted the results into a notebook. "Your Grace, did you eat all of your supper?"

Beth nodded. "Most of it. Not the lamb. It didn't smell appetising. I ate half of the peas, though. I'm sorry I'm not better about eating. It isn't because the cooks aren't talented. Please, tell them that for me. I simply cannot eat."

"I will, my lady. And your tea? Did you drink it? The milk also?"

"Yes, I drank both," Elizabeth answered wearily. "I hope that will please Mr. Treves. I so want to go home."

"He'll take it into account, I'm sure. Did your husband stop by earlier?"

"He did," she replied, more awake now. "He brought those roses. They probably had more vigour before he left them in a carriage for an hour."

Reston laughed. "At least he thought to buy them. Here now, I've brought your last medicine for the night. I know you're not fond of taking it, but the powder is meant to improve the quality of your sleep. I must say, ma'am, your colour is much better than when you first arrived."

"My husband's visits have a positive effect. That same powder again? I'll drink it, but it tastes awful."

"Medicine seldom tastes otherwise, my lady," she said, adding a dose of white powder to the glass and stirring in six ounces of water. "Now, you must drink all. We'll pray it stays down."

Beth grimaced as she sipped the bitter liquid, coughing at the taste—far worse than usual. She pushed away the glass, and wiped her mouth. "Oh, that is dreadful! Have you changed to a new powder? I'm very sorry, Mrs. Reston, but I simply cannot drink it!"

"No, we've not changed the powder. It's the same as always." Reston smelled the water, and her auburn brows pinched together. "This doesn't smell right. Here, now, I'll take this with me and change out your water whilst I'm about it." She looked into the pitcher. The liquid appeared dark in colour. "Not to worry," she said, although the nurse felt rising alarm. "I'll be back in a moment. Don't forget, now. Your handbell is right here, should you need anything." She started to leave, but then paused, turning back. "Duchess, the two constables who keep watch on your door. Did your husband dismiss them?"

"I—I'm not sure," she said, the small amount she'd swallowed already roiling in her delicate stomach. "That is…" she started, but she could say nothing more, for suddenly Elizabeth leaned over the side of the bed and vomited up the entire contents of her stomach.

The nurse set down the pitcher and glass and rinsed a cloth in a basin of cool water, using it to wipe the duchess's mouth and face. "I'm sorry, Your Grace. Your nausea has returned, it seems. Do you think your stomach wishes to rebel again? Shall I stay?"

Beth leaned back against the pillows, her face pale. "No. I don't think so. I'm very sorry, Mrs. Reston. I'd thought myself past all this nausea. Do forgive me for keeping you."

"You are the gentlest lady I've ever met, Your Grace. Now, you lie still, and I shall see to it that Mr. Treves is notified." She rang the handbell, and in a moment a second nurse answered. "Keep watch over the duchess, Mrs. Kemper. I shan't be long. And where are those two constables? I've a question for them."

"They were asked to move, Mrs. Reston. A message from Leman Street, I think. They keep watch near the east entrance now."

"What sort of nonsense is that? Very well. Stay here, and I shall see to it. No one enters this room unless it's myself, Lord Haimsbury, or Mr. Treves. Is that clear?"

Reston left and walked quickly towards Treves's hospital office, praying the hard-working surgeon hadn't yet left for home.

CHAPTER THIRTY-TWO

The city and Metropolitan police had worked the crime scene at the Exchange for three hours before Charles called it a night. He charged Arthur France to continue the investigation along with Reid, and Fraser's team. Fred Abberline went home to his wife, happy to get a decent night's sleep for a change.

The bone-weary marquess hired a hansom and used the time to make notes to himself. He penciled a list of questions to ask the earl along with various instructions for their ICI agents as the mare clip-clopped along the cold cobbles.

"You must find all this quite discouraging," a raspy voice whispered from the air beside him.

A pair of yellow eyes materialised within the vibrating space, and surrounding the peculiar orbs, emerged a long face framed in coal-black hair.

"I don't recall inviting anyone to ride along," Sinclair said, praying his voice betrayed none of the shock he felt.

"Most humans would scream at so sudden and mysterious a visit. You are certainly different, Charles Sinclair."

"Which one are you?" he asked the intruder.

The strange creature laughed, and the air escaping his mouth emitted a squawking sort of sound. "How soon humans forget. I've come to see why you wanted to return to this pale world. It is so very dirty, don't you think? Filled with dust and excrement. And the trees and stones have no life at all! What a dismal place this London is!"

Sinclair wondered briefly if he'd fallen asleep. His limited experience with spirit creatures was mixed. Once on the road to Branham, he'd encountered three in quick succession, all apparently whilst in a waking dream.

"Have you remembered your name yet, Creature?" he asked as he recognised the irritating gatekeeper.

The birdman had fully formed now, and its humanoid body bounced upon the seat as the coach passed over a set of rough, iron tracks west of the rail goods depot. "Does this place always move like this? I do not like it!"

"You are travelling inside a horse-drawn carriage. What do you want with me, Nameless Spirit?"

"Nameless! You are a very rude man, Charles Sinclair, and I shan't tell you!"

"Fine, then. Get out."

"I shall leave in a moment, but first I shall offer a hint. What will you trade for it?" the gatekeeper asked greedily.

"Nothing. Get out."

"You are as discourteous here as in *Sebet Babi*, human! Very well, I offer this hint for free, but if you want to know more, you will have to provide a small payment. Agreed?" it tempted.

"I agree to nothing. Get out of my coach."

"You bluster, but I see curiosity upon your face. Do not deny it! You want to know why I've appeared, don't you?"

"Not really."

The creature's head tilted in the same way it had so often inside the stone maze. "Tis a pity about those men."

"Men?"

"The dead ones. They cry for vengeance, but it will never come. Not until their murderer is caught."

Charles suspected the gatekeeper of a plot to lure him into conversation. "Go away."

"Yes, yes, I shall. These poor fellows wish only for you to discover the name of the one who slew them, and then left them in such dreadful poses! How very embarrassing, don't you think? If this madman is not caught, he may continue. Would you sleep well then?"

"I sleep just fine, thank you."

"Such lies! You hardly sleep at all, Charles Sinclair. Hemsfield had a dream only last week of death. He wrote about it in a book. I think it's called a journal or a germal, or something like that. Probably all lies, for no one writes truth in a journal, am I right?"

Sinclair thought of his father's journals and of Beth's. Why would the bird creature mention journals? "I've no idea," he answered non-committally.

"Yes, you do. You know perfectly well what I mean," the bird-man insisted, his face an inch from Sinclair's. "Ask her."

"Ask whom?"

"The foolish girl. The one with the puzzle. Ask her about her father's real business at the Exchange. Ask about his partners and his new offices. Ask about *the note*."

"The note?"

"Exactly. Oh, but there is one thing more. Your faithless wife is in danger. The one in love with that Captain fellow. If you do not hurry, she'll find her way back to us. *Au revoir*, Prince Charles."

The body shimmered and started to fade, but just before the mouth and eyes vanished, the birdlike lips spoke six words: "*Beware the looking glass. She lies.*"

"What?" Charles shouted as it winked out of sight, leaving the human staring at nothing but air.

He glanced down, intending to pray, but to his shock, found the page of his notebook covered in dozens of strange symbols. Charles had no recollection of writing them, and they were in ink, not pencil. Red ink, at that!

The wound at the back of his head began to throb, and Charles felt that same irritating tingle near the nape of his neck, as though a thousand flies had landed upon his skin simultaneously.

The hansom passed by Leman Street, meaning the hospital was no more than ten minutes away. The bells of Christ Church sounded eleven, and a white bird flew at the right-side window as though hurled. It crashed into the mud-spattered glass with a loud thud. Impossibly, the wounded bird stuck to the dirty surface, and its dying eyes bored into Sinclair's as if to offer a warning. A red spot formed on its left wing, despoiling the white feathers with an ever-widening circle of death.

Despite the late hour, a dense flock of crows and ravens appeared from nowhere, rushing towards the coach in a cloud of black anger. The open-air design of hansom cabs offers the passenger an unobscured view of the road ahead, but provides no protection against a murderous flock of supernaturally directed birds. Charles put up both arms, crossing them over his face against the onslaught.

He could hear the ravens' calls and deep-throated shouts; the dysphonic screams of a million battle cries, and he shut his eyes, praying for aid.

The horse could also see the bloodthirsty birds, even though the driver could not. She reared up on her back legs, nearly upturning the two-wheeled coach, and then bolted forwards, thundering through a hail of sharp beaks and flapping wings at breakneck speed. All the while, the bewildered cabman furiously pulled on the leather reins to make her obey.

When the horse finally stopped, it stood two feet from the main entrance to London Hospital. Not one feather could be seen anywhere upon the coach's windows; not on the doors, lamps, or the coach's roof. The exhausted mare panted, relieved to have escaped the hellish onslaught. The cabman jumped down, his face florid with sweat and panic, to offer an apology to his white-faced passenger.

"Do forgive me, sir. I dunno what go' into that animal," the man blustered, his breath clouding the air. "She ain' never done tha' afore. No charge, sir. It's on the 'ouse."

Nevertheless, Charles handed the bewildered driver a sovereign. "Make sure your horse gets double oats, on me. She's a rare one indeed."

He rushed into the hospital, staggering slightly as he passed through the doors. The pale marquess made his way towards the duchess's room, but three feet past the porter's office, collapsed upon the gleaming floor tiles.

"Fetch a doctor!" the night porter shouted. Sister Reston had just left the duchess's room at the end of the main corridor, and she ran towards the fallen man.

The porter helped the peer into a sitting position, and the nurse bent to speak with him. "Lord Haimsbury, are you injured?"

"Birds," Charles whispered, his pupils wide and black. "It was the birds."

"Help me, Mr. Jellico," she ordered the middle-aged porter. "We'll take his lordship to the nearest open room. I believe the one east of the duchess is still empty."

Charles felt himself lifted and half-carried towards the same room where he'd earlier prayed and talked with Paul and the others, but as they passed the door to Elizabeth's room, he noticed a flicker of movement—like shadowy wings.

"Who's in there? Birds?" he asked. "No, no, I don't mean birds. Who is in my wife's room?"

"Dr. Gehlen, sir," Reston answered as they set him upon the bed's edge. The table they'd used earlier had been removed, and the room returned to its normal state. "Here now, sir, lie down and let the spell pass. I was told you suffered a serious head injury last Sunday. It's a wonder you haven't collapsed before this. There now, close your eyes, and I'll fetch a doctor."

Charles felt intensely tired, and though he had no wish to sleep, his eyelids refused to remain open and within minutes, he lost all consciousness.

Next door, unaware of her husband's condition, Elizabeth Sinclair lay pale and weary upon her bed, being examined by Anthony Gehlen. With Treves already gone home for the night, it was Gehlen who answered the emergency call. Reston had found the thirty-eight-year-old obstetrician reading a book in the porter's lounge, and he'd rushed to the duchess's room as soon as the nurse showed him the pitcher of dark water.

"Did I hear Charles?" Beth asked Reston as she returned.

"The marquess is back, yes, but he's speaking with his constables just now," the woman lied, not wishing to upset her patient. "Shall I stay, sir?"

"Where were those constables?" Gehlen asked. "They've been there constantly since the first day, and now they're not. I hope the marquess gives both a good dressing down!"

Reston pulled him aside and whispered, telling him about Sinclair's collapse and the mystery of the constables. "I see," he muttered. "Very well. Let me finish here first. Duchess, how much of your medicine did you drink?"

"Only a sip. It tasted awful. Must I continue to take it? I'd rather try sleeping without it. Once Charles is finished, he'll stay with me."

Reston offered clarification. "I do not believe the duchess retained any of the liquid, Doctor."

"Let's pray she did not," he answered darkly. "Speak to the porter, Mrs. Reston. Ask if they noticed anyone in the hospital that doesn't belong."

The nurse left to carry out the orders but did not close the door. "Duchess, tell me how your feel," Gehlen said gently. "Are you experiencing any abdominal discomfort? Any cramping?"

"No," she answered wearily.

He moved his hands along her stomach, noting its surprising roundness. "You're how far along, my lady?"

"Eight weeks today."

"That's very precise. Not even I can be so certain of a conception date."

"Yet, I can," she told him plainly. "Why? Are you worried? Have I done something wrong?"

He replaced the quilt across her shoulders and sat, taking her right hand. "You've done nothing wrong, Your Grace. Did you notice anyone in your room this evening? A visitor, perhaps? Not a nurse or physician. This person would have stood close to your bed and picked up the water pitcher."

"A nurse was here, but I remember no visitors."

"Sister Reston?"

"No, another nurse. Just before Mrs. Reston arrived. Tall, dark haired. She never spoke, but she did pick up the pitcher. There was an odd smell. Like a strong, disagreeable mint."

"And how much of the water did you drink?"

"Not very much. It made me quite sick, but then I've felt nauseous the past few days. Now that the coughing has ceased, it's replaced by a noncompliant stomach."

He checked her pulse, grateful for its steady beat. "You may find the nausea grows worse, my lady, but it will eventually subside. Eight weeks," he said thoughtfully. "The morning sickness started early?"

She nodded. "I'd not call it morning sickness. It lasts all day sometimes."

"Dizzy spells?"

Beth nodded again. "For several weeks, yes. I'm quite unsteady at times. Is there something wrong? Why do you look so worried?"

"It's my job to worry about my patients, Your Grace. There is nothing wrong that cannot be cured with rest. I prefer not to administer a sleeping aid. Are you able to fall asleep without one?"

"Yes, if Charles is with me. When he's finished talking to the constables, would you ask him to come in, please?"

He stood and bowed politely. "Of course, my lady."

Gehlen exited and turned left, then left again, entering the hospital room where Sinclair lay. He found Reston sitting with the marquess, her grey eyes watching for signs of illness or injury.

"He's in a light sleep," she told Gehlen. "I believe he'd awaken if you wish to speak to him, Doctor."

Anthony drew a chair close to the narrow bed and sat into it. "Lord Haimsbury?"

The detective stirred, his eyelids slowly opening. "Yes? Who are you?"

"Anthony Gehlen, sir. We spoke earlier today."

"Yes, that's right," he said, sitting up and wiping his eyes. "Did I fall asleep?"

"In a manner of speaking. I'm told you suffered a blow to the head a fortnight ago. Have you a headache now?"

"A slight one."

"Do you suffer headaches often?"

"More often than I'd like," Charles answered honestly. "What time is it?"

"Half past eleven. Dizziness?"

"No, not that I recall. Why am I in bed?"

"You had a slight spell earlier, sir. May I?" Gehlen asked as he felt the back of Sinclair's head. "You still have some swelling here. Does this hurt?" he asked, pressing lightly against the healing wound. Charles responded with an unintentional gasp, for the pressure—though gently done—felt like an ice pick.

"As I thought, you've left your sickbed far too soon. From what little I know of you, Lord Haimsbury, that doesn't surprise me. Michael Emerson is your physician?"

"Yes. He's looked after me since the fire on the eighteenth, but he's in Edinburgh."

"He did a fine job stitching up the wound, but he should never have permitted you to return to work this early. I'll write up my observations and leave it for him to read when he returns to London. Treves mentioned that his brother has taken ill, and that Emerson may be away for some weeks."

Charles lowered his feet to the floor. "Yes, but don't blame Emerson. He tried to keep me in bed. I'm stubborn. Sister Reston said you were in with my wife. Is she all right? Is there something I should know?"

Gehlen weighed the cost of telling Sinclair versus not telling him about the constables' dereliction, but decided to allow the detective to regain strength first. "The duchess is tired and asks if you would stay with her again tonight. With your permission, I should like to spend a little time with her tomorrow."

"Of course," Charles said, standing. "Is Lady Cordelia still in hospital?"

"So I'm told. As I mentioned to you this afternoon, Treves is her primary physician, along with a growing roster of influential city men. Why?"

"Because I must speak with her right away."

"I'm sure the lady is sleeping, Lord Haimsbury," Sister Reston argued as she took his elbow.

"Nevertheless, I must speak with her. It cannot wait."

He took the steps slowly, but over the course of several minutes, Charles regained his balance. "Thank you, Sister. When I'm finished speaking with Lady Cordelia, someone will need to remain with her, for I've very distressing news to deliver. Her father, Baron Wychwright, is dead. Murdered in the city."

Olivia Reston gasped in shock. "Murdered? Oh, that poor girl! Yes, of course, I'll have a nurse sit with her."

As they entered the corridor, Sinclair noticed Beth's door stood ajar with no men near it. Turning back towards Gehlen and the nurse, his voice took on a harsh tone. "Where are the constables who are supposed to keep watch on my wife?"

"We're not sure, sir," Reston admitted. "The porter mentioned they had moved to the east entrance."

Sinclair's struggled to keep his temper. "Who told them to move?" he shouted.

"Sir, I'm sure there's an explanation."

"Not one that will satisfy me!" he answered sharply. "Find them and send them to the porter's office. Tell them to wait. I'll deal with them presently." He took a breath. "I am sorry, Mrs. Reston. It isn't your fault."

"I understand, sir. What else may I do to help?"

"Nothing yet, but I'll need to use your telegraph when I'm finished with Lady Cordelia."

Inside Wychwright's room, Charles found the girl awake within the darkened space. The drapes stood partially open, with a one-foot gap that allowed the rounding moon to cast a beam of silver across the floor.

"Is it morning already?" she asked. "Oh, Lord Haimsbury. Excuse my dullness. I was having the oddest dream about birds."

He crossed to the bed and sat. "Birds?"

"Yes," she answered, wiping her eyes. "Love birds. Very pretty. Why are you here?"

"I'm sure it was a lovely dream. Forgive me for disturbing you, Delia. I'm afraid I bring troubling news. Can you be brave for me?" he asked her, taking her hand in his.

"I'm generally not very brave. Must I be?" she asked, her high-pitched voice trembling.

"I'm afraid you must."

Charles hated delivering news of a loved one's death to family. He'd done so hundreds of times in thirteen years with the police, but each time felt as difficult and awkward as the first. What he had learnt in all these terrible moments was that no words sufficed. Preparing the loved one never softened the blow, but only delayed the inevitable pain of it all. Cutting straight to the awful truth allowed the shock to commence without delay, and hence moved all the quicker to eventual acceptance.

"Delia, I'm afraid your father is dead."

He'd expected her to cry out, to shout, scream, to wail in despair, but instead the eighteen-year-old merely sighed. "I see. Was it a heart attack?"

"No. His death came at the hands of another. Someone took your father's life, which makes it my job to find the killer and see he pays with his life."

"Father was...*murdered?*" she asked, paling.

"Yes. I'm going to send a telegraph message to your mother and have a policeman escort her to the hospital."

"No, no, please, I'd rather go home. May I go home?"

"So long as your doctors approve it. I can send an officer with you."

"Thank you," she answered softly. "Mother will likely fall apart, and she'll not want anyone to see her cry. I'll send word to my brothers. Two are abroad, and it may take them several days to receive the letter and travel here. We'll have to delay the funeral."

"Think about those things tomorrow, Delia. I am very sorry. If you need anything—anything at all, let me know, and I'll see to it."

Her lower lip began to quiver, and she squeezed his hand. "That's kind of you, but I think I'll be all right. It's time I grow up. Father always wanted me to grow up."

Charles recognised the look of shock, and rather than leave her, he drew the grieving girl into his arms. "I think he'd understand, Delia," he whispered. "You needn't grow up yet."

The tears started in earnest then, and Cordelia Wychwright sobbed like a small child into Sinclair's shoulder for a very long time. Not once did the detective suggest needing to leave; not once did he complain. Instead, he held her sweetly, whispering strength to her all the while that she wept.

11:55 pm – Consultants' Lounge

The two constables stared sheepishly at their shoes. After Charles sent several telegrams, including one to Commissioner Monro and another to Paul Stuart, he turned his mind towards investigating the matter of the duchess's door. Dr. Anthony Gehlen had taken the detective to a quiet room used by visiting physicians, where the shamefaced police constables listened to the newly promoted commissioner's outrage.

"How can this have happened!" Sinclair shouted. "How does a poisoner enter my wife's room and contaminate her water pitcher without anyone noticing? Where were you, gentlemen? Why did you abandon your post?"

"It was the note, Superintendent—I mean Commissioner, sir," the shorter answered cautiously. "We weren't shirkin', sir. The note gave us new orders, and we tried to find you to confirm them, but you'd already gone, and it seemed best to follow rather than disobey. We'd no idea what would happen, Commissioner. Honest!"

"A note?" Charles repeated, blinking his eyes to clear them, for the mounting headache moved from the back of his head to behind his eyes. "Do you still have this note?"

Police Constable Bright nodded and fished in the pocket of his dark blue tunic. "Here, sir. It looks just like your signature, sir."

Charles sighed. The typewritten note was on Leman Street stationery and read: 'New Orders. Relocate to East Entrance immediately.' The fabrication was signed in blue ink, 'Det. Supt. C. Sinclair'. The penmanship matched the commissioner's hand perfectly. "Did neither of you notice that it's signed with my previous rank? What am I now, Constable Bright?"

"A commissioner, sir. Commissioner of Intelligence."

"Yet it says?"

"Detective Superintendent, sir," he continued, his voice growing evermore soft with each syllable.

"I suggest you remember that, as it may come up during your next review. Who gave you this note?"

"A woman, sir. One of the nurses. She said you handed it to her as you left. It made a bit o' sense, as you'd been in the hospital earlier, and as I said, it does look like your handwriting, sir."

"Describe her."

"Tall, dark hair. Sort o' handsome for a nurse. Many hereabouts are plain, but this lady wore rouge and face powder, which surprised me. Most nurses don't."

"Constable, this woman, would you say that she was English?"

"No, sir. Though I cannot say where she might come from. Her accent sounded foreign. Spain, maybe. Or Italy."

"I reckon it's Italy, sir," the other constable interrupted. "We got a family of Italians living on the floor below. Me an' my wife, I mean. The woman looked like them, too. Dark eyes like a gypsy but with real white skin. Those black eyes looked right through me, ya know?"

"I know all too well, Constable Calhoun," he told the youth. *Why had Serena di Specchio impersonated a nurse?* "This is not over, but for the present, you're to return to your post. I'll not charge you with dereliction, as you thought yourselves following my command, but in future do not alter your behaviour unless you receive a new order from me, in person. Is that understood? I do not issue orders through notes!"

"Yes, sir," both men answered in unison.

The marquess left the lounge and returned to his wife's chamber, noticing a familiar voice coming from Cordelia's room. "Paul?"

The earl looked up as Charles entered. Wychwright had finished dressing, and the earl was helping her with a warm cloak. "I'm taking her home. I'll return tomorrow morning after breakfast. It's already been a long night for you, Cousin. Rest if possible."

Aubrey took the girl's arm and a porter carried the two cases to a waiting coach near the north entrance.

"Thank you, Lord Haimsbury," she whispered as she passed by Sinclair.

"You promised to call me Charles," he reminded her.

"Yes, that's right. Charles. Thank you. You're both very kind. Far nicer than I deserve."

"Have a doctor look after her, Paul," he told his cousin. "She's in shock."

"I will. Goodnight."

The earl left with the grieving woman, and Sinclair entered Beth's room. Charles found her turned on her side, sleeping peacefully. Gehlen stood nearby, having stopped in to make sure the duchess hadn't become sick again.

"May I have a moment? Outside?" he asked the marquess. "The porter's office, I think."

A nurse remained with the sleeping duchess, and the chastised constables took up their former post on either side of the door.

Once inside the porter's office, Gehlen spoke directly. "I apologise for the near-miss with your wife, sir. We will, of course, cooperate, in any way, to get to the bottom of it."

"Have you examined the water in her pitcher?"

"I have. The nurse thought it familiar when she smelled it, which is why she brought it to my attention. The odour is instantly recognisable to anyone familiar with the herb. Pennyroyal."

Sinclair nearly flew apart. "Pennyroyal! That is an abortion drug used by prostitutes!" he shouted.

"Please, Lord Haimsbury, I beg you to lower your voice. It's late, and we have patients in need of rest. Despite the obvious attempt, there is no damage. Your wife's sensitive stomach caused her to disgorge the entire amount almost immediately. She has vomited several more times since, and I find no indication that the herb affected her adversely."

"You know that this was an attempt to induce a miscarriage."

Gehlen nodded. "Yes, though I cannot imagine why someone would wish to do so. Your constables were removed from her door by way of a ruse, which allowed the perpetrator to enter without fear of being observed."

"She will be visited soon, for I know who she is."

"Then your investigative skills are as remarkable I've been told. Any person who would try to slay the unborn in this hospital deserves punishment to the fullest extent that English law can exact."

"I intend to make sure she receives all that is coming to her," the detective said, thinking of his unborn daughter. *But she was fine, when she helped me find my way through the stone maze. Georgie said she was ten-and-a-half. She seemed healthy and happy. I have to hold onto that! Lord, please, help me to hold onto that!* "And this poison will cause no harm?" he asked.

Gehlen had several thoughts at once. "Did Mr. Treves speak to you of our suspicion?"

"Briefly. Have you had a chance to examine my wife?"

"I have, but I'd like to make a more thorough, objective assessment when the duchess is no longer under duress. My cursory exam leads me to believe she carries more than one child. I've yet to be wrong with an early diagnosis of twins. Although, I said a singleton once, and the lady gave birth to twin boys. One was much smaller, which may have caused the confusion."

"Twins," Sinclair whispered. "How can you know?"

"At this point, I operate on my own experience with other mothers of twins. The extreme symptoms which manifested so early are sure signs, but also her abdominal distension is greater than it should be for eight weeks. It is eight weeks, correct?" he asked. "Not fourteen or even sixteen?"

"No, it is exactly eight weeks today."

"That's what the duchess told me. Her very words, in fact. How can you be so certain? I do not imply impropriety, so forgive me if it sounds as though I do, but very few parents know the precise date of conception."

"Our situation is unusual," he answered. "The one and only time I ever lay with the duchess was the eighth of October, and she was a maiden. Because our wedding ended with an abduction and chaos, we've not been intimate as husband and wife."

"October eighth? A doubling of the number eight, and it may be a doubling of the fruit of that night. Strange, particularly as this year is a trebling of the same number. 1888."

"I'd not thought of that. Strange, indeed. Doctor, because of what happened here tonight, I prefer to take my wife home tomorrow. Emerson may be away for many weeks yet. I wonder if I might impose upon you to visit my home, should we need your advice?"

"Of course, but isn't Lord Salperton the lady's physician?"

"Yes, he has been, but his specialty is the mind. Beth may wish to keep him, despite that. However, if he seeks a consult from a specialist, may we call upon you?"

"Anytime. Also, I'd suggest hiring a nurse. One who understands the specific needs of women carrying more than one child."

"Might Nurse Reston be available?" Sinclair asked.

"That is up to Sister and Mr. Treves."

"I'll speak to both tomorrow. Thank you. Thank you for all you've done for Beth—and for our children, no matter the number," the marquess said, smiling at last.

"It is my honour. Now, I'll leave you. You've the look of a man who needs to sleep."

Once Gehlen left, Charles sat on the edge of the bed, feeling Elizabeth's forehead. Cool and moist. As every other night, he set his coat, waistcoat, holster, shoes, and socks inside the closet. Then, he opened the blankets and climbed into the bed, pulling her into his arms. Weariness tugged at his eyelids, but he had no wish to fall asleep. He wanted to enjoy the warmth of her, the comforting nearness of her for a little while first. To keep awake, he mentally walked through all the steps that had led to where they now stood.

Trent had taken Elizabeth with the aid of a magic mirror. Someone had killed Trent and then hurled him out of the window, certainly a superhuman of some kind, or more likely a spiritual being. Beth had then escaped with the help of Prince Anatole, who took her to his castle. For reasons yet to be made clear, the mysterious Russian hired Salperton to look after the duchess, but insisted she remained in danger, refusing to allow Henry to tell anyone of her presence.

With Trent dead, who would want to harm the duchess? Di Specchio? Why would she try to cause Beth to lose their babies? Is it possible she knows about the twins? If she knows, then Redwing knows.

And what about Hemsfield and Wychwright? Hemsfield's killer showed tremendous strength, and Wychwright's demonstrated daring as well as cunning. Both victims were found by servants inside locked rooms. Sir Albert Wendaway's build was slight, and Charles very much doubted him capable of suspending the dead weight of a two-hundred-pound man from a high ceiling. If the baronet participated in the late earl's murder, then he had help. However, Wendaway's alleged attack on the baron's daughter spoke to motive. Had Wychwright learned of the assault and delivered an ultimatum to Albert? Had he threatened to report him to the authorities?

Then again, Reid's notations on Ida Ross's list indicated other murders as well. Anatole had warned of war.

Is one of the Watchers behind it all? And where is Romanov?

He longed to ask Lorena MacKey, but the physician had fled Queen Anne House, leaving no clue to her new location.

The first thing we do is find MacKey.

As he puzzled through these thoughts, his eyes perceived movement in the far corner of the room, next to the closet. A shadow lengthened along the wall, and a pair of black wings spread across the ceiling like ink pooling upon parchment. Charles discerned a scratching sort of laughter; the voices of a million crows.

Beware the looking glass. She lies, the creature had told him. *Di Specchio. Her name means 'looking glass'. Is that the solution to the riddle?*

He drew Beth into his arms and held her close as he shut his eyes and began to pray.

CHAPTER THIRTY-THREE

9:02 pm - Tuesday, 4th December

At Charles's insistence, Elizabeth was moved to Haimsbury House the following afternoon. Her overall health was judged no worse than before the attempted poisoning, and Treves agreed to Sinclair's request for his wife's dismissal. Elizabeth's lungs had healed well whilst in hospital, she'd gained three pounds, and despite the near miss with the Pennyroyal, her eyes were bright for the first time in many days.

To celebrate her delayed arrival in their new home, Sinclair arranged a family gathering, and the happy group enjoyed a casual supper served in the Cumbria drawing room, followed by an hour of games.

"I'll say goodnight," Drummond told his nephew. "You two newlyweds deserve some time alone. I'll see you tomorrow, son."

"You're welcome to stay," Sinclair urged the older man. "Della's promised to read a new poem."

"That sounds lovely, but she can read it to me tomorrow as well as tonight. I'm taking my sister with me. Tory and I have some plans to make regarding the reception for your investiture ceremony."

"I still can't imagine myself a duke, sir."

"You'll get used to it," Drummond laughed, slapping his nephew on the back.

Charles walked his uncle to the main doors of the grand home. "Thank you, James. This has been a long time in coming, but it's worth the wait. And we may have a surprise to announce soon."

"Another new title?" Drummond asked, rubbing his hands together happily.

"In a way," he said, thinking of himself as 'the father of twins'.

"Can you give me no hints?"

"No, sir. No hints."

"Aye, well, I'll let you keep your secret—for now."

Baxter helped the duke with his overcoat and hat, motioning to a footman to call Drummond's coach forward in the gravel park.

"Goodnight, Princess!" Drummond called into the large drawing room.

There was a moment's silence, followed Della's small feet upon the tiles. She raced to the door and threw open her arms. "Goodnight, Uncle! Beth says to tell you she also says goodnight. Cousin Charles has ordered her not to leave the sofa."

"And Elizabeth complied? Your Cousin Charles is a remarkable man to have tamed so fierce a woman so very quickly, Della. Give us a kiss."

She giggled as the six-foot-tall duke bent down. "Your moustache tickles," she told him.

"You'd best get used to it. Apparently, your cousin is growing one to compete with mine, and with a beard as well! I may grow mine again," he mused, rubbing his jawline. "It's been a decade since I had a beard. I wonder if my chin has any dark hair left in it."

Charles shook his uncle's hand. "Goodnight, sir. You are always welcome here. No need for an invitation."

"I'll let you enjoy your privacy for a few days before making a nuisance of myself. Baxter, come play a game o' chess with me soon. Booth's never been a fan o' chess, and Tory cheats."

"I should be honoured, Your Grace."

The duke left, and Sinclair reached for Adele's hand. "With your brother elsewhere tonight, you and I must provide entertainment. Shall I sing?"

She laughed. "I've heard you sing, Cousin Charles. Perhaps, it's best if I read my poetry."

"Well said," he replied as they returned to the drawing room.

"What poem have you chosen for us?" Elizabeth asked.

"One from my new book," the eleven-year-old answered. "Let me know when I may begin. Poetry sets a mood, and I'll not want it interrupted with kissing."

Charles laughed. "Shall I kiss my wife many times to get it all out of my system, then?"

"Yes, I think you should."

The marquess kissed Elizabeth sweetly, thrice, and then drew her into his arms. "There, all done for now."

He and Elizabeth sat quietly, the fire's yellow light flickering across their happy faces as they listened.

"*Once upon a midnight dreary, while I pondered weak and weary; over many a quaint and curious volume of forgotten lore. While I nodded, nearly napping, suddenly there came a tapping,*

As of some one gently rapping, rapping at my chamber door. Tis some visitor, I muttered, tapping at my chamber door—Only this and nothing more," Adele began. "This is rather strange, Cousin Beth."

"I'd call it atmospheric," the duchess answered. "Continue reading, darling. Don't break the mood."

"Very well. *Ah, distinctly, I remember, it was in the bleak December.*" The youngster stopped, her hand upon the illustrated page of the book. "Isn't that odd, Cousin Charles? It's December as I read this, and it's been very bleak. I like that word. Bleak. It rhymes with beak."

"Perhaps, you should write poetry, Della," he suggested. "I've never read this poem. You say it's by Poe?"

"Yes," she said, closing the book slightly to examine the brown leather cover. "*The Raven and Other Poems* by Edgar Allen Poe," she read out. "Why was Mr. Poe such a depressive man?"

"Did you say raven, Della?" Charles asked, the simple word sending a chill though his frame.

"Yes, that's the title of the book and the poem. Why?"

"No reason," he said quickly, but the improbable coincidence felt deliberate and contrived; not by Adele, but by something less friendly. "Do read some more."

"Let's see, I'll start where I left off. *Ah, distinctly, I remember. It was in the bleak December; and each separate dying ember wrought its ghost upon the floor. Eagerly, I wished the morrow—vainly, I had sought to borrow from my books, surcease of sorrow—sorrow for the lost Lenore.* What does surcease mean, Cousin Beth? I've never heard of that word."

"It's an Americanism, I think," she told her young cousin. "I imagine it means the same as cease. He's seeking an end to sorrow."

"Oh, I see. It's all quite gloomy, though. No wonder he wants an end to it!"

"Many poets write sorrowful prose. Poe was a tortured soul, darling," the duchess explained. "Why did you choose *The Raven* for our entertainment tonight?"

Della shrugged. "Honestly, I thought it would be much more stimulating than this. I once read one of his mystery stories all about pirates and gold treasure, and I thought a poem might be exciting, too. This one is hardly that. Why ghosts? His poetry is very different from Mr. Tennyson or Mr. Wordsworth."

"Poets choose lots of topics for their verse, Della. Pirates as well as the supernatural," Beth explained.

"Why the supernatural?"

"I suppose writers seek to understand that which cannot be seen, but all too often they insist God be removed, as if he is optional. I really have never understood it."

"How can God be optional?" the girl asked.

"Many a so-called artist considers our creator little more than an invention of man," Charles told her.

"And this poem is about the supernatural? Is this raven a demon then?"

Sinclair had no wish to speak of bird demons, but he also preferred to keep the evening's conversation light. "I've no idea. I am but a thick-headed policeman in the company of two beautiful ladies, therefore, I do not care about foolish poems or birds. I'm content with the life given me."

Della closed the book and walked to Sinclair's chair. "Cousin Charles, you're very sweet, and your head only appears thick because you have two of them, which means you have twice as much knowledge!" she added, giggling.

Charles jumped to his feet and picked the girl up, swinging her high into the air. "And for that you must be tossed until you are dizzy!" he teased. "Or perhaps, I shall tickle you until you beg for mercy!"

Della burst into a shower of laughter and then dashed back towards Mary Wilsham, who sat nearby crocheting a pair of gloves. "Aunt Mary, you must protect me!" she called, hiding behind Wilsham's chair.

The former housekeeper, now a permanent part of the Sinclair family, shook her greying head. "Now, now, little Della, I cannot protect you from Mr. Sinclair, and you know it well enough. I've no idea how that funny poem goes, would you read it out to me?"

Adele thought for a moment, but then ran back into Charles's arms and kissed his bearded cheek. "Yes, I'll read it to you, Aunt Mary, but I must forgive my cousin first. He is just so very happy to have Beth home that he forgets himself. I'm no longer a child, Cousin Charles. I shall be twelve next summer, and that is when most of my friends have gone away to finishing school."

Beth's dark brows shot up. "Oh no, not already, Della! Besides, I imagine your governess will have something to say about that, or have you convinced your Uncle James to reprieve you from Mrs. Chandler's tutelage?"

"Mrs. Chandler has returned to Scotland," Della announced. "Since I am to live with you and Cousin Charles, I no longer require a governess; that is what Uncle James said. May I, please, enroll in finishing school next year?"

"We'll discuss it with your brother. Paul is still your legal guardian, but we shall do all we may to persuade him," Beth promised.

Adele rushed over and gave her a kiss. "Oh, thank you! Come, Aunt Mary, I'll play a new song for you," she said, tugging on the older woman's hands and leading her from the drawing room.

Charles sat down next to his bride. "Alone at last," he whispered, touching her face. "I'm so glad to have you home, Mrs. Sinclair. Shall we stay here and watch the fire or go up?"

"I am content to do either," she told him. "So long as you're with me, I want for nothing, Charles."

"Then, as it's nearly ten, we should probably go to bed. I promised Treves and Gehlen that I'd make sure you got plenty of sleep. Otherwise, your doctors will scold us both."

"Must we move? It's so pleasant here."

"I fear we must, darling. Remember, you took a vow to obey me."

She laughed. "So I did, but, promise me that if I must retire early, that you will join me."

"Do you think Tory would object?" he teased.

"I think she would encourage it. You know…" she began, looking towards the doorway to make certain no one lingered nearby.

Charles read her mind. "Shall I close them?"

"Please."

He shut both panelled doors. "There, all alone. What is it you were about to say?"

She snuggled into his arms once more and gazed into the bright fire. "On our wedding day, when you and I arrived at Drummond House, do you recall that Tory had me meet her in a side room?"

Charles nodded, stroking her dark curls. "I do. It required me to fend off an unpleasant encounter with Albert Wendaway. A detestable man who deserves a visit from me."

"Because of Cordelia, you mean?"

"Let's speak of this tomorrow. It's far more than what he did to Delia. Wendaway may be involved in multiple crimes, but that's nothing new with him. May we keep to pleasant topics?"

"Yes, but if there is an unpleasant topic you're avoiding, I'd hear it, Charles. You've had a tiny cloud following you about all day. I thought it nothing more than concern for my health, but I begin to see it's more than that."

"I promise to tell you everything tomorrow. Finish your story, darling. What did Tory wish to share with you?"

"Advice."

"Advice?" he asked, laughing. "I cannot imagine what a spinster might say to a woman who has just married!"

Beth tweaked his wrist.

"Ouch!" he cried, feigning injury. "That hurt!"

She kissed it. "I doubt that, but you mustn't assume you know all about a person, even if you are a fine detective. I'd always thought of Tory as a prudish spinster, too, but I know better now. That day, she admonished me to cherish you always, not because you're her nephew, though she is very glad to have you back in the family, but because you love me so well. You see, Tory once loved a man with all her heart, but they never married, and she regrets it to this day. It's why she's remained unmarried."

"I apologise, Beth. I had no idea. When was this?"

"She was very young, when it happened; as young as thirteen. I know that she was only fourteen, when she left Grandfather's castle to live with his widowed sister, Charlotte Adelin, the Dowager Countess du Loire. Charlotte offered to provide finishing lessons and introduce her niece to society, but I never realised the real reason until Tory told me. You see, she'd fallen in love with a servant in Scotland, a groom named John Reynolds, and her father disapproved. I never met my great-grandfather, but I'm told he was very strict. Tory said she loved this young man, desperately loved him, and that they'd planned to elope to Glasgow, but her father found out and dismissed the boy from service. A month later, Victoria learned she'd fallen pregnant, and she was sent away to Paris to have the child."

"Oh, Beth, that's tragic!" Charles exclaimed. "But where is the child now?"

"Stillborn, but even if the girl had lived, she'd have been sent to a private orphanage in Switzerland, far from Victoria's reach. That's what was done in those days. It makes me sad to think of it. Tory said that, even if you hadn't been the long-lost Sinclair heir, she would have encouraged me to marry you, because true love is rare. And it is, Charles! What we have is so very rare! I pray we never stand in the way of it, if any of our children ever falls in love with... Well, with someone my great-grandfather would have considered unfit. Who are we to interfere in true love?"

"Would you have married me had I been just a policeman?" he asked, looking at her with wide eyes. "Truly, Beth, would you?"

She held his hand, touching his wedding band as she spoke. "Yes! Ask the duke if you don't believe me. I told him that I loved you, all those years ago, after my sixteenth birthday—though I think he knew even before, because I spoke about you often enough. I told him I wanted to marry you, and do you know what he said? He could have argued that I was promised to Paul, but he never even mentioned it. Not once. Instead, he told me that any man who protected and loved me, and whom I loved, would earn not only his respect but also his love, and that he would welcome you as my husband. His only concern was that you were still legally married. I'm sure that's why he sent me to Paris. Despite all that, I know that Grandfather liked and respected you even then, and since that day, he's come to love you, not because of your titles, my darling husband, but because of your character."

He drew her close, his arms 'round her waist. "Beth, do you know that I very nearly kissed you that day at Aubrey House? But I feared Paul might walk in on us, and he'd have made certain I never saw you again. When you left for Paris, it broke my heart. I assumed you were lost to me forever."

"Oh, Charles, I wanted you to kiss me! Couldn't you tell? I thought my heart was going to leap out of my chest when I saw you that day! Ever since, all I've wanted was to be your wife, and now I am. We were always meant to be together, Captain."

He kissed her cheek. "I love you more than any poet could express, Elizabeth. So very much, but the night has grown long, and it's time your Captain took you to bed."

She laughed as he carried her through the foyer, past the stairs, to the electric lift. He set her down briefly to shut the scrolled metal grating. "Keep close to me," he said as the motor engaged. "The cage still jerks and sways a bit. I'm having the electrics men look into it this week."

As soon as the lift reached the first floor, he drew back the grating and took her into his arms again, carrying her along the west corridor to their apartment.

"Are you sure I'm not too heavy?" she laughed. "I am getting fat, you know."

"Yes, you must weigh all of eight stone now, but if you weighed twenty, I'd love you all the more," he said as they entered the apartment.

"Of course, you do carry three of us."

"Three?" he asked.

"Your wife and two children. An entire family of Sinclairs in one package!"

"A very beautiful package at that, Mrs. Sinclair," he answered as they passed into the bed chamber. "Now, I shall settle you into this soft bed and leave you to sleep."

"Leave? Charles, don't go, please!"

"I'd assumed you're too weary, Beth."

"You and I have waited a fortnight to begin our married lives, Charles. Please, stay with me."

He placed his bride on the bed, and then sat down next to her. "No, I mean, yes! Of course, I realise that, but Beth, I make no promise about how I might behave."

"I think that is allowed now, husband. We are married, after all."

For weeks, Charles had imagined the moment when he could at last share himself with her, fully and completely—becoming one with Elizabeth—but he suddenly felt fearful.

"You're certain it won't harm the babies?"

"I asked Dr. Gehlen specifically about that. He said, barring anything unforeseen, that we should be able to enjoy a healthy wedded life, but added that he routinely cautions couples expecting twins to abstain at four months."

"Then we have two more months?"

"We do, Captain."

He removed his paisley waistcoat, and switched off the electric lights. "Shall I finish changing in my bedchamber?"

This puzzled the duchess. "You could, if you prefer, but you needn't leave because of me. I can change in the bath, if you wish privacy."

Suddenly, he felt like a youth encountering intimacy for the very first time. It made no sense. *I'm thirty-three years old! What am I afraid of? Hurting her? Hurting the babies? Or is it something else?*

"It's just easier," he muttered, leaving the chamber and passing through the bath and dressing area to the master's chamber. Sinclair shut his eyes, his back against the closed door that now separated them.

What is wrong with me? Any other man would already be making love to her!

"Charles?" she called from the other side of the door. "Darling, perhaps, we should wait. If you're too tired, I understand. You've slept very little this past week, and you're still recovering from your injury. Perhaps, you should rest tonight. There's no rush. We have a lifetime, after all."

He said nothing, a hundred thoughts arguing with one another inside his head. *Do I fear disappointing her? Disappointing myself? Good heavens, man, stop being an idiot! She loves you, and this is what you've prayed for these four years!*

"Darling? I'll just go to sleep on my own. Go to bed and rest. Honestly, I understand completely. I love you, Charles. With all my heart and soul, I love you," she whispered through the thick wood.

Charles could picture her standing there, and he knew her words were heartfelt. Amelia would have judged him harshly, even taunted him as fearful or weak, but not Beth. Never had God created such a gentle woman as this, and he was making her wait. Why?

He opened the door and lifted her into his strong arms.

"I'll rest better with you beside me," he whispered as he carried the duchess back to her bedchamber. He set Elizabeth upon the soft bed and gazed at her ethereal beauty, marvelling at the miracle before him. "I don't deserve such joy, but I bless God for it."

Since the night in Scotland, when a strange potion had forced them both into a situation that led to the creation of new life, Charles had often relived it in dreams. Nothing in those pleasant reveries compared to the passionate beauty of this night. Since the dawn of time, few couples had ever joined so closely, so intimately, so spiritually united, that time itself seemed to stop for an entire city.

But this night, it did.

Many would greet their morning eggs and toast with strange recollections of having dreamt of living miracles walking London's streets. The sun would rise behind a pillowy bank of friendly clouds, as though worried that his rays might waken the dreaming couple who held one another within their marriage bed. Westminster's dogs would sleep long and late, and impassionate cats refrain from chasing mice and birds, hushed into silence, their meowing ceased. That night, across the parish and surrounding, a mist of incredible peace blanketed all citizens, animals, and even the houses with rapturous joy, and for a little while, all was right with the world.

It would be a night of miracles, and for Charles Sinclair, making love to Elizabeth would heal his mind and body as nothing else in all the world ever could. As their hearts sang together in a single, melodious refrain, all his fears vanished.

In the quiet of a moonlit night, a new era had begun.

CHAPTER THIRTY-FOUR

Wednesday, 5th December, 1888

Exhausted from their night of bliss, Charles and Elizabeth slept late, not awakening until after ten. As he opened his eyes, the marquess smiled at finding the duchess lying beside him. Over their heads, entwined hearts painted on the underside of the tester bed's canopy reminded him of what he'd gained.

"Thank you, Lord," he whispered. "Today is another miracle."

Elizabeth turned towards him, her slender arm crossing his chest. She opened her eyes, asking sleepily, "Is it morning already?"

"It is the first day of our married life, my darling. Our true life, I mean. And today is my first full day as commissioner of this new branch."

"Must you work today?" she asked.

"Not right away. Salisbury and Matthews are my only bosses, you might say. I rather doubt they'll mind if I delay starting," he said, pulling her close. "Shall we have breakfast up here? Do you feel up to eating?"

"Not yet," she said, her stomach complaining. "Tea sounds fine. With peppermint, if it's not too much trouble."

He left the bed and crossed to the fireplace. "It seems cold in here."

"It's warm in bed," she tempted him.

"So it is," Charles answered, smiling, "but any warmth is because of you, not the heating. These new radiators are supposed to heat the rooms evenly, yet there are cold spots. This corner is freezing!"

She sat up, looking at him as he stood there, her eyes bright. Neither wore a stitch of clothing, and Beth began to laugh. "Perhaps, your lack of attire is the cause of your lack of warmth, Commissioner Sinclair."

Charles laughed, too, as he found his discarded trousers and pulled them on. He lit the gas in the fireplace, and then returned to the rumpled bed. "Are you complaining of my lack of attire?"

"Of course, not, my lord. I think you're quite handsome in your natural state. I've seen museum statues with less perfect lines. It strikes me that you could serve as a sculptor's model."

"Shall I model for you, my love?"

"As often as possible," she answered. "I've never been very successful at sculpture, though. Tis a pity, for your face has the sort of lines that cry out for fine marble."

He leaned across the bed and kissed her twice. "Even with the beard?"

"Even then," she told him. "Will you keep it?"

"If you want," he answered. "I could shave or let it grow to my chest like Salisbury. My grooming is constrained only by my lady's pleasure."

Elizabeth smiled. "Consider your lady pleased."

He grew more amorous, but someone knocked on the door, and a deep, male voice called hesitantly. "Sir? Are you and the duchess ready for breakfast?"

Charles shrugged. "We'll continue that later, wife," he whispered. Then turning, he called out, "Thank you, Mr. Baxter! We'll take tea in our parlour, if that can be arranged."

"Very good, my lord. I'll bring the morning papers as well, just as soon as Mrs. Paget prepares the tray. Do you prefer Darjeeling or Ceylon?" he asked through the closed door.

Sinclair rose from the bed. "Wait a moment!" he told the butler. Beth also left the bed and entered the bath.

Once there was no danger of embarrassing the duchess or the butler, Charles opened the chamber door a crack. "Thank you for your patience, Mr. Baxter. I'll have coffee, and the duchess prefers Darjeeling but asks for peppermint to soothe her stomach. Might that be possible?"

The butler grinned. "Ah, yes, the morning is always the most difficult time for expectant mothers, or so I'm told. Very good, sir. As it's your first full day as commissioner, shall I assist you with a shave?"

Charles ran a hand across his darkened chin. "No, not today. The duchess likes the beard. I may keep it. Has anyone called this morning? The earl?"

"His lordship sent a message. In fact, you've received four telegrams and two delivered notes. Also, a large basket of flowers arrived half an hour ago from Lord Salperton."

"Flowers? How thoughtful. Bring everything but the flowers up when you can, Baxter. Put the bouquet in the foyer to make sure the duchess sees it."

Pleased that his charges seemed content, the butler departed with a spring in his step.

Charles knocked on the bathroom door. "Beth? May I cross through, or do you prefer I use the other door?"

"Sorry," she answered. "Give me a minute."

The moment passed, and the door opened. Elizabeth's colour had paled, and she was wiping her face with a wet cloth.

"Darling, are you unwell?"

"No, just pregnant," she sighed. "Was that Baxter's voice?"

"Yes, and we're having tea delivered shortly, with peppermint. Is there any way I can help?"

"Alicia's still visiting her mother, which means I have no lady's maid. Would you help me dress?"

"I'll do my best," he laughed. "Give me five minutes first, though."

Charles crossed to the master's chamber and changed into a pair of pyjama bottoms and dressing gown, and then joined his wife once more.

Beth had selected a quilted velvet dressing gown in peacock blue, and he held the locks of her long hair as she slipped her arms into the sleeves and buttoned the front.

"I've always loved the way your hair curls. Is it natural?"

"I fear it is. Alicia uses a heated flat iron to straighten it for special occasions. Did our daughter have curls?"

"She did—or rather will have. I'm still wrestling with how to describe that experience, but I'm convinced you and I were in an actual place. For one thing, Georgianna called me a duke, which I'd thought a mistake at the time, but she said it was something from our future, and that she wasn't supposed to tell me. Apparently, the future version of myself warned against revealing too much."

Beth's eyes rounded with worry. "You'll become Duke of Drummond? Are you telling me that my grandfather will die before 1899?"

"No, darling, forgive me! I should have been more precise. I suspect your grandfather will outlive us all. I have never known a man more vital than James Stuart. Actually, Georgie called me Duke of Haimsbury."

"There is no such title."

"There is now," he said. "Or rather, there will be. Let me tell you about a very strange meeting."

"Are you saying I shall have a new title, husband? Duchess of Haimsbury?"

"You will, but allow me to tell the story in my own way, wife. As I left the London on Monday, a very odd fellow whistled to gain my attention. I'd never seen the man before, yet he insisted I join him. He would not take no for an answer, so I entered the coach and soon found myself at a men's club."

"What sort of men's club, Charles? Not one of those disreputable ones, I hope!"

"Nothing of the sort. Quite reputable, in fact. The Oriental. I asked the stranger why he'd brought me to a club to which I had no qualifications, and he led me upstairs to the Mauritius Room. Inside, I met a lady."

Beth's eyes widened. "You met a woman at a gentlemen's club? Please, don't tell me that you've strayed already, husband! I shall have to seek my solicitor's advice, or better still call for Baxter, who will soundly thrash you for such unkind behaviour!"

"No need to distress our butler, darling," he replied, patting her hand. "Not a whit. The lady in question wears a crown, you see, though she did not bring it with her that afternoon."

"The queen?"

"The sovereign, yes, but you, my darling wife, are the only queen who matters to me," he said, kissing her cheek.

"Finish the story, before this queen rings for her butler!"

"Very well," he laughed. "Have you, by chance, seen any newspapers of late?"

"No, why?"

"There's a story that's shown up here and there, which implies Her Majesty is illegitimate and hints at the existence of a royal bloodline with greater rights to the throne."

She grew serious. "Charles, are you referring to the inner circle? To our family?"

"Yes," he answered, "but you mustn't worry about it. I assumed the reports all invention or even speculation. Someone with a vague notion, hoping to sell papers, but it turns out that the story was whispered to Fred Best by none other than Prince Albert Victor."

"Eddy? Why would he do that, Charles? Eddy hasn't a political bone in his body!"

"I cannot speak to that, but Her Majesty admitted her own complicity in the plot. It's quite complicated, actually, but the bottom line is that she wishes to make me a duke and has asked me to serve on the privy council."

Rather than rejoice, Elizabeth grew agitated. "Did you say yes?"

"I've given no firm answer other than asking if I might talk with you and Uncle James about it. James found no issues, and he and Tory are already planning a party. Do you object?"

"I'm not sure," she replied seriously. "It's all too strange! I've been told again and again that the document which our ancestors signed must always be kept secret. You remember how much I avoided telling you this when we met in October. It's remained a secret in order to protect the children born to both lines. Her Majesty knows how hard we've tried to keep others from learning of it. Why would she make it public?"

"She has her reasons, which are politically motivated, and she's not making the document public, exactly. Look, it's best you ask her yourself. Oh, that reminds me, Her Majesty asked if she might join us at Branham for Christmas."

"I see," she said as Baxter entered with the tea, a selection of biscuits, a silver pot filled with strong coffee, and handful of telegrams. "Good morning, Mr. Baxter. Thank you for accommodating us."

"It is my pleasure, my lady. Shall I pour?"

"I can do that," Charles offered. "Is this the entire collection of messages?"

"It is, sir, and here are the morning editions for your perusal," the butler added, removing the broadsheets from beneath his left elbow. "Lady Victoria has returned and asks if we will be sending flowers, sir."

"Flowers?" Beth asked. "To whom?"

"The baroness, my lady," he answered before Charles could interrupt. "In condolence for Baron Wychwright's untimely passing."

"His passing? Charles, did you know about this?"

"I did, darling, and I'd planned to get 'round to telling you. I should have done last night. It was just that you looked so happy to be home. I didn't wish to spoil it."

"Oh, poor Cordelia! After everything else she's suffered, to have this hit her as well. Charles, we must send her a card. No, we should visit. Baxter, would you fetch me a bit of paper and a pen?"

"Of course, my lady. On Haimsbury stationery or Branham?"

"Haimsbury. Black ink. And a lap desk, in case I spill. Thank you."

The butler left the tray and departed to find the items in the marquess's study.

"Charles, how did the baron die? He looked quite healthy to me the last time I saw him. Is there something I should know?"

"It wasn't a natural death."

"Not natural? An accident?"

"That is yet to be determined," he said, preferring not to reveal the truth. "The case belongs to the city police and Sir James Fraser."

"Shall I ask him, as you refuse to offer a clear answer?"

She started to stand, and he took her arm. "No, Beth, please, remain here. Yes, I investigated it, and as you are highly intelligent, I'm sure you can deduce that a crime was involved. I'm afraid the baron was murdered."

She fell back to the sofa, despair overtaking her face. "Poor Delia! Oh, Charles, this is awful! I really must speak with her. Perhaps, I should go there this afternoon."

Baxter knocked as he re-entered the private drawing room. "Sir, I do hate to interrupt your morning, but a somewhat impatient constable awaits in our foyer. He has a message from the police commissioner."

"Tell the constable I am with my wife, Baxter. He will have to return to Whitehall without a reply."

"Well, sir, I did tell him that, but he insists that Commissioner Monro will not take no for an answer. The young man asked whether or not you have read the telegrams, my lord."

Charles reached for the stack of messages. Three came from Whitehall. One from Aubrey. He opened his cousin's first. "The earl asks me to meet him at White's on St. James's Street. He does not say why." He opened the first of the Whitehall messages. "It's from Monro. He says to meet him at White's as soon as I can get there."

Beth sighed, realising she'd be eating alone. "I take it the others ask you to meet them at White's?"

Sinclair opened the second and third Whitehall telegrams. "Salisbury. Yes, meet at White's. And this other is from the Home Secretary. The same. Darling, I am sorry. Can you forgive me?"

"If all these men seek your input, Captain, how can I deny them? Go and save the world from crime."

CHAPTER THIRTY-FIVE

12:01 pm

White's Gentlemen's Club had occupied the centre of St. James's Street since 1778 and was the oldest, and some said most prestigious, gentlemen's club in the entire metropolis. Originally, established on Chesterfield Street in 1693 by Francesco Bianco as a hot chocolate emporium, the popular political playground soon switched from serving chocolate to tea and after moving to its current location, became the unofficial headquarters of Tory government.

The chimes of Westminster had just sounded midday as Charles arrived. Granger opened his door, and the new commissioner left the Haimsbury-Branham coach and entered the Palladian style building. The smartly attired peer handed his hat and coat to a liveried butler. "I'm expected," he told the sober-faced servant, showing his warrant card.

"Commissioner Sinclair, of course. This way, sir."

It took several minutes to wind their way through the busy corridors and sedate decor of the smoking parlours. Charles walked past several familiar faces, including a few he'd met at his wedding. These men nodded in recognition, and the numbers grew as he and the usher approached their destination. Most of the men standing near the murder scene looked nothing like peers or businessmen, but rather like policemen.

"In here, Charles," James Monro called from the doorway of a drawing room. The barrel-chested police commissioner stood beside Paul Stuart, and around the panelled room were Prime Minister Robert Gascoyne-Cecil, 3rd Earl of Salisbury; Henry Matthews, Home Secretary; and oddly enough, Sir Reginald Parsons, the mysterious chief clerk of the House of Lords.

Aubrey wore a grim expression. "Forgive us for calling you out this morning, Charles. I assure you, it is urgent. This crime will reach all the papers before evening, making it imperative that we learn as much as possible before members, or worse yet, reporters destroy the scene. You know everyone here, I think."

"Yes, I do. What's happened?"

"Sometime 'twixt three and eight o'clock this morning, a woman found her way into the club. The porters, footmen, and butler all insist that no servants admitted her, yet she lies dead in the room just beyond this in company with Lord Peter Andrews. Andrews was last seen alive by a fellow member shortly before three o'clock. That member hopes to keep his name out of the papers, as you might guess, but he is available for questioning."

"Who?"

"Edward Milesborough. He's MP for Whitstable, and he stays at the club whenever Parliament's in session. Now, it's thought that Andrews died first and then the woman, for her body was still relatively warm when the cleaner discovered them both at eight o'clock."

"Peter Andrews. Why is that name familiar?" Charles asked as the prime minister joined them. "Good morning, Lord Salisbury."

"Charles, thank you for coming. We hated to disturb you, but as you can see it's rather a mess. A Division simply won't do, although Monro suggests they should handle enough of the investigation to keep Dunlap pacified. This is far too sensitive and requires a more experienced hand than Joe possesses. I should like your new intelligence branch to take charge. Consider this your first official case."

"If I may ask, then, sir, why is Henry Matthews here? Surely, Monro's presence is enough."

"The Home Secretary and Andrews were close friends. Both belong to this club, you know. Charles, this must be handled delicately and discreetly. Andrews has recently spoken out in support of a new bill that would give women the vote."

"I don't see a connexion. That bill is controversial, to say the least, but it's hardly a reason to kill a man," Sinclair noted. "And the woman? What has she to do with it?"

"That is why it is so very delicate," Stuart explained. "Her name is Monica Wiltmore, a well-known suffragette, and most probably his lordship's mistress. As with the other murders, the victims were found inside a locked room. And, as with Lord Hemsfield, Andrews also belonged to club known to our family all too well. One whose symbol is a bird."

"Redwing."

"Precisely. I've wired James and asked him to convene a meeting for seven at your home. We should be able to work through the evidence by then. I'm sorry for pulling you away from Beth. I'm sure the two of you hoped to enjoy a quiet day."

"If this is Redwing, then we work in her cause, Paul. How is Cordelia?" he asked as the two stepped into the murder scene.

"Devastated. One of her brothers arrives from Carlisle today. Edward Wychwright, the youngest and probably the only decent one of the three. William serves in the Army, posted currently to Afghanistan, and Thomas is a perpetual student of life in Paris. I sent them telegrams, but only William had responded as of last night. I promised to call on her this afternoon."

They'd entered a smaller drawing room, where decades of conversation still whispered in the air like debating, political ghosts. Green wallpaper covered three of the walls, broken only by a pair of windows that looked eastward onto a large gravel park and green space. Charles took in all the details before advancing further.

The peer's body lay at an acute angle with the fireplace, his head against the fender. Had there been no other trauma, one might assume he fell and struck his head, but the lack of feet or hands made that an impossible deduction. Each had been removed, and the carpet near the wounds was soaked with congealed and drying blood. A three-foot long ceremonial sword, stained to the hilt, protruded from his chest, rising up from a gash that ran from chin to bowel.

The unfortunate woman fared little better. She lay face down beside the man, her arms bound behind her back, a curved blade inserted into the thoracic region of her spine, two inches above her heart. She died slowly, in agony, barely able to breathe.

"This is hellish," Charles said as he stepped towards one of the windows. Beyond the park, he could see a three-storey building with a large marquee. "We have a perfect view of the entrance to the Egyptian Theatre. Isn't that the same place where you encountered Rasha and di Specchio?"

"Yes, on the last night I saw Susanna Morgan alive," Paul answered sadly. "And before you ask, I've assigned Galton's team to search for Morgan. Matthew Laurence sailed for Ireland last night. He promised to wire as soon as he has news regarding O'Brien."

"You've been busy," Charles told his cousin. "Regarding the search for Morgan, tell Galton to start with Urquhart."

"I've already done so," Paul informed his friend. "I thought I'd pay the builder a call tomorrow to discuss the weather."

"Oh, no. You're not to meet with him, Paul. Consider that an order. Once we have a dossier of every aspect of that worm's life, I'll handle the interview."

"You think I'd hurt him? Really, Charles," the earl grinned, removing his gloves. "I'd hardly touch him at all. A broken arm or a cracked jaw, at most." Returning to the task at hand, Aubrey stood over the victims, shaking his head. "None of this makes sense. We know Hemsfield and Andrews were Redwing, but what about Wychwright? How is he involved?"

"The note in the baron's pocket might be a clue. I've issued a warrant for Wendaway's arrest. If he's Redwing, then that may be the link."

"Perhaps, but why? Is murder the only means to solving disputes, or is there something we're missing?" Aubrey asked his cousin. "And why here? With this woman? Surely, they could have slain Andrews when he was alone. Is the woman involved? Is her death a message?"

"Possibly. But if it's a statement, who is the intended audience? Us? The police? Other members? Is it bloodletting for ceremonial reasons or intended as a warning?" Charles asked. "I'm still trying to puzzle out the Tarot card you found."

"I suspect someone in Redwing hopes to lay blame on Romanov. Where is he?"

"I find myself actually wishing he'd show," Charles answered, examining the room and staging. "Has anyone searched his pockets yet? Also, we should look for any occult items."

"Like the Hand of Glory candle France found at Hemsfield's murder?"

"Yes. Exactly like that."

Paul bent beside the man's body, trying to keep the blood from staining his boots. "I'd assumed A Division would have searched him when they responded, but apparently not."

"When did A arrive?"

"At nine, so I'm told," Stuart answered. "Clearly, Dunlap's constables require lessons in crime scene investigation. Here are coins, a pearl button, and a latch key. Why would he carry that?"

"To unlock his house, presumably."

"No, he wouldn't. Lord Peter keeps two houses. One in Mayfair, and the other in Marylebone. Both are large and well-staffed. Such men never unlock their own doors."

"Then, it may unlock another house," Charles suggested. "One not his own."

"Exactly. Look, I'll go to the Mayfair location and speak with his butler. We may find something in a diary. Have you met Reggie Parsons yet? He's called the chief clerk at the Lords, but that's hardly sufficient. The man's a summary of governmental secrets in a Regency suit."

"Yes, we've met. Parsons, his extraordinary suit, and I had a very interesting exchange on Monday, actually," Charles told his cousin. "I'll explain later at the meeting. If you're going to Mayfair, then I'll speak with the steward here and ask if our victim kept a room at the club. The latch key might fit that lock, rather than a house. Also, I'll find out if Andrews belonged to any other clubs."

"And the woman?"

"I doubt she stumbled into an assassination. More likely, she's involved. I count three, used whisky glasses. Who enjoyed the third?"

"A very good question," Paul said, sniffing the amber liquid remaining in one of the glasses. "Glenfiddich. A young whisky maker, but not bad."

"How can you tell it's Glenfiddich?"

"I grew up around fine whisky, Charles. One develops a nose for it. Before you speak with Milesborough, get the steward's story. It's possible they may not align. Someone let this woman into the club after hours. One or both may know if she visited before, although it may require financial incentive to jog the steward's memory."

Charles smiled. "You employ underhanded methods, Lord Aubrey. I only have ten pounds on me, though. How much does it cost to jog a steward's memory?"

Paul withdrew his wallet and handed his cousin fifty pounds in small denominations. "Twenty ought to do it. That's two month's wages for most men. Oh, before I forget, I've told Cordelia that any family members coming to London for the funeral may stay with me, if they require lodgings. Her mother's house is somewhat small."

"Queen Anne's available, if they require more space. I'm sure Beth would be happy to offer it."

"Thank you, Charles. Poor Delia's in shock, but her mother's not helping in the least."

"I'm sure the baroness is in shock, as well," Sinclair suggested. "Losing a husband suddenly is difficult enough, but losing one to murder is devastating."

"That might be true for a woman in love, but the baroness always seemed cold towards her husband. She's taken to bed and claiming a bad heart. All those doctors hired to care for Cordelia now flutter 'round the dowager baroness's door."

"Dowager? Oh, yes, I imagine the eldest son now inherits."

"William gets it all. Houses, land, and what little money poor old Wychwright managed to keep back from his spendthrift wife. Forgive me, it's poor manners to speak unkindly of her just now, but I find the woman insufferable."

"Could it be you care more for the daughter than you want to admit?"

The earl said nothing, merely raised an eyebrow.

"Paul, I've a few things to tell you about recent days that add up to trouble. Not only these murders, but other things. Very odd things that portend great danger."

"I can look after myself, Cousin," Aubrey assured him. "If odd things have happened, then any danger is most likely directed towards you, not me. See you this afternoon. Six, if not earlier."

The earl passed by Salisbury as he exited.

"Aubrey's leaving already?"

"He's off to conduct enquiries in Mayfair. Tell me, how well did you know Lord Peter?"

"Moderately well," Salisbury answered, his long beard wagging along with his chin. "Andrews was made a lifetime lord a few years ago. He led the negotiations in Cypress, you know. In '77. Couldn't have been more than thirty at the time."

"He looks older than forty-one."

"I believe he'd been ill. He missed a few meetings now and then, always sending regrets due to poor health. I'm sure his doctor could confirm that."

"Do you know his physician's name, sir?"

"Unless he's changed, it's Alexander Collins. Odd sort of duck. An alienist, I think, which may be appropriate in Peter's case. He behaved rather strangely in Cypress. Conducted some sort of occult ritual there with a goat. An Orthodox priest made complaint to our consulate, causing serious ripples that very nearly ended the negotiations."

"A goat?"

"Yes, so I heard. I can't tell you any more than that, but it involved a great deal of blood. Derby was foreign secretary then. He might be able to shed light on it. He's a Liberal Unionist now, I'm sorry to say."

"Would Lord Derby still be in London?"

"Certainly. Parliament doesn't adjourn until the middle of the month. If there's debating to be done, you'll find him in the thick of it. He keeps an office at the Lords. I'd suggest introducing you personally, but I rather expect he knows who you are, Charles. You're becoming quite a broadsheet celebrity."

Sinclair sighed. "Yes, I spoke with a great lady of mutual interest regarding those broadsheets on Monday."

"Sorry I had to miss, but I was contending with other matters. That good lady sought my input before and after the story reached Fred Best's huge ears, and do stop calling me 'sir', Charles! You'll be a duke soon, and perhaps even more, if that lady gets her way."

"I haven't said yes, Robert."

"Oh, but you will. That lady is persuasive and impatient. She awaits my report as to what's happened here, so I must be going. I hope you'll stop by my office this week. I've a few questions to pose before our next cabinet meeting. As Commissioner for Intelligence, you'll sit with me on those meetings. I did tell you, I hope?"

"You did, sir. I mean Robert. I'm setting up an Intelligence Office at Loudain House. The carpenters have completed the renovation of the ground and first floors. We could meet there, if you like. Will Friday be soon enough?"

"I should think so, but wait. When is your investiture ceremony? Isn't it Friday?"

"Next Friday. The fourteenth."

"Well, then, we'll meet this Friday, then. In the meantime, let me know if you require anything from me. Give my best to the duchess."

As Salisbury left the room, Charles glanced out the window at the façade of the Egyptian, thinking of Susanna Morgan. *Is she alive?* If so, then she might be able to explain the bloodbath taking place amongst Redwing's membership. He worried about Lorena MacKey. Would her body be the next one discovered?

Where are you, Lorena? he worried.

As he left the window, a thought occurred to him, and Charles knelt beside the bodies to examine the murder weapons. The sword's heavy hilt leaned towards the dead man's slack face, but the blade was stuck firmly in his spine. Sinclair found it odd. If the killer used the sword's point to slice the torso, then wouldn't the hilt be angled *away* from the head?

"Wandering onto my patch again, Sinclair?" a man's voice asked from behind the peer's back. Still kneeling, Charles turned to see who that man might be. It did not make him happy.

"Your patch, is it?" he asked the policeman. "That's no longer true, Dunlap."

Superintendent Joseph Dunlap's anger could not have been more apparent if he'd worn it as a hat. "This is twice you've invited yourself to one of my cases, Sinclair. You've no excuse now, however. You are a *former* Scotland Yard superintendent. A civilian with no more rights to a crime scene than my mother."

"Your mother might prove more insightful, Joseph. As to why I'm here, I was invited by the prime minister as well as your superior. Monro is still your superior, is he not?"

Dunlap practically growled. "We'll see about that!"

"I rather doubt you'll remove Monro from his post no matter how outraged you pretend to be," Charles said as he gazed at the ivory hilt of the sword. "And if you do not stop contaminating the crime scene, I shall have you removed."

"You'll what?!" the police detective shouted, his hands clenched.

"You heard me. When I'm finished, you and your men may prance about and despoil it all you like, but for the moment, I'm trying to concentrate, and you're blocking my light."

"We'll see whose light is blocked!" Dunlap blurted as he spun on his heel to find Monro.

Charles paid the man's histrionics no heed at all. He withdrew the leather notebook from his jacket pocket and opened it. Before his eyes was the collection of strange symbols in red ink; the ones he'd discovered just prior to the raven attack on Monday evening. To his very great surprise, he only now noticed that some of the symbols revealed a pattern. Three sets of three, and he'd seen them before.

"Good gracious!" he exclaimed as the significance became clear. These same three symbols were carved into the ivory handle of the sword as well as the wooden handle of the knife, but they'd also been written above the windows at the Hemsfield crime scene. He circled the symbols in the book and whispered a quick prayer of thanks as he took to his feet.

After passing by Dunlap, who was in the middle of a vociferous conversation with Monro, Charles crooked his finger at the police commissioner. "May I have a word?"

Monro didn't bother to excuse himself, but merely walked away whilst Dunlap was still talking.

"Have you found something?" Monro asked, hopefully.

"I think so, but I need to confer with someone first. If you'd keep Joe Dunlap from mucking up the crime scene in the meantime, I'd appreciate it."

"Certainly," the police commissioner answered. "I know your branch is separate from mine, Charles, but if you'd share anything substantive with me, I'd appreciate it."

"Of course, James. The Intelligence Branch and the ICI will, in no way, compete with the police department. Rather, it's my hope that we'll complement one another."

"Thank you," Monro answered, shaking Sinclair's hand. "And congratulations on the new appointment. I suppose I should call you Commissioner from now on—if not something grander."

"Commissioner of Intelligence is as high as I plan to rise," the marquess answered. "I've no aspirations beyond that."

Sinclair left and followed an usher back into the morning air, where the sun had finally decided to emerge from behind the cloudbank.

"Where to, my lord?" Granger asked as Charles approached.

"Fulham. Montmore House."

Hamish Granger whistled to the team of Friesians. The crested coach shifted into motion, and high above, a white owl followed.

CHAPTER THIRTY-SIX

1:56 pm - Montmore House Sanitarium

Henry MacAlpin washed his hands in the porcelain sink, his thoughts far away. He'd spent the better part of the day working through a tall stack of correspondence from colleagues, followed by conversations with resident patients, and now he hoped to find half an hour to eat before leaving for Westminster.

"Sir, Miss Doe is uneasy again," his nurse said from the doorway to the surgery. "May I increase her medication by half?"

The earl sighed. "I'd so hoped she would settle by now. No, let's not increase it yet, Mrs. Winstead. Let me speak to the lady first."

He dried his hands and left the brightly lit surgery and climbed two flights of stairs to the corner apartment currently occupied by a woman with amnesia. Known only as 'Miss Doe', she'd been committed to Montmore House by a judge who'd declared the well-dressed female *non compos mentis* due to erratic behaviour at Chelsea Station. She'd only lived at the private asylum for three days, and in that time had said nothing, nor had she acted out in any way. If the nurse thought the medicine required increase, then it was possible the anonymous woman had begun to recover her senses.

"Good afternoon," he said cheerfully. The rooms Doe occupied had served as his grandmother's residence during Henry's childhood, and he never entered without thinking of Eleanor Stuart Campbell's peaceful smile and rose-scented soap. "I do hope you're making yourself at home. Is my staff taking good care of you?"

She looked no more than thirty, possibly younger, for her eyes had a haunted expression that masked true years.

"Are you in pain? Hungry? Thirsty?" No reply. "I've introduced myself before, but it's a very forgettable name, so I'm happy to repeat it. Henry MacAlpin. May I ask yours?"

The woman sat upon the edge of the sofa. Were this any other peerage home, she might have looked merely weary or perplexed, but as this was a madhouse—albeit a private one—it made her seem so much more.

"Do you remember coming here?"

"Here?" she repeated.

Henry drew a chair close to the sofa. "You have a lovely voice. An unusual accent. Are you Irish?"

"Irish?"

He sat back, disappointed. Hearing her speak had made Henry hopeful. Most likely, however, she merely echoed the last word spoken. *What is it about this woman that so touches me?*

"Your red hair is lovely, but do I see dark strands beneath?" he asked as he moved closer. "I shan't hurt you, but do you mind if I touch your hair?"

She began to tremble, but allowed the gesture. Henry had very good vision, and he discerned dark roots beneath the cloud of copper tresses. "You prefer this shade, I take it. I agree. The auburn tones play up the paleness of your skin. I see from your records that you've eaten very little since becoming our guest. Lack of sleep can cause any number of maladies, including poor appetite. Strange beds always make me restive. I wonder, are you sleeping well?"

"No."

Finally! A non-repetitive response!

"I'm very sorry to hear that," he answered calmly. "Is our house too noisy? I fear that Mrs. Calhoun sometimes calls out in her dreams, and Miss Abernathy has a tendency to snore rather loudly. Is that why you do not sleep?"

She reached for his hand, her large eyes pleading. "Help me."

The plaintive words broke Henry's heart. "Of course, I'll help you. I shall do all within my power to help you. Can you tell me anything about yourself? What is the last thing you remember?"

Her right hand went to her face, stroking the right temple as though trying to stimulate memory. "Pain. A coach. No, wait. Something else. Cruel laughter."

"Unpleasant memories, to be sure. Is the pain associated with the coach? Did something happen to you inside a carriage?"

Her overall appearance was far too refined and healthy to identify her as a prostitute. Salperton wondered if she'd been assaulted. The crime was all too common in the parish, and such trauma might easily cause a confused mental state.

"I don't know."

He'd now heard enough of the woman's speech to recognise the accent. "You're American. Rather exotic hereabouts, but it matches your exotic beauty. Forgive me if that sounds forward. It's intended as admiration, nothing more."

She smiled, and the tension disappeared, revealing a younger face. *She's quite beautiful.* "You've a lovely smile. I'd be honoured to see it more often, Miss...?"

"Stuart," she whispered. "Violet Stuart."

"Is that so? Then we might be related! My grandmother was a Stuart. I'd no idea we have American cousins! My branch hails from Scotland, of course, as you can probably tell from my accent. It's much diluted from that of my childhood, grown more English sounding, so my father says. I attended school near London, you see, though my medical studies were in Edinburgh. How long have you lived in England, Miss Stuart?"

"I'm not sure. I can't remember. You're from Scotland?" This last question had a hint of hopefulness to it. Henry wondered if perhaps the woman had friends there.

"I am indeed. Inverary on Loch Fyne. It's an isolated fishing village, and my father owns most of it. I hate speaking ill of anyone, but my father's never been easy to get along with. I travel there twice a year, on his birthday and at Christmas. Oh do forgive me. I've prattled on about myself. Very rude of me. Have you ever been to Scotland?"

She shook her head. "I don't think so."

"It's beautiful, though outside the cities, it can be quite lonely. This is Montmore House. Did I tell you that already? Built in 1731. My grandmother loved the gardens, and she added a variety of roses, which she used to make her own soap. I miss her very much. My mother died when I was quite young, and she left me this house. Sometimes, I can almost hear Grandmother and Mother talking. Whispering secrets. Do you ever hear such things, or am I being fanciful?"

"I hear them. Sometimes, but not in this house. This house is quiet. Your name is Henry?"

"Yes. Named for my father. It's the way it's done in many of the old families. Do you have family in England?"

"I'm not sure. I think so. A cousin."

"Then we shall have to find this cousin and bring him for a visit. Or is the cousin a woman?"

"Not a woman."

"Are the two of you close?"

He watched her face as she absorbed the suggestion. If Violet did have a male relative nearby, then he would have to make sure her injuries weren't caused by this 'cousin' before allowing any visits.

"Miss Stuart, do you remember anything else before you came here?"

"No, should I?"

"I wish you could, for I want to help you. You do understand that you are a patient?"

"Am I? Why? Was I injured?"

"I'm still trying to determine that. I'm told that you were found at Chelsea Station, near the King's Road entrance. You had no identification, and as you seemed disoriented, a considerate stranger called the police. They brought you here."

She looked all about the beautifully furnished bedchamber. "This doesn't look like a hospital."

"No, as I said before, it is a lovely old house passed to me when my mother died. You're in my grandmother's old rooms, and she loved yellow, which is why there's so much of that colour in the decor. We have a blue room available, if you don't like yellow."

"No, yellow's nice. How long have I been here?"

"Three days and four nights. Are you hungry? I'm told you've eaten very little. Perhaps, it's the cuisine. Have you a favourite food? Mine is curried lamb cooked rare, roasted corn, and celery *au gratin,* when I can get it. A strange combination, to be sure, but then I'm unmarried and set in my ways. I rather think a wife might refine my taste in food. And yours?"

"Pheasant with truffle garnished potatoes," she said. "When I can get it."

He laughed and tapped her hand gently. "Then, I shall ask my cook if pheasant and truffles might be added to our menu. Do you enjoy music?"

"Yes."

"We've a fine Erard grand piano in our main parlour. Just tuned, and its keys are dusted daily, though seldom played. Do you play?"

"I'm not sure. I think so."

The nurse knocked on the open door, surprised to hear the conversation. "Sir, shall I have a footman bring luncheon?"

"Will you eat, Miss Stuart?" he asked her. "Even though it is not likely to be pheasant?"

"Yes, I will. I'm hungry."

"Excellent! Mrs. Winstead, have we any idea what Cook has prepared for us today?"

"I've just seen the menu, sir, and it's cress soup, beef medallions, potatoes in cream sauce, and beets. She can also offer sliced beef sandwiches, consommé, and fruit."

"Does any of that sound appetising, Miss Stuart?"

"All of it," she whispered. "I don't suppose that's very ladylike of me."

"Nonsense! It's a delight to hear!" he declared, taking to his feet.

"Forgive me, sir, but Mr. Saunders asked me to tell you that a gentleman has called."

"Thank you, Nurse. Miss Stuart, I've enjoyed our conversation. I shall visit you again tomorrow morning."

The physician bowed politely and left the apartment. The nurse shut the door, asking in a whisper, "Shall I lock it, sir?"

"No, not this time. Let's see how our guest responds with a little freedom. Who is my caller?"

"He didn't give his name, sir."

Salperton descended the curving staircase and entered the library. The immaculately dressed caller wore black trousers and a charcoal grey coat trimmed at the lapels in silver satin. His waistcoat matched the silver with a subtle check over grey. A gleaming gold watch hung from a fine chain, decorated with an acorn fob, symbol of the House of Stuart. He had black hair that curled slightly at the collar, startling blue eyes, and a two-week-old beard and moustache that accented his athletic face with equally dark hair.

"Lord Haimsbury, as ever you command a room as though born to royalty, and I mean that in many ways," Henry exclaimed upon entering the library. "I consider myself smartly attired as a rule, but you set the tone, I think. May I ask the name of your tailor?"

Charles Sinclair smiled as he took a chair. "May I?"

"Yes, please!" the earl said, taking the chair's match.

"You met my tailor last week," the marquess told him. "Martin Kepelheim, but he's far more than the finest haberdasher in London, as you'll soon discover."

"So your Cousin Paul has hinted," Salperton answered. "I must say, this is an unexpected pleasure, but I pray your visit doesn't mean the duchess has suffered a relapse."

"No, not at all. My wife is much better, thanks to you. She asks whether you might visit us soon. Beth calls you her very dear friend."

"That is kind of you to say, and I cherish that title above all others. I'd planned to call on you both later today. I received a very interesting telegram from Lord Aubrey, in fact. One might even call it a summons."

Sinclair laughed. "My cousin is never subtle. I take it he's invited you to this evening's circle meeting?"

"So I understand, though he didn't spell that out, but then he wouldn't. The earl may lack subtlety in some things, but in school I found him secretive to the point of frustration! Sir Thomas Galton is less so. The three of us had a very pleasant time catching up the other night, though much of what they told me has very dark associations. Redwing, I mean. I believe I've learnt most of the basics of the inner circle's mission, and I find it all fascinating! It supports theories I've held most of my life regarding the spirit realm and our interactions with it. You play chess, I assume?"

"Yes. I'd be a poor mathematician, if I didn't."

The viscount laughed. "I imagine you would, but even a mathematics genius would find it difficult to comprehend the complicated game played by the spirits. Fallen against unfallen, with God as commander on one side, and the person we call the Devil on the other. At least, that is how we describe this chess match, but I believe it's far more complicated than that. Our game is played in two dimensions—forwards and back, but the spiritual game of chess must surely be played in many dimensions at once. Perhaps, six, eight, even ten or more! We cannot see or understand it all, because the interplay these spirits have with our material world is limited by our point of view. St. Paul called it seeing through a glass darkly."

"I've never heard it described better, Henry. I've only been involved in the circle for two months, but in that short time, I've experienced things that defy human understanding, and a few might qualify me as one of your patients! It sometimes brings me to despair, to be honest. But the Lord has compassion on my trembling heart, and your words serve to remind me that it is *he* who fills the chairs 'round our table; he who orders our steps. My friend and cousin, you are most welcome! Only God knows why you chose not to join the circle long ago, but it's clear that the Lord's timing is always perfect."

"So it is, and I am honoured to be called your cousin. Second cousins, I think. I don't know about you, but I'm famished. Will you join me?"

"Thank you, no. I have far too much to accomplish before this evening's meeting. I've come here professionally as well as personally. Paul and I are investigating a series of murders related to Redwing, or so we believe. I wonder if you recall seeing these symbols recently?"

Sinclair opened the leather notebook and showed Henry the page filled with red symbols.

Lord Salperton's high forehead furrowed. "May I?" he asked, reaching for the book. He took it to his desk and sat, deep in thought perusing each line with care. "Now, these on the third line down are most interesting. I see you've circled them. You know, I believe I have seen them before, but I cannot recall where. Recently, surely. Carved, however, not written. Perhaps on furniture?"

"Do all of them look familiar or just the third line?"

"I can't really say. Those on the top, perhaps. Are they Egyptian?"

"I don't think so. The circle has obtained ancient texts with what Ed MacPherson calls Sumerian symbols, but these vary slightly."

"Sumerian writing? How very interesting! Wait, I remember where I saw them! It was at the castle! The main gate had these very symbols engraved into each of the stone pillars. I know because I passed through that gate a dozen times, trying to get out."

Charles smiled. "I'd hoped you'd say that. It occurred to me today that I'd seen them there as well, but so much has happened since, I feared I was mistaken."

Henry continued to examine the page. "Very strange. Is this writing connected to a crime? Perhaps, the murder you mentioned?"

"Two murders, actually. They were written in blood above the windows at one, and carved on the murder weapon at another. When do you plan to come by, Henry? We begin at seven, but it's likely we'll go late, particularly if my uncle calls for after dinner drinks, which he will. You're welcome to stay over, if you like."

"Ah, yes. Cousin James. Stay over? I might consider it. I understand Count Riga and the others are living there."

"In the dower house. Paul's sister has already made friends with them, and she's teaching Mr. Stanley to speak French."

Henry smiled. "I've never met Paul's sister. I look forward to making her acquaintance."

"Then you'll stay?"

"I just might! I could leave here almost immediately. If I'm to stay in Westminster overnight, I'd like to pay one last visit to a new patient first. She's only just begun talking, you see, and I want to reinforce the conversation."

"How many patients live here?" Charles asked.

"Presently, there are five. I like to keep the numbers small. I require no payment. Those who can afford it make up the shortfall for others. The Salperton inheritance left me quite well off, and I'm happy to open the doors to those who would otherwise be led away to harsher places."

"Have you ever heard of Castor Institute?"

"Alex Collins? Yes, he's a colleague, though not a close one by any stretch. I don't agree with his methods. Why?"

Sinclair returned the notebook to his pocket. "I thought I'd pay Dr. Collins a visit. His institute has come to my attention far too often lately to be coincidence. I wonder, if you'd consider coming along?"

"I'd be delighted! It will be my first circle assignment, you might say. Did you hire a hansom or bring one of your own coaches?"

"I brought a coach. My last hansom experience left me rather exposed," he answered cryptically. "I'll explain at the meeting."

Charles stood. "Shall I wait here?"

"Yes, if you don't mind. I promise to take but a moment. Charles, I wonder if we might stop by the castle on our way through Fulham? I'd like to see those gates again."

"Henry, you read my mind."

The viscount returned to the upper floor apartment and spoke briefly to his new patient. Violet Stuart had already received her luncheon tray and was enjoying a sandwich. He explained that he'd be away overnight but that Mrs. Winstead would be available should she need anything. He encouraged her to visit the music room and engage in conversation with the other patients.

After a short discussion regarding evening medications with the nurse, Henry collected his medical bag, a clean shirt and socks, and joined Charles inside the Haimsbury-Branham coach.

The two men left the drive, completely ignorant to the fact that only two floors above, watching from the confines of her bedchamber, Violet Stuart—once known as Susanna Morgan—watched the marquess and his cousin leave, wondering why the tall man with the beard looked so very familiar.

Sir Clive Urquhart rarely felt anything akin to fear, probably out of hubris rather than bravery, but as of this moment, the diminutive builder felt absolutely terrified.

"Another!" he exclaimed to his guest. "How many more will die before you admit it, Lord Raziel? Someone is killing us, and it must be one of your kind! Have you unleashed another of your hellish friends in London, or is the madman you call Saraqael to blame for this bloodbath?"

Several of Redwing's Round Table members had gathered at the builder's Grosvenor Square mansion, including their most powerful ally, Raziel Grigor, called Prince Alexei by the uninitiated humans of English government. The ancient elohim had patiently listened to the humans squabble amongst themselves, quietly sipping a cup of herbal tea.

"Will you not at least say something in your defence?" Alexander Collins insisted. "You claim to be all powerful, but your brother makes a mockery of you whilst murdering us!"

"I've made no claim to being omnipotent, Dr. Collins, and I resist the idea that Sara is a madman. Mad yes, but hardly a man. It is a problem of language, but as he now inhabits a flesh and blood human, I see your point. As to the accusation that I've unleashed another of my kind, I beg to differ. You and your Round Table performed the ritual that released Sara from his prison. Not I."

"Pah!" the portly builder dared argue. "We merely followed your instructions, Lord Raziel, and at your insistence! Tis *you* who wants to unlock the mirrors and mazes. *You* who seeks to bring about hell on earth. I begin to doubt our alliance with you, if you must know. You promised us riches, and instead we are hunted like rats!"

As with others of his elohim class, Raziel enjoyed taking human form when conversing with the clay-based inferiors of the material realm. He considered them little more than useful chess pieces, to be moved and removed, according to his will. The fallen angel's humanoid appearance was intentionally taller than nearly all sons of Adam, with eyes of cold blue that caused shudders of fear when required, but as he'd happily discovered, considered irresistibly mysterious by the daughters of Eve. He focused these ice-blue orbs upon Urquhart with such intensity that the frigid stare caused the man to visibly shrink.

"Do not speak to me of riches!" Raziel shouted. "Have I not made you a wealthy man, Sir Clive? Do not all of you stand as betters amongst the rabble of London? Would you have obtained lucrative government contracts without my help? Those subtle whispers into the ears of prominent men have availed you much increase. You boast of your wealth within your exclusive men's clubs, and then go home and wallow like fat pigs in your very expensive sties!"

He stood, towering over the group. "Those of your number who have died provide the blood required for the next phase of our plans, but the bloodshed needn't continue. I've no intention of destroying anyone who follows me."

Clive gulped, his fat Adam's apple bobbing up and down beneath the tight silk collar. "*You* killed them?"

"Indeed. Did you think me charmed and tamed like a pet? Did you imagine that you are in charge? My plans are subtle and beyond your capacity for thought, but they require nourishment. Only a few more deaths are required to unlock the next mirror, but we run out of time. The ceremony must take place on the solstice. We have but two weeks."

Collins gulped. "Are you saying this bloodshed will continue?"

"Of course."

Urquhart began mopping his moist face with a silk kerchief. "How many are a few, Lord Raziel? And must these deaths be our own?"

"Not necessarily. As to the number, I prefer not to reveal that."

"But we are safe?"

"Those who follow me will rise to glory, those who choose to follow Romanov or even Sara, will die. Simple, isn't it?" He poured another cup of tea, sipping thoughtfully. "A team of archaeologists from the British Museum have proven useful. I've endowed their expedition to Normandy to excavate Lord Araqiel's prison. I require his key to open the Realms of Fire."

"Fire?" the alienist moaned, wondering just what he'd gotten himself into.

Raziel paid him no heed. "Plans within plans within ancient plans begin to unfold and reveal themselves to me. The hidden guardians emerge, hungry for plunder."

"Forgive me, Lord Raziel, but your words make no sense!" the builder worried, his collar growing ever tighter.

"My words are not meant for you to understand," he told the distraught human. "Do as I ask, and all with be well, but the plans must proceed at my pace—my command. Who released the information about Sinclair to the press? I never sanctioned that."

Each looked to the other suspiciously. "I cannot say, my lord," Sir Robert Cartwright snorted. "Not I. "

Honoria Chandler tapped cigarette ash onto the rug. "Hell if I know."

Dr. Malford-Jones, Serena di Specchio, and her new paramour Sir Albert Wendaway stared as though turned to stone.

Alexander Collins was busy mentally weighing the odds of survival for any who opposed Raziel. Now, after realising he had few choices, the alienist suddenly blurted out an opinion.

"Lord Raziel is in charge, is he not? We invited him. Perhaps, you should temper your words carefully, Clive."

"My words? *Mine?*" Urquhart shouted in response, rushing to accuse the alienist. "You are the one who called this meeting in the first place, Alexander! Twas you who blamed Lord Raziel, not I! You are a sniveling, self-serving, little worm!"

Serena di Specchio chose charm as a weapon. "Even a worm has a use, Clive. Displacing the dirt to allow flowers to grow. Fertilisation comes to mind."

"A decomposing body makes a very good fertiliser, madam!" Sir Clive shouted. "I place no trust in either of you! You may both be in league with this hellion!"

"Hellion?" Raziel echoed, his voice resounding with a mockery of wounded vanity. "I take exception to that epithet. I do not live in the nether regions, but rather here, in the city that rules the world. As to trust, I've led you thus far, have I not? Trent took you in an altogether pointless direction that nearly brought you to ruin. Trust in me. I will lead you to the top of the mountain itself!"

"By way of the grave!" Urquhart shouted, his handkerchief soaked in cold sweat. "I am weary. We make no progress, and it is clear that our plans are lost. Finding the other mirrors is a fool's errand now. If three Watchers make such trouble, how dare we add to their number? My friends, we must abandon these dangerous ways before we are all fish food!"

"I am still here," Raziel complained, tapping his foot against the floor tiles. "No one else need die. Only those who oppose me. How difficult is that?"

Every face paled, even di Specchio's.

"Good. Now, we must continue with my plan to release the prisoners. We need all thirteen Watchers to unlock the final gates and return the earth to its glory days. The faithful will stand beside me and reign as kings and queens. Is that not worth all you have to offer?"

"Glory days? Glory for whom?" the builder dared to ask.

"Glory for those to whom it *rightly* belongs," the creature answered obliquely. "Do you doubt me?"

"I think your plans will lead to the ruin of us all! Redwing has existed for centuries without your guidance, Lord Raziel. I think we return to those days, eh? The Round Table idea of Trent's has divided us, to be sure. It is time we unite again beneath the brand of the wounded wing," he told the others. "We form a new table, with a new leader."

"And who might that leader be?" di Specchio asked. "You? Why? Because you are a man?"

"Men have always led the group. Women have their place, but not as leaders."

"I suppose England's queen might have something to say about that," Raziel suggested, his eyes on the tea in his cup. "Well, it's been enlightening, but I do have a life outside Redwing. Do continue bickering, won't you? I could leave you a few knives, if it helps to reduce your numbers. The fewer members remaining when I commence the next phase, the easier it will be to assume *full* control, so be careful whom you slander. An adder that bites its own tail poisons only itself."

He vanished from sight, the teacup hanging in midair for a few seconds before crashing to the floor. The tea stain spread upon the carpet in a strange shape, and as he stared at the widening shadow, Sir Clive realised that it formed the wings and body of an enormous raven.

CHAPTER THIRTY-SEVEN

Stavely House - No. 4 Fitzmaurice Place, London

"My brothers arrive in two days—well, two of them, anyway," Cordelia said as a somewhat somber butler carried a tray of desserts into the drawing room of the Wychwright's London residence. "William is very important in the Army, of course, and Thomas is a much admired student in Paris. He's very bright."

The eighteen-year-old had a shocked expression that troubled her guest. Elizabeth Stuart Sinclair had arrived half an hour earlier, and since then, Delia had talked almost nonstop, as though terrified to close her mouth and take a breath.

"And your third brother?" the duchess asked politely.

"Ned? He's in Carlisle. Father always loved Ned best, even though he's the middle son. Isn't that odd?" She paused, as though trying to sort through troubling thoughts. "Father... He's dead, isn't he?"

"Yes, I'm afraid he is," Beth answered gently. "When does your Aunt Margaret arrive? Isn't she going to help with the arrangements?"

"Yes, I imagine so. Mother's not up to it. She's taken to bed and will not leave it. Should I contact Parliament about my father? Is that my job? William is the new baron now, I suppose, but who will take over as MP?"

"I'm sure the Lake District will have a special election to select a replacement."

"Yes, I suppose so. How did he die? Father, I mean. Was it—was it quick? He didn't suffer, I hope."

The duchess set down her teacup and moved to the sofa beside the girl. "You shouldn't think about that right now, Delia. There's time for all that later, when you're stronger."

"Yes, I suppose you're right. I never expected my father to die, but if he did—when he did, I assumed it would be something more natural. Heart attack or something. Murder simply isn't done, is it? Not to peers. Who ever heard of such a thing?"

"I have," Beth answered softly. "My mother didn't die a natural death. A terrible man killed her, and I saw it happen. But, Cordelia, the pain of it all has faded with time. You'll find that, one day, you'll recall only the happy memories."

Tears welled up in the young woman's eyes, and she unconsciously reached for a dessert from the tiered silver tray. "These meringue tarts are quite good. You should try them. Lemon with raspberry cream. Father loved these. They were his favourites."

She bit into the tiny confection, tears streaming down her pink cheeks. Elizabeth reached out and took the grieving girl's hand. "Courage, Delia. You're not alone. You have friends all 'round you."

A footman stood silently in the open doorway, waiting for a moment to speak.

"Yes?" Beth asked the man, seeing that Delia failed to notice.

"Lord Aubrey has arrived, Your Grace, and asks to visit."

Delia's eyes turned towards the footman at last. "Paul is here?"

"Yes, my lady."

She brushed bits of sugar and cake from her hands. "Send him in at once, Parker."

Paul Stuart had chosen a somber suit of dark blue, cream silk shirt, and a grey waistcoat. His chestnut hair was pulled back and conservatively tied, and he'd even shaved his beard. Seeing Cordelia's hopeful face, the earl immediately went to her. Without speaking a word, that simple gesture caused a cascade of emotions within both women. Cordelia snapped out of her shocked fugue and let loose a torrent of tears, and Elizabeth perceived something which caused a strange mixture of joy and heartache: Paul Stuart, demonstrating love and support to another woman.

"I should go," she said, standing.

The earl released Wychwright from the embrace, suddenly aware of the duchess's presence. "No, Beth, stay. Please. I'm sure Cordelia needs support from both of us."

The girl looked thunderstruck. "Do I? Yes, yes, of course I do. Excuse me, I should see if Mother's awake."

Without another word, she bolted from the drawing room, and Paul turned to Elizabeth. "Did I say something wrong?"

"No, of course not. I think I'm to blame. I'm rather extraneous, you see. Delia's in shock, and you're far better at comforting her than I."

Elizabeth started towards the foyer, but the earl took her hand. "Are you angry with me?"

"No. I think you and Delia deserve some time alone. Besides, Charles sent word that Henry MacAlpin is with him, and they hope to arrive by four. It's nearly three now. I should get back to the house."

Her fingertips left his, and a part of the earl's heart began to ache. "You're angry," he declared. "Tell me what I've done."

"You've done nothing. Nothing at all. It's obvious that you've begun to care for her. I'm only trying to be considerate."

"I've what?" he whispered, stunned.

"Don't deny it, Paul. I know you very well."

His blue eyes widened. "Not well enough, apparently. Beth, I am being courteous to a woman who needs as many friends as possible. That is all."

"If you say so," she answered, turning to leave.

"Please, stay."

"I'll see you later," she answered. "Please, tell Delia goodbye for me."

"You are as stubborn as your mother at times!" he exclaimed, his eyes clouding with rising frustration.

The insensitive comment caused her face to lose all colour, and Elizabeth answered softly, her eyes downcast. "Then I beg your forgiveness," she muttered before rushing from the room.

He followed after, catching her just outside the main entry, but two coaches had pulled into the narrow drive, and an older, well dressed couple, followed by a young man and two children, were climbing the portico steps.

"Lord Aubrey!" the woman called. "Duchess, we'd no idea you'd be visiting. How are my sister and Cordelia doing?"

"Good afternoon, Countess," Aubrey said politely to Lady Cartringham, his eyes on Beth. "I fear the baroness has taken to her bed, but Cordelia's receiving. As you can imagine, both are devastated. Is that Ned with you?"

"Yes, and his children. They stayed with us last night, since this house is somewhat small. His wife Brenda remained in Carlisle. Family troubles." The countess whispered the final two words so the children wouldn't overhear. "He and I are here to plan the service. Are you leaving?"

"Paul's staying," Beth explained. "I'm afraid I have a guest arriving at four."

"A guest? You look pale yet, Elizabeth," the countess told her. "It may be too soon to entertain guests."

"This one is my physician, but also a friend. Paul, I'll see you later."

Aubrey caught up with the duchess before she reached the first step. "No stairs, Beth," he reminded her. "Here, let me." The earl took her arm and led the duchess to the coach.

Once at the door, he apologised. "Please, forgive me, Beth. I should never have said that about your mother—or you. Today of all days, I'm sure your mind turns to that dark time. The baron's murder only reminds you of losing your parents to murder."

"My parents?" she asked. "Mother yes, but Father's death was an accident."

"Of course it was," he answered quickly, trying to cover the blunder. "But a shock nonetheless. Darling, you're wrong. I am not overly fond of Cordelia. She is just a friend."

"Yet you shaved for her."

He smiled, finding the comment odd. "Didn't I shave for you as well? Your wedding, remember? I'd do so again, anytime you asked. Princess, there is no room in my heart for another woman. Not yet. Perhaps, one day, but it still aches for another." Tears rimmed her eyes, and he squeezed her hand. "Beth, I will always love you. Until the day I die."

"I know," she whispered, entering the carriage.

"Don't leave yet, Shipman," the earl told the driver. He hopped into the interior. "I cannot allow you to go until I know everything is as it should be with us. Beth, no one is happier for you than I, but I'm still adjusting."

"As am I," she answered. "It's selfish of me, I know, but..."

"But what, Princess?"

"I've always thought of you as mine, Paul. My knight who rides in to rescue me anytime I need him, but I must let you go. You'll soon ride away and find another to rescue. I think it's only now hitting me."

"You're jealous?"

Her dark eyes blinked as the truth took hold. "I suppose I am."

Stuart's smile returned, and he kissed her hand. "No need, Princess. I'll always be there to ride in, should you require it. Your favour is the only one I seek."

"Forgive me," she said, wiping tears. "My emotions are all over the place lately. I'm being cruel to you, and you don't deserve it."

"I would much rather be treated cruelly by you than kindly by anyone else."

Her eyes widened. "Why?"

"Because I love you. Now, go home and relax before Henry arrives. Margaret is right. You're overdoing, and it's straining you emotionally."

He kissed her cheek, and Elizabeth's smile finally returned. "Your face is less scratchy without the beard."

"So you've told me many times. Shall I remind Charles that you prefer smooth chins?"

"Go away now," she laughed.

The earl jumped out of the coach, waving to Elizabeth as the horses trotted away from the house. As he climbed the steps, he pondered his cousin's words. Was it possible that he *did* care for Cordelia?

One of the two children dashed past him as Paul entered the house, and the earl had a momentary glimpse of his own future.

A peer's greatest duty is to produce an heir, his late mother had told him many times. *A son to carry on the name and title.*

Paul had always assumed Elizabeth would give birth to that son. Despite the ache in his heart at losing her, the handsome Scot realised he had a duty to the eleven earls who'd lived before him: to find a suitable bride, marry, and produce an heir.

CHAPTER THIRTY-EIGHT

Stephen Blinkmire's favourite aspect of Queen Anne Park was the variety of wildlife. It was late afternoon, and the gentle giant sat upon a stone bench near the far western edge of the north gardens, tossing toast crusts into the rippling water. A pair of Mute Swans swam towards him, curiously looking at their visitor. To the north-west, beyond a wildflower meadow, Blinkmire could see a family of fallow deer, and the bare-limbed Copper Beeches of James's Woods were alive with squirrels, nuthatches, finches, and jays. Upon the tallest branch of the nearest tree, a white owl watched, its magnificently plumed head cocked to one side.

"Even in the cold, the park is pleasant, is it not?" a deep voice asked from behind Blinkmire's back. The giant turned about, for he felt certain the voice sounded familiar, though he couldn't place it.

The voice belonged to a very tall individual with long dark hair that fell loosely upon his broad shoulders. He wore fine clothing from an earlier age, and his appearance had a faint shimmer to it which hurt Blinkmire's sensitive eyes.

"Prince Anatole?" Stephen asked.

"Hardly. I am his much more interesting, far handsomer brother."

Standing, the befuddled Blinkmire started towards the stranger, but in a flash the man stood beside him. *I don't remember moving*, Stephen thought.

"You didn't move. I did. Your bravery is considerable."

"Bravery?"

The intruder's lips curled into a sardonic smile. "Some call it that, but is it really? I think your courage is overrated."

He started to reply, but the creature's eyes altered in a most peculiar way, turning black as night, and its mouth lengthened into a cavernous and impossibly long oval. Stephen felt as though the creature were swallowing his thoughts, and he instinctively thrashed about with his bandaged hands to protect himself. An intense cold overwhelmed his brain, as though a thousand needles of ice plunged deeply into his head, and he felt himself yielding to the trespasser's probe.

Where is he? the attacker asked angrily. *Where is Anatole?*

"I don't know!" the helpless victim whispered in agony. "Please, leave me!"

Tell me where he is!

"I beg you, please, I do not know where His Highness is!"

Highness? Highness! I sit higher than that insolent traitor! Tell me where he is, and I'll reward you with a new body. One of beauty, one that women do not deride. One they will admire.

"I want nothing from you!" Stephen cried out, his head ready to explode.

Though the torture seemed to last for many minutes, it actually passed betwixt the tick of one second to the next. Just when Stephen thought he could endure no more, the intense pain ceased, and the invader vanished.

"Stephen?" Count Riga called as he approached. "Are you all right?"

The giant felt as timid as a mouse, and his bandaged hands trembled. "No," he answered, his voice barely audible.

Riga crossed the gravel as swiftly as his hunched back could manage, and he placed a comforting arm on his friend's back. "Tell me."

"You won't believe me," the other insisted.

"I should never doubt you, my friend. Tell me. What did you see?"

"I'm not sure. I thought it was Prince Anatole, but he was hardly that! He used some form of magic to get inside my head—in my mind—oh, he is a very dark person with a capacity for infinite cruelty, Viktor. I have never in my life been so frightened! Not since the boys teased me back in Ireland."

"Let us speak no more of it for the moment," Riga said gently. "Perhaps, the events of this week have been too much, my friend."

"Yes, perhaps."

They returned to the dower house together, saying nothing. Riga's eyes kept careful watch on the shadows beneath the bare fruit trees and evergreens. Red berries ripened on long stands of holly, and blue ones on junipers. It seemed to the count that these looked more like blinking eyes than fruit, but he said nothing to his friend.

In a moment, they passed through the west entrance to the graceful home, and as one of the cooks shut the door, a pair of birds—one black, one white—overflew their heads, unnoticed.

The two birds landed on the slate roof of a field stone dovecote near the northern edge of the vegetable garden. The black bird shimmered as its form altered, becoming the creature who'd so frightened poor Blinkmire.

The other, a white-feathered owl reshaped itself into a fiery bird of prey, its massive claws rending the intruder's humanoid body with stripes of crimson.

The two enemies performed this hideous ballet again and again. Several times, the black-winged creature managed to inflict slight injury to the white defender, but never enough to force it into breaking off the attack. To those with 'eyes to see' into the mirror realm of *sen-sen*, the match was heavily weighted towards the white champion.

"Enough!" the interloper shouted. "I yield! I yield!"

The white bird refused to break off the attack, and its blazing claws tore into the foe's cold eyes again and again. No humans saw the supernatural battle, and in the end, the black-winged hellion returned to the Stony Realms to lick its wounds.

The victor rose up high into the air, bound for the roofline of Haimsbury House, where it re-emerged into the human realm and transformed once more into the snowy white, guardian.

4:01 pm - Castor Institute

Alexander Collins returned to his office, still stinging from Raziel's reproof. He'd only just settled into the desk chair, when a uniformed nurse knocked on the door. "You've guests, sir."

"I've no time for visitors, Mrs. Cadbury. Unless they are on fire or bring barrels of money, I am far too busy!"

Winifred Cadbury did not move. "Neither applies, sir, but..."

"But what?" he shouted.

"One possesses a warrant card."

Collins gulped, wondering what fresh hell had come his way. "The police?"

"Commissioner Sinclair, sir. The warrant card says Intelligence Branch, Home Office."

The alienist stood, smoothed his dark hair, and pasted on the sort of smile he would wear for a visitor bringing barrels of money. "Send him in."

Charles entered along with a second man, whom the physician recognised at once. "Henry MacAlpin, isn't it? From Montmore House. And I presume this is Commissioner Sinclair. Do come in, gentlemen."

The detective took a seat, joined by Salperton, and the two men offered disarming smiles of their own. "Dr. Collins, I paid a visit here a few weeks ago regarding the Victoria Park murders, but I spoke with Dr. Kepler. I was told you were engaged elsewhere that day."

"Yes, that's right. Kepler mentioned it," Collins answered, feigning ease. "Is that the reason for your visit today, Commissioner? I'm afraid we know nothing about those crimes."

Charles waited five seconds before responding, using those seconds to assess the physician's appearance: tight pupils, beads of sweat along the upper lip, and a slight tick to the left eye.

"That is strange," he replied in the sixth second, "for your institute and even your name keep coming up in my investigations. For instance, I'm told a man escaped from here, yet you failed to report the incident to the police. Why is that, Dr. Collins?"

"An escape? No, Commissioner, I'm sure you're mistaken. Our patient count is checked daily. No one has left our wards without a release from one our physicians."

Henry entered the conversation. "That is very odd, Dr. Collins, for you see, I've been treating a man who insists he was a patient here for many months. I should love to see your records. I'm sure his name is listed, as you must have issued a release."

"His name?"

"I fear the fellow must have been a vagrant or perhaps a victim of memory loss, for he was only given a number whilst here. Number Thirteen."

The unexpected shock precipitated by those two words caused the skin on Collins's face to lose all colour. The left eye's tick rate increased, the nose twitched like a rabbit's might, and his upper lip commenced a strange sort of curling motion. Charles quietly observed the curious display, and he noticed other telltale signs. Profuse sweating along the hairline, shallow breathing, and the soft thud of a tapping foot upon the floor carpet.

Salperton pushed onward whilst Sinclair watched the alienist squirm.

"Yes, this fellow, Number Thirteen, told me some fantastic tales, Alex. Claimed he'd been held captive in your lower levels and given harsh chemicals that altered his very humanity. Of course, you and I understand how mental patients can be, isn't that right? Imaginative is a kind way to put it. It's easily disproved. Just let the commissioner see your records, and then escort us through these lower wards of yours."

"Lower wards?"

"Oh, yes. They're famous amongst our profession! I remember seeing plans for this building when I studied at Edinburgh. Designed by Abraham Compton, correct? Castor Institute's considered a shining example of a modern facility. I'm sure you're quite proud of it. Whilst Sinclair looks through your books, I'd love a tour."

Collins had not one idea in his head. Not one thought that could extricate him from the Gordian knot before him, except the solution his namesake, Alexander the Great, had employed.

Cut through it.

Without further delay, Alexander Collins collapsed onto the floor and started jerking his arms and legs, and even going so far as to bite the inside of his cheek to draw enough blood that it could escape his pale lips.

Charles watched the performance with very little reaction.

"I see you're busy," he said, standing. "Henry, if you'll make sure of the doctor's vitals, I'll call for a porter."

"Porter?" the viscount asked as he knelt beside the pretender.

"To carry Dr. Collins to my coach. I'm sure my old friend Fred Treves will be happy to admit a fellow doctor, but as we wouldn't want to risk anyone barging into his hospital room, I'll place a pair of constables on the door."

Before the clock struck five, Alexander Collins had been carried to the clever marquess's coach, conveyed to London Hospital, and placed into a narrow bed, safeguarded by Constables Antram and Bright.

"He's to have no visitors," Sinclair ordered. "Not even policemen. If I discover either of you has left this door before your relief shift arrives at midnight, you'll find yourselves cleaning latrines for Edmund Reid for the next year. Is that clear?"

"Very clear, sir," they answered.

Catching Frederick Treves's eye as he and Salperton left, Charles explained the reason for the admission. "I cannot take the chance that Collins is genuinely ill, Fred. If you'd perform a full examination, I'd appreciate it."

"You believe he's malingering?"

"I do. I believe Dr. Collins is hiding something. Do the full work-up. Top to toes, and if you can keep him restrained, all the better."

"Restrained? Wrist ties?"

"Either that, or I cuff him to the bedframe. I'll stop in first thing tomorrow."

Sinclair and MacAlpin then departed the hospital, and headed for Westminster.

Moments later, Anthony Gehlen tapped his colleague on the shoulder. "What was that all about?"

"A favour for our new Intelligence Commissioner. Apparently, he suspects Alex Collins of deception. We're to perform a complete examination of all systems, particularly anything that might cause an epileptic seizure."

Gehlen laughed, his eyes glinting oddly. "Ah, well, not my area then. I'll leave it to you and your anatomists. See you for supper later?"

"Yes, I'd like that."

Treves entered the new patient's room and shut the door.

As he stood there, watching, Anthony Gehlen's human mind slept whilst the clever thief wandered about his memories looking for ways to make use of his new 'human suit'. Alexander Collins's name had no entry here, but Saraqael recognised the alienist from the meeting at the Empress. If he could find a way to enter Collins's head, then he might retrieve memories of other meetings. He might even discover information about Raziel.

Wait, he thought as he stood inside Gehlen's well-ordered memory stack, *wasn't Collins the fool conducting the human alteration trials? Perhaps, I'll give these experiments a little nudge in a new direction. Fashion them in my image, so to speak. Who needs clumsy wolfmen, when other, far more interesting combinations are available?*

"I say, gentlemen, why are you guarding this door?" he asked the constables.

"Superintendent—no, I mean Commissioner Sinclair placed us here, sir. Are you one of the doctors?"

"Oh, yes, I certainly am. Dr. Gehlen. I start teaching in the next term. You're?"

"Bright and Antram," replied John Bright.

"It's a pleasure," the Saraqael-controlled Gehlen said, shaking their hands. "I shan't be visiting with Dr. Collins right away, for I've a few records to review first, but then I'll return this evening. See you both then?"

"Aye, sir," Bright replied.

"May I bring you coffee with a bit of Irish added for spice? By then, I'm sure it would go down very well."

"We're not supposed to drink on duty, sir, but thanks all the same," Antram told the pretender.

"Such a pity. Meat pie, then? Lemonade?"

"That'd be lovely, sir," Bright answered quickly.

"Excellent. We'll all share a repast, and then I'll perform my examination. See you later. Sevenish, I should think."

He turned about, and Saraqael abandoned the 'suit' in favour of more freeing transportation. Unseen, he rose up to the ceiling, crossed through each floor, and then emerged from the roofline before spreading his wings. Taking the form of a great raven, he quickly crossed east London.

His destination was Castor Institute, and his plans took shape as he flew.

CHAPTER THIRTY-NINE

5:53 pm – Haimsbury House

"Henry, it's so very good to see you," Elizabeth told the physician as he reached for her hand.

"Forgive me for being so late. I believe your husband wired that we'd arrive around four, but we stopped along the way, you see. I hope I've not made you rearrange your plans at all."

"I fear my husband's estimation of time is not always precise, but he has little control over crime. His message said you and he would arrive together."

"Ah, yes, we intended to arrive together, but Charles had to stop by Loudain House first. He said he'd catch a hansom as quickly as possible. You'll have to make-do with me for now, I'm afraid."

Salperton wore a tweed jacket and waistcoat over simple wool trousers. He seldom thought about dress, though he could afford the finest, and he wondered if he shouldn't have worn evening clothes. Elizabeth's attire was elegantly formal, whilst his evoked country walks and shooting matches.

"I hope you'll forgive me, Duchess," he said as they walked through the broad foyer. "I'm a bit of a mess. I'd only finished my rounds when your husband called on me. From there, it was all a sort of whirlwind. He's a remarkably busy man."

"Far too busy, but as the wife of a detective, I find ways to occupy my mind and my time. Thank you for the flowers, Henry. They add colour and beauty to our entry. How did you know I like pink roses?"

"I confess I asked your cousin. The bouquet is to welcome you home. Your cheeks are as pink as those flowers, Elizabeth. Really, you are resplendent. I cannot tell you how it pleases me to see you looking so well!"

Beth laughed and took his arm. "That's kind of you, and you are hardly a mess, Henry. Did you hear the news about Baron Wychwright?"

He nodded as they entered the smaller, Eden River drawing room. "Yes, it's tragic. I suppose I should pay them a call this week."

"I visited them today. It's why I'm dressed formally. Poor Delia. She's heartbroken."

"Quite so. And the man's widow as well, I should think. Losing a loved one is never easy."

They sat down together on a wide sofa, where a gleaming table had been set with cakes, fruit, and cheese. A footman entered, carrying a large silver tray. "Are you ready for the tea now, Your Grace?"

"Yes, Hampton. Thank you."

The young man placed a covered pot on the table and lifted the quilted linen cosy, revealing a large blue and gold china pot bearing a heraldic crest. "Shall I pour, my lady?"

"Allow me," Henry insisted.

"Thank you again, Hampton. Leave word with Mr. Baxter that Lord Haimsbury is delayed, will you?"

"Of course, Your Grace," he said, bowing before leaving.

Henry lifted the monogrammed china pot. "My mother always said a true gentleman is willing to serve, even in a tea room. This set is lovely, Beth, and the crest unique. An H and B, entwined with a heart. Haimsbury and Branham?"

"Yes," she answered. "It was a wedding gift from our Aunt Victoria. The duke had the crest designed for our combined houses. It's on our coaches, our tableware, linens, practically everything. Grandfather made certain to place visible reminders of our union throughout the home."

"The duke is very thoughtful."

"And very loving. You know, there are several interesting points to the design that may have escaped the heraldry artist's notice."

"Such as?" he asked as he poured tea into the cups. "Before you answer, what shall I add to yours? You look rather like two sugars and a splash. Am I right?"

"How did you know?" she asked.

"It's an old trick. Most ladies take milk, and very few consider one cube enough, whilst only a handful will say three. If you'd contended with me, I'd have confessed my lack of insight." He added two sugar cubes and milk to her tea and the same to his own. "We're alike in our taste, it seems," he said, handing her the cup. "I think you and I are alike in many ways."

"I'm happy to say we are."

"So, tell me about this crest. I love heraldic symbols. Oft times, the artist adds coded secrets to them, but he's generally aware of their meaning."

"Look closely at the handle of the pot and cups. As a Stuart descendent, you'll recognise the oak and acorn motif."

He laughed. "A Jacobite emblem. A reminder that the Stuart acorns would one day grow into a mighty oak again. What else?"

"Within the centre of the scrolled initials is the symbol of the inner circle. It's beautifully hidden, but if you look closely you'll see it. As you're a circle member now, I can tell you, but ordinarily, I'd be forced to secrecy."

"I fear that I cannot see it. My eyes are usually quite sharp, but... Oh, wait. There are gold letters here. P and S? Is the S for Sinclair?"

"Oddly, enough, it might well be, but we'd always assumed it stood for Stuart. I'll let Charles and my grandfather explain the rest at the meeting later."

"Stuart," he repeated thoughtfully. "You know, Elizabeth, I talked with one of our cousins only this afternoon. From an American branch. I'd not thought we had any cousins across the pond, but apparently we do."

This caught her attention. "An American cousin? Where did you meet her?"

"Actually, I shouldn't have said anything. I endeavour to keep the identities of my patients secret. Poor thing's lost most of her memory. In fact, I only learnt her name today. She's recalled that much, at least."

"Her accent is American?"

"Indeed. I'd dearly love her to find friends and family again. Find herself! I cannot decide what it is, but something about her touches my heart."

"Your gallant nature is roused."

He laughed. "Perhaps. I wonder if you'd come visit. Or Paul. You might even come together."

"I'd be happy to visit, and I'm sure Paul would agree to it. She offered no other insights?"

"She told me she has a cousin here, but she cannot name him yet. I'm sure she will, though. It may take a bit of time. I thought we could arrange a musical evening. That way it can look as though your visit is incidental."

"I should be happy to help in any way, Henry."

"That's kind of you. I must say, Beth, you and Charles are very generous with your time, but also with your home. I confess that is another reason I was late. I paid a quick call on our patients before coming here. I was surprised at how very large the dower house is! The one at our castle is a dinky place. Scarcely enough room for a mouse, let alone an entire company of guests."

"I hope they're settling in well. How is Mr. Blinkmire?"

"Frazzled," the viscount answered. "He had a very strange encounter near the pond this afternoon. I rather think it was one of your gardeners, but apparently the man said something that upset our Blinkmire rather badly."

"One of my gardeners? No, they'd never intentionally speak unkindly to anyone! Did he describe the man?"

"He did, actually, and it sounds remarkably like Prince Anatole. I wonder what's happened to our former host, anyway? As tall as Romanov is, I cannot imagine another like him anywhere in London. Of course, he's unusual in many other ways. Don't you agree?"

The duchess didn't reply at first. The mention of a stranger on the grounds had sent a chill through her hands, and Elizabeth had a dark premonition. For the briefest of seconds, she felt as though eyes watched her, and cold waves of fear ran through her bones.

"Beth? I say, you've gone all pale."

"Excuse me," she said, setting the cup on the table.

She started to stand, but the movement occurred just as an intense wave of nausea passed through her body, causing her to pitch forward. Salperton managed to catch her, and after helping her back to the sofa, rang for the footman.

"Have you eaten today?" the physician asked.

"Yes. No, wait. I'm not sure. Probably. I think I had a slice of toast and a biscuit."

Hampton returned. "Yes, my lady?"

"Your mistress is ill. Would you bring me a moist towel, please?"

The servant left, and Henry sat beside his hostess, assessing her condition. "Your pulse is rapid and far too irregular. I've said something to upset you, and I can guess what it was. Forgive me, Beth. You now worry that something unnatural wanders about your estate. Isn't that so?" She nodded. "Duchess, I promise you that I've noticed nothing unusual about this house or the grounds."

"You've seen nothing? No spirits? No intruders?"

"Nothing at all, Beth. Blinkmire asked me the same thing, but I tell you that all is well. Do you wish to talk about it?"

"Not really. Henry, is it normal for an expectant mother to... To imagine things?"

He smiled as he held her hand. "I'm not the best one to answer that. It's more Gehlen's territory than mine. What worries you?"

"Something at Lady Cordelia's home. I saw a great owl, and I've noticed it before. For weeks, there's been a white owl following me. Even at the castle, it would sometimes sit outside my window."

"Owls are hardly an uncommon sight in London. With all the vermin running about, we should be grateful to them."

"This isn't an ordinary owl, Henry. An owl's eyes are amber, but this one's are blue."

"A bird with blue eyes? I'll admit, it's unusual, but not impossible. The animal kingdom has a wide variety of forms."

"I suppose it could have occurred in nature, but why do I feel as if it's *watching* me? Oh, I'm making no sense. Ever since the castle fire, it feels as though the air in London is thickening. Growing darker with a venomous miasma, just like the air in that awful place with all the ravens."

"The place in your dream?"

"You know it wasn't a dream, Henry. You told me that you could see me there. Ask Charles. He was trapped there as well, and he believes it's real. Is it possible that something followed me when I escaped?"

Hampton returned with the towel, and Salperton placed it on Elizabeth's forehead. "You're overwrought, that's all. Tell me, young man," he asked the footman, "has your mistress eaten today?"

"I cannot say, sir. Shall I speak with the cooks? Mr. Baxter is next door conferring with Mr. Miles regarding this evening's meeting."

"Ah, yes, I'm attending that. Baxter's the butler here?"

"He is, my lord."

"Ask the cook to send up something light. Soup, if you have it. Anything easily digested. She really must get something nourishing into her stomach that will stay down."

"Right away, sir."

The young man hurried off towards the kitchens, and Salperton continued examining his patient. "How's your breathing? You don't wear a corset today, I hope."

"Yes, actually, but only because I had but one dress suitable for calling on a bereaved friend. This one, and the waist is now too small."

"Don't move," he ordered her, leaving the drawing room briefly and crossing into the wide foyer. "You there," he called to a passing parlour maid. "Miss. Forgive me, what is your name?"

"Ada, sir."

"Ada, I just sent a footman to fetch a bite to eat for the duchess. Would you deliver a message to him?"

"Aye, sir," MacKenzie replied.

"Ah, you're Scottish. I should have realised some of the staff would be from our neck o' the woods."

"That's right, my lord. Glasgow."

"A lovely city. Ada, would you be so kind as to tell the footman to bring the food to the duchess's chamber? She is in need of rest, and I'm carrying her up."

"There's an electric lift, my lord. I can show you where it is."

"How very modern. Wait here!"

He dashed back into the drawing room. "Beth, lean on me. I'm going to take you upstairs and make sure everything's as it should be." The two of them followed Ada to the lift. The maid quickly taught Henry how to operate it.

"Just move the handle to number one, sir. The corridor leading to the master apartment is to the right, just off the lift. The duchess can direct you from there. My lady, shall I bring tea?"

"Yes, thank you," she muttered, her voice strained, for a very odd sensation had entered Elizabeth's delicate frame. Her heartbeat pounded in her ears, and she could sense a heaviness all around. Darkness settled in her eyes like a collapsing tunnel, and from the centre of the tunnel arose the cawing of birds.

The ornate lift slowly rose to the first floor, but Beth had fainted by the time it stopped. Henry carried her into the corridor to the right, wishing he'd asked for further directions from the maid. From beyond a corner, he could hear a dog barking, and as he made the turn, he nearly tripped over a brown and white terrier.

"Samson! Bad dog!" Victoria scolded the animal as she appeared two steps behind the dog. "Oh, good heavens! Whatever happened? It's this way. I just left their apartment."

Henry allowed the duke's sister to lead the way, and in a few minutes, he'd set the duchess upon the beautiful bed. "You're my Cousin Victoria, I take it? Dr. Henry MacAlpin. Just call me Henry. I'd shake your hand, but I'm a bit occupied, you see. But your timing could not have been better. I fear the duchess fainted in the lift. Has she eaten anything today?"

"Hardly a bite," the woman answered. "Her appetite is very poor. Is she feverish again?"

"No, but something overwhelmed her sense of balance. Has she suffered many difficulties of late?"

"A great many. We told Treves and Gehlen, of course. Elizabeth hasn't been herself since late October. When I asked Dr. Gehlen about it, he muttered something about how it all made sense, but it makes no sense at all! Are expectant mothers always this sensitive?"

"Some are," he said, loosening the clasps of the high-necked silk gown. "Do you mind shutting that door? I'll need help removing this jacket."

"Yours or hers?"

"Hers, of course. Removing mine would hardly make sense at all. Elizabeth told me that she wore a corset today. It's a very bad idea with a quick-growing pregnancy."

"*Quick*-growing? What on earth do you mean by that odd remark?"

"Hasn't Charles told you?" he asked.

"Told me what?"

"It's really not my place..." Henry backpedaled.

He was unfastening the hooks that secured the tight-fitting jacket in place, but the spinster objected. "If you don't mind, allow me to do that. I realise you're a medical man, but there are some things that I simply cannot alter my views upon, and seeing a man undress a woman is one of them. Go into the parlour and allow me to do this."

The physician backed away and did as the strong-willed Scotswoman asked. In less than ten minutes, she called him back into the bedchamber. "I do apologise, but I find modernity a bit much at times. My brother told me you'd joined the circle. Aren't you somewhat early for our meeting?"

"Yes, but Charles asked me to come early to look in on Beth. We'd just started tea, when she suffered a faint. No, actually, that's not precisely what occurred. I mentioned a strange man who looked somewhat like Anatole Romanov, and Elizabeth grew unsteady. She fainted shortly after. That's probably the footman with the food," he said as someone knocked. "In here, young man," he told the youth. "Set the tray there at the end of the bed. We'll see to it that the duchess eats. Please, thank the cooks for me."

"I will, sir."

The door shut behind the servant, and Salperton took a look beneath the silver domes. "Broth and toast. Perfect. Elizabeth, can you open your eyes?"

"Yes," she said, trying to sit. "Did I hear Tory's voice?"

"Your aunt helped with your clothing. That's why you're in a sleeping dress now. I recommend you rest for an hour, but first you must eat." He brought her the tray and helped her to sit up straight. "No chairs. If you feel faint again, it's best you're already in bed. Eat every bite, if you can manage it."

"I'm not sure I can, but I'll try. Tory, will you stay with me?"

"Of course."

The door stood ajar, and two black dogs entered, followed by the brown and white Parson's Terrier.

"Bella! Briar! Do stay down now," Victoria scolded the Labradors. "Beth, you must discipline your dogs."

Despite Victoria's reprimand, all three animals leapt onto the wide bed and formed a protective ring around the duchess.

"Charles wants them in here, Tory," the duchess answered. "They've formed a sort of friendship. Rather like a canine inner circle."

"Yes, so I see. Henry, I hear voices. See if that's Charles, will you?"

Salperton left the room, and the formidable lady turned back to her niece. "Tell me what really happened downstairs. What caused you to faint?"

"I'm not sure. It's probably nothing, Tory. Henry's been very helpful. Don't scold him. With Emerson away, I need a doctor nearby."

"Yes, but not one who's in love with you," she told Elizabeth plainly. "Anyone can see it! Surely, Charles realises it."

"Henry isn't in love with me. He's my friend. That's all."

The door opened again, and Charles Sinclair entered.

"It's time you got home, Charles Robert!" Victoria exclaimed. "Tell your wife to rest. She had no business paying calls today. She's only just out of hospital."

"Why, thank you for the lovely welcome, Tory. If I might have a moment alone with my wife, I'll be happy to tell her that."

Victoria Stuart shrugged. "You are hopeless! Come, Henry. Tell me about your family and how it is we're cousins. I'll see you downstairs, Charles. See that she eats."

The two left the bedchamber, and Sinclair sat on the edge of the bed, careful not to disturb the dogs. "I see your canine protectors keep watch. What happened in my absence? You seemed well when I left this morning."

"Nothing happened. I'm merely tired. I hate to admit it, but Tory may be right. Perhaps, I shouldn't have called on Cordelia this afternoon. It's worn me down, I think."

"Something is wearing you down, but not any condolence call. There's something you're not willing to speak aloud," he whispered. "Shall I stay here with you?"

"Of course not, Charles. You've work to do, I'm sure." She stared at the food. "I really cannot eat this. Would you ask someone to take it away?"

"Nothing at all?" he asked, touching the curling hair that fell along her face. "Not even one bite? Our children need nourishment, darling. If this doesn't appeal, then let me find food that will. If it's in the city, I'll fetch it for you."

"Please, Charles, I just want to sleep. I'll eat it later."

He took the tray and set it on a low table near the fireplace. "I'll come up as soon as we're finished, little one."

He kissed her cheek, and she slid down into the quilts. The dogs moved closer, and before Charles had shut the door, the human and her three furry companions had all fallen asleep.

CHAPTER FORTY

"Henry, I'd like to take you on a tour, if you've the time. We can talk as we progress," Charles told his second cousin as the two of them entered the library of Haimsbury House. "The other members won't start arriving for half an hour, I shouldn't think. You remember Martin, of course. Tailor, spy, and consummate philosopher."

Kepelheim stood near the room's carved Languedoc marble fireplace, a glass of claret in his right hand. The tailor's ample cheeks rounded as he set the glass on the mantle and extended his hand to greet the newcomer. "Good to see you again, Lord Salperton. I look forward to sharing all those talents with you. Also, I'd hear more about your own talents. You have a unique view of the world."

"Politically, you mean, Mr. Kepelheim?"

"Martin, please. In fact, you used to call me Uncle Marty when you were small. I've never had children of my own, but I do love them. No, the viewpoint I mean is a spiritual one. I've often wondered if the blood confers such abilities. As with your mother, you see into the hidden realms."

"I would happily give that gift to another, if the Lord allowed it," the viscount answered, "however, he has yet to do so. If that strange gift is useful to the inner circle, then I'm happy to share it. Charles tells me that you helped prove his inheritance rights."

"I played a small role," the shorter man answered. "Charles, did I overhear an offer to take our viscount on a tour? I'd love to come along, if I'm not intruding."

"I'd hoped you'd be willing to go with us, Martin," the marquess said. "Shall we begin with the ballroom?"

"Are you sure?" Kepelheim asked warily. "That room has very dark associations, as you'll recall."

"That's precisely why I want Henry to see it. If his vision is as clear as I believe, then I want to know if any shadows linger in that room. We'll stop by Mrs. Partridge's office and borrow her keys, and then take the lift from there."

After a short conversation with the housekeeper and a slow ride upwards, the three men arrived at the ornate doors to the grand ballroom. To his surprise, Charles found them unlocked.

"Now, that is strange, if not disturbing. I've left strict orders that this room remain locked at all times. The only time it's to be entered is for cleaning. Baxter's completely reliable, which makes it all the more odd. I'll ask him about it later," he said pushing open both doors. "Shall we?"

Henry stood his ground, remaining in the open doorway. "Perhaps, we should stay out here."

Charles had already stepped into the room, and he turned back to engage his guest. "Why?"

Kepelheim remained with the viscount. "Henry, what do you see?"

"Something that makes no sense," Salperton answered. "Tell me what you see, Charles. Describe the room to me."

Haimsbury found the behaviour puzzling. "It's a typical ballroom, I suppose, though I've not visited all that many, and all of them within the last two months. Three-storeys high with murals covering nearly every square foot of the ceiling—the parts that aren't stained glass, of course. A hundred feet wide, I imagine. Half again as long. There are six gilded mirrors along each side of the room, and light is provided by equally grand chandeliers, six in all. The floor is the same red and white marble tile in many of the rooms elsewhere."

"Rouge Languedoc and white breccia," Kepelheim said. "Your grandfather visited Versailles in his youth, and vowed that he would one day build a mansion to match it in London. On a smaller scale, he accomplished just that. Few men in England could have afforded such extravagance, but your grandfather never put a foot wrong when it came to business. The ninth marquess took an already vast fortune and multiplied it many times over. You might say this house is his epitaph."

"So I've read," Henry said, "but that is not what I see. Not even close. The room is hardly gilded, and the mirrors are not at all ordinary. They look more like unfriendly doors made of shining black. The walls are covered in vines, and the ceiling glass is broken and open to the sky. I am sorry," Henry added, turning away, "I cannot bear to look any longer! The entire room is filled with spirits!"

Sinclair could see none of this, but he wondered if these spirits might present themselves to him, if he crossed to the centre.

"Charles, go no further!" the viscount shouted as he rushed after his friend. "Stop!"

The marquess paused. "Why?"

"There are shadows all about the floor, and a great serpent with vertical scales upon its spine writhes beneath your left foot. This room is host to darkness beyond anything I've ever seen before!"

"Who are you?" Charles asked the room's inhabitants.

A whisper kissed his cheek, and a woman's voice answered. "An old friend. Remember?"

The chill of death ran through his body, and Sinclair felt her hands upon his shoulders, caressing his arms, his chest, thighs, touching him everywhere.

He leapt backwards, nearly stumbling into Salperton.

"What is it?" Kepelheim asked.

"Nothing. No one."

Sinclair left the room quickly and shut the massive doors, his heart pounding. "Martin, there's a parlour intended as a private room for ball attendees next door. I need to sit."

The two men helped Sinclair to the drawing room, and Charles took a seat in one of several dozen large chairs that lined a gallery wall, hung with portraits of previous marquesses.

Henry sat beside him. "What startled you?" he asked his second cousin.

"A voice I've not heard in years. It may have been my imagination. We'll end the tour, I think. Sorry."

"Yes, I think that's a good idea. Look, Charles," Salperton told him, "I've no wish to see what I do, but that room needs to be cleansed."

"I'm sure you're right. Martin, would you speak with MacPherson about anointing it after this evening's meeting?"

"Of course, my friend. Shall I fetch you a brandy?"

"No. I just need a minute." Sinclair glanced at Salperton. "You've seen these things your whole life? How do you remain sane, Henry?"

"Faith. My mother taught me that faith in Christ is our primary weapon against these creatures. It may sound simple, but then God's truths are simple, whilst also complex beyond our comprehension. Even given an eternity, scientists would never plumb their depths, yet a small child accepts them through faith."

Sinclair smiled. "I said it at the hospital, and I repeat it now. The Lord fills our chairs with his choices, his warriors."

"Hardly that," Henry argued, "but it's kind of you to consider me such. You and Aubrey are the warriors. If I'm anything, it's a humble squire."

"Shall we return to the library, or have you regained enough vigour to continue the tour?" Kepelheim asked his friend.

"I'm much better, thank you, Martin. Let's leave this area and explore the portraits in the long gallery. It's not far."

The trio left the ballroom antechamber and passed into the east wing of the rambling mansion, but once they'd turned the corner, the ballroom doors shivered and then opened, as though something had just left and now walked freely within the house.

CHAPTER FORTY-ONE

7 pm – Haimsbury House Library

Darkness had fallen across the elegant chimneys of Westminster, and many of the regal borough's citizens dressed for an evening out, gossiped about the latest string of fires and high-profile murders, or shared a drink and a smoke at their exclusive gentlemen's clubs. Unbeknownst to these preoccupied Londoners, inside one of the largest and newest private mansions, the members of England's most important organisation gathered to discuss matters that would affect every man and woman alive.

Haimsbury House library soared two storeys high, illuminated by a gleaming, four-foot-wide, cut crystal chandelier. Six matching wall sconces mirrored the chandelier's design; each with multi-faceted rock crystals suspended from their gilded and branching arms. The library contained no windows to distract from the structural beauty of the interior. Pedimented, mahogany bookshelves lined the north and south walls, each filled to bursting with classics, biographies, histories, Bibles, novels, dictionaries, and row upon row of journals and diaries.

The fireplace and entry walls contained no shelving but were decorated in brightly coloured murals that depicted scenes from Sinclair family history. This vibrant panorama radiated outwards from a curious central image, positioned just to the left of the fireplace. The spectacular interplay of oil and plaster had always fascinated visitors, and many of the members now offered theories as to its meaning.

"Is that Cumbria?" a tall man in a frock coat asked. "I don't recall ever seeing it looking like this."

"I believe it's the area where Rose House now stands, but long before the house was built," observed a smaller man in a hand-tailored coat of dark wool. "Ah, here are our stragglers! Edmund, do come in. I believe our marquess is about to open our fellowship," Kepelheim informed them. "Come, Dr. Whitmore, you and I must find chairs before all the sturdier ones are taken."

The men and women of the circle had been enjoying the magnificent space and sharing stories of their interactions with the man who now led them, when the ringing of a handbell called them to order.

"If you'll all, please, take your seats," their leader called. "We've a great many items to cover before we enjoy supper."

Edmund Reid and Arthur France took the last two chairs at the table, and Charles Sinclair called for the doors to be shut. "If you'll do the honours, Mr. Baxter, we'll begin."

The impeccably dressed butler bowed. "I shall be pleased to serve, my lord. If someone knocks, shall I answer?"

"I imagine so, but as we're all in here, I doubt anyone will. Good evening, everyone. I'm pleased to call us to order in my family's house, and now that my wife is in it, it begins to feel like a real home. Uncle James, would you lead us in prayer?"

Every head bowed, and Drummond petitioned the Lord. "Saviour of all who call upon your name, we do so, now, with humble hearts and minds. Not long ago, a day of rejoicing turned into a night of great despair, and it looked as though we might lose both Charles and Elizabeth, but through all of that anguish, you were ever in control. Since that dreadful night, we've come through the darkness into a bright and glorious morning. Charles has recovered, our girl is home, and our family continues to expand with the addition of a beloved cousin. We know that you brought Henry to us, and I personally want to thank you for using him to keep Beth alive."

He paused, and though everyone's eyes were shut, all were certain that the stalwart duke was weeping. Strong hands clutched at those of their uncle, and both Paul and Charles silently prayed for James Stuart.

Unbeknownst to the gathering of men and women, a white owl perched directly above them upon the steeply pitched, slate roof. Whilst the duke prayed, its head tilted to one side, as though listening. As the heartfelt prayer rose up to God's throne, the owl's great wings reached out into the chilly evening air, and it began to circle the mansion, scanning the mortal and immortal realms for signs of intruders.

After many moments of silence, Drummond continued.

"It's all too much for me sometimes, my Lord! Too much! I've seen many miracles in my lifetime, but this one reaches into the depths of my soul! I thought I'd lost them both, and I think it might have killed me, but that was never your plan, was it? These hands, these wonderful hands within my own bring me more joy than any man's heart can hold. Thank you, Lord! Thank you. I ask your forgiveness for my lack of faith, for my fears. We few here tonight form a ring around Beth and Charles and Paul. These three young people bear the brunt of the enemy's attacks, and I ask that you prepare all of us to protect them. Though we fail you daily, we ask that you might turn even our failures into victories, according to your perfect will. We ask that your Spirit overshadow our gathering and guide us as we seek to understand the wiles of the human and spiritual enemies of your kingdom. We seek neither power nor glory for ourselves, but submit to your will alone. May our words honour you, may our hands serve you, and may our conversation ever and always seek to praise you. In Christ's blessed and most powerful name we ask it. Amen."

"Amen," all echoed.

James wiped his eyes, a weary smile spreading across his lean face. "Don't worry, son. They're happy tears," he told Sinclair. "Very happy."

The detective stood behind his uncle's chair. "My friends, this wonderful man is our patriarch. When I first met the duke years ago, I instantly loved him. Who doesn't? Discovering that he is my uncle and Paul my cousin marked a turning point in my journey. James serves as my mentor, and Paul is my dearest friend. Our family bears a burden and a mission, one fraught with danger and disappointment, but also filled with wonder and countless joys. I consider myself living inside a miracle—a true miracle!—and no matter what darkness may overshadow, I know that our Lord's light will never cease to shine."

"That's right, son," James Stuart answered. "It's a joy to look at these two faces, these two cousins. Both love the Lord and serve him with all their hearts, souls, and minds. I ask you, can any man be richer?" He turned to Sinclair. "Son, I'm grateful to our King for his protection upon you and Elizabeth. My experiences in this long war pale to your own, and you've lived less than half my years. Yet, I fear your greatest tests still lie before you. I'll be seventy next May, which should make me wiser, but the older I get, the more foolish I feel." He laughed as he wiped the last tears from his face. "I've no particular agenda, son, merely rambling as an old man is expected to do. You're head of our circle. I'll let you lead the conversation."

Charles gazed at the assembly of professional and peerage companions as he returned to his chair. "Thank you, James. The Lord is indeed good. It means more than I can ever say to sit beside you, Paul, and all these fellow servants. It's my hope that we'll meet regularly from this moment forward. We'll do so here, for the present, but eventually I should like to move all circle activities to Queen Anne House."

Paul raised his hand. "Charles, I thought we'd decided to use Loudain House. Has that changed?"

"No, the ICI agents and Intelligence Branch operatives will use Loudain for training and as headquarters, but the leadership will keep offices at Queen Anne. I've already discussed this with Elizabeth, and it's made her very happy, as it allows me to work nearby. The drawing rooms and main library will be furnished as offices, but the apartments will remain living spaces for whenever we host guests. We'll make no structural changes, of course, because Queen Anne is part of our first child's heritage."

James began to smile broadly, causing his salt-and-pepper moustache to twitch. "A son, you think?"

"Yes, James, I believe we will have a son, but also a daughter, though I cannot say which will be firstborn."

The faces 'round the table reflected a mixture of mirth and confusion, and the marquess explained. "I'd planned to discuss this later, but perhaps now is best. It is a strange tale, but I assure you that it's all true. As James mentioned in the prayer, my wedding night didn't turn out as I'd expected. William Trent abducted Elizabeth and carried her to my old house in Whitechapel. We mounted a rescue, but our team was nearly stopped by a ferocious pack of wolf hybrids—a topic we must discuss at length tonight. I applaud the bravery of everyone who took part in that battle. I know some of you sustained injuries, but even those who didn't must surely have nightmares about it. I know I do.

"When the earl and I finally reached the house, it had caught fire. My memories of what happened next are rather imprecise, but I believe I tried to enter the house and was knocked unconscious."

"You were thrown against an iron post, Charles," the earl told him. "The way your head bled, I'd feared we'd lost you."

"I cannot remember that, but I suppose it's not surprising. However, that injury put me into a coma for seven days. I don't know if everyone who sleeps in such a twilight world travels, but I did. And I was not alone in those travels. It turns out that, during that same time, Elizabeth also lay in a deep sleep of sorts, for she'd taken to bed with a high fever, caused by exposure to the frigid cold that night. Whilst in our individual states, she and I shared a visit to the same place, a hellish realm of living stones and sentient trees. Huge blackbirds populated the air, and most could talk, though their hideous language sounded nothing like English. I could, however, understand and converse with one of these birds, a creature that called itself the gatekeeper. This very annoying gatekeeper had the ability to transform from bird to a human-like appearance."

"You called it annoying," Edward MacPherson noted. "How so, Lord Haimsbury?"

"Annoying in its persistent ambiguity, I suppose, but also in its utterly frustrating riddles," Charles answered. "You see, these living stones formed a high and very complicated maze of concentric stone rings. Each ring could only be accessed by selecting one of seven gates, which would then lead to the next ring within the maze, and so forth. Each ring had one true gate, whilst the others led to oblivion. One wrong turn, just one mistake, and I'd be forever lost. However, this noisome gatekeeper told me that if I navigated the maze without error, it would lead me to the centre, where a cottage stood. This tiny house would, in turn, take me home."

Charles reached for a glass of water. Cornelius Baxter, sitting near the back beside Reggie Whitmore, raised his hand. "My lord, per your request, I set out only water for the meeting, but if you prefer tea or something stronger, I'd be happy to fetch whatever you wish. I've decanted several choices for after supper."

"No, thank you, Mr. Baxter, water is sufficient. I'll keep my head clear for the present. When we've finished our discussion, then we'll all indulge in a meal and after dinner drinks. I'm told Mrs. Anderson has prepared a delicious selection of dishes, and if the aroma is any indication, her sister baked fresh bread and cakes this morning." He emptied the glass and poured it full again from the carafe. "As I was saying, the cottage was my only means to escape this awful place, but with seven choices, multiplied by seven stone rings, it felt like an impossibility. The bird-like gatekeeper repeatedly asked for payment in exchange for a hint, and his eyes fell upon my watch again and again."

Charles held up the Sir John Bennett to show the members. "It is a fine watch, but hardly unique. One might buy it at any jeweller's shop. However, my wife had this watch engraved for me, and I would never part with it. Not ever, for her words touch my heart and strengthen me, each time I see them. So, my dilemma was this: Find my way through the stone maze with no instructions. A daunting task, and I worried that I should fail. Therefore, I prayed for guidance."

Sinclair smiled, and his blue eyes grew wistful. "The Lord works in mysterious ways, and never more mysteriously than during that long, terrifying night. After praying, I heard a sweet voice, asking me why I was crying, and when I looked, I saw a child. A dark-haired girl in a white dress with pink ribbons. She looked identical to Elizabeth at eleven years old."

"As she looked when you first met her," Reid observed. "Are you saying the Lord brought you the duchess as his answer?"

"In a way," Sinclair replied, "but not exactly. I asked the girl her name. She told me it was Georgianna, and she called me Father."

Drummond's mouth and its moustache companion slowly widened into a massive grin. "Charles has told me this tale before, but it always gives me chills. This Georgianna claimed to be your own daughter, come to help you. Is that right, son?"

"Yes, sir. That's right. My daughter Georgianna is—or rather will be—just as precocious, bright, loving, and fearless as her mother. She informed me that many of the things she knew about my future were to remain secret. Apparently, I shall one day tell her all about this event, and she'll spend years learning everything she can about this stone world through dreams. I cannot tell you what a strange experience it was, but Georgie—she informed me that very few call her Georgianna—well, she remained completely calm and focused the entire time, and she led me to the cottage refuge. Once there, she had to leave, but promised to tell the future version of myself all about our adventure."

"Aye, that sounds like our Beth," Drummond laughed. "Georgie, is it? She sounds like my kind o' girl! I'll wager I taught her everything she knows."

"I've no doubt of that, sir, and I suspect that much of her persistent nature will be formed by you," Sinclair answered with a smile. "As I said, Georgie insisted she must go, so after bidding my future daughter goodbye, I entered this haven, where I found a pleasant woman, who called herself Hope. She asked who had brought me, and I mentioned Georgie. This Hope explained that the children never enter the house."

"Children?" Whitmore asked. "Plural?"

"Yes, plural," Charles replied, smiling again. "It will become clear in a moment, Reggie. All around this quaint house, were carvings, paintings, and even needlework images of entwined hearts, but at first I didn't notice that two other hearts, wrought in gold, were within these larger hearts. After I gained my bearings, Hope told me that a woman had arrived shortly before me, and that she slept in the next room."

"Elizabeth," MacAlpin said softly.

"Yes. My beloved wife. God had answered my prayer in a way that still seems impossible, yet Beth tells the same story. Only her guide through the maze was a boy, who looked, according to my wife, like a younger version of myself."

"Twins!" Drummond shouted, excitedly. "A boy and a girl! But has it been confirmed?"

"Yes, sir, I believe it has. I spoke with Treves and this new specialist, Anthony Gehlen, and both men believe Elizabeth's rapid physical changes, as well as early and very strong symptoms of nausea and balance problems, indicate twins."

Drummond jumped to his feet and pulled his nephew into a fond embrace. "Son, that is the best news this old man's heard in a month o' Sundays! Two wee ones who look like their parents. Two ta teach all I know 'bout fishin' and huntin'!"

"Two children who must be protected at all costs," MacPherson warned the group.

Henry MacAlpin stood. "May I speak?"

Charles cleared his throat as Drummond returned to his chair. "Of course. Do forgive me, everyone. My manners fail me. You heard the duke mention an expansion to our growing family, a cousin, in fact. Allow me to introduce that cousin. Dr. Henry MacAlpin, 7th Viscount Salperton. Henry, feel free to speak."

"Thank you, Charles," he began as he stood. "I am honoured to serve at this table amongst such a remarkable circle of Christ's warriors. As Charles mentioned, my late mother was the duke's first cousin, making the earl, Charles, and myself second cousins. In fact, Paul and I've been friends since Eton. He and Sir Thomas Galton always bested me at fencing and boxing, but I usually got my own back when it came to the sciences."

Galton laughed. "Ah, but you showed up the earl more than once on horseback, Henry. Polo is surely your sport."

"That's kind of you, Thomas, but untrue. I'm a rather poor athlete, but the Lord has given me other abilities to make up for the lack. And before I explain those gifts, let me say that I agree with Gehlen and Treves. I think it very likely that the duchess is carrying twins, which makes it doubly important that she rest as often as possible. I've come to know that gracious lady a little in the past week, and she strikes me as singularly brave, but also rather persistent."

Paul laughed. "Stubborn is the word, Henry."

"Well, I shouldn't wish to say so, but I shall call her tenacious. However, I suspect that aspect of her personality derives not from an unruly nature but from a lifetime of endurance. I shan't get into fine details, but I understand her experiences. My own are similar. My mother died when I was six. For all of her life, Mother saw angels and sketched and even painted what she perceived. I'm not sure how it all works, but I seem to have inherited that ability. However, I don't see angels in the way she did. I see other things. Dark spiritual entities and living shadows. I can sense them, whenever they're nearby, and I understand the burden it places on a person. It weighs you down, brick by hellish brick, until it feels as though you cannot even rise from your bed some days. The duchess sees the world this way, and I marvel that she's survived with her mind intact. However, if my understanding of the Plantagenet twins is correct, then does it not strike you as curious that she now bears twins? Paul and Sir Thomas tell me that Redwing plans to use any children born to Charles and Elizabeth for their own purposes. Twins give them a double opportunity. Twins began all this, and twins may conclude it. Rather like a snake eating its own tail."

Charles agreed. "Henry, you may be right, but I choose to rejoice rather than despair. I cannot explain how a child, not yet born, can rescue her father, yet it happened. I am convinced that it all truly happened. Georgie's positivity and energy are a reality, and they cause me to conclude that she will thrive, as will her brother." He took another sip of water. "Now, let us move to other business. Everyone who plans to serve as an agent for the ICI, please, raise your hand."

Paul Stuart, Edmund Reid, Arthur France, Sir Thomas Galton, Sir Anthony Meadows, Lord Malcolm Risling, Sir Percy Smythe-Daniels, Algernon Winters, and Sir Ralph Epperson raised their hands.

"Thank you. Counting myself, that makes ten of us. If you'll take a look at the ICI information in your folders, you'll see there are three tiers to the organisational structure. Command, Central Operations, and Field Operations. The duke will be our primary advisor, and he asked me to serve as Director General, but Salisbury and Matthews have created this new Intelligence Branch for the Home Office and asked me to head it. Therefore, Lord Aubrey will serve as DG in my stead, and I can think of no man more qualified. The earl will liaise with the Home and Prime Minister's Offices, as well as with my branch. I'll inform Her Majesty, as required. Our founding Commander of Operations is Sir Thomas Galton. He'll select men to oversee three branches of field operations: London, Kingdom, and International. Most of our investigations will occur in London for the present, but it is quite likely that some will take us beyond the metropolis into greater England and even other countries. Thomas, I trust you to select the best men—or women," he added with a nod towards Victoria and Diedra Kimberley, "for the job. Each of those who raised a hand should plan to recruit ten others whom we may trust with our lives. These will undergo an extensive background investigation, no matter what their connexions to us, and those who make the final cut will begin training at Loudain House in two months.

"My contractors have already begun the transformation, and by then it will be model of efficiency. Today, we commence our first assignment with a smaller membership. The Prime Minister asks us to unmask the killer or killers behind a series of recent murders in London. Edmund Reid has further information, and I'm placing Lord Aubrey in charge, warranted by both the Intelligence Branch and the ICI. I suggest someone with contacts in publishing keep watch on any pertinent newspaper articles. Lord Salisbury is painfully aware that two victims attended Redwing meetings, but he hopes that fact never reaches the public. It's our job to make that hope a reality. Paul and I shall meet with all agents at Queen Anne tomorrow morning for our first briefing, when we'll discuss the investigation in depth. Ten o'clock in the main library. It is imperative that we discover who is behind these murders and how they connect to Elizabeth."

"Do you think they do?" asked Henry.

"If Redwing is involved, then they must. Now, to another topic, this mirror used by Trent to take Beth. Is it still inside the shed behind Queen Anne?"

"Why wouldn't it be?" the earl asked. "No one has moved it."

"That doesn't preclude it from travelling," Charles argued. "I put no limitations on our enemy's abilities. Lorena MacKey begged me to destroy it, but I doubt doing so would be an easy task. Is the shed guarded? If not, then a human might have removed it, or perhaps..."

Henry's hand went up again, and he stood. "Forgive the interruption, Charles, but Mr. Blinkmire told me that a very strange person gave him a rather nasty fright earlier today. Blinkmire isn't the sort to be easily intimidated, yet this man did so. Stephen described him as looking a great deal like Prince Anatole."

"Like Romanov?" Paul Stuart asked. "He's been annoyingly absent since the fire. I begin to wonder if he didn't start it! Why is it he constantly interferes in our lives?" The marquess started to object, but the earl would not allow it. "No, Charles, do not defend him! The Russian cannot be trusted, no matter how many times he offers friendship. My experience in political matters outweighs your own, and I tell you that Romanov plays our government and us like a virtuoso!"

"Yet, the prince did rescue the duchess," Salperton argued. "I place no particular trust in this fellow either, Lord Aubrey, but thus far he's proven an ally."

"Even Lucifer can appear as an angel of light," MacPherson warned the gathering. "We must not seek guidance or advice from the spirit realm."

"I agree," Sinclair said, "but let us return to Mr. Blinkmire's visitation. Henry, you say this man looked like the Russian, but he was not. How did Blinkmire know the difference?"

"Our friend has known the prince for many years. Romanov rescued him when Stephen was sixteen. And, let me remind this assembly, that the prince also rescued Ida Ross as well as others. I do not make excuses for him; I merely ask that we keep an open mind. Blinkmire said this stranger called Anatole a traitor. Perhaps, we may begin there."

Both Charles and Paul stared at the viscount.

"Traitor? That is how Raziel and Rasha refer to Romanov," the earl told them. "Charles, we've seen nothing from Rasha since the wedding, and Raziel, his so-called father, has wandered these grounds before as though he owns them. Do you think he'd dare do so again?"

"Without a doubt. These creatures have the ability to appear and disappear at will, as if crossing from one world to the next. And Reid insists that the prince's horseless carriage arrived in similar fashion. How do they manage it? Is it science or magic?"

"We might call it magic," MacPherson answered, "but then inventions we consider commonplace today might be called magic by our ancestors. It's likely these spirit beings have knowledge of creation's secrets well beyond our own, but we must never seek knowledge from them. That is the mistake Adam made. Most will lie and try to cajole us into surrendering our free will, just as this gatekeeper tried to coax Charles into trading his watch for instruction."

"And the mirror?" Sinclair asked. "Dare we keep it on the grounds?"

"I vote we destroy it," the earl said. "If such can be done."

MacPherson offered an opinion. "If this mirror was created through demonic knowledge, then it may not yield to any manmade science. Lord Aubrey, do I remember a plot you told us involving a series of mirrors? Might this be one of them?"

The earl stood to address the members. "Susanna Morgan told me of such a plot. She may have lost her life because she betrayed their plans to me."

"Yet, Sunders doubts the body was Morgan's," Reid reminded the earl.

"Regardless, I owe Clive Urquhart a visit," Stuart declared.

"Careful, Paul," Sinclair warned his cousin. "If Susanna is dead, it is up to God to avenge it. Not you."

"What plans did this woman reveal?" Henry asked.

"A plan to release an entire cadre of evil by unlocking thirteen mirrored prisons," Aubrey answered. "Susanna told me little more than that, but she implied that human blood, provided by the Ripper murders, fueled the ritual to unleash one of these Watchers."

The clergyman shuddered visibly. "Watchers! Trent was a great fool and paid the ultimate price for his folly! Believe me, my friends, mortal men are no match for one of these beings without God's aid! They can travel from realm to realm as quick as lightning, and most of the original two hundred formed ranks within Eden's first rebellion. We know very little about the Watchers, or Grigori as some texts call them. They are created beings, and as such, must have limits. However, they surpass us, just as we surpass the animals. Yet, one day, when we stand in the heavenly council as co-rulers with Christ, St. Paul tells us that we shall judge these angels. Therefore, they both fear and hate those who serve Christ. That is why we must employ all the spiritual weapons within our arsenal, not just material alone. Else we will fail."

Martin stood. "If I may, I should like to tell a story about mirrors. A number of years ago, I travelled to Cumbria to visit Rose House, the Haimsbury family seat. The duke was serving in Crimea at that time, I think."

The duke shook his head. "If this is 1860, I'd already gone to Paris by then, Martin."

Kepelheim nodded. "Ah, yes, so you had. In fact, did you not also attend the negotiations, Your Grace?"

"I did. As did Paul's father and Charles's."

Sinclair set down his wine glass. "My father worked in government?"

Drummond touched his nephew's hand fondly. "Your good father also served as a spy, Charles. In fact, his mind was much like yours, designed to solve puzzles. There is much of Robby Sinclair in you, son."

Charles sighed as he rubbed the back of his head. "I wish I could remember him. What little Martin helped me recall of my childhood only whets my appetite for more."

The tailor gazed at the circle's leader knowingly. "I imagine all of those memories will return to you one day. This particular visit was in June of 1860, and your father had just returned from the negotiation table. He'd left the delegation early to attend your birthday, in fact. Your father hated being away from home, but he was often forced to do so, usually for circle reasons. I met him at Rose House, and as usual we all celebrated together. My birthday gift to you that year, Charles, was a set of silk handkerchiefs with your courtesy title, Lord Loudain, embroidered upon them. Your small nose was always running. I'm pleased it has since stopped."

Charles smiled. "I'm relieved to have outgrown it, Martin."

Many at the table laughed as Kepelheim took a sip of water. "So, I am at Rose House, and whilst there—a week perhaps—a most strange fellow visited your mother. Rose House sits upon a hill overlooking the Eden River Valley, forty miles southeast of Carlisle. Your father had gone into the city to visit a bereaved friend, and when he returned, he ordered the visitor to leave. Your father's behaviour was most unusual, as he was generally a tolerant man with guests. I wish I could tell you more, but neither your father nor mother told *me* more, which means I'm limited in what I may convey. However, I do know this: That night, your father told me privately, that he wished that *damnable mirror* had never come into his house! He used that very phrase, and I repeat it only to express how angry your father was. Robby Sinclair seldom swore, yet, he did so that night, numerous times. I'd never seen him in such a state!

"Naturally, I asked him what mirror, and he said the one that came as a gift for you on the day of your birth, Charles. It sat in your mother's bedchamber for many years, but in the spring of 1860, it was moved to your nursery. I remember seeing it there, and I tell you this mirror looked *exactly* like the one we found in the duchess's chamber."

"Could it have been the mirror used by Trent to exit into Whitechapel?" Aubrey asked.

"I think it possible. You see, we'd assumed only just the one existed back then, but I looked for the mirror when I was there last week, Charles."

"And did you find it?"

"No."

"My poor mother," Charles said wearily. "Was she also subject to the same horrendous visitations and perils that plague my wife?"

"Not exactly. Your mother seldom spoke of these things, but your father often saw visions," the tailor answered, "and at the time, it puzzled me, for most in the circle have always assumed it was the union of the Stuart and Plantagenet blood that the enemy longs for, but we know better now, do we not? When Paul's brother Ian was murdered, Patricia had no choice but to marry Connor. That led to Elizabeth, who descends from both twins, and she is both Stuart and Plantagenet. But since then, we've learnt that it has always been Redwing's plan to use Charles's blood, for he descends from Stuart, Plantagenet, and Sinclair. It may have a French connexion, for the Sinclairs reach back to ancient France and certainly to the founding of Normandy, but according to some sources the line also descends from another. I shan't say more until I have proof, but it's clear that Redwing has been manipulating marriages and births for centuries, if not millennia. And though we appear to play into their hands, as some would say, we do so with open eyes!

Sinclair's head began to throb, and he took another sip of his water. "Go on, Martin."

"As I say, that summer, your father was very angry, and he insisted this man leave. I only saw him once, Charles, just the once, but I must tell you, my friend, that he looked very much like Prince Anatole."

Charles felt the blood drain from his face, and Paul's hand was instantly upon his arm.

"What?" Charles asked weakly, his head pounding. "Are you saying that Romanov also befriended my mother? That *he* gave her that mirror?"

"I cannot make that claim. I say again, I only saw the man once, but he was the same height as Romanov—an unusual height to be sure—with dark, shoulder length hair, as the prince wears his, and eyes of icy blue. The only difference is that this man at Rose House wore a beard and moustache. Other than that, they are strikingly similar."

"Raziel," the marquess concluded. "If not Anatole, then it must be that sadistic creature! Romanov is ambiguous, but feels more fair than foul. It must have been his brother. What happened next?"

"It cannot have been Raziel," MacPherson argued. "Wasn't he imprisoned inside the Mt. Hermon stone until 1871?"

"Yes," Sinclair whispered. "You're right, of course. I'd forgotten. But if not Romanov, then which was it? Is there another of these creatures?"

"That is a question we must answer, Charles," Kepelheim replied. "That day, your father called the man out, and this fellow shot your father dead."

Charles jumped to his feet, his eyes round. "One of these creatures killed my father? And what of my mother? Was there no one to help her? Is that why she ran?"

"Sit, my friend, sit, and I'll continue. You look ready to collapse!" Kepelheim implored with much concern in his voice. "You're still recovering from a nearly fatal blow to the head, remember?"

Charles took his seat, looking to Paul. "I'm fine, Cousin. Martin, was there no one else there to help my parents when this happened?"

"A footman stood nearby, and he tried to assist me with medical aid, but your father's injuries were too severe. I did my best, but even my skills are limited. No one else witnessed the act itself, you see, and I later read a report from the local magistrate who took testimony from the footman. This murderer, for that is what he was, met your father without allowing him a second, a breach of all rules of dueling. I know this, for I saw no one acting as second when I arrived.

"I awoke to the sound of the first shot, and your mother and I ran to the garden, reaching it no more than two to three minutes later at most. As we ran, a second shot sounded. When we entered the garden, this fiend stood there smirking, holding a weapon which still smoked, and your father upon the ground, his own, unfired pistol in his hand. I administered all the aid I could, but your father's wounds were too severe, both bullets entering very close to the heart. He spoke only a few words into your mother's ear, I know not what, but she grew pale and ran to the house right after.

"This murderer fled almost immediately, or so I assumed, for the footman told me he'd disappeared, though I did not see the man leave. The magistrate was at a loss. He couldn't pronounce it murder with only one witness, and the suspect had vanished, figuratively, if not literally. Your mother left with you for Drummond Castle that very afternoon, and I accompanied both you and her there, staying until she ordered me to leave. I begged her to allow me to remain, but Angela said she wished to grieve alone. I sent letters at once to Paul's father and to the duke, both still in Paris, and to Victoria, also in Paris."

The duke reached for his nephew's hand to offer comfort. "As you can imagine, Charles, Tory and I were shocked to learn of it. All three of us rushed back to Glasgow on the next ship, but by the time we arrived, your mother had already fled the castle, taking you with her. The rest you know—or you know as much as we do. What we do *not* know, nor can we fathom, is what hold this creature had over Angela that would cause her to run from her own family. Martin, if the mirror we possess is the same as the one given to Angela, must we destroy it, or may we study it? Perhaps, even use it as a lure."

"I defer to Dr. MacPherson for that," the tailor said, resuming his chair.

MacPherson stood once more, adjusting his spectacles. "I should resist any attempt to use the device, Your Grace, unless God makes it clear that doing so is in His plan. These mirrors open doorways into a world which we are commanded not to pursue. The pagans seek power by engaging in such dark rites, but we who follow Christ lean upon *his* power, not our own. Opening these portals is a very dangerous activity. God may open such doors as he wishes, but man should never do so. I vote to destroy it."

Charles agreed. "I believe destruction is best, as well. But will doing so send a message to anyone on the other side of this doorway?"

"It may, so for now, let's leave it in storage," the duke decided. "I've placed a Bible in with it, and also covered it with scriptures and had MacPherson anoint it with holy oil. For now, I think it's safe, so long as we leave it boxed up."

"And I'll put a twenty-hour guard on the shed," Charles said. "Reid, have you anything to report on Hemsfield?"

"Nothing new," the inspector said, standing. "Did I hear that you've arrested Dr. Alexander Collins?"

"Not arrested, precisely. I've placed him at the London for observation and examination. Henry and I went to the Castor with questions regarding Lord Peter Andrews and other strange links to that institute, but Collins appeared to have seizure. I asked Treves to ascertain whether it was genuine or contrived. I plan to call on Treves early tomorrow morning."

The meeting continued, each man or woman offering a report regarding the Redwing murders, as they were now calling them, but also a series of arson fires. The earl kept notes regarding their locations and assigned Galton to visit each.

An hour passed in this manner, and as the clock struck half eight, a hand rapped upon the library doors. Baxter rose to answer. The members could hear him whispering with the caller, and he turned to face the marquess. "Sir, the duchess begs leave to join us."

"The duchess?" Sinclair asked, unable to believe it. "Elizabeth never asks to attend these meetings. Does she say why?"

"Only that she must speak to all of us."

"James, do we allow this?" Charles asked his uncle. "Paul has told me of a time when Beth attended a meeting and experienced hellacious attacks from the enemy. I will not allow that again."

The duke thought carefully before replying. "Paul, what do you think?"

Aubrey's face hardened with resolve. "I rarely refuse Elizabeth anything, but I agree with my cousin. I've no wish to repeat the event at Drummond Castle. Charles, may I speak to her?"

"Yes, of course."

The earl left the meeting and joined his cousin in the outer room. "Beth, why do you ask to come inside? I thought you feared such things."

"Paul, I must speak to you. To all of you. It's important."

He took her hand and led her away from the doors. "Darling, I worry what may happen. We've heard word of a spiritual attack on the grounds, and I cannot permit you to put yourself or the children you carry at risk."

"Do you think I would ever put my children at risk? I wish only to help them, Paul. Please, I've had a dream which I think is very important. It concerns Charles."

Aubrey sighed heavily, realising he had no choice. "Very well, but, Elizabeth, you must promise to leave if you feel anything unusual, and even if you do not, and we insist you go, then you must promise to accept our decision."

Her heart-shaped face turned up to his, the dark eyes large and honest. "I promise. I'll follow your every order."

They entered the library, and Charles stood. "It seems my persistent wife has won the argument. Darling, come here and sit beside me."

The duchess walked 'round the long table until she reached the head, where Charles offered his own chair. "I suspect this is how it should be," he whispered, kissing the top of her head. "You have been at the centre of inner circle lives since your birth, Elizabeth, and at the centre of mine since '79. How may we serve you, little one?" he asked sweetly.

"That's kind of you, Captain. I do not claim to have any special significance to this membership, but it is generous of you to say so. What I ask from all of you is that you give me your ears, for only a short while. I've just awoken from a very important dream. As some of you know, I've experienced many dreams in my life, and whilst some are obviously only that—a dream—others imprint themselves upon my mind and heart with a living vengeance. This one falls into that category," she began. "Some of you know that my father sometimes brought me to London when I was a girl. I never quite understood why he would take me on overnight trips without Mother, but I assumed it because of a need to meet with government ministers and the like."

Paul and Charles glanced at one other. Both knew the real reason Connor Stuart might have taken Beth from her mother now and then, for Patricia Stuart's ongoing affair with Sir William Trent had commenced very early in their marriage.

Beth continued without noticing either man's expression—or at least, she said nothing, if she did. "In '75, Father came home for Christmas, and he remained through the end of January. During his last week in England, he brought me to London, and we stayed at Queen Anne. Mother remained behind in Kent, for she'd suffered from migraines the entire holiday. Father thought to occupy my time with a shopping trip. Charles, as you know, Grandfather kept watch on all the Sinclair properties as the closest relative, and therefore had keys to all your houses. What you may not know is that my father also had keys. Including the ones to this house. That weekend, he brought me inside."

"Connor brought you into *this* house?" Sinclair asked, dumbfounded. "Why has no one ever told me? James, did you know about this?"

Drummond also seemed perplexed. "Princess, are you remembering correctly? Connor said nothing to me."

"I don't believe he would have told you, Grandfather. If you'll let me finish, it will become clear, I think. As I said, that weekend—a Friday, in fact—Father and I finished breakfast, and he asked me if I wanted to take a walk. It was a beautiful day, though quite cold. He made sure I was warmly dressed, and we walked, hand in hand to this house. Charles, I can see by your expression that you find this story irritating. You wonder why I've never told you, don't you?"

"Actually, yes," Sinclair admitted. "When I took you through before the wedding, you never said a word."

"I wasn't hiding anything, Charles, if that's what you're thinking. It is one of many things in my past which I could not recall—until now, that is. The dream dislodged the memory."

Paul interrupted. "Beth, is it possible this dream implanted the memory?"

"You think me imaginative? That is typical of how you've treated me my entire life, Paul, but I did not imagine this. If you'll allow me to finish, I think you'll understand, and perhaps even believe me!"

"Forgive me, Princess," the earl whispered, for he feared her tale might bring on emotional distress. "Yes, do go on."

As though sensing her need, Cornelius Baxter delivered a glass of cool water to his mistress. "My lady, I hope you'll forgive the impertinence, but you look parched. And, for the record, I believe you. I remember that weekend trip to London, and I'd be happy to corroborate, but this is not my story to tell."

"Thank you, Mr. Baxter, it is not impertinent at all. You are a dear for thinking of it, and once my tale is finished, if my cousin requires proof, then he may seek your corroboration."

She sipped the water and continued with her account. "We entered Haimsbury House through the south doors. I'd never been inside before, but I'd known the house sat near ours for a long time. I used to play in the gardens near the south entrance. The Haimsbury dower house has a lovely little folly in its garden, especially built for children. I used to call it the Hänsel and Gretel house, for it looks like something out of a fairy tale. The south conservatory entrance surprised me, for I'd no idea how enormous it was. Haimsbury House encompasses more land than Queen Anne, and to a child, its wings seemed to stretch out forever. We roamed the entire mansion, except for the ballroom, which Father said I must never enter. He called it an accursed place."

"I wonder, Your Grace, did Lord Kesson explain why he might call it that?" Kepelheim asked, thinking of Salperton's vision.

"No, not in my hearing. When we finished our tour, he brought me back into this room. The house hadn't been occupied for over fifteen years, and the floor and furnishings had thick layers of dust upon them, but this room had none of that. Not one speck of dust could be seen anywhere. I mentioned it to Father and even asked if he'd had the room cleaned, but he had no explanation for it. He showed me the books, and told me that they must not be moved or relocated. He was adamant about it. Then, he took me to this wall," she said, standing and walking towards the grand Languedoc marble fireplace. The duchess placed a hand upon the mural to the left of the fireplace. "*This painting is important*," he told me. "I asked why, and Father explained that it was a pictorial history of a very important family called Sinclair."

Kepelheim crossed the room and stood before the painting. "Connor called this painting a history?"

The duchess nodded. "Yes. Does that mean something to you?"

"It does indeed. If I may interrupt your remarkable story for only a moment, Your Grace, I believe I can expand upon this history. Do you mind?"

The duchess had begun to feel a heaviness all about her, and she nodded. "Yes. Please, do, Martin. Mr. Baxter, I hate to ask, but if there is any tea, I'd certainly take a cup."

"Right away, my lady," the butler answered, rising to leave the room.

Kepelheim pointed to the beautiful mural. "The artist who painted this was an Oxford friend to the ninth marquess. A man named Gustav L'Eauvive. The central image is of the Eden River that flows through Cumbria, but it's pictured around the year 500 A.D. You'll note that there is a very interesting animal painted beside the river. And next to the animal is a large stone structure. It is not a castle, as some might assume, but rather a stone maze."

Charles left the table to look more closely at the painting. "I find the idea of a stone maze unsettling after what Beth and I experienced." He grew concerned for the duchess's safety. If her dream was of this painting, then the reference to a maze was not coincidental. "Elizabeth, I think you should step out of the room."

She started to object, but then remembering her promise to Paul, she relented. "Very well, but I've not finished my story. Will you listen to me once Martin is finished?"

"You may tell me the rest in the drawing room," he told her, taking her arm. "I shan't be long. Martin, would you wait until I return to continue?"

"Of course," the tailor said, bowing to his friend. "Take all the time you need.

The newlyweds left the library, and Charles escorted her to a large parlour known as the Normandy Room. The ceiling here was lower than the library's, only twenty feet, but the plaster walls bore colourful paintings of the French countryside, particularly the region near the River Epte in Île-de-France, the origin of the Sinclair clan. As with the library, the fireplace surround was of carved rouge Languedoc marble, and it sat betwixt life-sized portraits of Charles Sinclair I and his wife, Henrietta Charlotte.

"In here, darling. I'll let Baxter know where to find you."

"Must you leave?" she asked, her eyes downcast. He couldn't tell if she was angry or sad.

"Beth, what is it?"

"Paul still thinks of me as a child," she whispered tightly. "I hope you do not."

He sat beside her and kissed her cheek. "Hardly. You are very much a woman. I didn't insist you leave because I doubted you, Beth, but because I fear for you—and for our children. That maze still haunts me, and I worried that Martin's mention of another maze might distress you. For the record, I believe every word you say. Every single word." She began to cry, and he pulled her into his arms. "What's all this? Why the tears?"

"I'm being silly, I know, but it's a feeling. Like a great heaviness falling across the world. It started this morning, after you left. I slept very well last night, but today, with each passing hour, this awful oppression grows. Charles, I'm worried something's going to happen. I felt this same way just before the wedding, do you remember?"

"You kept asking me about snow. I remember that, but Beth this feeling doesn't necessarily mean another tragedy will occur."

"But it did snow that night, and I still don't know why I kept asking you about it. I've these strange pictures inside my head of horrid looking creatures, blood, and snow. Charles, I shouldn't be afraid, but I am."

He tightened his arms 'round her. "I won't let anything happen to you, little one. If it costs my life, I'll protect you."

"Don't say that!" she exclaimed, her face paling. "Please, Charles, you must never promise that! I cannot lose you. I simply cannot!"

"Do you trust in the Lord?" he asked her sweetly.

"Yes, but..."

"No modifiers. It's a lesson I'm learning. Trust means leaning completely upon him. And if he chooses to let us fall, then we trust that it is for our good that he does so."

She shivered, and he found a small blanket folded into a basket near the fireplace. "Here," he said as he put it around her shoulders. "I'm not sure you're fully recovered yet. Shall I ask Henry to take a look at you?"

"No, I'll be fine in here, but before you go, will you let me finish my story?"

"If you can do so without returning to the library."

"Very well. The painting has a secret. That's what my father told me. There's imagery that asks a riddle. The answer is hidden, and the key to answering the riddle is in a book, found on the tallest shelf in your library. The book has gold lettering and red leather binding. He said that a tall man would one day remove the book from the shelf, and that the secret would reveal itself."

"You recalled all that from a dream you had today?"

"Yes. My father spoke to me in this dream, Charles. He looked so young! I'd never seen Father looking so well; so peaceful, so very happy! He told me that you and I were meant to be together, and that we would have many children. Then, he told me to remember our trip here when I was a girl. When I awoke, the lost memories had returned to me. You do believe me, don't you?"

"Of course, little one. And I believe the Lord has given you this dream for his purposes. I look forward to meeting your father one day, but for a season, I'll serve and protect you to the best of my abilities. I love you, little one. I love you so very much that it hurts sometimes. If ever I lost you, I would truly die inside." He kissed her lips, stroking her cheek tenderly. "Despite your objection, I'll ask Henry to make sure of your health, and then Victoria will come sit with you. Where is Della?"

"She and Mrs. Wilsham are visiting the dower house. And before you ask, they did not travel alone. Mr. Granger drove them, and he'll bring them back when the visit is ended. Della and Ida Ross have become friends, you see, and Mary already knew her, of course."

"Della and Mary are wonderful ambassadors, are they not? However, if they're not back within the hour, I'll send a footman to fetch them for supper. Rest a little, and after we eat, perhaps Della will play for us."

Charles passed Baxter on his journey back to the library, and he informed the soft-hearted butler that the duchess awaited tea in the Normandy Room and that afterward, he should re-join the circle for the rest of the meeting.

As he neared the library doors, Sinclair could hear several voices, apparently arguing. He entered to find Reid, Kepelheim, Kimberley, and Paul Stuart in a heated debate about the recent murders.

"I leave you for five minutes, and you devolve into this?" he asked his friends. "I promise that we'll discuss these new murders tomorrow at Queen Anne. Anyone who wishes to attend is welcome. For now, I would hear Martin's explanation for this painting, and when he's done, I'll reveal what Beth just told me."

The argument ended, and the combatants returned to their chairs. Martin Kepelheim removed the spectacles from his ample nose and polished the lenses with a linen kerchief.

Sinclair waited another moment. "Thank you. Now, Martin, do you know why this maze is depicted? What is its meaning?"

"A very good question," the tailor said as he placed the eyeglasses back onto his nose, "and one I once put to your father, but even he lacked concrete evidence, which makes our duchess's dream all the more important. Connor Stuart and Robby Sinclair were very close friends, and they shared theories and research which we still need to decipher. I can tell you this: No such structure sits there presently. Only Uther's ruined castle remains."

Paul joined his cousin and Kepelheim beside the muralled wall. "Martin, I know I've been to Rose House, but I was so young that I can't recall much. I always thought the Pendragons arose in Cornwall."

Sinclair focused on the strange images, trying to remember anything his father night have told him. "I wish my memories would return. Martin, what is this animal standing next to the maze? It looks a bit like a dragon."

"A dragon would make sense, given the proximity to Uther's castle. This, however, is not a typical dragon, but rather a very interesting chimeric creature," the tailor replied as he brushed his hand across the paint. "It is a dragon's body with three heads, rather like lions."

"Yes, but there are horns coming out of the lions' heads," Aubrey observed.

Edward MacPherson left the table and joined the others, adjusting his own wire-rimmed spectacles as he squinted at the wall. "Red-eyed lions, at that. The waves of the river are not ordinary either. They form black wings, Charles."

"I need to sit," Sinclair said, leaning heavily against the wall. Aubrey took his cousin's arm and guided him back to the table. Charles looked decidedly unsteady as he regained his former chair.

"Thank you, Paul. It's grown warm in here."

Baxter had returned from delivering the tea, and he now filled a glass with water and brought it to his friend. "Drink this, sir. May I ask, my lord, when did you last eat?"

"This morning, I think. Thank you, Baxter." The marquess drank half the glass and set the remainder on the table. "That helped. What's that?" he asked, taking to his feet once more and crossing to the painting. "See here? There's a legend written above the maze. It looks like clouds, but they're actually letters."

He looked closely at the spiralling image, touching the rough paintwork. The image was unusually warm. Though the room was heated by two steam radiators and a large fireplace, the plaster wall should have felt somewhat cool. A fine brush had painted a series of words within the sky above the maze.

"*A bhios a 'cumail a' gheata*," Aubrey read aloud.

"Is that Gaelic?" Sinclair asked.

"Scots Gaelic," Paul answered.

"It's a riddle," the marquess remarked. "Beth told me the mural contained a riddle."

"Yes, I believe she's right," Martin replied. "Lord Aubrey, can you translate it?"

The duke spoke Gaelic better than anyone. "Allow me. Roughly, it asks, *Who keeps the gate*? Son, might this be connected to the gatekeeper you told us about?"

"Quite likely. Beth told me the rest of her dream just now. She said her father mentioned a riddle written on this wall. She said a book in this library would reveal the answer."

"Did she offer a hint?" Paul asked. "There must be a thousand books on these shelves."

"She said it was on a very high shelf, and the book is bound in red leather with gold lettering. Connor told her that a tall man would one day find the book and reveal the answer to the riddle."

"You're certainly a tall man," the short-statured tailor remarked with a smile. "Six-foot-three and a whisper."

"Yes, but the earl is just as tall. However, Reggie Whitmore is taller than either of us."

The aged physician laughed. "I doubt the duchess's father referred to me, Charles! No, this is your house. I'm sure you're that tall man."

The entire membership began to scan the shelves, every eye searching for a book with a red spine.

"Got it!" Aubrey shouted, pointing towards the topmost shelf on the north wall. "Third from the left, Charles."

Sinclair rolled a library ladder to the location and climbed to the platform. "Our Pendragon theme continues. It's a copy of *La Morte D'Arthur* by Malory. The spine shows the publisher as Southey, dated 1817. Shall I take it down?" Charles reached towards the book. His fingertips brushed the embossed lettering, and a strange electric surge ran through his arm and downward into his entire frame. Without any instructions, the marquess pulled the top of the book towards the room, tilting it so that it leaned outwards at a forty-five degree angle.

To everyone's shock, the muralled wall sprang open towards the room.

"Looks like an invitation to me," Aubrey said.

Charles descended the ladder. Electricity still hummed inside his cells, and the mocking voice of the raven creature, who'd so tortured him in the stone maze, echoed in his brain. His fingertips felt cold, even though his forehead seemed to boil. A dozen voices spoke at once, and he slowly managed to sort through them, isolating that of his cousin.

"Charles? Are you all right?"

"Let me take a look," Henry said, pushing through the anxious membership. As he reached Sinclair, the viscount stopped in his tracks. "Charles, don't move. Everyone out. Now!"

Confusion overtook the gathering, but Kepelheim managed to restore a sense of crazed calm. "Let's do as Henry asks, shall we? Perhaps, Mr. Baxter will offer us a beverage selection in the Cumbria Room whilst we wait."

The butler stared at his employer, not wishing to leave, but the tailor tapped his friend's arm. "Cornelius, help me, please. If Henry says we must leave, then we must. He has clearer eyes than ours."

"Yes, of course. The Cumbria Room is three doors down and on the left of the main corridor," he told the gathering. "It's a magnificent chamber, is it not, Mr. Kepelheim?"

"It is indeed," Martin gabbed as he took Victoria aside. "Someone should go to the duchess and remain there with her."

"I'll go. Mr. France, will you accompany me?"

The young inspector looked to Reid for permission. "Go on, Arthur. After all, it's your primary job. Come back in half an hour."

"Yes, sir."

The company scattered into several groups, most of them following Baxter, a few others remaining in the hallway near the library doors.

Inside the closed room, the duke turned to Salperton. "Will someone tell me what just happened?"

"Sir, we are not alone in this room. A tall figure stands beside the fireplace, and he is pointing at Charles."

Sinclair looked as though he'd fallen into a trance. He slowly turned towards the phantom. Henry described what he perceived for the two blind Scotsmen.

"James, I've no idea what this apparition is, but he is dark-haired and quite tall with an athletic build. He wears a high collar, dark blue ascot, a paisley waistcoat in claret red and blue, dark trousers, no jacket. He's appears to be talking."

"Talking? Do we dare speak to him?" the duke asked.

Paul Stuart had no intention of allowing his cousin to greet a ghost, and he stepped in front of Sinclair. "Charles, look at me!" he shouted, using both hands to shake his cousin.

Sinclair said nothing, his wide eyes fixed upon the figure near the fireplace.

"Whom do you see, son?" the duke asked.

"It's my father. He showed me the passageway when I was a boy," the sleepwalker said. "I remember now."

"Your father? Are we to enter?" Paul asked.

Charles nodded. "Yes. That's what he says. The answer stands within."

"James, hand me that candlestick, will you? It's quite dark in there," Aubrey asked his uncle.

Henry MacAlpin gripped his cousin's arm. "No, Paul! You have no idea what's in there!"

The earl smiled. "Exactly."

Aubrey stepped into the darkened space, holding the candlestick high. The walls of the secret corridor were smooth and finished. Sconces that once held candles were set into the lath and plaster. The passageway continued long past the library and turned a corner approximately fifteen feet to the earl's left.

"It's an old servants' passage," he called out to the others. "Most of our homes have these, though they go unused now. I'm surprised Charles's grandfather included them in so new a house."

Henry remained with the marquess. "Charles, what else do you hear? I can see your father, but I cannot hear him."

"He says to look at the wall."

"Paul, is there anything on the wall?"

Aubrey held the flickering candle as he walked along the side shared with the library. "No. Nothing. Wait."

There was a long pause.

"Paul?"

Nothing. No reply. Not a sound.

James Stuart had no intention of waiting any longer. He entered the dark passageway, only to reappear seconds later, his face contorted in desperation. “He’s gone!”

CHAPTER FORTY-TWO

Paul Stuart had passed through a second, secret panel into a hidden chamber. His beeswax candle painted the small room with a flickering, yellow light. To his right, the earl discovered a gas sconce mounted slightly above eye level. Even at his height, the tall Scotsman had to stand on tiptoe to find the gas switch. He turned it slightly and used the candle to light the invisible vapour. The new lighting source shone upon three companion fixtures, one on each wall, and he went 'round the room to light these as well. Standing now inside a well-illuminated chamber, Aubrey marvelled at what he'd discovered.

"The room's a book," he spoke aloud. Every surface, including the ceiling had been overwritten in a language unknown to him. "I wonder if it's a code," he mused.

"So there you are," his uncle's voice called from the open panel. "We'd feared the ghosts had taken you!"

Paul laughed. "No, only curiosity. Sorry, James. I should have come back as soon as I discovered the second panel. What is this room? I don't recall hearing Charles talk about it."

"We'll have to ask him later. Henry's worried about your cousin, as am I. Is this more Gaelic?"

"No. At least not a form I've ever seen before, but it has a similar appearance. I think the room's a mixture of all kinds of languages. See there? In the far corner, just above the light? It looks like Greek. Over there, it looks more like Middle English. French there, German here, and over there by the entry, something resembling Russian."

"Babel," the duke said. "Son, I think you've discovered an architectural representation of something very dark. What do we know about Charles's grandfather?"

Paul set the candlestick on the only piece of furniture in the entire space, a circular pedestal made of carved marble. "I'm the wrong person to ask. I'd assumed you would know."

"Come, let's go back to the library. This room feels wrong."

"Very well, but I want to return here later," the earl answered as he began turning off the gas to the sconces. "It's a bit like a tomb in here, and... Wait a moment. Did you notice that?"

"What?" Drummond asked.

"The reflection of this candle. The panel we entered has closed slightly, and there's a mirror on this side. See?" Paul cast the candle's light towards the wall shared with the passageway. As he moved the candle, the dancing flame also moved, but not in a clean line; more in a rippling fashion. "

"It's definitely a mirror of some kind, though not silvered glass or mercury," he told his uncle. "There's no natural light in this room, which makes it difficult. Is this part of the wall, I wonder?"

He placed his left hand on the mirrored surface, and to his shock, it passed through!

"I don't like this at all," Aubrey muttered. "We're leaving—now."

James stared, his dark eyes filled with worry. "And we're not returning without a Bible and MacPherson."

They gingerly pulled the edge of the panel to open it wide enough for their exit, and then the two Scotsmen re-entered the passageway. In a moment, they're returned to the library.

"I'm relieved to see you," Charles said, his colour improved. "What did you find?"

"Secrets. Charles, we need to talk to Martin. He's the circle's historian. I want to know more about your grandfather."

"Is the meeting over then?" the duke asked his nephews.

"Yes, I think it's best we adjourn for the night and eat. I'll look in on Beth."

The four men left the library, and Charles summoned Baxter to lock it. "I want no one to enter that room for the present. Not staff. No one. And especially not the duchess."

The circle members wouldn't return to their discussion of the Sinclair history for many days, because three more murders would consume every waking moment of Sinclair's time. But as the company dispersed that night, the skies over the two estates glistened like a mirror. A white owl left the roof of the dovecote, flew over the Queen Anne House gates, and in a flash, lengthened into its normal, human appearance.

No one noticed the transformation. Standing just beneath a street lamp, his long dark hair pulled back with a scarlet ribbon, Anatole Romanov hailed a hansom for London Hospital.

Far away, beneath the foundations of Istseleniye Castle, the earth began to rumble. Ravens gathered upon the broken ramparts, their glassy eyes fixed upon a circular rock that covered an ancient portal. The stone had been placed there by Samael long before the castle's keystone was laid, and he'd placed wards and locks upon it through multiple inscriptions and spoken phrases.

The high gates that served as guardians to the castle's interior park began to shiver, the repeated Sumerian triplets glowing red. A pair of yellow eyes materialised within the magnificent stones, and around these, a shadow took shape. No longer did the gatekeeper fear the forbidding fortress. His plan to escape the confines of the Stone Realms had worked, brought forward by clever manipulation of time and timelessness.

The birdman hopped through the wall's stone guardians and into the gravelled park. He hadn't obtained permission to leave his prison, which meant he could be summoned to return at any moment. He had but one chance to alter the rules in his favour.

But he'd need assistance.

From her.

The demonic bird, who'd once been fully human, glanced skyward. "Do you see me?" he called to the indifferent moon. "I've done all you asked. Cast your eye upon me now and grant my petition!"

Not yet, came the reply. *But soon. You must be patient, my ancient friend. Before I can release you for good, my three knights must ride forth. The first will emerge when Night's long hours yield to Day's dominion. The next, when Day and Night cohabit as one. The third will complete the ride, thirteen moons later. For now, my beautiful bird, sleep. Sleep beneath the stones and wait a little lon-*

ger, and when all is done, we shall gain the throne and rule the world. All must be done in its own time.

The gatekeeper cawed and flapped its wings, sighing. "How I detest Time!" it cawed in disgust. "And this infernal city is nothing but clocks and bells, but we'll soon fix that, won't we, my lady? We'll shatter Time forever!"

He popped out of view, and the only eyes to see it were that of a grey mouse, but the miniscule observer had no chance to tell his many friends beneath the brambles that bordered the woods near the cemetery. Before the tiny bit of mouse flesh could reveal his secrets, he'd be digested inside a black cat, who would later find itself the victim of a rabid dog, who'd then be shot by a rat catcher on his way home for Sunday dinner.

The rat catcher would die that very night, burnt in a fire set by a crazed escapee from Bedlam. The police would find the arsonist wandering amongst the castle's charred stones, absent of clothing, and shouting of a thousand demons living inside his brain.

No one would believe him.

Save for one man.

Dr. Henry Robert Stuart MacAlpin, 7th Viscount Salperton, who'd visit the lunatic as a courtesy to a fellow physician. And from that moment forward, everything he thought he understood about time, truth, and the inner circle would be turned on its head.

End Book Four

Coming in September, 2018
Book Five of *The Redwing Saga*

ABOUT THE AUTHOR

Science, writing, opera, and geopolitics are just a few of the many 'hats' worn by Sharon K. Gilbert. She has been married to SkyWatchTV host and fellow writer Derek P. Gilbert for nearly twenty years, and during that time, helped to raise a brilliant and beautiful stepdaughter, Nicole Gilbert.

The Gilberts have shared their talents and insights for over a decade with the pioneering Christian podcasts, *PID Radio, Gilbert House Fellowship,* and *View from the Bunker*. In addition to co-hosting SkyWatchTV's flagship interview program and *SciFriday* each week, Sharon also hosts *SkyWatch Women* and *SkyWatch Women One-on-One*. She and Derek speak several times each year at conferences, where they love to discuss news and prophecy with viewers, listeners, and readers.

Sharon's been following and studying Bible prophecy for over fifty years, and she often says that she's only scratched the surface. When not immersed in study, a writing project, or scouring the Internet for the latest science news, you can usually find her relaxing in the garden with their faithful hound, Sam T. Dachshund.

Learn more about Sharon and *The Redwing Saga* at her websites: **www.sharonkgilbert.com** and **www.theredwingsaga.com**

OTHER BOOKS BY SHARON K. GILBERT

Ebola and the Fourth Horseman of the Apocalypse (non-fiction)

Blood Lies: Book One of The Redwing Saga (fiction)

Blood Rites: Book Two of The Redwing Saga (fiction)

The Blood Is the Life: Book Three of The Redwing Saga (fiction)

Winds of Evil (fiction)

Signs and Wonders (fiction)

The Armageddon Strain (fiction)

Contributing Author:

God's Ghostbusters (non-fiction)

Blood on the Altar (non-fiction)

Pandemonium's Engine (non-fiction)

I Predict (non-fiction)

When Once We Were a Nation (non-fiction)

The Milieu: Welcome to the Transhuman Resistance (non-fiction)

Made in the USA
Columbia, SC
23 August 2021